IAN IRVINE

A TALE OF THE THREE WORLDS

THE
FATE
OF THE
FALLEN

Volume One of
THE SONG OF THE TEARS

orbit

www.orbitbooks.net

ORBIT

First published in Australia in 2006 by Penguin Group (Australia),
a division of Pearson Australia Group Pty Ltd.
First published in Great Britain in 2006 by Orbit
This paperback edition published in 2007 by Orbit

A CIP catalogue record for this book
is available from the British Library.

ISBN 978-1-84149-469-2

Papers used by Orbit are natural, recyclable products made from wood
grown in sustainable forests and certified in accordance with the rules of
the Forest Stewardship Council.

Typeset in Veljovic by M Rules
Printed and bound in Great Britain by
Mackays of Chatham plc
Paper supplied by Hellefoss AS, Norway

Orbit
An imprint of
Little, Brown Book Group
Brettenham House
Lancaster Place
London WC2E 7EN

A Member of the Hatchette Livre Group of Companies

www.orbitbooks.net

CONTENTS

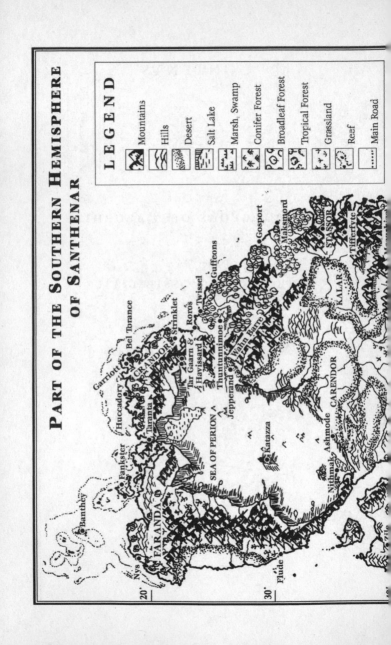

PART OF THE SOUTHERN HEMISPHERE OF SANTHENAR

LEGEND

- Mountains
- Hills
- Desert
- Salt Lake
- Marsh, Swamp
- Conifer Forest
- Broadleaf Forest
- Tropical Forest
- Grassland
- Reef
- Main Road

Maps by the author

ACKNOWLEDGEMENTS

I would like to thank my editor, Nan McNab, for all her hard work and insights. Thanks also to my agent, Selwa Anthony, for guidance and counsel in all sorts of ways. And to Cathy Larsen for the lovely design, to Janet Raunjak for patiently answering all my queries, and to my publishers Laura Harris at Penguin Books and Tim Holman at Orbit Books for support over many years and millions of words. I would also like to thank everyone at Penguin Books and Orbit Books for working so hard on all my books and doing so well with them. Not least, thanks to my family for putting up with me while I write these bloated epics.

NOTES

The Calendar: Santhenenar's year is about 395.7 days (adjusted to 396) and contains twelve months, each of them thirty-three days.

Ell: An ell is a small (and approximate) measure of distance, about the length of a finger joint.

League: A league is about five thousand paces.

Span: A span is the distance spanned by the stretched arms of a tall man, roughly two paces or six feet.

PART ONE

THE DUNGEONS OF MAZURHIZE

ONE

After checking that the loop-listener in the corridor was facing the other way, Nish gouged another line into the damp wall of his cell. 'Three thousand, nine hundred and fifty-nine days.' Tomorrow would make it ten years, and his sentence in Santhenar's grimmest dungeon would be over. Tomorrow meant the beginning of a worse nightmare.

Ten years in prison leaves scars on the toughest of men, but Mazurhize wasn't just any prison. It had been designed to break the most treacherous and irredeemable criminals of all: those who dared to oppose the Almighty, the Most Exalted One, the God-Emperor himself – Jal-Nish Hlar.

Nor was Nish just any prisoner, for Jal-Nish, his father, had sentenced Nish to Mazurhize as the first act of his vicious and tyrannical reign. Nish's only way out, once his time was up, was to swear absolute obedience – to become his father's lieutenant and enforce his every cruel whim on a world exhausted from a hundred and fifty years of war, then shattered, at the moment of an unexpected victory, by the loss of the Secret Art.

With callused fingers Nish crushed out his glowing rush-light before the snoop-sniffer down the corridor detected it, and lay back on the reeking straw to run through his feeble plan again. The mould got up his nose but he suppressed a sneeze. Down here, sudden noises provoked violent retaliation.

Tomorrow was his doomsday and he wasn't sure he would pass the test. Be strong, Nish told himself. Father will taunt and belittle you, as he's done all your life. You've got to stand up to him.

If only it were that easy. During the war Nish had overcome terrors few people had ever faced. He'd been a leader of men in several hopeless struggles, yet through sheer determination had triumphed. He'd stood up to the most powerful people in the land, for what he believed in. But those successes were long ago and the loss of everything he'd fought for, and everyone he'd cared about, had brought him low. The stifling tedium and mindless brutality of prison had completed his fall and, though Nish had spent years strengthening his will and building up his courage for tomorrow, he feared it wouldn't be enough. He'd also need all the luck in the world, though luck had been running against him for a long time now.

His plan was simple. If he could keep his cool under the most extreme provocation, he might get a chance to snatch the two sorcerous quicksilver tears which were the mainstay of Jal-Nish's power. But he'd have to remain focussed. Jal-Nish had never been a great mancer, but with the power of the tears he didn't need to be, while Nish had only the smallest talent for the Secret Art.

And what he did possess – a certainly clarity of sight, an ability to see through surface deceptions to what lay at the heart – had slowly developed from the alchymical compulsion his father had cast on him when he'd thrust his son's hands into the tears long ago, in a previous attempt to bend Nish to his will.

Nish had spent years honing his tiny gift, using everything he'd picked up about the Art from the great mancers he'd known, and he *thought* he'd found a way to use the tears against his father. Evil men never believed themselves to be evil; they invariably thought that they were doing the world a service. If Nish could forge his clearsight into a

4

weapon and reflect it into Jal-Nish's innermost soul, surely even *he* must see what a monster he'd become. There had to be some good left in his father, surely.

If it worked, the realisation might paralyse Jal-Nish long enough for Nish to snatch the tears, if he had the strength. Starvation, beatings and solitary confinement had left him a shadow of the man he'd once been. And though his rage burned as strong as ever, Nish was terrified that he'd break, as he'd broken in the past.

The self-doubt was crippling, the consequences of his probable failure unbearable. Jal-Nish would send him back to this stinking cell for another decade and Nish didn't think his sanity could survive it. His iron-hard determination began to waver. Nothing could change the past, so why not agree to his father's demands? Why not become his lieutenant and eventual heir to all Jal-Nish had created? Nish ached for what his father had offered, yet he couldn't bear the thought of giving in to the monster, of becoming like Jal-Nish in any way.

His eyes adjusted to the dark. His cell was a cube four paces by four and four high, the walls solid granite blocks, the roof a single slab of slate with water seeping from dozens of brown-stained cracks. Without thinking, he positioned himself to avoid the drips, for this was the lowest level in an inverted pyramid of dungeons, and the seepage was stained by piss and blood from the cells above.

An emaciated rat warily poked its head up at the other end of his straw. Normally Nish would have slain it with a lump of rock and eaten it raw, to keep the hunger pangs at bay for another day, but hunger would help strengthen his nerve for the morrow. Besides, he felt a kinship with the rat, which was as skinny as he was. It would find nothing to eat in Mazurhize unless it got to a dead prisoner before the guards discovered him.

He tried to banish the self-doubt. Be strong. Stay focussed and keep to the plan. You'll only get one chance. Don't waste

5

it. You're his son and that counts for something, even with Father. The future of Santhenar depends on you.

But his own frailties undermined him every time.

'Judgement day,' wheezed the asthmatic guard, turning a huge brass key in the lock. 'Get up!'

Nish, startled awake, rolled over in the damp straw and swore under his breath. He'd planned to rise early to prepare himself, but the scarlet-clad Imperial Guard were already standing in two rows of three outside his door.

He stood up, too suddenly, for his head spun and he had to bend over, pretending to brush straw off his rags, until it steadied. Nish cursed his frail flesh. Today he must put on the act of his life. Jal-Nish despised weakness in any form, but most especially in his youngest son.

At the door Nish looked left towards the base of the stairs where the prison's most effective sentry stood, a master wisp-watcher. From its broad stone bowl, threads and tendrils wisped up to form the iris of a rotating, all-seeing eye that never slept, never blinked, could see even in this dim light, and reported all it surveyed to the tears. As Nish passed beneath its lifeless gaze, feeling like a man with a target painted on his back, he heard a faint, eerie buzz. It was *sending*, telling the tears that he was on his way.

He shivered as the snoop-sniffer drifted above him, along the ceiling, trailing its glistening brown sensing cords like a decaying jellyfish. It had been created specifically for the ninth and lowest level of Mazurhize, and its movements were constrained so it could never leave. Only this snoop-sniffer, inured by constant exposure to the unbearably putrescent reek, could pick out other faint aromas that might be evidence of treachery. And Jal-Nish, despite holding all the power in the world, was always on the lookout for treachery. It was the thing he feared most, apart from public ridicule. And death.

The snoop-sniffer's cords boiled out towards Nish, recognised the smell of the Imperial Guard, then plopped down

6

again. Nish looked right towards his father's other sleepless spy. Dangling from the dripping ceiling, an ethereal bile-green cord ended in a noose the diameter of a human neck, twisting back and forth in the draught like a corpse dangling from a gibbet – a loop-listener. Within the loop, light reflected off thousands of drifting black specks which danced to the faintest sound, as sensitive as the ears of a bat.

They climbed stair after stair and tramped corridor after corridor until his knees were wobbling. There was no need for it – Jal-Nish could have fetched Nish to his palace through the sheer power of his Art, but that would be too easy and wouldn't give the right impression. It wouldn't display Nish to the staring world. Nor would it prove Jal-Nish's power and majesty, and he never missed an opportunity for that.

Finally they reached the surface, emerging from a stone stair onto a vast and featureless expanse of paving with gigantic, tower-mounted wisp-watchers at its four corners. Mazurhize Prison lay entirely underground, to heighten the contrast with Jal-Nish's Palace of Morrelune, half a league away across the paved plain and framed by the rearing mountains immediately behind it.

Morrelune had the form of a pyramid, though an airy, delicate one. Nish had never known his father to display good taste or an appreciation of beauty, but Morrelune was stunningly beautiful. It too consisted of nine levels, tapering upwards. Each had the form of an open temple supported on many columns arranged in interlinked circles. There were no walls in Morrelune, not even in the topmost level, roofed over with a spire that pierced the heavens, where Jal-Nish held court. The God-Emperor, at the height of his power, kept even the weather at bay there.

The bright sunlight made Nish's eyes water and, as they tramped across the warm paving stones, he began to feel faint. It was a mild day in late autumn but there had been no seasons in his cell at the nadir of Mazurhize, just an eternal dank and foetid chill, and the sun felt as if it were frying his brains. His knee trembled but Nish willed it to hold out, for there was still a long way to go. Ten years you've prepared for this day. Keep to the plan! Endure!

The stairs of Morrelune proved a greater challenge, for they were not just steep, but the risers were twice the height of normal steps and even his tall guards strained to climb them. For Nish, a small man, every step was a mini-battle against his father. Surely the design was deliberate; Jal-Nish didn't need to use the stairs.

Though his muscles were screaming, Nish did his best to maintain a confident, careless air until the final flight, but halfway up it his legs gave out and he collapsed, gasping. The guards sneered, then hastily checked over their shoulders. Nish was the son of the God-Emperor, after all.

Fight on! Damn them one and all. He scrambled up the final steps on hands and knees, all dignity lost. The guards thrust him forwards and turned back smartly. His father must intend this to be a private confrontation.

The topmost level was entirely open, its golden stone glowing like sun-warmed honey, though parts were concealed by the intersecting circles of columns. The polished floor shone, the columns were waxy smooth, and there were one or two rugs on the floor, but little furniture and no artworks save for a single plain tapestry suspended from the ceiling. Jal-Nish did not require ostentation in his personal quarters. There were no wisp-watchers here either. This close to the tears, none were needed.

Two-thirds of the way across, at a circular table carved from green stone, sat his father. Nish caught his breath. Jal-Nish was writing and did not look up. Nish hesitated, his throat dry, then forced himself to go on.

Jal-Nish had once been a stocky, almost plump man, bursting with life and vigour and a charm Nish had envied, but all that had been sacrificed to a seething bitterness at his mutilation, a burning thirst for vengeance and a ruthless determination to prove himself by clawing his way to the top, no matter what it took.

Nish often asked himself how his father's corruption had come about. How had the troubled child, then the stern and unyielding father, become the irredeemable monster that Jal-Nish now was? What had been the fateful choice from which there had been no going back? How and why had Jal-Nish crossed that gulf? And how close was he, Nish, to the same abyss?

Jal-Nish looked up. His figure was now hard and spare. His curly hair was as thick as it had ever been, though the rich brown had faded to a peppery grey. He still wore the platinum mask he'd made long ago to cover the ruin a lyrinx's claws had made of half his face, but he had two arms now. The amputated right arm had been replaced – flesh-formed with the power of the tears, Nish assumed. That bitter day on the ice plateau was burned into his memory. Jal-Nish had begged to be allowed to die, but Nish could not bear to lose him. He'd pleaded with Irisis to do whatever was necessary to save his father. She'd cut off his arm at the shoulder and sewed his face back together, and from that moment Jal-Nish had been determined to destroy her.

If he could replace an arm, why hadn't he been able to repair his face? Nish stopped a few spans away from the table and attempted a tentative probe with his feeble clearsight, but discovered nothing.

His father laid down his pen, raised his new right hand, a trifle mechanically, and, to Nish's left, the air formed a curving mirror a couple of spans high and wide. 'Look at yourself, my son.'

Nish resisted as long as he could, but he hadn't seen his own reflection in ten years, so he looked. He was filthy, for there was no water for washing in Mazurhize. The caked grime could have been scraped off him with a knife, while his matted hair hung down past his backside. There were

9

streaks of grey in it, but even worse, it appeared to be receding at the front, though he wasn't yet thirty-three. He was as thin as string, his back was bent and there was a defeated look in his brown eyes. The mirror also showed a miasma surrounding him like a foetid cloud, his reek made visible.

He looked away, overwhelmed. Jal-Nish didn't have to say anything. How could such a shambling wreck as he think to defy the God-Emperor?

'Ten years you've served,' said his father, 'and it has gained you nothing. You know I'll never bend, Cryl-Nish, so what say you now? Will you stand at my right hand and help me rule unruly Santhenar, or do you still defy me?'

Every day of his imprisonment Nish had imagined this moment and tried to prepare himself for it, but now realised he could never be ready. A thousand times he'd weighed up his three choices: to defy his father, go back to Mazurhize and eventually die there in squalid futility; to swear fealty and serve him, surely to become as degraded and brutal as Jal-Nish. Or to follow the flimsy plan and try to seize the tears for himself, though that hope was fading rapidly. Even if he did gain them, the tears would probably withhold their Arts from him. There had been plenty of time for Jal-Nish to bind them to him alone.

There was a fourth alternative: to swear fealty, but break his oath and work in secret to bring his father down, though how could he hope to deceive the master of deceit himself? And if Nish used his father's methods against him, could he claim to be any better?

He didn't want to think about the final option – to take the coward's way out and end it all. After Jal-Nish had executed beautiful Irisis, the love of Nish's life, he'd sworn a binding oath and he couldn't go back on it.

There has to be a purpose behind her sacrifice, he had raged to the shocked crowd in the town square, *and I will make it my own. I will survive whatever this monster does to me. I will endure, and you must endure with me, for the coming years are going to be the cruellest in all memory.*

Let the name Irisis become a rallying cry for the resistance. Let the resistance grow until not even the tears can stand against it. And on that day we will tear down this evil tyrant –

'There *is* no resistance,' said Jal-Nish as if he'd read Nish's mind. And for all Nish knew, perhaps with the power of the tears he *could* read minds. 'I control the known world. My wisp-watchers stand in every village marketplace, my loop-listeners on every street corner, and my snoop-sniffers creep into the darkest corners of the underworld. I have secret watchers too, and they speak to the tears daily. Nothing escapes me, Cryl-Nish.'

Nish knew that much already. His guards often boasted of the grip their dread master held on the world, though they looked over their shoulders when they said it.

'You're all alone, Cryl-Nish.' Jal-Nish smiled behind the mask – Nish could tell from the way the muscles moved in his father's exposed cheek – before he went on, brutally, 'Every one of your old allies is dead.'

Nish reeled. His one sustaining hope was the belief that some of his friends still worked in secret to bring Jal-Nish down. But if they were gone –

'Moreover, there's not a trace of the Secret Art left on Santhenar, apart from my own. I've sought out all the old Arts, incorporated the best of them into the tears and destroyed the rest.' Jal-Nish smiled thinly, then added, 'And I've made sure no one can use them but me.'

Nish tried to conceal his growing panic. It was hopeless. He was defeated before he began, so what was the point of trying? Indeed, what was the point of anything?

Jal-Nish glanced to his left, towards a pedestal rough-sawn from black meteoritic iron. Above it, floating in the air like melon-sized balls of swirling, shimmering quicksilver, and emitting a low humming sound, were the tears that had been formed by the explosion of the node of power at

11

Snizort twelve years ago. They were darker, more swirling, complex and ominous now, and Nish felt his gut tighten at the sight of them.

The humming rose slightly in pitch. 'The Profane Tears. I call the left-hand tear Gatherer,' Jal-Nish went on, 'for it's set to gather every detail that my watchers, listeners and sniffers uncover; both the public ones and those that are hidden, secret, *invisible*. The right-hand tear is Reaper, which enforces my will in all things. Gatherer and Reaper are the perfect servants: ever watchful, utterly trustworthy, and they ask nothing of me. Can you hear the song of the tears, Cryl-Nish? One day Gatherer and Reaper could be calling to you.'

Nish shivered. The teardrop-shaped globes were made of nihilium, the purest substance in the world, and one that held the print of the Art more tightly than any other. The Profane Tears had brought only ruin since the army-annihilating moment of their formation. Just days afterwards Jal-Nish had stolen them, slain everyone who knew of their existence and, at the end of the war, when every node on Santhenar had been destroyed, all the Secret Art became his. With the tears he held absolute power, and if no one else could use them he could never be beaten.

'They've changed,' said Nish, unable to tear his eyes away.

'As I absorb the old Arts into the tears, they grow. And I'm close to achieving my ultimate goals, Cryl-Nish. So very close.'

'What goals?' Nish croaked.

Jal-Nish just smiled. He could be lying, though his words had the ring of truth, and black, uncontrollable despair washed over Nish. He was all alone and there was no way out.

Jal-Nish's one-eyed gaze softened, an odd thing in itself, then he said gently, 'My son, my only son, you're all I have left. Why have you forsaken me?'

12

Nish stared at him. His sister, who was two years older, had died in childbirth many years ago, but as far as he knew, his brothers were still alive. 'What's happened to my brothers?'

His father's jaw knotted. 'Dar-Nish died of the flesh-wasting disease in the last days of the lyrinx war. Mun-Mun was slain by rebels seven years ago, and Vigg-Nish had an apoplexy last summer and never recovered. None of them gave me grandchildren, and I can no longer father children.' Jal-Nish stared blankly at him, and Nish was astonished to see a tear in his eye, though it was swiftly drawn back in. 'I have only you now.'

'Why didn't you tell me?' Nish said dully. He hadn't been close to his brothers, who took after their father in all important ways, but nonetheless he felt the wrench, the emptiness.

'I couldn't bear to speak of it.'

'And Mother?' She had repudiated Jal-Nish after his maiming but Nish had always hoped she'd go back.

'Never mention her name!' Jal-Nish hissed. 'She's dead to us. She doesn't exist!'

'Dead?' said Nish. 'You haven't . . .?' The thought was so awful that he couldn't follow it through.

'She lives,' grated his father. 'She doesn't deserve to, after the callous way she abandoned me when I needed her most, but I'll allow no one to raise a finger against her.' With an irritable gesture, he dismissed the topic.

'What is your choice, Cryl-Nish? Will you bow before me, be my first lieutenant and do my will in all things, without question?' His eye grew liquid with yearning. He'd treated his sons harshly but family was the one thing he'd cared about, and now only Nish remained. 'Do so and I will give you wealth undreamed of, the most beautiful women in the world, and power second only to my own. Everything you wish for can be yours, and all you need do is say one word.' Jal-Nish swallowed, then said softly, 'I need you, Son. I'm so alone and I can't fight on by myself forever.'

The pleading tone, and the admission of weakness, shocked Nish. 'What do you mean, "fight on"?' he said sceptically.

'Don't judge me. You have no idea of the vicious creatures that lurk in the eternal void between the worlds, desperate to get out, but I do. I've seen them with the tears, and every one of them hungers for the prize: the jewel of worlds that is Santhenar. They can only be kept at bay by a strong leader with the whole world united behind him. The least hint of rebellion and they'll swarm over us.'

Nish did know of those perils, better than most, and it gave him pause. Santhenar had been troubled by the void before. Several of the mighty Charon had come here in ancient times, and Santhenar had been invaded some two hundred and twenty years ago, when the Way between the Worlds had been opened. Thranx and lorrsk had briefly terrorised the world before being exterminated, but the huge winged lyrinx had thrived in remote corners of the globe and, once their numbers had increased, begun the war for Santhenar which had lasted for a hundred and fifty years.

They were gone now, to bring order to the beautiful world of Tallallame, and Nish found it hard to believe that Santhenar was again under threat. It wasn't easy to escape the void, and his father's claim had the ring of self-justification. The assertion was easily made and impossible to disprove. Yet Nish clung to the hope that he'd been right and his father wasn't irredeemable. That there might still be some good left in him, and that he, Nish, could save his father from himself.

'How do you know, Father?' Jal-Nish was happy for the world to see him as a black-hearted monster, but he needed his one surviving son to know that he'd acted in a noble cause.

'I'm not mad or deluded, whatever you think. The tears told me.'

'Told you?'

14

'Gatherer can see far beyond the boundaries of the world; and out in the void a terrible threat is growing.'

Nish's scepticism must have shown on his face, for Jal-Nish's eye grew hard. 'If I must fight alone, I will. Deny me and you'll rot in your stinking cell for another ten wasted years, but nothing will change. No one else can use the tears – save you, Cryl-Nish, if you prove yourself. With their power I don't weaken and I'll never grow old.' Nish saw a faint hesitation there, a shadow in his father's eye as if the inevitable decline into old age bothered him. 'Rather, my wits and strength increase every day – unlike yours.'

Nish glanced in the mirror and involuntarily clenched his fists. He couldn't endure ten more years of such degrada-tion, but he was coming to think that his plan had been self-delusion. His father was a monster who could not be shaken by the darkness in his soul, for he knew it already. That left Nish with only one alternative.

Yet how could he betray all he held dear by swearing to his father? He felt that temptation more strongly now than ever. Nish had always been ambitious; as a young man he'd dreamed about making something of himself, having the world look up to him, and pleasing his demanding father too. And *even now*, after all Jal-Nish had done to him, Nish still felt that urge. He didn't think he would ever be free of it. As Jal-Nish's lieutenant he'd have power, wealth and, most of all, respect. He'd been respected after his heroic deeds at the end of the lyrinx wars, but no one could see him as he was now and feel anything but contempt. He was the lowest of the low, and Nish so desperately wanted to rise again.

But at what price? There was always a price, with his father. What cruelty, what evil, what brutalities would he require Nish to carry out to prove his loyalty, or just for Jal-Nish's own amusement?

'You haven't had a decent meal, a flask of wine, or a woman in ten years,' said Jal-Nish softly. 'You always were a man of strong appetites, Cryl-Nish. I know how much your lusts mean to you, for I was like that too, before the tears burned all that out of me. Just say the word, my son.'

Nish squeezed his eyes shut, for they were burning and his mouth had flooded with saliva. He was overcome by the mere thought of good food. He ached, he *yearned* for it, but he fought down the urge as he'd done so often.

He would not become a disciple of his father, which left only one choice, to attack, even though there could be only one outcome – utter ruin. The temptation eased and Nish tried to form a new plan. Could he lie convincingly to Jal-Nish, the world's greatest liar, then get close enough to snatch the tears and cut his father off from their power? He didn't have much hope for this plan either, for he wasn't sure he could use the tears if he got them, but he had to try.

'Father,' Nish said, and the words were so bitter in his mouth that it took every ounce of control to say them without vomiting in self-disgust, 'I will bow before you and do your bidding in all things, without question.'

Again Jal-Nish's cheek twitched, but before Nish could move, his father held up his right hand. 'Forgive me, beloved son, but you'll understand that I must test your word. I trust *you*, of course, yet faithless men with black hearts have sworn to me before.'

'Test me?' said Nish. A chill spread through him. His father knew everything; he couldn't possibly deceive him.

'It's the smallest trifle,' said Jal-Nish. 'Just look upon this image as you swear to serve me.'

He reached out towards the right-hand tear, whereupon Reaper pulsed and swelled until a filament streamed out of it, to hang in the air before Nish. It slowly formed into one of his starvation-induced hallucinations, only far more real. This one showed his beautiful Irisis on her knees, gazing lovingly up at him, but before he could look away the executioner's blade flashed down, ending her life and his dreams. He saw the horror of it, over and over and over, and though he fought harder to contain himself than he'd ever fought before, to ignore the provocation, Nish snapped.

'I'll never bow to you!' he screamed, propelling himself forwards so violently that he took Jal-Nish by surprise. Leaping onto the table, he hurled himself at his father. 'I curse you and all you stand for, and I'm going to tear your evil world down.'

He got so very close. He had his hands around Jal-Nish's throat, below the platinum mask, before Jal-Nish could move. But as Nish's hands closed on something hot and inflamed, his clearsight saw right though the mask to the horror that lay beneath and which, for all his father's power, he hadn't been able to repair. As Nish's fingers tightened, Jal-Nish shrieked. Involuntarily, Nish's grip relaxed and the instant it did, he was lost. It wasn't in him to harm his father and Jal-Nish now knew it.

He tore free, knocked Nish onto the table and stood over him, breathing heavily, the mask askew. But again Jal-Nish hesitated. He must care!

'You little fool. I did everything for you.'

'You had me whipped!' Nish choked. 'You killed Irisis. You sent me to the most degraded prison in the world –'

'You were weak; a prisoner of your *feelings* for others.' Jal-Nish spat the word at him. 'What I've put you through has made you strong, as all I've suffered has made me what I am. I've given you the strength to become the man you've always wanted to be – a leader like me.'

'I despise everything you stand for. I'll never –'

Jal-Nish didn't hesitate now. He thrust one finger towards Reaper, which brightened and grew. As the song of the tears rose to a shrill wail, pain such as Nish had never felt sheared through his skull. It was an agony so complete that he couldn't think, couldn't act, couldn't even stand up. He rolled off the table onto the floor, curled up into a tight shuddering ball.

Dimly, Nish saw his father wipe his throat fastidiously

with a silk cloth and adjust the mask. 'Traitorous son! Once more you betray me, as your mother did, and everyone I've ever trusted, and most of all, *her.*'

He stabbed his forefinger towards a hanging curtain, which slid out of the way. A crystalline coffin stood behind it, its walls and lid as clear as if they were made from frozen tears. The coffin drifted towards them, stopped an arm's length away and stood on end.

Nish looked through the lid and screamed. Inside lay the perfectly preserved body of his beautiful Irisis, unchanged from when he'd last seen her alive. Unmarred save for the thread-like red seam where her severed head had been cunningly rejoined to her body. Her eyes were looking right at him and he imagined that her pupils dilated, though that wasn't possible. She had gone where no living man could follow.

'I was wrong about you, Son. You still don't have the strength to take what you've always wanted. Before you can be reforged, you must go back to the furnace. Ten more years,' said Jal-Nish, and walked away without a backwards glance.

TWO

Maelys shivered, turned the page, moved her cushion closer to the embers, then closer still. Books burned hot but unfortunately not for long, and once the last of her clan's ancient library was gone, the creeping mountain cold would surely freeze them solid.

Unwilling to think about matters she was helpless to change, she went back to the story, trying to memorise every word before her precious, forbidden book of tales ended up in the fire. *Tiaan and the Lyrinx* was a wonderful tale but, because of the way her mother and aunts were muttering around the cooking brazier, Maelys was finding it increasingly difficult to concentrate. They were always chattering, though lately their talk had grown urgent, calculating. They were plotting something and she knew she wasn't going to like it. Bent over the fuming brazier with their lank hair hanging across their faces, they looked just like the three evil witches in Snittiloe's scurrilous tale.

Maelys's little sister, Fyllis, who was playing with some carved animals in the corner, sat up suddenly, head to one side. Maelys jumped, for she knew that look. Not again!

Her hand crept towards the egg-shaped taphloid hanging on its chain between her breasts, well hidden there, even from her family. Though only the size of a chicken's egg, it was heavy. Its surface was smooth yellow metal, neither gold nor brass. Pressing hard on the round end opened it to reveal the dial of a clockwork moon-calendar.

The taphloid had been a secret gift from her father when she'd turned twelve, but it never needed winding, and that was strange. Equally strange were the other little numbered and lettered faces that only appeared rarely and fleetingly. She had no idea what they were for, but it was the only treasure she had left and Maelys felt safe whilever she wore it. Her father had warned her never to let anyone see it, and never to take it off.

The women stood bolt upright, three staring statues carved out of gnarled root wood, then Maelys's mother, Lyma, jerked her head. Maelys darted to the door, pulled the hanging blanket down so not a glimmer of light could escape, then eased the door open to look out into the ruins.

A pang struck her at what the God-Emperor had done to their beautiful home. Her ancestors had dwelt here for thirty generations, carefully managing their alpine orchards, tending their flocks and forests, and extending Nifferlin Manor whenever the rowdy clan grew too large for it. When Maelys had been little she'd had the run of a dozen halls, a hundred rooms, and had been welcome everywhere. With twenty-eight young cousins to play with it had been a carefree time, despite the war and the loss of so many uncles and older male cousins. But when the war ended, instead of the peace everyone so longed for, the God-Emperor had come to power, and in a few brief years Clan Nifferlin had lost everything.

Now the menfolk were dead or in prison, the women and children scattered or enslaved. The manor had been ransacked a dozen times, its walls torn down to the foundations. Anything that couldn't be carried away had been smashed. All that remained were these three rooms, and only the one Maelys and her family cowered in had a complete roof.

Something skittered across the sky; the little hairs on her arms stood up, then she heard gravel crunch on the road.

'They're coming!' she hissed. Maelys slipped inside and bolted the door, not that it could hold out the God-Emperor's troops. Nothing could.

'Fyllis?' said their mother urgently.

Fyllis was staring at the door. She winced at the first shout outside, winced again as a sledge-hammer smashed into the wall of the next room. Putting her hands to her temples, she began to hum under her breath and the room blurred as if fog had drifted under the door.

It wasn't fog, but a subtle *shifting* of reality. Too subtle, for now hammers were thudding all around, sections of plaster and gilt ceiling smashing on rubble, pieces of wall collapsing. Their orders must be to bring down every last remnant of Nifferlin Manor. How they'd crow when they found the cowering women, the girl and the child cringing here, and gloat over the reward.

'Hey,' said a soldier's voice just outside. 'There's a *door* here.'

'Can't be, or we'd have seen it last time,' said a more distant voice.

The latch was rattled, then a hammer thudded against the timber. The bolt held, though the door couldn't take many such blows. 'Hoy! Lantern-bearer,' yelled the first soldier.

'Fyllis!' hissed Lyma.

Fyllis glanced at her mother, took a deep breath, squeezed her head between her hands and the fog thickened until all Maelys could make out was a faint glow from the fire.

'Don't see no door nor wall,' said the second soldier. 'You're imagining things. It's just old magic lingering in the ruins.' His voice went squeaky as he said 'old magic', then he continued, 'Give us a hand to knock down this chimney. Seneschal Vomix wants the place razed.'

'I definitely saw something and I'm not going to the torture pits because we didn't find it. I'm calling in the wisp-watcher. Hoy, scrier – over here!'

Maelys felt the cold creep up her legs. Fyllis's talent couldn't hide four walls and a roof from a wisp-watcher, not this close. The fog thinned momentarily and she saw something she'd never seen before – stark terror in tough old Aunt Haga's eyes. Maelys looked away. If Aunt Haga had given up there was no hope at all.

An axle squeaked as a cart was hauled their way, its iron-shod wheels crunching through the rubble, and Maelys made out the faint, hackle-raising buzz of a wisp-watcher. As it came closer, she began to feel that familiar unpleasant itchy sensation inside her head, along with a distant raspy whisper that she could never make out.

'Back, you useless dogs,' said the scrier in a dry, crackling voice. Maelys smelt a foul odour, like burning bones. 'Give the *watcher* room.'

The soldiers scrambled away across the rubble and the buzz rose in pitch. She struggled to control her breathing. Her mother was panting. Fyllis let out a little gasping cry. The buzz became an irritating whine.

A sudden wind wailed around the ragged fragments of wall, muffling the wisp-watcher for a second, but it returned louder and more chillingly than before. Outside, the hammers had fallen silent.

It knew they were here. It was playing with them, deliberately delaying, storing up their torment for its master's pleasure.

'Nothing!' crackled the scrier. Another whiff of burned bones drifted under the door. 'I didn't think there could be. It was just the soldiers jumping at ghosts again. Get on with it – Seneschal Vomix has a lot more *watching* for us tonight. Bring down that last bit of wall.'

The cart creaked and grated away. A fury of hammers attacked the masonry nearby, chunks tumbled with a series of thuds, then silence fell.

Maelys got up and went for the door. 'No!' hissed Aunt Haga.

Maelys stopped. Everyone was staring at Fyllis, whose face had gone blank. She swayed from side to side. Her mother steadied her, then Fyllis looked up, bestowing a childlike, innocent smile on them as if it had all been a game. Returning to the corner she took up her animal figures and soon was immersed in her play as if nothing had happened.

Aunt Haga drew her two sisters over to the brazier and began to whisper urgently. Every so often, the three would turn to stare at Maelys before putting their heads down again. She tried vainly to ignore them but the knot in her stomach grew ever tighter.

Maelys was woken from a restless sleep by her mother's cracked sobbing. Lyma often wept in the night when she thought the girls were asleep. Maelys scrunched up into a tighter ball, for her straw pile was always furthest from the embers and her toes felt as though ice crystals were growing on them.

At the movement Lyma broke off, and Maelys heard a rustle of clothing from the direction of the hearth as the three women turned to stare at her. She pretended to be asleep.

Lyma took a long, shuddering breath. 'Why did it have to be Rudigo?' she whimpered. The girls' father had fallen into the God-Emperor's hands long ago and was now dying in Mazurhize.

'Get a grip on yourself!' hissed Aunt Haga. 'We've been over this a hundred times. The cursed clan talent put him in Mazurhize, and just be thankful none of us have got it, or we'd be as dead as our useless husbands. Who would look after Fyllis then? Not *her*, you can be sure, the trouble-making little slattern.'

Her aunt meant Maelys, of course, and she could feel the sisters' hard little eyes on her. They blamed her for every misfortune and Maelys didn't understand why. She worked

23

harder than any of them, never complained, and always thought of Fyllis before herself. Maelys felt as if she had to make up for some awful crime, though for the life of her she couldn't think of anything she'd done wrong. Even as a little girl she'd been a dutiful, obedient child.

'Just be thankful *she* hasn't got a talent,' said Aunt Bugi venomously. 'Imagine the trouble the little cow would have caused us if she did have one.'

Until the war ended, having any kind of ability for the Secret Art had been a precious, special gift, but since the God-Emperor came to power it was more often a death sentence. Maelys squeezed her eyelids tightly closed, clutched her taphloid to her chest and gave thanks that she had not a skerrick of talent.

Lyma began to sob again and this time her sisters couldn't console her. Maelys wanted to cry as well, but she wasn't going to give in to her loss. Someone had to be strong and it always fell to her.

They ate a frugal breakfast of cold mash speckled with chopped, mouldy nuts. After washing up, Maelys put the last crumbling stick on the fire and returned to her book, though she couldn't concentrate.

They had only survived this long because of Fyllis, or rather her instinctive talent for deceiving Jal-Nish's wisp-watchers, and the mealy-mouthed aunts had nothing but praise for her. Their father had been on the run since Maelys was twelve and she'd only seen him fleetingly over the next four years, but he'd finally been taken by the Militia three years ago and was now dying in Mazurhize, three days' walk away down the steep mountain paths. Rudigo wasn't expected to last the week, though, after grieving for him so long, she mainly felt relief that his torment would soon be over.

Her last two surviving uncles, Haga's and Bugi's husbands, had disappeared when Maelys was thirteen, not long after they'd passed a loop-listener, and their bodies had never been found.

The farms, estates and vineyards of Nifferlin had been confiscated when she was fifteen, and two years later the manor had been torn down, save for this small section which Fyllis had, in some incomprehensible way, *hidden* even from the wisp-watchers. But they kept coming back.

Even though it meant death to be found here, Haga and Bugi had refused to leave their ancestral lands. Lyma had no choice but to stay with them, for she had nowhere else to go. Maelys and her mother had dug out the demolished pantries and storerooms but their last storage bins had been scraped bare in early autumn. The family now survived on what they'd gleaned from under the nut trees, though the last mouldy barrel would be empty by mid-winter. And then, unless a miracle happened, they'd starve. Maelys still didn't know what Clan Nifferlin had done to offend the God-Emperor.

She smoothed down her threadbare skirt, rubbed a goose-pimpled arm and turned another page, though she hadn't taken in the previous one. She longed to be like the brave heroines in the tales she loved – those girls and women who could fight any enemy and cheerfully resolve every crisis. They were clever and resourceful as well as brave.

Unfortunately, Maelys had grown up expecting to marry well, then manage her home, estate and vineyard. It was all she knew, but that prospect was long gone. No respectable man would have her now. The family was tainted.

The muttering died away; her mother and aunts turned to stare at her again. Maelys, unsettled, ducked her head, watching from the corner of her eye until they turned back to Fyllis, smiling, stroking her hair and offering her the last of the honey nut cakes made from a honeycomb Maelys had found while gleaning in the forest. She salivated but there would be none for her. Even Maelys's mother treated her like a servant. What had she done to make them resent her so? It was as if she were cursed.

Maelys tried not to resent her little sister, but it was hard sometimes. Fyllis was eight, eleven years younger than Maelys, and they were as different as two sisters could be. Fyllis wasn't clever but she was exceedingly pretty – an ashy blonde, blue-eyed, golden-skinned beauty who one day would be as tall, slender and elegant as their mother had been. And as the heroines of my tales always are, Maelys thought ruefully.

She took after their father. Maelys was little and pale, with hair as black as char, eyes the colour of bitter chocolate and eyebrows so dark they appeared to have been brushed on with ink. And she was inclined to be buxom, which was most unheroine-like.

As she turned the next page, her mother and aunts stalked across and gathered around her like fluttering birds – all beaks, claws and long, bony shanks. Her mother plucked the book from her hands and cast it into the fire. Maelys started up with a cry of dismay but the aunts pushed her back on her stool and held her down until she gave up the struggle.

'We can't take any more,' said beaky Aunt Haga, staring at her, head to one side. 'Your time has come, girl.'

'The men have let us down, as men always do,' said fluffy-jowled Aunt Bugi. 'It's up to the women now.'

Maelys thought that was a bit rich, since the men of the clan had died in agony trying to protect them or, in the case of her father, were soon going to die. She didn't say anything. The three sisters were immune to any opinions other than their own, and they'd put her down so consistently since her father fled that she knew they wouldn't listen to her now.

'It's up to you,' said Lyma, the youngest of the trio. She still managed a hint of elegance, though hard times had

26

turned her once slender figure to stringy sinew and wasted muscle, and she was losing teeth. 'You've got to save the clan.'

Though Maelys was a dutiful daughter, and she'd been expecting this for months, a chill ran through her as she confronted the relentless aunts. They must be planning to marry her off to some disgusting old lecher, or worse, one of the brutal sub-sub-minions of the God-Emperor. Whoever it was, there was nothing she could do about it. The aunts had worn out what little influence they'd maintained a year ago, pleading vainly for her father's life. Maelys was their only hope and if she failed her family they wouldn't survive.

'Who is it?' she quavered, watching the pages of her precious book curl up and blacken in the fire. Tears formed in her eyes – at this moment, losing the book felt worse than the other, somehow. 'Who do I have to marry? It's not . . . Seneschal Vomix, is it?' She shuddered with disgust.

He'd spoken to them on the road once, on their way to market when she was eleven. Vomix was a thin, ill-favoured man whose yellow eyes had seemed to look right through her clothing, and she'd hated it. Maelys had likened his face to the rear of a boar, but thankfully he hadn't heard. She'd since learned that he was responsible for enforcing the God-Emperor's will in this province, a task he carried out with unnerving relish.

'Vomix!' snorted Aunt Bugi. 'You've got tickets on yourself, girl! He may be a vicious brute, but he's a powerful man who can have any girl in his domain. He wouldn't look twice at a little dumpling like you.'

After living on such meagre rations for the past year, Maelys couldn't be described as plump, but the name hurt.

'Forget those dreams,' said Aunt Haga. 'They're not for you, any more than the silly adventure tales you're always mooning over.'

'Or scribbling in your sad little diary,' sneered her mother.

27

'You're just like your father. He had too much imagination and look where it got him.'

Maelys stood up abruptly. 'How dare you read my private book!' she cried, breast heaving. 'And you've told *them*?' She glared up at the bony aunts.

They pushed her down. 'Of course I've read it!' snapped her mother. 'If we're to survive I have to know everything. We all had a good laugh before we put it in the fire.' Maelys choked, but Lyma went on, 'Though then we had an idea. We're sending you on your very own quest.'

The backs of her hands prickled. 'Me? Where am I going? What am I supposed to do?'

'It's a vital mission, Daughter,' said her mother. 'A secret journey.'

'It's a plan so bold and desperate, no one but us could ever have thought of it,' cackled Aunt Haga, who held a supreme opinion of the sisters' collective intelligence, and especially her own.

Maelys gave her a look that said, What would you know? In all your life you've never done anything but gossip.

Lyma slapped her across the face. 'Show respect for your aunt! The lineage of Nifferlin is one of the oldest in the east, girl. We're privy to secrets you've not imagined in your wildest scribblings, and never forget it.'

'Even a dreamer like you must know about the God-Emperor's son, Cryl-Nish Hlar,' said Aunt Bugi. 'And how his ten years were up two weeks ago.'

Maelys rubbed her cheek, where she could feel the welts left by her mother's hard fingers. Of course she knew about Nish, which was the name the common people called him. She'd first been told the dreadful *Tale of Nish and Irisis* when only nine, and it had moved her more deeply than anything she'd ever heard.

She'd read a brief, banned version of the story many times since, though not even her all-seeing mother knew that. Maelys pored over it in secret and hid it carefully in an

28

old pot in the orchard afterwards. If only she'd left her diary there as well.

'Nish was one of the heroes of the war,' she said softly. 'As well as an architect of the audacious plan that ended it, and all by the age of twenty-two.' And he had given up everything for love – no, for just the memory of his dead love. Maelys's romantic soul was so touched that tears sprang into her eyes every time she thought about the story. Nish was strong. No matter how bad things got, he'd never faltered, and she admired that kind of courage more than anything, for it reminded her of her father. Nish would have had his own place in the Histories, had not Jal-Nish abolished and burned them. 'What did he do when he got out?'

'The fool refused his father's offer, tried to seize the sorcerous tears and was sent back to rot in Mazurhize for another ten years,' Lyma said contemptuously. 'What a waste.'

She didn't mean a waste of Nish's life – Lyma didn't give a fig for him. It was the opportunity that had been wasted. But Maelys's admiration for Nish only grew. He was steadfast beyond all other men; he would never yield; never bend from the principles he held dear. Myth, rumour and, recently, prophecy held him to be the Deliverer who would save the world from the wicked God-Emperor and usher in a golden age of peace and prosperity.

'Truly, Nish is a saint,' she murmured, though she was not so credulous as to think that he *could* save the world. Jal-Nish was all powerful and could never be beaten. But if only . . .

Lyma and her sisters exchanged incredulous glances. 'He's a moron,' Lyma rasped. 'A selfish little runt of a man who deserves everything he's got.'

The tall aunts often called Maelys a runt, and the insult made her feel closer to Nish.

'Can you feed your sister with *principles*?' sneered Aunt Bugi. 'Can you clothe her with *honour*?'

'Can you shelter and protect your clan with dead icons?' said Aunt Haga.

'Yet there's a chance,' said Lyma. 'Assuming that the child . . .'

Again the aunts exchanged those ominous glances. Maelys wasn't sure if they were referring to her or Fyllis. No, surely not Fyllis. 'What is it?' she cried, feeling quite bewildered.

'It's a bold, far-reaching plan,' said Aunt Haga, again studying her in that head-to-one-side, bird-like way. 'But quite desperately dangerous.'

'It's treachery, sedition and heresy all rolled into one,' said Aunt Bugi quietly. 'Scheming to overthrow the God-Emperor himself. And should you fail, Maelys, we'll die in the most excruciating agonies his torturers have ever invented.'

Maelys's heart missed a couple of beats, then began to race. Everyone knew about the rebellions of a few years ago, and the savage brutality with which they'd been crushed so as to teach the whole world a lesson.

'Dare we?' said Aunt Haga. 'Dare we risk all to gain all? Indeed, is the girl up to it?'

She definitely meant Maelys this time. No I'm not, Maelys thought desperately. How could anyone think I could be? I've never been anywhere, never done anything outside the estate, never been trained to use weapons. I'll be caught, tortured in the most fiendish ways, tell everything and then we'll all die.

'She's a dreamer and a *romantic*,' sniffed Aunt Bugi, peering short-sightedly at Maelys. 'And yet, if she can be prevailed upon to use it, she's got a good head on her shoulders.' The backhanded compliment was the first she'd ever given Maelys but it came too late. Maelys had been undermined so often that she had no confidence in herself.

'We're dead if she can't!' said Aunt Haga.

'What is it?' Maelys was finding it hard to breathe. 'What have I got to do?'

'Cryl-Nish is the only man who has a chance of over-throwing his father,' said Lyma. 'But first we've got to get him out of Mazurhize, to his supporters.'

'What supporters?' said Maelys, but they didn't answer.

'And then ensure his gratitude,' said Aunt Haga with another assessing glance at Maelys.

'What do you mean, "we"?' said Maelys.

All three sisters looked towards the corner, where Fyllis was moving her carved figures about, singing, a vacant look in her eyes.

'No!' whispered Maelys. 'You can't even think –'

'Why was Fyllis blessed with the talent,' hissed Aunt Bugi, 'if not to restore Clan Nifferlin to its rightful position?'

'She can deceive the wisp-watchers, and even fool the loop-listeners for a time,' said Aunt Haga. 'The God-Emperor believes his spying devices because he can't bear to trust his officers. It gives us our chance.'

'Do you realise what he would do to Fyllis if he caught her?' said Maelys. 'How can you take such a risk?'

'Because we've nothing left to lose,' her mother hissed. 'What do you think her fate will be, *and yours*, once we're not here to protect you? That day grows ever closer, Daughter.'

Maelys looked down at her fingers, which were knotting themselves in her lap. She'd known it for months, though it had been easier to hide from the unpleasant truth in her beloved books than face up to the future. But if someone had to be sacrificed, she knew her duty. It wasn't going to be Lyma or the aunts, and it couldn't be Fyllis. Maelys was strong and if this were to be her fate, she would have to endure it, though she felt sure she was going to die horribly, for nothing. No one could outwit the God-Emperor.

'What am I to do?' she repeated dully.

'We're starting down the mountain tomorrow –' began Aunt Haga.

'Why so soon?' Maelys liked to put unpleasant things off as long as possible.

31

'We've little food and no wood. And if Jal-Nish sends his son to another prison, far away, or Cryl-Nish dies . . . it's got to be now.'

'Once we get there, we're taking Fyllis to Mazurhize to see her father,' said Lyma. 'We have permission for that, before he dies.'

'I'd like to see Father too,' said Maelys plaintively, 'for the last time.'

'You can't. You'll be waiting in the foothills above Morrelune Palace.'

Aunt Haga added, 'During the visit Fyllis will wander off – no one would suspect an eight-year-old girl – and get Cryl-Nish out of his cell without alerting the wisp-watcher. She'll lead him up and away to you.'

'Then what?' Maelys was appalled at the risk Fyllis would be taking. 'And what happens if something goes wrong?'

'Don't worry about us,' said her mother, as if Maelys's only concern could be for them. 'Fyllis will shelter us until we reach our hiding place.'

Leaving me to fend for myself, Maelys thought. It didn't seem like much of a plan. There had to be more that the sisters weren't telling her. 'Why risk trying to free Nish anyway? Why can't we all go away together?'

'To live like peasants in a mud hut, in terror of the God-Emperor's whim?' snapped her mother. 'You forget where you come from, girl. Clan Nifferlin cannot bend to this evil man.' She looked over her shoulder as she said it. 'It's our right and duty to recover everything we've lost. We owe it to our clan Histories.'

Or die trying, Maelys thought. The sisters were obsessed with the clan's heritage, and its fall. 'Where am I supposed to take Nish? Assuming Fyllis succeeds, I mean?'

'You'll lead him up through the rice terraces to Cathim's hut. You remember Cathim?'

'I don't think so.'

'He's your third cousin on your father's side; a great red-bearded bull of a man,' said Aunt Bugi.

'Him!' Cathim had frightened Maelys when she was little, for he'd been so loud and hairy, so wild and boisterous, hurling her high and catching her only at the last second, roaring with laughter all the while. She couldn't remember when she'd last seen him.

'Cathim's a good man. He knows the secret mountain paths, and where the hidden wisp-watchers are, too. He'll take you and Cryl-Nish north to Hulipont, to Ousther.'

'Who's Ousther?'

Again Aunt Bugi looked over her shoulder, and lowered her voice further. 'He's the leader of the Defiance; he'll help Nish achieve his destiny and become the Deliverer.'

'I didn't know there was a Defiance,' said Maelys.

Aunt Haga smiled thinly.

'What if the guards catch us?' said Maelys. 'What if something happens to Cathim? How am I supposed to defend us against armed soldiers?'

Aunt Haga's bony fingers caught Maelys's chain and jerked the taphloid out from between her breasts. 'With this, you little fool!'

Maelys reeled. How had she known? 'How?' she said weakly.

'I'll tell you when you need to know.'

Maelys's heart was thumping. 'Why do I have to go with Cathim, anyhow? I'll just be in the way.'

'Because once you're safe in Hulipont, girl,' said Aunt Bugi, 'you'll use your feminine wiles to bind Cryl-Nish to our clan, forever.'

'What do you mean, *bind* him?' said Maelys. Nothing they said made any sense.

The aunts looked incredulously at Lyma. 'But surely . . .?' said Aunt Haga.

Lyma shook her head. 'Maelys . . .' She trailed off, embarrassed.

33

Haga thrust Lyma out of the way. 'The tears came at a price, though it was one the God-Emperor paid willingly, for he had four sons and it didn't matter that he could father no more children. Now only Nish survives and his father wants grandchildren desperately.

'By binding Nish,' she said, harsh as an old crow, 'we mean getting his baby into your belly. Not even Jal-Nish will touch us once we're his only family. Indeed, he'll raise us higher than Nifferlin has ever been. And it's all up to you, girl.'

'If you fail in your duty, we're dead,' Aunt Bugi added, unnecessarily. 'And you won't have long to do it, for we'll have to leave our new hiding place at the end of winter.'

Horrified, Maelys put her hand over her mouth. Not only was Nish the last surviving son of the God-Emperor, but a mighty hero and an honourable man. Though she'd loved the stories she'd read about him, he was as far above her as the stars outreached the sparks in the fireplace. Besides, using womanly wiles to seduce and trap a man was wicked and deceitful, and her father had brought her up to be honest. But as her gaze fell upon little Fyllis – so innocent, so pretty, so vulnerable – Maelys knew she had to do it no matter how wrong it felt.

'What if he doesn't like me?' she said plaintively.

'He's a man, isn't he?' said her mother. 'One who hasn't been with a woman in ten years. And you can be . . . attractive enough, when you make the effort.'

'Well, I dare say she could be *made* presentable,' said Aunt Haga, prune-mouthed. 'For those who like that sort.'

'After ten years in Mazurhize, a camel would look beautiful to Nish,' Aunt Bugi said spitefully. 'You do understand the feminine arts, don't you, Maelys?'

'I don't recall Mother explaining those to me either,' snapped Maelys, embarrassed. She knew about the physical act of mating, of course – no one could grow up on an estate, learning the care and husbandry of animals, without doing

34

so. But of the arts between a man and a woman, of flirting, charming and seducing, she was painfully ignorant.

'Oh, for goodness sake,' said Aunt Haga, scowling at Lyma. 'Come here, girl. And pay attention. I'm only going to say this once.'

THREE

Nish felt sure he was going mad. Weeks had gone by since the confrontation with Jal-Nish, but the same thoughts kept cycling endlessly through his mind and he could not get rid of them. How could he have been such a fool as to attack his father; and why, after all his planning and preparation, had he allowed Jal-Nish to get the better of him so easily? Why hadn't he gone for the tears? Most alarming of all, where had that ungovernable rage come from? Perhaps he was more like his father than he'd thought.

Closing his eyes, he tried to will himself to sleep, to forget for a few brief hours, though sleep inevitably led to a single dream – beautiful Irisis, perfectly preserved by his father's sorcerous Arts in that crystalline coffin. From his first waking moment each day Nish longed to see her again, even in death, though the moment she appeared in his dreams he could focus only on the thin red line around her throat. There was nothing so lovely that Jal-Nish could not corrupt it, or use it to torment his recalcitrant son.

He could still feel echoes of the pain Reaper had inflicted on him, yet Reaper had barely touched him. Nish moaned and began to rock back and forth in the straw. The brief taste of freedom had only thrown his degradation into sharper focus. Every man had a weakness and Jal-Nish had found Nish's. During the war he'd shown courage in the face of impossible odds; he'd endured pain and privations that would have broken many a man, but he couldn't face the numbing nothingness of prison any longer. When strength was most needed, he'd lost it.

What if he were to batter at the door until the guard came, then beg to be taken to his father again? If it would have done any good Nish would have done so, but Jal-Nish had sentenced him to ten more years and he *never* went back on his word. Besides, the choice his father offered would be just the same. He was trapped.

The rage surged again; once more Nish gave way to it, and to dreams of violent, bloody revenge, but this time the urge to smash and destroy built up until it became uncontrollable. Had Jal-Nish walked into the cell at that moment, Nish would have torn him apart and laughed while he did it; he could not have stopped himself.

Once the rage had worn itself out, leaving him gasping in the stinking straw, the realisation sickened him. No matter what he'd done, Jal-Nish was still his father and he must not harm him. Besides, he couldn't be beaten, and if Nish kept trying, it was going to drive him insane. There was no choice but to repudiate his ringing promise to the world, even though it meant betraying Irisis's memory.

He fell back in the stinking straw, overcome by despair.

Someone passed by in the dark, though it wasn't one of the heavy-booted guards. Nish's ears, sharpened by isolation, picked up the rustle of soft cloth, the pad of small feet. He caught a whiff of soap, a kind he hadn't smelt since he'd been sent away from home as a boy, and he almost choked at the memories it produced.

The footsteps turned back. Something slipped through the bars, hit the floor with the tiniest *tkkk* and the visitor had passed by. Trick or trap? Nish didn't move until his world settled back into its stony silence. He could barely make the object out. It was like a pale straw, or a rushlight, but why would anyone toss a rushlight into his cell?

He was permitted light for a few specified hours a day, to read such instructional books as were deemed suitable – his father didn't want Nish turning into a vegetable – but evening was lights-out and he'd be flogged if the snoop-sniffer caught him burning a rushlight.

He picked it up, and could vaguely make out writing along it, though it was too dark to read the words. It didn't feel like a trap, though. He checked that no watcher was observing him directly, made a careful spark with his flint striker to light his stub of rush from earlier, and examined the writing.

I'm coming for you at the tenth hour. Be ready.

The guard had changed a while ago so it was after six in the evening. Nish scraped the writing off and ate the crumbs, crushing the brief hope as he extinguished the light. It had to be a trap. His father was a sadistic monster who, in the early days of his reign, had allowed rebellions to fester and grow so he could have the pleasure of grinding people's hopes into the dust. He wanted Nish to dream of escape, then exact a devastating punishment.

Or did he just want to raise the hope and let it come to nothing? There was no end to his malice. Damn him, Nish thought. I won't react in any way. I won't even think about escape. *I won't!*

But he couldn't stop himself.

The minutes dragged as they'd never done before. Nish could tell the time from the sound the wisp-watcher emitted: a chilling, low-pitched whine every six minutes as it rotated to scan the stairs, then turned back to the corridor. The meandering snoop-sniffer dragged along the ceiling with a slippery slither, but the loop-listener at the other end of the corridor hung from its stand as silently as a corpse.

The tenth hour finally came; nothing happened. Nish felt an urge to pace his cell, but stayed where he was in case watcher or listener detected the movement and became suspicious. He closed his eyes and lay back on the straw, cursing himself for falling prey to hope.

Then it came again – that soft footfall and a waft of fine soap. Nish held his breath. Could it really be happening? Of course not. Yet if it *were* his father, something did not ring true. He searched his memories and eventually it struck him. It was the soap – children's soap, the kind that did not sting the eyes – and only wealthy people could afford it. What was such a child doing in Mazurhize?

The oiled lock turned smoothly, the door opened and someone small slipped through. It *was* a child, a slender, pretty blonde girl of eight or nine; he could tell that much by the pallid green glow emanating from the distant loop-listener. She came across, innocence itself, and held out her hand to him.

'Will you come, Cryl-Nish?' she said softly, though not so softly that the loop-listener wouldn't hear.

Terror clutched at his heart – for her. What reckless fool had sent her on this hellish errand? Jal-Nish wouldn't hesitate to torment a child, or even kill one, and the prettier and more innocent she was, the more pleasure he would take in it. Since his maiming he'd developed a particular loathing for beauty and revelled in his power to destroy it.

Nish could feel a moan rising in his throat, but choked it back. 'Please go,' he whispered, using a low, breathy tone that the loop-listener wouldn't pick up from a distance. 'I don't want you to come to any harm.'

She chuckled. 'I know how to fool the watchers and the listeners, silly! Hurry up or we'll be late.'

Late for what? That traitor, hope, rose in him again, but he didn't ask.

'Oh!' she said. 'I forgot. Mother sent you these. They were Father's.'

She handed him a cloth bag. Inside were two pairs of knitted socks plus a pair of worn boots. He put them on.

They were a good fit apart from pinching a little on the outsides, and it was this which convinced him that it was really happening.

'Come on.' She held out her hand.

He took it and went with her. Nish knew they wouldn't get away, but even a few minutes' freedom would be a highlight in his unchanging existence.

'What's your name?' he said as they reached the door.

'Fyllis. Shhh now.'

Her blonde hair was an aching reminder of Irisis, all they'd made together, and what they might have . . . He couldn't think about such things; it was too painful. Instead he focussed on the child and for the first time in ten years forgot his own troubles. He was terrified for this slender, serious little girl, so proud of the job she'd been entrusted with, so oblivious of the risk. Fyllis couldn't imagine what Jal-Nish would do to her, but Nish could.

She edged through the door and turned towards the wisp-watcher. The filaments of its iris stirred and its black centre contracted to focus on them. Nish felt the painted target again, but on her this time, and his skin crawled as he imagined the alerts going off in the guardhouse and in his father's palace.

'It's watching us,' he said out of the corner of his mouth. 'Run!' Run where?

Fyllis jerked his hand as if she were cross with him and kept walking, wearing a slightly vacuous smile. He kept on as well, for he couldn't abandon her, whatever the next few minutes held. Besides, there was no turning back now.

They passed beneath the wisp-watcher and began to climb the stairs, and only then did Nish realise that it wasn't making its normal buzzing noise. Whatever it was seeing, it wasn't sending it to other wisp-watchers, or to the tears. His heart surged – maybe this child *could* fool them, and if the wisp-watcher didn't store what it had seen to send later, Jal-Nish would never know how Nish had escaped.

He was running far ahead of himself. Mazurhize was thick with vigilant guards, and many other kinds of traps and defences. Perhaps Fyllis did have a talent for fooling his father's uncanny devices, but she couldn't conceal their escape from sharp-eyed human sentinels.

At the top of the first flight, Fyllis stopped. Letting go of Nish's hand, she made a tube with her curled fingers and peered through it, up the stairs and down, then along the dimly lit corridors. They were longer here, for each higher level was larger than the one below it. Shortly she took his hand again and continued up, repeating her action at the next level and the one after. Nish couldn't imagine what kind of talent she was using. He'd been told that all Arts had been lost when the nodes were destroyed, save his father's, but clearly that had been a lie. He found a little hope in that, too.

At the fourth level, Fyllis peered through her rolled fingers again, started then snatched at Nish's hand and hauled him along a dark corridor, almost running, until she came to a cell whose door stood ajar. She pushed him inside and crouched behind the door.

'Shhh!'

He was panting from the effort of keeping up – with a kid! Nish squatted down beside her, trying to breathe slowly, to control his rising panic.

'You're very smelly,' said Fyllis.

He was sweating, despite the chill. 'Sorry, they don't give us water for washing. What's going on, Fyllis?'

'The aunties are making a fuss over on the other side.'

'Aunties!' Nish had to restrain a peal of hysterical laughter. An attempted rescue by a little girl and a bunch of mad aunties? Was he dreaming a farce?

She patted his hand, as if *he* were the child. 'Don't worry. They're very clever.'

He could see the disaster coming and there was no way to avoid it. Little Fyllis was going to die horribly, along with

41

her ridiculous aunts, all their friends and associates, and every one of her relatives down to the fourth cousin. When his father made an example, no one *ever* forgot it.

Something went thud, like a heavy weight being dropped some distance away. Fyllis began to count under her breath.

'Where are we going?' said Nish.

She shook her head, kept counting, and when she reached thirty, crouched in front of him and put her hands over his ears. He didn't ask what she was doing; he knew it wouldn't make sense anyway.

At forty, she screwed up her pretty face.

And then the world fell in.

FOUR

Maelys knew something had gone wrong. The aunts had set off their only weapon, a long-hoarded rimlstone, and the *brainstorm* it had caused had faded ages ago. The rendezvous time had long passed but there was still no sign of Nish. Fyllis must have been caught, and the aunts too.

She crouched in the dark, almost weeping with terror for them, and rubbing her throbbing temples. Aunt Haga had said that the brainstorm couldn't harm anyone in their clan because of a peculiar gift they had, yet its implosion had been like boiling oil poured through a hole into Maelys's head. That agony had passed in a minute or two, but now she had a splitting headache and her thoughts were fuzzy, as if she'd gone a night without sleep.

On the good side, since she was hiding in the foothills half a league from Mazurhize, it must have hurt everyone down there far worse. She prayed that it had brought down Jal-Nish as well, though she didn't think that was likely. If anyone on Santhenar were protected against the Secret Art, he was.

Maelys still didn't know how the aunts had done it. Aunt Haga had been more offhand than usual about their plans, saying only that the rimlstone was a clan treasure charged with power long ago, so it wasn't affected by the destruction of the nodes. Jal-Nish had sent out his scriers to hunt down and destroy all such devices, but their rimlstone had been so well hidden that it had gone undetected.

Crunch. The sound, as if someone had broken a piece of slate underfoot, came from further up the slope. It must be a sentry pacing down the ridge, and he'd probably come straight past. No, it sounded like a squad of them. The whole area must be patrolled. Her quest was going to fail before it began. She would let the whole family down and confirm their worst feelings about her.

Maelys realised that she was breathing heavily but still couldn't get enough air. Quiet, before they hear you! She tried to talk herself out of the panic, but she'd never done anything like this before; how could she elude the God-Emperor's eagle-eyed guards? If she moved, they'd hear. If she stayed where she was they'd walk right over her. The very idea of her rescuing Nish was a joke. She'd be caught before he even got here, and what would happen to Fyllis then?

She scanned her surroundings, though it was too dark to make out more than the outline of the steep slope rising up to the endless mountains the family had climbed down over the past three days. Anyway, she'd already looked over the area at sunset. The dry ridge contained a few scanty bushes, none big enough to hide her from the most cursory search, and was littered with fragments of flat rock which made it almost impossible to move quietly. Scattered boulders and a few angular, rearing outcrops of slate were too far away to conceal her.

The footsteps were crunching down the path. Why had she waited so close to it? And why hadn't she moved when she'd first heard them? They were only a hundred paces away and every step made her slim chance of survival slimmer. Maelys bit her finger until it hurt; it helped to control her panic. She didn't think there was any hope but she was going to do her pathetic best. Think! Was there anywhere at all she could hide?

The rocks and bushes were too far away; she'd never get there in time, but ten or twelve paces from the other side of the path she recalled a little shallow depression, not much bigger than a crumpled eiderdown. If she lay down in it and pulled her coat over her, it might blend into the dark surrounds sufficiently to hide her. But could she get that far, unseen, unheard?

The sentries were tramping down, not making a lot of noise but not hiding it either. And why should they? The God-Emperor's guards acted as though they owned the world.

You're hesitating again – go now! It was hard to force herself to action, for daring and desperate deeds were far outside her experience. Maelys took a careful step towards the path she had to cross, feeling the grit squeaking under her boots and her heart battering at her ribs, then another step. She was beside the path, and about to step onto it, when from the corner of her eye she caught a movement further up.

She froze. If she could see him, surely he would see her too. Should she run? Hide? Wait to die? Whatever she did, it was bound to come to the same thing in the end.

Maelys urged herself on. Morrelune was out of sight behind the curve of the ridge, and if she kept low she wouldn't make a silhouette against the dark lower slopes. She stepped onto the path, feeling like a rabbit in the sights of an archer. The little dip, just a stone's cast away, felt as remote as the moon.

She concentrated on lifting her feet and putting them down carefully, trying to make no sound, though the rasp of gravel underfoot sounded like army boots, her breath like wind echoing through a cavern, her heartbeat like pounding hooves.

Maelys had just reached the other side of the track when a cry echoed down the slope. 'Hoy, what do you think you're doing?'

She went rigid, one foot raised, nearly wetting herself with panic. A scream was building up and she felt an overwhelming urge to bolt, heedless of the noise it would make.

45

She turned stiffly, like a statue rotating at a neck joint, to stare up the slope. She couldn't see anything. Keep going, you damn fool. Never give up. Maelys edged sideways, her boot scraping across a rock, and cringed at the sound.

Boots skidded on grit and she knew she'd been seen. They were running after her; she imagined their long shining blades out, ready to disembowel her, but this time she kept going, using their noise to cover her own small sounds, and when she was a few paces beyond the path Maelys realised that she'd been mistaken. A man laughed – a bray like a donkey – and another grunted with his exertion. It sounded like two guards wrestling. It was just horseplay, for she made out a thudding blow, then a low, angry voice, one used to command.

'Two days in the iron-toothed stocks each! And if it happens again, I'll register your charges with the seneschal – *fools*! Sentry duty for our glorious God-Emperor is an honour for scum like you, and never forget it.'

They began moving down again, no more than thirty paces away now. Maelys crouched lower, lifting each foot carefully and putting it down delicately. Five steps to go; four; three; two. She gained the tiny hollow, feeling its sparse grass sighing under her boots, pulled off her coat and went down on hands and knees.

The leading sentry crested a hump just up the slope as she settled on her belly and drew the coat over her with a bare rustle. Maelys lay still, breathing into a fold of fabric to stifle her panting, striving with every ounce of will to stay calm in the face of a terror that was getting worse every second. She couldn't take any more. Not one little thing.

The first two sentries had gone past and the next was approaching when something crawled onto her neck. It had an awful lot of legs and its feet left a tickling itch behind. She caught her breath, praying that it would crawl off again, but it continued down the side of her throat. There it seemed to disappear, only to reappear between her breasts. It had crawled down the chain of her taphloid. It felt like a centipede, and some were venomous. Maelys couldn't do anything about it, for the next guard was approaching, some distance behind the first two, and if she made the slightest sound or movement he'd pick it up.

The centipede was now butting into her compressed cleavage, the bristles on its back segments pricking like needles. She could feel its tiny feet hooking into her skin and tugging as it tried to move forwards. Afraid it was going to bite or sting, Maelys raised her chest ever so slightly. The centipede crawled through the gap, then as she moved, it bit her on the soft swelling of her breast.

Maelys went rigid, squeezing her eyes shut against tears of pain and clenching her jaw to stop herself from crying out. It took a superhuman effort, but she managed to suppress all but a tiny squeak. The instant she made it, she went cold inside.

'What's that?' called a sentry further up the path.

'I didn't hear anything,' said another man, below her.

'It was a little squeaking sound. Like someone in pain.'

'Men in pain don't squeak,' said the man below her. 'They yell. It must have been a bat. Bats squeak; and mice. Come on. I'm hungry.'

'Light a lantern and search the area,' said the sergeant coldly from above. He tramped down. 'Good sentries never ignore a sign, no matter how innocent it sounds.'

This was it. She was finished. No, run, you fool! But Maelys couldn't; she stared at the tall shadows, paralysed. A sentry unhooked a lantern from his pack, raised its glass and struck a flint striker at the wick, snap, snap. She couldn't do anything but lie there with her whole breast throbbing, waiting for them to take her.

A stray breeze carried the smell of lamp oil to her, and the men's sweat. She felt sick. The lamp caught, the glass was lowered with a metallic *tock*, and its light grew.

'Hey!' called a sentry from well down the path. 'What's going on down at Morrelune?'

'Sentry?' called the sergeant.

'All the lanterns of the God-Emperor's palace have gone out. And at Mazurhize too.'

The sergeant cursed as if afraid he'd be blamed for it, then took off down the path, skidding on the grit in his haste. One of the men let out a muffled groan. 'Come on!' the sergeant roared. 'Weapons out and eyes peeled.'

Maelys followed their footsteps all the way down and out onto the parade ground before silence resumed and she found the courage to get up, breathing heavily. She flicked the centipede out of her shirt and moved well away from the path in case someone came back to investigate.

Something had gone wrong, and if Fyllis hadn't been caught already she soon would be, with the sentries running around and raising the alarm. The attempted rescue was a disaster; a fiasco.

She rubbed her stinging breast and grimaced. Maelys couldn't even feel good about her narrow escape, for she'd done nothing clever nor brave. She'd panicked at the first crisis and showed no resourcefulness whatsoever. The best that could be said was that she hadn't given up. Only blind luck had saved her, but it wasn't going to help her next time.

Still no sign of Nish. Maelys's fingers crept to the taphloid, her only defence if she were taken. It was driven by a small crystal at its core, and if that were forced to implode in a certain way, which Aunt Haga had explained, the reverberations should disrupt the linkage between Jal-Nish and any spies, watchers and devices close by, long enough for her to escape. Both crystal and taphloid were forbidden objects and meant her death if she were caught with them, though in the circumstances that hardly mattered.

Aunt Haga had cautioned Maelys not to implode the crystal except as a last resort, for the taphloid would help to

48

shield her from the eyes of the enemy, at least from a distance. But more importantly, it contained a secret that would be vital when she got to Hulipont. Maelys hadn't been told how to unlock that secret; evidently it was too risky for her to know before she'd reached safety.

She fingered her purse, which was empty apart from a golden bracelet, the only thing of value her mother had been able to give her. Its links would buy food for the long journey ahead, if she were frugal. She felt dreadfully unprepared.

The lanterns of Morrelune were still out, though Maelys could hear shouting in the distance. Her gut tightened painfully. This was madness. Her mother and aunts must have been out of their wits to think of such a plan, and she and Fyllis were going to pay for it.

Something scraped on rock, not far below. Could Fyllis have got through after all? Maelys whirled, her eyes searching the darkness, but couldn't see a thing. She eased the small pack on her back and took a tentative step down the track. The sound came again. She moved towards it, trying to stay calm, though her palms were sweaty. The homespun trousers were already chafing the insides of her thighs. Generally she wore a gown but her mother had insisted she dress as a boy. Maelys could see the sense in that, though even with her breasts bound and her plaited hair coiled and fastened under a broad-brimmed hat, she didn't look like one. Her figure was too womanly. She wasn't comfortable, either; her chest hurt.

'Fyllis?' she said softly, though Maelys didn't expect her sister to answer, for she wasn't supposed to come this far. The plan had been for Fyllis to leave Nish at the edge of the paved area, then scurry the other way to meet Lyma and the aunts and escape in a different direction while Nish climbed the track to meet Maelys.

Straining her eyes, Maelys thought she could make out

something pale bobbing below: Fyllis's hair? It was just an adventure to her. Oh, to be so young and innocent again. That faint image might be the last she'd ever see of her little sister.

Maelys hesitated. She'd been ordered to stick to the plan but it had already gone wrong. Should she go down? Suddenly the lamps of distant Morrelune flickered on, surrounded by haloes from the ground mist, then swelled enormously, lighting up the God-Emperor's palace like a golden wedding cake. If Jal-Nish had been hurt by the brainstorm, he was over it and the hunt was on.

Fyllis could be in trouble. Maelys began to creep down the winding path, trying not to make a sound, though that was impossible on the dry, gritty ground. She reached the bottom of the ridge and it *was* Fyllis, lurching along supporting a larger shape on her shoulder.

Maelys's heart jumped. 'What are you doing here?' she hissed. 'You were supposed to leave him –'

As Fyllis turned, Nish slipped off her shoulder and fell to the ground.

'The spell hurt him, Maelys. I tried to shield him the way Aunt Haga showed me but it didn't work. I couldn't think of anything else to do,' she said anxiously. 'I couldn't leave him there, could I?'

Maelys's stomach knotted. It had all been for nothing and they'd be found within minutes. 'No, of course not,' she murmured, putting an arm around her sister. Fyllis should never have been put in such a position. 'Let me think.' She heard an uproar in the distance. The guards of Mazurhize must be recovering from the brainstorm; there was no time left. 'Go to Mother, quick! Leave him with me.'

As Fyllis turned away, another pang struck Maelys. 'Wait!'

She took Fyllis in her arms, sure she'd never see her again, sure that this was the end of everything.

'What's the matter?' Fyllis had begun to squirm in her tight embrace. 'Are you crying, Maelys?'

'No,' she lied. 'I'm just sorry to see you go.'

'But we'll be together again once it's all over . . . won't we?'

'Of course we will.' Maelys couldn't afford to upset her sister's innocent belief that everything was going to be all right. 'Off you go now – and be careful.'

'Don't worry about me,' Fyllis said casually. 'Bye.'

Maelys watched her go with such a lump in her throat that she could hardly draw breath. Fyllis's pale hair appeared and disappeared as she darted along the ragged base of the ridge towards its end, then blurred into the night and she was gone.

Nish's foot rustled in the gravel. Maelys wiped her eyes and bent down. He was moaning and a faint bubbling sound came from his throat. She couldn't see him clearly but his smell was unpleasantly strong and she felt let down. Surely this helpless, filthy wretch couldn't be the hero of the lyrinx wars, and the world's Deliverer?

She made allowances. He'd been starved and beaten in prison, and was still suffering from the brainstorm. It wasn't his fault. A prisoner had no control over his life.

Lights bobbed in the distance. 'Nish?' she said softly, going to her knees beside him. Should she even call such an important man by a nickname? No – no time for such silliness. 'Nish, come on.'

He came upright, eyes reflecting the lights of Morrelune glassily. 'Who – you?'

'Shh!' She lifted him to his feet.

He thrust her backwards, breathing in ragged gasps. 'Go away, Father – take her – with you. Can't be tempted – by *her*!'

Had he so lost contact with reality that he couldn't tell a flesh-and-blood person from a phantom? And what did he mean by *her*? It sounded like an insult, as if he thought her ugly. 'Nish –'

He bent, felt on the ground and came up with a rock in

his fist, swinging it at her. Maelys ducked then, afraid he'd brain her, hit him on the jaw. It wasn't a hard blow but he went down and began to twitch.

Horrified at what she'd done, she bent over him. 'Nish, I'm sorry –'

'Where – am – I?' he said weakly.

'Nish, you're safe. You're with me now. I'm Maelys.' Safe – if only he knew!

He moaned and tried to crawl away. 'Leave me alone, Father.'

The poor man was quite deluded. 'Nish, I'm Fyllis's sister.'

The name calmed him, thankfully, but it was taking too long and they were making too much noise. 'Take my hand. I'll help you up.'

He tried to get up but fell down again. 'Legs – don't work.'

The paved area around Mazurhize was suddenly lit with an unpleasant greenish light, while an eerie humming set her teeth on edge. The huge, tower-mounted wisp-watchers were talking to the tears again. Jal-Nish must have racked them up to their highest setting and they would soon begin to scan the darkness all around. Not even a fieldmouse would be able to move undetected then.

But she couldn't be the one who gave up. Maelys crouched down, took Nish under the arms and lifted him to his feet. He was half a head taller than her yet didn't weigh much more than Fyllis. The poor man had been starved; no wonder he couldn't resist the brainstorm. She gave him her shoulder and set off up the winding, gritty path again, knowing they'd never make it.

'Where – taking?' he said listlessly.

'Up through the rice terraces to Cousin Cathim. He'll help us get away.' But all the delays had cost too much time. They should have been nearly there by now.

At the top of the ridge she looked up the dark mountain slope. The moon hadn't yet risen and the stars shed barely enough light for her to see where to put her feet. She mentally

52

traced her route up through the terraced paddy fields. Aunt Bugi had made her rehearse it on a rough map until she'd known it perfectly, but attempting the real thing in darkness was another matter entirely.

Maelys was used to climbing, for she'd lived in the mountains all her life, but Nish was an awkward burden to support and already her arm and back were aching. She kept moving, performing her duty to her family. More than that, it was an honour to rescue the God-Emperor's son, the man who was to become the Deliverer, and she would not shirk it.

On she went, and up, swapping a silent, stumbling Nish from one shoulder to another as she wound through the maze of terraces cunningly built to catch what little moisture fell on these arid slopes in the rain shadow of the mountains.

After an hour or so, while taking a brief rest, she saw three trails of lights moving steadily up the slope to her left. The troops were after her and climbing a lot faster than she could. Panic made her choke until she realised that they weren't following her at all. They didn't know she was here. It took a while to calculate where they were heading. They were converging inexorably on Cathim's hut and they were going to get there first.

'Quickly, Nish!'

He pushed her away, weakly. 'Leave me alone, Father.' He'd relapsed into delusion.

'Nish, I'm Fyllis's sister, remember?'

Again her name calmed him and he made an effort for a minute or two, though by that time he was panting so heavily that she was afraid the distant loop-listeners would pick it up. She couldn't take the risk – she'd have to carry him.

She was used to carrying heavy loads, too, but not this heavy. Maelys managed to heave him over her shoulders and continued, staggering under his weight and trying not to make a sound. The troops were only a few hundred paces away now, almost level with her. Cathim's hut was further across, along the dry-stone wall between the terraces to her left, though she couldn't see it in the dark.

She stopped for a moment to catch her breath. Nish was squirming on her shoulders but she daren't put him down for fear she'd never lift him again. Her calves were burning and her knees felt alarmingly rubbery.

He let out another muffled groan. 'Hush!' she said softly, putting her hand to his lips. He went still and she wondered if that had been a liberty.

Something passed across the sky to her right, making a rasping flutter that raised her hackles. Could it be a *flappeter*, one of the God-Emperor's legendary flesh-formed horrors? Hunters in the air would make escape impossible. Maelys couldn't think what to do. She wasn't considered an adult yet; she wasn't used to taking command, or being responsible for everything. It was beyond her.

The soldiers were gaining and she was beginning to feel really panicky. She prayed that Cathim had a Secret Art of his own or all was lost. She had to put Nish, and herself, in his capable adult hands.

Putting on an extra burst, she thump-thumped along the embankment, making too much noise. Might she get there first after all? She dared to think so, until a squad of soldiers swarmed up over the terrace wall to her left, starlight making pinpoints on their polished, horned armour, which was individually formed to fit each soldier by Jal-Nish's uncanny Arts.

They were only fifty paces from the hut, a few hundred from her. Cathim was finished. She was on her own now. Maelys began to back around the corner of the terrace wall, scanning the night in every direction, and upwards as well. She couldn't hear the flapping now. Was that good or bad?

Suddenly a bellow of rage echoed across the terrace, and Cathim's hut was lit up from half a dozen points at once as the surrounding troops unshuttered powerful storm lanterns. She saw an open doorway, the door torn off its hinges, and a great bull of a man struggling with an armoured trooper.

The trooper was hurled into the front rank of soldiers, knocking two down, and Cathim surged forth swinging a double-bladed woodcutter's axe in scything blows that cut down a fourth trooper, then a fifth. For an instant Maelys thought that he might win through but three troopers converged on him, thrusting out long, three-pointed tridents. They pinned him, he shimmered mauve for a second and, with a ringing roar, he fell.

Maelys turned away, feeling sick. Her cousin was going to suffer a terrible death and she couldn't help him. But before he died, under the brain-searing torment of Reaper he was bound to reveal Nish's destination, Hulipont. All was lost.

Maelys fought an urge to lay Nish down and run for her life. After all, his father would never harm him; at least, not the way he would her. But she'd given her word, and to abandon him now would be a betrayal of both duty and trust.

There was no point heading for Hulipont, which would take weeks to reach and would be captured long before she could get there. Her only option was to head up into the mountains and try to hide before it was too late, though she didn't see how that could work either. By dawn Jal-Nish would have a thousand soldiers scouring the mountainside – maybe ten thousand.

Nish began to whimper. She put one hand on his forehead and he stopped at once, but it didn't help. Her panic was getting worse, her heart crashing back and forth in her chest, her knees barely holding her up. It had all gone wrong from the beginning, as she'd known it would.

'I can't carry you any further,' she said hoarsely. 'Can you walk, Nish?'

After a hesitation she felt him jerk his head, so she eased him to the ground. He swayed; clutched at her arm. Maelys debated what to do. Should she implode the taphloid, as she'd been told to do in an emergency? If she did, the secret within it, vital for her survival later, would be lost.

No, the soldiers were too far away; they wouldn't be affected. It would just tell the accompanying scriers where to look for her.

'This way, Nish.' Taking his arm, she headed along a stony, little used path between two terraces towards a large pond, hoping their tracks wouldn't show on the hard ground. She could just make out a patch of reeds or rushes in one corner of the pond.

Nish was moving like an old man, but she daren't hurry him in case he collapsed. She stared down the slope, trying to track her hunters by the starlight winking off their armour. It was her one advantage. The God-Emperor liked his troops to stand out, so their appearance would strike fear into all.

Maelys could see plenty of reflections now, moving up the mountain in lines that extended all the way back to the barracks behind Mazurhize. Could the scriers be tracking her? The aunts had said not; her taphloid would shield her, at least from a distance. But the aunts had been wrong about Cathim . . .

A breeze carried the smell of water to her and it reminded her of a hiding place used by the heroine in one of her favourite tales. Maelys plucked a handful of rice straws. 'This way, Nish. Over the edge and down into the water. Can you swim?'

'Enough to save myself.' He sounded a little stronger, more normal.

'You're better than me, then. I can't swim a stroke.' Stupid, stupid! You've got to *encourage* him.

She led him down the slope then across onto a rock shelf that ran into the water. Sitting Nish down, she took off his boots and stinking socks, which she stuffed into the oilskin pouch containing her spare clothes. Wet footwear would be deadly up here at this time of year. She did the same with her boots, then her coat and jacket, pulled the drawstring, tied it to her pack and slung the pack on her back.

The water still retained some warmth from the afternoon sun, thankfully. At Nifferlin, a thousand spans higher than here, it would have been frozen by now. She waded out until it reached her shoulders, then drew him to her. 'Hold on.' Nish was twitching again and his eyes were the size of eggs. 'I'm Fyllis's sister, remember?'

He nodded stiffly; the twitching eased to a tremor. Maelys led him around the curve of the pond towards the rushes, careful not to get out of her depth. Her feet skidded on the sludgy bottom and it was hard to stay upright. They reached the rushes, where at least she had something to hang onto, though she had to be careful not to break the stems – the troops would check every sign. She kept Nish behind her in case he flailed at the rushes, pushed her floating pack into their centre, and waited.

The water felt cold now and was leaching all the warmth from her body. Nish's teeth were chattering. She folded over a couple of straws and thrust them into his mouth. 'Bite on these.'

He did so and the chattering stopped. She could hear the approaching soldiers; they were making no attempt to disguise their movements.

'We've got to go under, Nish. Can you breathe through a straw and let out the bubbles among the rushes?'

'Don't – think so.' His teeth were starting to chatter again, poor man. He was just skin and bones, and he'd chewed through the straws.

'I'll help you. Quick, out there where we'll be hidden behind the rushes.'

Maelys eased her way between the clumps, pulling Nish through the water behind her like a sodden pillow, floating with head back and just his nose and mouth out of the water. At least he couldn't cause too much trouble that way.

She reached the outer fringe of the rushes as the first lantern appeared over the rim of the terrace. Moving into shelter, she put her mouth to Nish's ear. 'We're going under now. Hold your breath. I'll look after you.'

Maelys wasn't sure she could but he nodded with a jerk that created a little splash. She held the straws in her mouth, ducked and pulled him under. He sank at once but she found it hard to stay down. Holding him with one hand, she grasped a clump of rushes below the water with the other. It kept her from floating up though she couldn't use her straws.

She found his right hand and curled his fingers around the rush clump, praying that he'd have the sense to hold on. He did, so she did the same with his other hand. Poking the straw ends above the water, she drew breath.

It proved surprisingly difficult to draw air down the thin straws, and it made a faint whistling sound that worried her, but she got a breath, then pulled Nish closer to her. She had to feel for his mouth; she couldn't see a thing underwater.

She slid the straws in but he bit through the ends, and they were her lifeline. She pulled his face hard against hers, sealed his mouth with her own and blew most of her breath into him. He jerked again.

His lips were almost dead with cold, and he didn't move until she pulled away, yet Maelys felt acutely uncomfortable. It felt intimate, wrong, even though she was doing it to save his life, and it reminded her of the greater intimacy, the far greater wrong that she had to do with him if they ever got away.

FIVE

Suck and blow. Suck and blow. Maelys was doing it automatically now. It felt as though they'd been in the water forever, though it couldn't have been more than a quarter of an hour. Her head was aching and she was shuddering from the cold, but Nish wasn't even shivering. Was he sinking into a coma from which he would never wake?

One of her cousins had died of exposure when she was seven and she could still picture him lying by the fire, so pale and deathly cold. Nothing they'd done had been able to warm him. She dared not take the risk with Nish; she had to go up even if it meant being caught.

Squeezing his hands tightly around the base of the rushes, she gritted her teeth and drifted up, trying to break the surface as gently as she could. A breeze feathered the still water; on her wet skin it felt icy. Maelys floated, blinking water out of her eyes. It was darker now, for gauzy cloud covered the stars directly above. She couldn't make out anyone on the pond wall to her left. Nothing on the right side, either, though the central portion of the wall was partly concealed behind rushes. That's where they'd lurk if they thought Nish was hiding in the pond.

No, if they even suspected he was here they'd have come in at once, no matter the cold. What was a little discomfort compared to the wrath of the God-Emperor? Her teeth began to chatter. Maelys clenched her jaw. She'd have to risk it. She couldn't endure the cold any longer.

Nish! It had been more than a minute. Maelys took a deep breath, went down hastily, drew his rigid body to her and blew the whole breath into him. His lips were freezing. Had she killed him? Panicking, she pulled him to the surface, grabbed her floating pack, then dragged him through the reeds and heaved him onto the rock. 'Nish?' she whispered, shaking him.

He didn't answer; her heart turned over. She felt his cheeks, his throat and then, again feeling that she was taking a liberty, under his arm. Detecting a faint warmth there, she put her ear to his chest. He was breathing, though very shallowly, and was so cold that he might die. She spread her heavy winter coat on him, knowing it wasn't enough. When someone got this cold they couldn't generate enough warmth by themselves. She had to do it for him. She slipped under the coat and lay on him, pulling him tightly against her.

It was lucky he was unconscious, for the position was acutely mortifying. She lay there, rocking gently from side to side, feeling her cheeks flaming and the cold wind licking at her wet neck, until eventually she began to feel warmth at chest, belly and thighs, where they touched.

As she rolled off, Nish gave another little whimper. That was better. She stripped off his wet rags, thankful for the dark, and pulled her spare pair of pants on him. Her shirt wouldn't fit over his broad shoulders but she managed to get him into her jacket and put his boots on. He was shuddering fitfully so she wrapped him in her coat as well. 'Can you walk?' she said, shivering in her wet clothes and wondering how *she* was going to cope. The cold was just bearable here, but further up it would be freezing.

'Hungry.' His teeth began to chatter.

Cathim had been providing supplies for the journey and all Maelys had were some soft biscuits made from dried fruit and nuts pounded together. She fed him one, then another.

'Beautiful food,' he said hoarsely, and starlight touched a tear on his eyelash.

Truly, he must have been starved. She gave him another of the precious biscuits. 'Come on. We've got to get right away from here.'

They climbed the slope, rested briefly in a little dip then headed along the next ridge, which ran up into the mountains proper. It was hard, slow work, for Nish was so weak that she had to support him most of the time, but every step was another step away from Jal-Nish and widened the area he'd have to search.

A long time after that, but still a few hours before dawn, Nish ground to a halt and Maelys couldn't get him going again. She was rubbing his cold face and hands when she heard the raspily unnerving flutter she'd noted earlier. Pulling Nish against her, she held him still and searched the sky. Was that a shadow passing in front of the stars? It was hard to tell.

Before she could move there came a wild swirl of wind and a shrilling wail of triumph. A beam of lantern light touched her, then a flappeter – one of Jal-Nish's flesh-formed monstrosities – dropped out of the dark and began to hover just a few spans above them. How had it come so close without her hearing it?

Nish cried out in horror and Maelys had to choke back a scream, for she had heard dreadful rumours about flappeters since her childhood.

She drew Nish backwards across the slope but the flappeter kept pace without effort, its feather-rotors scooping at the air like egg-beaters and blasting cold gusts into her face. There was nowhere to run, nowhere to hide. The barren mountain slope offered no concealment.

She looked up, shielding her eyes, as a man's voice called, 'Surr, I've found him!' The flappeter had a rider and he was leaning forwards, his fist outstretched, evidently speaking to someone via a glistening loop-listener.

'Found who?' This voice was distorted to a glutinous hiss

61

by the loop-listener but it sent shudders through her, for it reminded her of something unpleasant from her childhood. 'Identify yourself and your location, fool!'

'I'm Rider Hinneltyne, on Flappeter Rurr-shyve, surr. I'm right above Cryl-Nish Hlar. It's definitely him, though he looks in bad shape. He's with a boy, about twelve.'

'A boy!'

'Yes, surr. They're not armed, Seneschal Vomix, surr.'

Seneschal Vomix. Maelys felt sick with horror.

'Excellent,' said Vomix. 'The God-Emperor will be well pleased.'

'Can you send another flappeter for the boy, surr?'

There was a short pause. 'Not at the moment. Secure them, Rider Hinneltyne, but ensure not a hair of Cryl-Nish's head is harmed. I'll send a squad to escort him down. Where are you?'

'On Nusimurr Mountain, surr, just to the west of Ironbar Col. And the boy?'

'Teach him his first lesson but don't damage him. Our God-Emperor has reserved that joy to himself.'

The rider drew back his fist; the loop-listener went dull and he looked down into Maelys's eyes. She shivered and pulled Nish backwards, studying the hovering flappeter.

Even in the dimly reflected lantern light it looked bizarre. It was three times the length of a horse, but had an elongated body like a dragonfly, covered in large scales and bristly hairs. A pair of oval discs stuck up at the tail and four pairs of thin legs ended in scythe-like hooks.

One pair of luminous compound eyes were the size of large melons, another pair no bigger than lemons. Its triangular head was crested with two pairs of horns, a long curved pair which protruded sideways and a short straight pair extending forwards. But its wings were the greatest oddity of all, if they could be called wings, for they didn't belong on any creature Maelys had heard of.

There were two sets, one above the other, sprouting

above the rider's head like feathered rotors from a stalk, as thick as her thigh, which arose from the middle of its back. Each feather-rotor had three long, curved, scythe-like blades driven by great muscle bunches below the stalk, and they spun rapidly, the rotors tilting and the angle of the blades changing all the time to keep the monstrosity in the air.

The flapping flutter was constantly rising and falling, an unpleasant sound that set her nerves on end, and the creature breathed with a revolting wet sucking gurgle. Its reek, as pungent as a squashed stinkbug, stung her nose.

'Stop right there!' shouted Rider Hinneltyne, swinging the flappeter around to stay above them.

'Get ready to run, Nish,' she said in a low voice, praying that he was capable of taking in their situation. She let go of him but he wobbled then slumped to his knees.

Maelys almost wept with frustration. She had never been attacked before and had no idea what to do. She couldn't carry Nish, nor could she abandon him. She backed away so the rider couldn't take them both at once, feeling on the ground for a stick, a stone or anything she could defend herself with, but the rocks littering the slope were either too big to throw or too small to do any damage.

The flappeter dropped sharply, its rider snorting in triumph. Maelys ran a few more steps, snatched up a stone the size of a plum and hurled it up at him. It missed. Even as a child she'd not been one for throwing stones. She was feeling for another when the flappeter swooped at her, tilting sharply. Rider Hinneltyne thrust one fist forwards and it disappeared for a second, then a double-beat of the feather-rotors blasted her off her feet, sending her rolling across the stony ground.

She scrambled up, dropped the stone, snatched another and hurled it at one of the creature's large eyes, but it had already darted away towards Nish. 'Nish!' she shouted, 'Look out!' not realising that the leather-clad rider had dismounted until he threw himself at her.

Ducking low under his outstretched arm, she ran. He was a big man, head and shoulders taller than her and powerfully built, but slow-footed and lumbering, as if not used to moving on the ground. Maelys stayed ahead of him, though she wasn't sure how long she could keep it up. Her legs were very tired. As she turned to check on Nish, the flappeter, its pairs of bristly legs spread, came down on top of him, knocking him to the ground. Reversing the beat of its rotors, it slowly rose, holding him between four of its legs. The moon was just rising, silhouetting the creature's bristles and, creeping down the legs towards Nish's limp form, many small shapes like saucer-sized lice.

This was the fatal moment. Nish was lost and, even if she got away from the rider, Vomix's troops must track her down. Her only hope was to implode her taphloid. Maelys hesitated, though only for a second. She couldn't go much further. There was a stitch in her side and her knees were giving out.

She jerked on the chain as she ran, tearing the taphloid from between her bound breasts and pulling it over her head, recalling the way Aunt Haga had instructed her to implode the crystal inside it. But that would cost her the only treasure she had left . . . She darted back towards the rising flappeter as Hinneltyne came at her. Nish was struggling now, the lice swarming on him. And the taphloid held secrets she'd need later on. She pressed its hidden catch, shook out the crystal and thrust the now-dead taphloid back where it came from. She shot a glance over her shoulder.

The rider was only a few paces behind, grinning as if already counting his reward. Not if she could help it! Maelys thought herself into the heart of the crystal as she'd been taught, then imagined turning it inside-out and all the power stored within it long ago vanishing in a burst of fury. Come on, crystal, come on! Hinneltyne threw himself at her but she ducked again and darted the other way, skidding on gravel. At last the crystal grew hot in her hand. Spinning on one foot, she hurled it down onto a rock directly between herself and the rider.

The crystal cracked and red fire glowed along the crack lines, though it was instantly sucked inside with a zipping sound. The crystal burst asunder, setting off a *disruption* that rang through the air in all directions, sending a flurry of enigmatic images through her mind. A spear of pain wiped the images out of memory before she could take them in. She lost a few seconds and came to, staggering across the mountainside with the moon glaring into her eyes.

The rider was crouched ten paces away, holding his head between his hands, swaying from one foot to the other and moaning piteously. Where was Nish? She couldn't see the flappeter. Had it gone already?

Something made a shuddering, sucking gurgle above and behind her; there came a series of violent flutter-flaps and she whirled to see the flappeter spinning wildly, now on its side, now upside down and desperately trying to stay in the air. The feather-rotors tangled and it crashed into the slope, rolled over, still holding Nish between its bristly legs, and lay still.

Had she killed it? Surely not; it hadn't fallen far, nor all that hard. Nish was struggling weakly but didn't seem able to free himself from the barbed hooks that ran up its legs. She watched it warily, afraid to approach in case it caught her too.

Maelys didn't want to go near it, for it was powerful enough to tear her legs off, but this was her only chance to free Nish. Dare she try? Taking that first step required what little courage she had left. She was willing herself to take another when Rider Hinneltyne groaned and forced himself to his feet. He reeled towards her, teeth bared in a grimace of agony, eyes like luminous holes in the moonlight. The disruption had hurt him badly but nothing short of death could make him give up such a prize.

Maelys wasn't used to thinking on her feet and instead of

bolting, she froze. He fumbled a knife from a belt sheath – a long, curving blade with something shining in the hilt, and held it up so she could see it. It matched the unnerving glitter of his eyes, but now something was wrong; he didn't look like the same man at all.

Hinneltyne lurched towards her, swaying from side to side, the knife hacking at the air. What was the matter with him? He was acting like a man insanely determined to kill her, despite Vomix's orders. The disruption must have robbed him of his wits, much as the earlier mindstorm had done to Nish.

The flappeter reared up to her left and let out a shrill cry of pain, whereupon the rider fell to his knees, mouth gaping, his cry echoing its suffering. Could rider and flappeter be linked in some way, so that each felt the other's pain?

She had to attack while he was down. Maelys threw herself at him and managed to wrest the knife out of his trembling hand, but before she could get away his eyes focussed and he swung the other fist, cracking her on the jaw so hard that it knocked her sideways.

Tears sprang to her eyes as she fell, jaw throbbing. Her head spun. She scrambled away blindly on hands and knees, the knife clacking on the stony ground, nearly dropping it as she came to her feet and ran. He hurled a stone at her. It just missed – he seemed to be recovering his coordination.

Maelys was on her last gasp and couldn't run any more. She turned, watching him warily. He hurled another stone, which caught her below the breastbone, knocking the wind out of her. She doubled over, wheezing.

He moved a few steps towards her, only to stumble as the flappeter let out another cry. Maelys backed away, though this time he rose at once, looking even more witless, and hurled another stone at her face. She wove out of the way but it cracked into her upraised left elbow and her arm went numb. Maelys forced herself on, sobbing with pain and terror. Where was the knife? She'd dropped it. She grabbed it with her good hand as the rider came for her, big hands out-stretched, eyes fixed on her throat, snarling like a beast. If she didn't stop him he was going to kill her. It was a life-changing moment. Maelys had never contemplated harming anyone before, but there was no choice now.

She took a wild slash at his hands. He swayed out of the way, then kicked out at the knife, catching her on her numb fingers. He kicked again, trying to knock the knife out of her hand, but missed and the blade skated across his shinbone. He gasped; the flappeter reared up, letting out a sympa-thetic wail, and he convulsed, but shook off the momentary loss of coordination and went for her throat again. Maelys's knees were giving out; she couldn't last another minute.

He must have been trained in knife fighting for he avoided each slash easily, slow though he was. She swiped at his hand, missed; brought the knife up and hacked down at him. He knocked her arm out of the way, carelessly, con-temptuously. Hinneltyne wasn't afraid of her, and suddenly Maelys ran out of steam. She watched him come, knowing he was going to take her and unable to do anything about it.

He laughed wildly, lunged. His big hands encircled her neck and his thumbs dug into her windpipe, trying to crush it. She gasped, flailed wildly, knowing she was doomed, then more by luck than skill got a wicked hack into his corded neck. The point of the blade went right through the jugular vein into his windpipe. Hinneltyne made a sucking gurgle, his fingers relaxed, and in a spray of blood he fell.

Six

Maelys reeled away and fell to the stony ground, unable to tear her eyes from the ghastly sight of the man she'd killed. The blood flow was just a trickle now, but his severed windpipe was still sucking and bubbling. His arms and legs twitched and went still; the sucking stopped, then in the distance she made out a shrill keening as if the flappeter was grieving for its rider who would link with it no more.

She'd killed a man; taken a life. Nothing would ever be the same. Maelys rolled over onto her back. She felt awful. Her jaw ached, her chest and stomach were a mass of pain, her throat was bruised and as the life returned to her numb forearm she felt a sharp pain in her right index finger where he'd kicked her. It felt broken.

The flappeter wasn't moving now, but neither was Nish, still trapped between its legs. She was making her way to him when she noticed a light, a long way down the mountain to her left. No, a line of lights – the troops Seneschal Vomix had sent.

The flappeter lay still, its breathing tubes squelching every so often. Mucous dripped from them and the acrid stink was stronger here. 'Nish?' she said softly.

He mumbled something incomprehensible. He was held within a tepee of four or five legs, each the length of a tall man. They were no thicker than her wrist, and covered in a horny substance through which wiry bristles protruded at intervals, terminating in retractable hooks. A series of thorny outgrowths, each the length of her little finger, ran up the front of each leg, and Nish was caught in these.

As she tried to pull him out, something bit her on the little finger. Maelys jerked her hand away but the giant louse didn't let go; its fangs were still embedded in her finger. She brought the knife up sharply, skewered it through the back and flicked it away. Her finger was burning now.

Nish was covered in the creatures; dozens were crawling across his face, trying to push into his mouth and probing at his nostrils. She dropped the knife and attempted to ease the flappeter's legs out of the way. They were rigid, as if the muscles had locked when the creature collapsed, but by heaving with the weight of her body she managed to pull them apart.

She was bitten three more times before she had formed a gap large enough to ease Nish out, wiggling him this way and that to free him from the snagging thorns. She dragged him a few steps and checked on the lights, which were noticeably closer. And what if Vomix got hold of another flappeter? Panic rose at the thought but she choked it down and went at Nish's giant lice with her knife, flicking them off and stamping on them. After she'd killed a few the rest scuttled back to the flappeter.

Nish had been bitten many times. His face was dotted with little flecks of blood and rising lumps. She felt him over, front and back, making sure that none of the creatures had hidden inside his clothes or forced themselves into his mouth.

'Nish, the soldiers are coming up the mountain. Can you walk?'

'Gruummmp!' He didn't move, and when she heaved him to his feet his legs collapsed. He was really cold; he could die of exposure higher up. And without her coat, so might she.

She pushed up his eyelid; his eye stared blankly out.

Maelys felt sick. What else could she do? Yet a little core of defiance remained in her. She couldn't bear to think of Fyllis in the God-Emperor's hands; she had to keep going.

The rider's leathers were fur-lined, just what Nish needed. Trying to avoid looking at the mess she'd made of Hinneltyne, she began to strip off his jacket. It was bloody down the front, stank of sweat and swam on Nish. She put her own coat back on. Maelys considered Hinneltyne's pants, couldn't face the thought of removing them, then decided that she was in no position to be squeamish.

She pulled them down over his massive thighs. It was surprisingly hard work, for he had gone floppy and it was difficult to lift his legs. After hacking the pants legs to the right length she dressed Nish in the leathers, pulled the sleeves down over his hands and folded the ends back in.

Maelys took Hinneltyne's boots, mittens and belt, ran it around her waist twice and buckled it on. The mittens would be useful if she did get away. He wore no rings or money belt, though below the ragged opening in his throat a leather thong ran down into his blood-matted chest hair. Something glowed faintly green there.

Drawing it out by its thong, she wiped the blood off on a fold of the rider's undershirt. It was a little oval brooch or amulet whose shape vaguely reminded her of a flappeter, though its jade eyes were slanted rather than spherical and the feather-rotors were represented only by indentations.

The body of the amulet was metal, perhaps brass, with intricate patterns which she couldn't make out in this light. It had four pairs of hinged metal legs folded beneath it. The horned head, and the tail, were also tucked under. As she cleaned it the glow from its jade eyes faded, though it did not entirely go out.

She touched the underside of the amulet with a fingertip. Her head spun and the skin over her entire body burned, as if little flames had sprung up there. White streaks flashed in her inner eye then her head steadied and the burning sensation faded to a hot tingle that fluttered back and forth before slowly disappearing.

The flappeter sucked in a gurgling breath, its legs twitched and flexed, and she felt a dull pain in her right elbow. Now she sensed a simmering alien rage – surely the creature's rage at the loss of its rider. The amulet must have made a mental link between her and it, and she had an insane idea. Could she take command of it, even escape on it?

Maelys shied away from the idea. She'd never been brave or daring. As a kid, while the other children had been off on rambles, diving from rocks into hidden pools or walking across ravines on tree trunks, she'd preferred to sit under a tree, reading or daydreaming. But this time she was going to take command of her situation. She had to.

She touched the amulet again. Once more the flappeter gave a small cry, though this time Maelys didn't feel anything unusual. She went to the fallen beast, gingerly. Its legs were still tangled and jerking spasmodically, as if the disruption had also affected its coordination and it couldn't work out how to untangle them. She studied the pairs of legs, biting her lip, afraid to touch the beast since it had regained consciousness. And the soldiers' lights were much closer now.

Hauling Nish onto the rear saddle of the flappeter between the saddle horn and a pair of saddlebags, she tied him on with a coil of thin rope looped there. Her broken finger was swelling but there wasn't time to attend to it. She jammed Nish's feet into the rider's fur-lined boots and tied them above the ankles so they wouldn't come off. Taking hold of one of the flappeter's legs, she tried to ease it out of the way. It resisted, then suddenly gave. As she fell forwards, it snapped back from the knee joint, thumping her in the midriff.

Maelys landed hard, hurting all over. Had it attacked because she'd touched it, or because she wasn't its rider? Its

71

legs were clacking against each other as they thrashed, its long body heaving sinuously and the scales making a dry rustle.

Rolling onto its side, it forced itself to five or six of its feet and gave a little stagger like a newborn calf. Its long neck curved around and it stared at Maelys for a moment, then bent its legs, snapped them straight and shot into the air. The lower feather-rotor spun, the creature hovered, then the top rotor turned as well and it began to climb.

Maelys cried out in dismay. It was going to fly away with Nish, back to its master. She ran a couple of steps and shouted, stupidly, 'Come back!' It lifted out of reach but suddenly the upper feather-rotor jammed and, emitting a shrill wail, it crashed back to ground. Again she felt that twinge in her elbow, though sharper this time – *its pain*.

She approached it, careful of teeth, tail and legs. One of the feathered blades of the top rotor was sticking up. It had landed on it earlier and must have damaged the blade in the fall. If it couldn't fly, all was lost.

Maelys had never been closer to giving up than at that moment. She'd been thrown headfirst into a violent world she knew nothing about, where none of her skills were much use, and nothing she did made a difference in the end, so what was the point? Why not leave Nish and run for her life; there was a tiny chance she'd get away.

Why not? Because she'd given her word and that was sacred to her. Her father lay dying in Mazurhize because he'd refused to break his promise and betray a friend, so how could she do otherwise? The thought of being taken, though, of Seneschal Vomix's all-seeing eyes roving across her body, his slimy fingers all over her, was almost enough to make her change her mind. No! She would keep trying, to the very end.

Could she do anything for the beast? Maelys had been looking after animals all her life, because the care and health of an estate's stock, birds, fish and bees was vital to its

72

survival and prosperity. Though she'd never seen a flap-peter before, there might be a way to gain its confidence.

Moving slowly towards it, keeping in clear sight of the compound eyes, she began to hum, just three notes, the deepest she could manage, shifting smoothly from one to the next. It watched her with that unblinking insect-like stare, but when she was only a few paces away the elongated tail whipped around and would have broken her legs had she not sprung out of the way.

Any injured creature might have done the same but at least she understood farm animals. The flappeter, however, was Jal-Nish's creature, perhaps made in his image, and she couldn't hope to gain its trust so quickly. Even horses had to be broken to the saddle and that took ages. But time was short, and if she was going to be caught she'd sooner be killed by this alien monstrosity than by Jal-Nish's torturers.

Flappeters were rare and valuable. There were only a few of them and if one's rider were sick or injured, surely another rider must be able to use it. The amulet might be the key. Taking it from her pocket, she squeezed it in her hand as the rider had. Its folded metal legs gave a twitch, the glow of the jade eyes brightened fractionally and she sensed the flappeter's rage and pain once more. It drew breath hard, then raised its long neck to study her, and Maelys sensed that something had changed between them.

Clutching the amulet tightly, she approached the tail. The neck bent, the eyes following her all the way, but this time it allowed her near. Good so far. She rifled through the saddlebags, looking for anything she could use to tend its injuries. She found food, spare clothing, a tent, bedroll and camping gear. Could the tent pegs be used to splint the rotor blade? She didn't think she could tie them on tightly enough.

At the top of the food bag lay three forearm-length sections of bamboo or cane, full of a sweet, sticky juice whose smell made her salivate. She poked the knife through one and licked her fingers. It was sweeter than honey, but fermented and strongly spirituous.

Slipping the sections under her arm, she tore one of the rider's shirts into rags, cut more strips from the surplus leather, peed into his mug and soaked the strips in it. Holding the amulet again, she climbed onto the front saddle and caught hold of the sheathed stalk. The lower feather-rotor was at her shoulder height while standing up, the upper one above her head. The moon was bright now and she could see that the damaged rotor blade had a distinct bend; either a break in the bone (assuming this creature had bones), a greenstick fracture or at best a bad sprain.

The flappeter's body was covered in thick scales but each rotor blade had a thin, leathery skin out of which the feathers were extruded from horny collars. As she felt the hot swelling of the injury the flappeter let out a ringing cry and tried to heave her off.

She hooked her arm around the stalk and hung on until the beast went still, trying to work out how to fix the injury so it could fly. Had it been any normal farm animal she would have known, but the flappeter had been created by the abominable evil of flesh-forming, from the bones, tissues and organs of any number of creatures, fashioned to suit the God-Emperor's perverted whim.

A cry echoed up the slope. Could the troops have seen her? The lanterns were surrounded by mist haloes now, so probably not, but there wasn't time to think things through. All she could do was let her fingers work instinctively. If she could get the creature into the air and away, even for half a league, it would give her a faint chance.

Maelys hung the thong around her neck and thrust the amulet deep into her cleavage, hoping that skin contact would suffice. As she felt along the injury the flappeter writhed and its tail arched up towards her. She hastily pulled her shoulders forward, compressing her breasts until she felt the warmth of the amulet between them. The metal legs

74

unfolded against her left breast and she nearly screamed. It felt like a huge, hard spider there. Maelys drew a deep breath, clenched her fists and restrained the urge to claw it out and bat it away into the darkness. After a long, shuddering moment the flappeter relaxed and the metal legs slowly folded again.

She wiped her brow, then, trying to maintain pressure on the amulet, began to manipulate the feathered blade. She was used to working by feel; it was ages since her family had been able to afford candles.

The blade wasn't broken, for it didn't have bones at all. Beneath the skin and feathers was a flattened, horny shell like the leg of a crab, though it was as flexible as a thumbnail. An oddly hinged joint in the middle was dislocated and felt badly sprained. She eased it back, ignoring the creature's flinch, allowing the internal tendons to pull the joint together then rotating the two sections this way and that until she could feel them slipping into place.

That was the easy part. Now she had to immobilise the joint so it would not dislocate under the strain of flying, yet allow the blade to rotate as it should, with as little pain as possible. No simple splint could do that, for even if she bound it on so tightly that it cut off the circulation it would eventually fail, and if that happened in the air they would die. But perhaps a two-part splint might serve.

She split one piece of bamboo in two and rubbed its spirituous contents over the lacerated area around the dislocation; it would help to stop it becoming infected. After carving out the ends to fit perfectly over the blade she padded the insides with cloth. The flappeter was stirring and the metal legs of the amulet twitching again, so she swiftly bound the bamboo on with the strips of pee-soaked leather, stretching them as tightly as she could. As the wet leather dried it would shrink, binding the bamboo on more tightly.

Maelys felt the repair; it was as good as she could manage. She slid back to Nish, who was still comatose, though warmer than he had been before, and breathing steadily. Time to go, assuming she could make the flappeter move.

She slid forwards into the rider's saddle, drew the amulet out, squeezed it in her fist and said, 'Go, flappeter.'

It didn't move. 'Fly!' It did not react at all. 'Get going, beast!' Then, 'Please.' It just stood there on its many legs, its neck turned, staring at her with those paired eyes.

Was she supposed to call it by name? Hinneltyne had used its name when speaking to Vomix but Maelys couldn't remember it. *Rurr*- something. Or was she supposed to say a prayer to the God-Emperor first, or give a special order or signal? It could be anything. How was she supposed to prevail over its alien consciousness?

There didn't seem any way to find out. Maelys slumped in the saddle, feeling her suppressed panic rising again, and watching the soldiers' lanterns creep ever nearer, when she noticed a brain-like protuberance at the back of the creature's elongated skull.

It looked rather like a second brain grafted onto the first, and arising from it was, unmistakeably, a little loop-listener, its faintly luminous bile-green noose no bigger than a rat's neck. The dark specks within the loop were still now. The rider had leaned forwards and spoken to Vomix through it. Could Vomix have ordered the flappeter to keep her here until the troops arrived?

Behind the loop-listener was a small, fleshy bowl, from the centre of which rose, on a stub of stalk, a round disc filled with shimmering threads. At first she thought it was a kind of wisp-watcher, though it didn't have an iris. The threads appeared to be in random motion, and neither was it making that characteristic buzz.

Suddenly the specks inside the dangling loop began to sparkle. 'Hinneltyne, where are you? Report immediately.' It was Seneschal Vomix.

So the front organ wasn't a loop-listener at all, but something greater and more dangerous. Maelys had no name for it but would call it a speck-speaker. Hinneltyne had used it to talk to Vomix. And when Hinneltyne didn't answer, what would Vomix do? Try to take direct command of the flappeter?

The flappeter's head reared around at her and the serrated jaws opened, though then it seemed to hesitate as if waiting for an order which hadn't come. 'Don't!' she whispered, foolishly. The speck-speaker shimmered, sending her words to Vomix and, thoughtlessly, sure he'd ordered the beast to attack, Maelys whipped her knife out and severed the loop from its stalk.

Something that wasn't blood spurted out, yellow-grey in the bright moonlight. The flappeter screeched and lurched sideways, its hooked feet scrabbling on the stony ground. The metal legs of the amulet snapped out and it scuttled across her left breast, over the nipple then down towards her armpit before it was brought up by the thong. This time Maelys did shriek; she couldn't stop herself.

The flow ebbed, the wound skinned over and the pressure in her mind diminished so suddenly that she almost fell out of the saddle. The flappeter's rage eased as well, although now she felt its overwhelming grief at the death of the rider it had been bonded with. No, not so much grief as *loss*. The bond with its rider had made it complete, and if it didn't soon replace that bond it would go mad. Had she freed it from Vomix's shackles only to torment it unbearably?

The amulet bent its legs, clinging by their points to the outside of her breast. She plucked it out and was reaching towards the wisp-device with the knife, wondering if she should cut it away as well, when an intimation made her draw back. What if that were the way the beast was controlled by the rider? She recalled Hinneltyne thrusting his fist forwards a couple of times, and once it had seemed to disappear. She clenched the amulet in her fist and thrust it through the wisp-filled circle.

Her fist disappeared, then fire ran along her nerve endings all the way up her arm, around the back of her head and into her skull, and Maelys experienced the strangest feeling of *connection*, as if she were an extension of the great beast she was mounted on. She felt many things: its core-deep pain for its dead rider; a dull ache from the splinted rotor blade; a sharp pain and a sense of loss from the stub of the severed speck-speaker; a dull emptiness in its gut, and other emotions too dark and alien for her to comprehend.

She heard shouts now, and about twenty soldiers appeared out of the fog a few hundred paces away, plodding in their heavy armour up the slope.

'Go, Flappeter!' she cried, whipping her hand out.

Are you taking on Hinneltyne's contract, little one? said a deep, shivery voice inside her head. She looked up to see its eyes fixed on her. The moonlight reflected off them in geometric patterns.

Maelys didn't know what to say. Presumably *contract* meant the bond between flappeter and rider. No time to think; she had to take the risk. 'Yes, yes! I'm taking on the contract.' She felt its relief; its pain and loss seemed to ease.

Are you strong enough? You seem young and callow to me.

'I killed your rider.' Why had she said that? 'I cut you free of Vomix. I fixed your rotor blade. I'm strong.'

You'd better be, for if you falter I'll devour you and take the amulet for myself. You do know that, don't you?

'But you owe me –'

Never make the mistake of thinking I'm human. I was made without any human frailties. I owe you nothing.

'Then why are you talking instead of eating me?'

It didn't answer. It must need her for the moment, though she was worried about the consequences of cutting off the speck-speaker. Had that weakened it? Or by ridding it of the bond to Vomix, and perhaps Jal-Nish, had she offered it the chance of freedom?

'What's your name, flappeter?'

My name is Rurr-shyve, amulet-bearer.

'Go, Rurr-shyve,' she said desperately. 'Take us to Hulipont, please.'

Hool . . . eee . . . ponttt . . .

It didn't move and her panic was rising again. Threats were no way to get the best out of a creature, though Rurr-shyve was a monster created by the God-Emperor to oppress people, and perhaps threats and brute force were the only things it understood.

An arrow whistled overhead. The soldiers were just within range; soon their marksmen would be able to pick her off. Maelys thrust her fist through the circle of the wisp-controller, feeling the heat grow along her arm and the inside of her skull warming up. 'Go to Hulipont, Rurr-shyve!' she said in the most commanding voice she could manage.

She raised her hand and felt the thin legs flex. They folded down until she could have stepped onto the ground, then snapped upright, catapulting the flappeter three or four spans into the air with such force that the blood drained away from her skull. Her belly churned, she tried desperately to avoid throwing up, then the lower feather-rotor began to spin, the upper one too, scooping the air down in huge blasts. It was like standing in a gale. The flappeter shot higher but it didn't turn north, in the direction of distant Hulipont. It began to head east, directly towards the God-Emperor's palace, and though Maelys wriggled her hand this way and that in the wisp-controller until every nerve in her body was singing, she could not divert it from its path.

SEVEN

Maelys had tried reasoning, and failed; she had even pleaded with Rurr-shyve, but it had cut itself off from her. How Jal-Nish must be sneering at her frantic efforts to escape. What pleasure he must have taken from the foolish hopes she'd raised after overcoming each new obstacle. Perhaps he'd allowed her to do so, knowing that her final, irrevocable failure would be all the more crushing.

There was one last way to frustrate him. It wasn't in her to harm Nish, and Maelys was now resigned to Rurr-shyve taking him back to his father, but she might still save her family if she had the courage for it. If she threw herself off the flappeter from a great height her body would be unrecognisable.

Suicide was such a terrible wrong that Maelys could barely contemplate it. Not in the worst of times had she fallen prey to despair, and she wouldn't choose death to avoid the God-Emperor's torturers; it wasn't in her nature. But if there were no other way to save her family, did duty require her to take her life? It was a question her simple moral outlook wasn't equipped to answer, though if Jal-Nish took her alive he'd soon torture the names of her family out of her.

Maelys couldn't see any alternative but to die. After all, she would defend her little sister with her life, and that would be accounted a noble sacrifice. Was defending Fyllis by taking her own life so very different? She felt that it was. The one was showing courage in the face of desperate odds, the other, taking the easy way out. Yet if her survival meant Fyllis being tortured, surely Maelys had to make the sacrifice . . .

She didn't want to die. She'd do anything to escape such a fate. The flappeter was so high now that in the distance she could see the pinpoints of the lights of Morrelune. The flight wouldn't take long and there was no point putting off her end, in case Jal-Nish took steps to prevent it. She had to do it now . . .

But first she must make sure Nish was all right and say goodbye, even if he couldn't hear her. She couldn't go without doing that. Slipping her feet out of the stirrups, Maelys climbed backwards over the saddle horn, hanging onto the straps as Rurr-shyve bounced on the air currents. The moon was high now, shining on Nish's face. He looked younger, more at peace, and cleaner too. Immersion in the pond had soaked the worst of the filth off him.

His cheek was cold but his throat was warm, and so were his feet inside the fur-lined boots. He would survive, a small miracle in itself. If only he wasn't going back to his father. Well, she'd done her best and it hadn't been enough, but that was how things were fated to be.

Maelys turned away bleakly, turned back and, on a whim, bent and kissed Nish on the lips. It was the most shocking liberty, one that made her cheeks grow hot, but even a condemned prisoner was allowed one last request.

As she sat back, Nish's eyes opened, he looked up at her sleepily and smiled. 'Maelys,' he said, and the name was like poetry on his lips. 'You saved my life.' He sat up, looking around in wonder, and his voice grew stronger. 'You stole a flappeter from its rider, and you're *flying* it?'

'He – he came at me with a knife. It was sheer luck that I – I killed him.' She couldn't bear to think about it.

'But only a trained, *talented* rider can compel a flappeter. Are you a mancer, hidden from my father all this time?'

'I'm just an ordinary gir– boy.' She hoped he hadn't noticed her slip, though it didn't matter now. 'I – I'm sorry, Nish. I did everything I could but I've failed. I – goodbye.' She turned to climb over the saddle horn but he caught her arm.

'What are you doing?'

She pointed dumbly towards the lights. 'I can't control the flappeter and it's taking us back to Morrelune. If I'm identified, you know what the God-Emperor will do to Fyllis. I've – I've got to jump . . .'

He didn't let go. 'No you don't.'

'But it's my duty.'

'I understand all about duty, Maelys, *and the way people use it against you*. We're not finished yet. It'll take half an hour to get to Morrelune in this headwind. How did you take command of the beast?'

A wave of relief washed over her. Nish had been a leader of men; he'd know what to do. She hastily explained how she'd splinted the feather-rotor blade and compelled the flappeter into the air. 'I was going to cut off its wisp-controller too, in case your father could use it to take control from afar. Perhaps I should have.'

'If you did that it might not be able to fly.' He thought for a moment, then said in a low voice, 'My guards often talked about flappeters. Of all Father's created creatures, they're the wildest and most wilful beasts; they don't even serve *him* willingly. He should never have given them intelligence. They resent the bridle; sometimes they refuse to obey and he's had to threaten them.'

'How?' asked Maelys listlessly, watching the lights of Morrelune come ever closer as the flappeter descended, and feeling a pain in the pit of her stomach.

'I don't remember,' said Nish, oblivious to her torment.

She was glad about that. It had nothing to do with him and she didn't want him trying to talk her out of what she must do. Maelys began to ease her boots from the stirrups, took a deep breath and tried to go calmly and with dignity. Old people, children and even babies were robbed of life every day. Her death did not matter. There wouldn't be any pain.

But I don't want to die! It was a scream from the depths of her being. She clenched her fists on the saddle horn and tried to ignore it.

'Severing!' cried Nish.

'What?' She settled back in the saddle. The question and answer would gain her another minute.

'The guards said Father had threatened reluctant flappeters with *severing*.'

'Severing what?' she asked quietly, so Rurr-shyve wouldn't hear.

'I don't know.'

Maelys turned forwards to study the flappeter in the moonlight, then lowered her voice until it could barely be heard above the *thup-thup* of the feather-rotors. 'Rurr-shyve spoke into my mind and told me its name, so perhaps Jal-Nish meant severing their consciousness. No intelligent beast could bear that.'

'Yes, that must be the answer. But how would Father do it?'

Maelys was staring blankly at the bulbous protuberance at the back of the flappeter's skull, like a second brain grafted behind the first, when it hit her. 'What if that's a second brain for flight, or consciousness? The two must be connected in some way, and if they were cut apart –'

She gave Nish a meaningful look, wanting him to take charge and do this terrible thing to Rurr-shyve, but he flopped backwards in his saddle, white-faced under the water-smeared dirt. He was having a relapse.

'I – I'd better do it then,' she said.

'Tie on first,' he said faintly. 'Flappeter – won't like it.'

She tied the last of the thin rope around her waist, checked the knots twice, then fastened the free end to a ring

83

on her saddle. Maelys inched forwards until she could reach the bulge, but as soon as she drew the knife Rurr-shyve bucked wildly and turned upside down.

Maelys, taken by surprise, fell off and heard the line creaking as her weight pulled on it. If it gave, all her troubles would be over. Her head hung just above the whirling feather-rotor and if it struck her she'd die.

The knot pulled so tightly around her waist that she could scarcely draw breath. The flappeter was falling, the feather-rotors now driving it down. They stopped then spun the other way, whereupon Rurr-shyve let out a cry, its pain setting up sympathetic echoes in Maelys's mind.

The damaged feather-rotor slowed; the other one sped up to compensate and the flappeter flew on, upside down. Perhaps Rurr-shyve wasn't game to try another manoeuvre in case the injured blade gave. She wiped her brow, then noted the thin legs unfolding, the hooks and barbs extending. They couldn't get her from here, but once the beast turned right-side up, leaving her hanging beneath, they'd have her.

She sheathed the knife and locked the thong over it so it wouldn't fall out. Gripping her lifeline in both hands, she watched the flappeter carefully. Nish's eyes were on her but he was too weak to help.

The lower rotor reversed; Rurr-shyve doubled up its long body and twisted so as to come upright. As it rolled, she heaved on the lifeline with all her strength, slammed into the saddle and clung desperately to it. But she couldn't stop to get her breath; she had to do it now, else sooner or later Rurr-shyve would rid itself of her.

Scrambling up its neck, she whipped out the knife, raised it high then stabbed it into the valley between its skull and the protuberance. The knife cut through the horny scales, sank in the length of her little finger and stuck. Rurr-shyve let out a shivering peal of agony that reverberated up and down her nerve fibres. Maelys hung on with her thighs, snatched out the legged amulet with her free hand and thrust it backwards through the wisp-controller. Pressing down on the knife, she shouted. 'Stop, Rurr-shyve! Stop or be *severed!*'

The flappeter went still, apart from a thrumming of its folded legs against its lower body and a quivering of the discs on its tail, then hovered on its spinning feather-rotors. She could feel the great muscles that drove them clenching and contracting between her thighs.

Who are you, little Maelys? The voice in her mind was far more menacing this time.

She raised the knife. 'Wh–what do you mean?'

I only took you on because you had the same aura as Rider Hinneltyne. Lacking that aura, I would have torn your head off and sucked your brains out through your nostrils.

It pronounced the last word as *nossstrrillllsssss*, and Maelys shuddered. 'But you offered me his contract.'

No, I asked if you were taking it on. But his aura is gone now. You deceived me, little Maelys. Only people with a talent for the Art produce an aura, and every aura is unique, so how could you have Hinneltyne's then, and now none at all?

'I have no idea,' she said, feeling as though she were sinking ever deeper into a pit. 'I know nothing about auras and I don't have a trace of talent.' Yet if that were true, how had she commanded Rurr-shyve, and how could she hear its mindspeech now? 'All I did was break my crystal –'

And killed my rider! Rurr-shyve hissed. *You broke the bond between us: you hurt me cruelly as you severed his contract. And without his aura, your contract is null.*

'What are you going to do with me?' she whispered, understanding nothing save the dreadful peril she was in. The balance of power between them had shifted again and she couldn't see how to get it back.

I don't know, little Maelys. It cocked its head as it hovered, slyly observing her. *I can't say how long it will take.*

'What . . . do you mean?' She sounded like a mewling kitten. She had to take control and she had to do it now.

To learn all I need to know about you – all you're good for . . .

It was playing with her mind and she had to stop it. She pressed the knife down again, hard enough to hurt. 'But you did take the contract on, Rurr-shyve, and you can't repudiate it now that a bond has formed between us.'

Rurr-shyve spun in a tight circle, so fast that she felt dizzy. *How little you know about contracts, or flappeters.*

This time she jammed the knife right in, and gritted, 'Turn around. Head west until we're out of sight, then north for Hulipont. Any diversion, any tricks and I'll sever you.'

It was probably too late, but there was still a chance that poor Cathim had held out, or had died before revealing the destination. If she could reach Hulipont quickly there was still a tiny hope for Nish, and her family.

Rurr-shyve said no more, but Maelys could feel the creature's rage in every thump of the rotors. Its breathing had taken on a raspier squelch, its underside gave off visible pulses of the stinkbug stench which had burned her nose earlier, and its tail kept curling out as if to sweep her off. It hated its creator, but it hated her even more, and if it ever got the chance it would make her pay.

However, Rurr-shyve did what she'd demanded. It turned, steepened the angle of its feather-rotors and climbed away from Morrelune, west up the slope of the mountain. Once the lights of the palace disappeared, Rurr-shyve turned north.

She experimented with the wisp-controller. Raising or lowering her palm compelled the flappeter to climb or descend, while right or left motions directed it to starboard or port. It didn't want to obey, and she could sense its resistance all the time, but for the moment it seemed to have no choice.

Flying the flappeter proved to be exhausting, both physically and mentally. Even when she wasn't actively directing Rurr-shyve, Maelys could feel the mental strain of the bond between them, and she had to concentrate every minute.

She was quite desperately tired now, for it could not be long until dawn, and every bone and muscle ached. Even so, she could not relax in case she went to sleep. Her bitten finger was swollen like a sausage and her myriad bruises throbbed. She had splinted her broken finger as best she could, using strips of leather and a piece of bamboo, but it hurt all the time.

Nish was sleeping again. She extracted a couple of biscuits from her pack by feel and nibbled at them as they flew north. She'd been too busy to notice the cold since the flappeter appeared, but now it struck her to the bone, and the higher Rurr-shyve climbed the worse it became. If she'd been riding a horse it would have helped to keep her warm, but this creature was as cold as a corpse.

Maelys pulled her coat around herself, envying Nish the fur-lined leathers and his being able to sleep. Remembering the mittens, she pulled them on, which helped, and drew the collar up around the back of her neck.

Her eyes slipped closed; her head drooped. She raised it drowsily, realised that she'd almost fallen asleep and shook herself. If she so much as dozed the flappeter would turn back. Her lids drooped again. She was so tired that not even the cold could keep her awake. She pinched her arm, twisted and looked around.

And jumped, for a pair of bulbous green eyes were shining behind her. She blinked, rubbed her eyes and looked again. Nothing. She was imagining things. Nonetheless, she turned Rurr-shyve sharply, just in case.

Nish let out a wail and began to struggle against the cords holding him in his saddle. As Maelys turned to see what the matter was, with a *thapper-thapper-thap* another flappeter shot past, so close that she felt the icy blast from its feather-rotors. It had come out of nowhere and disappeared the same way.

Leaning forwards, Maelys tapped her knife on the protuberance, then thrust the amulet through the wisps and said, 'Fly, Rurr-shyve. Fly for your very life.'

She felt a tingle of alien laughter and Rurr-shyve sent, *My life isn't in danger, little Maelys*, but it put its head down and the feather-rotors spun a little faster.

Dread made pinpricks across the backs of her hands. How did it know her name? Because Nish had said it earlier. And Maelys had also mentioned Fyllis. The two names would be enough to identify her family, so she couldn't let Rurr-shyve go at Hulipont. Would she have to kill it too? How quickly her sheltered life had changed.

'Perhaps not your life,' she lied to the beast, 'but your consciousness is at risk.' She raised the knife.

Rurr-shyve blasted a pungently green, eye-stinging mist at her. She covered her eyes until it had dispersed, then looked back nervously. It didn't seem possible that they could have lost the other flappeter so easily, though she could see no sign of it. She checked the angle of the moon through the filmy cloud. They were still heading north, at least.

Rurr-shyve broke into clear air and suddenly there were flappeters all around. She could see their big green eyes shining wherever she turned, four or five sets of them, and there was no way this injured beast could outrun them. 'Go down!' she yelled over the icy wind, expecting Rurr-shyve to refuse.

Down? Away from Hulipont?

She hesitated, but only for a second. If she headed directly for it they might guess the destination. 'Yes, away. Go low; see if you can find some fog.'

Rurr-shyve went into a vertical dive, dropping so fast that the wind tried to tug her out of the saddle and she had to whip a bight of her safety line around the saddle horn. Not far above the mountainside they plunged into mist, where Rurr-shyve levelled out and streaked away west. She wondered how it could fly safely in such conditions. Did it have additional senses, like a bat? Could other flappeters track it the same way?

She didn't see the pursuit again, and after half an hour of winding flight the mist disappeared and the sky began to grow light ahead of them. Rurr-shyve continued but, as dawn broke, four flappeters spiralled down out of the sky, their riders pointing crossbows at her.

Again Maelys froze; she just wasn't used to thinking on her feet. The mist had gone and the sky was free of cloud. There were mountains all around, their upper slopes bare rock and patches of ice and snow which offered no concealment. The flappeter gave a coughing grunt which appeared to indicate amusement.

'Forest,' said Nish.

'What?'

'Tell it to head for the forest.'

She looked where he was pointing, down into a deep valley winding between two towering peaks. The valley bottom still lay in darkness but a smudge on the lower slopes must be forest, stretching further than she could see.

'Go down to the forest, Rurr-shyve,' said Maelys.

It kept on until she tapped the flat of the knife on its scaly hide, then peeled off and dived, sending a spasm of sympathetic pain though her elbow at the strain on its injured rotor blade.

'Where does that valley lead?' she asked over her shoulder.

'I don't know,' said Nish. 'This isn't my country. But flappeters don't like flying through forest.'

'Why not?'

'It's too easy to get hurt – or killed.'

'I wouldn't think your father would care about that.' The instant Maelys spoke, she wished she hadn't mentioned Jal-Nish.

After an uncomfortable pause, Nish said, 'He'd order his

riders into any danger and they'd have to obey. But flappeters aren't so easily swayed. How can Father reward them; or punish them, for that matter? He needs them too much. They're difficult to create, he's only got a few and they're sensitive to each other's pain.'

'How do you know?'

'In the lowest level of Mazurhize there was nothing for my guards to do, and they talked about every topic that wasn't forbidden. Father liked people talking about flappeters – his most difficult and fearsome creation.'

Nish was right about their sensitivity. Maelys could feel the pain of Rurr-shyve's damaged rotor blade all the time now, and its brittle loss at Hinneltyne's death still nagged at her.

The light was growing stronger now, extending down into the great valley and touching the canopy of the looming forest. Spindly, windblown trees were scattered across the upper slopes, but further down they became giants. She saw no sign of habitation: no clearing, track or dwelling.

Rurr-shyve was straining, tiring. Its triple hearts were going thump-thump-thump, its feather-rotors creaking and, worryingly, a hot inflammation was growing at the site of the dislocation, which was stretching and contracting with every whirl of the rotor. The splint was working loose and sooner or later must give.

The sudden dive had taken their pursuit by surprise, allowing Rurr-shyve to gain ground, but the other flappeters were rapidly catching up. The leading beast was not far behind and its rider, a small, wiry man with a leathery countenance, was leaning sideways, half out of his saddle, pointing a crossbow around the feather-rotor stalk at her. The bow wavered back and forth but, with an irritated gesture, he thrust his hand through the loop-listener and urged his beast on.

'He's afraid he'll miss and hit Rurr-shyve,' said Nish. 'Or me.'

'But he's happy to kill *me*,' Maelys said dully.

'If that's what his master has ordered. Father rewards those who serve him well, but any failure, any mistake, any unfortunate accident incurs his wrath.'

The other three flappeters were spreading out to come at her from all sides. 'I'm doomed, then.'

'I see it as a weakness,' said Nish. 'His servants live in terror of making a mistake but, for most of them, that fear outweighs the hope of reward. It doesn't encourage them to show initiative. They follow orders and, when something goes wrong, the most cunning blame someone else.'

The wiry rider leaned out on the other side, the crossbow wobbling back and forth as he tried to find his target, but again he put it away.

'I don't suppose there's a crossbow in the saddlebags?' said Nish.

'I wouldn't know how to shoot one anyway. I've never –' She bit her lip. 'I'd never harmed a living person, before today.'

'I was good with a crossbow, once. Have a look.'

You're closer, and you're doing nothing! She bit down on the flash of irritation and felt backwards in the bags, not daring to take her eyes off Rurr-shyve. She encountered clothing, food packages, a hatchet and rope and, finally, tucked into a side pouch that she'd missed earlier, the wire and stock of a crossbow plus a lumpy bag of quarrels. She handed them to him.

Nish steadied the bow on his knee and began to turn the crank. He gave it three turns, jerked it a bit further, then stopped, looking up at her with such chagrin that she felt for him. He was too weak; there wasn't enough tension in the wire to send a quarrel from one end of the flappeter to the other.

'Look where you're going!' he snapped.

She turned hastily but there was no obstacle ahead of them, and if there had been, Rurr-shyve would have avoided it without any action on her part. Three of the flappeters

91

were close behind but slightly above, and couldn't fire for fear of hitting the feather-rotors. The fourth beast had gone out to her left, diving until it came level. Its rider was the wiry man who'd been aiming at her before, and she saw his savage grin, for she'd done exactly as he'd expected. He fired at her face.

Rurr-shyve jinked left again, the quarrel whirred past her left ear and the rider cursed. She jerked her hand to the right and Rurr-shyve shot directly into the path of the fourth flappeter, which darted upwards to avoid her, forcing the others to swerve wildly. Maelys dropped her wrist; Rurr-shyve put its long neck down and laboured for the trees.

She took it low and fast down the steep slope, which was dotted with trees between a series of great out-thrusting buttresses of stone. Unfortunately, the concealing forest was too far away. Three flappeters were still following and she wasn't going to make it.

'Give me the bow, quick!' she hissed.

He handed it forward, somewhat reluctantly. 'Have you ever used one, lad?'

'Of course not!' She held it as she'd seen him do and wound the crank. She managed two full turns then, forcing hard, another half turn, and a quarter, until the wire creaked. Maelys passed it back. 'Will that do?'

'How did you do that?' he muttered.

She'd shown him up and he didn't like it. 'Is it enough?'

'It's good. Nearly as good as I –'

'Can you – can you hit one of the riders?' More killing.

'I could have, once.'

A mad plan came to her. 'See that great rock stack down there?' It was the size of a small castle, with half a dozen jagged pinnacles on top, but she'd seen a narrow cleft between the uphill side and the mountain slope. 'I'm going to fly in low on the uphill side, dart through the cleft and, once we're hidden from view, turn suddenly and come at them over the top.'

'What if the cleft doesn't go all the way?' he said faintly.

She didn't answer, knowing if she thought it through she wouldn't have the courage to attempt it. 'As soon as we turn, be ready to fire.'

He looked back. 'They're only a few seconds behind.'

'Ready?'

'I'm ready,' he said hoarsely.

She squeezed the amulet hard and thrust her wrist through the loop, down and to the left. Rurr-shyve went hard left and she felt a sharp pain in her elbow at the stress on the rotor blade. She was gambling that the other flappeters wouldn't take the risk of following through the cleft; that they'd turn at the last minute and go around. They'd better. She could feel Rurr-shyve's resistance. It didn't like the look of the narrow passage, and nor did she. One mistake and they would die.

There was no choice and risks were meaningless now, but she could sense its fear. She tightened her will over Rurr-shyve, forcing it to obey the contract. They raced down, just skimming the slope, swerving around trees and over small outcrops. She flicked a glance over her shoulder. The other flappeters were closer. She tilted Rurr-shyve a fraction, heading directly for the cleft. She daren't look back now.

'What's going on, Nish?' she gasped.

He didn't answer. Then finally he said, 'They're going the other way.'

'Yes!' She curved Rurr-shyve down, fighting its impulse to avoid any situation that could injure it. The cleft was narrower than she'd thought; the feather-rotors were going to smash into the rock!

Rurr-shyve went sideways at the last second and Maelys drew her hand out. Her directions would only hinder it here. She let it fly on instinct, ducking as it wove along the winding cleft. Then they came around a corner and faced a solid wall of stone.

The pain in her head swelled enormously. Rurr-shyve let

out a cry; Nish shrieked, and Maelys felt as though her arm was being bent backwards at the elbow.

She cried out. The feather-rotors spun the other way, then Rurr-shyve straightened up and arched suddenly until its tail almost touched the back of its head. Maelys watched in horror, sure the rotors would smash into it. But the flappeter slowed suddenly, skimmed the lower part of the cleft, its leg pairs snapped straight against a boulder and they were catapulted vertically so hard that Maelys went dizzy.

Rurr-shyve shot up out of the cleft in a whirling cloud of feathers. Maelys clutched her stomach. Nish was white-faced. She directed the flappeter sharply to her right, her elbow throbbing, and they came hurtling up and over the top of the rock stack between the pinnacles as the other flappeters flashed past, below and to the right, one, two, three, flying nose to tail. She couldn't look back – she just prayed that Nish could do enough with his one shot to give the enemy a fright.

The crossbow snapped. For a moment she thought he'd missed completely, and so did he, for he groaned, but the thin rider on the leading beast slumped sideways and his hand must have flicked up as it slipped from the loop, for his flappeter tried to stand on its tail in mid-air. It slowed so rapidly that the one behind was too close to avoid it.

As it slammed into the first, the feather-rotors of the two beasts locked, then sheared off. The leading rider was already falling when a whirling blade cut him in half. The other man was sent flying into a boulder, head-first. The two beasts, still locked together, thundered into the slope further on, tumbling over and over and causing a minor avalanche before coming to rest in clouds of dust a few hundred spans further down.

The third flappeter let out a screech and shot left, narrowly missing a pinnacle, with its rider wailing in sympathetic pain. Maelys could feel it too – she hurt all over and felt the most crippling sense of loss, though she had no idea *what* she'd lost. How much worse must it be for flappeters and riders who'd been linked for years?

Nish passed the bow forwards; she wound it absently and circled above the rock stack, watching the remaining flappeter, which was wobbling in ragged spirals a few hundred spans away while its rider tried to regain control.

She pointed the crossbow at him, whereupon he weakly brandished a fist and turned away. Maelys headed down for the safety of the tall trees and, once they were a good half league into dense forest, brought Rurr-shyve to ground.

It stood there on shaky legs, its long neck drooping until it touched the ground. Its feather-rotors sagged. Their tips had been plucked bare and the injured blade was so swollen that the bamboo splint was embedded in it, but Jal-Nish had created flappeters to be nothing if not resilient.

Scrambling off before it collapsed, she helped Nish down. They were on a shallow slope broken by a series of steeper banks where the exposed soil was deep red. The forest was so tall and dense that no sunlight reached the ground. It was almost dark here and the misty air had a faint greenish tinge. Maelys caught hold of a low branch. Her knees felt weak.

'Well done, lad,' said Nish, shaking her hand. 'I would not have thought it possible.'

Maelys lowered her head, thrilled at being praised by such a great man, but not knowing how to respond to it. She hadn't been praised for anything since her father had fled. And she had done well, despite everything, perhaps because she hadn't allowed herself to think. She'd just acted on the spur of the moment. Nish had done well too. 'Thank you,' she murmured, looking up at him shyly. 'That was a brilliant shot.'

'With a lot of luck behind it. I couldn't do it again.'

She waited for him to take over, but he didn't say anything else, so after a pause she said, 'We've got to find a safe place to camp. Rurr-shyve can't go any further. And we need water.'

'There'll be a river further down but I wouldn't camp there. They could come on us from any direction. Go that way until we come upon a stream, boy, then follow it up.'

Maelys bit her lip. Being called 'boy' was galling; it undermined his praise. Yet Nish had been a hero of the war and a leader of men, and he thought she was just a kid, so she made allowances.

She called Rurr-shyve on, and after about ten minutes of creeping between the trees they came upon a rivulet at the bottom of a rocky gully, running down a steep slope. She followed it up to a point where the gully was impassably choked with scrub and small trees. They mounted again and Maelys directed Rurr-shyve to hover over the trees until she found what she was looking for – a secluded glade covered in ferns and moss, by a rocky pool.

The instant they settled, Rurr-shyve's feather-rotors flopped down and it seemed to shrink in on itself. Its tail thudded into the ferns, its inverted knee joints quivered, folded suddenly, and it thumped into the ground.

Extending its neck, it took a long slurping drink from the pool, leaving the surface streaked with strands and clots of smelly yellow mucous. It tore up a barrelful of ferns by the roots and fed them through its grinding plates, dirt and all, before laying its long neck down, head tucked back under it. The compound eyes dulled, though its jaws continued to move and a bulging sac under its neck churned and squelched.

Every so often it gave a heave, regurgitating shovelfuls of ground-up fern into its maw, and chewed over them until brown strings of saliva surged out, accompanied by indescribable stenches.

'Get it tied down, lad, or it'll be off while we sleep,' said Nish after watching it for a while. 'Or worse.'

She should have thought of that, and it was a boy's job to carry out the menial camp chores, but again Maelys felt diminished. She scurried to do the job, wishing he could appreciate her for who she really was. The ropes in the bottom of the saddlebag had metal collars attached. She fastened one around Rurr-shyve's neck where the scaly carapace was scored, the other at the tail, and fixed the free ends to the trunks of two stout trees so it would have freedom to browse.

Then she slumped onto the ground, well out of reach, and tried to think what to do next. Nothing came to her; she was too exhausted. She knew in her heart that it was too late to head for Hulipont, but there was nowhere else to go.

She looked up to see Nish's eyes on her. Maelys coloured and turned away. The great deeds she'd accomplished so far had been easier than dealing with him. She felt embarrassed about the little intimacies of before. How could she have treated the great war hero, the son of the God-Emperor, so familiarly? She couldn't even look at him.

'There's food in the saddlebags,' she said hoarsely, staring at the ground. Nish wasn't over the brainstorm yet and she should have served him, but she couldn't manage it.

He nodded formally, wobbled to the saddlebags, holding the loose leather pants up with one hand, and took out the food bag. Nish must have been ravenous but he ate delicately and in small portions. He held the food bag out but she shook her head, too embarrassed to approach him.

After drinking from the brook, well above the pool Rurr-shyve had befouled, she washed her face and hands. Taking the rider's fur-lined cloak from the other saddlebag, she wrapped it around herself, lay on a moss-covered patch of ground a safe distance from the flappeter, and Nish, pillowed her head on her little pack and tried to sleep.

The sheath was digging into her hip. Maelys unbuckled the belt and laid it beside her, the knife close to hand. She closed her eyes again, but now became aware of how chafed her bound breasts were. She glanced at Nish, who was looking her way, and coloured. Sooner or later she would have to reveal that she was a girl, but not now. She gritted her teeth and tried to will herself to sleep.

That didn't work either, for her mind began to replay the scene with Rider Hinneltyne after the disruption had driven him mad. She kept seeing the knife hacking into his neck and the blood bursting out. So much of it, and all due to her.

Maelys tried to think about other things, though it was a long while before she could. She could smell the creature's foetid breath from the other side of the clearing, sense its burning hatred of her and its longing to tear chunks from her flesh with its serrated maw, or beak.

What was the contract between flappeter and rider, anyway? It must be a bond developed by Jal-Nish to make sure the beast could be controlled, though how could *she* fulfil a contract she didn't understand? Once Rurr-shyve recovered from the loss of its former rider, it would probably attack her for the interloper she was.

Even after she drifted off to sleep, its presence made dark shadows at the edges of her mind, and she dreamed that Jal-Nish was exerting all his energies to seize back control of it.

EIGHT

Nish dozed briefly, then snapped awake to see the green eyes of the flappeter on him. He didn't think his father's creature would be able to harm him, though how could he be sure? There was something wrong about it; something he couldn't fathom, because it wasn't like any other creature.

Its very existence made his father a hypocrite, for flesh-forming was an alien Art the lyrinx had used in the war, and for that reason Jal-Nish had regarded them as an abomination. He had done everything he could to wipe them from the face of the world, so why was he using their Arts now?

Nish sat up. He felt wide awake, fully rested, and having good food in his belly gave him the most marvellous feeling of well-being. He glanced across at the boy, who was sleeping soundly, wrapped in the rider's cloak. Why had he done all this, and why had Fyllis been involved at all? Nish remembered her face clearly, and her quiet, confident manner, as if it were a game and she could come to no harm.

No, not a game; a serious responsibility she'd been entrusted with because she was the only one who could do it. That was the strangest thing, and for the first time in many years Nish felt a glimmer of hope. Fyllis had revealed a crack in the all-powerful façade his father had erected.

He tried to recreate the past night in his mind. Everything was clear up to the point where she had pulled him into that empty cell and put her hands over his ears to protect him. But from what?

After that his most prominent memory was pain; pain that sheared through his head and robbed him of his senses. He vaguely remembered throwing up, then being led somewhere, but he couldn't see or hear for ages. He recalled his feet thudding against paving stones, and her warm hand in his, then nothing until he'd come to his senses staggering up the mountain with the boy.

There was something odd about the boy. He looked about twelve but acted like an adult, and he must also have a native talent. Nish had a vague memory of breathing underwater, surely a hallucination, then some intimacy that made him squirm, and the next he knew he was trapped in the flappeter's legs and it was trying to carry him away.

Nish recalled the rider towering over the boy, knife in hand, followed by a dull red flash and more pain, worse than the first time. He had been blind, helpless, trapped; insects had been crawling all over him, sucking his blood, trying to get into his mouth and nose.

But the boy had risen to every challenge, escaped every attack and even taken control of a flappeter. Clearly two children, no matter how talented, could not have done all that by themselves. Could the lad be a wizard in disguise? Nish didn't think so; the boy seemed too gentle; too kind. He was just a servant, but who was the master? Jal-Nish must have a powerful enemy who was now showing his hand.

The flappeter stirred, rotated its feather-rotors half a turn and raised its head. Nish's skin prickled. He couldn't read anything in its eyes, but he'd heard plenty about the nature of flappeters and their feeding habits. They could live on just about anything, including rotting wood and the stinking sludge at the bottom of duck ponds, but they had a particular liking for live flesh. What motivated this one – hunger, curiosity, pain? No, Rurr-shyve was no longer in his father's thrall, for Maelys had cut off its speck-speaker. Nish shivered as he thought through the implications. Did it yearn for freedom? If it did, not even he was safe now.

Rurr-shyve began moving back and forth, testing the ropes. Nish eyed the knots, praying that Maelys had tied them securely. The ropes must be enchanted to prevent flappeters from biting through them.

Rurr-shyve tore up a clump of ferns as if they were lettuce and began to grind them to paste, slimy saliva dripping from the gapes of its maw. Ferns were poisonous to most creatures but it seemed unaffected.

Nish noticed that his hands were filthy, despite his time in the water. His nails were long and splintered, his matted hair hung down his back and his stench was as great a pollution of the sweet air of the glade as Rurr-shyve's noisome belches. His odour was an unpleasant reminder of prison, and of a life controlled by his father; he could change that, at least. He rose, unsteadily, for his head felt slightly disconnected from his body, and stumbled across to the boy, who was sleeping soundly, head pillowed on his clasped hands.

Taking the belt, sheath and knife, Nish went upstream until he found a pool in the rocks. He hacked his hair off until it was just the length of a thumb joint, cut his beard even shorter, trimmed his nails and cleaned them with the point of the knife. Then he took off his clothes, sank into the cold water and scrubbed himself with handfuls of sand until his prison-pale skin was red and every speck of ingrained dirt was gone.

After washing Maelys's pants and jacket he left them hanging on a branch to dry, but put the fur-lined leather pants back on. They swam on him and he needed the belt to hold them up. He left the coat behind, since the forest here was no colder than his cell in Mazurhize. Donning his socks and boots, he turned up the slope, revelling in his freedom to do the simplest things. Freedom! It was the most precious gift of all.

Above him, a rocky spur rose out of the forest. Nish

began to climb it. He needed to see what lay beyond and reassure himself that, for all his father's power, there were parts of the world over which he held no sway.

His legs hurt from last night's climb, but that was good too. He was free; he could feel again. He took pleasure in every sensation, even his weakness and exhaustion, for these were under his control. He could get his strength back.

The top of the pinnacle was scarily steep but Nish forced himself to attempt it. Perhaps his father could not be beaten, but he didn't control the whole world, or Nish. If Nish couldn't fight Jal-Nish, he could go far away to a place where his father's sway didn't hold, and make himself a new life as an ordinary man. It was the only hope he could allow himself.

His racing heart was skipping beats from the unaccustomed exertion. Nish flopped onto a mossy ledge ten or fifteen spans below the top. He was nearly at the treetops here, and thus far he'd been concealed by overhanging branches, but once above them he'd be visible if anyone was watching from further up the mountain, or from the sky.

He climbed on, slowly now, for he was very tired. The pinnacle was taller than it looked and his earlier euphoria had begun to fade. He was even weaker than he'd thought; it would take months to regain his former strength.

Then, edging around a sharp horn of rock, Nish felt the sun on his face, the clear, scented air in his nostrils, and his eyes stung with tears. Sunshine; fresh air; freedom – they were such simple pleasures, but what else did a man really need? There was no need to go further, so he sat down, well clear of the edge with his back to the rock, gazing across the gigantic valley.

It had to be many leagues wide, for the forested slope on the far side was blue with distance, and the valley ran upstream and down even further, untouched by human hand. With a sigh, he lay back on the ledge and closed his eyes, allowing the tension to seep out of his legs, relaxing his whole body as he'd never been able to relax in prison, trying

102

to think of nothing at all. That wasn't easy. He'd always been the slave to an overactive mind.

But now, with the cool rock beneath him, the warm sun on his face and a pleasant tiredness in his limbs, the world disappeared and for a brief while he could be an ordinary man again. There was not a cloud in the pale sky; no sign of life apart from a hunting bird wheeling in the distance.

Nish was dozing off when his sluggish mind realised that it couldn't have been a bird, for it was too long and the wrong shape. It was a flappeter, searching the forest, and his dungeon-pale skin would stand out against the dark stone.

Cursing himself for a fool, Nish eased back out of sight. He didn't think the beast could have seen him, but where there was one there would be others. Of course his father's reach extended to this wilderness; it probably covered the entire world and he, Nish, would never be able to get away from him.

Despair bowing his back, he went down the pinnacle as quickly as his shaky legs would allow. By the time he reached the bottom he was starving again, so he hurried towards the camp site, collecting the remaining clothes on the way.

Before he got there an irrational dread crept over him, that he'd find the boy slain and a force of soldiers waiting for him, and it grew stronger with every step. He told himself that he had nothing to fear but his own terror, and that his father's power was no greater than people allowed it to be, but Nish didn't believe it. Jal-Nish held all the power in the world and no one could ever beat him.

Beset by feelings of approaching doom, Nish was almost to the camp site when he heard an odd, snorting rumble. His hackles rose; he eased the knife out, holding it low in front of him the way he'd been taught during the war, noting with faint surprise how his muscles remembered what his brain had forgotten. He began to creep down the steep slope, taking advantage of every tree and bush, scanning the ground in case he kicked a stone or cracked a stick under-foot.

The sound grew louder. Nish slid in behind a tree above the camp site and peered around it, then relaxed. The flap-peter was sleeping, head tucked under its long neck again, making the beastly equivalent of a snore.

The boy lay still and the camp site looked just as it had when Nish left it. He was about to move when Rurr-shyve gave an extra-loud snort, waking the boy, who jerked upright and looked around wildly. His hat fell off, revealing long black hair plaited and coiled on top of his head. Nish didn't think anything of that, for it wasn't uncommon for men to wear their hair long, and he'd occasionally seen warriors plait it and tie it up before battle.

The boy rubbed his chest, grimaced and looked furtively around the camp site. What was he up to? Not seeing Nish, he unfastened his shirt and began to pick at a cloth knotted around his chest. The knots were tight and it took a minute or two to untie them. He drew out a long strip of linen, sighed in relief and rubbed his chest again, though not in the way a boy would. Definitely not.

For Nish had glimpsed, unmistakeable even from this dis-tance, two pale, plump breasts. Maelys was a girl, of course. And thinking about the hair, the voice, the way she'd moved, he wondered how he could ever have thought otherwise, even in the dark. Not a young girl either. No child could have had the presence of mind to do all she'd done.

Nish couldn't help himself, for he hadn't seen a woman in ten years. He just stood there, staring like a yokel, instantly and painfully aroused. Then Maelys looked up and saw him.

She cried out, whipped her shirt closed and flushed a bril-liant, glowing red. He turned away at once, thinking that it made her even more of an enigma. Definitely not an expe-rienced young woman. His beautiful Irisis had once gone into battle with her breasts bared like a warrior queen of legend, but there had been no woman in the world like Irisis . . .

That wasn't a thought he wanted to pursue. Nish came out from behind the tree, bowed his head and said thickly, 'I'm really sorry, I thought you were a boy . . . I should have called out.'

'It doesn't matter,' she lied, going even redder, if that were possible. She didn't look at him, just kept staring at the ground. 'How could you have known?'

He came across slowly, reassessing her. An unusually modest young woman, even for these prudish times, and once again he wondered what she was doing here. She looked too fresh and innocent to survive alone in the harsh world. It must have been sheer luck that she'd killed the rider. She'd shown resourcefulness during their escape, but if Jal-Nish's troops caught her she'd be broken so thoroughly that she would never recover. He couldn't have that on his conscience. She had to be sent home to her family.

'Thank you for all you did last night,' he said. 'I would not have thought it possible, but now –'

She nodded stiffly. 'I was just doing my duty.' She managed a fleeting smile. 'You seem better.'

'I feel so much better.' He rubbed his clean, spiky stubble. It didn't feel like him at all and that was good, too. 'You can't imagine what it's like, not to bathe for ten years.'

She looked down again, the colour starting to fade. Maelys was an attractive little thing; almost pretty with that ink-black hair, flushed skin and shining eyes – but so young. And his father's spies were nearby.

'I saw a flappeter circling, from up there.' Nish pointed. 'They're looking for us.'

She took a deep, shuddering breath. 'Then we're trapped.'

'The forest goes as far as I could see. If it's dark tonight –'

'There's nowhere to go!' she cried, clenching her little fists helplessly. She told him about Cathim, Ousther and Hulipont.

'Who's Ousther?'

'I don't know. The aunts didn't tell me.'

Nish frowned. She wasn't making sense. 'What aunts? You'd better start from the beginning – from the pretty little girl who got me out.'

Maelys looked hurt, as if he'd implied that she were plain, though she hastily concealed it. She explained, and as the story came out – the crushing of an ancient clan, the women struggling for survival in the one room left to them, the aunts who refused to bend to the tyrant, Fyllis's unusual talent – the knot in the pit of Nish's stomach tightened.

'I don't understand what your clan's downfall has to do with me.'

On the pinnacle he'd foolishly succumbed to the hope of an ordinary life beyond his father's reach. Maelys's tale shattered that hope. There *was* no great conspiracy against Jal-Nish; no powerful enemy preparing to take him on. Nish remembered the aunts now; Fyllis had mentioned them. He was trapped in a farce constructed by three mad old women. He bit down on hysterical laughter.

'Because you've got to become the Deliverer,' she said, as if that were obvious.

'The Deliverer?' The knot tightened painfully. 'What's that?'

Maelys gave him an odd look. 'Before you went to prison, you vowed to return and save the world from your father.' With eyes shining, she quoted his ringing declaration back at him, word for word and with exactly the emphasis he'd used when he'd spoken it after Irisis's death. It took him right back to that awful day, the worst of his life, and Nish couldn't bear it. He screwed up his eyes, trying to block out the sound of her voice, desperate to escape the memories.

Maelys stopped abruptly. When Nish opened his eyes she said simply, 'All Santhenar has been waiting for this day. Everyone remembers your promise, and we've all been praying that you would escape from prison and save us from the God-Emperor. You've got to become the Deliverer. You're the only hope left in the world.'

She was looking at him with such wide-eyed, innocent trust that he wanted to throw up. His father couldn't be beaten and it would destroy him to try; that's why he'd decided, back in Mazurhize, that there was no choice but to repudiate his promise. How dare she! He had to put the past behind him.

'Then the world has no hope at all,' he said, despising himself for the oath-breaker and coward that he was, 'for I can't do it.'

NINE

Maelys, watching Nish stumble into the forest, picked sightlessly at her binding cloth. It had never occurred to her that he would break his word. What could the matter be? She carefully avoided the thought that he was a coward, or that the stories about his heroism in the war had been made up. Who was she, an inexperienced girl whose only knowledge of the world came from books, to judge such a great man?

He'd been through too much, and must also be suffering from the *brainstorm* and the *disruption*. She should not have pressured him. If they escaped she would nurse him back to health, and only then remind him of his duty. Yes, that was the best way. He must become the Deliverer; no one else could. But the doubt had been raised and, try as she might, Maelys could not quite banish it.

The aunts wouldn't want her to become pregnant to a coward and oath-breaker, surely? Or would they? If the God-Emperor took Nish back, the baby would be his only grandchild and would save Clan Nifferlin. That was the only thing that mattered to the aunts.

She sank down among the ferns, head in hands. Everything was so difficult. She had no idea how to bring Nish out of his dismal withdrawal. She didn't know much about men, for the men and youths of her clan had all been killed or driven away when she was still a girl.

For the past two years there had only been her mother, the aunts and Fyllis, and the aunts never stopped talking about the follies of their dead husbands, or pointing out the superiority of women in all important matters. The bitterness helped to mask the pain of all they'd lost, but it didn't assist Maelys in understanding what was the matter with Nish. She was so used to being blamed when things went wrong that she felt sure it was her fault. She had to discover what really ailed him, then help him to recover. He had to do his duty and so did she.

Later Maelys took off Rurr-shyve's splint, applied salve to the broken skin and re-fastened the sheath carefully so as to better support the injury, yet cause as little pain as possible. That night they took to the air again, flying at treetop height across the forest, and though they saw flappeters high up, silhouetted against the moonlit sky, Rurr-shyve was not seen against the dark canopy.

After that it was overcast for days and she had to fly in daytime, for night flying in these rugged mountains became too dangerous. There had been no sign of pursuit for the past three days, nor any evidence of human habitation. All Maelys had seen were the towering mountains on either side and the forested valley winding between them. However, Rurr-shyve was, for the time being, compliant.

Flying hadn't become any easier, though. It was always exhausting, and she never got over her urge to scream whenever the amulet unfolded its legs and began to creep about inside her shirt. She couldn't keep it anywhere else, though, for unless it was touching her skin or in her fist, she couldn't control Rurr-shyve.

As the sun was setting, in the distance Maelys made out a long clearing and a pattern of cultivated fields on either side of a river, then a large village set on a heart-shaped rise partly enclosed by a meander. She turned away at once, flying low and close to the dark mountain slope, and brought

Rurr-shyve down between a series of rock spires where a luxuriance of ferns and moss offered good grazing, plus shelter from the cold wind.

The village couldn't be seen from here but she guessed it was half a league away. An hour's walk, in the dark, as long as the country wasn't too rough. She mentally traced a route to it, down the ridge then through the forest to the edge of the clearing.

They set up camp in silence, after which Nish began to pace around in a ragged circle, head down. He did it every night and it was driving her mad.

'Is something the matter, Nish?'

'I need to think things through.'

He said that every night as well, though she couldn't imagine there was anything left to think about, after all his years in prison. It was time for action, surely, but Nish appeared to be recycling the same despairing thoughts over and over. She had to shake him out of it.

'We should go down to the village and ask for help.'

'What help can they give us?' he said dully. 'My father's reach extends across the known world.'

'So his servants say, but we're a long way from Mazurhize now and maybe he hasn't bothered with such a remote village as this.'

'No detail, however small, escapes my father's eye.'

'We've got to *do* something, Nish! We can't run forever . . .' Maelys didn't go on, sure he'd think she was criticising him. But the time was rushing by. It was almost winter now. Her family would have to come out of hiding at winter's end, if not sooner, and once they did, Jal-Nish must find them. She had to convince Nish to become the Deliverer long before that, to gather a protective host of followers around him and begin the uprising. To strike before his father expected it, then use Nish's reputation to raise the world against the God-Emperor.

It sounded easy, when she put it that way, but it wouldn't

be. Jal-Nish had spies everywhere, and many people would be prepared to betray the fledgling revolution out of fear or greed. How could she know who to trust? She'd have to rely on Nish's experience and good judgement. Maelys avoided thinking too hard about that irony, but she had to begin making him into the Deliverer right away.

The fires of the village were just visible in the distance and Maelys had an idea. What if she put him in a position where he had to act? It felt sneaky and wrong, but what choice did she have?

'I'm going to go to the village . . . to get fresh food.' She coloured at the half-truth but he didn't notice. 'Will you come with me?' Please, please do. She didn't want to go by herself.

'You go. It's not far. I've got to think,' he said abruptly, walking away.

She felt like shouting at him – it's past time for thinking. You've got to do something! But she didn't; respect was ingrained in her. Besides, they did need fresh food, if any was available, though Maelys wasn't hopeful at this time of year.

Ducking out of sight, she dressed in her boy's clothes, bound her breasts as flat as they would go – not very flat – and buckled the cut-down belt, and the knife, around her waist. She took a single gold link out of her bracelet, for payment, leaving the rest of it in her pack.

Maelys pulled the chain of the taphloid over her head, feeling a mental wrench as she took it off for the first time since she'd been given it. All of a sudden she felt naked; exposed. But after all, it was useless without the crystal. She put the taphloid in her pack as well, but kept the amulet inside her shirt. She dared not leave it behind in case Rurr-shyve got it.

The flappeter stirred in its slumber, then settled down again. Nish sat on a rock, staring at the clear sky.

'I'll be off then,' she said, still hoping he would come. She felt uneasy at going alone, and afraid that she'd make a fool of herself at the village, for she planned to appeal to the villagers on behalf of the Deliverer. It would go much better if he were there. Once they saw Nish, they couldn't help supporting him.

Nish grunted but did not look around. Maelys felt a wild urge to hurl a clod of dirt at him, but suppressed it and set off down the hill. It was growing dark, though a full moon was rising and there would soon be plenty of light. Besides, she was used to walking in the dark.

It was rough going down the ridge and she had to descend parts of it backwards, clinging to the knobbly rock. After a quarter of an hour she reached the edge of the forest and here the walking was easier, between tall, widely spaced trees with just an understorey of knee-high bracken. The moon had risen high enough that an occasional shaft slanted in through gaps in the canopy, and shortly she hit upon a narrow but well-used track probably made by small animals. It led in the general direction of the village so she followed it, trying to work out what to say when she got there.

She'd never spoken in public but Maelys was sure the words would flow when she needed them. Surely it couldn't be that hard to appeal to the people? No village in the known world was untouched by the God-Emperor's cruel whim, so once she told the villagers that Nish was here, and reminded them of his famous promise, they would surely flock to him.

Then Nish, fired up by their support and loyalty, would finally take on his life's role – he wouldn't have any choice. He'd probably be angry at first, though Maelys shied away from thinking about that. One day he'd thank her for it.

She smiled as she walked. It felt good to be doing her duty, and helped to overcome the nagging voice which kept reminding her that she'd done nothing about endearing herself to Nish. I can't do everything at once, she rationalised.

112

I've got to give Nish time. Let's get the Defiance underway first.

Her main worry was that the villagers would have gone to bed by the time she arrived. If she had to wake them they wouldn't be in a good mood. She walked faster. Ahead the path divided, one branch heading right, the other off to her left.

After checking the angle of the moon, Maelys took the right-hand track, climbed a long, gentle slope and on the downhill side reached the edge of the forest. Below and to the left she saw lights in the distance. A large blaze looked like a bonfire; smaller ones scattered around it would be lanterns. The villagers must be celebrating a festival or a wedding. She couldn't believe her good fortune.

Slanting across the cropped grass, she hit upon a beaten path and followed it until she reached the edge of the village, a broad, straggling circle of two-storey houses and simple huts. The bonfire blazed in the centre and she could hear singing and clapping; a large group of people were dancing while others carried blazing torches on poles.

Maelys moved between two huts and stood in the shadows, watching the revelry and wondering how best to approach them. About thirty pairs of young men and women were dancing in an oval around the bonfire, while a smaller circle of girls skipped to a tune played on bone flutes beyond the fire, and a straggle of boys were clapping away to her left. A throng of adults, perhaps a hundred strong, stood to the back, clapping and chanting.

She couldn't see either a wisp-watcher or loop-listener, which made her feel better – clearly Jal-Nish didn't have them in every village in the world. Should she wait until the dancing stopped before making her appeal? No, if she were discovered they might think she was a spy. Maelys began to feel anxious and, knowing it wouldn't help, took a deep breath, stepped out into the lighted circle and called, 'Hello.'

The chanting and clapping broke off; the dancers froze in

113

position and everyone stared at her. There was not a welcoming face among them and suddenly the words she'd been rehearsing slid out of her mind.

A tall, stringy old man limped out of the throng. He was clad in homespun pants and baggy, dun-coloured shirt, and wore a long sheepskin coat with the wool on the inside, fastened with thongs, plus a cap made from animal fur with a long grey tail wrapped around his neck like a scarf. His weathered skin was seamed and he had but five or six yellow teeth.

'What are you doing here, boy?' the headman said in a deep, throaty voice, as if suffering a bad cold. He stooped to squint at Maelys. 'What is your clan?'

'I – I –' She couldn't think what to say. She looked from face to face, desperate for inspiration, but found no interest, kindness or tolerance – just dumb hostility that she'd interrupted their celebration.

The old man clenched gnarled fists. 'Your Histories, boy!' The crowd were slowly moving forwards.

Just say what you've come for! Taking a deep breath, she looked him in the eye, but raised her voice to speak to them all. 'I am the emissary of Cryl-Nish Hlar, *Nish*, the son of the God-Emperor, and he speaks to you all.'

As she paused, there came an audible intake of breath from the adults. The old man took a hasty step backwards. One of the smaller children screamed and others began to cry. Perhaps mentioning the God-Emperor's name had been a mistake. Maelys hastily went on.

'Nish,' she repeated loudly. 'The great hero of the war against the lyrinx, and the bitter enemy of his father, who imprisoned him for ten years.' They stared at her, blank-faced. 'Enemy' hadn't done her any good either. Why hadn't she thought her speech through on the way and rehearsed it in the forest? She struggled on. 'Nish, who promised to return and become the Deliverer.'

Maelys began to quote his famous last words before he

was dragged off to prison, but they didn't come out the least bit inspiring. They sounded like a lesson out of the Histories, and she could see that she was losing these dull, stolid folk. Living so far from anywhere, they must be suspicious of strangers, and while they knew of the God-Emperor's dread power it was beyond imagination that his son should come to their insignificant little village.

That thought made it even harder to find the right words, but she tried again. 'The *Deliverer* has come and he needs your aid. Will you help him begin the uprising against the God-Emperor . . .'

No, no! Why had she said that? She should have told them why it was important to aid Nish, and what they would get out of it. She could see in their faces that she'd offered them nothing but their doom.

'We're loyal worshippers of the God-Emperor, here, and he knows it,' grated the headman. 'We shall worship his Son, too, if the Father asks it of us, but we will never support the Son against the Father, who has given us the food we eat and the mead we drink, blessed be his name. Be off, tempter.'

'Blessed be his name and all his works,' echoed the crowd fervently.

Surely they didn't think Jal-Nish had sent her to test their faith? 'But I haven't come from the God-Emperor to tempt you into betraying him,' said Maelys. 'I've come from his son, Nish.'

'That's a lie,' said the headman, advancing on her, 'for the Son is held in prison for his crimes against the Father. Begone back to your master, lad, and tell him so. Tell him that, even should every other village on Santhenar rebel, the hamlet of Byre remains steadfast. Jal-Nish is our God-Emperor now and for all time.'

'For all time,' hissed the crowd, in tones that sent worms wriggling up Maelys's spine.

The headman was close now, and though his back was bent, he towered over her, treating her to a blast of sour mead fumes. 'Were you a man full grown, I'd beat you black and blue for such blasphemy and send you to the God-Emperor in chains. Scurry back to your master, boy, whoever he is. Beg him to surrender to the God-Emperor's mercy before he condemns you both.'

'Please listen.' How could she convince them that she was in earnest? Risking everything on a last desperate appeal, she said, 'My master is Cryl-Nish Hlar, the son of the God-Emperor, and he curses Jal-Nish's evil name. The God-Emperor is a stinking liar, a disgusting, deformed monstrosity who should have been slain long ago. I –'

She could not have chosen worse words. The entire village, from the most withered crone to the smallest child, let out a collective gasp of horror, then the adults surged forwards, brandishing sticks and clubs.

'Wait!' she cried, but they kept coming. 'Listen –'

'Blasphemous dog of a boy!' cried the headman. 'How dare you take the God-Emperor's name in vain?'

'The lout is a spy and a rebel who threatens us all,' rasped a woman from the crowd. 'He must be taught a lesson such that the God-Emperor will never question our loyalty. Beat him within an ell of his life and cast him out to die.'

'Put out his eyes,' said another woman, her own black eyes flashing in the firelight.

'Sear the mark of the traitor bone-deep across his brow,' said a third.

'No!' cried Maelys. She should have turned and run for her life, but she still thought that, if she could just find the right words, she could sway them. 'You've got to listen –'

The headman held up his hand and the crowd hung back like a pair of dark wings unfurled behind him. 'The rebel must be taught a stern lesson, but he must also live, that the God-Emperor hear of our loyalty, and how we repay those who dare to tempt us. We *shall* burn the mark of the traitor bone-deep into his brow, and beat him too, though not badly enough to cripple him. Take the scoundrel.'

It was hopeless. Maelys whirled and bolted, but hadn't gone ten paces before she was tackled by a flying youth. She hit the ground hard and felt her binding cloth slip off. She tried to scramble to her feet but the youth's hand locked around her ankle and before she could kick free two more lads piled onto her.

Maelys stopped struggling, for they were strong farmhands and any one of them was her match. She went limp, hoping that they might relax and give her an opportunity for escape.

The first youth twisted her arm up behind her back until she had to bite her lip to avoid crying out, then turned her around and proudly forced her into the light. It was brighter now, for the lantern-bearers had closed into a circle around her. Her breasts bounced with every movement and they couldn't possibly miss it. Under the God-Emperor's rule, women were seldom beaten as harshly as men, but they were punished in other ways . . .

The headman stared at her, an unnerving gleam in his eye. He gestured to the youth, who let go of her arm and moved back, though only a step.

'A girl,' he said wonderingly, reaching out towards her chest but dropping his hand at the last moment. 'That's another matter entirely.' He licked his flaking lips. 'I can use a girl.'

Maelys took an abrupt step backwards and came up against the youth, who thrust her forwards again.

A bent old woman, even more aged than the headman, came lurching out of the crowd and delivered him a blow to the side of the head that sent him staggering sideways. 'You'll use her for nothing, you old fool,' she said in a cracked hiss.

She stared at Maelys as if she could see into her soul. Reaching out with a dirty, trembling finger she touched Maelys on the lower lip, but whipped her hand back smartly. Her eyes narrowed. 'That's no innocent maiden, but a witch-slut sent to tempt drooling old men and weak-minded youths.'

She glanced over her shoulder towards the shadows to the left of the bonfire, and Maelys's heart gave a lurch. Her eyes had been dazzled by one of the pole lanterns and she'd missed it before, but from this angle it was terribly clear – a wisp-watcher mounted on a tall post was pointing directly at her. How could she have been so careless?

The headman began muttering to the crone, though Maelys couldn't make out what he was saying. She ran through her options. Wisp-watchers could see but not hear, and she didn't see a loop-listener anywhere. Since Jal-Nish didn't know her name and hadn't seen her face, why would he be interested in some little conflict in an insignificant village? On festival nights, full of drunkenness and revelry, there must be thousands of fights, so she hadn't given Nish away, yet.

'She's a temptress,' the crone hissed, prodding the headman in the chest with brown-stained nails, 'and if we don't get rid of her she'll destroy us all.'

'What do you mean, Gyghan?' said the headman, giving the wisp-watcher a fearful sideways glance. It was slowly rotating so its unblinking gaze swept across the village centre every few minutes.

'The God-Emperor must have sent her to test us, to see if we remain faithful to him no matter what the temptation, and already you fail the test. Men!'

'What are we to do with her?'

'Kill her!'

Maelys's blood turned to ice. What a fool she'd been. Why hadn't she listened to Nish? How could she have thought to come here and manipulate him so crudely? She was doomed as surely as if she had fallen into the God-Emperor's hands.

The headman's eyes kept flicking back and forth between the crone and the wisp-watcher, with occasional furtive glances at Maelys's breasts. He kept shaking his head.

118

'But . . . but if she *has* come from the God-Emperor – we can't kill one of his servants.'

'He would expect no less of us,' said Gyghan the crone. 'What cares he for one servant when he has thousands? But he cares very much to know that his people remain faithful, no matter the temptation. The witch-slut preaches blasphemy and treachery. Once the ritual purifications are done, she must be slain as set down in the sacred books. The truth about her treachery must be burned into her body from forehead to toe, then she must be bound with chains and thrown in the river to drown.'

'We have no chains.'

'Then use rope and stones, idiot man! Begin.'

He stood there, hesitantly. 'Can we not burn her on the bonfire?'

'Burn a witch-slut here and her soul will be set free to haunt Byre until the end of time. Strip her down to a loincloth, before the Eye of the God-Emperor, then lash her to withies bent into a great circle.

'My women will mix a barrel of the red earth from the river bank with thrice-blessed well water, and every man, woman and child must hurl the sacred mud at her until she is coated with it. Only when the mud dries and cracks from her slut-heat is she to be taken down and the words of treachery burnt into her with the red-hot poker.' Gyghan raised her voice. 'Bring the witch-slut to the Eye.'

Two brawny youths seized Maelys and hauled her after the crone, who was hobbling around the left-hand side of the bonfire, walking on the outsides of her feet as if it pained her to place them flat on the ground.

A young girl ran in, looking scared but determined. She reached out, drew back, reached out again and pinched Maelys painfully on the upper arm before darting away, grinning gleefully. Two more girls came from the other side, not quite as scared this time, pinching and poking Maelys, and then children ran from everywhere. Her arms were stinging by the time she'd been hauled around to the other side of the bonfire, where a battered wooden post protruded from the ground. It looked unnervingly like a whipping post and stood in the direct view of the Eye.

The crone shooed the children away and motioned to the youths to hold Maelys steady while four equally aged and snaggle-toothed women gathered around, inspecting her like a piece of meat on a butcher's block.

'Please,' Maelys begged, 'you've got it wrong. I –'

Gyghan slapped her across the face. 'Be silent, witch-slut.'

Shortly a group of men came up from the river bank, dragging a number of willow boughs. The headman consulted the crone, who conferred with her followers then selected two long, slightly curved branches. The men stripped the twigs and side branches off, curved the boughs into three-quarter circles and bound them together where they overlapped to form a hoop a span and a half across, then tied it to the whipping post.

Maelys had to act now. Once they tied her to the hoop she was doomed. Wrenching her right hand free, she thrust it into her shirt and whipped the amulet out. Holding it out before her she roared, 'Rurr-shyve, Rurr-shive!' The amulet's jade eyes began to glow, picking out the tracery of the flappeter's outline on the side facing her.

She rotated it so everyone could see, taking care to conceal it from the all-seeing wisp-watcher, which had swung in her direction. It remained silent, thankfully, but if it began to buzz, it would be *sending* what it saw to the tears.

The metal legs of the amulet unfolded, and the youths holding her choked and backed away. The crowd backpedalled as well; a child began to cry. The headman stood his ground for a moment before taking two steps backwards, then running. The crowd surged after him towards the houses, all save for Gyghan.

'Stand firm,' she quavered. 'This witch-slut has no power over the god-fearing.'

'Oh yes I have!' cried Maelys. If they were to call her witch, she'd act a witch to the best of her powers. She raised her arms to the heavens and roared, 'Rurr-shyve, come for me, and if anyone from this accursed village stands in your way, smite them all the way into godless eternity.' Her words sounded desperate, so she attempted a wild cackle. To her ears it sounded shrill, false and frightened.

However, the crone paled and turned to stare in the direction of the pinnacles and the camp, invisible in the darkness. The amulet grew warm in Maelys's hands and for a moment she felt that sense of *connection* she'd had when she'd ordered Rurr-shyve to fly, and it had obeyed. She strained to reach it, to order it to come for her, though she felt sure she could not contact it from such a distance. Nothing happened; the connection slowly faded. Her arm shook and the tracery on the amulet began to fade. She'd failed and she was going to die.

Gyghan read her face. With a spreading, gap-toothed leer, she said, 'The God-Emperor's beasts refuse to answer her call. It's proof that the witch-slut lies. Strip her! Bind her to the hoop.' A gaggle of leering youths and hairless old men rushed forwards. 'Back!' she cried. 'No lustful fool of a man shall touch the temptress.' She gestured to her crones.

The men and youths retreated, torn between fear and resentment. Six crones advanced on Maelys, avoiding her eyes. She turned to run but a wall of youths blocked her way to freedom. She turned back, charged the crones and knocked the first two out of the way, but someone tripped her and she fell. Immediately the crones swarmed over her. She kicked and punched, desperate to get away, but there were too many of them and, despite their age, they were strong and wiry.

Two crones held Maelys's arms until her struggles had exhausted her; another two stood on her shins. The remainder tore the shirt from her body, sneering as they exposed her, then cut away her other garments until all she had left were the rags of her trousers. Perhaps exposing the rest of her would prove too great a temptation.

They hauled her across to the hoop and bound her to the withies by her wrists. Long cords ran from her ankles to the lower rim of the circle, were stretched tight and bound there. They didn't touch the amulet, though. They seemed afraid of it.

'Well you might be afraid,' said Maelys, loudly enough for everyone to hear, 'for if you harm me you doom yourselves. My flappeter is coming, and once Rurr-shyve is finished with Byre village, no one will ever live here again.'

A great wail went up from the crowd but Gyghan raised a shaking hand. 'The witch-slut lies. The witch-slut must die. Prepare the sacred mud.' She turned to her fellows. 'Headman, cleanse the pokers in the hottest part of the bon-fire so we can burn the corruption and evil out of her. All hail to the God-Emperor.'

'All hail to the God-Emperor,' echoed the villagers.

Maelys jerked furiously, tearing the skin of her wrists, but the ropes didn't give an ell.

TEN

Nish was so immersed in his troubles that he hardly noticed the passing of time. He ate some dried meat from the saddlebags, washed it down with rank water from a water skin and resumed his vigil. Where could he go that his father would never find him?

Unfortunately he had only the vaguest idea where he was. Mazurhize and Morrelune lay in the southern section of the mighty mountain chain that ran up the east coast of the continent of Lauralin, not far from the coastal city of Fadd, but it was a land Nish knew only from maps. And after days of flying, much of it in cloud or fog as they followed the winding valleys, he was lost.

Maelys's original destination of Hulipont was in the mountains north of the ancient Aachim city of Stassor, but he must assume Hulipont had been taken by his father by now. There was no refuge at Stassor either, for the city had been forbidden to all outsiders for more than a thousand years. Besides, after the destruction of the nodes and the failure of the Secret Art, even eternal Stassor could have crumbled.

There must be places in Lauralin too empty, remote or rugged for Jal-Nish to bother about. Many Aachim had gone to Faranda at the end of the war but Jal-Nish probably held sway over them as well. However, Meldorin Island, where the war began a hundred and sixty years ago, had been abandoned to the lyrinx in the last years of the war and must still be a largely empty land.

But Nish didn't want to hide from Jal-Nish. He wanted what ordinary people had – a measure of freedom to live their lives without interference. He couldn't live in fear of his father, constantly looking over his shoulder.

There were more distant lands on the other side of the world, where he doubted his father had ever been, but he had no way of reaching such places. Rurr-shyve could cross small mountains and narrow seas but not oceans, since it had to land several times a day to feed. And even if he could take the flappeter, what could he do about Maelys? She had to be protected until she could be returned to her family, though unfortunately Maelys didn't know where they were hiding.

Nish was immersed in these gloomy thoughts when Rurr-shyve reared up so suddenly that the top of the small tree it was roped to whipped back and forth, shedding twigs and leaves on his head. Lowering its tail, it used it as a lever to raise its long neck as high as it would reach. Its head darted back and forth, sniffing the air. Its compound eyes took on a ruddy gleam in the firelight and it sucked air through its breathing tubes with a revolting snotty gurgle. After holding that pose for a minute the gleam faded and it sank down again.

There was no way of knowing what had disturbed it; the creature was too alien. Nish was recalling his travels in Meldorin, and trying to think of the best place to head for, when it occurred to him that Maelys had been gone rather a long time.

The moon had moved a third of the way across the sky since she'd left, so the best part of four hours must have passed. More than enough time for her to walk to the village, spend an hour there and walk back.

Still, she wasn't a child. She'd eluded his father's Militia, controlled an alien flappeter and killed its rider, a man armed and experienced at hand-to-hand combat. What harm could she come to? he rationalised. He paced back and forth across the camp site, still thinking about Meldorin, but his thoughts kept returning to Maelys and he realised, to his chagrin, that he'd changed his previous view of her capabilities to suit himself.

A young woman, out alone in the dark, was never completely safe from villains. Or she might have fallen and broken her leg. Even a twisted ankle could be fatal in this wilderness, where savage creatures hunted day and night. Should he go after her? But there was no path to the village and she might have gone any way, so how would he find her?

Nish resumed pacing but his unease grew. What could possibly have delayed her? He peered between the pinnacles in the direction of the village but saw nothing save a faint fire glow. He scrambled up the tallest pinnacle, which was hazardous in the dim light. The glow was a bonfire and he made out smaller sparks of light moving around it.

The wretched girl was probably gaping at some third-rate tumbler cavorting around the bonfire. He would give her another hour. Nish had just climbed down when Rurr-shyve reared up again.

For Maelys to control the beast, there had to be a connection between her and it, and if one suffered the other felt it. On the way here, he'd seen her flinch each time Rurr-shyve let out a cry. Was it now reacting to her pain?

'Rurr-shyve,' he said quietly, unfastening the ropes, packing them away and going to the front saddle, 'Maelys is in trouble. I'll have to direct you down to her.'

The flappeter gave a snorting gurgle, as if to say, *You don't have the talent.*

Nish knew he didn't, but he climbed on, put his hand through the hoop the way he'd seen Maelys do and said, 'Fly, Rurr-shyve.'

Rurr-shyve snorted more snottily, but did nothing. After

sitting there for a minute or two, feeling like a fool, Nish got off and refastened the head rope around the tree. 'You'd better hope I return safely,' he snarled as he began to tie the second, 'for if I don't you'll be shackled here until you die of thirst. And good riddance.'

The flappeter lunged at him and he had to leap smartly out of the way, though Nish felt sure it couldn't harm the only son of the God-Emperor. At least, reasonably sure . . . He *hoped* it couldn't, anyway, though with its untrained rider missing, his father's prohibitions might not hold at all.

Taking the crossbow out of the saddlebag, he wound it as far as his strength would allow. He'd been exercising hard since the escape, and now managed to rotate the crank a full turn further than previously, though not as far as Maelys had done. A direct hit would certainly disable an opponent or a wildcat, and possibly kill it, though he wouldn't be able to wind the crank quickly enough to deal with a second attacker. It was better than nothing, though. He thrust the leather bag containing the short crossbow quarrels into a deep pocket.

Standing on the rocky edge, Nish put a hand to his ear but heard nothing save Rurr-shyve's gurgling. He headed down. Rurr-shyve trumpeted. He kept going but the sound was repeated, loudly and urgently, and the feather-rotors went *thuppetty-thup*. Rurr-shyve never used them when tied down, for fear of catching a rotor blade in the ropes. What was the matter?

He clambered up again. The flappeter was hovering a span and a half off the ground, straining the ropes tied to the two small trees until they slid up the trunks. If the relatively small branches gave, the ropes might pull up and off.

'Stop!' Nish brandished the crossbow but Rurr-shyve spun its feather-rotors faster, until the rope tore through the bark of the small branch on the left-hand tree and slipped free. If it managed the same with the other rope, it could get away.

'All right! I'll untie you, but you'll have to let me lead you like a dog on a leash, and if you try to get away I'll put a bolt right through your rotor.'

Again that gurgling snort, and Nish was sure he detected amusement this time, but the flappeter came to ground and waited while he untied its tail and put the rope in the saddlebags. However, as soon as he'd untied the head rope from its tree, Rurr-shyve sprang, lifted three or four spans in the air and dragged Nish over the edge.

Letting out a squawk, he clung desperately to the rope as it carried him out into mid-air a good ten spans above the steep slope. He could feel the line slipping through his fingers, and if he fell from here he'd be killed, or as good as. He tried to loop the line around his wrist but it was too taut.

'Rurr-shyve!' he gasped as the flappeter carried him even higher, 'Put me down. I'm slipping.'

There was no mistaking its malicious amusement this time. Rurr-shyve kept flying straight ahead. The rope burned as it slipped through Nish's fingers and his arm was cramping from the strain. The flappeter dipped sharply; Nish swung through the air in a figure-eight, just managed to hold on as the rope looped out then swung back and, as he shot past the rocks crusting the steep slope, dropped sprawling onto them and tumbled into a crack, whacking his head and nearly taking an ear off.

He expected the flappeter to race away, but when the stars had gone from his eyes Rurr-shyve was still hovering above him, the end of its tether moving in a lazy circle, its breathing tubes squelching in merriment. Nish struggled out of the crack, caught the rope above his head, swiftly made a loop in it and pulled it around his waist.

Instantly, Rurr-shyve was off again, sweeping down the slope so quickly that he couldn't keep up. He was continually lifted in the air, legs windmilling, then dropped until his feet dragged across earth, rocks and grass, and through spiky shrubs, before being jerked up again so hard that he left his dinner behind.

Finally they reached the gentle slope at the base of the ridge. Nish expected Rurr-shyve to take off and drag him through the tops of the trees, but it merely continued at the same height and pace. He was now running like a man hauled by a racehorse, stumbling, falling and being dragged on his knees, or full length or on his backside, until he was battered and bruised all over and his legs would no longer hold him up.

Rocks loomed up and, afraid that he'd be smashed into them, he untied the rope and skidded across the ground, sure that would be the last he'd see of the flappeter.

Rurr-shyve kept going for a few seconds, then curved around and hovered, allowing the tether to loop itself over Nish's shoulder. He swatted it away and flopped onto his back, his heart thumping so erratically that he was afraid it would tear open.

The rope dragged across him, as if Rurr-shyve wanted him to take hold of it again. He brushed it away. 'I'm sure that was very amusing,' he panted, 'but I'm not playing your game any more. You've got your freedom, so fly away and be damned.'

Rurr-shyve kept looping around, pulling the rope across Nish's face until he remembered an earlier conversation with Maelys about the binding of such creatures. Because she'd been able to take command of Rurr-shyve with the amulet immediately after its rider had been killed, his contract and link must have transferred to her. Presumably Rurr-shyve couldn't go free unless it either retrieved the amulet from her, or she died.

Nish knew that the bond between flappeter and rider was meant to prevent a flappeter from conniving at its rider's death, though it could happen where the rider was weak, new or poorly trained. Since all of those factors applied to Maelys, and she'd slain the true rider, Rurr-shyve must resent her even more. He, Nish, would have to be careful once he found Maelys in case Rurr-shyve tried to kill her and snatch the amulet.

He'd better be ready to thwart it before it struck. On the other hand, Rurr-shyve could probably sense where Maelys was. Nish slung the crossbow securely on his back then fastened the rope around his middle and braced himself, expecting the flappeter to take off with a jerk. It was watching him with those great globe eyes, but this time it moved ahead at no more than a fast walking pace, the whirring feather-rotors taking most of the weight off its spindly legs.

The passage through the forest took longer than he would have liked, for once inside it Rurr-shyve had to be careful to avoid vines and overhanging branches. Nish was worried now. If Maelys was still at the village, she must be in some kind of trouble. He didn't think she was the kind of girl to be distracted for hours at a village fair, but then he knew so little about her.

Approaching the edge of the forest, he looked down at a blazing bonfire circled by the whirling sparks of dancers carrying torches, and a spasm of fear clenched his heart. He unfastened the rope. Rurr-shyve rotored up into the darkness and disappeared. As soon as it had gone he regretted letting it go; at least it would have struck fear into the credulous villagers.

He unslung the crossbow, forced the crank another half-turn until it dug painfully into his palm, then seated a bolt in the groove. After making sure that the bag of quarrels was within reach he began to creep towards the village.

A two-storey dwelling lay straight ahead, with smaller huts to left and right; a narrow alley ran between them. He headed for it, sliding noiselessly along the wall of the house to the end, where he would have a clear view of the circular area within. Judging by the smell of manure, the villagers stabled animals below their living quarters.

He reached the end of the alley and peered out into the

lighted circle. A tight cluster of people stood down the far end, beyond the bonfire. It didn't look like a festival gathering. He was trying to work out what they were doing when everyone surged to the left, revealing a small brown figure suspended from a hoop mounted vertically on a post.

No, not a figure, a model made out of clay. He let out his breath, but the figure raised its head and he glimpsed patches of pale skin between the brown. It was Maelys, thickly covered with mud, and a group of children ran forwards together, hurling more handfuls at her. She cried out, squirming as she tried to avoid them, but every throw hit. What had she done to turn them against her so violently?

'Enough,' said a squeaky old voice. 'Bring the red-hot pokers.'

Nish's heart gave a painful lurch. At most he could kill two of them, but if he did the villagers would tear him to pieces. The only alternative was to declare himself as the son of the God-Emperor, though that would reveal him to Jal-Nish, for Nish could see a wisp-watcher in the distance.

He hesitated, though only for a second. Whatever happened next, he couldn't allow them to harm an innocent girl. Nish swallowed, raised the crossbow and stepped into the light. He was about to shout his name when something struck him hard on the elbow. The crossbow flew out of his hands, struck the ground and went off. Someone shrieked from the crowd and everyone swarmed around a falling figure.

A fist seized Nish by the collar, a sharp point dug into his back, and a hoarse voice said, 'Don't try anything.'

He couldn't resist, for his arm had gone numb. Before he took in what was happening, Nish had been dragged across to the hoop by a fellow as strong as a blacksmith, stripped to a rag wound around his loins and bound upside down to the hoop, his feet beside Maelys's head.

'Stop!' he cried thickly, feeling the blood running to his head. 'Don't you realise who I am? I'm Cryl-Nish Hlar –'

An old man lurched across and smacked him in the mouth. 'Liar and blasphemer! How dare you rouse us to rebel against the God-Emperor?'

'But I didn't . . .' Surely Maelys hadn't tried to enlist their aid in a rebellion? How could she think to begin an uprising in such a remote village? How think it at all, the little fool!

The old man whacked him again. 'How dare you take the sacred name of the God-Emperor's Son!'

A gaggle of old women approached, wailing and tearing at their clothing. Four of them carried a thin crone with straggly hair and a wound in her side, still seeping. Her clothes were drenched in blood and Nish knew she was going to die. In the war he'd seen death enough for a hundred lifetimes.

A cry went up. 'The blasphemer shot Gyghan deliberately, and she a helpless old woman. Kill him!'

Nish's face was swelling with blood, his pulse pounding in his ears. 'But I didn't! The man behind me knocked the crossbow out of my hand. I wasn't even holding it when it went off. You must have seen . . .' He scanned the crowd for the fellow but it was impossible to tell, upside down. 'Look at me!' he said desperately, despising himself for having to invoke his father's name. 'Can't you see my father, Jal-Nish, in me?'

A fistful of mud struck him in the face, going into his open mouth and up his nose. He gagged and tried to spit it out but dribbles of muddy saliva ran into his eyes. He blinked enough out of his right eye to see.

'Liar!' shrieked one of the crones, the shortest and most hideous person Nish had ever seen. 'We've seen the graven images. Cryl-Nish Hlar is a young, handsome man, the image of the God-Emperor, and you're an ugly scrawny runt!'

'It could be him . . .' began another elder, who was white-haired, black-gummed and toothless.

'If it was,' said the headman, 'the wisp-watcher would have recognised him and the God-Emperor would have

131

appeared in a clap of thunder to save his Son. Since he has not, it's proof that this wretch is an impostor.'

'He couldn't get here that quickly!' cried Nish. 'Please –'

'He – must – die,' slurred the dying crone.

'Kill him, kill him, kill him,' chanted the squat woman, and the rest of the villagers took up the chant.

The headman nodded. 'The impostor must be slain in the prescribed way, else the God-Emperor will believe we condone blasphemy.' After studying the staring circle, he raised his voice. 'Put out his eyes with the red-hot irons. Sear the marks of the traitor into his face and body. Treat the witch-slut the same way, then weigh them down with stones and cast them into the river.'

Nish tried to tear himself free but he was too well bound. He let out a muffled groan. More muddy dribble ran into his eyes.

Something touched him on the shin. Maelys had stretched out her fingers. 'Courage, Nish. Our doom is set, but at least we can try to face our deaths with dignity.'

'Only a fool who's never felt pain could say such a stupid thing,' he snarled.

'How do you know what I've suffered?' she said quietly.

'Before they've finished with us we'll be screaming in such agony that we'd betray our own mothers to stop it.'

Maelys looked down at him with such reproach that he regretted his words at once. She could imagine their final agonies as well as he could, and she was facing them far more nobly. How had Father turned him into such a coward?

Out of the corner of his eye Nish saw a man approaching with a long, glowing poker, white-hot from the bonfire. Nish shuddered, but managed to steel himself. Face your end with dignity.

'I'm sorry,' he said. 'I'm so sorry, Maelys.'

'So am I,' she said. 'I've been such a fool, Nish.'

The last thing he saw before he closed his eyes to block

out what was coming was the flappeter shooting across the sky, the firelight burnishing the undersides of its whirling feather-rotors and picking reflections from its compound eyes. He thought he made out a faint, distant cry of triumph. It would soon be free at last.

ELEVEN

There had been plenty of time for Maelys to regret her stupidity. She had hung on the hoop for the longest hours of her life, with the whole village staring at her, watching the crones mixing red ochreous mud in a cauldron, adding various witchy powders, fluids and pastes, and chanting a dirge as they stirred the mess. Once they were satisfied with their concoction every villager took a hand in pelting her with the stinging muck until she was coated with it.

They slowly rotated the hoop on the whipping post so the bonfire would dry the mud into an even coating. She couldn't imagine why that mattered, and whether the ritual had some sorcerous intent prescribed by the God-Emperor for blasphemers or was just a local superstition. However, once the mud baked on they didn't bother to repair the places where pieces flaked off. Evidently it had completed its part in the ritual.

But no regret was so bitter as when Nish appeared between the houses. *Turn back*, she prayed, at the same time hoping that he could pull off a miraculous rescue, like the hero he'd once been. But he neither turned back nor noticed the shadow creeping up behind him, and before she could work the dried mud from her lips to cry out a warning, he'd been disarmed and taken.

Even then it didn't occur to Maelys that Nish would be in danger. She assumed that, once he told the villagers who he was, they would bow down before him and he would come to his senses and take on the mantle of the Deliverer.

Only after Nish was condemned did Maelys realise just how catastrophically she'd blundered. She'd undone all the good she'd done in helping Nish to escape. No, she'd made things immeasurably worse.

While Nish had been in prison, the world could hope that one day he would fulfil his promise. Now hope was going to die in this insignificant village and the God-Emperor himself could not prevent it. Even if Nish had been recognised in the images sent by the wisp-watcher, it would take many hours for Jal-Nish's nearest lieutenant to get here, and since wisp-watchers weren't able to receive messages, he couldn't order the headman to stop the executions. By the time he arrived it would be too late for anything but to wreak terrible vengeance on the poor, foolish people of Byre.

And her actions, her choices and her failures would be responsible for their deaths, and for robbing Santhenar of hope. To say nothing of seeing the man she'd admired above all others tortured to death before her eyes. It was the worst moment of her life.

Maelys watched them approach with the pokers, already regretting her reproachful words. She hadn't suffered much, as it happened – at least, not physical pain – so who was she to criticise Nish?

Below her, he was tugging against his bonds, though they didn't budge. His face had gone purple from hanging upside down and he'd torn the skin around his wrists and ankles. Threads of blood trickled up his legs and his bulging eyes were fixed on the pokers that would put out the lights forever.

Maelys couldn't bear to watch, but she couldn't close her eyes to his fate either. She tried to think of something to say. She had to support him but could find no words that would help. 'Nish –' she began.

There came a shrill cry from above her, something shot across the village square, and her hair was buffeted by a blast from Rurr-shyve's feather-rotors. The villagers cried out in fear and backed away, save for the two with the pokers. They stood their ground, staring up at the dark sky as they tried to work out what this sign meant.

Maelys's hope faded as quickly as it had appeared. Rurr-shyve must have come for the amulet, possession of which would give it its freedom, and since she was about to die it no longer had to serve her. Indeed, it was free to kill her once it snatched the amulet and, after all she'd done to it, Rurr-shyve probably would.

A great cry went up. 'It's the God-Emperor's flappeter,' wailed the crones. 'The prisoners were telling the truth. Set them free. Hurry!'

Someone moaned, and the sound spread though the throng, swelling like a low note on an organ. People began to run back and forth.

'Quiet!' roared the headman, crouching by the fire, head in hands.

'They're doomed and he knows it,' Nish said quietly. 'The village was about to commit an unforgivable crime against the Son of the God-Emperor, and the wisp-watcher saw it all. There's nothing they can do.'

'Then we're saved,' Maelys said, sagging with relief.

The headman sprang up. 'Tear down the wisp-watcher! Bring down the flappeter as well. Gather your livestock and all the food you can carry then burn the houses. We must flee for our lives, into the wilderness.'

'What about the prisoners?' quavered a young man, all bravado gone. 'Maybe if we set them free the God—'

'Do you think he'll show us mercy *now*? There is no mercy in the God-Emperor, only revenge for those who've harmed him in the smallest measure. Wait till the wisp-watcher is down, then kill them.'

The poker-wielders thrust their implements back into the

bonfire. Ropes were looped around the pole on which the wisp-watcher was mounted. It began to buzz furiously; bluish auras crackled across the bowl below its iris, drifting around it before fizzing out. A band of youths heaved on the ropes, some shouting in exhilarated defiance, but most silent, wide-eyed and shaking.

Earth cracked and crumpled at the base of the pole; lightning crackled from the tip of the iris. The youths moaned and allowed the ropes to go slack, but the dwarfish crone hobbled forwards and beat them about the shoulders until they heaved again.

More earth moved and, with a furious crackle, the wisp-watcher crashed to the ground, the rim of its bowl carving a crescent into the dry soil. The youths let out a ragged cheer, followed by a full-throated cry of defiance. The tiny crone pointed to the river. Two youths ran forward and tried to lift the wisp-watcher. One seized it by the rim of the bowl, the other by the dirt-encrusted base of the pole.

'Don't touch it!' screeched the crone.

It was too late. The youth who'd touched the base threw up his arms, arched backwards until his groping hands caught hold of his heels and locked as rigid as a wheel. Formed into a circle of flesh and bone, he began to roll down the slope towards the river, his head flopping and bouncing at every obstacle. Another youth tried to stop him but as soon as he touched the first he too whipped backwards into a living, helpless circle and began to roll away.

A third youth cried out and ran to help, but others restrained him and everyone watched in silence as the two young men rolled into the river. As they touched the water they both let out eerie, identical wails and began to thrash their arms. They floated for a while, churning in circles, then began to drift away with the current. The wailing from one youth was cut off by a bubbling noise as his head went under. The other sank without a sound, and there was

137

silence apart from the cracking of the bonfire and a dull fizzing coming from the wisp-watcher.

The youth who had touched the rim was stuck fast, his eyes white holes in his head. He screamed, arched his back and managed to tear one hand free, but held it up to his eyes and screamed again. The tips of his fingers were glowing, there were luminous bands across his fingers where he'd been held fast, and the skin and flesh appeared to be peeling back to reveal the bones inside.

He tore the other hand free. The skeletal fingers were bending into curls like twigs in a fire. He held out his hands to his friends, pleading for help, but no one dared go near.

Someone shouted and pointed towards the river. The youth turned that way, his knees wobbling and twisting sideways, but after a couple of steps he turned around again and lurched back towards the wisp-watcher, holding his bloody arms out beseechingly. The bones in the palms of his hands were showing now, and his shrieks grew so loud and agonised that Maelys's scalp crawled.

All the villagers were staring at the youth. A pretty, beardless lad had even taken a few steps in advance of the crowd, but stopped, afraid to approach. The glow from the downed wisp-watcher brightened; its iris was twisted and fluttering like a candle flame.

The youth let out a cry that might have been mistaken for ecstasy and began to trot towards it, though as soon as he touched the iris he screamed and turned away with the bones of his forearms emerging from the dangling flesh. He'd only gone a few steps before he turned back, holding out his arms again, and so the macabre dance continued, forwards and back, forwards and back.

A great shudder took him. He managed to tear free and threw himself to the ground, clawing at the dirt in an effort to drag himself to the water, but his finger bones broke off. He rolled over and began to hump himself backwards towards the iris like a caterpillar crawling across a leaf.

His feet passed into the circle and burst into flame. He tried to resist the pull but his muscles kept propelling him back. He tilted upright like a pole pulled to the vertical, half man and half animated skeleton, stood in the circle for a moment then slowly shortened as his flesh sloughed off and the unsupported bones collapsed. His disembodied skull remained for a while, mouth gaping, but no lungs remained to give it breath. Then, in a sudden flash, it crumbled into separate bones.

'To the river with it, quick,' hissed the crone.

The staring crowd caught its collective breath, then the youths took hold of the ropes again, very gingerly, and dragged the wisp-watcher down the slope, leaving a smoking, stinking trail behind it. Each time it passed over a living plant the leaves burst into brief fire.

The remaining villagers followed, keeping well out of the way. The youths hauled the watcher to the water and, under the direction of the headman, levered it in with sticks. It hit the water and sank like a rock, though from her perch Maelys could see a glow on the surface of the water. The water bubbled; a dark stain spread outwards and the currents could not shift it.

Someone let out a hollow victory cry but no one else joined in. The villagers drew back, alarmed that the wisp-watcher lay there, a blight upon their village and a grim reminder of their unforgivable crime.

The headman pointed up to the bonfire; the villagers headed towards Maelys and Nish, speaking in low, fluttering voices. A group to her left, mostly youths and young men but with a few girls among them, were urging each other on, clutching sticks and rocks. They wanted revenge but dared not look directly at Nish, perhaps afraid he shared the powers of his father.

Another group of youths on the right appeared to be urging caution, while a spokesman for the villagers shouted, 'Leave them! We must fly before it's too late.'

'Stop!' The tiny crone extended a trembling finger at the whipping post. 'They brought this curse upon our village. Though they've cost us everything, we're not creeping away from Byre on our bellies. The God-Emperor has abandoned us and now we're doomed. Doomed! Yet we were proud once, and we'll abandon Byre in pride, not cowardice.' Her eyes flicked nervously towards the bubbling water as if she expected Jal-Nish to rise up out of it. 'Kill the witch-slut!'

'What about the Son of the God-Emperor?' the headman said in a voice barely audible above the crackling of the fire.

'The God-Emperor will crush us like roaches, but we'll make him pay. Kill the Son! Kill them both!'

After a long hesitation, the crowd roared, 'Kill them!'

The poker-wielders withdrew their instruments. The ends of the pokers were white-hot for a couple of hand spans. The two men headed for the whipping post, heads bowed, afraid to look into the eyes of the God-Emperor's son.

The shorter of the two, a stocky bald fellow with a squinting left eye, stood by the post, breathing heavily as he tried to find the courage for this monstrous sacrilege. The other man, stringy and as leathery as Rurr-shyve's saddlebags, waved the poker half-heartedly towards Nish, but his arm jerked it back. Maelys felt the heat of it on her ankle. Nish flinched and screwed his eyes shut.

'Put out their eyes!' shrieked the crone.

As they started forwards, Rurr-shyve dropped out of the sky between the villagers and the bonfire with a trumpeting shriek, hovered and swung its long body in a circle around its rotor stalk. Its scaly tail slammed into the crowd, battering adults and children out of the way. Villagers screamed and ran in all directions.

The two men stared at the huge beast, a creature out of their nightmares, and the pokers drooped in their hands. The headman climbed to his feet, wiped blood off his face and shouted, 'Kill them! Guards, hack the beast to pieces!'

The villagers were not armed but a group of men and youths ran for the houses. The crowd began to hurl clods of earth and small pebbles which bounced harmlessly off the creature's hide. The stringy man gathered his resolve and thrust his cherry-red poker at Nish's right eye. Nish jerked his head out of the way, desperately.

'Hold him,' the fellow said hoarsely, with a fearful glance over his shoulder at the flappeter. It was rising again, its feather-rotors kicking up clouds of dust as it moved.

The man with the squint took Nish's head in his shaking hands and held him, but before the stringy fellow could do the gruesome business Rurr-shyve's serrated beak tore his hand and forearm off. With a toss of its head, hand and poker went spinning through the air.

The squint-eyed man thrust his poker at Rurr-shyve's neck and the red-hot metal hissed as it burned through the scaly carapace. Smoke puffed up. The flappeter swung its head sideways into the man's midriff and Maelys heard ribs break as he was hurled across the dirt towards the bonfire. He crawled away, moaning.

The villagers were heaving up stones from outside the door of the largest house. The men and youths were creeping back, brandishing mattocks, scythes and picks. Not even Rurr-shyve could fight them all at once, though it didn't need to. All it wanted was the amulet, and Maelys dead.

It lifted and came at her, its paired legs extended as if trying to snatch the amulet. Maelys flinched but Rurr-shyve caught hold of the ropes binding the hoop to the post with its foot hooks and rose sharply. The hoop creaked and cracked but the post held.

A broken chunk of paving stone came whirring through the air, just missing her hip. The crowd tore up another slab and began attacking it with a hammer, breaking it into useable pieces.

Rurr-shyve heaved again. The ropes groaned; the hoop cracked and rotated on the whipping post, tilting Maelys to the left. The armed men were moving in a spreading line towards them, trembling and trying to urge each other on. Despite everything, Maelys pitied them, for their peaceful village life was over and it was unlikely any of them would escape Jal-Nish's vengeance.

Rurr-shyve spun in a circle, still gripping the ropes. A flying rock struck it hard on the upright discs of its tail, knocking it sideways. It recovered, heaved again and with a shudder the whipping post tore out of the ground. Rurr-shyve lurched upwards, labouring under the weight as stones whistled underneath its trunk. One of the bindings of the willow hoop pulled apart and Maelys's foot ropes slipped free, leaving her swinging agonisingly from her wrists, with every lurch tearing more skin away.

The burly leader of the attackers raced towards them, swinging his scythe in wicked slashes. Her bare feet were dangling from the lower curve of the hoop, which was opening wider all the time. If the scythe didn't get her, the next lurch was likely to drop her right into the middle of the attackers.

A lump of rock struck Nish in the belly. He convulsed but was held fast by his bonds. Maelys slipped further; the scythe whistled by so close that it could have cut her toenails. Rurr-shyve, struggling to lift the heavy post, wasn't climbing quickly enough.

One of the youths, bolder than the others, came racing across, sprang and caught hold of the base of the whipping post. His weight almost dragged Rurr-shyve out of the air. The feather-rotors went *flutter-thump* as they tried to hold it up; the willow hoop groaned and its two halves opened wider, lifting her above the post and out to the side. Maelys could feel the hoop separating; she was going to fall.

The youth pulled himself up the post, clinging with hands and knees. He reached the top and attempted to drag her down, but the rope binding the remains of the hoop to the post slipped free and he fell with it. Rurr-shyve lurched upwards, carrying the hoop by the bindings, and Nish. The half Maelys was tied to separated. Her wrists slid free and she fell into the crowd.

The villagers swarmed at her, and she knew they would tear her apart. Rurr-shyve might be bound to save Nish, but it would welcome her death. She was staggering to her feet in a hopeless attempt to defend herself when Rurr-shyve dropped sharply, Nish held between its pairs of legs, and spun in a circle on its feather-rotor stalk. Its whirling tail sent people flying, then it caught Maelys by her rags and heaved her up. Another foot hook snapped around her upper thigh and it lifted her sharply, swaying through the air.

A hail of rocks and clods of earth arced up at her. A hoe just missed her dangling foot, a lump of wood caught her painfully on the knee, then the flappeter whirred up out of the light of the bonfire and the missiles fell away. It was completely dark here, for the moon had crept into thick cloud moving in from the west.

A minute or two away from the village, Rurr-shyve dipped down again, dragging them through the cold river until all the mud was gone and they were gasping for breath, before turning in the direction of the pinnacles. Maelys heard its gurgle of amusement.

'Why did you save me?' she panted, 'when you could have taken the amulet and gone free?'

I'm compelled to look after the Son. I can't go free.

'But you didn't have to save me.'

It's easier with a rider. The God-Emperor made us that way. Besides, I'm partial to human flesh. I'm saving you up.

Maelys didn't think Rurr-shyve was joking.

Nish didn't say a word all the way back, or even after the flappeter had set them down by the embers of the camp fire. She hung in the creature's hooks for a while, scrunched up and trying to cover herself. He wasn't looking at her, though. Nish was staring into the dark, his jaw knotting and unknotting, in the grip of some powerful emotion.

143

As soon as he turned away she scurried into the shadows, retrieved her pack and dressed in her spare clothing, thinking that they'd be fleeing any minute. However, Rurr-shyve settled, devoured a spiny bush then tucked its head under its neck and its eyes dulled. It didn't move, even when Nish fastened the tethers.

'Hadn't we better go?' she said tentatively.

'Once it's rested,' he said tersely.

She dropped her head, though after all she'd put him through, he had a right to be angry. 'Yes, of course.'

She covertly watched him dress his thin body, overcome by her emotions. Nish had risked his life for her, a little nobody. He was staring at her now, his eyes smouldering in the firelight. What was he thinking?

Maelys went across, forced a smile and sank to her knees in front of him. 'Nish, thank you so much –'

'What did you think you were doing back there?' he burst out, spit flying onto her shirt in his fury.

'I – I – had to get food . . .' She dared not admit what she'd really been up to.

He leaned forwards, red-faced. 'You lying little toad! You went down to try and start a rebellion in my name, *without saying a word to me*. How could you think that would work? You're the stupidest little fool I've ever met, and that's saying a great deal.'

'But you must –' she began.

'No!' he said savagely. 'No, no, no! Did you really think they'd rally to me just because you told them my name?'

'Yes,' she squeaked. 'Because ten years ago you promised to come back and overthrow your father. The whole world is waiting for you to make good your promise.'

'Is it? How can you be sure? And even if it is, *what about me*? What if I'd changed my mind, or discovered it was impossible? How dare you try to manipulate me? You're as bad as my father.'

It was as if he'd struck her. Maelys felt the blood draining away from her face. She swayed on her knees then tried to scramble away, but he caught her arm and went on.

'And even if I were disposed to start a rebellion, *which I'm not*, I certainly wouldn't begin it here. What can a couple of hundred peasants do in the middle of nowhere? When Father catches them, and he must, he'll destroy them to the last woman and the last child. And it will be your fault.'

'I'm sorry,' she whispered. She couldn't face him; couldn't bear to think about what she'd done. How could her good intentions have gone so wrong? 'I thought –'

'You didn't think. You're a stupid, naïve little child. And worst of all, you've undone all the good you did in helping me to escape.'

'What?' She couldn't think straight; didn't have a clue what he was talking about.

'The wisp-watcher!' he hissed. 'It saw me and Rurr-shyve. Now Father knows exactly where I am and he'll already be after me.' He dropped his head into his hands. 'I'd sooner have stayed in prison, with no hope, than to be given hope then robbed of it so brutally. I wish I'd never heard your name.'

TWELVE

Nish scowled at Maelys's stricken face, then stalked off into the darkness, shaking. How could she have thought that the villagers would believe her sorry tale, or follow the Deliverer anyway? They had little to gain from doing so, everything to lose, and now they'd lost it. Within a week the survivors would be screaming in his father's torture chambers.

What did Maelys want from him anyway? Nish knew she was after something, for he'd spent years among the most cunning manipulators in the world and could tell when he was being used. No girl's clumsy deceptions and awkward half-truths could deceive him; he'd seen through Maelys's story days ago. If she didn't want something from him, the absurd aunts who'd sent her did.

Not so absurd, come to think of it. Fyllis *had* got him out, relatively unharmed. And Maelys *had* overcome every obstacle, including ones Nish couldn't have defeated. It was all the more incomprehensible that such a resourceful and level-headed girl (thinking of her as a girl made things so much easier) should have acted so rashly. What was she really after?

Yet . . . when he thought about it, Maelys was so quiet and shy that it was inconceivable she could be working on her own behalf. She must be acting out of duty to her clan. Her ancient clan had nothing left to lose but their lives, and such proud folk might account their lives of little worth when reduced to such a mean existence. But they had everything to gain if Nish did overthrow his father.

It all became clear. The aunts were prepared to risk everything on this reckless gamble, knowing that if they lost they'd suffer the cruellest fate the God-Emperor could contrive for them.

Ah, but if they won . . . Just for a moment, Nish allowed himself the glorious dream – that he might take his father's place and dispense justice tempered by mercy with an even hand, revered by all his subjects as he worked to change Santhenar to a better, fairer place.

And he *would* reward Maelys's clan beyond their imagination, for Nish never forgot his friends. He followed that delicious dream as he stumbled through the dark, until he put his foot down and there was nothing underneath it.

His heart lurched and he threw himself backwards, just in time. When he'd recovered, Nish felt around in front of him, thinking that he'd come to the edge of a cliff, but it was just a ledge about a span high.

Still, he might have broken an ankle. He sat on the edge and hard reality pushed his daydreams away. Well he might admire the aunts' gamble, but there was no place in his mind for dreams and no room in his heart for hope. He'd cut himself off from its miseries and hope's treacherous cousin, expectation. He would look for nothing more than the life of an ordinary man, would expect nothing save to live from one day to the next. If he expected nothing, he wouldn't be let down again.

His thoughts returned to Maelys, and how he'd struck out at her. To his shame, Nish discovered that he'd enjoyed taking out his bitterness on her; hurting her had helped to ease his pain. He saw the stricken look in her eyes and felt sick. Prison had changed, no, *lessened* him. He'd spent so long immersed in his own troubles that he'd lost all feeling for others.

Maelys, at least, had acted selflessly, out of duty to her family. Yes, she *had* tried to manipulate him, in her awkward, girlish way, and it had turned out disastrously for the villagers, yet their elders had made the choice to blind and kill him, when they could have held him for the God-Emperor's minions. They'd brought it on themselves.

And he had to learn to look outside himself. He was deeply in Maelys's debt. He owed her his life and the chance to live again. He had to make it up to her.

Apologising wasn't going to be easy and Nish didn't want to do it, for he was a proud man who found it hard to admit his failings. Never admit a weakness. That had been another of his father's harsh childhood lessons. Why me? he kept thinking as he headed back, and had to remind himself again – so soon – to get out of his self-absorption. He rehearsed various forms of apology as he stumbled through the dark, but finally decided on the simplest, 'I'm really sorry'.

Approaching the camp site, he hesitated outside the circle of firelight. Rurr-shyve was still sleeping, assuming that what it did at such times was sleep. Who could tell? Surely only his father could see into the mind of the alien beasts.

Maelys was sitting well back from the fire, in the shadow cast by the discs of Rurr-shyve's tail. Her arms were wrapped around her chest and she was rocking back and forth, humming softly and staring at the scrubby grass between her bare feet. She looked as though she'd been crying.

Something rustled to his left and she looked up eagerly. Nish hadn't noticed it before, but with that pitch-coloured hair and pale skin, and the lush but compact figure, she reminded him of the girls from his homeland in distant chilly Einunar.

Nish felt a sudden pang of nostalgia for home and family. Because of the war, he'd been sent away from home at the age of sixteen to become a prentice artificer in one of the newfangled clanker manufactories. He hadn't seen his mother, his sister or brothers, or Einunar since his eighteenth birthday. Now his siblings were gone and he had no idea how to find his mother. He felt utterly alone. Maelys was the only person who'd cared about him and, despite her folly, he'd treated her shabbily.

She looked around, uncomfortably, as if aware that she was being watched. Nish didn't want her to think that he was spying on her. He probed with one foot until he encountered a dry stick and stepped firmly on it. She jumped at the sound and he went forwards, making plenty of noise, so he wouldn't frighten her.

She turned to face him, her knees together modestly as if she were wearing a skirt rather than pants, and gave a little smile, so tentative yet so full of yearning. He paused in mid-stride, for it lit up her face, turned her from being an attractive girl to a beautiful one, and suddenly it struck him.

Nish wasn't one of those men who thought every woman who smiled at him desired him. In his youth he'd discovered, cruelly, that they did not, though by the end of the war he'd learned to read men and women. The look in Maelys's eyes was unmistakable. She didn't know she was giving herself away, but it was as clear as daylight to Nish.

She was developing a romantic fondness for him (he shied away from the word *love*, which he couldn't even bear to think about). But any kind of romantic yearning was unbearable to him now.

He did like Maelys, who was warm-hearted, generous and brave, and he was truly grateful that she'd done so much for him. *But she wasn't Irisis*, the love of his life, his obsession ever since her death, and the only woman he wanted. He couldn't even think of Maelys – so little, quiet and shy, the very opposite of Irisis – in that way.

149

As he stepped into the firelight, she rose to her feet and her face lit up. 'Nish,' she began, 'I was so worried –'

There could be no future for the two of them, so it was better to crush her feelings right away, even if it made her hate him. It would be simpler if she did.

'I deeply regret what I said earlier,' he said formally but without a trace of warmth, 'or at least, the way I said it. You tried to manipulate me and it went terribly wrong, but I should have been more measured.' He couldn't address the other issue, though: his broken promise. 'I must also thank you for all you've done for me,' he went on in clipped tones, and saw the light fade from her eyes. 'I will never forget it. But don't think that I feel anything more for you than *gratitude*. I never will, for I am in love with a beautiful woman before whose memory all other women pale to insignificance.' He glanced around awkwardly. 'Get your gear ready. We're going.'

He regretted the words the instant they'd left his mouth; it was clear that he could not have wounded her more cruelly if he'd spent a year planning it. She flushed, then drew herself up to her meagre height and said with trembling pride, 'I have no idea what you're talking about. I'll be ready in two minutes,' then whirled and fled into the bushes between the pinnacles.

He heard her retching as if she were bringing up her heart, but shortly she staggered out again, wiping her mouth on a tuft of grass, and began stuffing the camp gear into her pack.

Long before Nish was ready she was standing by the flappeter, avoiding his gaze. He couldn't look at her either, so he shook Rurr-shyve from its slumber and unfastened its tethers. By the time he'd finished, Maelys had packed his gear and swung herself up into the front saddle.

He climbed into the rear one, which took every ounce of his strength, and slumped backwards, keeping as far away from her as he could. She took hold of the amulet, her back rigidly erect, put her wrist through the wisp-controller and urged the beast into the air.

Nish fastened the safety line around his waist and closed his eyes. It was as if he'd kicked the faithful dog that had saved him from drowning.

THIRTEEN

Maelys couldn't speak for an hour or two – it hurt too much – but after that she remembered her duty and forced herself to put her feelings to one side. What mattered was her family, especially Fyllis, and Maelys would make any sacrifice to ensure their safety.

She tried to understand why Nish had acted so meanly. Had the years of confinement brought out his true character, or had it broken him? The latter, she told herself, for Maelys could not allow herself to believe she'd been so wrong about him.

Yes, he must be a broken man and, before he'd learned how to deal with his sudden freedom, she'd pressured him to become the Deliverer. It had been too much. How could she have been so arrogant?

The flappeter darted left, into a cloud. It was nearly dawn now and she was exhausted, but she still had to find a safe hideout, and soon. The God-Emperor's minions must have been on their trail for ages.

As she went over the events of the evening, Maelys realised that Nish had been right. Five people had died because of her stupidity; the community of Byre had been destroyed and the villagers would be hunted down and punished. If she hadn't gone there, Byre might have continued unchanged for another hundred years.

And yet, that hurt less than Nish's rejection. She wiped

her eyes, allowed Rurr-shyve its head and they fled into the dark.

Rurr-shyve was flying slowly down a winding, forested valley while Maelys looked for a safe place to land, for the sun was up already. As they passed over the crest of a hill she saw a large village spread out across the curve of the river, straight ahead. She wasn't going to go anywhere near this one.

'Turn away, Rurr-shyve.'

Rurr-shyve kept going. Since the rescue, the balance of power had shifted. The flappeter never refused an order but it took longer to obey, and went out of its way to make things uncomfortable for her. And once they camped, whenever she turned her back she could feel its compound eyes boring into her, their malice and their hunger. One day . . .

'Turn away!' she shouted, afraid of being seen.

The flappeter curved across the village square before banking right. People cried out and pointed, and a wisp-watcher rotated to watch which way they went.

Rurr-shyve snorted though its breathing tubes, and after another half league turned back to the river. 'Fly on,' Maelys snapped. 'We can't stop here.'

Rurr-shyve is thirsty. It put its head down, landed on a high, grassy bank, folded its paired legs and slid down. Before Maelys realised what it was up to it plunged deep into the river.

The water was so cold that it took her breath away, and she couldn't swim. She tried to push to the surface but her left foot was caught in the stirrup. She could feel her chest tightening, her air running out, and the urge to thrash wildly was uncontrollable. Nish gripped her shoulder hard and she managed to resist her panic.

She was just easing her foot free when Rurr-shyve sucked in a bellyful, snapped its legs upright and burst through the surface in a deluge of water. It then sauntered – there was no other word for it – downstream to a point where the bank was low and walked out.

Maelys slid off, dripping. *Rurr-shyve is hungry.* It swung its head around and up to her, nuzzling her chest with its hard mouth.

She sprang backwards, wiping clots of slimy brown drool off her coat.

Juicy eating there.

'You can't eat your rider!' she cried. 'It'd hurt you too much.'

Rurr-shyve shook with what she interpreted as laughter. *You don't understand, little one. If I eat you, it won't hurt me at all. There's no loss, you see.* It began to crop the lush grass and tall rushes.

She didn't say anything. Rurr-shyve was testing her. Maelys had to find a way to reassert her mastery, though she couldn't think of one.

The following evening she was looking for a camp site when, without warning, she began to hallucinate that she was flying around the ceiling of one of the God-Emperor's torture chambers, looking down at bloodstained instruments and brutalised bodies. Rurr-shyve swerved wildly and the hallucination was gone.

'What's the matter?' yelled Nish.

'Must have dozed off,' she muttered, thinking that it had been caused by lack of sleep, and headed for the nearest landing place, a windswept island in a frozen lake.

After dinner she went directly to her blankets and slept, but soon found herself in a different nightmare. A vast parade ground, like the one between Mazurhize and Morrelune, was carpeted with thousands of people, all lying on their faces clad in nothing but loin rags. The masked God-Emperor was stalking back and forth on their backs, flogging indiscriminately with a stiff right arm.

154

She must have cried out and woken herself, for Nish was sitting up in the rider's sleeping cloak, staring at her in the dim firelight. Pretending to be half-asleep, she settled down.

The night after that she had a similar nightmare, twice, the second time so vividly that she woke, bolt upright and running with sweat. She could still hear the sound of the whip striking flesh, though none of its victims had made a sound – that wasn't permitted. There was an unnerving moaning sound in her ears, though it took several moments before Maelys realised that it was coming from her own throat.

Nish was on his feet but she couldn't face him at such a moment of weakness. She dropped down, pulled her coat over her head and lay under it, shaking, until his footsteps moved away.

The nightmare she had before dawn was much worse, for it featured Nish as a strutting popinjay, giggling while he watched people being tortured and executed. She woke shuddering, but the dream did not fade as her others always had. It remained perfectly clear and kept repeating all day.

Was she seeing the future? She knew how tempted Nish was, for she'd heard him crying out in torment when he thought she was asleep, refusing his father's offers. What if he succumbed?

She was breathing so heavily that Nish woke and came to her. She tried to push him away, striking his chest with her fists, but he held her wrists until she collapsed back into sleep, and she was only vaguely aware of him kneeling by her, watching over her for what remained of the night.

They flew west then north along the mountain chain between the highest peaks into a remote, uninhabited land. Maelys didn't have a destination in mind, though she was aware that, further north, the mountain chain broadened and became even more rugged. In that uncharted mass of

155

towering mountains and hidden valleys they must be able to find a safe hiding place, at least for the winter.

Nish had barely spoken to her since they'd returned from the village. He spent his time on the ground exercising furiously, trying to regain his strength, though when flying he just stared into space, taking no interest in his surroundings. He hardly slept and seemed to be sinking further into depression. His promise didn't seem to mean anything to him now. Nothing did, save running away. She couldn't bear to think of him as a coward, but what other explanation was there?

And yet, though still weak and ill, he had gone down to Byre to rescue her, so how could he be a coward? Could it all be her fault for pushing him too hard before he was ready? It must be. His father had broken Nish and, before the world could hope for deliverance, he had to be put back together again.

What about her other duty? Despite the rejection, Maelys had to try again. His feelings for his dead lover were an unhealthy obsession brought on by ten years of solitary confinement. She had to help him overcome them, too.

Rurr-shyve turned sharply left, then right as she directed it through a rocky slot. It was late afternoon and the flappeter was fighting a headwind so strong that it hurt her eyes and made her nose drip. Rurr-Shyve's rotor-blade injury was healing well but Maelys was afraid the strain would dislocate it again.

Flying conditions would have been better at a higher altitude but they had to stay low, winding along each valley, for the cold was so intense higher up that Nish couldn't endure it.

Could *fleshly deprivation* be part of his trouble? The prune-mouthed aunts had often spoken scornfully about men's appetites, and Maelys wondered if doing that duty with him might be the best way to get through to him.

Her heart began to race. Apart from the time when she'd

caught him staring at her bosom, he'd studiously avoided looking at her figure, and it was clear he was never going to make any kind of approach.

The aunts had also sneered about how easily led men were, through a woman's wiles. Maelys wasn't convinced; her father had been a strong man who knew his own mind, but she couldn't see any other option for herself. Since Nish was never going to make the first move, she had to try and seduce him.

The sun was low now. She went over what Aunt Haga had told her as she searched the barren landscape for a safe camp site. The sides of the valley sloped steeply here and were covered in grey scree with an occasional spindly bush. She hadn't seen a cave in days, and they couldn't camp on the windswept slope where there was neither water, shelter nor fuel for a fire. Further ahead the river angled through a gorge that looked even more inhospitable.

Rurr-shyve was labouring now and couldn't go much further, for it hadn't fed well in days and was starting to eye her ever more pointedly. It turned the corner, fighting the strengthening wind, and entered the gorge. The sun disappeared.

Maelys pulled her coat more tightly about her, thinking that they'd have to camp on the slope no matter what, which at least would put off her seduction duty for another day, when the gorge opened out into a steep, forested valley. To the left a series of caves extended along a band of white rock.

Rurr-shyve put its long neck down and headed for the river. After it had drunk and fed on a wiry water weed strung with float bladders that crackled and popped as it chewed, Maelys tethered it in the shelter of some rocks while Nish went up to the caves to set up camp, silent as usual.

She climbed up and inspected the caves. The left and middle ones were just shallow niches that the wind eddied through, but the right-hand cave was deeper, with a high, sloping roof that would convey the smoke out, and it was dry and sheltered from the wind by a rock buttress shaped like the rear half of a buffalo.

'We'll sleep warm tonight, for once,' she said. And protected from Rurr-shyve's alien stares. She couldn't possibly seduce Nish with it looking on.

Nish was shivering fitfully. 'I don't think I'll ever be warm again.' He began carrying armloads of dry wood up and stacking them for the fire.

While he got it going Maelys cut more wood with Hinneltyne's hatchet, extending the stack in a curve so their sleeping environment would be as cosy as possible. She fetched water from the river and gathered a shirt-full of mussels, twisting them off rocks just below the water's edge. There were no fruits, vegetables or nuts to be gathered at this time of year, though she did find green herbs in a boggy patch by the water.

Then, as the sun set, black fish began to jump near the shore and, accomplished gleaner that she was, on the fourth try she scooped one out of the air with an improvised hand net. It was a handsome fish, large enough for both of them, so she quickly gutted it, wrapped it in the herbs and took it up with the other provender to cook in the coals.

It was the best she'd eaten in months, and Nish appreciated it too; he didn't leave a scrap and licked his fingers afterwards. She poured him tea she'd made from one of the herbs, took a mug for herself and settled back until he'd finished it. And then . . . No, first she needed to bathe. She'd avoided doing so for the past few days because it had been so cold, but she couldn't bear to come to him unclean.

'I'm going down to the river to wash,' she said.

He continued staring into the fire, so she took the fur-lined cloak and went down to the water, immersing herself in it for as long as she could bear the cold. As she came out, Rurr-shyve lifted its head and gave her a long stare. She hastily turned her back, dried herself on her clothes, rinsed them and wrapped herself in the cloak.

It won't work.

She spun around. Rurr-shyve was just an outline in the starlight but it was still staring at her. 'Go away!'

He's not for you. You know he isn't.

'Shut up and mind your own business.'

It is my business. It was laughing at her again.

She went up, heart thudding, jaw clenched, mouth dry. Nish hadn't moved. She gave him a tentative smile. He didn't smile back and her heart sank. She couldn't do it; but she had to. After hanging her wet clothes on a length of cord stretched between two rocks, she warmed her freezing hands and feet at the fire. Her feet were blue and took ages to warm up, yet her face felt hot, inflamed. It felt strange to be naked under the cloak, and dangerous, like setting off on a journey to a foreign land without a guide.

No, Nish would be her guide. She knew from the stories she'd read about him that he'd been a gentle, loving man, though she'd seen precious little of it. She sat down beside him, though not too close.

How to begin? You must be subtle, Aunt Haga had said, though not too subtle, for men can be slow on the uptake. Talk to him, show him you like him, praise him. Haga had also explained the merits of wine in seduction, for both parties. Maelys wished she had some now.

Talk to him, but what about? It had to be something positive. After the way he'd reacted the other night she was reluctant to bring up his failed rescue at the village.

'I've read your tale many times,' she said quietly, edging a little closer and turning to face him. The cloak fell open from ankle to knee and she hastily twitched it closed, though she needn't have bothered. He kept his eyes averted.

'What tale?' he said, turning to her in puzzlement.

'The *Tale of Nish and Irisis.* It's famous . . .'

It was the worst thing she could have said, for at the

159

mention of Irisis's name such pain racked him that she had to look away. He doubled over and began rocking back and forth.

Tonight was not the night, though her relief was tinged by guilt. After a while she edged closer, reached out and touched him on the shoulder. 'Nish, are you all right?'

He shuddered and straightened up. 'Who wrote our tale?'

'The teller, Mindelmy. It was the last tale he wrote; he was beheaded for it. I first read it when I was a kid.'

From the look on his face, he still regarded her as one. 'What does it say . . . about me, I mean?' His eyes warned her not to mention Irisis again. 'If you can remember it.'

'I've read it so many times I could recite it word for word. It tells of your part in the last three years of the war. It's a forbidden tale; I could have been put to death for having it.'

'Even as a child?' he said wonderingly.

'Even so.'

'And yet you still read it; kept it?'

'Yes.'

'You must have been a brave little girl.' The compliment sounded condescending, though she didn't think he intended it to be. 'So Father has forbidden anyone to talk about my life,' Nish mused. 'He can't tolerate the thought of a rival . . .'

'You were a great hero of the war . . . and because of the way the tale ends –' Why had she mentioned that?

He didn't react this time. 'You mean the promise to over-throw my father.'

'Yes. But everyone knows it now. Would you like me to recite some of the tale?'

'How long is it?'

'Five hundred and ninety-two pages.'

'Another time,' he said, less gruffly than before.

It gave her heart. Perhaps she might be able to go through with her plan after all. Praise him. 'You must have been brave too.'

'I was terrified out of my wits most of the time. I'm not naturally brave at all. I often had to force myself to go on.'

'That's what bravery means,' she said quietly. 'I have to force myself too. Every minute of every day. And even now,' she said, almost inaudibly.

His ears were keen. 'What do you mean?'

Maelys blushed. 'Nothing,' she lied. 'Everything is so very hard. This journey; finding food; the future . . .'

'Tell me about yourself, Maelys,' he said kindly.

'There isn't anything new to tell. I told you everything before.'

'I don't remember much; because of the brainstorm, I dare say.'

She went back to the beginning, telling him about her clan, though not its name or where Nifferlin was, just in case he was taken back to his father. She described the manor, her happy childhood marred by the loss of so many young men in the war, and the nightmare that followed after the God-Emperor seized power.

She paused but he didn't say anything, so she went on to talk about her expectations once she was grown up – to marry well and run her manor, farms and orchards, and how those dreams had gradually been crushed, the clan name falling so low that all hope of a respectable liaison was lost.

'I never gave up hope,' she said, staring into the fire. 'Not completely. But now . . .'

Suddenly Maelys felt overcome and began to weep for all she'd grown up to expect as her right, but could never have; for ending up on this dismal flight to nowhere that, realistically, could only end one way; and most of all for being forced into this deceitful position with the man she'd so admired, and even now was so far above her.

He patted her awkwardly on the shoulder. 'Come on, it's not entirely hopeless. We're free, you and I, and he hasn't found us yet. Here, dry your eyes.'

161

He pulled his hand up into the sleeve of his shirt and dabbed at her face with the cuff. She wiped her eyes, pulled the sleeve up and took hold of his wrist with her cold hand. His eyes softened, and for the first time she knew he really cared about her.

Do it, an inner voice urged her. It'll never be easier than it is now. He wants you. She swayed towards him.

'Maelys,' he said, holding his arms out. She went to him in a rush, raising her chin and tilting her head backwards so he could kiss her, but he moved to one side. She saw the puzzled look in his eyes as his face went past hers and he put his arms around her in a brotherly, comforting way.

It was going wrong, as she'd known it would. He didn't desire her at all. He was just being kind. Or had he failed to get the message? He gave her a squeeze, began to draw away, and Maelys knew she had to send him a signal he couldn't possibly mistake. She held onto him, breathed into his ear then licked it with the tip of her tongue as Aunt Haga had instructed her.

Nish recoiled so quickly that Maelys lost her balance, fell backwards and the cloak came open all the way. He sprang to his feet, staring down at her and breathing heavily.

'Cover yourself!' he said coldly. 'What kind of a woman are you – you know my heart is given to another. Don't *ever* come near me again.'

It was the most mortifying moment of her life. Maelys sat up, her treacherous face burning, jerked the cloak closed and nodded stiffly as Nish stalked away into the darkness. She wanted to do the same. No, she wanted to crawl into a hole and die.

She lay by the fire for ages, listening to his agonised cries echoing back and forth between the steep walls of the canyon. She couldn't have slept if she'd wanted to, for she was too afraid it would bring on another of those hallucinatory nightmares.

Finally silence fell, so complete that she began to feel

anxious about him. In this mood he might have done anything. She crept down to the river bank to make sure he was all right. There he was, sitting on a rock by the water, exposed to the biting wind, looking utterly desolate. His lips were dark – with blood?

'Nish,' she said softly. 'I'm so sorry –'

He turned to her, though his eyes showed no recognition. He was too far gone. 'Father still has Irisis,' he rasped. 'My beautiful Irisis, perfectly preserved in a crystal coffin, as though she's just sleeping. I've got to have her back.'

Maelys's skin crawled. He was out of his mind. She backed away but his eyes looked right through her.

FOURTEEN

Nish couldn't think straight, for the blood was pounding in his head like a drumbeat. How could Maelys have thought he'd be interested in *her*? How dare she insult Irisis's memory so?

His head began to whirl and his lover's face appeared to him as if in a dream, but it dissolved into the recurring nightmare of the execution, followed by the unbearable horror of her preserved body in the crystal coffin. He closed his eyes but the vision grew stronger and clearer until he could even see the thread-like scar where her head had been rejoined to her neck. He screamed, over and over and over, and couldn't stop until he began to taste blood in the back of his mouth.

It was a long time before he realised that the vision was gone. He sat down shakily, trying to focus on the reflections of starlight on the water, but saw Maelys instead, weeping on her knees, then on her back with the cloak fallen open like some cheap, perfumed strumpet.

But that didn't fit either. The attempted seduction was so clumsy that it was clear she'd never done it before and, from the awful look on her face afterwards, she hadn't wanted to. She didn't care for him; she was just doing what her aunts had told her, to doubly ensure his gratitude. It would have worked in the olden days, before Irisis.

He blinked and Irisis was back, her live and dead faces

tumbling over each other and sending such waves of longing and despair through him that he started screaming again, and couldn't stop until another vision abruptly cut off both his agony and his self-pity.

This time Irisis had her back to him and was walking up to the cave. She stopped outside, the firelight lighting up her golden hair, and shortly Maelys appeared, white-faced and stumbling. They stared at each other, then Irisis put out her arms and Maelys went to her. They clung together, then turned reproachful faces to him, and Irisis walked out of the cave and vanished. She'd never been there at all. It was just Maelys, standing at the entrance, staring down into the darkness.

He plunged so deeply into his mad obsession that, when Maelys came down and stood before him, she was no more real than the phantoms he saw everywhere. He didn't hear her speak, nor notice when she backed away, shaking her head in horror, though after she'd gone the visions slowly faded. Once he'd come to his senses, he felt calmer and more at peace than he had in ages.

Only then did he realise that he'd humiliated her in the most unforgivable way. The night grew intensely cold but Nish couldn't go back to the camp fire. He huddled on the shore, sheltering from the incessant wind behind Rurr-shyve, sickened by what he'd become. He had to put things right but couldn't see any way of doing it without raising Maelys's hopes. He couldn't bear it if she were to try again.

So he did nothing, and crept back into the cave at dawn, three-quarters frozen, silent, dead inside and cursing himself for the most craven coward of all – one who took his frustrations out on the helpless and innocent.

Maelys felt so humiliated that she couldn't meet Nish's eyes that day – she certainly couldn't speak to him – and she was grateful for the small shield of the saddle horn between them. He tried to talk to her several times but she leaned forwards until the rotor blast drowned him out.

That afternoon she was nodding off in the saddle for the third time when Nish leaned over the saddle horn, put his hand over hers and directed Rurr-shyve to go down. It came to ground in a glade by a rivulet, where stunted trees reared leafless black trunks to the sky. She sat in her saddle, too weary to move, while he tethered the beast and set up camp.

She was half asleep when he lifted her off and laid her on the ground on her spread cloak, and she was surprised to discover that he carried her easily. He was growing stronger every day. He made tea sweetened with black honey from an abandoned hive he'd found in the trees, and handed it to her.

'We'd better talk, Maelys.'

'If it's about last night –' She still couldn't look him in the face.

'It's not, except that I'm a pig and a boor and I'm deeply sorry.'

'Oh!' she exclaimed. 'It doesn't matter!'

Clearly she hadn't expected an apology. Did she truly see herself as having so little worth – or him as being so exalted? If only she could see the worms writhing in his soul.

'Of course it matters, but that's not what I want to talk about. It's your nightmares.'

'What I dream about is my own business.' She added pointedly, 'I wouldn't dream of asking you about your own.'

He squirmed, but continued. 'It's my business if it's my father getting at you.'

She rocked backwards. 'But . . . that's not possible.'

'He can do almost anything with the tears.' He peered at her as if trying to see inside her head. 'Especially to people whom he's recognised as having a talent for the Secret Art.'

She snorted. 'That's absurd.'

'Is Fyllis's talent absurd too?'

'We knew she had one before she could walk. But I don't even look like her.'

166

'Are you saying that no one else in your clan has a talent? That Fyllis's talent came from nowhere?'

She didn't answer at once. Such gifts were only talked about after checking that no one could overhear, or betray. 'Cousin Cathim had a small gift. And Father, I think. I heard Mother talking about it once to the aunts. That must be why your . . . the God-Emperor took him. But not me.'

'Maelys, I spent ten years listening to the guards' gossip. Flappeter riders need a talent to command their beasts, and to hear their mindspeech. Since you can do both, you *must* have a talent for the Art, hidden from you for your very survival – and I think Father is using it to send nightmares at you.'

A chill swept down her back. Concealing a talent from the God-Emperor's watchers meant a death sentence. Even *having* such a talent was usually fatal and she shied away from believing him – she didn't want to be special. Those gifts had destroyed Clan Nifferlin.

But if she did have one, what could it be? Fyllis hid the family from Jal-Nish by blocking his watchers and listeners from sending messages to Gatherer, while Cathim had been able to locate the secret wisp-watchers from their intangible wisps, but Maelys couldn't do either of those things. To have any talent was bad enough, but to be vulnerable to sendings from the God-Emperor was unbearable. Was he trying to drive her mad, or was it something worse?

Nish crouched down in front of her. 'You've got to uncover your talent, Maelys.'

She shook her head. 'I don't want it. It destroyed our clan.'

'It's for your very survival. And mine, if that still matters to you. You can't fight Father's nightmares unless you understand your own gift.'

'I wouldn't know where to begin. You've got to have a mentor.' How did she know that? 'Can . . . can you teach me?'

167

'Me?' He laughed hollowly. 'Hardly.' He began to pace in front of the fire.

Since he seemed to be finished, Maelys lay down and closed her eyes. She must have dozed, for the next she knew he was bent over her, shaking her arm.

'What?' she said drowsily, unwilling to rouse from such precious, dreamless slumber.

'Did your mother or aunts give you anything, or tell you anything about your talent?'

'No. Nothing.'

'Do you mean they sent you out on this perilous journey armed with nothing but your wits?'

She bit down on a snappy retort. He surely hadn't meant to be rude. 'I had my taphloid –'

'So they did give you something.'

'No, Father gave it to me when I was little.'

'Show me.'

Maelys drew it out. It was warm in her cold hand. She clenched it in her fist for a moment, for comfort, then passed it to him. 'It's a clockwork moon calendar. Its movement was worked by a little crystal but I had to implode it to save you, when the flappeter came.'

Rurr-shyve raised its long head. *You made me suffer, little one, and I haven't forgotten it.*

Maelys shivered at the memories, then went on. 'The aunts said it would help to hide me from the enemy, unless they got really close. They said it also held a secret that I'd need when I got to Hulipont, but I suppose it was lost when I imploded the crystal.' She looked at him anxiously.

'I wouldn't know,' said Nish. He studied the taphloid, front and back. 'It's a simple little thing.'

Like me, you mean. 'No, it's not. Sometimes other faces appear on it briefly, with odd characters and symbols on them, and moving hands, but I never knew what they meant or how to get them back.'

'Didn't your father explain it to you?'

'He just told me to keep it hidden, even from Mother and the aunts. They have no talent, you see. But they found out.'

Nish pressed the taphloid to his forehead and began to walk in a circle around the embers of the camp fire. Every time he went past the flappeter it raised its head, and specks of firelight were reflected in its cluster eyes.

'My clearsight tells me there's something here,' he said at last. 'Though I can't say what. I guess it's protected you by hiding the weak aura your talent creates. That's how Father hunts down people with talents; at least, those who can't conceal their aura.'

'What is your clearsight?' she asked timidly.

'It's hardly anything. Just an ability to see what's at the heart of things. Truths that have been concealed, things hidden. Unfortunately it doesn't tell me anything when I turn it upon myself.' He gave a rueful grin and rotated the taphloid in his hands. 'My guess is that it's meant to explain your talent to you, when you're old enough . . .'

'I am old enough!' She felt a mixture of emotions, among them eagerness and anxiety. 'Can you read it now?'

He gave a mirthless laugh. 'I don't think it's meant to be read by anyone but you.'

'But how?'

'You'll need a crystal that suits the taphloid, I expect.'

'Your father had them all scried out and destroyed.'

'Not even my father could scry out all the hidden crystals in the world.' Nish paused, gnawing at his lip, as if he doubted his own words. 'Though finding one will be another matter.'

'Well, if there are hidden crystals, the leaders of the Defiance will have them.'

'What's the Defiance? No, let me guess – some rabble who want to forge me into a weapon against my father so as to gain power for themselves.'

'I'm sure they're sincere,' said Maelys tentatively. Now he'd think she was trying to manipulate him again.

'I'm sure they're not! I spent the last years of the war among the most powerful and corrupt people on Santhenar, remember? I don't trust *anyone* who's after power, and especially not the hypocrites who claim that they only want it to do good.'

'But . . . surely to overthrow your father is a good thing? The people –'

'I used to think that, but I know better now. It's the common people who suffer most in a revolution, and no one gives a damn, least of all the scum who are making revolution in their name. Before my father could be cast down, the streets would be ankle-deep in blood, and for what? Just to replace one tyrant with another. Or worse, to plunge Santhenar into a civil war without end.

'Remember this, Maelys, whenever anyone preaches revolution to you. The worst and most capricious ruler in the world – yes, even my father – is better than civil war, or anarchy. Under my father's reign, the ordinary people live their lives largely unhindered. They may not be free, but at least they're safe. But when there's no one to govern, *everyone* suffers save the villains.'

FIFTEEN

Maelys was turning over everything Nish had said. The aunts *were* secretive, calculating and obsessed, but they weren't fools. If she needed to know about her talent they would have left a way for her to uncover it. Perhaps that's why they'd sent her to Hulipont, where the Defiance must have mancers who could teach her. Unfortunately that possibility was now closed.

The other alternative was to find a crystal, though the few crystals that had been hidden from the God-Emperor must be incredibly valuable now, and why would anyone waste one on her?

They were flying through misty cloud, its moisture condensing in little droplets on the bristles and spines of the flappeter, and in her hair. Maelys blinked drops off her eyelashes and looked around. Nish was asleep, wrapped in every garment he possessed but still shivering. She couldn't see anything through the cloud; they might not have been moving at all. Might even have been heading back towards the enemy whom, she felt sure, was still hunting them with the single-minded ruthlessness that had taken Jal-Nish all the way to the top.

She glanced at Nish again. Asleep, he looked younger, and fragile, but she reminded herself that he could be ruthless too. She put her hand in her pocket, where she now kept the taphloid to avoid its chain tangling with the amulet, for the comfort of touching it. It was as dead as before.

Rurr-shyve bucked in a sudden updraught and began to veer left and right, as if unsure which way to go. Maelys hastily hauled the amulet out and clutched it in her fist. The beast looked back at her, snorted, and steadied.

The amulet was warm in her left hand, the taphloid cold in her right. She drew it from her pocket and opened her hands, looking from one to the other. Were the eyes of the amulet a kind of crystal? They glowed faintly, and sometimes the amulet was warmer than it should have been. Occasionally it moved about inside her shirt, so it had to have a source of power. But was it stored power, or *sent* from the tears?

If sent, she could be in danger whenever she used it or commanded the flappeter with it. Was that how Jal-Nish sent the nightmares and hallucinations? And would she be in greater danger if she tried to use the amulet in another way?

With its legs folded, it might just fit into the taphloid's crystal compartment. She thumbed the hidden catch, opened the taphloid, then hesitated. If the amulet could link to the tears, putting it in might reveal the taphloid's secrets to Jal-Nish.

She closed the catch, afraid to take the risk, then opened it. But everything she'd done since she left home had been a risk, and not knowing what her talent was posed another. Making up her mind suddenly, Maelys thrust amulet and thong into the taphloid and closed it. The outline of the tiny door disappeared.

Rurr-shyve's head whipped backwards, it glared at her then turned sharply left and increased the beat of its feather-rotors. Alarmed, she withdrew the amulet; Rurr-shyve turned back onto its original heading. What could it mean? She wanted to ask Nish but he was still asleep. She put the amulet in. Again the flappeter gave her that look and turned onto the new heading.

Maelys realised that she was breathing hard. Had she given away their location to the God-Emperor, who was now calling the flappeter to him? Or had power from the amulet woken the taphloid and Rurr-shyve was now following its directions, to safety? She had no way of telling.

Logic told her to take the amulet out and never risk bringing it near the taphloid again. Intuition said that this was her only chance and she'd better take it. She weighed the first, immersed herself in the second. Which?

The taphloid was damp with her sweat. She wiped it on her coat, went to withdraw the amulet, then hesitated. It didn't *feel* as though Rurr-shyve were carrying her to the enemy.

She would take the risk. She slipped the taphloid back into her pocket.

A few hours later the flappeter broke out of cloud and she saw, ahead and to the right, a substantial town in the valley bottom, dominated by an enormous red and black citadel whose towers rose to jagged points. Her heart jumped. She'd seen paintings of the God-Emperor's bastions and this was clearly one of them.

'I made the wrong choice,' she said numbly to Nish. He'd woken earlier and she'd told him what she'd done.

He blanched, though he didn't blame her. Maelys withdrew the amulet but this time Rurr-shyve didn't change direction. It didn't react, even when she thrust the amulet through the wisp-controller and shouted at Rurr-shyve to turn away.

Shortly, however, she realised that if it continued on its present path it would pass the town half a league to the left. And it did continue, as straight as a line drawn on a map. They were too far away to see people in the streets, though a large wisp-watcher, mounted on the top of the tower and facing down into the market square, jerked upright as they made their closest approach then rotated to keep them in view as they went by.

173

To the very end, Maelys expected the flappeter to turn and curve back to the tower, but it kept on, ruler-straight, until town and tower disappeared in the haze behind them.

Only then did she release her death grip on the amulet and turn to Nish, whose knuckles were white against the saddle horn. 'What does it mean?'

'I don't know. Father loves playing with his victims, but I don't think that's what he's doing here. Did you see the way the wisp-watcher jerked? Our coming here was a surprise.'

'It's not now.'

Shortly after that they plunged into a valley full of cloud which Rurr-shyve could not climb above. They continued for an hour with the weather steadily deteriorating, into a headwind that grew ever stronger until Maelys had to squint to see at all.

Now they began to encounter vicious updraughts which flung them upwards and sideways so hard that once she was lifted completely out of the saddle and fell back only to find that it was no longer beneath her. Flinging out both hands, she just managed to catch hold of a stirrup and swung there until a white-faced Nish dragged her back. After that she kept her line fastened all the time.

By this time she had no way of telling what heading they were on, for the cloud was so thick that she could no longer tell where the sun was. She began to see fantastic shapes in the mist, like bizarre creatures forming and reforming as she went by. They appeared to turn and watch her out of sight, and she wondered if it *was* Jal-Nish trying to unnerve her. Had he also begun to assert command over the flappeter?

'I'm worried,' she said to Nish. 'We've never spent so long in cloud before. We could be anywhere.'

'I think we're still going the same way.'

Maelys wasn't convinced, but was too tired to argue. Her eyelids drooped. The past days had been exhausting; flying in this weather demanded the utmost powers of concentration even when she wasn't actively directing the beast. She could feel the strain on Rurr-shyve in every scale and bristle.

Three-quarters asleep, she failed to notice Rurr-shyve twitch convulsively, then cast a calculating glance backwards. Seeing Nish lost in his own world, and Maelys slumped over the saddle horn, it began, ever so slowly, to turn in a broad curve.

The flappeter burst out of the mist into clear air and the red and black citadel was less than half a league away. Maelys, startled awake, let out a shriek, for she could see the soldiers gathered on the flat roof beneath the gigantic wisp-watcher.

'Nish, quick!' she wailed.

'What's the matter?' he muttered drowsily.

She shook him awake. 'It's that citadel! Jal-Nish must have taken command of Rurr-shyve hours ago.'

He came half out of the saddle. 'Not from such a distance. It'll be one of his local seneschals. Fight him or Rurr-shyve will give us up.'

Casting him a nasty look, Rurr-shyve put its head down and streaked for the top of the citadel. Maelys stretched forwards, put the amulet through the wisp-controller and ordered the flappeter to turn back.

Not this time, little one. I answer to a higher power now.

'Is it . . . the God-Emperor?'

It made a gurgling chuckle through its breathing tubes. *Just his seneschal, little Maelys.*

'Not Vomix?' she breathed.

A servant most diligent in prosecuting his master's commands. He's marked for greater things, is your friend Vomix. This victory will set the seal on it.

'He's not my friend!' Maelys was feeling around in the saddlebags. The dead rider's blade had been taken from her in the village, and Nish had lost the crossbow there too, but she'd sharpened one of the iron-hard tent pegs to a wicked point. Ah, there it was.

You would be advised to make him your friend once we get there, little one, and do his will in all things. Vomix likes your type and you'll never have more need of an ally.

She drew out the tent peg, checked to make sure her safety line was tied securely and that there were no frayed patches, then sprang forwards and stabbed the tent peg down into the healed wound, right where she'd threatened Rurr-shyve with severing the other day.

'Where's your higher power now!' she hissed, twisting her free arm through the straps. 'Turn or I'll *sever* you.'

Rurr-shyve bucked so violently that her feet went up above her head. *You'll die if you do. And the Son.*

She pulled herself down again, gasping, 'I'm going to die anyway, so there's nothing to lose, and at least it'll be quick.'

What about the Son?

'It'll put him out of his misery.' She felt a physical pain inside her as she said it, but didn't dare turn to look at Nish. If she wavered now they were doomed.

The *thup-thup* faltered, but Rurr-shyve continued on. She pressed the point in. The flappeter shuddered and was trying to turn away when Maelys felt words in her head – no, they seemed to be coming *through* the creature to her. A hissing, mucous-slick voice, terrible in its power. And she recognised it.

FLY ON, RURR-SHYVE. FLY TO THE CITADEL AND TASTE YOUR REWARD.

It was a voice she'd heard twice before, though only once clearly, on the road to market when she was a girl of eleven, and Maelys had never forgotten it. It was Seneschal Vomix. She thrust harder, and Rurr-shyve bucked and twisted sideways, away from the citadel.

FLY TRUE, RURR-SHYVE. BRING THE SEDITIOUS BLASPHEMERS TO YOUR MASTER.

Maelys could tell from Rurr-shyve's spasm of rage that *master* had been the wrong word to use, and tried to take advantage of it. 'I'll sever you if you do,' she shouted over the wind, 'but I'll never be your master. A flappeter can have no master – with the possible exception of the God-Emperor himself,' she added hastily, in case Rurr-shyve had a genuine feeling for its creator, though she didn't think it did. 'But you, Rurr-shyve, are your own master and always will be.'

Over the pain, she felt its wry amusement. It did not reply, but continued its turn.

TURN BACK, TREACHEROUS RURR-SHYVE, raged Vomix. TURN BACK OR YOU'LL SUFFER THE WORST SANCTION ANY FLAPPETER CAN FACE.

Rurr-shyve kept going, but now Vomix seemed to realise that the rider was the problem, for he turned his attention to Maelys. His words oozed from Rurr-shyve into her mind, and they hurt so much that she cried out.

'What's the matter?' Nish said urgently as she flopped back into the saddle.

'It's Vomix, speaking into my mind through Rurr-shyve.' Her voice broke; the waves of pain were excruciating and she felt an irresistible urge to strike back, any way she could.

'Don't answer him, whatever you do.'

OH, HOW YOU'LL PAY WHEN I CATCH YOU. YOU'LL WISH –

She tried to hold back. Maelys tried really hard, and though she seldom lost control of her temper, it was as though something irresistible was urging her on; she couldn't stop herself. 'You'll never take me!' she screamed, brandishing the amulet at the tower. 'I'll die before I come near you, you slimy, stinking cur –'

Nish slapped his hand across her mouth. 'Stop!'

The voice was lower this time, more slippery-sticky. I KNOW YOU, DON'T I? WE'VE MET SOMEWHERE, LONG AGO.

Nish moved his hand to hers, squeezing it hard, and with an effort she regained control. Chills were running up and down her backbone, radiating out in all directions. Had she betrayed herself? She bit her lip, gave Rurr-shyve a warning jab in the side and tried to keep Vomix out. It made no difference.

I CAN GET TO YOUR MIND THROUGH THE BEAST, AND YOU CAN'T STOP ME.

'Be damned,' she said under her breath, and concentrated on control, hoping that would block Vomix out. 'Go back the way we were heading, Rurr-shyve.'

It did so. Maelys looked out for the cloud bank that had hidden them before, but it had blown away.

LOOK BACK, RIDER, WHOEVER YOU ARE. LOOK BACK AND DESPAIR.

'I won't!' she said through gritted teeth.

'Maelys?' said Nish anxiously.

She didn't answer, for she couldn't divide her attention any further.

I'VE A GOOD MEMORY AND I'M SEARCHING IT NOW. I'LL SOON DISCOVER WHO YOU ARE. LOOK BACK.

She let out a muffled moan. If he did identify her, he'd know her clan as well. She prayed that he wouldn't associate the child who'd spoken so rudely about him with her.

'Maelys,' said Nish, 'what can I do?'

Nish had proven himself in the war, in all sorts of ways. Of course he could help her. Without thinking she twisted around to look at him, but heard Vomix sigh, *AAAAH!* Half a dozen flappeters were rising up from the citadel. Her stomach knotted. A tired Rurr-shyve, already partly in Vomix's thrall, couldn't outrun fresh beasts eager for the kill.

I'VE GOT YOU NOW, LITTLE ONE. ALREADY DESPAIR'S FINGERS ARE CREEPING TOWARDS YOUR THROAT.

'Despair's fingers!' she sneered. He was no poet, but he knew how she felt.

'Maelys?'

'He's getting to me!' Rurr-shyve tried to break away. She hastily turned back to her duties with tent peg and amulet.

'Try to block him out.'

'But then I'll lose control of Rurr-shyve.'

She was already. The flappeter was slowing, twisting its

178

body this way and that, and not even the sharpest jabs made a difference now. Had it realised that she lacked the will to sever it? Had Vomix?

LOOK BACK, LITTLE ONE, AND SEE YOUR DOOM.

Maelys couldn't help herself; she looked back and saw flappeters rising up everywhere, hundreds upon hundreds of them: red ones, grey ones, black and gold ones, so many that they darkened the sky. Her chest cramped and for a few seconds she couldn't breathe. The tent peg slipped; she just caught it before it went over the side.

'It's no use, Nish. There are hundreds of them. We're beaten.'

He looked back, frowned, then unfastened his safety line, scrambled over the saddle horn and slipped into her saddle behind her.

'What are you doing?'

He put his hands on her shoulders and the pressure eased. 'Maelys, it's Vomix.'

'They're everywhere, Nish!' She had to bite down on a scream.

'Hallucinations! Father doesn't *have* hundreds of flappeters. I see to the heart of things, remember?'

He sounded so calm and, for the first time, so strong. Like the Nish of the tales she'd so loved. She still saw hundreds of flappeters but she had to trust Nish. Settling back in the saddle, she allowed him to put his arms around her, and it did help. The hallucinations were still there, the mucosal voice in her mind was as threatening as ever, but she no longer felt that she was fighting a mighty opponent all by herself.

Flappeter hallucinations appeared in every direction, surrounding them in a vast doughnut of whirring feather-rotors that began to form an enclosing shell, densest in front of them. Even Rurr-shyve seemed to be seeing them now, for the beat of its feather-rotors was faltering, its long neck turning this way and that as if it were afraid to go on.

179

'Keep going,' said Nish.

'Which way?' she wailed. 'I don't know where to go.'

He pointed ahead. 'That way.'

'But that's where they're thickest.' It was so hard to trust his eyes over her own.

AHA! I KNOW YOUR FAMILY, AND I HAVE THEM WITHIN MY GRASP. TURN BACK.

SIXTEEN

Maelys gasped and reached through the loop to turn the flappeter back. Nish caught her arm. 'What are you doing?'

'He's got my family! I have to give myself up.'

'He's lying. They must be a hundred leagues from here.'

'I can't escape at their expense.' Maelys knew it was a stupid, emotional reaction which would do no one any good, but she couldn't act any other way.

'What about me? You'll be giving me up too.'

She could think of nothing save Vomix getting his filthy hands on Fyllis. 'Not to death, Nish.'

'There are lives far worse than death.'

She squeezed her head in her hands. 'I don't know what to do. Whatever I choose it will be wrong.'

'Then keep on, because even if you give yourself up he won't let your family go. Father is merciless, but Vomix is depraved.' He thought for a moment. 'What did he say, exactly?'

She told him.

'But he didn't identify any of your family by name? Not even Fyllis?'

'No.'

'Then he's bluffing. Believe me, if he knew who they were, he'd name them and gloat.'

'And if you're wrong . . .?' Her stomach knotted with dread, for Fyllis.

'You can't believe a word he says. Father is the very God of Liars and his servants ape him in every way.'

And you're the son of the father. Would you sacrifice my family to your freedom? The noble Nish she'd hero-worshipped would not have, but she wasn't sure about this stranger. As she hesitated, Rurr-shyve slowed and looked back at her, and she could feel her control leaking away. The pursuing beasts were closing fast and she didn't know what to do.

'Maelys!'

Nish's arms were crushing her ribs. She turned; his teeth were bared, his eyes staring. He pushed himself up out of the saddle. What was the matter? Surely he wasn't going to jump? No, for he put his hands around her head and laid his forehead against hers. What was he doing?

A trace of his clearsight must have passed to her, for she recognised the mental paralysis as another of Vomix's Arts, and it faded. Giving herself up was pointless, whether he had her family or not. She seized back control. 'Fly, Rurr-shyve! Fly as you've never flown before.'

The beast seemed to leap forwards in the air. She pointed it at the dense knot of flappeters in front of her, holding her breath as they converged at a shattering pace, and flinching to avoid the impact, but at the very moment of collision the hallucinations vanished and Rurr-shyve streaked away.

It had the advantage of height over the six real flappeters, which were labouring up after them, and now began to lengthen its lead. By the time the pursuit reached their altitude Rurr-shyve was a good league ahead, though the fresher beasts soon began to peg back the gap. The town disappeared, then the tower. They were flying over rugged country now: steep ridges covered in scrub, topped with angled outcrops of grey limestone dotted with black sinkholes.

TURN BACK, TURN BACK . . .

Vomix was just a whisper in her mind now, easy to resist,

182

though her strength was failing with Rurr-shyve's, while the sympathetic echoes of its pain and fatigue were growing stronger in her. Her bones ached and it was all she could do to sit up. Her eyes were watering from the cold wind. She wiped them on her sleeve, trying to focus on what lay ahead – an oddly shaped mountain whose top seemed to have fallen in.

Rurr-shyve was tiring so rapidly that the end could not be long in coming. Thick, slimy lather extended in streamers from its mouth, while yellow mucous oozed along its neck in wind-blown threads from its breathing tubes. Every breath came with a gurgling suck and the feather-rotors were battering at the air rather than curving smoothly through it. The gap was closing too quickly. Maelys couldn't see any way of escape.

'Rurr-shyve is nearly done for,' she gasped, sagging against Nish. 'And so am I.' Her muscles were a throbbing mass of weariness. Her head felt fuzzy and it was incredibly difficult to concentrate. 'I can't take much more, Nish.'

He held her up. 'You've got to hold out. Just a few more minutes. Even one minute.'

What for? She did her best but she had nothing left. She felt as though she were consuming herself. 'Food, quick!'

He felt around in the saddlebags, then thrust a crumbling biscuit into her hand, one she'd baked the previous day from mashed grass seed, egg and honey. She crammed the whole lot in and gulped it down. A little strength came back. She spat out grass husks.

'Thanks,' Nish muttered as they were blown into his face. 'Sorry –'

TURN AWAY, RURR-SHYVE.

The flappeter's feather-rotors stopped for a second. This order was so overpoweringly loud that it blocked Maelys's thoughts and, before she'd recovered, the beast was turning away from the mountain.

Wearily, she forced it back.

'I *heard* that,' Nish said wonderingly. 'It must have hurt Vomix to have used such power. He's desperate, Maelys. But why, when he's within reach of his goal? It doesn't make sense.'

She didn't have the strength to answer. Holding Rurr-shyve on course, and enduring the echoes of its pain, were taking everything she had.

'What if we're close to some place he doesn't want us to go?' He scanned the landscape. Maelys's aching eyes saw nothing save scrubby limestone ridge country and the collapsed peak. 'Can it be that mountain? Keep straight on, Maelys.'

She gritted her teeth and endured the pain. The peak, from a distance, resembled drawings of volcanoes she'd seen in a book in the clan library, except that water gushed from a cavern a third of the way down, forming a stream linking a series of pools. It wound around the mountain three times, like the thread of a screw that grew ever wider, before disappearing into another cave near the bottom. The stream looked as though it had been deliberately carved into the mountain.

'It's just a volcano, Nish.'

'I don't think so,' Nish said thoughtfully. 'I flew over dozens of them during the war and none were like this. It looks –' He broke off, staring ahead over her shoulder.

Rurr-shyve broke away. Exhaustedly, Maelys turned it back on course. 'What . . . is . . . it?' She could barely choke the words out.

'They're almost on us. Go harder.'

Rurr-shyve shied away from the peak. She turned it back; it shied away again. Her amulet hand began jerking through wild arcs; the amulet's metal legs had unfolded and it began scratching at her closed fingers, trying to get out. Nish couldn't hold her arm steady. 'It doesn't want to go there, Nish.'

'Then that's where we've got to go; any way you can.'

'Doing my best,' she grunted.

'Force it, cajole it. Seduce it if you have to, but get us there.'

There wasn't time to dwell on his unfortunate turn of phrase, as a crossbow bolt whizzed well above – a warning shot. Nish stood up in the saddle, using his weight to hold her arm steady, and together they turned Rurr-shyve towards the mountain. As they neared the crest, a small walled village came into view, set in a depression on the far slope. People were working in terraced vegetable gardens. The top of the mountain had collapsed to form a kind of crater from which shimmering fumes – no, steam – wavered up.

Suddenly the flappeter shot forwards, though it took a few seconds for Maelys to work out why. 'Nish, Vomix's presence is gone!'

'Turn back to the crater,' Nish cried. 'I know what it is – it's all that's left of a destroyed node from the time of the war.'

'Then what's the use of it?' She turned Rurr-shyve sharply, watching the other six beasts. Once they cut across the angle, they'd be upon her.

But they didn't. They veered left, away from the crater, and curved in a great circle around it.

'I don't know,' said Nish, frowning. 'Unless . . . can it be that Vomix's power doesn't hold here . . .? It must be. Head for the village. Hurry!'

The flappeter began to turn, but suddenly the wind stilled, the world seemed to hold its breath, and silver lightning sheeted across the sky. Rurr-shyve let out a shrill cry and turned the other way.

'Turn back,' cried Maelys, but it didn't respond. Maelys pulled free of Nish, jammed the sharpened peg into the wound and threatened Rurr-shyve with severing, but it kept going as if she wasn't there.

'Harder,' said Nish, grim-faced.

'What is it, Nish? What's Vomix done?'

185

'It's Father! He must have been monitoring Vomix, and when he failed, Father took control through the tears. How could he do that from so far away? He doesn't want us to go near the crater, and that's the first good news I've heard in a long time.'

'Not if we can't get there,' Maelys panted. Her insatiable hunger was back, worse than before, but there was no food left.

'Try harder. To convince Rurr-shyve, you'll have to hurt it.'

She didn't want to be the cause of any creature's suffering, but better Jal-Nish's flesh-formed beast than her family, or Nish. Maelys thrust the peg in with all the force she could muster.

Rurr-shyve screamed and tried to buck her off. Nish, who had taken off his safety line earlier, went flying into the air, but his grasping hand caught hold of her line, which had looped out behind her. He clung to it with both hands, slammed down hard and thumped into the saddle as the flappeter tried to tie itself in a knot.

Untwisting with another great convulsion, it went humping and bucking away towards the other flappeters, which were now slowly circling the mountain half a league out, as if they didn't dare come any closer.

Maelys tried to crawl up the neck to prick Rurr-shyve again, but it was bucking too wildly, and now she began to feel pressure building in her mind, like shimmering cords trying to wrap themselves around her brain. A wave of dizziness swept across her as if the blood was being squeezed from her head; pain stabbed in her sinuses, then a drop of bright red blood splashed on the saddle horn in front of her. Another followed it and another, until her nose was streaming blood and it was running down her face and dripping off her chin.

She felt so dizzy she could barely stay upright. The peg slipped from her hand as she grabbed desperately for the saddle horn. 'Nish?' she croaked, feeling the cords tightening, her consciousness slipping away. 'Nish, what's he doing to me . . .?'

She made one last effort to take back control but her fingers lacked the strength to hold the amulet. It tore free from her hand and ran forwards as if it intended to scuttle up Rurr-shyve's neck. Unfortunately, at that moment Rurr-shyve lurched wildly. The amulet slid off the bloody saddle horn in front of Maelys, its metal legs scrabbling for a purchase on the scaly carapace, hung for a moment on one spike-tipped forelimb, then fell away.

Instantly, Rurr-shyve's long neck twisted around and it snapped viciously at her, the hooked tip of its serrated beak gashing her forearm. Maelys shrieked. Nish began to beat at it with one of the tent poles but Rurr-shyve put its head down and laboured towards the nearest of its fellows.

Everything faded into a pink mist in which all she could do was cling to the saddle horn, watching the blood running down her arm and mixing with the blood still flooding from her nose, and try not to throw up all over herself. 'Nish . . .'

Nish lunged for the amulet but missed, and it was lost. After beating off Rurr-shyve's attack with the tent pole, he shook Maelys, trying to rouse her. It was useless. Without the amulet, the beast was uncontrollable and she was doomed.

There was still a chance for him, though. Nish could sense his father reaching out towards him with a grudging admiration, that his surviving son had eluded the pursuit for so long and evaded every trap set for him. He wouldn't give Maelys any credit for that. Father's arrogance could not allow him to think that he'd been bested by a slip of a girl.

Had something changed for Jal-Nish since the encounter in Morrelune? Nish sensed his father's yearning, could feel the words slowly crystallising in his mind. *Come back, my son, and all will be forgiven. I need you – you're the only one who can help me now. Come, sit at my right hand and everything you desire shall be yours. You have but to name it.*

Nish was tempted, for he'd never heard his father plead before. Something had definitely changed. And his father *would* give him everything he asked for, for a price. Everything but the life of Maelys and her family, for he would see them as the blackest traitors. There was nothing Nish could do to save them, unless . . .

He didn't stop to think, but scrambled up Rurr-shyve's neck, clinging with his legs, then took hold of the wisp-controller and, with a mighty heave, tore it out by the roots. Rurr-shyve shrieked in agony, reared up until it was standing on its tail, then flipped over backwards and came upright again. Maelys echoed its pain in a rending cry that went on and on, before slumping in the saddle, unconscious.

The presence in Nish's mind vanished. Unfortunately, Jal-Nish's command of the flappeter failed with it, and Rurr-shyve's agony was so great that it lost control of its extremities. The feather-rotors jammed together and it plunged towards the rocky mountainside in an uncontrollable spin.

SEVENTEEN

The muscles that drove the feather-rotors were still bunching and contracting beneath him but the blades had jammed. As the flappeter whirled, Nish caught hold of the rotor stalk and, balanced precariously, heaved at the locked blades, which were shuddering under the strain but unable to spin. Each heave opened a small triangular gap between the feathered edges, until another driving contraction of the great muscles beneath him snapped it closed. On his third attempt, Nish was lucky to get his fingers out.

Just a couple of minutes to impact. He eyed the gnashing rims through which the feathers protruded. If he caught his fingers between them they'd be crushed to paste.

He slid down for the tent pole, scrambled up again and forced it between the locked blades at the point where Maelys's bamboo splint left a small gap. Standing on tiptoe with his arm around the thrumming rotor stalk, he thrust with all his strength. The splint cracked along its length and one side was propelled up in the air like a bolt from a crossbow. Nish caught his breath, but after all, what did it matter? The rotor blade only had to hold for one minute.

The feather-rotors slipped past one another and began to spin, slowing the descent, though Rurr-shyve's head was flopping from side to side and it was still whirling as it fell. Was there anything else he could do? Nish scrabbled along the tail, locked his ankles around it and bashed the vertical discs to the left. The flappeter came out of its spin but it was still falling.

Maelys had slid out of her seat as the beast rolled and was now hanging in mid-air by her line, one arm swinging. Rurr-shyve was humping and jerking spasmodically, and would soon slam into the mountainside hard enough to break every bone in their bodies.

It rolled to the left. Nish clung on with his legs and, below, glimpsed the stream curving around the mountain-side. Could he direct the flappeter into it? He pulled himself upright and, with exhausting heaves of the tail discs this way and that, tried to turn the beast towards the water. Down and down they plunged, falling too steeply now. They were going to overshoot.

He corrected the other way, overshot again, then Rurr-shyve's head jerked up. The feather-rotors spun furiously, stopping it in mid-air with a jerk that pulled Nish's stomach down painfully, then it began to hover about twenty spans above the ground.

Nish was just thinking that they might survive after all when the beast let out a shrill cry, the injured rotor blade dislocated above his head and the flappeter plummeted towards the rocks. Nish heaved desperately on the tail discs, managed to point the flappeter towards the stream, and they hit the water a few spans from the bank.

Rurr-shyve plunged all the way to the bottom, carrying them with it, then rolled onto its side and began to drift downstream with the current. The feather-rotors were still feebly trying to turn, churning the water to brown foam and moving the flappeter this way and that. Nish struggled free between their beats, kicked well away and reached the surface.

He couldn't see Maelys anywhere. She must be trapped underneath, still tethered by her line, unconscious. And she couldn't swim. He cursed, took a deep breath and plunged under, feeling his way down the long body. Something struck him on the cheek, hard enough to cut the skin. It was one of those giant lice, and there were others all around, abandoning their dying host, whose breathing tubes were sucking and squelching as it tried to breathe.

Rurr-shyve bobbed to the surface momentarily but the breathing tubes on its left side were still under the surface and it was sucking in water with each intake. He couldn't see Maelys and now Rurr-shyve was sinking again.

He dived and swam along its trunk. A convulsive thrash of the dislocated rotor blade whacked him on the back of the head. Nish kept going and made her out in the murky water, tangled among the twitching sets of legs. She was conscious now but couldn't free herself. Bubbles trailed from the corners of her mouth and one clenched fist was feebly beating at the legs.

Nish found where her line was caught around one of the thorny protrusions and slipped it over. He couldn't free her from it; there wasn't time to untie the knots. He yanked on the buckle that held down the front saddle and pulled it off. It began to float up, buoyed by air trapped in the saddlebags. Nish kicked away from Rurr-shyve, now rolling onto its back, and dragged Maelys up to the surface.

'Can't swim,' she gasped.

'It's all right,' he said soothingly. 'I'm a brilliant swimmer.'

'Liar,' she murmured.

Rurr-shyve, who was floating upside-down twenty spans upstream, gave a convulsive heave then went still. Maelys cried out and sagged in his arms. He hoped she'd just fainted; that Rurr-shyve's death hadn't killed her too.

Nish supported her with the buoyancy of the saddlebags while he scanned the sky. The flappeters were circling, still keeping their distance from the mountaintop. Their riders were urging them down but they kept shying away.

The water swirled around a fallen tree. Nish kicked hard to avoid becoming tangled in its roots. They were drifting downstream towards a set of jagged rocks, gathering speed.

191

Nish was thankful for the saddlebags; he couldn't have supported Maelys without them. He wasn't sure he could have saved himself. He felt terribly weak.

He was towing Maelys towards the shore when he realised they were on the wrong side of the river. If they were to have a hope of reaching the dubious safety of the village they'd have to cross the water. He began to kick outwards, though not very effectively.

Bubbles gushed from the saddlebags, which were losing buoyancy and tugging Maelys down. He felt around her waist but the knots had pulled tight under the constant jerking and he didn't have a knife.

He whipped the little taphloid out, flipped open its secret catch as he'd seen her do and began to saw at the rope with the metal edge. It wasn't an effective blade but he eroded the strands enough to snap the rope with a jerk. He dropped the taphloid's chain over Maelys's head, heaved her away from the sinking saddlebags and began to tow her towards the centre of the stream.

The current was stronger here, and boiling with eddies that tried to pull them under. Nish, never far from panic in the water, had to talk himself into staying calm. An eddy whirled them around then shot them out on the other side, fortunately closer to the far bank. Scooping desperately with his free arm, he managed to drag Maelys into the slower water and from there to the bank.

He couldn't rest now or he'd never get going again. Nish hauled her out, gasping. Her forearm was still bleeding, though it wasn't a dangerous injury, so he left it and scanned the sky. Two more flappeters were flying up from the south. They were larger and carried what looked like baskets suspended beneath them – troop carriers. Behind them, its brass fittings shining in the sun, was an object he hadn't seen for ten years, and it raised such ambivalent memories that for a moment he couldn't breathe.

It was an air-floater – no, this craft deserved a grander title, so baroque was its extravagance of shining brass, polished ebony and tar-sealed silk – an air-dreadnought; a flying vessel suspended from three gigantic ovoid balloons filled with explosively deadly floater gas, and propelled by three spinning rotors at the stern. Air-dreadnoughts had been common in the last years of the war, and Nish was responsible in a minor way, for he'd had the idea for hot air floaters in the first place.

According to the gossip of the guards at Mazurhize, only Jal-Nish and his most trusted lieutenants had air-dreadnoughts now, and they were only used to strike fear into the cowering populace.

This one certainly struck fear into Nish, for an air-dreadnought could carry fifty heavily armed troops. Creatures like flappeters, which depended on the Art, and even mancers might be afraid to approach the uncanny mountaintop, but his crack troops feared nothing save the displeasure of their master.

Maelys stirred and pink water dribbled from her mouth. Nish helped her to her feet. 'Come on. They're after us.' She swayed; caught at his arm. 'Can you walk, Maelys?'

She clenched the taphloid so tightly that her knuckles stood out. 'I think so.' Her voice was hoarse, reedy; her eyes unfocussed.

The first of the battle flappeters rotored towards them, and if it crossed the stream there was no hope of escape. It attempted to do so, but as it approached the stream its feather-rotors slowed almost to nothing and it turned away sharply, coming to ground further down. The other flappeter tracked it. Now the air-dreadnought was sailing up majestically, brightly armoured troops leaning over the sides, eager to hunt down the prize. Nish held his breath. Nothing could stop it now.

Then, a bare hundred spans out from the river its triple rotors stopped with a shriek of torn metal. The suspended troop vessel swung forwards on its cables, then jerked sideways as the wind caught the airbags. The craft lost way suddenly and was driven downslope by the wind. The pilot pulled the emergency floater gas release; the air-dreadnought dropped sharply and crunched into the rocks below the stream, hurling several men overboard. The remaining troops piled over the side.

'We'd better get a move on.' Nish took her hand and began to run, though before he'd gone fifty paces he was out of breath. Running up the mountain was beyond him, and Maelys, still dazed and in pain, could only manage a stumble.

Troops from the first flappeter were pounding along the far side of the river. Two went to their knees, pointing wickedly ornate crossbows at Nish and Maelys, while the others headed downstream towards the rocks where they might cross.

A bolt struck sparks off a boulder just above Maelys. Nish jerked her around in front of him, shielding her, and pushed her forwards.

'Stop or we'll shoot,' boomed a bemedalled officer.

Maelys froze. 'What are you doing, Nish?'

'They won't harm me, but they'll kill you. Keep going.'

There were at least seventy troops on the ground now, all clad in the iridescent, beetle-shell armour of his father's Imperial Militia, and the leaders were starting to cross.

On he laboured, and up. Crossbow bolts spanged off the rocks to either side; arrows whistled over their heads. None came too near, save when, after some ten minutes of desperate, scrambling flight, Maelys tripped and fell sideways out of Nish's shelter. A bolt slammed into a boulder between her clutching fingers, shards of stone cutting little crescent shaped gashes there. An ell either way and it would have taken a finger off.

Nish hastily hauled her in front of him, though he knew that a skilled archer, if prepared to take the risk, could go out to one side and pick her off. Behind them, he heard the officer shouting again.

They'd gained a few hundred paces while the soldiers slipped and skidded across the stream over the half-submerged rocks, though once they reached the other side they began to gain rapidly. There was still a steep climb to the low wall encircling the village, which surely couldn't hold these soldiers out long. The leading troops were going three steps to his one and would be on them within minutes.

He forced himself through the pain and ran harder, pushing Maelys ahead of him, but his .wasted muscles were giving out and she couldn't keep it up either. Ahead, a house-sized boulder offered temporary shelter. They rounded it and stopped abruptly.

Before them stood a tall, imposing man whose long black hair hung down past his shoulders. He had black eyes and a thin, hooked nose and, though only in early middle-age, the weathered skin of his face and neck looked as though someone had taken a wood rasp to it, for it was as corrugated as the bark of an old tree. He looked as solid as a tree, too, and utterly implacable.

'Go back!' he said in a deep, hypnotic voice. 'Whoever you are, you have no business here.'

'Sanctuary!' gasped Nish, staggering forwards.

'Go back!' The man thrust out his right arm and the loose sleeve of his robe slid up. His hands and arms were clad in skin-tight tan gloves made of leather so fine that it was almost transparent, extending up past his elbows. Nish felt a surge of power from the man's hand and his hair rose up, as it had once years ago when he'd been close to a stroke of lightning.

'This is Cryl-Nish Hlar. *Nish!*' panted Maelys. 'He's the man who will become the Deliverer. You've got to help him!'

The tall man went very still, then stooped, put one gloved hand under Nish's chin and turned his face upwards. Nish didn't know what to say.

'Cryl-Nish!' the man said, wonderingly. 'Many men have claimed to be him, but all have been fools or liars in the service of the God-Emperor. Betrayers!' he spat. 'But there is a test.'

Behind them, boots scrabbled on rocks and a pair of soldiers burst into view. 'Step away, old fellow,' one shouted, 'or you'll taste the steel of the God-Emperor.'

The tall man raised his right hand again, then pointed it at the soldiers. Nish saw nothing, but a shrill wailing hurt his ears and the troops fell down, blood pouring from their mouths and noses. 'Come,' he said. 'My name is Monkshart. The God-Emperor's power does not extend into Tifferfyte, but the steel of his soldiers' swords bites as hard here as anywhere.'

Part Two

The Pit of Possibilities

EIGHTEEN

Maelys mistrusted Monkshart from the moment she set eyes on him, though she couldn't have said why. It might have been the arrogant way he carried himself, for he was extremely tall, yet moved so as to make himself seem even taller. He walked stiffly, on just the balls of his feet, with his head tilted back to look down his long arched nose at her.

Or perhaps it was the fall of black hair, as carefully tended and glossy as any maiden's, that contrasted so sharply with the rugose skin of his face. The men of her land wore their hair close-cropped, save for highwaymen and other dubious characters, and she couldn't bring herself to trust a longhair.

It definitely had something to do with the look in his black and piercing eyes; eyes that seemed to shine when he turned them her way, and especially when he spoke. Not with lust for her, she felt sure. That was not his vice, but he spoke with a fervour that was maniacal in its intensity. Monkshart was a charismatic zealot whose people would follow him anywhere, but a dangerous man too, for once set on a path he would follow it unswervingly, no matter what or who got in his way.

Yet perhaps, despite her personal feelings, that made him the right man to lead the Defiance. And turn Nish into the Deliverer.

As they climbed up to the village, more troops appeared around the rock below them, followed by an officer wearing a plumed helmet. He inspected the bodies, studied the layout of the village then watched until Monkshart, Nish and Maelys crossed the wall. Why didn't he send his troops after them? Was he afraid of Monkshart, or had they been called back by Jal-Nish?

The sun was setting as Monkshart led them through the village, and everyone stared as they went by. The place was neat and tidy, the paths freshly swept and even the composting piles formed into neat circles, but every structure had an ill-made, temporary look.

The defensive wall was merely dry-stone rocks loosely fitted together as if by inexperienced hands, and would not have held the God-Emperor's troops back for a second. The houses must also have been built by novices, being the rudest of stone huts roofed with slabs of crumbling shale. The terraced gardens were mostly bare at this time of year, apart from a large patch of what looked like turnips and leeks.

The people were thin and work-worn; their dark, staring eyes had a feverish glint which bothered Maelys almost as much as Monkshart had. They looked haunted; trapped. And there was another odd thing. She didn't see any children.

A gaunt, ravaged young woman came stumbling out of the next but last hut as they went by, crying and tugging at Monkshart's sleeve. 'Surr,' she wept, 'it came again last night. It took Milli and we can't find her anywhere. I'm so afraid.'

He brushed her off. 'Phrune will deal with it, Ganni.'

She wailed and stumbled off. Maelys watched the girl go, feeling her own hackles rising. She expected to be taken to one of the huts but Monkshart led them up a set of steps rudely hacked into the stone all the way to the top of the mountain, then turned aside. Nish stopped suddenly and Maelys's heart lurched, for one step ahead the ground fell

200

away into the steaming crater, which was nothing like the pile of rubble she had expected.

Its almost sheer inner walls were mostly as smooth as glass, as if the rock had been melted in a titanic forge then trowelled flat, though here and there the surface was hung with glassy festoons and dribbles where molten rock had flowed then set. Directly across the crater, where the light of the setting sun struck the wall, the surface glowed in reds, purples and mauves. To her left it had a greenish hue, and colours shimmered across it like a film of oil on the surface of a pond. It was an uncanny place and she didn't want to go anywhere near it.

Maelys looked down and wished she hadn't. The walls fell sheer for a good hundred spans, below which the rising steam blotted out her view, though she glimpsed a blurred yellow flicker in the depths. A faint crackle reached her ears, in waves that rose and fell.

'What is this place?' said Nish softly, as if speaking loudly would be sacrilege.

Monkshart smiled thinly. 'Should you answer my questions correctly, you may ask your own. This way.'

He extended a long arm to his right, where a glass-smooth path, no wider than Maelys's shoulders, ran down the inside curve of the crater towards a structure she could not see clearly through the belching steam. All she could make out was a pair of red columns and what looked like a platform extending over the abyss. It was warm though – like sitting by the fire in a well-built house.

'And if we don't?' said Nish.

Monkshart jerked a thumb over the side, then gestured ahead. 'To the pavilion, if you please.'

Nish followed the glassy path, slowly and grimly. Maelys went next, treading just as carefully, for it would be easy to slip on the smooth glass underfoot, and fatal if she did.

Monkshart came a few paces behind and she resisted the urge to glance over her shoulder. She could feel his physical

201

presence smouldering behind her, as if he might burst into flame at any moment. The thought of him watching her made her acutely uncomfortable.

Nish gained the floor of the pavilion with a gasp of relief and headed towards the rear, putting as much distance as he could between him and the drop. Maelys stepped inside. The pavilion had a semi-circular floor, a domed ceiling the same shape, and five columns equally spaced around the curve of the semi-circle, all carved from the glassy rock as if by the hand of a master, then polished until they shone.

Clearly the novices who'd built the village had no part in making this place. A perfectly round opening at the rear led into darkness, while at the front a long plank of thick rock-glass extended out like a diving board between the second and third columns, over the crater.

'What's that for?' Maelys asked in a low voice.

'It's where those who fail my questioning take their last walk,' said Monkshart, and she knew he was in earnest. He motioned Nish to a stone chair to his right, Maelys to one facing it, and took the central chair. 'Phrune!'

'What?' said Nish, evidently thinking Monkshart was speaking to him.

A brown-clad shadow slipped through the round opening. 'Master?' said a treacly voice that made Maelys's flesh creep. Phrune was a baby-faced, chubby young man whose pale skin shone as if he'd been freshly oiled. His head was shaven, apart from a gleaming queue sprouting from the top, and his face was so plump that his eyes were mere slits. His lips were as red and pouting as a split blood plum.

Phrune gave Nish a cursory glance before turning to Maelys, studying her from head to foot then licking his swollen lips. Her eyes met his for a second and she felt a physical shock; a revulsion she'd never felt before. And yet she found it hard to look away, for his gaze clung to hers and held it against her will.

'Water for my guests, Phrune,' Monkshart said sharply, mechanically smoothing the gloves over his long fingers.

Phrune bowed low and, with another sideways glance at Maelys, oozed back through the opening. After he'd returned with a jug of tepid water and two stone beakers, and been sent away, Monkshart turned to Nish.

'You claim to be the son of the God-Emperor. You would do well to know that I served under Jal-Nish Hlar when he was scrutator, and during his exile in the last years of the war.'

'I wouldn't call it exile,' Nish snapped. 'He lost the battle of Gumby Marth through his own hubris, then ran away like the cowardly cur he is, leaving his army to be slaughtered by the lyrinx.'

Monkshart smiled, though Maelys couldn't read it. She knew that story, for it formed part of the *Tale of Nish and Irisis* and marked the time when Nish had first come into his own. Though he'd not led men before, he had taken command of the decimated army, single-handedly led the survivors against a superior force of the enemy, and broken through to safety. The battle had still been a crushing defeat, with most of a once proud army destroyed, but by the manner of the survivors' escape they had given hope to humanity in the darkest hours of the war.

'Sometimes a limb must be sacrificed that the body may survive,' said Monkshart. 'If you truly are Cryl-Nish, you would understand that.'

'*I* didn't cut off my father's ruined arm,' Nish said thickly.

'The tales say you did, after a failed attack on a lyrinx camp left him maimed.'

Nish's right cheek spasmed. 'The tales are wrong – I couldn't face it. I begged Irisis to do it to save Father's life, for one thing *she* never lacked was courage. She cut off the arm, sewed up Father's face and saved the life he didn't want, and from that moment on she was doomed.'

'What was the name of your little sister, who died just two weeks after birth?'

Maelys saw Nish start. 'How did you know that?' he said hoarsely. 'We weren't allowed to mention her name.'

'I was close to your father, once – until he became the God-Emperor. Answer the question, please.'

Nish took a deep breath. 'Hisly. My baby sister's name was Hisly and I was holding her when she died. She just stopped breathing. I was only five; I didn't know what the matter was, and by the time I ran to Mother it was too late. Father never forgave me. I was the least favoured son ever after, the one who'd let his precious daughter die.'

'But now, *if you are his son*, you're all he's got and he's forgiven you. Take off your coat and shirt, and your pants.'

'What?' croaked Nish.

Maelys felt the blood withdraw from her stomach. Had she been wrong about Monkshart? Was he a man of depraved appetites?

'I wish to see your scars,' said Monkshart.

'Why?' said Nish.

'Jal-Nish often talked about his youngest son, and all the heroic things he'd done in the war. He knew every scar on Nish's body, and I remember everything he said about them.'

'I don't see how he could have,' Nish said thickly.

'The wisp-watcher outside Nish's cell showed Jal-Nish everything he wanted to see. He'd spend hours and days with the tears, watching his son. And he questioned everyone who'd known Nish during the war. Jal-Nish was proud of his son and wanted to know every detail of his service.'

'My father was proud of me?' Nish said in an odd voice. 'I've not had a second's praise from him in all my life.'

'Nonetheless, he *was* proud,' said Monkshart.

Maelys felt a shiver run up her spine. Was the God-Emperor as obsessed with his son as Nish was with Irisis? If he was, it changed everything. Nish choked, then stripped off and stood before Monkshart in just his undershorts.

Maelys hadn't seen him unclad in daylight before, though she knew the story. The starkly pale skin of his back was

204

scored with faint mauve marks where he'd been flogged as a young man, and he had many other scars too; war wounds. He was shivering.

'Turn,' said Monkshart.

Nish did so. Monkshart squinted at him, his lips moving as if he were counting. From the corner of her eye Maelys saw Phrune appear in the opening. He was staring at her, and she knew what he wanted. Monkshart waved him away.

Finally, after several minutes, Monkshart nodded and said, 'You may dress now.'

Nish dressed hastily, staring up at the zealot, then suddenly Monkshart smiled like a wolf and thrust out his hand. 'Cryl-Nish Hlar, son of Jal-Nish, welcome to Tifferfyte.'

Nish tentatively offered his hand, which Monkshart clasped in both of his big hands and shook firmly.

'I know why you've come,' Monkshart said. 'My fame has spread, for I'm one of the few people on Santhenar who dares defy the God-Emperor. Perhaps the only one. Tifferfyte is an enclave of the forbidden Defiance, and Jal-Nish can't touch us, for there is a power here which not even his tears can fight. It frightens him that there's one place where his Arts do not hold, and he dreads what could come out of it.'

'But the steel of his soldiers' swords bites as hard here as anywhere,' quoted Nish.

'Not when they can't come near enough to use them. I've lain a protective halo around the mountaintop and no Art-powered device can pass through its outer boundary without my permission. No human may cross the inner boundary, which lies near where I met you, unless I allow them access. Let's get down to business. Ten years ago you swore to deliver Santhenar from your father, Cryl-Nish, and now you have your chance. I'm going to turn you into that Deliverer.'

'What if I no longer want to?' Nish gave Maelys a cool sideways stare, as if to say, you've got what you wanted. I hope you're happy.

'Of course you do,' said Monkshart.

Maelys lowered her eyes, almost fainting with relief. Beyond hope and almost by accident, she'd succeeded. Tifferfyte was the one place on Santhenar where Nish's father couldn't touch him, and Monkshart did have the drive and the passionate purpose to forge Nish into the Deliverer. Now if there were only a way to bring her family here, she would have done her duty. It was the only way Maelys could do it now; not even for her sister's life could she make another seduction attempt.

'Come to my quarters for refreshment, Deliverer,' said Monkshart. 'And after that, there is much to be settled before we begin the campaign.'

Nish rose. Monkshart took his arm. Maelys began to follow but the zealot stilled her with a glance. 'Who is she?'

'My name –' Maelys began, but Monkshart cut her off, gesturing to Nish instead.

'Her name is Maelys,' said Nish. 'She got me out of Mazurhize – at least, her sister did – and Maelys brought me all this way. I wouldn't be alive if it hadn't been for her. She killed the flappeter's rider and took control of it . . .'

'Maelys who?' said Monkshart icily.

She didn't like the way this was heading. Clearly, he thought her a nobody to be cast aside. She knew she looked a mess, in her muddy, tattered and blood-stained boy's clothes, with her hair hanging around her shoulders like a rat's nest and her boots squelching as she moved. But surely, she thought naively, Monkshart is pleased that I brought Nish to him?

Nish looked embarrassed. He didn't know her clan name, for Maelys had kept it back. The habit of secrecy was too deeply ingrained.

Monkshart turned those searing eyes on her and it was impossible not to tell him. 'Of Clan Nifferlin,' she said reluctantly, not expecting him to recognise the name. Though Nifferlin was an old clan and had been modestly well off before the war, it had never been a powerful or influential one. There was no reason why he should know it.

He looked up at the ceiling for a minute or two, and she gained the impression of a man searching a vast catalogue of memory for one small detail, then he focussed on her and his mouth turned down. 'Nifferlin? Unbiddable rebels all of them. Entirely unsuitable for the Deliverer. Phrune!'

Phrune put his head out through the opening. 'Master?'

'Take the girl to a suitable chamber and keep her there until I call for her.' He bent and whispered in Phrune's ear, though loudly enough for her to hear. 'He's lying, trying to protect the little tart. She hasn't got a speck of aura. She's only out for one thing and she's not having him.' He turned to Nish, saying in a normal voice. 'Come over here, lad.'

'Nish?' Maelys said, as Phrune took her by the arm with plump, slippery fingers. His shiny face looked as though it had been rubbed with lard. She tried to shake him off but he locked his fingers around her arm until the long, manicured nails dug in.

Nish stood his ground. 'Maelys is my friend. I owe everything to her.'

'Of course you do,' Monkshart said smoothly. 'Do you think I can't see her qualities? But for her sake as well as the Deliverer's, some matters are best kept private. Rest assured, Acolyte Phrune will take very good care of her. Won't you, Phrune?'

'Indeed, Master,' said Phrune, bowing deeply to Monkshart, then almost as deeply to Nish. His slippery fingers slid back and forth on Maelys's arm like the caress of an eel. 'I'll give her my most special attention and take care of *all* her needs.'

Jerking on her arm, he hauled her through the circular opening. Maelys looked back despairingly. Monkshart was afraid Nish would form an attachment with her and be diverted from the cause, and suddenly Maelys knew that she'd never be safe here. She would have to be on her guard night and day.

If only Monkshart knew, she thought bitterly. He's got nothing whatsoever to worry about.

NINETEEN

'The girl is a danger to the Deliverer,' said Monkshart after Phrune had taken Maelys away.

'Nonsense,' said Nish. 'She and her family saved my life and I'm in their debt.'

'She's unworthy of you, Cryl-Nish. And she wants something from you.'

Nish yawned involuntarily. 'So does everyone who believes in the Deliverer. Including you, Monkshart.'

'I admit it. I can't bear to see my world and my people suffering under this brutal monster – I beg your pardon, Deliverer. He is still your father.'

'There's no need to apologise,' Nish said stiffly.

'How dare he call himself "God-Emperor"!? For any man to set himself up as a god is blasphemy!' he cried, his bark-like face dark with passion. 'There is only one god –'

Nish stirred uneasily. Like most people on Santhenar he had little time for gods, whose dogma always seemed to reflect the mores of the societies that created them, and he was suspicious of anyone who tried to convince him otherwise. He kept silent, though. Monkshart had given him shelter, after all, and he was a powerful, dangerous man. Let's find out what he really wanted, and if they could work together.

'You must agree with me, Cryl-Nish?' Monkshart's hot eyes seemed to be trying to peer inside his skull.

'I have no truck with emperors,' said Nish. 'Especially not

self-declared ones. But for a man to declare himself a god is an abomination.'

Monkshart smiled thinly. If he'd noted Nish's careful answer, he chose to overlook it. 'And you *will* become the Deliverer?'

'Until I'm satisfied that I know who you are and what you really want, I won't commit myself to anything.'

'Very wise. Santhenar is full of liars, cheats, charlatans and false prophets.' Monkshart sat back in his seat. 'Ask of me what you will.'

'Who are you, Monkshart, and how did you come by such power?'

'I was a mancer in the war. Not one of any great distinction, let me assure you, though I'd worked harder than most to master my craft. I was just one among many warrior-mages in your father's army, until it was destroyed.'

'At Gumby Marth.'

'Quite so. We were both hurt in that battle, your father badly. He carried the tears away, and I carried him.'

'Despite all he'd done?'

'I wasn't pleased to be running away but I'd sworn an oath to him and I do not break my word lightly.'

Nish gave him a thoughtful glance. 'Yet you no longer serve him.'

Monkshart ignored that. 'Your father and I went into hiding and I nursed him back to health, over many months and three relapses. The last nearly killed him. He lay between life and death for seven weeks and I stood by him all that time, watching over him night and day.'

'Why didn't you let him die?' said Nish. 'The world would have been better off if you had.' To hear the words from his own mouth shocked him, despite everything his father had done since.

'I had to remain true to my oath, for if men are foresworn the whole world must come to chaos. Besides, humanity was losing the war and I saw a strength in Jal-Nish that I've not

210

seen in anyone before, or since. For all I knew, that strength might have meant the difference between survival and enslavement for humanity. I believed it did.'

'Yet you now oppose everything he stands for, so why should I trust you? Any man who turns his coat once is liable to do so again.'

'I turned no coat. I served your father all the while that he was consolidating his power, and until he declared himself God-Emperor, seven years ago. At that moment I told him to his face that he had broken the terms of my oath, and therefore the bond between us was void. I had sworn to a man, not a false god.'

'But he let you live?' Nish wondered if it was the truth. Perhaps Monkshart still served his father and this was another of his elaborate traps. How could he, Nish, tell?

'After I saved your father's life, he swore to never harm me save in self-defence, nor to take my Arts from me. He wasn't happy with my going, but he held to his word.'

'So how did you come by all this?' Nish indicated the crater with a sweep of his arm. 'Surely you didn't just *happen* upon it by some lucky coincidence?'

Monkshart ignored the sarcasm. 'Of course not. After all the nodes failed, your father had me search out every one of them and make sure.'

'That they had actually gone dead?'

'Yes, but more importantly, to check each dead node in case something had formed there at the moment of its destruction. You'll understand why.'

The tears, Gatherer and Reaper, had been formed when the Snizort node was deliberately destroyed in a particular and very special way, and Jal-Nish would have been desperate to make sure that no more tears, or other arcane objects which could threaten his power, had formed at any other node. 'And had there?'

'Oh no,' said Monkshart. 'No tears, at any rate, nor any other device of power. The tears are unique.'

211

'Then why are you here? Why hasn't my father driven you out, and your fledgling Defiance?' That was what Nish didn't understand.

'Until you came, he didn't know I was here.'

Nish's eyes narrowed. A while ago Monkshart had boasted about his fame spreading, but since Jal-Nish knew everything, how could that be true? 'Why not? Surely flappeters would have detected the strange . . . er, *field* here before.'

'There is no field, and besides, my protection halo wasn't activated until I saw your flappeter being pursued so desperately. Anyone who flew over Tifferfyte would have seen no more than an impoverished village, not worth bothering about.'

'Why didn't Father's troops follow us? Can your halo really keep them all out?'

'Possibly not, but remember Jal-Nish has had three terrible shocks at once. His long-lost former ally has just reappeared, and at a site of power like nothing Jal-Nish has ever seen before; his renegade son has joined that ally. What are the implications? Your father will think them through thoroughly before taking any action that might fail and damage his dread reputation.'

'What is the source of power at Tifferfyte?'

Monkshart shrugged. 'I don't need to tell you yet. All I'll say is that *Nothing goes to nothing*. No object nor device of power can ever be completely destroyed. All force has to go somewhere, and the former Tifferfyte node has been transformed into a place where the Secret Art, at least as your father understands it, no longer holds.'

'Ahh!' sighed Nish. 'And you plan to form it into a shield against him.'

'If only that were possible. The power of Tifferfyte doesn't reside in an *object* that can be carried around, like the tears. It's an *essence*, if you like, intrinsically associated with Tifferfyte. It only holds here.'

'Then what's the use of it?'

'It provides a refuge where I can help you to build your strength, as the Deliverer, unmolested.'

'What use is strength in the middle of nowhere? My father can only be overthrown in the heart of his empire.'

Monkshart hesitated, then looked deep into Nish's eyes, before nodding as if satisfied at what he'd seen there. 'Tifferfyte isn't a solitary outpost. The Defiance is strong and growing every day. People are flocking to our bastions in their hundreds, simply on the rumour that Jal-Nish's son has escaped. Already your father trembles in Morrelune Palace.'

'With derisory laughter,' Nish said sourly.

'He knows!' said Monkshart, bright-eyed. 'The whole world hates Jal-Nish and questions his legitimacy, and it burns him. He might be the most powerful man in the world –'

'He is!' Nish said fiercely.

'But he understands how quickly power can be lost. He's afraid of you, Cryl-Nish, for you're all he's got left and he can't injure you in any way.'

'He tormented me in prison without a qualm.'

'But never really harmed you. This is your chance, but you must seize it without delay. As long as you move swiftly and decisively, you'll always be one step ahead of him.'

'I'll need to see evidence to support your claims.'

'I would expect no less.' Monkshart drew a folded map from inside his cloak. 'The Defiance has nine secret fortresses in the east; these are their locations. We keep in touch by skeet. It's the safest way these days.'

Skeets were large raptors, used for centuries to carry messages because they were fleet and vicious. Nothing attacked them, save man, though they were a menace to train and use. 'How come my father, with all his spies and watchers, doesn't know where your refuges are?'

'They're well hidden in remote places, difficult to attack and easily defended.' He handed Nish the map.

It was just a sketch on rice paper, so it could be eaten in an emergency, presumably, but there were nine small marks on it with names beside them, and some were places Nish knew. One was Hulipont.

'Hulipont was Maelys's initial destination,' said Nish. 'Is it still in Defiance hands?'

'I had a skeet from there yesterday.'

Then Cathim must have died without revealing its name, so Maelys's family might also be safe.

While Nish was studying the map, Monkshart added, 'And we have other bastions in the east and north, not marked on that map.'

Nish handed it back, thinking furiously. Could he become the Deliverer? And could he trust Monkshart? He didn't see that he had a choice, for he knew too much to be allowed to leave, and if he didn't agree, would he and Maelys be allowed to live? He tried to see into the zealot with his clear-sight, but it felt blocked here. That wasn't surprising, since Nish's tiny talent had come from the touch of the tears.

'I know what worries you,' said Monkshart. 'It's all very well for the Defiance to have secret outposts, but what's the good of them if they never strike at the enemy? I have hundreds of agents in the west, spreading subversion against the "God-Emperor".' His lips twisted as he said the title, as if it were bile to him. 'Even now we're preparing for a strike against him. Within days we'll be ready to attack his citadel of Rancidore, which lies behind the range in the west. Perhaps you saw it on the way.'

'We passed by a town with a horned tower at its heart. That's where the flappeters found us again. And Seneschal Vomix.'

Monkshart frowned. 'Why has Vomix followed you all this way? He should have handed over to the Seneschal of Rancidore.'

214

'I don't know,' Nish mused. 'But he said he recognised Maelys –' As soon as the words left his lips he regretted them.

'Indeed?' Monkshart gave him a keen glance. 'How curious.'

'How do you plan to attack Rancidore with a few hundred hungry villagers? This place is so shabbily constructed, a flappeter's fart would blow it down.'

Monkshart allowed himself a superior smile; he'd expected the question. 'My chief Art is illusion – the only Art which has grown stronger since the nodes were destroyed. You saw what I wanted you to see, as does every flappeter and rider who passes overhead. Jal-Nish now knows there are rebels at Tifferfyte, and that they've assembled at the one place his power cannot reach. But he's not aware of how my illusionist's Art has been strengthened here. We have weapons enough to attack Rancidore, well hidden, and veterans of the wars to wield them.

'And whether Rancidore falls, or the attack is beaten off, or even if our forces are wiped out, the shockwaves will reverberate around Santhenar, growing ever stronger, especially when we announce that Cryl-Nish Hlar stands at the head of the Defiance, ready to fulfil his promise. Cities will fall to us on the strength of your name; peasants will rally in their thousands. Will you join us, Cryl-Nish, and help to tear down the abomination of the *God-Emperor*? Will you fulfil your promise, or will you betray the faith of your suffering people?'

Listening to the zealot's stirring words, and thinking about the array of other Defiance outposts, even Nish saw a glimmer of hope.

'Your father can't touch you here,' said Monkshart. 'Vomix has already withdrawn his forces to Rancidore.'

Nish looked up at Monkshart, feeling his despair lifting for the first time in years. A surge of fury went through him at all his father had done, and suddenly all his doubts disappeared and the resolve was there, almost as strong as when he had made the promise. 'I will!' he cried. 'Together we'll tear down the tyrant and restore freedom to Santhenar.'

TWENTY

Maelys tried to jerk her arm away but, though Phrune's fingers felt as greasy as lard, they'd locked like a manacle around her forearm.

'Don't pull away,' he purred. 'I can be a good friend to you, Maelys.'

'I don't need a friend,' she snapped, 'and if I did it wouldn't be you, you blubbery little creep.' She wasn't normally so forthright, but there was something about him that was *uggh*, disgusting.

He jerked her around to face him in the gloom and his bloated lips stretched into an unpleasant smile. 'You're in my power, so I'd advise you to cooperate. Unless you please my master, *and me*, well . . .' The smile almost cracked his face in two.

She managed to pull free. 'I have pleased him. I brought Nish here.'

Phrune went stock still. '*Nish?* I though you said Nisk before. Are you saying that man is Cryl-Nish Hlar, the son of the God-Emperor?' He let go of her arm.

'Yes he is. I rescued him and brought him here, and he's my very good friend, so I suggest you treat me nicely or you'll find *yourself* in deep trouble.' The last bit was wishful thinking but Nish was a noble man, deep down, and she felt sure he'd repay the debt. Anything to get Phrune off her back, which was just where he wanted to be. Maelys knew his type by instinct.

'Come this way.' He reached for her arm. She whipped it away. He dropped his hand and hurried down a glassy-walled corridor, motioning her to follow. Seen from behind, he waddled. After passing two doors he stopped at a third, pushed the stone door open and went in. Lighting a wall lantern with a flint striker, he said, 'Stay here. I will send a servant to attend you momentarily,' and rushed out.

The room was furnished with a bed formed from the same glassy stone. A jug stood on a small table beside the bed, though it was empty.

Maelys sat on the bed. On the rare occasions she'd thought about getting to Hulipont, she'd expected to be welcomed with open arms. She felt like a prisoner here.

Yet there was one consolation. In those last desperate minutes in the air she and Nish had been working together as if they were a team, even friends, and it had been wonderful. Then Nish had saved her, twice, and she knew that he did care for her. The coldness he'd shown her previously must have been a defence against being hurt. How could she have tried to seduce him so crudely? He must have been mortally insulted.

It didn't help her to do her duty, though. Despite all she'd been through, it was something Maelys could never stop thinking about. Her family was all she had and she had to provide for them. No one else would.

Shortly a barefoot serving girl, about fifteen, appeared. She was rather taller than Maelys, but thin, and her hair, though neatly brushed, was dull and stringy. 'Will you come with me, please, Lady Maelys?' she said in a soft voice, her eyes downcast.

Maelys didn't move. 'Where are you taking me?' She couldn't keep the anxiety out of her voice.

'To your bath, Lady Maelys.'

There was no good reason to refuse. One part of Tifferfyte would be as safe, or dangerous, as another. 'You don't have to call me Lady Maelys. I'm just an ordinary woman.'

'Yes, Lady Maelys. This way, please.'

'What is your name?' Maelys said.

'Girl!' she said, like an exclamation. 'You may call me, "Girl!", Lady Maelys.'

'I'd prefer to call you by your real name.'

The girl looked over her shoulder, then said softly, 'it's Jillazoun, Lady Maelys, but you can just call me Jil.'

Maelys followed her along the corridor which led away from the pavilion, then down several sets of steps. Walls, floor and ceiling were all carved from the same glassy stone. Shortly Jil turned left into an open chamber and Maelys heard the sound of running water. Jil pushed open a door, the rushing sound swelled and Maelys looked up in awe.

A large rock-glass basin, full to overflowing, was set in the middle of the room, thigh-high above the floor, and it was so big that a horse could have bathed in it. It was continually filled by water falling like rain from hundreds of holes, in the form of paired crescent moons, in the ceiling above its centre. The overflow ran in a sinuous channel across the floor before disappearing down a grated hole.

Maelys trailed her fingers through the water. 'It's warm!' She hadn't had a warm bath since she was a little girl.

'The fiery heart of the mountain heats it,' said the girl, plucking at Maelys's shirt as if to undress her.

It didn't feel right. There had been no servants in Nifferlin, for all the work had been done by members of the clan. 'I can undress myself. You can go now, thanks, Jil.'

The girl's lower lip quivered. 'How have I displeased you, Lady Maelys?'

'You haven't,' Maelys said more kindly, 'but I'm not used to being waited on.'

'It is the custom in Tifferfyte, Lady Maelys,' Jil said in a soft but dignified voice. 'I bathe everyone who dwells down here, save Monkshart.'

Maelys's curiosity stirred. 'Why not him?'

'He . . . doesn't like to touch or be touched, save only by Phrune.' Jil looked revolted.

'What happened to him? His skin looks –'

Jil glanced towards the door, then lowered her voice. 'It's said some spell or Art went wrong, a long time ago, but I wouldn't know. He has to wear those tissue-leather gloves and leggings. And only Phrune knows how to make them –' She broke off, as if she didn't want to think about him, and shook her head.

'You bathe Phrune too?'

Jil grimaced. 'Even him.' She added, softly, after again checking over her shoulder, 'If you do not allow me to bathe you, I will be beaten for displeasing you and my little brother will go hungry tonight.'

'I didn't see any children in Tifferfyte.'

'My brother is the only one. That's why it's such a sad place.'

'The villagers looked haunted,' said Maelys. 'What –'

Again Jil shook her head and Maelys, not wanting to make the girl more uncomfortable, didn't pursue the thought.

'Why are you here, Jil? Do you believe in the Deliverer too?'

'Everyone believes in the Deliverer, Lady Maelys. We had no family, save my big brother, so when he came to Tifferfyte in the name of the Deliverer, we came too. There was nowhere else to go.'

'I always wanted a big brother,' said Maelys with a sigh. 'It must be wonderful having him to look after you.'

'He . . . died, Lady Maelys.' Jil shivered. 'There's just me and my little brother now. I don't want to die for the Deliverer but we can never leave.'

'Do you mean you're not allowed to?'

'Er, yes, Lady Maelys.'

Jil's situation reminded Maelys of Fyllis, whom she would probably never see again; who might already be in the God-Emperor's hands. 'Then of course you must bathe me,' she said tiredly, and gave herself up to being waited upon.

Half an hour later, after the girl had scrubbed her clean and washed her hair, Maelys stepped out of the basin. Jil rubbed her dry, pulled a simple blue gown over her head – no more was needed in the balmy warmth of this place – brushed her hair and dressed the cut on her arm. Then she led Maelys back to her room, went out, and shortly reappeared carrying a jug of water and a tray containing half a loaf of brown bread, a large chunk of cheese, a length of sausage and a bowl of pickles.

Jil carved a perfect slice of bread, cut cheese and sausage into even pieces, piled them artistically on a slice, topped it with a spoonful of pickles and reached out towards Maelys's mouth.

'No!' said Maelys. The girl's lip quivered again, so she hastily went on, 'I am perfectly pleased with you, Jil, but I prefer to feed myself.' Something occurred to her. 'Am I allowed to punish a servant who displeases me?'

'Of course, Lady Maelys,' Jil whispered.

'And reward one who pleases me?'

'Yes, Lady Maelys.'

Maelys took the knife from the girl's hand, sawed off another slice and a few pieces of sausage and cheese for herself, then handed the remainder of the food to Jil. 'This is your reward for pleasing me. Feed your brother. You may go now.'

'Thank you, Lady Maelys.' Jil went out with her head held high.

Maelys sat on the bed and ate her dinner. How naïve she'd been to think that, once she'd delivered Nish to the Defiance, all her troubles would be over. They were only just beginning.

221

She'd already learned more than she cared to know about Monkshart and the kind of world he would create if ever he brought Nish to power. She didn't want anything to do with him, which was unfortunate, since he looked like the only person who could help her to uncover her hidden talent – assuming it was still there. Monkshart had said that she lacked any aura, so maybe she didn't have a proper talent at all, and suddenly she wanted it.

Maelys lay on her bed until midnight, brooding. Why did Monkshart resent her so? From the moment he'd looked at her she'd sensed an antipathy in him, and surely there had to be more to it than her relationship with Nish. She had to find out. Dare she spy on Monskhart? After her recent failures she was reluctant to use her initiative again, but if he succeeded in separating Nish from her, her quest would fail.

It took her a long time to find the courage. Opening her door quietly, she slipped down the passage towards the circular opening, barefoot, so she wouldn't make a sound. She could hear Monkshart and Phrune talking, though not what they were saying. Maelys was about to creep closer when one of the chairs scraped. Did they know she was here?

She scuttled back to her room, slipped inside and lay on the bed as if asleep, trying to control her heaving chest. Shortly Phrune came padding down the hall on his plump feet and appeared at the door, eyeing her in the dim light. The hairs rose on the back of her neck and she was still shuddering a long time after he'd left.

She wasn't game to go back, since he could return at any minute, and eventually Maelys dozed. Later – she did not know how much time had passed – she was woken by the unmistakeable sound of Phrune's feet on the floor of the hall: a wet slap as he put each foot down, and a faint squelch as he lifted it. *Slap-squelch, slap-squelch, slap-squelch*. The sounds stopped outside, his outline appeared in the door again and she could sense him trying to read her.

'Phrune?' Monkshart called irritably. 'Hurry up. You've still got to cream me.'

Phrune slap-squelched down to the opening and went out onto the pavilion. Maelys took a deep breath, gathered what little remained of her courage and followed, trying to avoid stepping on the damp smears he'd left on the floor. This time she continued almost to the opening. No point spying unless she could hear, and she didn't think being caught could make things much worse for her.

'It took a long time to go through the archives,' Phrune said with a hint of defiance. 'And I didn't find anything about *her*.'

'Give it here.' Maelys heard pages turning. 'Ah, Clan Nifferlin.' Monkshart muttered something she didn't catch. 'I was right about them. An old clan, neither rich nor important. Clever people, though with a talent for picking the wrong side in a conflict. Rebellious but mostly principled rogues . . .'

'And her?' said Phrune silkily. 'I could use her next, if you like . . .'

'Keep your hands off her!' snapped Monkshart, then added, as if mollifying Phrune, 'For the moment, anyway. I wonder about Maelys. She's a cunning little thing; she's got to be, and she'd encourage him to think for himself; to question.'

'And we can't have that, can we?'

'She's the last companion we want for the Deliverer. His consort must be beautiful, elegant, charming, and worthy in all ways to stand beside the Son of the God-Emperor. This greedy little slut doesn't even come close.'

'Either mentally or physically,' amended Phrune. Maelys imagined Phrune's tongue caressing his lower lip.

'Quite. The Deliverer's consort must be a lovely young woman, but the stupider the better. Also vacuous and easily moulded.'

'Though not by him,' said Phrune. 'Are you sure he'll take to such a one?'

'Jal-Nish often talked about his youngest son, in the olden days,' said Monkshart thoughtfully. 'Cryl-Nish is a lusty little beggar and women are his weakness. He can't resist them, can't get enough of them –'

'He's an ugly little runt. I'd be surprised if he's had three women in his life.'

'So we don't find him a consort yet. We ply him with willing girls, a different one each night, until he's so cock-struck he can't think of anything else. He'll soon forget the little drab. Get onto it tomorrow, Phrune.'

Maelys headed back to her room, feeling sick. She didn't want to hear any more about Nish, or herself. She looked into a small mirror on the wall but the woman reflected there was neither beautiful, elegant, nor, to her mind, charming. Irritably, Maelys blew out the lantern and threw herself on the bed.

Nish spent the next few days closeted with Monkshart, anxiously going over the plan for the attack on the city and citadel of Rancidore. Though he knew little about either the capabilities of Monkshart's troops or the defences of Rancidore, to Nish's experienced eye the attack seemed poorly thought out and unlikely to succeed. Monkshart was undoubtedly a charismatic leader but he was no general.

Unfortunately there was nothing Nish could do about it, since the little army lay hidden in the caves of Londe, ten leagues away, and Monkshart would neither allow him to go there nor put off the attack.

Since it was out of his control, Nish busied himself with planning for the Deliverer's campaign, though he found it difficult to concentrate. Monkshart planned to create an uprising, relying on his personal charisma, his undoubted talent for mancery and perhaps the strange power of Tifferfyte too, then move swiftly through the populous coastal lands, gathering an army of supporters behind Nish and stirring up rebellion everywhere, before falling on Morrelune like a storm.

It was a brilliant plan with several major flaws, of which the greatest was Nish himself. What if he failed, or broke, or simply didn't inspire people?

It was bad enough that he was taking on the most powerful man in the world, one whose attention to detail was as legendary as his ruthlessness, and moreover one who'd had ten years to perfect both his defences and spying networks. But when that man was his father, by whom Nish had always felt intimidated, and against whom he'd never felt that he measured up, he simply didn't believe that it was possible.

Furthermore, his father still retained that hold he'd put on Nish before the battle of Gumby Marth. It had lain dormant all this time but surely, as soon as he became the Deliverer, Jal-Nish would find a way to renew it and everything Nish had built so painstakingly would come tumbling down, to the ruin of all.

His father's forces had withdrawn to Rancidore and had not been seen since, nor had any flappeters approached the mountain. Monkshart took that as a good sign but Nish did not. He didn't believe that his father had given up, nor that he couldn't take Tifferfyte if he chose to.

Maybe Monkshart's Arts could slay a few soldiers from afar, or even a few hundred, but no renegade mancer could hold off an army determined to fight through despite the cost. His father wouldn't hesitate to lose most of an army storming the mountain if their deaths allowed the rest to get through. As they must.

Besides, Nish had spent years working with the greatest mancers in the world, and knew that all Arts were painful and exhausting to use, and caused debilitating *aftersickness*. If Monkshart tried to fight his father's army, alone, aftersickness would soon cripple him.

No, Father had withdrawn because he had a better plan.

Why attack too soon, and risk a morale-damaging defeat, when he could build up his forces to ensure an overwhelming victory at a time of his choosing?

Nish's other problem was that, even here, he could feel his father reaching out to him when he was half-asleep, trying to find a way past the halo of protection. Despite Monkshart's assertions, Nish didn't feel safe from Jal-Nish in Tifferfyte. Safer, perhaps, but not safe.

On the night before the attack on Rancidore was due to take place, Nish and Maelys were drinking tea in the pavilion with Monkshart, prior to retiring to their separate chambers, when a young messenger came bolting down the glassy path from the top of the crater. A strip of paper fluttered in his right hand and he was gasping as if he'd run all the way from Rancidore.

'Master?' he croaked. 'Master – the most dreadful news!'

He skidded to a stop at the entrance to the pavilion, but did not speak. Monkshart's head jerked but he continued to peruse the map in his hand, the picture of self-control apart from a tap-tap-tapping of his left foot on the floor. After a minute he looked up. 'Well?'

'Master, a skeet has just come from –' Catching sight of Maelys and Nish sitting in the shadows, he broke off.

Monkshart glanced at Maelys, frowned, and motioned her to leave. She began to rise, fuming, but Nish put a hand on her arm. 'She stays. What is it, messenger?'

The messenger, a slender youth no older than the servant girl, Jil, looked at Nish, paled, then turned away, confused.

'Yes, it's him!' thundered Monkshart, rising to his feet to tower over the lad. 'This is Cryl-Nish Hlar the Deliverer, and he's just as great and terrible as his father the God-Emperor. Read the message, cur, or he'll deal with you the way he does to all who oppose him.'

Nish scowled. 'I'm not like my father!' he snapped, 'and don't make me out to be.'

'The message, boy,' growled Monkshart, ignoring Nish.

The youth raised the strip of paper and began to read. His hand shook. 'These tidings come from the hand of Byalmon, Under-Steward of Hulipont.' He glanced at Monkshart but couldn't meet his fierce gaze. He licked his lips and read on, the words tumbling out in a rush.

'Sire, dreadful news. Hulipont has been captured and razed, and Ousther, the Chief Steward of the Defiance in the east, taken and tortured to death.'

Monkshart let out an inarticulate cry, swiftly bitten off, then motioned with a clawed hand for the youth to continue.

The youth's eyes were darting this way and that, like a rat in a trap, but he read on. 'But there – there is worse. As you know, the leaders of all our eastern Defiance outposts were at Hulipont when it was attacked, developing your campaign strategy now that the Deliverer is at large.' The youth's eyes slid towards Nish, then darted away. 'They – they've all been captured and, under torture, must reveal the names of the other rebels. Jal-Nish will take their outposts one by one, if he hasn't done so by the time you receive this.'

The youth gulped at the air like a stranded fish, before reading on. 'I, Byalmon, Under-Steward, take full responsibility for this disaster and now die by my own hand.'

Monkshart reeled, his eyes darted wildly around the pavilion, and then his jaw hardened.

'How dare you bring us such evil tidings, idiot boy!'

He sprang forwards, caught the youth by the front of his coat and raised him so high that his bare feet kicked helplessly a third of a span above the floor. 'The blasphemous God-Emperor must be toppled, and all who serve him, wittingly or unwittingly, must die. In the name of the Deliverer you shall suffer the penalty set down for all those who undermine the irresistible march of the Defiance.'

The youth began to wail. 'Please, Master. I only brought you the message that came from the skeet. My crippled mother –'

Nish leapt to his feet but before he could take a step, Monkshart, roaring like an enraged bull, threw the lad high out over the brink. He tumbled in the air, emitting a hair-raising shriek that had Phrune screwing up his face and blocking his ears, then fell towards the centre of the pit far below. His cry tailed off to nothing well before the ghastly pulpy thud came echoing up.

Maelys was so shocked that she couldn't say a word. How could Monkshart be so indifferent to the life of an innocent boy? And how could it have happened so quickly, and so finally? Abruptly, she doubled over and vomited her dinner onto the gleaming floor.

'This is the end of us, Monkshart!' Nish was choking on his rage. 'How dare you murder that innocent lad for telling you the truth. *And in my name!*'

TWENTY-ONE

Phrune stood in the opening, licking his bloated lips. 'That was a waste, Master,' he said, though Nish didn't think he meant the waste of a human life.

Monkshart was staring at his hands, which were held out in front of him, fingers hooked. The left glove had torn apart under the strain, exposing ruined skin which was red, flaking and weeping from hundreds of cracks. He turned towards Nish, his dark complexion as grey and waxy as a dead man's.

'Master, Master,' said Phrune, like a mother to a distressed child. 'It's over now. Come with me. I'll look after you.' He took the zealot's hand.

Without saying a word, Monkshart stumbled through the circular opening, Phrune padding beside him.

Maelys was swaying on her feet, staring sightlessly into the pit. Nish caught her arm. 'Come on.'

She pulled free, took a gasping swig from the water jug and rinsed her mouth with it. She dashed water into her face, wiped it with her sleeve and nodded. 'Where are we going?'

'I don't know.' His voice cracked. Leaving here was madness, but there was no choice. 'I won't stay to be manipulated by this monster. Have you got anything better to wear?'

She picked at the flimsy gown. 'The serving girl took away my boy's clothes but I still have my coat and boots.'

'Get them. You can't go mountain climbing barefoot. And a hat. What about a weapon?'

'Only a dinner knife.'

'It's better than I've got. Meet me back here in two minutes. There's no time to waste. Try not to look suspicious.'

She nodded and hurried away. Nish headed to his own quarters, pulled on socks, boots and coat, and returned to the pavilion, meeting no one on the way. Maelys was waiting there. The knife was thrust through her belt and her eyes were staring. They were back to where they'd started but she was with him all the way: leaving was the one honourable course left.

They started up the winding path, which was lit only by faint reflections from the walls, for it was after midnight now and the moon was veiled by cloud. Maelys went first, staring rigidly ahead. Nish felt an irresistible urge to look down into the pit, then wished he hadn't, for steam swirling around the cylindrical walls left a clear tunnel through the centre, like the eye of a hurricane. It was lighter down there; he could see the youth's broken body on a knob of rock. Nish's eyes veered away to a haloed glow in the depths, though he could not distinguish its source.

His stomach knotted and he hurried up after Maelys, knowing that he was acting like a fool. The messenger was dead; nothing could bring him back, and once they fled Tifferfyte they would quickly be taken by Vomix. Maelys would die and he, Nish, would be returned to his father, so what was the point?

Yes, Monkshart *was* a monster, but a strong one, and it would take the greatest strength to overthrow his father. Nish stopped. Was it really worth losing everything just to maintain his reputation? One or two people might praise his noble gesture, but the suffering masses of Santhenar would curse him for the fool who had offered them hope, then robbed them of it.

He was wavering when Maelys looked over her shoulder

and came back, treading carefully on the mist-damp surface. 'Better a fool than a knave,' she said quietly, as if she could read his thoughts. 'Come on.'

She gave him her hand and at her touch his doubts vanished. Choices that were so tortuous to him always seemed clear to her. 'A pair of fools! We'll find a way, somehow,' and such a wave of relief washed over him that he felt his eyes moisten. Never compromise your principles, he told himself. You're nothing like the God-Emperor, so don't fall into the trap of acting like him.

Maelys was a few steps below the rim when a triangle of moon peeped between the clouds, its single ray lighting her up like a princess ascending to her throne. She stopped abruptly, one arm outstretched as if she were posing for a sculptor.

'Go on,' he said in a low voice. 'We must be well away before –'

Her shoulders slumped. He climbed the next few steps then stopped, for a pair of burly guards, armed with clubs, blocked the path up. 'I'm Cryl-Nish Hlar, the son of the God-Emperor. Move aside.'

'Go back, surr,' said the leading guard.

'I'm the Deliverer,' Nish said furiously, 'and I'm ordering you to move.'

The guard took a step backwards but the fellow behind him clapped him on the shoulder and his resolve firmed. 'The Deliverer would not run like a dog at the first setback,' he sneered.

'Don't give in to them,' said Maelys.

Her faith in his abilities was touching, in the circumstances. Nish briefly considered rushing the soldiers, though she was blocking his way on the narrow path. Besides, the edge of a precipice was no place to launch an attack on two armed men.

'It's over,' he said dully. 'There's no way out!' He turned and stumbled back down the path again.

There was no sign of Monkshart, but Phrune was waiting for them in the pavilion with that sickening plump-lipped smile. 'It's the only way,' he said silkily. 'Steel can only be fought with steel.'

'You want to turn me into my father,' Nish said as they were led inside.

They spent the next day confined to their chambers, with guards stationed outside, but the morning after that Maelys and Nish were summoned to the pavilion. Monkshart was already in his chair, his eyes dull blobs the colour of black olives in deeply sunken sockets. He wore a new set of tissue-thin leather gloves, a fish-belly white this time. He gestured Nish and Maelys to the other chairs.

'Hulipont was the Defiance's most important bastion,' began Monkshart in a flat voice that lacked any of his earlier fire. 'It held most of our weapons as well as our entire store of banned uncanny devices, carefully shielded and husbanded over the past decade.' He broke off, staring into the pit, and a shudder rocked his long form.

'And without them the Defiance is impotent,' said Nish.

Monkshart turned those blackened eyes on him. 'It's a setback, but we believers always knew there would be obstacles on the road. With faith and determination we can overcome them. You can still become the Deliverer. Indeed, the need is greater than ever.'

'I wouldn't give you the time of day.'

'You will,' said Monkshart in a tone that made Maelys shiver.

'In any case,' said Nish, 'I can't begin an uprising on my own, trapped here. Even if Father is unwilling to approach Tifferfyte, which I doubt, he can simply encircle the mountain with troops and wisp-watchers, and wait until starvation forces us out. You may be able to knock down a soldier or two with your Arts, but there's no power in the world, uncanny or military, that can be used against the tears when he wields them.'

'I've already abandoned that plan,' said Monkshart. 'Besides, there's a power in the world which Jal-Nish cannot defeat, for every attack on it will make it grow stronger: the power of faith, the power of belief, that people can have a better life under the Deliverer.'

Maelys stirred uneasily beside Nish, but did not speak.

'After you murdered that poor boy the other night, no one will believe in the Deliverer either,' Nish said coldly.

'I acted rashly, it's true. I was too focussed on the ultimate goal. But Cryl-Nish,' Monkshart leaned forwards and the light swelled until his eyes were ablaze, 'you can only triumph by being as ruthless and iron-hard as your father. Can't you see that?'

'So to beat his father,' said Maelys, 'Nish has to become him? Then what's the point?'

Monkshart ignored her. 'You're not your father, Cryl-Nish, and never will be. Nonetheless, the people of Santhenar have been led by ruthless leaders since the Council of Scrutators was formed a century and more ago. It's all they know; all they can respect. You can be just as ruthless as your father. Indeed, you must, for there is no other way *now*. You must drive all the way to victory.'

'Or ruin,' said Nish bitterly.

'Or ruin,' echoed Monkshart. 'It's a hard road and we may well fail, though with faith, belief and determination –'

Nish was thoroughly sick of Monkshart's exhortations. He always spoke as if he were trying to sway a mob. The zealot genuinely wanted to overthrow the God-Emperor, but what did he intend to put in his place? 'I won't do it.'

Monkshart leaned back in his chair, staring at Nish, then crossed his arms. 'You will.'

'You can't force me. I'm the Deliverer, remember – the one who made the promise.'

'Your willing cooperation will certainly make things easier, for the people will listen to you and your oratory can inspire them. But if you force me, Cryl-Nish, I have Arts of

233

illusion and coercion that can make you walk and talk, yet leave your mind a blank.'

'I don't believe you,' said Nish. 'I know plenty about the Secret Art.'

'As it used to be, before the tears, perhaps,' Monkshart said, smiling blandly. 'And some Arts were more secret than others. My master taught me things about coercion that you can't even imagine.'

'I don't believe that any such Art can make me a credible Deliverer if I refuse to do it.'

'It will be difficult, certainly.' Monkshart rubbed his square chin. 'On the other hand, the people desperately want to believe in you, Cryl-Nish, and when I tell them how cruelly you've suffered at the hands of your father, and how he damaged you, I'm sure they'll make allowances for your incapacity.'

'You may turn me into a puppet, but I'll be fighting you all the way, and sooner or later I'll tear you down and feed you to the mob.' If only Nish could believe it himself, but he knew it was the hollowest of boasts.

Monkshart's fingers clenched and his eyes flashed, but this time he controlled himself, steepled his fingers under his chin and closed his eyes, remaining that way for several minutes. Then his eyes sprang open.

'Very well, I'll put that alternative aside for an emergency. Besides, I'd much rather you served me willingly.' He gave Nish a chilling smile.

'I won't.'

'Not under any circumstances?'

'None that I can think of.'

Monkshart's eyes roved around the pavilion, though Nish got the impression that it was just a gesture designed to draw out the tension between them. 'Not even to protect Maelys?' said the zealot softly.

Nish started. From the corner of his eye he saw her knuckles whitening on the arm of the chair. 'I –'

'Unless you serve me willingly,' Monkshart rode over the top of him, enunciating each word with care, 'I will give her up to Seneschal Vomix.'

Maelys let out a muffled cry, then straightened her back and lifted her chin. 'Don't do it, Nish,' she said, her voice fluttering. 'If it's my doom to be given to Vomix, I must be strong and suffer it. I ask only one thing of you. That whether you overthrow your father, or whether you go back to him, you do everything in your power to save my little sister.'

Nish turned an anguished face to Maelys. 'I can't let you –'

'You must, Nish.'

'I'll give you the night to think about it,' said Monkshart, 'but in the morning I will have an answer, one way or the other. Phrune!' he called, 'take them to their chambers and set the guards at the top of the path again.'

Nish sat in his chamber in the dark. Jil had come with his dinner earlier but he'd waved it away without a glance. He couldn't have swallowed it anyway, for there was a lump in his belly the size of a brick.

This time there was no honourable alternative. If he agreed to work with Monkshart he would be betraying everything he stood for, and he could only imagine the contempt Irisis would have felt for such a spineless capitulation. But if he refused, he would be betraying his only friend, who had given her all for him, to say nothing of his promise to Irisis and the world. He was trapped either way and he couldn't bear it any longer.

Besides, taking on the mantle of the Deliverer was pointless now that the other Defiance outposts had been destroyed. The struggle was hopeless; his father could never be beaten and it was futile to try. Even if, by some miracle, he could escape from here to fight again, he'd lost the will for it. After ten years of self-analysis Nish knew his own character intimately, but he couldn't do anything about his biggest failing, despair.

That left only one way out, the coward's way, and he despised himself for taking it, but he couldn't summon the strength to fight on.

TWENTY-TWO

Hours had gone by. After Phrune finally padded down the corridor, extinguishing the lanterns, Nish went to his door. It wasn't locked. He watched until the dull fan of light from beneath the acolyte's door was extinguished, waited a few more minutes, just in case, then returned to the pavilion. All was dark there too, save for the faint radiance from the depths of the crater.

He stood on the brink for a while, looking down and thinking about all that might have been, then took a step onto the glassy plank that stretched out over the abyss. The plank was a couple of spans long, but after his second step he could feel it bending. If he went much further he would slide off, and he didn't want his demise to be by default. It had to be a conscious, deliberate choice.

Besides, the plank was Monkshart's instrument of execution and it didn't feel right that he, Nish, should escape from his troubles that way. Going back into the pavilion, he stood at the far corner, looking up. A guard was just visible at the top of the crater.

Nish turned to the path that ran from the other side of the pavilion down into the depths of the crater. The dark was thicker here and he could barely make out the glassy rock beneath his feet. He went down slowly, trailing his right hand along the wall and feeling with each foot before lowering his weight onto it. Ironic, the lengths to which he was going to stay alive, so he could kill himself further down.

As his eyes adjusted, he began to see *into* the vitreous surfaces of the pit, which in daylight had exhibited such ever-changing, shimmering colours and patterns. Something moved there now – images just beyond the boundary of recognition, like straining to remember dreams after waking.

They worked powerfully on his psyche, though. At one point he found himself moved to such melancholy that tears pricked in his eyes, while another shadow-image spoke to him of all those great and glorious creations – priceless art, poems of the most exquisite sensibility, the Great Tales – lost forever during the reign of his father.

Shaking his head, Nish continued and, not far below, made out a smooth bulge protruding over the abyss like a glassy tonsil. Was that where the young messenger had met his end? It seemed probable. He made his cautious way to it, stepping extra carefully as he moved out onto the bulge, but the mess made by the impact had been cleaned away.

He sat on the broadest part of the overhang, which seemed a fitting place for him to meet his end, and to atone for the murder done in his name. Far below lay the still-fuming core of the destroyed node – its dead heart. What perversion of reality had the destruction of the node created here? He would never know.

There was no point putting it off, for the longer he postponed his end the harder it would be to act. Nish rose suddenly, took a deep breath then bent his knees to spring. As his feet left the floor, something jerked him away from the edge and he landed flat on his back on the bulge, hard enough to knock the wind out of him. The moment he got his breath back, Nish tried to throw himself forwards.

'Stop!' said Monkshart, and with three fingers of his other hand he tapped Nish across the forehead.

Nish was overcome by a dreamy lassitude and couldn't think what he was doing here, or what had seemed so urgent and final. It only lasted a few seconds but, when it passed, so had the urge to hurl himself into the pit.

He sat up, rubbing his throat, which felt bruised. 'How – how did you know I was here?'

'Sensing a self-destructive urge in you, I set Phrune to keep a covert watch.' Monkshart put a hand under Nish's elbow and easily lifted him to his feet, turning him away from the brink. 'Come with me.'

'Where?' said Nish numbly.

'Down to the dead heart. I do understand what you must be going through, Cryl-Nish, but that way is not and can never be the answer to your troubles.'

'There *is* no answer, save that life is an empty, futile torment.'

'On the contrary, there is *always* an answer, but first you must ask the right question. The dead heart of the node is the place to ask such questions, for it contains all possibilities and all things become clear there.'

With that cryptic statement Monkshart unshuttered a lantern and held it up in his free hand. Nish allowed the zealot to lead him down the path and asked no more questions, for he felt oddly empty of curiosity, or interest. What was to be would be.

The base of the crater was knobbed and speckled with glassy lumps, many of which had shattered to litter the floor with curved shards that crunched underfoot. Every sound was drawn out to extended echoes.

'Careful here, Cryl-Nish. The rock-glass floor is full of bubbles and the larger ones won't support your weight.'

It was hard to make out what Monkshart was saying through the echoes. He waved the lantern around. The floor ahead looked like froth set solid, though most of the larger bubbles, the size of melons, had collapsed, and the edge of one was blotched with unpleasant rusty stains.

Nish trod carefully after Monkshart, who was weaving his way towards a sump in the floor, about a span across, with walls of wavy, flowing, solidified glass. The glow he'd seen from above came from it. A wooden beam had been laid across the sump and a rope ladder was tied to the beam. Nish looked in but could not make out the bottom.

'Down there?'

Monkshart nodded stiffly. He looked tense now. 'If you would go first.'

Nish took hold of the top rung of the ladder and swung himself down. He should have been anxious, especially with the zealot above him, but he felt nothing. He climbed down slowly, trying to avoid looking at the increasingly tortured walls, which resembled a mural made of war victims. It was only five or six spans to the bottom, but by the time he reached it Nish felt as though he'd passed through a gate into another world.

The collapsed dead heart of the former node had the form of a cluster of gigantic bubbles blown into the glassy rock, though their thin inner walls had collapsed to a litter of shards. Even to Nish's deadened gaze, the place had an air of unreality. Layers of grey powder lay in an inward spiral centred on a murky hole – more correctly, an emptiness – in the floor. The powder might have been a form of the quick-dust which Irisis had once told him about – at any rate, his foot went straight through it – and a greenish miasma drifted above the emptiness.

Dark oozes seeped from cracks in the walls, like tar, though each had a mirror-shiny surface. Wisps and phantoms drifted up from the emptiness – fragments of alternative realities, perhaps, each struggling to come to fruition like starving beasts fighting over a corpse. The dead heart had an eerie feel, but there was something else about it, something he hadn't felt in a very long time, though it took a while to work out exactly what it was.

He felt lighter here, less burdened, as though a weight

had been lifted from his shoulders. No, not a weight, an *influence*. This place was completely free of the tears' influence. Not a skerrick of his father's Art could reach him here.

But as if to deny that comfort the moment he'd realised it, something began to seep into the edge of his consciousness, like an image which, no matter how quickly he turned his head, always remained just beyond the edge of sight. He tried to blink it away, thinking that it was his father after all, but it wouldn't go.

Nish sat down on the most solid and shard-free piece of floor, half expecting to float up again, and shook his head. The image faded but was replaced by another, clearer this time, of a small band of people walking through an icy wasteland towards a distant tower. It faded too, but his curiosity had returned.

He looked up through the hole. 'What is this place, Monkshart? You said all the nodes were destroyed.'

'They were,' said Monkshart, peering down at him, 'but as I told you, *Nothing goes to nothing*. No object or force can ever be completely destroyed – it can only be transformed into something else, and the Tifferfyte node was transformed into this place, which I call the Pit of Possibilities.'

'But it's not a place of power?'

'Not if you mean uncanny power, nor indeed any force that can be used to strike against the enemy. The Pit offers nothing but visions of possible futures.'

'Possible futures?' Nish sniffed. 'Like the charlatans' scrying bowls we used to read about in the Great Tales?'

'Not at all. Scrying bowls need not tell you any truth, but the futures you see in the Pit of Possibilities *must* include the true one, and once you discover which it is, a wise man will know how to make it come true.'

'Just like that?' Nish said sceptically. All prophecies had an out and here it was in the words 'a wise man', which could mean anything or exclude anyone.

'The future is never easy, not even with a map,' said Monkshart as if he were lecturing a stupid child. 'And even if the path to success becomes clear, it doesn't mean you can follow it. That depends on your strength, your resolution, your courage and your skill – not least in swaying others to do your bidding.'

'Then assuming you saw your own future in the Pit of Possibilities, how have your plans gone so wrong?'

'I saw where success lay, and failure, even to the loss of the other Defiance outposts. I took steps to protect them but I failed. I was distracted at the critical moment, and perhaps the enemy had a hand in that.'

'But surely, if you saw how to make your desired future come true, you would have seen all the ways that it could fail, and overcome them?'

'The Pit just gives glimpses of the future. It can't reveal every single obstacle on your road, else it would take as long to show it as it would to live through that future. Besides, the reactions of others in response to your decisions can wreak great changes. I'm a fallible man, I admit it. I allowed myself to be distracted and overlooked a minor event that later became critical. But all is not lost. In every second of time, new possible futures are created. It's up to us to make ours true – if it is within our power. It may not be. We may fail; I haven't tried to hide that. Will you look into the possibilities of the pit?'

Nish shook his head. 'I see no difference to other forms of fortune-telling, all of which prey on the gullible.'

'What have you got to lose, Cryl-Nish? Just look, and examine what you see.'

It was tempting, despite his mistrust of Monkshart. 'How will I identify my real future?'

'You'll know when you see it, I promise.'

'What if I can only believe in the future I want the most?'

'That's why *I'm* here, Cryl-Nish. I discovered the Pit of

Possibilities eight years ago, when I still served your father –'

'But you didn't tell him about it, even though you were his sworn servant?' It was another chink in Monkshart's battered moral armour.

'I was never his *servant*,' Monkshart said loftily, 'though I did serve. I've spent much of my effort and my Arts since that time, working out how to use the Pit of Possibilities. Enough talk. I'll wait up here, where I can wield my Art without being influenced by the possibilities, and make sure that you can tell the false futures from the true ones.'

Nish couldn't decide whether Monkshart was a charismatic charlatan, a scheming scoundrel or a dangerous fanatic, though it was clear he only wished to use Nish for his own ends, not for any higher cause. Nish had been used so often in his brief career that he could tell a villain on sight.

Yet that didn't mean Monkshart was a liar, or the Pit of Possibilities a trick. The most successful schemers were those who manipulated the truth as little as possible, and always retained a kernel of it in even their most outlandish tales. Perhaps the Pit of Possibilities did enable people to see the future, and there was an awful lot of future Nish wanted to see.

'How do I use it?'

'Its vapours are already working on you. Haven't you noticed?'

'I've seen a few images, as if from the corner of my eye, though they weren't very clear. But the harder I looked, the more they faded.'

'They'll become clear once I employ my Art and you allow your tension to drain away. You can't *seek* out the possibilities, Cryl-Nish. You have to abandon yourself to them and allow them to come in their own time. Are you ready?'

'I'm ready.' He wasn't.

'Sit down there, between the outer wall and the Mistmurk –'

'The what?' said Nish.

'That blur of nothingness with the green vapours above it. Careful! Don't allow any part of yourself to touch it, or even pass above it.'

'Why not?'

'Just don't!' Monkshart snapped. 'Lean against the wall, close your eyes and surrender yourself to the possibilities. I'll be by the top of the ladder.'

Nish felt a vague unease, but dismissed it. If Monkshart wished to do him harm he'd had any number of opportunities. He went to the wall, carefully avoiding the roiling Mistmurk, and settled back against the stone. Closing his eyes, he followed the creaking of the rope ladder until Monkshart reached the top and silence fell.

Utter silence, so complete that it made him uneasy; he realised that he'd reduced his breathing so it wouldn't make a sound. His thumping heart slowed; he relaxed his muscles one by one, gradually slumping against the wall, and waited.

Something green and shadowy appeared in the corner of his eye but as he tried to focus on it, it flicked back out of sight. Fool! Just let it come. He relaxed further, trying to remove all expectations from his mind, all hopes, even all dreams. Just let come what will come, though he couldn't rid himself of every vestige of unease, no matter how hard he tried. Something felt wrong; he really needed his lost clearsight now.

No possibilities came to him. Rather, Nish felt so unburdened and free of his father that he slipped into sleep, only to wake suddenly with tears streaming down his face, for he'd been dreaming about his beloved. Irisis was alive; the horror of her execution had never happened and they were going to be together for as long as they both lived.

He didn't open his eyes, wanting to maintain the dream

for as long as possible. Now Irisis was striding away from him, moving with odd stiffness, and he was hurrying after her, beseeching her to wait, but she broke into a run. He bolted after her, caught her by the arm and whirled her around, but she hid her face from him, and when he looked below her hands he saw the thread-like seam around her throat. He tried to pull her hands away, to tell her that it didn't matter, but she beat him off.

And as she did, one of her cheeks was uncovered and he saw a patch of corruption growing there. Nish recoiled in horror. He couldn't help himself, and a look of the most terrible regret crossed her face.

'I told you, Nish. Didn't I tell you?' she said sadly. 'It can never be.'

She began to walk away and this time he didn't go after her, just sat watching the familiar swaying walk, the lush hips . . . He couldn't bear it.

'Let her go, Cryl-Nish,' said Monkshart from above. 'By seeking an impossible possibility, you close yourself to the futures that could come true.'

'I didn't seek her out. She came in my dream –'

'Never allow yourself to dream in the Pit of Possibilities. Empty your mind, but you must stay awake.'

Nish slumped against the wall again, but could feel himself slipping towards sleep and yearning for what it could bring him, so he stood and tried to rid himself of the dream memories. It didn't work; unlike normal dreams they remained perfectly clear. The ache was too great, and in the end he had to forcefully purge the memories.

At once the futures began, so vividly that even the most absurd seemed as real as life. The first was mercifully short, for it showed him being torn apart on a great wheel, and Maelys burned alive while an angry mob danced around a bonfire and his father looked down, unmoved, from the back of a gigantic flappeter soaring through the rising sparks.

245

In the second he was a bald, bearded, toothless wreck, gibbering and dribbling in the cell where he'd spent the past forty years. This future was worse than the first but he steeled himself to neither reach for it nor shy away, but allow it to fade so the next one could come.

The third future showed that icy wasteland he'd seen earlier, though there was no tower in it this time. He was alone by a dismal shack, dressed in rags, exhaustedly wielding a wooden pick as he tried to break the iron-hard ground. A body lay on the earth floor inside the doorway of the hut, though Nish couldn't make out whose it was.

Death, madness or exile – he didn't need the Pit of Possibilities to tell him that those were his most likely futures, and little to choose between them. Was the imprisoned madman happy now, or had he suffered so grievously before going insane that he would sooner have died on the wheel? Had the exile found freedom, or was he as much a prisoner as the madman in his cell? Was the Nish being torn apart on the wheel the happiest of them all because it would soon be over?

Other futures came and went, some as clear as diamond, the others mere suggestions in the corner of his mind, but the alternatives always remained the same – exile, madness or death. He looked in vain for any other fate, including the option he'd been dreading for so long – the one where his father took him back.

And in every alternative that involved Maelys, her end was a bloody one. Was that because of the way Irisis had died? Could he not rid himself of that curse, no matter what he did? Or had sweet, generous Maelys been doomed from the beginning?

'Empty your mind, Cryl-Nish.'

Nish started. He'd been so immersed in analysing the possibilities that he'd forgotten about Monkshart. Was he sitting up there pulling the strings like a puppet master?

No more futures came. Surely that couldn't be all? There

246

had to be a good future for him somewhere, since he was so bound up in the one Monkshart was pursuing. Unless . . . unless Monkshart only needed him as a figurehead to get the Defiance rolling, then planned to betray him and seize power.

Another possibility began to form, slowly this time. He was walking in pitch darkness down what felt like a long corridor, and there was a loud drumming in the distance, like heavy rain on a shingle roof. As he continued the sound grew until it drowned out his thoughts, whereupon the darkness was replaced by brilliant light and he was standing on the steps outside a magnificent palace or temple, dressed in robes of red silk shot with gold.

Three steps below him, to his left, Monkshart stood with one upraised arm pointing towards Nish. The drumming grew again, though this time he recognised it as a vast crowd roaring in acclamation. Nish bowed, raised his right hand and they fell silent. And then it struck him with such force that his knees nearly gave beneath him.

He was the Emperor of Santhenar, beloved by all as he worked tirelessly to undo the damage of his father's reign and restore the world to a paradise where there was freedom, justice and opportunity for all.

Tears formed under his eyelids as Nish gave himself up to the possibility. He hadn't sought it; it had simply come to him, but Monkshart had been right. He *knew* this was his true future, or could become it. His life wasn't hopeless. This future might never happen; it *would* never happen unless he gave his all for it, and perhaps not then, but he had to try. It was what he wanted most in all the world, though he'd never before allowed himself to dream of it.

No more possibilities appeared; he'd seen all he was going to see. He felt transformed, his previous anguish replaced by a monk-like serenity. His destiny was clear at last.

'You saw,' said Monkshart as Nish bounded up the ladder,

247

so inspired that his body felt weightless. He felt that he could do anything.

'I saw,' said Nish. Then, hastily, 'But I was not the *God-*Emperor.'

Again that fleeting twist of the mouth. 'Of course not. No man may declare himself God. It is an abomination. Do you agree to become the Deliverer, then, and cast down the false god?'

'On one condition.'

'Only one?' said Monkshart.

Nish, thinking that he was being sarcastic, nodded. 'That you will never again give way to the rage that burns within you. You will do no more evil in the Deliverer's name.'

'What is evil, anyway? And what if it's necessary to do a small evil to prevent a greater one, or to achieve the greater good?'

'I fail to see how murdering that poor lad could prevent a greater evil.'

'If I told you, you wouldn't believe me, since you've already judged me. But I give you my word – I will meet your condition. And now I suggest we go up to our beds, for we have much to plan in the morning.'

'Monkshart?' Nish said as they were crossing the pavilion, for something had occurred to him.

'Yes, Deliverer?'

Nish smiled. For the first time, it sounded right. 'The Pit of Possibilities only showed me achieving my goal. It didn't show me any of the steps along the way. So how am I to know what to do when it comes to each choice?'

Monkshart frowned. 'You must seek the support of your advisors, then follow your heart or your head, according to the moment.'

It was the most useless piece of advice Nish had ever heard, but he suddenly felt so weary that he could barely keep his eyes open, so he merely nodded and turned away to his chamber.

Only as he was drifting off to sleep did Nish realise that he should have imposed another condition on Monkshart while he had the bargaining power – that Maelys be placed under his protection until she could be sent to a place of safety. Was that why she'd died in all his futures?

TWENTY-THREE

Two days had passed since Nish's return from the Pit of Possibilities, and Monkshart's attitude had changed towards Maelys. He treated her with polite deference, but she still didn't trust him. Even Phrune kept his distance now and said nothing offensive, though she often noticed his eyes on her when he thought she wasn't looking.

She wasn't convinced about Nish's envisioned future, either. He'd told her about it the afternoon after it had happened, while Monkshart and Phrune were up in the village. She hadn't said anything, for Nish looked a decade younger. There was colour in his cheeks for the first time, and a spring in his step she'd not seen before.

Maelys had intended to question him about that night, and how he'd ended up at the Pit in the first place, but she could never get him alone. Night or day, Monkshart and Phrune were always with him, deep in discussion over the coming campaign. They stopped talking as she entered the pavilion, glaring at her as if she were an interloper.

Her questions were answered with polite nothings, even by Nish. The afternoon after his vision in the Pit he'd been as excited as a child; he'd even hugged her, but since then he'd become progressively withdrawn, as if she had no more part to play in his life and they were going their separate ways like the most casual of acquaintances. It hurt, after all they'd been through together, and she began to wonder if

Monkshart had cast an enthralment over Nish to make him forget her.

Monkshart had made his feelings clear from the beginning – Maelys was unworthy of Nish, would distract him from his great quest and must be separated from him at any cost. Once that happened, she surmised, Monkshart's lies would destroy her in Nish's eyes, and even if his quest did succeed, her family would get nothing out of it. Indeed, they would be in as much danger as if Nish failed, and everything she'd done since leaving home would have been for nothing.

That couldn't be borne. She had to find a way to rescue the situation, though how could she possibly outwit such a cunning foe? She sat in her room for hour after hour with nothing to do but brood. Monkshart's sudden transformation to Nish's humble servant wasn't credible. He was up to something. She needed to know more about the Pit of Possibilities, and whether he could manipulate what was seen there. Perhaps he planned to betray Nish for the reward, or the God-Emperor's favour.

Or, most chilling of all, what if Monkshart had lied about his parting with Jal-Nish, and still remained loyal to him? Monkshart might have been put here to establish the Defiance, so as to lure all the malcontents and rebels on Santhenar into the God-Emperor's web. Everything he'd done might have been part of a long-range plan. How could anyone truly know?

However, two things were perfectly clear. First and most importantly, if she didn't act now, her family was lost. Secondly, and despite everything Monkshart had said, she felt sure that Nish's life was also in danger. He was being used and, once Monkshart gained what he was after, Nish would be disposed of – or given up to his father.

Wait – Monkshart's agony on hearing of the loss of the other Defiance outposts had seemed genuine, so unless he was the most consummate actor of all time, he couldn't be secretly serving Jal-Nish, could he? Yet since returning from the Pit of Possibilities, he'd looked like the cat lapping at the bowl of cream. How could that be, when he was trapped here with Jal-Nish's net closing on him? Two explanations came to mind. Either he was Jal-Nish's man, or he had a plan to escape. But if Monkshart did, he wouldn't be taking her.

Jal-Nish's attack could come at any time, so Monkshart must have a secret escape route. She had to get to Nish before they fled, and she could only do that when everyone was asleep, but each night Phrune locked her chamber.

'Jil?' Maelys said as the girl brought her dinner that evening, 'can you do something for me?'

'Of course, Lady Maelys.' She stood waiting.

'It's – it's my lover, Nish,' Maelys lied, colouring. She wasn't practiced in deception and had never spoken about such intimacies before, but was hoping that Jil's romantic nature would make her sympathetic.

'He's so handsome, Lady Maelys,' said Jil.

That wasn't how Maelys would have described Nish. Attractive was the best that could be said for him. 'And I'm a lucky woman. At least –' She put her hand over her heart and sighed heavily. 'Oh, Jil, they won't let me see him. Phrune says I've got to wait, and I do understand. Nish has to become the Deliverer. It's more important than anything I want, but . . .' Another sigh.

'Do you miss him, Lady Maelys?'

'More than I can ever say.' She took Jil's hand. 'If I could be with Nish tonight, just for a little while, I *hope* I'll be able to bear the terrible separation to come, when Monkshart takes him away to begin the Great Defiance and tear down the false God-Emperor. But what if . . . what if . . .?' Maelys choked, and it wasn't feigned. 'What if they fail and he never comes back?'

Jil's soft heart was touched, then a look of scandalised awe crossed her face. 'Do you wish to go to your lover's room? To – to *lie* with him, unwed?'

252

Maelys's face grew hot. It was always giving her away. 'I do,' she lied, though it wasn't really a lie. 'It might be the very last time I see him. Do you think I'm wicked?'

'I – no – he's the Deliverer, Lady Maelys!' Jil flushed, looked confused, then lowered her head. 'It's not my place to judge the doings of the mighty, but how could it be wrong, the night before he goes off to war?'

So tonight *was* the last night. 'I think so too, Jil.' Maelys lowered her voice. 'I hate to ask but . . . can you help me?'

Jil didn't answer straight away, but stared at the floor, shuffling her bare feet. Maelys could imagine what she was thinking. Jil's punishment would be dire if her mistress was found outside her room.

'I –' Jil began.

'I quite understand – it's too much to ask . . .'

'I will do it,' said Jil, looking hurt at Maelys's assumption. 'For the Deliverer, and for love. I'll come at the first hour after midnight, and again at the third hour. You must be back by then or it will go very ill for me.'

Maelys could imagine how ill. She embraced the thin girl. 'Thank you. You don't know how much this means to me.'

Something mischievous flashed in the girl's eyes. She grinned, then bowed and went out.

Maelys was exhausted, for she'd not slept well since she came here, but she was afraid to nap in case she missed the subtle sound of the key in the lock. The minutes passed like hours, and every one raised another problem. What if Jil didn't come? What if Phrune heard her, or Monkshart had already fled with Nish?

The key turned so quietly that she barely heard it. Maelys slipped off the bed and opened the door. The walls of the corridor were touched by slivers of reflected moonlight from the pavilion.

'You look beautiful, Lady Maelys,' said Jil.

In this light, at least. Maelys touched the girl's hand in

thanks then tiptoed barefoot to Nish's room. She looked back: Jil was staring at her, though Maelys couldn't read her expression. She opened Nish's door and slipped inside.

His room was pitch dark. She could hear steady breathing, so unlike his tortured sleep on the way to Tifferfyte. She took a step towards him then stopped, realising what she was about to do to him. To win Nish back to her side she must convince him that the future he'd seen was a lie, but that would destroy the only peace of mind he'd had in ten years. And what if she were wrong? What if that future truly was his destiny, and she prevented him from achieving it?

Maelys hesitated, one foot frozen in mid-step. If only she had her own map of the future. Then it hit her. She must take Nish back to the Pit of Possibilities and let him see for himself, without Monkshart's interference. If Nish saw the same vision, he could be sure it was the true one. But what if he saw something completely different?

Nish's steady breathing changed; the bedclothes rustled and he sat up. She caught a whiff of his masculine scent and her nerves tingled.

'Who's there? Is that you, Maelys?'

'Yes,' she said softly, wondering how he could tell. 'It's me.'

'What are you doing here?'

'I had to talk to you. I'm so afraid. They won't let me near you, Nish. They're isolating you from me so you'll have to rely on them –'

'I don't *have* to rely on anyone!' he said sharply.

She'd touched on a sensitive issue, evidently. 'I meant . . . Oh, Nish, they lock me in my room at night, and I'm terrified what they're going to do to me once you're gone.'

'They wouldn't dare harm you –' he began.

'How do you know? Monkshart has looked down on me from the beginning. I'm not worthy of you; I can't be allowed to distract you, and you know how ruthless he is. He'll order me thrown into the pit or –'

He drew a sharp breath. He'd been so caught up in

254

Monkshart's plans that he'd not given her a thought, and that hurt after all they'd been through together.

'Or give me up to Vomix. Once you're gone they'll be rid of me, one way or the other.'

He didn't reply, but he was breathing heavily now.

'You're the only friend I've got, Nish, and if you can't help me, I'm dead.'

'What do you want me to do?'

She felt her way forwards until her knees encountered the edge of the bed, then crouched beside it. Taking a deep breath, she said, 'I want you to come down to the Pit of Possibilities with me, and look again.'

A long silence, then he ground out, 'Why are you trying to bring me down?'

He always took things the wrong way. 'Nish, please.' She reached out, but at her touch he jerked his arm away. 'I'm not trying to bring you down. I care about you more than anyone, save only my little sister.'

'You're trying to rob me of the one good thing that's happened for me since Irisis was murdered.'

It was too much. 'Oh, stop whining!' she hissed. 'I think Monkshart sent you a false future in the Pit – the one he knew you wanted to see. Don't you want to know the truth? Or do you find his lies more comfortable?'

The bed shook and for an awful moment she thought he was going to strike her, then he drew back, in the grip of such powerful emotions that he was nearly choking. Maelys, appalled at what she'd done, said softly, 'Nish, I'm so sorry.'

'You mistake me,' he said eventually, fighting to control his voice. 'For an instant, you reminded me of my beloved. She wouldn't put up with my self-pity either.' She heard a rustle as he wiped his face on the sheet, and the bedsprings creaked. 'But Maelys, I've never before experienced such . . . serenity as I've felt since I came up from the Pit knowing where my true path lies. If I lose that, what will I have left?'

'If you lose it, all you've really lost was a lie,' she said. 'Yet if you go down to the Pit again you may come up with the truth. There's a comfort in truth, no matter how hard it may be, that you can never find in the most beautiful of lies. Will you come down now? I don't have much time.'

He got up, silently, and went out. She followed him down the dark path, but at the rope ladder that dangled into the Pit Nish hesitated, his face ominously lit by the glow from below. 'Go first.'

'Me?' Her heart lurched. 'Why?'

'I want to know what the Pit of Possibilities says about your future. And so, I'm sure, do you.'

She shook her head. 'No, I don't.'

'Surely you're not afraid?' he said gently.

She was; terrified to see something she wouldn't be able to face. Maelys felt sure the future was going to be short and tragic, for herself as well as her family, but as long as it was unclear she could cling to hope like the optimist she was. 'You're just trying to delay going in yourself,' she said desperately.

'I neglected you and I'm trying to make up for it. Off you go.'

There was no choice; she couldn't bear for him to think of her as a coward. 'What do I do when I get there?'

He told her, reciting Monkshart's warnings about the Mistmurk, and sleeping in the pit. Maelys swallowed, then slowly climbed down the rope ladder, inspected her surroundings uneasily, and settled herself against the wall.

'It takes a while,' Nish called down.

It didn't. She closed her eyes, and choked. She was looking down on the crater of Tifferfyte, where a gigantic army was advancing towards the foot of the mountain from all sides, in the moonlight. This future could be happening right now. Flappeters were circling not far out, while beyond them hovered three air-dreadnoughts, including a red and black monstrosity that she felt sure was the God-Emperor's personal craft.

Her viewpoint shifted; the image blurred and reformed. It was dawn now but the sky had clouded over and she couldn't see either flappeters or air-dreadnoughts through the misty rain. She could see the army, though, advancing up the mountain in an eerie silence.

The view shifted again, now extending down the slope as if seen by one of the defenders behind the rude stone wall surrounding the village, now looking left then right at the other guards. They were armed only with scythes, mattocks and hammers, and an occasional pitted sword or rustic bow. They wouldn't last ten minutes against this army.

And she was to die with them. Was it her looking out? It wasn't – the hands holding the mattock were brawny man's hands, with coarse black hair on their backs. She scanned the village but saw neither Monkshart, Phrune or Nish, and they weren't at the crest of the crater either. Monkshart must have fled with them, leaving everyone else to die.

The army raised their swords and pikes and, with a massed roar that Maelys could almost hear, charged. She wrenched her eyes open. The vision vanished and there was nothing in the chamber but the greenish miasma rising from the Mistmurk.

'Are you all right?' Nish called.

She was panting, but Maelys willed herself to stay calm. 'Yes. *I'm* all right; for now.'

He didn't ask what she'd seen, thankfully. She pressed her palms against the floor to steady herself and closed her eyes again. Maelys felt drowsy but she mustn't doze down here. If she leaned against the wall she would go to sleep. She got up and began to pace in a circle around the Mistmurk, not too close, but with her eyes open she couldn't *see* anything. She closed her eyes, walking carefully, and shortly began to see blackness streaked with occasional flashes of red.

That image lasted for ages, as she slowly circled, until she must have walked too close to the Mistmurk. A tendril of its coldness touched her bare ankles and her taphloid, which had been lifeless ever since she'd imploded its crystal, suddenly grew warm. An image drifted into focus, though it took a long time before she could make out what it was. It looked like a single red-raw eye staring through an oddly curved and twisted mask.

The eye moved, and she smiled as she recognised what it was – a man's face seen in a distorting mirror, like the funny mirrors she'd looked into when a travelling carnival had come to Nifferlin at the end of the war. Probably one of the lying futures, she thought, preparing to disbelieve it and move on to the next.

But it grew as though the man had drawn the mirror closer to him, trying to see right through it to whatever lay beyond. He pulled the mask away; for an instant his face became clear and Maelys cried, 'No!'

'Maelys?' Nish called. 'Do you want me to come down?'

'No. Yes. No, stay there!'

It was horrible but she didn't want to lose a second of it. It wasn't a distorting mirror, but a man's face reflected in a shiny drop, like quicksilver – it was Jal-Nish, using one of the tears! Jal-Nish, without the platinum mask that normally concealed the ruined half of his face, was searching for something in the tear.

She should have withdrawn right away, for he was a foe that not even the strongest mancer could face. But it *was* one of her possible futures and she needed to know about it. She had to know all of them and there wasn't much time. By now, Monkshart or Phrune might have realised that she and Nish were missing.

Maelys clenched the taphloid tighter as Jal-Nish's eye appeared to rush towards the tear. Its shiny surface blurred and everything went out of focus. He was inside the tear, or had melded himself to it, and for an instant she had a flash of insight into the corrupt mind of the man who controlled the tears.

Jal-Nish was gloating, for his mastery of Gatherer and Reaper was growing every day and he was close to finding the three secrets that would allow him to become invulnerable for all time: perfect knowledge of the Profane Tears; complete mastery of himself; and a clear understanding of the Art by which he used Gatherer and Reaper. And he believed he was close to gaining all three.

Maelys, feeling panicky, swayed backwards and the Mistmurk swirled about her legs again. The cooling taphloid grew hot between her breasts, then Jal-Nish, with a gasp, dragged himself out of his melding with the tears and looked around sharply, as if afraid he was being spied upon. Had he seen her? She moved hastily away from the Mistmurk.

She couldn't look at his ravaged face, but his eye bore a haunted look. The God-Emperor, despite holding almost all the power in the world, was afraid of something.

TWENTY-FOUR

Nish had sent Maelys in first so as to delay going down himself. If he was to be robbed of both hope and serenity he wanted to hold it off as long as possible, though the instant she cried out he regretted pressuring her.

She came up, covered in sweat and clearly shaken. 'What did you see?' he asked, helping her off the ladder.

'My first future showed your father's army attacking the village, and only men and youths with farmyard implements to defend it. They're going to die, every one of them,' she said bitterly, 'and the women too. There was no sign of Monkshart or his precious Arts. Or you. He must have fled with you, concealed by illusions.'

'Assuming it was a true vision,' said Nish, swallowing. 'Most of the possibilities in the Pit are not.'

'I *know* it's true, and it's my fault, just as the deaths of all those people in Byre village were. If I hadn't brought you here . . .'

'No one who opposes my father is safe, Maelys, and the people of Tifferfyte also knew the risk when they chose to oppose him. Besides, I brought *you* here. What else did you see?'

She wiped her sweaty brow. 'I saw –' Her voice went hoarse. 'I saw your father, without his mask, reflected in one of the tears. But then he seemed to go into the tear, to merge his mind with it, and . . .'

Nish's mouth was open. 'You saw *Father*? You actually saw him using the tears?'

'Worse. I saw *into* his mind; and what he was communing with the tears about.'

'How could you see him, yet he not see you? Why *you*, anyway? Why not *me*?'

Maelys looked slighted. 'He created your clearsight in the first place, Nish, so he'd hardly leave himself vulnerable to it. But he doesn't know me at all, and maybe I've been touched by Gatherer, distantly, via the link with the flapper. And I do have an unusual talent, it seems. Perhaps my taphloid has something to do with it, too. Besides, surely that's not –'

'Monkshart said the Pit of Possibilities was the one place the tears could not reach, and I felt it as soon as I went down – as if a great weight had been lifted from me. Father couldn't touch me there.'

'Nish –'

'So how could you *see* him? I wonder ... if the Pit of Possibilities shows our true futures as well as false ones, there can't be any constraints on it. If Father is in your future, it's got to show him.'

'But it didn't have to show him close up. It didn't have to let me into his mind.'

'I don't understand it either,' said Nish.

'Wait – could it be because I was holding my taphloid at the time? A patch of the miasma touched me and the taphloid seemed to ... *wake*.' She got it out, turning it over in her hands.

'I don't see how it could, unless there's a chip of jade from the amulet inside,' he said doubtfully. 'If Father's Art made the amulet in the first place, and he'd actually held it in his hands or empowered it with the tears, it might explain why the Pit of Possibilities was able to see into him.'

Maelys flipped open the compartment where the amulet had been placed, but there was not even a shard of jade in it.

'Unless it's the taphloid itself . . .' said Nish.

'How could it be? I've had it since I was little and it's never been anywhere near your father.'

'Hmn. What did you see when you looked into his mind?'

'I thought you'd never ask. Nish, he needs only three things to become invulnerable for all time: perfect knowledge of the tears; complete mastery of himself; and a clear understanding of the Art by which he uses Gatherer and Reaper. And he's close to gaining all three.'

Nish reeled and nearly fell down the hole; she caught his shoulder to steady him. 'If he succeeds,' Maelys hissed, 'there won't be anything the Deliverer can do, even with all Santhenar behind you. He's got to be stopped and there isn't much time to do it. Go down, Nish.'

'What's the point?' he said despairingly. 'The future Monkshart showed me must have been a lie, and there's no way out of here anyway.'

'I'll bet there is. Monkshart looked pretty happy the last time I saw him. Go down.'

He put one foot on the ladder, but stopped. 'Wait! I've just remembered something.'

'Yes?' Maelys said dubiously.

'When I attacked Father after he let me out of prison, he hesitated momentarily before attacking back.'

'So what?'

'He's not a hesitating man. Right or wrong, he never wavers.'

'Why is that so important?'

'It means that Father must still have a weakness, even if it's just that he cares about me, and if I can discover what it is there may be a chance to beat him after all.'

'For a moment I thought he'd seen me, at the end,' said Maelys. 'And for a second he looked afraid.'

'I'm guessing, but this is what I think he's worried about,' said Nish. 'Father has made out that he's invulnerable and all powerful, but he's not. At least, not *yet*. And despite all his power, he's terrified that he'll be overthrown and everything he's done will come to nothing. What he really craves is immortality, for what's the point of his great and terrible life if someone else will undo all his work once he's gone? Father wants to make a mark on Santhenar that can't be undone; one which people will still recognise in a thousand years. That's the immortality he really craves.'

'If he wants it so desperately, it's another weakness,' said Maelys. 'When it comes to the ultimate test, he'll do whatever it takes to ensure his work endures.'

Two weaknesses. It did Nish's heart good to discover them. He climbed down into the Pit of Possibilities and this time, the instant his feet touched the dusty, shard-strewn floor something felt different.

The maze of futures were foggy in his mind, all save one which was brilliantly clear. On a remote, rain-soaked plateau a long way north in this great mountain chain, something long hidden from his father lay waiting for him. The vision didn't say what it was, or precisely where it lay, though Nish felt sure he'd recognise the plateau once he saw it. In all his travels he'd never seen a landscape like it.

Though the scene was shrouded in drifting mist that didn't allow him to see the whole of the plateau at one time, its shape was clear. It rose out of the rainforest like a needle whose point had been cut off. It was so tall that its flat top lay in the clouds, and its sides were sheer wet black rock that would be a nightmare to climb.

Unfortunately it didn't seem that the change in his fortunes extended to Maelys, for she had not appeared in this new future either, nor her own. Nish scrambled up and told her what he'd seen.

'And Monkshart lied!' he ended, fighting mixed emotions. 'He manipulated the visions to show me just what he wanted me to believe. Come on!' He strode across the shard-strewn floor towards the path, and for the first time since escaping from prison he knew exactly what he wanted.

'What are you going to do?' Maelys said wearily.

She was plodding along behind him, looking as if she could barely stay awake. 'Find out how close the army is. Hurry!'

'That vision could have been weeks away.'

'I've a feeling the army has left Rancidore already and is only days from here.'

'Monkshart isn't acting as though it's near.'

'Perhaps all his spies have been rounded up. My fortunes have turned, Maelys,' he said quietly, 'and I'm going to ride my luck for as long as it lasts. I'm not going to be manipulated by Monkshart again.' Not by anyone.

He looked up as they came around the curve towards the pavilion, for a lamp was glowing there, and silhouetted against it at the top of the path stood the lying, manipulating, murdering zealot.

Nish's smouldering rage burst into flame, but he tried not to show it. He kept walking, eyes downcast as if caught somewhere he had no right to be, until he came within a few steps of the pavilion. Then, propelling himself forwards like a rock from a catapult, he drove the top of his head into Monkshart's belly with such force that the zealot was knocked backwards off his feet and cracked his head against the stone floor of the pavilion.

Diving onto him, Nish whipped the knife from Monkshart's sheath, tossed it to Maelys and hissed, 'Get into the shadows!' He dragged the dazed and winded zealot to the edge of the pavilion so that his head, shoulders and upper back hung over the brink, then raised his feet until he could feel the cloth of Monkshart's robes bunching against the edge.

Monkshart cried out, 'Phrune, help!'

Nish raised the zealot's legs higher and pushed him until he reached the teetering point. Something tore under his palms. Monkshart's legs were also encased in tissue-fine leather and the rents had exposed cracked, weeping skin.

264

Nish took a better grip and tried to ignore the creepy feel of it. 'Things have changed, Monkshart.'

Monkshart shuddered violently at Nish's tight grip on his ravaged skin, but managed to gain control of himself. 'Deliverer – if you kill me – Defiance must fail.' His eyes narrowed and Nish heard the pad of plump feet in the corridor. He glanced back, praying that Maelys was ready. If she failed him he would end up at the bottom of the crater with Monkshart, for this time he wasn't giving in.

'Put him down!' Phrune cried in a high, anguished voice, advancing through the opening with a little jewelled stiletto in hand. It was a woman's weapon but deadly enough for all that, and Phrune's glistening, babyish face was twisted, sick.

He came on carefully, the knife held low and steady as if he'd gutted people before, licking his swollen lips as if he'd enjoyed it. Nish realised that he'd miscalculated. Phrune was a viper who would enjoy maiming and mutilating, and unfortunately Maelys was on the wrong side of the opening. She couldn't jump him without Phrune realising she was there, and he'd carve her up without a qualm. Nish had to distract him.

With a roar of defiance, he heaved Monkshart's legs as high as he could reach. The bunched cloth began to slide across the edge of the pavilion as the zealot's weight pulled him down.

'Stop!' cried Phrune, slitted eyes staring. He took a step then froze, realising that the least wrong move could tip the balance beyond recovery.

Maelys sprang from the shadows, threw her right arm around his neck and dug the point of her knife in under his ribs. Nish, standing half turned and straining to hold Monkshart's weight, could see the fury on the acolyte's face, and the stealthy movement of his knife hand as he prepared to hack into her side.

'Put down the knife,' Nish said, 'or I'll drop your master

265

into the pit. Harm Maelys and he dies, and curse the consequences.'

Monkshart had gone as rigid as a board, but he'd regained
self-control, or perhaps come to an acceptance of his fate.
'Let it go, Phrune. The Deliverer has mastered me.'

Phrune could hardly bring himself to do it. It was touch
and go whether the lust for violence twisting his chubby features could be overcome, or whether he'd strike anyway.
The stiletto was shaking in his hand, inching into striking
position.

'Down!' choked Monkshart.

With an awful grimace, Phrune tossed the stiletto to the
side. Maelys jerked his head backwards then thrust him
stumbling the other way. Before he could recover, she
snatched up the blade, her breast heaving. She'd gone close
to being disembowelled, and knew it.

'Well, Monkshart?' said Nish. 'Will you swear to serve the
Deliverer this time?'

'I swear it upon my faith and holy purpose,' Monkshart
said thickly, his face a congested purple. The panic was
gone, and Nish could not help but admire his strength of
will, to say nothing of his resilience.

Nonetheless, he held Monkshart above the drop for
another half minute, reinforcing his dominance and even
taking a shameful pleasure in revenge, until his arms began
to shake. He hastily drew the zealot back from the edge and
allowed his long legs to drop to the floor. 'I'll be giving the
orders now, Monkshart.'

'Of course, Deliverer.'

Monkshart sat up, rubbing the back of his head, wincing
and inspecting his fingers. He wiped off the threads of blood
seeping through his torn gloves. 'You're a bold man, as the
Deliverer has to be.' He had so gained control of himself that
he revealed neither terror nor anger. He climbed to his feet,
indicating the chairs. 'Bring refreshments, Phrune; the best
we have. This is a moment to celebrate.'

Phrune, his eyes glittering with malice, jerked his head and went out.

'You don't believe I can change,' said Monkshart, sitting down and repeatedly smoothing the torn leathers to cover his inflamed calves. 'And why should you? But when you came to Tifferfyte, Deliverer, you showed none of the strength or determination needed to take on the mantle bestowed on you. To put it crudely, you weren't up to it. If the Defiance were to have any hope of success I had to take on the role of puppet master. It was a role I assumed reluctantly, and one which, now you've exhibited the qualities required, I'm happy to relinquish.'

'You're right,' said Maelys, holding the knife out low, blade upwards, in imitation of Phrune's expert stance. 'We do find it difficult to believe.'

'But not impossible,' said Nish, 'as long as you live up to your words. The balance has changed, Monkshart. We'll work together to overcome the God-Emperor, and I'll listen to your advice, but the final decision will always be mine.'

'Master.' Monkshart bowed his head.

He seemed genuine this time, but he always had. Monkshart was a consummate actor and a master manipulator. Nish decided to reserve judgement. All that mattered was that they be able to cooperate to bring down his father's realm.

'Don't listen to him,' said Maelys wearily. 'He'll say anything to get what he wants. Judge him by his slimy acolyte.'

Monkshart looked pained, though he said calmly, 'You're entitled to think that way, Maelys. I won't attempt to persuade *you*.'

'What happened?' Nish said shortly, looking at Monkshart's legs. Straw-coloured fluid was now weeping through the ruined tissue-leathers.

'The kiss of the tears,' said the zealot. 'Should you ever be in a position to take them, Deliverer, beware!'

'Father thrust my hands into the tears and they didn't hurt me. Did you try to steal them?'

267

Monkshart clenched his fists, then waited until he'd calmed himself before saying, 'I held to my oath to your father, as I've already stated. I – I dare say you're entitled to know. Jal-Nish would have shielded you from the kiss of the tears but he couldn't protect me. It was at the end of the battle for Gumby Marth, when he was defeated by the great lyrinx sorcerer, Anabyng, and I carried your half-dead father to safety on my back. He begged me to go back for the tears and, much against my better judgement, I did so. They were still singing with power from the monumental struggle and, in the brief minutes I held them before I gave them up to Jal-Nish, they burned me all over.'

'All over?'

'Inside as well as out!' Monkshart screwed up his eyes for a moment. 'Such pain,' he said in a faint voice. 'You cannot imagine it, Deliverer, for it was like no kind of burn I've ever had. It crisped me like a chicken's skin in a hot oven, even to the soles of my booted feet, and as you see, all these years later I still suffer from it. Only Phrune's balms can keep the pain at bay.'

Nish made a disgusted sound in his throat.

'I know what you think of him,' Monkshart went on. 'Poor Phrune repulses everyone he meets. He always has, and he can't understand why. I'm his one friend, and in return he looks after me as no one else can.' Self-disgust flickered in his eyes, then he added quickly, 'His potions and unguents are unique. Moreover, his enchanted tissue-leathers protect me from the torment of touch, and I can't do without him.'

He held Nish's eyes for some time, as if weighing him, before continuing, 'I wasn't afflicted by these rages before I touched the tears. And so you see, Cryl-Nish, the webs of obligation that tied your father to me were strong, layered, and complex. That's why he swore never to harm me. Ah, Phrune comes.'

Phrune bore a tray of tiny orange cakes and three rock-glass goblets whose bowls were no bigger than eggcups, each

268

containing a viscous yellow-green liqueur. Its luscious bouquet made Nish salivate. Phrune handed the goblets around, then offered the cakes.

Monkshart's eyes lit up. 'The very last of the aged *gellon* liqueur! A fitting way to toast the end of an era, since gellon is unobtainable now at any price.'

'And the beginning of a new era; the age of the common man,' said Nish sententiously, raising his glass and sniffing deeply before taking a small sip. 'That's good.'

'You're not joining us, Phrune?' said Monkshart.

'I see little to celebrate,' Phrune grated, casting a malicious look at Maelys, 'and there wasn't enough for four.'

'Very well!' Monkshart said sharply. 'I won't keep you from your bed. I know how much pleasure you take from your activities there.'

Phrune reacted as though he'd been slapped, then flounced out.

'To business,' said Nish. 'I've looked into the Pit of Possibilities, Monkshart, and what you showed me wasn't there.'

'Nonetheless, it is *one* of your possible futures,' the zealot said blandly. 'I judged it the only one that would convince you – the former irresolute you, I mean – that you *could* become the Deliverer.'

'I don't like to be lied to.'

'The God-Emperor must be cast down,' said Monkshart, 'and it can't be done by the weak or squeamish. Nor is there much time.'

'Less than you think. Vomix has a huge army surrounding the mountain and they could attack as soon as the morning.'

'No!' Monkshart sprang right out of his chair. 'The sentries would have told me. I saw it coming in five days' time –'

'Look again, Monkshart. It would be ironic indeed if your failure in the Pit of Possibilities cost the Defiance its only chance.'

'Phrune!' Monkshart bellowed down the corridor.

Phrune came running. 'Master?'

'Run up to the lookout, quick, and tell me what you see.'

Phrune dashed up the path and disappeared. Shortly an inarticulate cry echoed down, then he reappeared, staggering from side to side. 'The sentries are dead but there's no mark on them. And there are lights as far as the eye can see. A gigantic army surrounds the mountain, making no attempt at concealment, and I saw flappeters wheeling in the moonlight. We're undone, Master.'

TWENTY-FIVE

'Pull yourself together,' Monkshart snapped. 'He won't attack until his army is here. How close are the foot soldiers?'

'Two hours, I'd guess.'

'The Deliverer and I have much to do before we can take the secret way. We'll need at least that long.'

'If you know a secret way,' said Nish, 'you'd better get the villagers into it.'

'It's a dangerous path and there are . . . problems to be solved first,' said Monkshart. He glanced at Maelys, whose head was nodding. 'Such beautiful skin. It's as soft as I've ever seen.'

An odd turn of phrase, to Nish's mind, though he was too weary to pursue it. With the lateness of the hour, and all that had happened since he got up, and now the liqueur singing in his veins, he was finding it hard to concentrate.

'Her one good feature.' Phrune reached out to touch her arm but Monkshart shook his head. 'Shall I take her?' the acolyte went on.

'What?' Nish said thickly.

'To bed,' Monkshart said smoothly, rubbing a frayed patch on his left glove. 'Are my new gloves ready?'

'They tore in the tanning, Master. The charm goes wrong, sometimes. I –'

Monkshart went cold. 'I have to have them, Phrune.'

'I know. I've already begun –'

'How long?'

'A couple of hours. But if we had twice that, I could make you the finest gloves you've ever had. They would caress –'

'There isn't time,' Monkshart said regretfully. 'What a waste. I'll have to go with what you have. Take her, Phrune, and come straight back.'

'I'll do it,' Nish said hastily, knowing how Maelys felt about Phrune. He carried her out. Her eyes drifted open, she smiled, settled her head against his shoulder and didn't stir as he laid her on the bed and folded the covers over her.

'What if you were to send the Deliverer's true believers out to his defence,' Phrune was saying slyly as Nish returned, 'to sacrifice themselves while you lead him away, shrouded by an illusion created from the possibilities from the pit?'

'No!' Nish advanced on Monkshart. 'I'm not starting this campaign the way my father would. We're taking the villagers with us.'

Monkshart and Phrune exchanged pregnant glances, as if Nish was again displaying a lack of the required mettle. 'Alas, if only we could,' said Monkshart.

'Why can't we?'

'The secret way is perilous, even for the best prepared mancers. *Especially* for the best prepared, since those strong in the Art or in physical strength are more susceptible than the weak. The paths we must take are not entirely of this world, and so deadly that, without the protection of a certain potion, none of us could survive them. Unfortunately I've only been able to prepare enough for us.'

He withdrew a small box from a pouch and prised open the lid. Inside, a crystal phial was wrapped in blue velvet. Nish held out his hand and, after a brief hesitation, Monkshart gave it to him. Nish held the phial up to the light. It was half full – a couple of teaspoons at most.

'So all along you've been planning to abandon the villagers to their deaths!'

'Deliverer, you see evil where there is none. I never intended to leave here by the secret paths, because they're too *draining*. We were going to retreat down the steep western ridge-path, cross the stream at the Ford of Milbo and take refuge in the endless caverns of Spondee. We could hide from a dozen armies there, but with my spies captured and the mountain surrounded, that way is now impossible. Yet if the villagers surrender . . .'

'They'll die like the rebels they are,' said Nish. 'You know that as well as I do.' He expected Monkshart to tell some glib lie but the zealot surprised him again.

'Aye,' said Monkshart. 'There's no hope for them now.'

'But there is for us,' Phrune said with that sickly smile. 'They can give us the extra hour we need.'

'How?' said Nish.

'Your followers love you, Deliverer, and they'll willingly fight to the death for you. Indeed, they'll glory in their martyrdom, knowing that their deaths are helping to create a better future for their absent families, and the whole world.'

Had Monkshart said it, the words might have had a certain grandeur – a noble sacrifice – but from Phrune's mouth they sounded sick, as though the villagers' lives meant nothing and their deaths gave him a perverted pleasure.

'I won't –' Nish began.

'They're doomed, Deliverer,' said Monkshart softly. 'Would you deny them a chance to give their lives for the noblest cause of all?'

The zealot's arguments were self-serving, yet despite Nish's repugnance for the idea, he felt tempted. Having taken up the challenge of becoming the Deliverer, why not fashion something from the villager's deaths if they were going to die anyway? The coming struggle must cost thousands of lives and if he were too squeamish to face up to the consequences he might as well abandon the cause right now.

'Very well,' Nish said, feeling ill. 'But I'll go up and speak to them first, to offer them the choice. I won't sneak away like a cur – as Father did – leaving them to die.'

'Not like a cur, no, but you must come with me now,' said Monkshart. 'The circle is drawing ever tighter and there's much to do before we take the perilous paths. Phrune will speak to the villagers on your behalf.' He rose.

'What do we have to do?' Nish got up reluctantly, feeling as though he were being railroaded.

'I need to search out the secret paths, and that can only be done in the Pit of Possibilities. You must come too.'

'Why?' The late hour had caught up with him and Nish didn't have the strength to take Monkshart on again. The earlier struggle had cost him too much.

'The secret paths are like no way you've ever encountered, Deliverer. They don't like to be seen, much less used. They're deceitful; evil, some say, and if they get the chance they'll lead us to our deaths. A single traveller – yes, even one as clear-sighted as myself – can easily be led astray, but if we compare the paths we've been shown independently we'll see where any deceit lies. Make haste. Time passes swiftly in the Pit of Possibilities.'

'I'll get Maelys.'

'Let her sleep. A third presence is never advisable at the Pit, for conflicts inevitably arise and the possibilities become blurred. Phrune will signal as soon as the attack begins. Time enough then to gather her and take the deadly paths.'

They headed down the glassy track, and several times Nish found himself stumbling with weariness, but each time Monkshart steadied him before he could slip. At the bottom the zealot said, 'I'll go first. When I come up, I'll say nothing about what I've seen for fear of influencing you. Only after you climb up from the pit will we compare the paths we've been shown, to make sure we have the true one.'

Monkshart descended the ladder and settled himself against the wall of the Pit, where he sat motionless, eyes closed. Nish watched him uneasily, having no idea what to expect this time, but nothing happened for so long that, despite his myriad fears, he dozed.

He woke abruptly; Monkshart was shaking his shoulder. 'Your turn, Deliverer.'

Nish scrambled into the Pit but had only seen the vaguest blurry images of glassy paths when he was ripped out of the envisioned possibility by Phrune shouting and his feet slapping down the path.

'Master, Master!' he screeched.

'What is it this time, Phrune?' Monkshart said irritably.

Phrune's face appeared in the opening, eerily lit by the glow from the pit. Sweat was dripping off him. 'The army came up the mountain more quickly than expected, and a company of soldiers dropped from air-dreadnoughts into the village. The village has fallen and they're storming the crater even now.'

Nish began to run up the ladder. His foot missed one of the rungs, sending the ladder swaying wildly.

Monkshart cursed. 'But we need Cryl-Nish's view of the paths. Without it –'

'There's no time, Master.'

'Then we'll have to go with what I've seen, and that's not going to be easy. Stay where you are, Deliverer. The paths lead down from the Pit. Phrune, have you got my new gloves?'

'Of course, Master!' Phrune said.

Nish kept climbing. Thrusting his head up beside the beam which the ladder was tied to, he squinted towards the dimly illuminated circle of the crater's rim. A number of figures were silhouetted against the night sky, which had a red tinge now. 'I'll get Maelys!' he panted.

'She – she went up to the village, to see how close the enemy were,' said Phrune, with a glance at Monkshart. 'A band of soldiers landed all around her. She had no chance.'

Nish felt as though he'd been struck in the chest with a hammer. His feet slipped on the rungs and he caught on desperately. 'What are you saying. Is Maelys – *dead*?'

'I believe so, Deliverer.'

'You're lying!' Nish thrust past Phrune, knocking him flying onto the shard-strewn floor. 'I'm going up.' His whole chest was aching, his legs had turned to jelly and his eyes hurt. He couldn't believe it. How could Maelys be gone, just like that?

Suddenly Monkshart was behind him, gripping his shoulder. 'I know how you feel, Deliverer –'

'You know nothing about how I feel!' Nish cried. 'You don't know anything. Maelys!' he shouted, twisting free.

Monkshart caught him, holding him back easily. 'If you go up, Deliverer, all will be lost. Phrune, are you sure?'

Phrune picked himself up, fastidiously brushing the dust and shards off. 'Quite sure, Master. I'd reached the rim of the crater and was turning down the path to the village when an air-floater appeared out of the mist, above the houses. There were soldiers everywhere. I just had time to grab your . . . gear on the way down.' He hefted a canvas bag.

Nish wanted to drive his fist into Phrune's mouth and spread those red, self-satisfied lips right across his face. Why would Maelys go up to the village with an army approaching? It didn't make sense. 'And you saw her slain?'

'I lost sight of her among all the troops, but they were doing dreadful slaughter.' Phrune's tongue slid slowly across his lower lip, then back. 'They must have had orders to leave no one in the village alive.'

'Save Maelys,' Nish said desperately. 'Father would want *her* alive.'

'Possibly,' said Monkshart, 'though the troops wouldn't have expected her to be in the village. She would be just another rebel to them. I . . . I want you to be satisfied that's she's gone, Deliverer, but we don't –'

Shouting echoed back and forth across the crater, then a vast, familiar shape blocked out the ruddy glow from the burning village. An air-dreadnought was hovering directly above the crater and someone aboard was bellowing orders, though Nish couldn't make them out over the roar of the rotors.

'Into the Pit, quick!' said Monkshart in a low voice. 'He's broken my halo of protection.'

Nish stared up towards the pavilion, unable to believe that Maelys was gone and that there was nothing anyone could do about it. He had to go after her. He sprang, but Phrune blocked his way and Monkshart caught him around the waist.

Nish struggled but could not tear free. 'You're a proven liar and murderer,' he said wildly, 'and Phrune is a sadistic pervert. Why should I believe either of you? You've been trying to turn me against Maelys since we arrived.'

A lucky blow caught Monkshart in the eye. Nish tore free, danced around him and began to run up the path, but had only gone a few steps when Monkshart caught him again.

'She's gone, Deliverer!' Monkshart hissed, 'and the enemy will be on their way down within minutes. My potion takes a minute to work and if you rob yourself of that time, you're risking everything for nothing.'

'I don't abandon my friends,' Nish hissed.

'Shh!' Tall, blocky shapes were moving onto the top of the glassy path. Monkshart dragged Nish back towards the sump and forced him onto the ladder, shaking him. 'Listen! The Deliverer must do what is necessary to survive. There's no middle way – either you gain everything, or lose it, and if we don't fly now all will be lost. Go down the ladder.'

Nish didn't move but he couldn't fight, either. The burning resolve with which he'd overpowered Monkshart earlier was gone and he couldn't dredge it up again. He felt empty, sick.

'She's gone, Deliverer,' said the zealot softly. 'I can sense it.' He jerked his head at the pit.

Nish bowed his head for Maelys, then went down. His chest had a deep-seated throb now and his eyes were burning. At the bottom, Monkshart took the little box from Nish's pocket, pulled the stopper and held it out to Phrune. 'Just the merest taste on your tongue, remember? Too much is as bad as too little. Then count to fifty-five and go.'

Phrune tasted the potion, made a face and handed it back hastily. His lips appeared redder and more swollen than before. Monkshart's left eye was swelling from Nish's lucky blow. He handed the flask to Nish but Nish didn't take it.

'After you. I don't know what to do. I never saw any paths.'

'I know, and that's going to make it far harder.' Monkshart tasted the potion and passed it to Nish. 'Count to fifty-five then follow me. Tread exactly in my footsteps and keep an image of something you know well in your mind the whole time, else you'll lose the path. Or go mad.'

That wasn't reassuring. Nish was sniffing the top of the phial when there came a series of brittle cracks from above, like crossbow bolts smashing into the glassy floor. Someone shouted a furious order and the sounds ceased. He tilted the phial, allowing the thick liquid to surge onto his tongue. Too much! Ugh, it was bitter.

Phrune said, 'Fifty-five,' stepped forwards and dropped into the green, miasma-filled Mistmurk. The murk roiled and he was gone.

Monkshart was staring at Nish. 'Ready?' Nish nodded numbly. Monkshart clapped him on the shoulder again. 'Steady!' and followed Phrune.

Nish realised that he hadn't begun to count. It must be thirty seconds by now, surely? He counted down to fifty-five, took a deep breath and stepped into the Mistmurk.

Lights flashed before his eyes, then all senses blanked out, save one – he could still feel. He was falling, though very slowly, and had the oddest feeling that his arms and legs were dissolving into drifting vapour, before reforming. He landed on something soft and rubbery, bounced twice and heard an audible *snick* inside his head.

His senses returned; Nish made out a steep slope

corkscrewing down to the right and caught a flash of movement there. Realising that he was still holding the phial, he tossed it away and heard it break.

Maelys was gone. It hurt more than he could ever have imagined. He tried to fix her in his mind and use her as the focus he'd need to survive the uncanny paths, but she kept slipping away from him. He should have gone back to make sure, whatever the risk. No, he should never have come down to the pit without her. Why on earth had she gone up to the village?

Nish still couldn't focus on her, and finally, guiltily, he went back to the only memory that would never fade – Irisis. It helped at once, and he began to climb down into a maze of pathways.

Preoccupied as he was, for the first few minutes he barely noticed the strange world they were trudging through. Now he looked around. A myriad of tracks, many clearly impossible, stretched away from his feet in every direction, including straight up, straight down and out to either side, tilted so that their surfaces were vertical.

Each path moved and shifted with every step he took, though they were just transparent phantoms compared to the track he was on, which wound off into the murky distance ahead of him, clear and solid. There was nothing else, though – they weren't in a building, cavern or landscape – just the maze of paths.

Nish hadn't realised that the others were seeing things differently until Monkshart, who was leading, fell to his knees, groaning and shaking his head.

'What's the matter?' Nish said coolly.

'The paths! The infinite paths are driving me insane,' the zealot said through gritted teeth.

Nish was pleased to see that Phrune was suffering even more cruelly. Sweat was pouring down his round cheeks, his eyes were running with tears and his upper lip was shiny with oozings from his nose. He swayed from side to side as he walked, mumbling a dirge with desperate concentration as if, should he forget it, he would lose his mind.

'You can see?' Monkshart was rubbing his eye. The deep, bruise-dark sockets were swollen, the left one more than the right, and his corrugated cheeks were cracked and weeping.

'The path is perfectly clear to me,' Nish said with deliberate arrogance.

He had to take every advantage he could in the battle with Monkshart, though he wondered why he could see better than they could. Ah! His clearsight was back. Did that mean he'd passed beyond the influence of Tifferfyte? Perhaps, though his talent felt stronger and clearer now, as if it had been changed, perhaps even enhanced by passage through the Mistmurk. Was it showing him the most direct path towards his imagined future?

'You're not troubled by sickness, shooting pains or unsteadiness in the limbs?'

'The only thing that troubles me is the loss of my friend,' Nish said curtly, though that wasn't true. Whenever he focussed his clearsight hard to locate the path, his eyes burned and he felt the beginning of an ache at the base of his skull. Could that be aftersickness?

Monkshart ignored the bitterness. '*Seeing* here in the maze is another sign that you're the Chosen One.'

'Another sign?'

'The people need signs, Deliverer –' Monkshart's head whipped around, his eyes rolled sickeningly, but through sheer will he managed to steady himself. 'What's that?'

'Didn' hear anythin',' slurred Phrune.

Monkshart withdrew a small six-sided brass tube from a pouch under his arm, rotated a knurled wheel and raised the tube to his right eye, staring back the way they had come. He shook his head, whereupon his eyes rolled the other way. He staggered and had to clutch at Nish's shoulder. Rotating the knurled wheel another half turn, he scanned their path.

'Just as I thought,' he said grimly. 'They're after us already. I can't think how they got through the Mistmurk unscathed. Vomix must have smoothed the passage for them, though not even his mancery can carry them though this maze unaided.'

'Vomix?' said Nish. 'I thought it was Father this time.'

'I can read the stench of Vomix's aura from here.' Monkshart folded at the knees, managed to recover then blinked several times in rapid succession. 'I can't see how to get out. The potion, Deliverer.' He held out a shaking hand.

'I threw it away.'

Monkshart choked, then his eyes flashed. 'Fool, fool!' He seized Nish by the shoulders and began to shake him ever more violently as the murderous rage took hold of him again.

Nish choked; lights whirled before his eyes and in a flash of clearsight he knew that Monkshart was going to kill him. He kicked out vainly as he struggled to get a breath, but suddenly Monkshart let Nish fall.

Phrune was pulling the zealot away. 'Master, Master, what are you doing? Come away with me; allow me to soothe your torments and slake your needs.'

Monkshart knocked him flying. 'Not now, Phrune!' He swayed, then with a wrench managed to take control of himself. He walked around them in a stiff-legged circle, thumping his thighs with his fists, before coming back and jerking Nish to his feet.

'Forgive me, Deliverer. I don't know what happened there. It's the maze, the cursed maze. Why did you throw away the phial? You must have known we'd need it again.'

Nish felt like a stupid schoolboy. 'I wasn't thinking, save of Maelys left to die.'

'Another sign,' Phrune said mockingly. 'He's a false Deliverer; a fool.'

Monkshart was quite calm now. He quelled Phrune with a stare before turning back to Nish, looking troubled. 'I hope

281

you threw the phial hard into the maze where our enemies won't find it, Deliverer. For if they do . . .'

How could he have been so stupid? 'I – I just tossed it to the side,' Nish stammered. 'But I heard it crack.'

Monkshart's eyes flashed again; his fists opened and closed. The pale gloves were torn across the knuckles. 'Vomix will find it and he'll recover every drop. There was enough left to treat a squad of soldiers.'

'You said there was only sufficient for half a dozen people!'

'A necessary lie. Your path to victory will be filled with them, Deliverer. We can't cumber ourselves with the useless on the way or we'll never get there.'

'Those villagers were ordinary, decent human beings! People who've supported you all the way.'

'And they gave their lives so we could get away, which is why they were there. Come on. We must make the best we can from this mess, though I don't doubt Vomix's troops will be on us within the hour.'

TWENTY-SIX

Maelys was woken by shouting so loud that it hurt her ears. A dull ache throbbed behind her temples, her back felt bruised and something sharp was sticking into her side. She opened her eyes, sending spasms of pain jagging through her head.

It was still dark, but she wasn't in her bed or even inside the crater, for above her she caught a glimpse of stars through rushing cloud, and in the distance she made out the outline of a cottage. As she tried to sit up, such a spear of pain went through her head that she let out a gasp. What was she doing in the village? She remembered coming up from the pit, then the confrontation with Monkshart and, vaguely, sipping liqueur from a goblet. Later Nish had been carrying her to bed. She didn't recall anything else.

A cold breeze whirled across her bare skin. What was going on? Her gown was up around her neck. She was naked underneath it and she tingled all over, as if prickly fingers had been trailed up and down her body. She jerked it down, feeling the hot blood flood to her face.

The shouting grew louder; she made out battle cries, the clash of weapons and shrieks of agony. There was a strange taste in her mouth – no, an absence of taste; her tongue felt numb. Had she been drugged? Her thoughts came laboriously.

It was cold and drizzling. Maelys was wiping her face on her sleeve when she caught a lingering, sweetly oily odour there, masking something less pleasant – Phrune! He must have drugged her liqueur, sneaked into her room afterwards and brought her up here to molest. And then, left her to die.

A dream fragment rose up, unbidden. An abandoned stone hut, an odd, meaty smell like a butcher's stall, and a plump shadow bending over a vat. No, it was a cauldron warmed by a handful of coals in a brass brazier, and the figure was hooking something out of it, tissue-thin and dripping, checking it with his fingers then lowering it below the oily surface again.

The figure was disguised, perhaps by some kind of illusion, but Maelys knew who it was by the way he moved, and his smell. Phrune looked over his shoulder at her, the look of a jackal, then returned to the spell he was casting . . .

Later he'd knelt beside her, and ever so slowly drawn up her gown to expose her upper body. In the paralysis of the dream Maelys couldn't move to stop him. His face was in shadow but she could hear the distinctive sound of his tongue on his lips. He stroked her bare belly with one hand while with the other he was making an odd rasping noise, flicking the blade of a stiletto with his thumb. He touched the tip of the blade to her upper lip and giggled as she tried to shrink away.

Maelys managed to shake her head. Phrune lifted the knife, fastidiously, then held her jaw and made a small, careful cut at the top of her upper lip. Thick, shiny saliva beaded on his lower lip – he was drooling in anticipation. Maelys screamed, he reared back on his heels and she lost the nightmare, thankfully.

A rain of arrows rattled against stone roofs and walls. Someone cried out to her left. Maelys dragged herself into the shelter of the wall and managed to sit up. Her top lip was tingling. She felt along it, winced, then had to hold onto the wall at the sick realisation that followed. It hadn't been a dream – her lip was swollen and a thin scab extended along it, exactly where Phrune had run the tip of the knife.

She'd been quite wrong about him. His eyes hadn't been roving over her in a lustful way at all. Phrune wasn't a rapist or a pervert; he was a killer. Having the power of life and death over others, and using it, was what gave him his gratification. He'd been imagining the pleasure of her pain when he lifted her skin off in one piece, so as to please his master with the finest body-glove he'd ever had.

Maelys was suddenly struck by the gaunt face of the young woman, Ganni, who had appealed to Monkshart as they'd entered the village.

'Surr,' Ganni had wept, 'it came again last night. It took Milli and we can't find her anywhere. I'm so afraid.'

And Monkshart had brushed her off. 'Phrune will deal with it.'

No wonder the villagers looked so haunted. They were trapped here by Monkshart's halo of protection and mesmerised by his tales of the Deliverer coming to save them, yet whenever Monkshart needed a new body-glove Phrune stalked them in the darkness for their skins.

But Monkshart was a huge man, so how would the skins fit? Phrune's Arts must ensure that they were elastic enough to stretch over him, even from people as little as her.

Another fragment of Maelys's nightmare: something had interrupted Phrune and he wasn't happy about it, for he'd thrown her over his shoulder and raced down a rough, stony path, cursing all the way. She didn't remember anything else. How long had passed? Long enough for the damp chill of the village to seep into her. She looked around warily in case he was still lurking nearby, but couldn't see anyone. No, he wouldn't risk *his* skin in a battle that could only end with the village being wiped out. He'd be making his escape by now.

Clinging onto a low stone wall, Maelys pulled herself to her feet. Her head hurt so much that she could hardly think. Something whistled overhead; this time it sounded like a crossbow bolt. Dropping down, she squinted though a gap in the stones. She was just inside the wall on the downhill side of the village. Further down the slope she saw hundreds of lanterns and the moving shadows of the army. To her left a handful of villagers were fighting three armoured soldiers, hacking at them with hoes and scythes, though none of their blows were getting through.

A surgical blow took the arm off a yellow-haired villager, a measured thrust skewered him through the belly and he collapsed, screaming. Maelys hastily turned away, ducked down and began to creep up between the houses, looking for the path to the crater. As she rounded the wall of a tumble-down cottage she stumbled into five or six villagers. 'Come on,' she hissed. 'You can't fight an army.'

'We have always been prepared to die for the Deliverer, Lady Maelys,' said a small, gaunt man with a white wisp of beard on his chin. One eye glinted as it caught a lantern's reflection. 'And if you were a true believer you would die with us, to give him his chance.'

'But I don't want to die,' she said softly.

'Then run for your life and you might save it, though you'll regret it later.' He turned away scornfully and the others turned with him, proudly shouldering their scythes and mattocks. The poor fools. She wanted to scream the truth at them but knew they wouldn't believe her. They were too deeply in Monkshart's thrall.

She encountered another pair of villagers beyond the next house, but they spoke just as fervently; after that she didn't try to persuade anyone. She had a higher duty – to her family.

Something whirred high in the air. Maelys looked up, dreading that it was a flappeter, but the drizzle was turning to rain and she couldn't see anything for cloud. It hadn't sounded like a flappeter though. It had sounded much bigger.

Behind her a flash of light lit up the whole village, accompanied by a *crack-boom* that shook the ground. The wall of the cottage beside her collapsed suddenly and she had to leap sideways to avoid the tumbling stones. Further down, a woman screamed, high-pitched and tremulous.

Maelys looked back and wished she hadn't, for soldiers were swarming through a breach in the wall, their beetle-shell armour shiny in the light from a burning house. The villagers whacked uselessly at them with their agricultural tools and were cut down. If she didn't get moving she would suffer the same fate.

Maelys took off, which made her head throb even more cruelly, and had just lurched around the corner of the highest cottage when she ran into someone in the dark, knocking them off their feet. 'Sorry!' she said instinctively.

'Lady Maelys?'

'Jil? What are you doing here?'

'I live here,' she said simply.

Maelys made her out now. Jil picked herself up, and then a child – her little brother.

'But you're not planning to die for the Deliverer.' Maelys remembered that much. 'Come on.' She turned towards the crater path, and Jil followed.

'There's no way out for me, Lady Maelys,' Jil said so softly that Maelys barely heard her over the racket of battle, the crackle of burning cottages and the ominous whirring from above. 'But . . .' Jil pushed the boy at her. 'I risked everything for you. Please . . . take Timfy to safety. He's a good boy. He'll serve you well.'

Maelys took the boy, who clung to her, still half-asleep. He was thin, like his sister, and small, yet heavy in her arms. 'Where's Nish?'

'Gone, Lady Maelys. With Monkshart and Phrune.'

Her heart lurched. Did he truly mean so little to Nish? 'Gone where?'

'Down to the secret way out.'

'What secret way out?'

'I don't know. I heard them talking about it after Nish carried you to bed.'

'Hurry!' Maelys began to walk faster, though Timfy was growing very heavy and she felt oddly weak, as if the sleep potion had leached all strength out of her.

'I dare not, Lady Maelys. Monkshart –'

'Are you more afraid of Monkshart than you are of dying here?'

'Of course, Lady Maelys.'

Perhaps that's what had happened to the big brother Jil had so looked up to. Had Phrune taken his skin? Maelys's arms came out in goose pimples. What was she supposed to do if they did come upon Monkshart, Phrune and Nish? She never wanted to see Phrune again. She couldn't deal with such sick malevolence, but she had to find a way.

The whirring sounded again and something huge burst out of the mist above the village with a blast of chilly air. The craft was so gigantic that Maelys couldn't take it all in at once; couldn't believe in it. She'd never seen such a thing before, because she'd been too dazed to see the one that had followed them to Tifferfyte.

It had to be an air-dreadnought, the most fearsome craft in the world. A bronze-sheathed vessel roughly the shape of a longboat, three spans wide and fifteen long, was suspended from airbags so large that she could only see their lower curves through the streaming cloud. The airbags were held in position by a maze of rigging. Ropes dangling from the sides and bow of the vessel each held five clinging soldiers, ready to leap to ground. They wore the armour of the God-Emperor's Imperial Militia.

Jil made an incoherent sound in her throat. Maelys pushed Timfy into her arms and cried, 'Come on. Run!'

She bolted up towards the rim of the crater and, after a brief hesitation, Jil followed. Maelys looked back as they reached the edge. The Imperial Militia were dropping from the swaying ropes like shining fruit, some falling into a crouch to level their crossbows, others already running as they landed.

Jil came level with Maelys, caught her with her free hand and dragged her over the edge onto the narrow glassy path, the shrieks of the dying ringing in her ears. Jil's sandals slipped and she wobbled dangerously, but found her footing and headed down, still carrying her brother, moving faster than Maelys would have dared. She wasn't halfway to the pavilion when the whirring became an echoing roar and the air-dreadnought appeared above the crater, so low that its keel scraped the rim.

'Stop, girl with the black hair!' The voice sent shudders up her back – Vomix again. 'Stop or you'll be shot.'

Putting her arm across her face to avoid being recognised, she stumbled down.

A crossbow bolt caromed off the wall above her head, filling the air with powdered glass. She broke into a trot, her bare feet giving her a sounder grip this time. Another shot whizzed past to her left. Fortunately, shooting down at such a steep angle in the gloom would be tricky.

The pavilion lay just ahead. Maelys sprang between the columns into the welcoming darkness, skidding halfway across before she came to a halt. Jil was on the other side, holding her brother, who was squirming in her arms.

Maelys peered around a column. The armoured soldiers were at the top of the narrow path now, moving gingerly, for they were big, broad-shouldered men and their armour scraped against the wall as they moved. The air-dreadnought was hovering; fortunately it could come no lower since the airbags extended further than the width of the crater. More soldiers came over the sides, swinging back and forth on long ropes, though there was nowhere safe for them to settle but the edge of the pavilion far below, and they were having trouble manoeuvring them down.

She ducked across to the downward path. 'Lead the way, Jil.'

Jil was just standing there. 'You have no boots.'

'There's no time to fetch them!'

'You must have shoes, or you'll go lame. Run; it'll just take a minute.'

A minute would be too long. Maelys looked around wildly. How could she delay them? She sprang up, wrenched one of the lanterns off the wall, blew it out and hurled it up the path. It smashed about halfway up, though it wasn't light enough to see if it had spilled its oil.

She ran to her room, grabbed boots, socks and her little pack, hurtled back to the pavilion and started down after Jil.

'Faster, fools!' roared Vomix. 'They're getting away.'

The leading soldiers broke into a trot. They were only a minute behind. Jil was moving slowly now, for it was so gloomy here that the path could barely be seen. Maelys hadn't gone far when glass crunched up above and a voice roared, 'Look out!'

The second soldier, who was halfway down, had slipped on the oil. His feet went from under him and he began to slide down the path on his back, roaring in fear. The soldier below him realised his peril and began to run down the slippery path, desperately trying to get ahead, but the second soldier, sliding ever faster, swept into him from behind, knocking him off his feet. They went over the edge in a tangle of thrashing arms and legs.

The remaining soldiers stopped and began to mutter to one another. Vomix's voice came echoing down from the air-dreadnought, a cold rage that made Maelys shudder.

'After them. If they get away, you'll be impaled!'

Lanterns were lowered on ropes, casting the crater into bright light and deeper shadow. The soldiers continued, slowly and carefully. Maelys tried to put them out of her mind as she felt her way down.

Jil was waiting at the top of the Pit. Strips of its floor were illuminated as brightly as a moonlit night. Her brother stood beside her, looking around sleepily. He had a shock of tangled brown hair and a quizzical expression, and appeared about seven years old.

'I don't see any way out,' said Jil.

Maelys took a turn around the walls, feeling with her fingers, then spiralled in, looking for a concealed passage or door. Her foot struck something yielding in a strip of shadow and she smelt blood and offal – the two dead soldiers, still tangled. Thankfully, darkness hid what the fall had done to them. Fragments of beetle-shell armour crunched underfoot as she backed away.

Maelys found nothing that resembled a door, cave or opening of any sort. If the escape way had been rendered invisible she could do nothing about it. The only other alternative was the Pit.

'It must be down there,' she said, putting on a confident air for Jil. 'I'll go first.'

Jil nodded stiffly. Her eyes were huge and she was holding her brother so that he faced away from the corpses.

'Come on!' Maelys went down the rope ladder in a rush, turning aside at the bottom to leave space for Jil and Timfy. As she scanned the Pit, she could feel a number of dark possible futures swarming in the corner of her eye. Perhaps they came quicker the second time. She tried to rid herself of the grim images, but they wouldn't go.

The curved walls were solid. So was the floor, apart from the fuming Mistmurk, and even had Maelys not been warned about it she would have kept her distance. It had a dangerous, corrosive look, with roiling fumes bursting out of it at intervals, sometimes belching high like miniature thunderheads, at other times creeping across the floor as though the vapours were too heavy to rise any higher.

Something came crashing and smashing down, to burst upon the beam above the Pit. Shards of crockery, as if from an enormous pot, rained through the sump. A fragment fell into the Mistmurk, making it fizz and seethe. A soldier shouted, from not far above them, 'That's enough! They're down in a hole in the floor. We've got them trapped this time.'

291

Jil was squeezing Timfy to her chest, her face frozen. He squirmed as if he wanted to be put down; he didn't understand the danger. Maelys was beginning to panic again. She forced it back, still finding it impossible to believe that Nish would have run away and left her here to die.

'I don't know where they could have gone,' she said to herself.

'They went down the hole,' said Timfy. 'See?' He pointed at the Mistmurk.

She crouched down. A few threads torn from dark cloth were moving in an air current, caught on a splinter of glass just outside the wavering edge of the Mistmurk. They were the colour of Monkshart's cloak.

Maelys met the girl's eyes. There was a question in them. Above, a horde of soldiers was clattering down the stairs. 'I'm prepared to take the risk,' Maelys said.

Jil nodded stiffly. Maelys caught hold of her upper arm and together they jumped into the Mistmurk.

TWENTY-SEVEN

In an instant, the taphloid became burning hot between her breasts. Maelys jerked it out on its chain, holding it away from her in the darkness. Her skin crept as if she were covered in crawling ants, then began to burn as if it were peeling off. A wavering aura flashed into existence around her, then she felt a burst of excruciating pain and the aura felt as though it were being forced back inside her. Maelys cried out, snatched at the taphloid, which was no longer hot, and squeezed it hard for a moment. The aura faded and took the pain with it.

The boy began to moan; Jil shushed him. They were jerked sideways, then upside down, though they didn't actually seem to be falling. Maelys couldn't see anything now, even when her hand brushed against something soft and slick. She had no idea what had happened.

They hung in nothingness for about twenty heartbeats, then began to fall so quickly that the wind whistled around Maelys's ears. As abruptly, their motion slowed and they drifted onto an angled rubbery surface covered in little round knobs, bounced twice and slid down the slope for a good few spans before coming to rest.

Letting go of Jil's hand, Maelys grasped the taphloid again. It was cool, and it felt different. There still seemed to be some kind of life or presence within it, but it wasn't comforting now. The taphloid felt loaded; dangerous. She put it back into her cleavage, which stung, for the skin was blistered there.

The crawling sensation disappeared and she began to distinguish a maze of transparent paths, tunnels, bridges and stairs leading off in every direction, including straight up. They were in a labyrinth in which every path was intertwined with every other one, but each was also in ceaseless, jiggling motion.

No matter where she looked, nothing was still. It made her dizzy to look at it, and there was no way of telling the correct path, for none looked clearer, stiller or more solid than any other. Even the slope they were sprawled on appeared to be moving, though it felt stable beneath her. The hole they'd jumped through, the Mistmurk, could no longer be distinguished.

Beside her, Jil began to retch and tried to crawl down the barely tangible slope. Maelys held her back. 'Jil, if we're separated, we'll never find each other again.'

Jil brought up a thin green trickle and groaned. Maelys's stomach heaved in sympathy but she held it down. Timfy was on his feet, his eyes wide and mouth open in wonder. What was he seeing? It could be different for each of them; it probably was.

She took their hands. 'We've got to get away in case the soldiers come after us.' And they would. No matter how terrified they were of the Mistmurk, they'd be more afraid of incurring the God-Emperor's displeasure.

Feeling forwards with one foot, Maelys began to make her way down the sloping path, and with every step the three-dimensional maze shifted and wavered. She fought down the nausea until they reached a small unseen depression, then stopped, trying to work out if any path or direction were more real than the others. Unfortunately they all looked the same. Her ears popped and the rubbery ground quivered as if from a heavy impact, then another and another, though she couldn't see anything.

A man's voice spoke, shivery and echoing. It couldn't be far away though it appeared to come from all directions at once. 'Where have they gone?'

Jil opened her mouth to scream. Maelys hastily covered it with her hand. 'Shh! They'll hear.' She stared around her, trying to see where the soldiers had come through.

'What the blazes is this place, Sergeant Tink?' said another voice. 'Vardo, what's the matter?' A liquid choking and gurgling was followed by an angry curse and the smack of a fist against flesh. 'Disgusting pig! Why didn't you turn the other way?'

'What's the matter?' said the first voice, the sergeant.

'Vardo threw up all over me,' said the second. 'The swine always did have weak guts.'

Two more pops and the floor quivered twice. 'Here come the rest,' said Tink. 'Spread out and start looking for them, but don't lose sight of each other.'

'Cursed place,' said the second soldier. 'And curse the mancer who created it. Curse them all.'

'Shut your mouth,' hissed Sergeant Tink. 'Seneschal Vomix will be here in a minute.'

'I hope he can see better than I can,' muttered the second man.

'A mancer of his power will see straight through this maze,' said the sergeant. 'They won't get away this time.'

There were more pops, more quivers. Maelys's dizziness was getting worse. She thought ten people had come through the Mistmurk, or perhaps eleven, but the voices faded and though she could still hear them she couldn't make out what they were saying. The confusion of the maze was getting worse. People could go mad in here.

Timfy began to cry. 'Shh!' Maelys whispered.

'What's that?' said Vomix's unmistakeable voice, mucous-thick and sibilant.

'A whining brat,' said the sergeant. 'Down there . . . I think.'

'No, they're this way,' said Vomix, and he was closer. 'What's the matter with that man, sergeant?'

'The maze scrambled his wits, surr. Can't stop hurling his guts.' Tink chuckled mirthlessly.

'Get rid of him and call more men down.'

Maelys heard stumbling noises, more cursing and vomiting, and a mad cry. The sergeant said, hoarsely and slurring a little, 'That's three down, surr. This place is twisting the brains inside my head. I can't send them back, Seneschal Vomix, surr.'

'Why the devil not?'

'The hole closed over and I can't tell where it was.'

Vomix let loose with a series of vile oaths. Jil, who was swaying from side to side, put her hands over Timfy's ears. Maelys noticed that there was blood on his lip. 'What's the matter with him?' She pointed to his mouth.

'What have you done, Timfy?' Jil whispered, straining to focus. 'What's that in your hand?'

It was a small crystal bottle, the kind used for perfume or potions, with the top broken off. Maelys reached out for it but Jil said, 'It's Monkshart's. I've seen him with it.'

'What's it for?'

'I don't know. Did you drink it, Timfy?' Jil's voice went squeaky.

'Just a little taste. It was horrible.'

Maelys and Jil exchanged glances. 'I don't see why it would be poison,' said Maelys, 'and if he only had a little bit . . .'

'You don't know what they're like.' Jil's eyes were wide and staring. She squeezed her brother so tightly that he cried out, then upended the broken flask against her fingertip and raised her finger towards her mouth, though she was so uncoordinated that it took three attempts to reach it. She licked her finger and shuddered.

Maelys did know, but there was no point adding to Jil's torment by saying so. She took the flask, which had a strong

296

fruity smell, so cloyingly sweet that it made her salivate. As she took another sniff, the shifting maze solidified a fraction and her dizziness faded momentarily. Could it be –?

'Down there!' slurred the sergeant, his voice coming from one direction, then another. 'Seneschal, this way!'

Maelys turned around twice, but couldn't see anyone. Suddenly a huge soldier burst out of a fold in the fabric of the maze behind Jil, swaying from side to side, his head whipping back and forth as if that were the only way he could see clearly. He grabbed Jil and Timfy but staggered and fell to his knees. His eyes were rolling in circles; chunks of vomit clotted his iridescent chest armour, but he didn't let go.

'I can *see*,' Jil mouthed.

Maelys hesitated no longer. She had sucked down three or four thick, intensely bitter drops when someone thumped onto the floor behind her and a hairy, bony hand snatched the phial. Another hand snaked around her side and caught her by the left breast, but instantly the taphloid grew hot and he jerked his hand away with a gasp of pain.

'What did you do?' whispered Jil, staring at Maelys.

She shook her head; she had no idea.

Her vision began to clear. Seneschal Vomix was dancing around in a circle, shaking his hand furiously. 'You little cow!'

'What's the matter?' said Tink.

'Bitch has a very odd aura. Touched mine and it seemed to turn inside out. Ah, that hurt.' He studied his hand, which appeared to be swollen. His yellow eyes were looking in two directions at once. He swayed, held the phial up and blinked at it, slowly and owlishly. Maelys tried to slide away but his boot came down on her foot, pinning her to the path.

He sniffed the phial. His eyes widened and he tried to shake the potion onto his palm, but the phial was empty. With a roar of rage he made to hurl it away, but thought better of it and broke it against his boot. Picking up the pieces, he carefully licked the potion off the inside of the largest. After a good few seconds his eyes uncrossed.

Handing the remaining shards to the big soldier, Vomix bade him do the same, though the sergeant was so far gone that his tongue was bleeding in four places before he'd finished.

'That's the last of it, unfortunately,' said Vomix. 'Better hope it's enough to get you and me out, Sergeant Tink.'

'What about my men?' said Tink.

Three soldiers were slumped on the ground further up the slope; others could be heard stumbling about, making increasingly incoherent noises. Maelys prayed that they'd collapse as well.

'They'll have to follow as best they can, though the maze madness will take them all, I'll warrant.' Vomix didn't sound as though he cared. 'Can you see?'

'Better than ever,' said Tink. 'I can see double!' He laughed hysterically. 'What about you, surr?'

'I'm all right.' Vomix swayed, scowling at Maelys, who was still trying to get her foot free, then thumped her in the side with an elbow. She felt a rib creak. Dizziness hadn't affected his aim. 'Bitch took the last of it.' He tore off her pack, pawed through it, pocketed the golden bracelet and tossed the pack to one side. She wrenched her foot free and lunged for the pack. He kicked it out of sight. 'Know you, don't I?'

Maelys's blood ran cold.

'I remember now,' he said slowly. 'An insolent brat who didn't know her place. It was on the road to market – what, six years ago. Or seven? Where was that?' He pretended to think, but Maelys was sure he knew and was enjoying tormenting her. 'Oh yes, on the road down from the manor of that upstart family, Clan Nifferlin. You must be Maelys, the rude little girl who compared my face to a boar's arse.' He reached down for her but thought better of it. 'You brought your clan to my attention that day, and doomed them as surely as if you'd pissed in the face of the God-Emperor.' He snorted like a pig.

'I was just a little girl,' she croaked. 'I didn't mean anything by it. That can't be why . . .'

'You drew my attention to your clan, Maelys of Nifferlin. I took a closer look and didn't like what I saw – a concealed, illegal talent for the Art, allied to an arrogant and rebellious nature that made Nifferlin a threat to the God-Emperor. I plucked the troublemakers one by one until only three stupid old women survived, and the little girl, and *you*. I was going to have you for myself.' He reached down to twist her nipple but again jerked his hand back. 'But the five of you vanished and not even the wisp-watchers could tell what had happened to you.'

Vomix seemed to be trying to recall those times. 'How could five people vanish so utterly? Your mother and aunts had no talents; my torturers tested them thoroughly.' He let out an evil snort. 'And I don't think it was you. To ride a flappeter you must have a talent, but that's not the kind that can conceal an escaping family.

'Ahhh . . . odd incidents spring to mind at the ruins of Nifferlin – searches that found nothing though the soldiers swore to seeing things. You were *still there*, hidden by the fifth person – the blonde girl. Oh, I especially like extracting secrets from pretty little girls. The God-Emperor will make me a high lord this time.'

Maelys's blood was clotting in her veins. No wonder her mother and aunts had treated her so badly – the downfall of Clan Nifferlin had been all her fault. All doubts about right and wrong, or doing her duty with Nish, disappeared. She'd doomed her clan; only she could save what was left of her family. Neither Vomix nor the sergeant could be allowed to leave the maze alive. And if she did get out she must do whatever it took to make up for that childhood stupidity.

'Not if you let Nish get away,' she whispered, trying to distract him.

Vomix thumped her on the back, though not hard enough to do any damage. She noted that he was being careful not to touch her with bare skin. 'He won't, because you're going to lead me to him.'

'I don't know where he is. He's run away.' She immediately wished she hadn't spoken; Vomix might see no further use for her, or the others.

'I don't believe you. He can't be that far ahead, can he, Sergeant?'

'Just minutes, according to Vardo. He saw three men running down the path as we left the air-dreadnought. Vardo had the keenest eyes in the guard.'

'Where is Vardo? Get him down here right away.'

There was a short pause. 'He was the first to succumb, surr. He's the man you ordered up. He wasn't moving, the last I saw of him. A good man at your back in a battle, was Vardo.'

'No good now, though, is he?' Another snort. 'Can you see the true path, Sergeant?'

'I can see a hundred paths, surr, and I can't tell the difference between any of them.'

'I only see five clearly, but I don't know which one to take. And the soldiers are useless. Maelys?'

'I see seven paths but I can't tell which one is true,' she whispered.

'Lying bitch!' Drawing a long, heavy gauntlet from a belt hook, he struck her across the face. 'You're letting him get away. What about you, girl?' Vomix clouted Jil over the side of the head.

'It's all whirling,' wept Jil, choking with terror. Timfy screamed and thrust his face into her shoulder.

Vomix scowled, pulled out a dagger and was about to cut her throat when the sergeant said, 'We may need her later, surr.'

Vomix lowered the knife. 'Are you defying me?' he said dangerously.

'What if the brat's the only one who can see? We won't get any sense out of him if you've just slaughtered his sister.'

Vomix slammed the knife into its sheath. 'You're right, of course. In places like this, sometimes weakness can mean strength.' He wrenched Timfy's head back. 'Well, brat!' he roared, spit flying onto the lad's cheeks. 'Can you *see*?'

The boy tried to pull away. Vomix jerked him back and slapped him with an open hand. He began to wail.

'Surr,' said the sergeant, 'I don't think –'

'Soldiers don't think,' said Vomix in a deadly voice. 'Beating is the only way to get the best out of a brat.' He raised his hand.

The sergeant caught it and held it in an unbreakable grip. 'Stop, surr!'

Vomix's other hand flashed to the dagger. 'Get your filthy hand off me –'

'I am a sergeant in the God-Emperor's Imperial Militia,' said the sergeant. 'And I'm not required to answer to any man, even you, surr, who is acting against my lord's wishes.' Tink turned to Maelys. 'You've got your wits about you, girl. Make the lad speak, for all our sakes.'

Maelys managed to coax Timfy from his sister's arms and took him a little further down where he could still see Jil, but not Vomix nor the soldiers. 'Timfy,' she said, 'can you tell which way to go?'

'Of course,' he said. 'Can't you?'

'No, I'm not as strong or clever as you. Nor as brave.' Timfy swelled a little. 'Jil and I need you to show us the way out so we can get away from the bad men. Can you lead the way, Timfy?'

'I want my sister.'

'I'll call her.' She waved at the sergeant, who brought Jil down. Vomix followed, glowering, then two staggering, cross-eyed soldiers. There was no sign of the others and she imagined what it must be like for them, lost in an unreal place they could not understand, then abandoned by their comrades to madness and death. The Imperial Militia were brutal thugs who doubtless deserved to die but she could still feel pity for them, dying alone down here.

Timfy strode ahead, proudly and confidently, as if he were walking along the road through Tifferfyte. Maelys could see the path he trod, though it was just one of many arching up, plunging down or curving around in circles, with nothing to distinguish it from any of the others. Behind her one soldier sounded as though he was trying to bring up his intestines. The other wailed and ran up a smoothly curved wall, managing several leaps before he fell backwards onto the path, twitching but unable to get up. The sergeant knelt beside him for a moment, until Vomix angrily called him on.

'Any soldier who falls must be abandoned, sergeant, else the potion will wear off and we'll be trapped here too.'

Only Vomix and the sergeant were with them now, and the sergeant was lurching like a drunken man as his small dose of potion wore off and the wild magic of the maze took an ever stronger hold. Vomix, unfortunately, seemed little worse than he'd been at the beginning, for he kept casting charms on himself to ward off the multiple visions. Each charm appeared to hurt him more than the previous one, though he soon recovered. Afraid to touch Maelys now, he drove her on by pricking her back with his knife, muttering dire threats should she lead him astray.

Maelys endured it as best she could while she tried to work out what had happened at the Mistmurk. After she'd arrived at Tifferfyte, Monkshart had told Phrune that she had no aura at all – and therefore, no talent. But after touching Maelys, Vomix had been stung or burned by her odd aura. Had passage through the Mistmurk changed her in some fashion?

She didn't think she could keep going much longer. The

potion was wearing off and she could see so many intersecting, quivering pathways that her mind had begun to rebel and reject all of them, even the one she was standing on. She felt giddy all the time and was having trouble telling up from down. Jil had bound a strip of cloth over her eyes: only terror for her brother kept her on her feet.

Vomix's rage was swelling all the time. Prevented by the sergeant from harming Timfy or Jil, he took it out on Maelys, though he was careful only to touch her with the gauntlets. He was grunting and gasping; strings of slobber dangled from the dense black stubble which had sprouted on his chin. Maelys felt sure he was being driven mad by the maze, and aftersickness from the dangerous charms he was using to keep it at bay.

Wait – none of them really mattered to him, but Nish did, and if Vomix brought Nish back unharmed it would make him. So if she could offer him that hope there might be a chance . . .

'A light, a light,' she lied, pointing in a wavering circle, forwards. 'Nish, help –'

The maze hadn't affected Vomix's reflexes. He sprang at her, knocking Jil and Timfy out of the way, and slapped his reeking gauntlet across Maelys's mouth and nose.

'You'll live to regret that,' he hissed. Thrusting her sprawling, he peered into the maze. 'Where's the light? I don't see it.'

'There.' She gestured to where a narrow grey path appeared to coil up and over, before plunging down precipitously. 'Halfway down the further slope.'

'I can't see anything,' Vomix growled.

'You can see it, can't you, Timfy?' Maelys said desperately, knowing that Timfy would say no and then, likely as not, Vomix would plunge his sword right through her. 'Can't you?'

Timfy looked up and said, with the perfect innocence of a child, 'I saw the light ages ago. It was climbing up but now

303

it's going down again.' He pointed somewhat to the right. She could have hugged him.

Vomix looked from Timfy to her, breathing heavily, then back to Timfy. 'You pointed further left,' he said to Maelys.

'No, that way.' She described another shaky circle in the air, her arm trembling so badly that she could barely hold it out.

His eyes narrowed, but a spasm racked him and bile-green saliva trickled from the corner of his mouth. He managed to gasp, 'Follow the light, and be quick about it.' He made a gesture as if blessing himself, renewing the painful illusion-breaking charm. 'Aahhh!' he roared, doubling over and holding his stomach.

Maelys moved backwards to safety, knowing that he'd lash out the moment he'd recovered. If she could keep him at bay long enough, aftersickness must build up until he couldn't resist it.

As she turned away, a gauntleted blow drove her to her knees, then Vomix spat a green gob beside her. 'Liar!' he roared, jerking her up and around to face him. 'My charm tells me that there is no light. How dare you coax the boy to lie for you?'

He swung another wild blow, which glanced off her shoulder. 'But you *know*! You've known where Cryl-Nish and the traitors were all along and you've been leading the boy astray so they could escape.' He reached out with the knife. 'You'll show –'

Maelys couldn't take any more. She lunged, bringing her right knee up so hard between his legs that she felt something burst. He shrieked and collapsed on top of her. She thrust his vomit-crusted face away, wriggled out from under him and flicked a glance to her left. The sergeant had his sword out but his eyes were crossed and he kept jerking his head left and right, as if that were the only way he could focus. It was the only chance they'd get.

'Run for the light!' she hissed in Timfy's ear.

304

Timfy didn't move. 'Jil?' he said anxiously.

Jil's nose was running and she was staggering like a new-born calf. Maelys caught her around the shoulders. 'Run ahead, Timfy!' she hissed. 'Show us the way. If we can get out of sight the bad men won't be able to find us again.'

He took his sister's hand and began to pull her along as fast as she could stagger. Maelys looked down. Vomix was still squirming on the ground, making a thin squeal like an animal chewing its leg off to escape a trap. His knife was in its sheath, partly under him. She had her hand on the hilt when he rolled over onto his side and drew his legs up. His eyes were screwed closed, and if she snatched the knife and buried it in his heart it would all be over.

She reached for it but it was now trapped under him and she wasn't game to roll him over; he didn't look completely incapacitated. Besides, she didn't think she could kill him in cold blood, monster though he was. It was a weakness she might come to regret but it wasn't in her to do it. Maelys backed away.

The sergeant began to lurch after them, now in a rush, now wobbling from side to side, but his path was like an ant meandering across a sheet of paper and he soon began to head in the wrong direction.

She didn't look back, though shortly she heard a shriek when Vomix realised that they'd escaped. Why hadn't she used the knife?

On Maelys staggered, and on. Hours had gone by since they'd escaped, and the maze was brightening by the minute. She felt weak from hunger and thirst. Jil was as blanched as an almond and her cracked lips were bleeding.

Only Timfy was unaffected, but there seemed no end to the maze and Maelys had lost hope of his finding a way out. Soon, when she could go no further, they were all going to die here.

Jil sat down suddenly and covered her face with her

arms. 'Can you see the way, Timfy?' Maelys said, as she had many times before.

'No,' he croaked. 'But the light is getting brighter.'

'It must be daytime outside,' she murmured.

'No, the *light* is getting brighter.'

'That's what I just said – *what* light?'

'The light I've been following.'

It took an agonisingly long time to take in what he'd said. 'You mean there *is* a light? I thought you made that up.'

Timfy looked shocked. 'Only bad people tell lies.'

'Sometimes good people have to . . .' She didn't have the energy. 'Where is it?'

His thin arm pointed. 'There.'

The maze shifted sickeningly as she tried to focus, as if it were responding to her feelings and deliberately trying to frustrate her. She squinted, which helped a little, so she closed one eye. Everything settled down and she saw a small, jiggling yellow point in the distance, though it made her nauseous to focus on it and she couldn't have followed it far.

'Are we getting closer?'

'No. It's going faster now.'

'I don't suppose you can find a quicker way through the maze?'

He licked his lips, but didn't answer for some time, as if afraid he'd get into trouble. 'I know how to get out.' He wasn't looking at her, nor at his sister, who was now lying on her side with her knees drawn up.

'How did you discover that?'

'I saw it ages ago.'

She couldn't restrain herself, snapping, 'Then why didn't you tell me?'

Timfy jumped backwards and she regretted it instantly. 'The bad man told me to follow the light and I was scared . . . scared he'd hurt Jil.'

'Sorry, Timfy. I'm not cross with you.' Going down on her

306

knees before him, she took his hand. 'Do you think, if we went straight to the way out, we could get there by the time they do?' She nodded in the direction of the light.

'We'll get there first.'

'Good boy. I'll carry Jil. Lead the way, but don't go too fast.'

He waited until she had heaved Jil over her shoulder, then set off proudly, taking a path to their left which she hadn't realised was there. It went down steeply and became a blocky, square staircase. She followed as best she could, trying not to think, squinting through one eye so as to block out the shifting paths. They went along a springy track, like a sheet of rubber stretched across a gorge, waded through something invisible that dragged at her legs, then climbed a long incline to a lookout shaped like a segment of an orange, enclosed on the curved side by a shoulder-high wall with a warm, fleshy feel.

Maelys peered over. Most of the alternative paths had disappeared and the others had faded to barely visible lines, but the true path was clear now, and other details were becoming visible for the first time. The track wound back and forth down a steep slope to a small rest station consisting of four columns and a pointed roof. Below that, another path running from the right joined theirs and it turned towards a transparent tunnel, beyond which she thought she could faintly see something real – trees and rocks.

'Is that the way out, Timfy?'

'Yes.'

'We'll wait down there under the roof,' she said, weak with relief. There was no reason to seek shelter since there was no sun in the maze, no weather, not even a sky, but it looked safer there. 'It's not far now, Jil. Do you think you can walk?'

Jil opened her eyes, winced at the brightness and looked around, more alert than she'd been in hours. The wild

307

power of the maze must be weakening as they approached the exit. 'Yes,' she croaked. 'I think I'll be all right now.'

Maelys took her arm. They went down slowly and settled onto the floor of the way station. There was no dust. She put her back against a column and closed her eyes, thinking about Nish and what he'd say when he saw her. She refused to believe that he'd left her behind deliberately. There had to be another explanation. She prayed that there was.

She must have dozed, for an unexpected sound jerked her awake. Jil was asleep on her back, breathing through her cracked lips and snoring softly. Timfy was snuggled up to his sister, also asleep. Since the other path went right past the way station and no one could go by without seeing them, Maelys hunched herself up, getting as comfortable as she could, and closed her eyes.

She was just dozing off when the sound came again, though this time she recognised it for what it was. It wasn't Jil snoring, but a snorting chuckle. She scrambled to her feet, heart pounding, as a man stepped out from behind the far column of the way station. Seneschal Vomix grinned, snapped his fingers and her legs went rigid.

'How . . .?' she managed to gasp. Her lips had gone as stiff as old rubber.

'I knew you were hiding something,' he gloated, moving closer but careful not to touch, 'so I set a trap and you fell right into it. Did you really think you could disable *me* with such a crude blow? I let you get away; I knew one of you would lead me to Cryl-Nish.'

'How did you find us?'

With another click of his fingers, a shining thread appeared in the air, looping back and forth across the pavilion then halfway up the hill. It began at her back and ended in a coil in his hand. He tossed it in the air and it vanished. He must have put the spell on her when he'd thumped her on the back.

'It was as easy as following a line,' he sneered. 'You don't become the God-Emperor's seneschal without knowing every trick there is.' Glancing towards the exit, he smiled. 'I'll have my full strength back by the time your friends come by.'

TWENTY-EIGHT

Vomix took them up the track to a point where he could
see the other path without being seen, then disappeared, shortly to return supporting the sergeant, who
looked as though he'd fallen down a set of stairs.

His nostrils were caked with blood, he'd lost four front
teeth and his face was so bruised and swollen that he could-
n't see out of his left eye. He limped along, supporting
himself on the point of his sword, though from the blood
seeping from the toe of his right boot he must have skewered his foot at some stage. But he looked alert again. It
would not be easy to get away a second time.

The seneschal let him fall and the sergeant slumped on
the ground, breathing raggedly. 'Pull yourself together,
Sergeant,' said Vomix, stirring him in the ribs with a boot
toe. 'You militiamen are supposed to be tough. They'll be
here in a few minutes. And don't breathe so damn loud.'
Shading his eyes with his hand, for the light was brightening
all the time, he stared back into the transparencies of the
maze.

Maelys couldn't see anyone coming, though she didn't
doubt that they were. However, she couldn't warn them for
she could neither move nor speak. Jil lay where Vomix had
dropped her, eyes closed. The boy was slumped against a
rock, fast asleep, and Maelys hoped he'd stay that way
through the coming attack. He'd done more than anyone

310

could ask of a child, and seen more than any child should see.

Shortly, staring down at the other path, she saw something move in the distance. They were coming. Her gut tightened and her heart began to race. She tried not to react, but Vomix, watching her, grinned like a hyena. Hauling the sergeant to his feet, Vomix worked hairy fingers over his head in what Maelys assumed to be a rejuvenation spell. The sergeant immediately stood up straighter, though he still needed the support of his sword.

'Go down to the ambush point,' said Vomix. 'Keep under cover.'

He looked ghastly too, though aftersickness hadn't weakened him as she'd hoped. He cast another restorative charm on himself, which drained the blood from his face and made his lower lip droop like a cretin's, and turned down the boulder-strewn slope after Tink. He and the sergeant settled into their ambush, slightly above the path.

Maelys could see Nish clearly now. He was stumbling with weariness, though he looked better than the other two. Monkshart's tall form was doubled over, his head almost at ground level and his arms flopping like dead weights. The long pale gloves hung off in shreds, exposing the weeping skin of his arms.

Her stomach heaved at the sight of Phrune, for he resembled a flabby, glistening balloon, apart from his cheeks, which sagged like a bloodhound's. His shaven hair had grown rapidly in the maze; a dark mat, half the length of Maelys's thumb, now surrounded the oiled queue. She couldn't bear to think about the things he did, or the other services he provided Monkshart. How could any man become so debased?

'Nish!' she tried to shout, but just the barest wisp of sound emerged. It didn't even wake Jil.

Maelys tried again, trying so hard to shout that it hurt her throat. 'Nish, turn back. It's Vomix; an ambush.' No sound came forth this time.

311

Vomix turned his head sharply and she saw that his teeth were stained red. She shouted her warning again and again, until her throat was raw, but never managed more than a raspy scrape. Just once Nish stopped, cocking his head to the left as if listening but, evidently hearing nothing, continued. He was only a few spans from the huge boulder behind which the ambushers lurked. Looking towards the transparency that marked the barrier between the maze and the real world, Nish laughed in relief.

Behind the rock, the sergeant raised his sword and a chill went through her. Tink didn't look like a man preparing to take prisoners and she prayed he hadn't been driven mad in the maze.

Nish couldn't tell how long they'd been lost in the maze, though it felt like all night and half the next day, and he'd had nothing to eat or drink in that time. Monkshart hadn't packed food or water, expecting that the transit would take no more than an hour, but as they'd wandered helplessly with no idea of how to get out, twice more he had succumbed to those murderous rages.

Both times they were directed at Phrune, fortunately, but Nish felt ever more alarmed. Monkshart's power, allied to that passionate purpose and mesmerising charisma, made him one of the most potent people in the world, but the rages gave him a deadly unpredictability.

On three occasions, early on, Monkshart had sensed Vomix and his men nearby, but each time the zealot had managed to conceal his little company and the paths of pursued and pursuers had diverged again. Yet Nish's worst fears hadn't come true: there had been no sign of pursuit in many hours and finally Monkshart allowed Nish to have his head, since he could still see a clear path and it appeared to be going somewhere.

Nish could see little but the path, since relying on clearsight all this time had dulled his normal senses. The base of

312

his skull throbbed, his eyes felt as though hot peppers had been ground into them, and he couldn't concentrate on anything more complicated than placing one foot in front of the other. If this was what aftersickness felt like, he was glad he lacked a talent for the Art.

Now the exit lay just ahead. Not even Monkshart knew where they would emerge, though he'd said that distances travelled through the maze were greater than in the real world, and they might come out anywhere on the continent of Lauralin. Nish prayed it was on the other side of the world from Morrelune.

Nish! It wasn't a voice, just the faintest of echoes whispering through the spaces of the maze, and at first he thought his tormented mind was playing tricks on him.

He stopped but couldn't hear anything, and neither Monkshart nor Phrune had reacted. Nish continued, trudging on aching, blistered feet. He couldn't remember when he'd last walked so far without a rest, and his only thought was of passing the barrier and getting out into the real world which, thankfully, was becoming clearer every minute.

It came again, *Nish!* and a note in it was an aching reminder of Maelys. Could she be calling him from beyond the grave? Were such things possible in the unreality of the maze? Clearsight didn't offer any answers.

He didn't hear the ghostly call again, and was moving on when the back of his neck prickled and a jag of white fire hurled Monkshart backwards, skidding him across the rubbery ground. A huge, blood-covered sergeant lurched out from behind a boulder to their left, waving his sword like a madman. Phrune yelped, ducked under the sword and hacked at the soldier's groin with a stiletto. He missed, though a short red gash appeared on the sergeant's thigh. Phrune didn't look like a fighter but he was as quick and deadly as a viper.

Nish looked around for the source of the blast. The maze

313

shimmered in front of him, blocking his way to the real world, though he couldn't see what was behind it.

The sergeant grunted and attacked with a measured horizontal slash that shaved off Phrune's queue, giving him a tonsure. He looked stupidly at the horsetail of dark hair, which had settled on the path as if it had grown there, then lunged. It looked as though the knife was going to carve right through the sergeant's belly but he bent backwards and the blade only sent buttons flying.

Phrune lunged again, cutting a streak across the sergeant's other thigh. The sergeant speared the point of his sword at the acolyte's face. Phrune wove sideways then screamed as the blade sliced off his ear. Another lucky blow?

No. The point flicked out again, taking the other ear off just as neatly, then sliced Phrune's nose from bridge to tip. The soldier was playing with him, and Nish couldn't blame him for it. Phrune stumbled away, squealing like a stuck pig, and shortly a brief sparkle lit up the surroundings as he forced himself through an intangible barrier and passed out of the maze.

Nish slowly raised his hands. 'I'm Cryl-Nish Hlar, son of –'

'I know who you are, lad,' panted the sergeant. 'I'm a sergeant of your father's Imperial Militia and you'll come to no harm from me, but don't move. You're going back to Morrelune.' He looked the other way.

Monkshart had recovered and was slowly beating Vomix down. The seneschal was still firing bolts of uncanny force, though aftersickness appeared to be taking its toll, for they were feeble and the zealot avoided them easily. Monkshart raised his hands high and his expression slowly set hard as he prepared a killing blow.

Nish didn't see the sergeant move, but a knife flashed from his hand, its hilt striking Monkshart on the right temple, and he fell without a sound. Vomix lurched across, picked up the knife and was about to plunge it into the zealot's eye when the sergeant caught his hand.

'The God-Emperor will not be pleased if you kill the man who once saved his life.'

Taking the knife, he slid it into its sheath, then tore the sleeve off Monkshart's coat, exposing the ravaged skin of his arm. The sergeant gagged him with part of the sleeve, pulled the coat over his head and bound it down tightly to blindfold him. Before Monkshart had recovered, his red-raw fingers had been fastened together so he could work no spell, and his hands tied behind his back.

Nish should have run, but he was so dazed from overusing clearsight that he couldn't think clearly. He stumbled for the exit but Vomix blocked the way, and before Nish could get by, the sergeant had taken him from behind. Tink swiftly bound Nish's hands, gagged him and tied his coat over his head.

'Lead them out, Tink,' Vomix gasped. 'Let's see where we've ended up. I hope the maze hasn't taken us too far.'

Nish prayed that it had. He felt the sergeant's strong hands working at his bonds. 'I've tied you to Monkshart so there's no point running. This way.' Tink turned Nish around.

'Keep a sharp eye out for that cur of an acolyte,' said Vomix, who was recovering. His resilience was astonishing. 'Though I'll bet he won't stop running until he reaches the Great Ocean.' He snorted. 'You're alone and friendless, Cryl-Nish. You'll be back in your father's hands before you can say torture chamber. I'll catch you up,' he said in a lower voice to the sergeant, then muttered something that Nish did not catch. He heard Vomix walking away.

Nish began to walk, despair rising up his throat like bile.

Maelys watched helplessly as the brief battle went one way, then another, until Phrune fled and Nish and Monkshart were taken. It was all over in a couple of minutes and, though there was nothing she could have done, she bitterly regretted letting Vomix live, earlier. If she'd had the courage to stab him to the heart when she'd had the opportunity, she and Nish might now be out of the maze and on their way to safety.

Vomix lurched up the slope, grinning from one side of his sick mouth to the other. 'I always win in the end,' he said, jerking her towards him. 'The God-Emperor will reward me beyond all measure for what I've achieved today. And do you know what I'm going to ask for, as part of that reward?'

'What?' She managed a painful croak.

'You, little Maelys. I'll ask Jal-Nish not to damage you, outwardly. I wouldn't like my pleasure in you to be marred in any way. And then I'm going to break you in. Do you enjoy pain?'

She didn't want to communicate with him in any way, for that was all part of his game, but if she didn't respond she'd suffer for it. She jerked her head.

'You will. In my bedchamber, ecstasy and agony are inseparable. You'll come to beg for it.'

Down below, the sergeant was leading Nish and Monkshart through the barrier. Their outlines sparkled, wavered a shimmering yellow, then became shadows beyond the transparency that blended with all the other shapes and shadows. Maelys wondered if she could stir up trouble between them. It was worth trying.

'You'd better keep an eye on the sergeant,' she croaked, all she could manage. 'He has no reason to love you.'

'We both serve the same master.'

'But does Sergeant Tink want to share the credit for this victory?'

He smacked her in the mouth with a gauntlet. 'Don't treat me like a fool.'

He clicked his fingers and the paralysis was gone, though she still couldn't speak above a whisper. He began to drag her down the path, kicking Jil in the ribs on the way past. She woke dazedly and he snarled, 'Bring the brat. Don't make a sound or he dies.'

The barrier had barely any resistance as they followed the path through it – it was no harder than pushing through a soap bubble, and that was peculiar. Where was the maze country anyway, and how could it be separated from the real world by such a fragile barrier? Maelys stepped out into the normal world, into a sweltering wave of heat and humidity. The air was sticky and scented with a rich muskiness that was unfamiliar. Perspiration burst out all over her.

Ahead and down the slope, a wall of tall trees with huge, moss- and fern-covered trunks cut off all view of the distance. Behind her a curving outcrop of grey granite formed a broken cliff, a good thirty spans high, which curved in either direction further than she could see. There was no sign of the transparent barrier though she felt sure it coincided with the granite cliff. Its surface was pocked with fern-covered crevices and long wet fractures, while a shear zone at the base had eroded away to her left leaving a mossy overhang. Tall ferns and glossy-leaved shrubs luxuriated in the damp soil along the bottom.

Vomix was feeling the cliff, doubtless trying to work out how such a powerfully uncanny place as the maze could exist without the God-Emperor knowing of it, and trying to find a way that he, Vomix, could profit from it. Was the maze part of the Pit, or had it been created separately by Monkshart? Or was it a place apart? Either way, Monkshart must be a mancer of rare and enigmatic talents.

Vomix might also be thinking that Monkshart had been Jal-Nish's friend, and that Jal-Nish had sworn never to harm him. What if Monkshart turned his coat again? Jal-Nish might welcome him back and, in exchange for the secrets of pit and maze, might reward him with favours that rightly belonged to his faithful Seneschal Vomix, who had never wavered.

Vomix eyed Monkshart's broad back, licked his lips, then eased the dagger in its sheath, caressing its bone hilt. He looked around and Maelys hastily averted her eyes. A man who contemplated killing his master's former friend could permit no witness to such thoughts.

He dragged her across to a sapling in the shadow of the cliff, swiftly bound her to it, and tied Jil nearby. Vomix didn't bother with Timfy. 'Don't make a sound,' he hissed.

She still couldn't speak loudly enough to call to Nish. Maelys watched Vomix walk along the base of the cliff to the sergeant, who stood with Nish and Monkshart. Nish did not know she was within a hundred leagues, or even alive, and she had no way of telling him.

Vomix pointed to the granite wall. 'Climb up that cleft. See if you can see a landmark.'

The sergeant nodded. 'Keep a sharp lookout. The acolyte –'

'He won't get past me.' Vomix led the prisoners away around the curve of the cliff.

The sergeant walked along to the cleft and began to climb. He was gone some time, but when he came trotting along the base of the cliff from the other direction he was grinning. 'I recognised a citadel tower just a league away, for I served there once, as a common soldier. It's Gundoe.'

'Gundoe!' said Vomix. 'But that's . . . that's a hundred leagues north of Tifferfyte, at least.'

'Closer to two hundred, as the skeet flies. It's not far south of the city of Guffeons.'

'How did we come so far? It would be weeks of walking in the real world.'

'A question the God-Emperor will want answered,' the sergeant said dryly.

'Keep an eye out for the acolyte. He's a dangerous man and he may have friends nearby.'

'He'll need a lot of friends to make any difference. I flashed a message to Gundoe, using the Imperial Militia's secret signal, and they answered. They'll have a mounted squad here within the hour.'

318

TWENTY-NINE

Half an hour had gone by and Maelys was counting down the remaining minutes with increasing desperation. Jil and Timfy were a good ten paces away, while Nish and Monkshart had been taken by the sergeant out of sight around the base of the cliff. The troops would be here soon, and no one escaped from the army's custody.

Maelys told herself not to give up hope. Surely there must be a way to use her dangerous new aura against Vomix? She was fantasising about that when she realised that she'd touched him earlier, in the maze. She'd put her hands on his face and pushed him away, yet he hadn't reacted, so her aura can't have been powerful after all. Her faint hope faded.

But what if it hadn't been her aura at all? What if the taphloid had stung him through her shirt? It had grown burning hot as she'd passed through the Mistmurk, and she'd glimpsed an aura around herself, though only for a second. Yes, that had to be it. The passage must have changed the taphloid in some way, and if she could trick him into touching it with his bare skin, it might distract him long enough for her to attack.

Vomix was heading down into the forest with a handful of dry grass, undoing his belt buckle. She hoped he suffered from constipation, like Aunt Haga. If he did, there might be time for this last desperate gamble.

'Timfy!' Her whisper came out almost normally. Vomix's spell must be wearing off at last. 'Do you think you could untie me?'

He trotted across, but Vomix's knots were cunningly tied and Timfy didn't have the strength to undo them. 'I'm sorry, Lady Maelys.'

'Keep trying,' she said distractedly, for she'd seen something moving on the shadowed part of the granite slope above and to her right. Who could it be? She couldn't make it out, though the mounted troops couldn't come that way. There was no sign of Vomix yet.

Someone dropped to the ground on her other side and she smelt a familiar sickly sweet and oily odour. Her head whipped around. Timfy scuttled out of the way.

'Phrune!' What was he up to? Better not say anything about being left in the village, or his night-time activities. Let him think she knew nothing; it might give her a small advantage. 'I thought you'd run away.'

'That's what I wanted everyone to think,' he said in a thick voice. 'Run away to fight later, that's my motto.' He gave her a sour grin. 'How did you get here, anyway? I wouldn't have thought you had it in you . . .'

'There's more to me than meets the eye.' Her voice was a little stronger now.

'Oh, indeed.' He looked her up and down as if measuring her for one of his master's body-gloves.

Maelys shuddered and looked away hastily, unable to disguise her revulsion. With the top of his head shaven down to red-speckled skin, two bloody holes where his ears had been and a cleft through the end of his nose which exposed its crusted insides, Phrune was more repulsive than usual. A shiver of fear passed through her. 'What are you going to do?'

'Since you and I are such good friends,' he caressed her arm with plump, oily fingers as he spoke, 'I'll be relying on you to create a diversion.'

'How?' she croaked, trying to pull away.

He drew a stiletto and Maelys shrank back, for her previous nightmare came flooding back as if it were happening now, but Phrune slipped the stiletto between her wrists. The bonds parted and the blood pulsed into her numb hands, making her fingers tingle. He slid the back of his hand across her cheek. 'Such beautiful skin. It would be a pity to waste it. I'm sure you'll think –'

He broke off, pressed a small knife into her hand and vanished into the shadows. Seneschal Vomix was making his way up the slope, a long way from where he'd entered the forest, moving quickly but quietly.

He gave her a cursory glance as he passed, then headed along the granite bulge towards Nish and Monkshart. Maelys couldn't see them from where she stood, though she'd heard Vomix talking to the sergeant earlier and knew roughly where they must be.

She surreptitiously tested the blade as she debated what to do. It was blunt; Phrune wasn't taking any risks with her. Phrune was a treacherous dog who couldn't be trusted, though for the moment their interests coincided. Could she sneak up on Vomix? Her heart began to race. Not a chance; as soon as she moved, he'd see her.

She had only one option, though it made her sick to think about using a child that way. So don't think about it, just do it. She drew out her taphloid and called softly, 'Timfy?'

'Yes, Lady Maelys?' He came across.

'Could you touch this and tell me if you feel anything? Be careful though.'

He stroked the taphloid. 'It's beautiful. It feels nice.'

'It's a taphloid, and it's always looked after me.' She guessed it only affected people with an ability for the Art. Vomix had said that his aura had felt turned inside out, so what if . . .?

'Can you do something important for me? Something no one else can do?'

'Yes, I can.' He lifted his chin.

'Could you give this to the bad man, Seneschal Vomix, and tell him you found it?'

'But I didn't find it. You had it all the time.'

Maelys sighed. Timfy was too well brought up. 'Close your eyes and hold out your hand.'

He did so. She put the taphloid on his palm and closed his fingers around it. His hand dropped a fraction under its weight.

'Open your eyes.'

He opened his eyes, and then his fingers. 'You just found the taphloid in your hand, didn't you, Timfy?'

He smiled. 'Yes, Lady Maelys.'

'So can you tell the bad man you found it?'

'Yes, Lady Maelys.' He trotted off around the curve of the granite wall, proudly.

Maelys felt ill. If Vomix realised what the taphloid was meant to do he would slay the lad out of hand, but what else could she do?

To her left, Jil was staring blearily at Maelys as if trying to work out what she was up to. Suddenly the colour drained from her face. 'Timfy!' she called in a voice as weak and cracked as Maelys's own. 'Timfy, come back! Maelys!' she hissed, 'I'll never forgive you!'

'It was the only way. Do you seriously think that monster will let any of us live?' Maelys said quietly. It wasn't a defence, for she didn't have one, but she owed Jil an explanation.

An agonised cry rent the air; *Vomix*. Maelys hurled her cut ropes away, stumbled to Jil and began to saw at her bonds. Jil's eyes flashed sparks, and as soon as her hands were free she began punching, slapping and tearing at Maelys's face with her nails, then snatched the knife and stumbled around the corner.

Maelys went after her, head ringing. She rounded the bend and stopped dead. Vomix was reeling about, holding Timfy's hand which still clutched the taphloid, and making a dreadful keening wail. The seneschal's face was so contorted, seemingly by his agony, that the skin had torn at cheek, left ear and brow. Blood ran down in curtains, dripping off his jaw. He kept shaking his swollen right hand as if trying to rid himself of the taphloid, but his hand had locked so tightly around Timfy's, and around the taphloid, that Vomix couldn't rid himself of it.

Her father must have set it up to conceal her small aura, but passage through the Mistmurk had transformed it and now, when someone with a different talent touched the taphloid, it reversed their aura agonisingly. Vomix was swinging from side to side, stabbing the air blindly with his sword. Maelys caught her breath – it would take only a single blow to slay the boy. Jil was hopping from one foot to another, waving the knife but unable to get close.

Maelys had to put things right; she had to stop Vomix even if it meant attacking him with her bare hands. As she stumbled towards them, Sergeant Tink came pounding along the cliff from the other direction, shouting, but Vomix couldn't take anything in save the deadly, tormenting device attached to his hand. He managed to open one eye, raised the sword in his left hand to plunge it into Timfy, and Maelys couldn't get there in time.

She snatched up a broken stick, hurled it at him like a spear and for once her aim was true. The jagged end caught him in the ribs, low down. He staggered and his sword drooped.

Jil sprang forwards, hacking at Vomix with the knife. He swiped the sword at her, knocking the knife out of her hand, but the sword slipped from his bloody fingers. Jil, with a look of dreadful determination, snatched it up, raised it high and hacked off Vomix's right hand, the one holding Timfy and the taphloid, above the wrist.

Vomix screamed thinly and reeled towards the cliff, running at it as if intending to run up it vertically. He crashed to the ground, rose with blood pouring from his mouth, nose and stump, and began to climb the crevice the sergeant had gone up earlier. Screaming hysterically, Jil prised the bloody hand off Timfy's and flung it after Vomix. Phrune, who stood further on, clapped his hands over his ears – shrill sounds appeared to cause him pain. Jil threw her arms around Timfy, squeezing him tightly, then wrenched the taphloid out of his fingers and hurled it at Maelys. The heavy little device struck her on the forehead so hard that she blacked out momentarily.

She came to on the ground, seeing double. Jil was running for the trees, her brother in her arms. In the distance, Phrune stepped out of the shade and hurled a stiletto at the sergeant. The blade took him in the right eye and he fell dead. Maelys was lying on the damp ground with her vision going in and out of focus when she made out Vomix at the top of the cliff, flailing madly with his truncated arm as if at an invisible enemy. He stepped off the cliff, plummeted into a ravine and she lost sight of him.

Maelys couldn't stand up, but if she didn't hide, Phrune would kill her too. Catching the taphloid by its chain, she dragged herself to the base of the cliff, towards the undercut partly concealed by ferns. She was wriggling backwards into the low space when Phrune appeared.

He bent, gingerly touched the fallen taphloid with a knuckle, then jerked away as if he'd been stung. His eyeballs rotated in their sockets and his mouth gaped. Maelys grabbed the chain and humped backwards but, before she could get inside, Phrune put his boot on the taphloid. He crouched down, took a rag from his pocket, folded it around the taphloid and tore the chain out of her hand.

Maelys felt a physical wrench as the taphloid passed into his keeping. She felt naked without it; exposed. Was her aura now visible to Phrune? She had to get away and hide. She dug her boot toes into the base of the crevice and pulled herself backwards a hand's width, then another.

Phrune wrapped the device in several folds of cloth

324

which he bound on securely with cord and stowed the package in a pocket. Maelys was really frightened now, for her head and shoulders were still exposed. He drew another stiletto and reached out for her throat but his eyes revolved again and Maelys snatched the knife.

She swiped it at him then humped backwards into the undercut, which was no higher than a bookshelf. It was cool and wet. She continued crawling backwards, holding the knife out in front of her. Phrune went down on hands and knees, but he was still shaky. She slashed at his face; he scrambled backwards out of sight.

Distantly, Monkshart gave a muffled cry. 'Phrune, Phrune!' Shortly she heard Phrune stumbling away.

Maelys had just enough presence of mind to pull the dangling ferns back in place to cover the entrance, then laid her cheek in the mud and closed her eyes.

THIRTY

After being tied up and having his coat bound over his face, Nish found it hard to follow what was going on, apart from the moment they crossed out of the maze into the real world. He recognised it instantly, because of the sudden assault on senses that had been confused and deprived for a day and a night. Not only the sounds of nature: water trickling down rock; a bird calling in the distance, its trill ending in a whip crack; wind in the tops of tall trees. But also the smell and feel of the real world: pungent wafts of leaf oils that previously he'd only smelt in unguents from the tropical north; a humidity that was all the more stifling because he couldn't loosen his clothes or uncover his face; the solidity of the ground beneath his feet.

Even more striking, however, as he passed through the slight resistance of the maze boundary into bright, burning sunshine, was the sudden relief of the pressure of the maze which had been in his mind all the time.

The sergeant bound Nish and Monkshart to separate trees and ordered them to remain silent. They had no choice, being gagged so tightly. Nish was standing in the hot sun and soon tickling sweat was running down his chest and back.

Before long the sergeant came back with a dipper of water. He loosened Nish's gag and allowed him to drink his fill, then restored the gag. To his left, Monkshart was gulping down his portion. Some time later Nish heard the sergeant and Vomix talking, and discovered that a squad of soldiers would soon be here.

He fought down panic. He must be stoic about his fate, since there was nothing he could do. His luck had run out. He closed his eyes, sagged against the bonds and managed to doze.

In battle, Nish had heard men dying in every imaginable form of violence, but the cry of agony that roused him was unlike anything he'd ever encountered. It was an agony of the soul, as if the man's very life essence was being ripped out of him, twisted into its negation and forced back in. Shivers rippled along Nish's arms; would he be next?

The sergeant yelled, 'Seneschal, what is it?' but Vomix didn't answer. The screaming sank to a quavering moan.

A child cried out then Nish made out a woman's hoarse voice. 'Let him go, you brute. Let him go.'

The moaning was cut off by the thump of a sword blade shearing through flesh and bone. Nish knew that sound too. Vomix screamed, though this time it was just normal human pain. Nish heard running feet; someone grunted, then a body thudded to the ground not far away.

He wrenched at his bonds, expecting to die. Nothing happened for some minutes, then the ropes were cut and the coat lifted off his head. He was dazzled by the brilliant subtropical light for a few seconds, then Monkshart cut the gag and Nish looked around, blinking. A bloody-faced, mutilated Phrune was heaving a stiletto out of the eye socket of the sergeant, who lay in the ferns at the base of a granite cliff. There was no sign of Vomix.

'I thought I heard a woman and a child.' Nish rubbed his sore mouth where the gag had cut into it.

'Fled, and good riddance,' said Phrune in a thick, oddly flat voice, the sound issuing from his gashed nose as well as

327

his mouth. He wiped the blade fastidiously on the sergeant's shirt and stowed it in a sheath strapped to his left calf, under his trousers. 'Come on. The troops will be here any minute.'

'What happened to Vomix?' said Monkshart, giving Phrune a shrewd glance.

'He fell off the cliff, up there,' said Phrune, pointing.

Monkshart's gaze followed his finger. Nish's did too. The drop into the ravine was a good ten spans and almost certainly fatal, but –

'I'll believe he's dead when I see the body,' Monkshart said quietly, rubbing his raw arms. He pulled the sleeves of his coat down over his hands, wincing. His corrugated face was criss-crossed with pain lines.

A horse whinnied distantly. 'This way,' said Phrune. 'Quick! And don't leave any tracks.'

They followed him down into the forest, being careful to leave no footmarks. Nish had an awful lot of unanswered questions but now wasn't the time to ask them.

An hour later, when they were well away into the forest, Monkshart drew Phrune aside into a wall-like copse of trees, saying over his shoulder, 'Stay here, Deliverer, while Phrune attends my skin.'

Nish nodded and lay on the decaying leaf litter, staring up at the sky. He was too weary to move. He heard muffled cries of pain from the copse, but must have dozed, for the next he knew Monkshart was standing over him, his cheeks gleaming with lotion, wearing a new set of tissue-leather gloves and looking just like his old commanding self.

They spent the rest of the day creeping through a forest of gigantic, widely-spaced trees festooned with vines and creepers, watching every footstep. They walked upstream or down along the bed of every stream they came to, and took extra care to leave no marks on the banks where they came out. Finally, at sunset, Phrune announced that they'd lost their pursuers.

'Vomix was scum,' Monkshart said, 'But he was also the God-Emperor's personal envoy, and Jal-Nish won't give up until he finds him.'

'It'll take him days to get here,' said Phrune, 'and in the meantime the soldiers won't learn anything.'

'Why not?'

'I used a charm to hide what happened back there. Enough to confuse minor mancers.' Phrune drew the zealot away and spoke quietly in his ear, watching Nish the whole time. Monkshart didn't look pleased. 'Very well,' he said at the end. 'I must know what she saw down below but there's nothing we can do to find out now. But they'll find the servant girl and the child.'

'I cast a temporary glamour at them too, so they'd get away, undetected.'

'That was uncommonly big of you, Phrune. I wonder why you didn't just slit their throats.'

'A generous impulse, surr, since they'd saved our lives.' Phrune smiled mockingly at his lie. 'The girl had Vomix's sword and wasn't afraid to use it, and he was still at large. By the time he went over the cliff, she'd bolted with the brat and there wasn't time to run them down.'

'No matter. Her tale will help spread the news about the Deliverer,' said Monkshart. 'It's time to put the plan in motion.'

He didn't look like a man who'd walked a day and a night without sleep, nor suffered such bouts of confusion in the maze. He was burning with zeal again, and Nish felt uneasy about it.

'What plan is that, Monkshart? I'm in charge, remember?'

'Of course, Deliverer,' said Monkshart blandly. 'And the first part of the plan is to find a safe refuge, wouldn't you agree?'

'Where do you have in mind?'

'I don't know this land but we're a long way north of Tifferfyte, near the city of Guffeons. I suggest we head there, and on the way I'll try to contact our allies. Let's put some distance between us and the soldiers, Deliverer.'

Nish couldn't argue with that, so after a frugal meal of withered berries he fell in behind Phrune. They tramped through the night until he was so weary that he couldn't keep his eyes open.

Not long before dawn, Monkshart and Phrune set up camp at the top of a stony ridge while Nish slumped against a rock out of the wind. They ate fat wood grubs baked in the ashes of the fire, spitting out the tiny hooked segment spines and the gritty mouth parts, drank stagnant water from a pool at the base of the ridge and finally, blissfully, wrapped themselves in their coats and slept. Nish didn't even dream.

He was woken by whispering in a singsong accent he didn't recognise, though it wasn't Monkshart or Phrune. Had they been discovered already? He schooled himself to remain still. It was mid-morning and he could feel the sun's heat through his clothes.

'Can that really be the *Deliverer*?' a youth whispered in awed tones.

'Shh, you'll wake him,' said another, a young woman. 'The poor man. He looks so thin, so tormented.'

'The Deliverer has suffered mightily for his people,' said Monkshart. 'The God-Emperor treats his son as cruelly as any rebel or criminal. See how he had Cryl-Nish flogged when he was still a boy?'

Nish felt his shirt being drawn up, and there came a collective gasp as the scars were revealed. He sat up, irritably jerking his shirt down. He didn't like his body being on public view, and especially not his whipping scars, which he still felt ashamed about. He'd richly deserved that punishment, the callow, unpleasant youth he'd been at the time, and wanted to forget it.

Eight people stood in a semi-circle around him, peasants

dressed in brown homespun. Most were young – three young women and two youths – but there were also two older men and a tall but shrivelled, white-haired crone.

His overwhelming urge was to snarl at them but Nish bit down on it. 'Good morning,' he said with forced politeness, wondering how they'd found him so quickly. If the word had got out already, his father's troops must know it too, and the garrison wasn't far away. 'How did you know I was here?'

No one spoke. They looked too awed, until one of the girls, a buxom, sturdily built lass with black hair and laughing eyes, said boldly, 'Master Monkshart came for us, surr, so we could worship –'

'Worship!' Nish bellowed, forcing himself to his feet and directing a furious scowl at the zealot. 'You went down and rounded up these . . . peasants in direct contravention of my orders, to *worship* me?'

The peasants took a collective step backwards, save for the crone and the young woman. She bit her lip, but did not lower her eyes as the others had. The crone was watching him, though he couldn't read her expression.

'Not exactly,' Monkshart said blandly, 'though at the nearest village I did seek out those who believed in you.'

'Why?' Nish could hardly contain his rage.

Monkshart drew him aside, saying quietly, 'The God-Emperor knows you're at large, Deliverer, and it won't take him long to discover where you came out of the maze. You've been lucky, uncommonly so, but you can't rely on it. You've no choice but to begin the uprising, and for that you must have supporters. These are the first. If you act the part here, by tomorrow the word will be spreading as fast as people can walk. Faster! Within a week you'll have a small army, and you'll need one. It will take an army of bodies to protect the core of the Defiance from your father's wrath.'

An army of living, breathing and disposable shields, he

331

meant, and Nish was having none of it. 'I'm not hiding behind anyone!' he snapped. His earlier moral flexibility still bothered him. There had been little choice but to leave the villagers of Tifferfyte to die, but Nish felt ashamed that he'd agreed to it with so little protest. He felt complicit; tainted.

'Then, what is *your* plan, Deliverer? Do you have one?'

Nish's only plan was to give Monkshart and Phrune the slip as quickly as possible and make his way to the rain-shrouded plateau he'd seen in the Pit of Possibilities, but he wasn't going to give the merest hint about that. He never stopped thinking about it, though.

'I thought not,' said Monkshart quietly. 'You'd better go along with *my* plan, Deliverer, for without it we'll be screaming in the God-Emperor's torture chambers before the week is out. Go to your followers and sway them, and do it quickly, for they're looking uneasy. Once they lose faith they'll start to focus on the perils of following the Deliverer, and soon someone will decide that there's more to be gained by betraying you than supporting you. They cannot be allowed to lose faith. The Defiance must either grow like an avalanche, or fail and be crushed. There's no middle way.'

He was right. It was the only course and for as long as Nish was stuck with Monkshart he'd better follow it. Could it work? He had no idea. Nish took a deep breath and turned back to his followers. Could eight people really start a revolution? Or would they, and all who followed them, fall to his father as every other rebel had?

It reminded Nish that Maelys had seen into his father's mind, and that he believed he was close to becoming invulnerable and immortal. He had to be stopped, every second counted and for the moment Monkshart's way was the only way.

Nish noticed that Phrune was staring greedily at the buxom young woman, his tongue flicking across his lips. Nish felt an urge to kick his feet from under him, but he suppressed it. If he were to become the Deliverer he had to make use of whatever tools came to hand, even Phrune, though he felt cheapened by the man.

Nish looked into the eyes of each peasant in turn, then focussed on one. Not the lass with the flashing eyes, to whom he was instinctively drawn, physically at least, but the crone with the thin white hair and a face as seamed as saddle leather. Her eyes were clouded and he guessed that she was nearly blind, but they never left his face, as if she were searching for something in him. If she found it, she would sway the others.

'Just over ten years ago,' he said softly, so they had to stretch forwards to hear, 'we won the war that humanity had been losing for a hundred and fifty years. And despite the conniving and treachery of some of the most powerful people in the land, we won it honourably.

'We did not crush our enemies, thus making them hate us all the more. We made peace with the lyrinx, who had sprung from humanity in the distant past after being exiled to the void for their beliefs. We gave them their own world, Tallallame, to wrest back from savagery, and they took it and departed in friendship. The invading Aachim, sadly weakened by the folly of their leader, we gifted with the desert land of Faranda to make it bloom. Once all that was done, we sat down to plan a new and better world, *for everyone.*'

No one spoke; no one fidgeted. Their hungry eyes were fixed on him. 'But in the very moment of our victory, peace and freedom were snatched from us by my father and his sorcerous tears, Gatherer and Reaper, aided by the folly of one of the heroes of the war who caused all the nodes in the world to explode, one after another.' Brilliant, unhappy Tiaan. He wondered what had happened to her. Dead at his father's hand, he felt sure. 'We tried to stop Jal-Nish but we allies were scattered, slain or taken.

'My father didn't just want supremacy, though. He also

wanted revenge and he hated my beloved Irisis most of all. She should have fled with the others but Irisis could never run away. She gave her life to save mine – the greatest gift any person can give – and remained nobly defiant to the end. When Father had her slain, I swore to endure the worst he could put me to, for however long it took. I swore to help build the resistance in her name.'

His voice strengthened. 'I swore that one day I would return, and that together we would tear down the tyrant and all his evil works. That promise has troubled me ever since, for I am just a man, no braver than any of you. Many times I've wavered, and many times my courage has failed me, but the day has come and here I stand, ready to fulfil my oath. The Defiance has been formed, and *blooded*. The villagers of Tifferfyte, two hundred leagues to the south of here, gave their lives just the day before yesterday so we could win free.'

There was a stir of disbelief in the crowd.

'It's true,' Nish said, looking into the cloudy eyes of the old woman. 'We travelled two hundred leagues in one day, *on foot*, from the Pit of Possibilities at the dead heart of an exploded node of power, a place not even the God-Emperor's Gatherer and Reaper could reach, all the way to the cliffs near Gundoe. And how did we do it? Through an unknown force; a new Art the God-Emperor knows nothing about. He told the world that he held all the Arts there were, didn't he?'

Nish looked to each of the villagers in turn, and they nodded.

'That's what Father said, *and he lied*. Why did he lie?'

No one answered.

'Because he's afraid!' Nish boomed. 'He's terrified that we've recognised his one weakness and know how to attack him.' Suddenly Nish felt Monkshart's curious eyes on him. Better not go any further down that path; he didn't want the zealot to wonder about what else Nish might have seen in the Pit of Possibilities.

'Yes, my friends, there *are* other Arts in the world, and other powers too. Yesterday we used one to walk the maze, two hundred leagues beneath the very roots of the mountains, on a path no man or woman has ever dared tread before.

'But not alone. We were hunted all the way by Seneschal Vomix, the most feared and hated of all the God-Emperor's lieutenants, at the head of a squad of the Imperial Militia. Now the militiamen lie dead in the maze, and Vomix fell where we came out of it. The God-Emperor's servants *can* be defeated, and so can he. He *will* be defeated if we can just hold to our purpose.

'Separately we're nothing. Together we will make the Defiance into an unstoppable force that will sweep from one side of Santhenar to the other. Together we will topple the God-Emperor, destroy his evil works, and create the new and better world that we've been crying for since the end of the war. Together we will do this, my friends.'

Nish reached out to include them all, met the eyes of each in turn, and bowed his head. He'd never been much of an orator, and in his ears the speech sounded awkward, uninspiring; an appeal it would be easy to ignore.

But it must have had something, for the old woman clapped her hands, once, and as though they'd been waiting for her approval, the peasants let out a roar of acclamation, then rushed forwards to touch him. She followed slowly, but as her fingers met the back of his hand he sensed something in her with his enhanced clearsight.

She was more than a nearly blind old woman – she was a *mover*, one who could help to shape the future, his future, and it was no accident that his steps from the Pit of Possibilities through the maze – *his* vision of the path – had brought him out near her village.

Monkshart was talking to a grizzled peasant, perhaps the headman of the village, when the old woman turned away, stumbled and caught at Monkshart's arm. He broke off, staring into the distance, though once she'd steadied herself he resumed as though nothing had happened.

After they'd gone, Monkshart clapped Nish on the shoulder. 'A competent address in the circumstances, Deliverer. Your sincerity made up for your inadequacies as an orator and a trifling charm of my own made the difference. Under my tutelage you'll improve with every oration, and before we stand on the golden steps of Morrelune you truly will be the Deliverer, in word as well as in deed. Now we must move, swiftly and unpredictably.'

The peasants went back to their village and Monkshart pressed on, following random paths the choice of which he confided to no one. Nish never went near a village, for they all had wisp-watchers and some would be secret ones, but Monkshart slipped away each time they camped, to return with more and ever more awed peasants, *believers*. His charisma had turned the bloody slaughter at Tifferfyte into a noble sacrifice and a clarion call whose echoes reached further every day.

On the second day dozens came, while the day after that, hundreds gathered to hear Nish speak and touch him if they could. By the fourth evening Monkshart no longer needed to leave the camp, for the word was spreading like an avalanche.

At the end of a week the camp was surrounded by thousands of true believers who had brought tents, supplies, weapons and some mounts, and most never went home. Nish's hoped-for quiet march had become a noisy pilgrimage that must have been ringing alarm bells all the way up and down the east coast.

But it got worse. The pilgrims were beginning to treat him as a kind of messiah, bringing crippled children to be blessed and pleading for favours of every kind, including the kind that he longed for desperately but could not bring himself to accept – the young women whose eyes followed him everywhere he went, and whom he was constantly having to eject from his tent in the middle of the night.

Being treated as a messiah was the last thing Nish wanted, and he now realised that Monkshart had been using him all along. But what did Monkshart really want?

THIRTY-ONE

Maelys woke with such a desperate headache that, for a minute at least, she wished she had died. She opened her eyes, which hurt even though it was dark. Or had she gone blind? She remembered being hit on the forehead and Phrune coming after her, though the memories after that were fuzzy. She tried to get up but it felt as though the weight of a mountain were holding her down.

Closing her eyes, she slumped onto the muddy rock and drifted back into an exhausted sleep. Whatever Monkshart and Phrune had planned, there was nothing she could do to stop them.

The next time she woke it was daylight and her mouth was so dry that her lips crackled when she licked them. Her head felt better though. It hardly ached at all.

She couldn't see anything but the green outlines of ferns – she was still under the shelf-like overhang. Maelys wriggled out through the ferns and was reaching instinctively for her taphloid when she remembered Phrune taking it. It had seldom left her hands since her father had given it to her. She felt a pang of loss, though she was too desiccated to shed a tear for the only treasure she'd had left. Besides, it had done its work. The image of Vomix convulsing as he desperately tried to rid himself of the taphloid would never leave her.

She didn't quite understand that; didn't have the energy to think about it either. Maelys stumbled out into brilliant sunshine that hurt her eyes and crept along the base of the cliff in the shade, looking for water. She was sure she'd heard it trickling earlier, and around the curve came upon a moss-covered buttress of granite, facing south, threaded with tiny ribbons of water from a seep. She lapped at them like a dog, washed her face and hands, wet her hair, and pressed herself against the surface until her gown was saturated.

Sitting with her back to the wall, she tried to work out what to do. Nish, Monkshart and Phrune must be long gone, though she couldn't tell if they had escaped or been captured. The lush herbs and ferns along the base of the wall had been trampled flat by a host of men with big feet, the soldiers from Gundoe Citadel.

Nish was gone without ever knowing that she was alive, or what she'd done to save him. And he'd been so close. At one point she could almost have reached out and touched him.

Jil had fled with Timfy and Maelys couldn't blame her. Using the boy against Vomix had been unforgivable, even though it had saved all their lives. And perhaps Jil had thought she'd killed Maelys, and had fled to avoid being taken for punishment.

They were all gone. She was alone and friendless. Half of her mission had succeeded, the other was an utter failure. The only consolation was that both Vomix and the sergeant were dead, so her identity was safe; and her family.

She turned back to the streaming wall and lapped at it until her belly was full, then headed down into the forest, avoiding the tracks made by the soldiers.

Going nowhere.

After an hour or two she came to a pebbly stream, just deep enough to lie in with her nose sticking out. The water was tepid and hardly cooled her at all, but it was a pleasure to

339

scrub herself clean, clothes and all. Afterwards she tramped the banks on both sides, searching for Monkshart and Nish's trail, but if they'd come this way they had hidden it carefully. After weaving a broad-brimmed sun hat from reeds, she continued, heading north, since the plateau of Nish's true future lay that way.

There was no sign of winter here. The nights were pleasantly mild, and only in the hours before dawn did she ever feel cool, but the days were sweltering and unbearably humid for someone who had lived all her life in the cool southern mountains. She couldn't imagine what it would be like here in summer.

The plants were unfamiliar too, though on the second afternoon she discovered a bramble thicket behind an abandoned cottage which held enough late fruit to gorge herself on, and fill a basket woven from dry grass. The morning after that she tickled a fish out of the river and ate it raw, even the eyes. It was flavourless and full of tiny bones that stuck in her teeth, but she was too hungry to care.

Late in the afternoon she made out a village downstream on the far side of the river. Remembering the doom she'd brought to Byre and Tifferfyte, Maelys didn't approach it at once. She followed the river down until she was opposite the village, then sat under a tree, watching what went on there and trying not to think of her empty belly.

She had nothing with which to buy food, for Vomix had stolen her bracelet before he'd kicked her pack away into the maze. She could work for food if there was work to be had, or she could beg, though beggars were often taken before the wisp-watchers and picked up by the next patrol, for the God-Emperor's workhouses.

Maelys had no choice. She didn't know where to find Nish's plateau, so she'd have to ask, which would immediately put her at risk. Besides, though she was resourceful enough to find food where it was available, and to hunt small animals, feeding herself would take most of each day. She could make rude

340

shoes from hide when her boots wore out, though untanned leather would stink and not last long. However, she couldn't replace her gown which, after another week of travel, would be as stained and battered as any vagabond's. Then people would treat her like one and drive her off.

She scanned the village again. She couldn't see a wisp-watcher from here, though there was bound to be one. However, a crowd of people were setting up trestles in a shady meadow by the water, below the high upper bank of the river. People were often more friendly on market day, at least until they'd sold their goods and drunk too much sour wine. Maelys headed for the ford.

But it wasn't market day and no one was drinking. They were listening to someone standing halfway up the sloping bank, out of sight of the wisp-watcher. The villagers were tall, lean and dark-skinned, nothing like her, and she expected them to push her away. One or two people gave her curious glances as she edged into a space in the crowd, but they didn't look unfriendly.

The speaker was an old woman with white hair and a leathery, seamed face, and she was concluding a speech.

'. . . when the Deliverer spoke, his tale brought tears to my old eyes. He has come a long way to find us, my friends, and suffered grievously to get here, but he never faltered.' She took a breath.

'Ten years we've groaned under the yoke of the God-Emperor. Ten years he's been killing or taking our *talented* ones, never to be seen again. For ten years his brutal officers have abused our sisters, wives and daughters. And for ten years we've had but a single hope – that his son would return as he promised to do, and overthrow the father.

'The Deliverer has honoured us by beginning his campaign in our beautiful Campanie. Now it's up to us to honour him. Will we rise up to support the Deliverer, or cower in our beds and allow the God-Emperor to tighten his grip on the world until all hope is lost?'

She looked over the gathering with clouded eyes, as if staring into the future, and Maelys felt a shiver run up her spine. This old woman, and others like her, had the power to make Nish's campaign, or break it.

'It will not be easy. Many of us will die, more will suffer, and we could well fail.' Her eyes moved back and forth across the crowd. 'Or be betrayed. Or,' and now the chill covered Maelys's entire back, 'we could betray the Deliverer and the Defiance to the God-Emperor and be rewarded beyond our wildest dreams.'

Again she scanned the crowd and her eyes appeared to settle on Maelys for a moment before moving on. 'We could betray him here and now, though how would we sleep in the jewelled beds the God-Emperor rewarded us with, knowing that we'd robbed the world of the one good thing it had left – hope? I could not! We've never kowtowed to authority in Campanie. We've never given our allegiance willingly, save to those who earned it. We're rebels and proud of it, so let us do something, here and now, to make our children proud of us. The Deliverer needs us. Let us go to him. Let us begin the Defiance, right here. Right now!'

The crowd seemed to draw in a deep breath, and hold it. Only the old woman looked calm – no, serene – as if she already knew what their response would be.

Suddenly everyone in the crowd thrust their right arms high. 'The Deliverer! The Defiance!'

Maelys did the same, without hesitation, caught up in the intensity of the moment. 'The Deliverer! The Defiance!'

She lost sight of the old woman as everyone began leaping about, shouting, yelling and embracing one another, and even her. Then a big man clapped twice, and the racket broke off.

'We have work to do,' the old woman said hoarsely, and two men helped her down from the bank.

The people went back to the village in ones and twos. Maelys was climbing the high bank, planning to ask if she could work for her supper, when she noticed the upper curve of the iris of a large wisp-watcher between the cottages. It wasn't pointing towards her but she hastily turned away, shielding her face with her arm, and ducked out of sight.

She was wondering what to do when she sensed someone watching her. She stiffened involuntarily, then made to climb down towards the river.

'Stay where you are, girl.' It was a man's voice. 'Turn around.'

She considered running but there were villagers between her and the ford, and they'd easily catch her. She half-turned, shielding her face again.

'Turn around!' the man said.

'Leave her to me, Vixil,' said the old woman from below. 'Off you go.' The man turned for the village at once. The old woman laboured up the bank. 'You've come a long way, girl, yet you don't look like a traveller.'

'W – what do you mean?' said Maelys.

'I'm not blind yet. You're born and bred in the misty mountains of the south coast, if I'm not mistaken.' The old woman touched her hair. 'Only the mountain dwellers of that region have such silky ebony hair and such creamy skin. From the shape of your face and the way you speak, I'd say you were a native of the province of Fadd, and not long left home.'

The old woman was no fool. The city of Fadd was only a week's walk down to the coast from Nifferlin Manor, and Fadd Province included the mountain spine where Maelys had lived all her life.

The old woman touched Maelys's cheek with a dry hand, but drew back at once, looking thoughtful. 'Yet your complexion is unmarred by sun and wind. Had you trudged hundreds of leagues from the south, it would not be.'

'I might have ridden,' Maelys said faintly. 'Or come by ship.'

'You don't walk like a rider.' She lifted the back of Maelys's

343

hand to her nose, sniffing it. 'And you've never seen the sea. You dwelt in the mountains all your young life and never travelled before this, yet here you are, looking as fresh as if you'd just left home.'

Maelys snorted, for she was dirty, sweaty, ragged and unkempt. She didn't ask how the old woman could tell so much about her. It was worrying enough that she could. 'What are you going to do to me?'

'Perhaps I'll take you with me – at least until I unravel your mystery.'

'Take me where?'

'To follow the Deliverer, of course.' The old woman's eyes were clearer now. 'All the way, as long as my legs can carry me.'

'But . . . you're . . .'

'A frail old woman who hasn't got long to live.' She laughed. 'I've buried three husbands and worn out four lovers, and all my children died in the war. I've no one to answer to, I'm tough as ironwood and I'm going on the great adventure of my life. Nothing can stop me save only Death, and do you think I'm afraid of her? I'll see the God-Emperor brought down first, or all hope lost.'

'Have you seen Nish – the Deliverer?' Maelys said, a trifle too eagerly. 'Is he all right?'

If the old woman noticed the slip, she didn't comment on it. 'He looked well enough, considering all he's been through. I *think* he has the mettle for it.'

'But . . . after what you just said . . .'

'The future is not fixed and can never be, no matter what fool or seer tries to tell you otherwise, *nor* what is seen in pool or pit. Even in the very moment of victory one random action can undo all, and the Defiance is a long way from its first sniff of victory. But we *will* defy the God-Emperor. Not for the likelihood of victory, but rather because the trying gives us hope, and without hope, life is no more than living death. What is your name, girl?' she rapped out.

344

'It's Maelys,' she said without thinking, 'and I'm *nineteen*.'

'Therefore not yet of age, and still a girl. I'm seventy-eight.' The cloudy eyes roved over her. 'You know him, don't you?'

'I – I –' How could she tell? 'The Deliverer, you mean?'

'Don't treat me like a fool, girl! I can see it in your eyes. You know the Deliverer and you want something from him.'

Maelys bowed her head, afraid of this old woman who saw everything so clearly, despite her clouded eyes. 'I know him,' she whispered.

'I'll take you with me, just to see what happens. It could be rather amusing. But tell me no lies.'

THIRTY-TWO

The old woman's name was Tulitine. She didn't say where she had come from, but Maelys gathered that she was a wise woman well respected in these parts for her herb lore, as well as for clear-sightedness in other ways unsaid.

Tulitine left the village at dusk, along with twenty-two believers who were off to follow the Deliverer. They separated a few hours later, and Tulitine, Maelys and Rog, a muscular, smiling farmhand who slept in the old woman's tent, took a wandering path, and she spoke at every village on the way. Consequently three days had passed before they reached the secluded valley where Monkshart had camped for the night. They arrived at the ridgetop on the eighth day after Maelys had emerged from the maze, in the mid-afternoon.

She looked down into the grassy valley, drew a sharp breath and threw herself out of sight. All the upper slopes were covered with tents, hundreds upon hundreds of them, crammed into every available space between round rocks and copses of umbrella-shaped trees.

'Is something the matter?' Tulitine limped up to her, leaning on a black, knobbly walking-stick. Rog followed with her gear.

'There's an army down there.'

Tulitine reached the top and looked over, moving her head from side to side as if that helped her to see better. 'Indeed, and it's ours. That's the Defiance, girl.'

'But . . .' Maelys looked up at the older woman, who stood taller, even though her back was bent. 'There are thousands of people down below, and it's only been a week since you met Nish.'

'I've been to twelve villages, calling on everyone there to join the Deliverer and fight for our freedom. Some of my friends are doing the same, as are many of the people they've swayed, and Monkshart himself. How many people would you say are down there?'

Maelys studied the scene. People were swarming everywhere and, for an instant, hope flared in her heart. If the Defiance could grow so quickly, maybe it was possible to overthrow the God-Emperor after all. 'Too many to count. Three thousand? Four?'

'I'd heard six thousand this morning, and more are coming all the time.'

'But the God-Emperor must know about them. They're not even trying to hide.'

'Oh, he knows, but why should he be in a hurry? He's never been beaten, and the Defiance presents him with the opportunity and the pleasure of teaching his realm another lesson. If he attacks tonight or tomorrow, the rebellion will end right here.' Tulitine turned to Rog. 'I'll take your arm for the journey down, if I may. My old knees find it harder going downhill than up.' She looked up at him, smiling girlishly, and Maelys could have sworn that the old woman fluttered her eyelashes.

Rog grinned and closed his big brown hand over her veined fingers. 'No one could take better care of you than I will, Tulitine, by day or by night.'

Maelys's euphoria passed as quickly as it had come. The God-Emperor had gigantic armies which were well-equipped, disciplined and highly trained. He had battle mancers, flappeters, air-dreadnoughts and all kinds of devices powered by the Secret Art, to say nothing of the tears themselves. He could never be beaten.

347

As they came down out of the scrub into an open meadow they were intercepted by two guards, though as soon as they saw Tulitine they bowed, smiled and turned away. Everyone knew the old woman and respected her, but it felt lax to Maelys. How many spies and agents of the God-Emperor were already in the camp? All he had to do was snatch Nish away, then fall upon the leaderless Defiance and butcher them. She shivered, though it was another hot day.

'Where is he?' The tents were all shapes, sizes and colours, and there was nothing to say which one was Nish's. She felt a sudden tightness in the chest, a shortness of breath. 'Where's Nish?'

Tulitine took her by the arm, drew her to one side and waved Rog ahead. 'Shh! From what you've told me, Maelys, which isn't as much as you might have, Monkshart and Phrune must not learn you're here, or else they'll finish the job they began in Tifferfyte.'

'But . . .'

'You told me that Monkshart won't allow the Deliverer to form attachments which could distract him from his purpose. And there's something else about you – something dangerous. I'm not sure what it is but Monkshart must have sensed it too.'

'Oh?' Maelys wondered about that. 'But I've still got to see Nish.'

'And so you shall, though not openly. Maelys, listen. You may think of me as a silly old herb woman, but I'm wise in the ways of the power hungry. Treachery is the God-Emperor's must valued weapon and it's how the Defiance is most likely to come undone. Trust no one.'

'Not even you, Tulitine?' Maelys's family had squabbled constantly, but clan loyalty was everything to them and betrayal unthinkable.

'What makes you think you can trust me?'

'We've been talking for days. I know that you're wise, and kind –'

'Am I,' said Tulitine coldly, 'or have I just put on a suitable face? Many mancers and illusionists could disguise their true selves to look like a harmless old woman. Who am I really, girl? What do I want, and how far will I go to get it?'

Maelys reeled backwards. 'But . . . but if I must suspect everyone I meet, what's the point of hope, or friendship . . . or life, for that matter?' She regarded Tulitine with her dark eyes, then said furiously, 'I trust my judgement; I do trust you, whatever you say to the contrary!'

Tulitine sighed. 'That's the only answer. You must trust your judgement above all else. Of course you can trust me, child. After all, how could an old woman like me harm anyone?'

Maelys smiled at that. Some of the most evil deeds in the Histories had been committed by crones as venerable as Tulitine, and they both knew it.

'What about Nish?' she said plaintively.

'Since you haven't seen fit to favour me with your full confidence, about either him or yourself, I have nothing to say.'

Maelys flushed. She hadn't told Tulitine her clan name, nor of her second duty to her family. 'We've been through so much together and I think . . . I –'

'You think you love him, though I doubt it's more than a girlish infatuation. Either way, trust him least of all.'

Maelys felt insulted. 'He's a good man!' she snapped. 'And I'm not a child, so don't treat me like one.'

'Then don't act like one,' Tulitine said mildly.

'I'm sorry. I didn't mean to be rude. I'm not normally –'

'I know that. You can't offend me, child,' said Tulitine. 'But I've touched Nish, so I know him almost as well as you do. Better, in some respects. He's a good man and a worthy Deliverer who will do his best to fulfil his promise, if the world will let him. But beware! He's subject to forces that would tear any normal man apart. His father works on him in all sorts of uncanny ways, seeking to tempt and compromise

349

him. And Monkshart who, though few knew it, was the God-Emperor's most powerful sorcerer and ally before he turned away –'

'I didn't know that!' cried Maelys. 'He said he was just a minor mancer.'

'And you believed him, though you had every reason not to? Monkshart, formerly called Vivimord, was the highest of the God-Emperor's lieutenants, with everything he could ever want save the one thing he could never have. Yet he gave it all up – for what?'

'On a matter of principle, Monkshart said.'

'And you believed him?' Tulitine repeated.

Maelys didn't say anything this time.

'I also touched Monkshart, or Vivimord. I can't be sure about him, though men like Monkshart seldom change. I suspect he wants what only Nish can deliver him, and he'll bend every iota of his intellect, will and mancery to the task of getting it. How can your friend resist these two opposing forces? Nish must bend one way or another or, like the tree that tries to resist the hurricane, he'll be torn apart.'

Maelys was silent for a long time. 'What am I to do? I've got to know if Nish callously abandoned me, or if he was duped by Monkshart.'

'And you'll feel better for knowing the truth?'

'I've got to know,' she said stubbornly, 'whatever the truth. And if Nish is in such danger, I've got to help him.'

'What if your presence would only make things worse?'

'I don't know!' she wailed. 'But I've got to do something.'

'Yes, you must. Go and sit under that tree, and watch,' said Tulitine. 'I'll find all-covering robes for you, as if you were a Healer of Flammermoul.'

'Won't that seem suspicious?'

'Not at all. The Healers are forbidden to show their faces, and no one with any respect would dream of asking them to. You'll be quite invisible, and you can keep an eye on Cryl-Nish while you busy yourself with good works. But you must not go so near that Monkshart will recognise you. Or Phrune. Or Nish, for that matter.'

Something occurred to Maelys. 'What about you, Tulitine?'

'What do you mean?'

'You say you understood Monkshart simply from touching him. What if he understood you, too? You could be in as much danger as I am.'

'Old women are never in as much danger as young ones, for we have so much less to lose. Don't worry about me; I take good care of myself. And there's Rog to look after me.' She turned away.

But Rog was just one man. And no matter how clever Tulitine was, how could she be a match for the man who'd formerly been the highest of the God-Emperor's lieutenants?

Maelys, swathed in the shapeless green gown, headpiece and veil of a Healer of Flammermoul, spent the next two days tending the sick and injured. She knew how to act the part, for Aunt Bugi had been the clan healer and Maelys had helped her since she'd turned seven.

There were many sick among the Defiance, mainly due to foul water, and injuries were common, generally from fighting, drunkenness or snakebite. Her first patient was suffering from all three, and her duties kept her so busy that she had no time to dwell on her own problems. She hadn't seen Tulitine since they'd arrived, and didn't know whether she was also in disguise or had left the camp.

Monkshart led the ever-growing Defiance in a wandering curve centred on the city of Guffeons, which was situated on the coast. It took over an hour to get going each morning and the caravan stretched for the best part of a league, scouring the land of everything edible as it passed. He seemed in no hurry to reach Guffeons, if that were his destination, for Campanie was fertile and well populated. Here he could recruit more followers in safety, or so he told the assembled Defiance.

351

Maelys, however, felt oppressed; the enemy was out there somewhere and her dread grew stronger every day. How could this ill-disciplined and poorly armed rabble hope to keep the God-Emperor's crack troops at bay?

On the tenth day, not long after noon, they camped on a tongue-shaped hill with rugged country at the back and swamp to either side, chosen because it was easy to defend. It was a long haul to get water, though. Maelys was wearily climbing the steep slope from the swamp with a bucket in each hand, sweating rivers in her confining clothes, when lightning struck the rocks at the back of the camp and the skies opened.

Before she reached the hilltop she was soaked to the skin and the camp had become a muddy, steaming wallow. The downpour flooded the floor of the tent she shared with half a dozen other women, though an hour later the clouds had blown away and it was blisteringly hot again.

She spent most of the afternoon tending twin brothers who had chopped down a dead tree for firewood but felled it on top of themselves. They had fifteen broken bones between them and it took most of the afternoon to set them and dress their injuries. Once they were sleeping she pulled the hood over her face, drew her veil up and went, as she did every day, to stand at the back of the crowd of supplicants who were milling outside the Deliverer's tent, hoping to gain audience.

Some she recognised as having been in waiting for days, while others were given audience without delay. She wondered why. She could just make out Nish in the shadows well inside the large tent, separated from his followers by four burly guards.

She was trying to get a better view when she saw Phrune seated in a little canvas foyer. His facial injuries had been rudely repaired and he glowed with self-satisfaction, which could only mean one thing. She hadn't noticed him in the camp before and such a surge of hate and disgust went through her that she choked. The man next to her gave her a curious look.

She hastily turned away, her thoughts racing. Monk-shart's tissue-thin body-leathers only lasted a few days before they had to be replaced, so Phrune must be up to his nocturnal activities again, stalking the young and innocent for their flawless skins.

It took two circuits of the vast camp site before she felt steady enough to go back. And Phrune had her taphloid. That was the worst thing of all. She couldn't bear to think of the only possession from her childhood, the gift of her dead father, in Phrune's depraved hands. What if he or Monkshart could look inside it and see the memories or lessons her father had hidden there for her? She had to get it back.

The supplicants were still milling in the blistering sun. Phrune interviewed each of them at length, chose those who would be permitted to see the Deliverer, and turned the rest away.

One young man had been refused every day since she'd been here, yet he always came back, standing on tiptoe to try and catch the Deliverer's eye. He was tall, with close-cropped brown hair and pleasant, regular features. He might have been called handsome save that his cheeks were hollow and he had a pinched look about him. He'd been worked too hard, with seldom enough to eat, she thought. Still, the world was full of such people, including herself.

Exhausted, she put him out of her mind and headed towards her sodden bedding for the briefest of naps, but all she could think of was her taphloid in Phrune's hands and the impossibility of getting it back.

THIRTY-THREE

By the tenth day the Defiance had grown to a force of eight thousand, though Monkshart's envoys and rumour-mongers told of twice or even thrice that figure. Most were armed with bows, swords or spears hidden since the end of the war, and they appeared to be a formidable force, from a distance.

But Nish had once commanded an army and was dismayed by what he saw. Of his eight thousand, many were beardless youths and young women who had never held a weapon before, while almost as many were middle-aged or old. They weren't feeble but their reactions were slow, their eyes weak and their muscles wasted. Less than a quarter had any battle experience, and that dated back to the war. Monkshart had made officers and sergeants from the best of these and set them to train the remainder, though it was not going well. They simply could not impose army discipline on the unruly peasants.

There had been no word of his father. No spies had been taken in the camp nor been seen watching it, and Monkshart's growing network of informers had heard nothing of any army on the march. The garrison at Guffeons, a force large enough to annihilate the Defiance, remained in its barracks. No flappeter had flown over the camp in all this time. Why not? The whole world must know he was here by now, so why was Jal-Nish holding back?

His crack troops would carve through the Defiance like a knife through cheese, and Nish pointed this out to Monkshart daily, but the zealot brushed aside his criticisms. Monkshart wasn't concerned about casualties; indeed, he seemed to welcome them for their use in his increasingly well-oiled propaganda machine.

Nish wanted to take charge of his forces and train them properly, but Monkshart had other work for the Deliverer and Nish couldn't sway him. He'd lost that dominance he'd had after coming up from the Pit of Possibilities, couldn't get it back, and felt the failure keenly. If he couldn't even assert control over the zealot, how could he hope to succeed when the Deliverer faced a real challenge?

The one issue on which Monkshart had given way was in the selection of the camp each evening. Nish chose each site to be as defendable as possible, though successful defence required discipline above all else, and he had an untrained rabble.

Every morning at five, when it was still dark and pleasantly cool, Monkshart took Nish to a guarded tent pitched well apart from the others and tutored him in oratory. First off, Nish had to improvise an address on a minute's notice. As soon as he finished, Monkshart tore it to shreds then demanded another, on a different topic, which he dealt with just as cruelly, followed by a third and a fourth. An hour of such toil left Nish wrung out, but Monkshart had barely begun.

He handed Nish a scroll, closely written on both sides. 'What's this?' Nish said sourly, 'One of yours?'

'It's Rulke's famous speech to the assembled Aachim after he single-handedly took their world from them. Read it once, remember it then deliver it as he would have done. It'll be a nice contrast to the rambling orations you've been tormenting me with.'

Nish did his best with Rulke's hauntingly lyrical words, but muddled the beginning, left out the middle and trailed off at the end without ever making Rulke's most important point. He didn't need to see Monkshart's barely controlled rage to know that he'd been embarrassingly bad.

Next he was given one great speech from the Histories after another, each of which he had to remember and deliver, perfectly, after a single reading. The zealot savaged each of these performances as well, and so the morning went on until Nish was hoarse and his mind numb. Monkshart never pronounced himself satisfied; the highest praise Nish gained, and that was seldom, was that his oratory had been almost adequate . . . for a beginner.

After a short break in mid-morning, Nish wrote the oration he would give to the assembled Defiance that afternoon, though it generally took a dozen drafts before Monkshart expressed a modicum of satisfaction. Nish found this labour even more trying, being unaccustomed to writing his thoughts down.

In the early afternoon he held court in a sweltering tent, meeting delegations and pleaders for favours, sorting out disputes and, where required, dispensing justice. He hated this most of all. He felt like a pretender to his father's throne, and nothing could have been more calculated to bring the God-Emperor's wrath down on the Defiance. Why was he holding back?

Once the day began to cool, Nish addressed the multitudes after Monkshart had whipped them into a fervour with his brilliant oratory. Nish didn't try to compete – if he'd practised every day for a decade he would not have had half of Monkshart's skill. He kept his words simple and his message direct – he'd given his promise and he was here to deliver it. Together they would cast down the God-Emperor and create a better world.

It seemed enough, and afterwards he walked among the Defiance, despite Monkshart's objections that it was now better to remain aloof. Monkshart wanted to control him, but equally wanted to control who met him. As Nish moved

356

through the camp he could see Phrune and his marshals forming barriers between him and those undesirables Monkshart didn't want him to meet, and Nish didn't have the strength to fight that battle as well.

Afterwards he returned to the tent with Monkshart and Phrune to continue work on their strategies and tactics for the campaign.

Finally, generally after midnight, Nish went gratefully to his guarded tent, where every night he had to eject a comely young woman from his bed, and once a brace of them. He sent them away as politely as he could, though they, or others, often reappeared in the night. He ordered the guards to keep them out; they nodded, winked, slyly tapped the sides of their noses and did nothing. Apparently Monkshart personally interviewed and selected each young woman according to what he knew of Nish's tastes.

Each time it was harder to send them away; he could feel his resolve weakening daily, and damned Monkshart for manipulating him in yet another way. Nish took a surly pride in not having succumbed. Yet.

Nish shot upright in his bed, heart pounding. The ululating shrieks seemed to be plunging right at him, rising in pitch as they came.

He had taken to sleeping in his clothes as an extra barrier against the night intruders. He thrust his feet into his boots, laced them up and ran outside. The camp was dimly lit by the night's dying fires, which gave enough light to show a flappeter hurtling down towards his tent. How had it known where to find him? There must be a spy in the camp.

It rocked in the air, levelled out and raced towards him, its pairs of legs extending like a black spider's. Nish, slow to realise its intentions, threw himself to the ground as the flappeter shot overhead. A foot hook snagged in the back of his shirt, jerking him into the air and carrying him along, swinging wildly.

Its rider was leaning over the side, grinning in triumph. Taking Nish had been easier than he could have dreamed. The other pairs of legs were reaching towards Nish and he had to get free now, before they took an unbreakable grip. He thrashed his arms, kicked his legs, and felt the thin fabric of his shirt tear.

It slipped along the hook but unfortunately snagged on a seam, which held. Nish threw his arms up, wriggled violently, and the shirt, which was large and loose, began to slip free. Another foot hook caught it. Nish punched it out of the way. A third came at his face; he wove to one side, gave a mighty thrash like a fish trying to escape from a hook, tore free and fell onto a nearby tent, collapsing it onto the people inside. A woman's voice cried out in terror; another joined it, and another.

Rolling off the heaving canvas, Nish came to his feet. He couldn't see the flappeter that had attacked him but another was sweeping down on the row of tents. Catching a set of tent ropes in its hooks, it tore the pegs out of the ground, dropped the tent on the one next door and continued down the line, ripping up more tents and dropping them on others, on the panicked people milling in the dim light, and onto the camp fires. Nish saw people carried high into the air and flung away like missiles before the flappeter, its momentum spent, feather-rotored away.

The other beasts had done much the same. Fires sprang up all over the camp. People, many naked from their bedrolls, were screaming and running in all directions. Now arrows and crossbow bolts began to fall out of the sky as the unseen riders fired down at them. In the densely packed throngs, many missiles struck.

'Spread out!' Nish shouted. 'Take what cover you can,' but in the din no one heard him.

Was the attack just meant to unsettle them, or was it cover for something larger? There had been no news of an army on the march, though even as far back as the war some battle mancers had been able to *cloak* a large force of soldiers. He wove his way to the edge of the camp and looked over the steep side of the hill. He couldn't see anything, not even with the clearsight which was still holding back on him since leaving the maze.

He moved down the slope, torn shirt flapping, until the racket from the camp faded. The wet ground squelched beneath his feet. Nish scanned the darkness. What was that? It sounded like a faint, rhythmic murmur. He turned his head this way and that, trying to make it out above the distant clamour from the camp. He continued down; the murmur was fractionally clearer here, and suddenly he knew what it was.

It was the massed tread of a marching army and they couldn't be far away. He scrambled up the slope to find the chaos unabated. Monkshart was bellowing orders but for the first time in his life no one was taking any notice. If someone didn't take command the Defiance would die here today, and he, Nish, was the only one who could do it. But first he had to have a battle plan.

He ran down the long ramp of the hill. They had one single advantage – he had chosen the camp site carefully, overriding Monkshart who had wanted to stop by a stream in a location that was almost undefendable.

The camp lay at the top of a flat hill with a curve of steep, rocky country at its back, and no army would choose to attack up those difficult slopes, though a squad of climbers might. Forwards, the hill ramped towards the plain in a narrow neck on either side of which were sharp slopes with marshland at their bases.

The army would have to attack up the neck. He was a third of the way along it now, crossing into a shallow dip. His boots sank to the ankles in sodden earth and his plan crystallised. The army would be attacking uphill on wet soil which would become muddy as they tramped through it, then through this boggy dip. Above here the neck narrowed before flaring out at the top of the hill.

He pulled his boots out of the sticky mud with an effort, and backed up onto solid ground. The enemy's formation, compressed at the narrows, would not be able to attack *en masse*, so if he could get his ragtag forces into position in time they would have another small advantage.

The flappeters had only made one pass and Nish didn't think they would be risked in the coming battle. They were too scarce and valuable, while men's lives meant nothing to Jal-Nish. Nish judged that the army was close to the bottom of the hill and could be here in ten minutes.

He wasn't sure he could even restore order in that time; the Defiance sounded close to panic and if he couldn't gain control right away it would be too late. Once they got wind of the army they would abandon their weapons and flee. Could he do it? He had to try; and after all, he'd led his men in equally hopeless battles during the war.

Nish ran back to the camp and snatched sword and shield from a guard who lay groaning on the grass with an arrow in his belly.

'To me!' he roared, leaping onto one of the dinner trestles and banging his sword against his shield. 'Now is the hour of our greatest need. Your Deliverer needs you. To me!'

Their sweating faces reflected the firelight as they turned his way, just a few at first, then more and more as he continued to bang sword on shield. It wasn't light enough to read their faces, though he sensed that he hadn't got through to them. Another aerial attack could see them panic and bolt; news of the enemy certainly would. They were at the point where the actions of a few hotheads or cowards would decide the fate of all. He had to get to them first.

'Quiet!' he roared, and this time they stopped talking. They were used to listening to him in silence, thankfully. 'Any man or woman who speaks while I'm addressing you will be banished from the Defiance.' He eyed them, his glance sweeping over the crowd. 'Are you with me?'

'Yes,' they said unconvincingly.

'I said, *are you with me*?'

'Yes, Deliverer!' the crowd roared.

He took a deep breath. 'The enemy army is at the foot of the hill.' He pointed with his sword. 'They think we'll run like dogs, but they don't realise we've lured them into a trap!'

A shiver passed across the face of the crowd. He'd hit on the right approach by accident, but he still had to convince them.

'That's right, a *trap*! I chose this battlefield carefully. To beat us here, the enemy would need three soldiers to our one and they don't have the numbers. I, your Deliverer, will captain you against them. Follow my lead and we'll drive the God-Emperor's army into the swamps to drown. Once people hear of the Defiance's great victory, the whole world will rise up against the tyrant.

'Follow your Deliverer! Defiance, this way!'

Nish leapt off the trestle and ran towards the neck, not looking to see if they were following. He couldn't afford to show any uncertainty. After an agonising silence he heard the first feet behind him, and then the rest of them. But five minutes had passed, and they had to reach the narrow part of the neck well in advance of the enemy. It would take time to order his raw troops into defensive formation. More time than he had.

The fires cast a faint illumination down the slope; enough, as Nish reached the narrows, to show the dark mass of the army moving up the base of the neck. He continued to the centre of the dip, feeling the saturated ground sinking under his boots, then went backwards onto the slope above it, which had shed the rain and remained solid underfoot. It was the best defensive position he could hope to find.

'Spearmen,' he called, 'come forwards; form a triple line here.' He swept his sword back and forth across the neck. 'Swordsmen, form ranks behind the spears. Whatever happens, don't move until I give the order.'

The spearmen began to straggle into position, but they were so damned slow! Nish's throat had gone dry; he could hardly speak. 'Hurry, the enemy is on the march.'

He jogged back through the lines to the rear, showing himself to as many of his troops as he could and trying to look the part of the Deliverer. He didn't feel it. He felt sure they were all going to die.

'Archers!' Nish indicated the slightly higher ground to left and right, further up the hill. 'Take position there and there; be ready to fire over the heads of our troops. Don't shoot until I give the order.'

He sent scouts to keep watch from the rocky heights behind the camp, in case a detachment circled around and attacked from the rear.

Monkshart came running down the slope, dark robes flapping about his long shanks. 'What on earth are you doing, Deliverer? You can't risk yourself in battle.'

Nish brandished his sword and Monkshart stepped aside smartly. 'I lead the Defiance,' Nish shouted, raising his weapon high so the firelight blazed off it. 'To victory or to death!'

'Victory or death!' roared the Defiance, putting themselves between him and the zealot.

Nish headed back towards the front line. Monkshart drew his own weapon, though he didn't follow. Nish recruited a dozen boys and girls to act as runners, for his orders would not be heard over the din of battle, and crouched behind a spindly bush. The enemy were halfway up the neck now, advancing more rapidly than he'd expected.

He wouldn't have driven troops that hard, since the slippery climb would soon exhaust them in their heavy gear. And since there had been no sign of an army from the lookout last night, they must have made a forced march to get here. They would have been weary before they began the climb – another small advantage to the Defiance.

The leaders were so close now that he could make out individual soldiers. Nish sent runners back, ordering his archers to fire at once, and again as the enemy reached the top of the slope below the dip, then to be ready for hand-to-hand fighting.

He signalled his front-line troops to crouch down. They did so, clutching their weapons. Dawn was breaking and he could just make out their faces – fearful but, he hoped, resolute. The archers fired over their heads and the ragged volley opened up a few gaps in the enemy's front line, though not enough to make a difference to either side. He prayed they'd do better with their second volley, though massed archery fire required careful training and they hadn't had it.

An enemy officer ran out ahead of his fellows, waving his sword and urging them on. If Nish had brought a crossbow he could have picked him off. The army broke into a plodding run. Good! They'd be exhausted by the time they got to the dip.

The enemy archers fired from the flanks and a dozen of Nish's spearmen fell. A fresh-faced youth, the camp joker, began to scream in agony and jerk at the arrow in his belly. Other soldiers were moaning, wailing, begging for help. It could be enough to demoralise his green troops.

'Stand firm,' he cried. 'Fire!' he roared, running out into the open and brandishing his sword above his head. His archers fired again, though with no more impact than the first time. Return arrows whizzed by. He hastily dropped flat.

The advancing army reached the dip and began to labour, but the troops pressed on, their boots churning the wet earth to sticky clay. It would make the dip harder for those behind to cross, but Nish's previous optimism was fading rapidly. The enemy was a strong, disciplined force and, despite the advantages of position, he didn't think his troops were going to survive the initial onslaught. Once the enemy broke through their lines, the Defiance would be finished and so would he.

The light was growing rapidly now. Nish could see the insignias on the soldiers' shields, and the look in their eyes, for many of them had their helms up, the better to see.

Their archers fired a second volley. Arrows whizzed above him, tearing a bloody hole through the centre of his defensive line. Their spears were pointing in all directions, his troops able to think of nothing but their dead and dying friends. The first experience of bloody battle was always shocking, even for well-trained soldiers. Nish could see his troops' morale wavering. They were staring at the approaching tide in horror and if he didn't act now they would turn and run.

'Defiance!' he shouted, leaping to his feet. 'Rise up for your Deliverer. Rise up and come at them.'

The spearmen came to their feet in a sinuous wave and began a stumbling, shaky advance. The enemy were now churning through the dip, moving ever more slowly and wearily as the sticky clay clumped on their boots, making every step a labour. The front line now covered the slope and was jamming up as those behind continued to push forwards. Their archers could no longer see past them to shoot.

'They're bogging down,' cried Nish, waiting for the spearmen to reach him. 'They can hardly move.' He raised his sword. 'At them.'

They split to go around him and he went with them, sword out, knowing that the enemy wouldn't recognise him and he could die at any moment. His heart was pounding but he felt perfectly calm and clear-headed. He would wield his third-rate force as well as he possibly could and if he failed, if he died here, it would be the end of all his troubles. And maybe his death would inspire others to resist, as Irisis's death had been his inspiration and driving force. Either way, he would go with a smile on his lips.

He felt the ground soften beneath his boots. He was on the edge of the muddy patch. He took a step backwards onto firmer ground. 'Here we stand! The Defiance!'

'The Deliverer!' roared his troops, thrusting out their spears, and for the first time he knew they were with him all the way.

The grim-faced, staggering army came onto them and there was no more time for thought as they struggled and fought and slipped and died in the greasy clay that was soon sticky with spilled blood, brains and entrails.

Nish hacked and slashed, cutting up at the tall soldiers, his sword going into a groin here, a ribcage there. He twisted to tear out the blade then jerked sideways as a giant of a man hacked down at him with a two-bladed war axe. It shaved threads off his shoulder seams then buried itself to the handle in the clay. The soldier wrenched furiously at it but the suction was so strong that it wouldn't budge. He tried to step backwards to get a better heave but his boots had worked down into the clay and before he could pull them free a spear took him in the throat.

The enemy's whole front line had fallen now and, trapped in the sticky mud, those behind them made easy targets. Nish's spearmen started to advance. He ordered them back. 'Stay here, on solid ground. Let them come onto your spears.'

The enemy, ordered to clear the rebels as quickly and brutally as possible, trampled over their dead and dying comrades and continued driving onto the spears, and dying before they could reach their enemy. Their officers were so far back that they hadn't realised what the problem was.

The soldiers couldn't bypass the dip without crossing onto the steep sides of the neck above the marshes, which would put them at an even greater disadvantage. They had to scramble over their dead and dying comrades, and as they did they were cut down by the spearmen or the archers, now firing from the rises further back.

The army's archers still couldn't fire for fear of hitting their own men, but gaps were opening in Nish's front line as the relentless attack continued. Half his spearmen had fallen; the others had to be replaced with fresh troops or the battle would be lost. The enemy dead were now so many that they would soon form bridges over the bog, and if their superior troops were allowed to reach solid ground in any numbers they would sweep his amateurs away.

'Spearmen, fall back! Swordsmen, to the attack.'

His forces, fired up from seeing the enemy taking such terrible casualties, advanced in a rush. Nish stayed with them; having taken on the role of the Deliverer, he could do no less. He felt no fear; he didn't care whether he lived or died. All that mattered was to drive the enemy troops back, and deliver a blow to his father's pride that would inspire the suffering world.

But first he had to keep the enemy in the mud. It was time to take the battle to them. 'Advance!'

He sprang forwards up onto the carpet of bodies, and his swordsmen followed him in a cheering, screaming wave that drove the exhausted enemy back down the dip into the churned ground where, trapped in the sticky mud and with the soldiers behind them pressing forwards and leaving them nowhere to go, they died by the thousand. The carnage was sickening. The memories would stay with him until he died, but there was no choice. It was kill or be killed.

'Fall back and drop to ground,' Nish ordered, sending two pigtailed runners, wide-eyed girls no older than twelve, scuttling low to tell the archers to fire at will.

His swordsmen fell back, dropping into a crouch on solid ground above the mound of dead. Though his archers were not trained to fire *en masse*, many were skilled hunters, and in the growing light they exacted dreadful slaughter on the soldiers trapped in the mud.

Peering over the wall of bodies, Nish tried to work out how the battle was going, but he couldn't see well enough. He crawled up onto the death carpet, over corpses and live men twitching and moaning from ghastly wounds, and gazed down the slope.

He estimated that the enemy had numbered about ten thousand, a force that on a level battlefield would have annihilated his six thousand ill-trained fighters. His father's army had lost half their number, dead or dying, with perhaps another two thousand too badly wounded to fight. Few of those would survive the march back to their garrison. But that still left three thousand, more than enough to destroy his ragtag force if he lost control of it, or made one mistake.

Nish didn't think the enemy's officers would allow the army to retreat, since they would be treated like deserters and executed. For Jal-Nish's troops it was victory at all costs, or decimation. How could he capitalise on that?

'They're weakening,' someone shouted from behind him. 'At them!'

Nish's head whipped around. The speaker was a huge, burly peasant, a giant of a man. A natural soldier, he had slain at least a dozen of the enemy and now had the blood lust burning in him. He sprang forwards, swinging his sword above his head. 'Charge!'

'Charge them!' The cry echoed through the ranks and the front line of swordsmen surged after him.

'Stop!' Nish cried, but they didn't hear him above the roar of battle.

The folly of one man could swing the tide to disaster, for once they climbed into full view on the mound of bodies the enemy archers would cut them down. Nish came to his feet and, as the peasant went charging past, swung the flat of his sword into the man's belly, knocking the wind out of him.

'Stop!' he roared, advancing on the others, who were leaping up onto the pile, and flashing his sword at them. 'That's what they want you to do. It's a trap!'

One soldier ground to a halt, then the rest, and they turned and scuttled back to their line. As the burly peasant went to his hands and knees to follow, Nish smacked him across the backside with the flat of his sword, to reinforce the fellow's shame.

Nish was about to step down after them when something struck him sharply in the back, knocking him off his feet. He'd been hit by a long arrow, angling into his back muscle in the region of his lowest right rib, but he struggled up, not feeling any pain.

He could feel blood running down his back though and, even if the injury wasn't mortal, it would soon weaken him. His knees felt shaky and a mist passed before his eyes. Nish clung desperately to one thought – before he fell, he had to ensure victory, and victory was still far from certain.

It was hard to think straight, but he must. He tried to concentrate and a desperate plan came to mind. The enemy had seen him fall and must know that, whoever he was, he'd led the battle so far. If he could convince them that the rebels were totally demoralised by his 'death' . . .

He staggered off the pile of bodies and fell down into shelter. It really hurt this time. Worse, his entire front line was staring at him, aghast, the soldiers' weapons drooping in their hands.

'Messengers and officers, to me,' he croaked.

They didn't move. What was the matter with the fools? Nish's eyes met the eyes of the huge peasant and he jerked his head at the fellow, as if to say, come here; make up for your folly.

The huge peasant jumped up. An arrow shot over his head. He crouched down and ran forwards, picked Nish up as easily as if he were a child, and scuttled back with him.

'Hold me up.' Nish felt a chilly weakness creeping over him. The peasant tugged at the arrow, sending a spasm of agony through Nish's back. 'Leave it,' he choked. 'Get my officers and messengers.'

They gathered around and he explained his plan. They looked shocked, disbelieving. 'Just do it, in the name of the Deliverer,' he said limply.

The officers went to their troops, the messengers darted back and forth. 'Ready,' came the signal.

Nish nodded. That hurt too. His archers laid down a covering fire. The huge peasant hefted Nish in his arms, taking care not to disturb the half span of arrow protruding from his back, then carried him towards the rear like an honoured dead.

Nish's soldiers retreated with him, then formed into a mass in the centre of the neck where it broadened just below the camp. The ones on the outside threw down their arms, and all began to mill about. A great wailing filled the air.

Monkshart came running up to where the huge peasant stood, still holding Nish. The peasant had carried him to the archer's rise on the right hand side of the neck, so he could keep the battlefield in view.

Monkshart paled at the sight of the bloody wound, then rapped out, 'Bring him back to my tent, soldier.'

'No!' Nish said urgently, feeling his focus fading. He willed himself back to full alertness. He had to hold out for long enough to enact the plan, and hopefully spring the trap. No one else could do it; certainly not Monkshart.

It seemed to grow dark suddenly. Nish tried to speak, though it was hard to form the words. 'Tell me what's happening, soldier,' he said in a gritty croak. 'Every detail.'

'They're starting to advance,' the huge peasant said in a deep burr. 'Their archers have just fired a volley but it went overhead, into the tents.'

'Tell our troops the Deliverer says to throw down their weapons and look panicky.'

'Troops –' roared the peasant.

'Don't tell the enemy as well, you bloody fool. Send runners.'

They were sent. Nish's sight returned for a few seconds, just long enough to see the enemy moving more quickly now, but faded once more. 'What's . . . happening?'

'Our archers are firing again,' said the peasant. 'Half the enemy front line has gone down but they're coming on.

They're halfway across the dip; going slowly now; bogging down.' He paused for a good while. 'They're almost to the pile of bodies. They're climbing the pile. The first of them are jumping down onto solid ground. Do I give the signal?'

'Not – yet,' said Nish, cursing his weakness. How could he fight a battle when he couldn't even see? 'How many are on solid ground?'

'A few hundred. They're coming slowly; they're so weary they can barely walk.'

'Good. How many have fallen to our arrows?'

'About the same number.'

'Not enough,' Nish whispered. 'Give the first signal, soldier.'

He felt the soldier raise his arm. 'Done, surr. Our men are still moving backwards.'

'Excellent . . .' Time passed. Nish had no idea how much. He felt so very weak and listless. He couldn't care about anything.

'More than half their army is on solid ground now. They're about to attack, Deliverer.'

'Wait,' said Nish, though he was no longer sure of himself. The plan was slipping away with his consciousness. 'Now!'

He felt the soldier slash his arm down, there came a great roar and the ground shook as the enemy made a last effort.

'Our troops are grabbing their fallen weapons, surr. They're forming into a wedge in the centre of the neck. The enemy are coming at them. They're attacking. *They're getting through!*' The peasant said no more for agonising moments. Nish could hear the man's pounding heartbeat, but could not feel his own. 'No, they're splitting to go around and attack our boys from both sides. They're going to –'

'Third signal,' Nish whispered.

The soldier whipped his arm up again. 'Our soldiers are attacking furiously, surr. The enemy are fighting back but they can barely hold up their swords. Now our women and children are coming at them from between the tents. The enemy are still fighting – they're doing bloody slaughter on us, surr! I think . . .

'No, our spearmen have moved out on either side, to cut them off. Our swordsmen are going at their flanks, driving them backwards, backwards . . . Oh, surr, surr!' cried the burly peasant, shaking Nish in his arms, pain from the waggling arrow breaking through his lassitude.

'We're pushing their flank right back, over the edge. They're breaking! They're breaking, surr! They're running down the steep slope towards the swamp. They'll never get out of there. The left flank are breaking too. They're over the edge. Our archers are moving into position. It's over, Deliverer, surr. We've beaten the finest the God-Emperor's Imperial Militia could send at us. Oh, surr!'

The huge peasant was shaking, laughing, crying and dancing, and Nish felt the man's tears falling on his cheeks as he slid into unconsciousness.

THIRTY-FOUR

Maelys was so tired that she hadn't realised the attack was happening until the tent was torn away in a maelstrom of snapping canvas and flying tent poles and pegs. A knotted rope whacked her so hard on the right cheekbone that she was bound to get a black eye out of it. All around her, people were screaming or crying out to each other. No one knew what had happened; everyone feared the worst.

'Be quiet!' Tulitine's voice sounded nearby, and such was her authority that everyone fell silent. Unshuttering a lantern, she directed a narrow beam around her. She was clad in healer's robes, like Maelys's, though of a darker green with a black sash.

'Stop whining!' Tulitine said disgustedly to a group of women huddling around someone lying on the other side of the tent floor. 'We always knew the God-Emperor was going to attack the Defiance, and now he has. Get your weapons and prepare to defend the camp.'

'Vula is dying,' sobbed a frizzy-haired woman about Maelys's age. 'It's not fair. She never hurt anyone.'

Tulitine crouched down by the tall girl who lay flat on her back with the splintered half of a tent pole embedded in her throat. Maelys came around the other side. The girl was choking but there was no point trying to remove the pole – it had torn through the arteries in her neck and a bucket of blood had pooled on the ground beneath her. As Maelys watched, the choking stopped.

Tulitine closed the girl's eyes with her fingers. The frizzy-haired woman began to wail. Tulitine whirled, slapping her across the face so hard that it knocked her head sideways.

'This is war, girl. Ever since you left your village you've been boasting about how brave you are, so stop whining and get to your position. And if you have to die, *which you probably will*, do it with a dignity worthy of the Deliverer.'

In short order, Tulitine organised the defence of the tents and sent teams to beat the fires out and shovel earth over the cinders. A healers' tent was set up, cloth torn into rags and cauldrons of water put into the fires to boil. The attack had caused dozens of injuries, and arrows as many more. The dead were humped to the back of the camp and laid out next to the rocks. The living waited.

Maelys stood at the opening of the healers' tent, tension drawing the knots in her belly ever tighter. The fall of arrows had stopped and the enemy army was at the foot of the hill. Before she'd left home, reading about adventures such as this had been her lifeblood, but being in one wasn't the least bit exciting. It was violent, brutal and, worst of all, random. She'd hadn't taken that in before, but it could as easily have been her lying dead with a tent pole in her throat, or Tulitine, *or Nish*.

He was leading his troops from the front, and as a hero of the lyrinx wars Nish was probably the best person to do so. She stood up on tiptoe but could only see the dark mass of ill-trained Defiance defenders waiting for the attack that would roll right over them. The God-Emperor's troops had a fearsome reputation. They'd never been beaten in battle, and they'd had plenty of time to prepare, so how could this puny rabble hope to hold them back? Though Maelys was optimistic by nature, she couldn't find any hope. The sides of the hill would run red with the blood of the Defiance and then the enemy would push through to the women and children.

The children and old women would die, the young women only spared to be used the way soldiers used women in war, then slain or dragged off to the God-Emperor's interrogation pits.

She fought down an urge to abandon her post and run, but even if she had been minded to, it was already growing light and there was nowhere to hide on the grassy plains. No one would be allowed to survive to tell the story of the Deliverer and his Defiance. There would be no tales of courage in the face of impossible odds, or small heroes defying the all-powerful God-Emperor, only of Jal-Nish's crushing might.

Maelys was reminded of Nish's words on the way to Tifferfyte. 'It's the common folk who suffer most in a revolution, and no one gives a damn, least of all the people who are making revolution in their name.' She wondered if Nish were remembering those words now as he watched the peasants die.

Another flight of arrows rattled around them and someone gasped. The woman who had been working beside her just a few minutes ago lay thrashing with a red-and-black-feathered arrow in her belly. Maelys knelt beside her, studying the wound, then cut off the arrowhead protruding from her back and began to pull the shaft out, but before she had drawn it all the way the woman was dead.

Maelys dragged her to one side and returned to the flap. Dawn was spreading across the sky. It would not be long now. The ground shook as the army pounded up the hill.

'Hoy, Healer, over here.'

There were a dozen healers here now, but Maelys was as skilled as most, and ran to help. Two women were heaving an old man onto a trestle table. He had deep, ragged gouges across his back and shoulders – flappeter wounds – though unless they became infected he would survive. She carried across a bucket of hot water and began to clean the torn flesh with steaming cloths.

Other casualties were brought in and she was soon so immersed in her work that she scarcely gave a thought to what was happening outside, though she could not block out the screams of the maimed and dying.

A massed roar went up, a sound that sent a shiver down her back. She washed her hands yet again, wiped them on a clean rag and turned away from the young man she was bandaging. The battle must be over, the Defiance lost.

Taking a knife from the table, she went to the flap, expecting to see the enemy flooding towards her. It was bright daylight now, the sun just rising, but all she saw were the blood-covered rebels whooping and embracing each other.

Even after the healers began laughing, weeping and cheering, Maelys couldn't take it in. They'd won? How could it be possible?

A messenger girl came running and caught Maelys by the hand. 'Healer, Lord Monkshart bids you come, quick!' She began to drag Maelys towards the neck of the hill.

'What's the matter? Who is it?' But there was a pain in the middle of her chest, just under the breastbone, and it grew stronger all the time. She knew what the girl was going to say.

'It's the Deliverer, Healer. He took an arrow in the back.'

Pain speared through her from front to back. 'But he's all right?'

'Just come.'

The rebels had gathered along the sides of the hill, leaving the centre open, and for the first time she saw the full horror of the battle. Bodies lay everywhere, where they'd fallen, while down at the narrowest point of the neck the dead made a wall waist high and a good forty paces wide. She couldn't see how far down the slope it extended but there had to be thousands of bodies in it.

It was the most gruesome sight she'd ever seen, and

already flies were swarming. Carrion birds wheeled high above and more were joining them every minute.

Then she saw him. A huge soldier held Nish in his arms, and even from fifty paces away she could see the long arrow in Nish's lower back and his sagging head. He looked so small, so frail, so dead. She gathered up her skirts and ran.

Before she got there, Monkshart stepped out from behind the giant, and Phrune from behind him. Maelys faltered, then continued. Nish needed her help. She was one of the better healers here, and she had been called. She couldn't turn back now, though they were bound to discover her identity and then she was done for.

Head bowed so her hood would fall forwards, she continued past them and began to examine Nish's wound. Monkshart's hand caught her upper arm and jerked her painfully towards him. His hand reached out to push her hood back. His eyes were glittering.

'If he dies, Healer –'

THIRTY-FIVE

'Unhand her, Monkshart!' Tulitine's voice came like a whip crack. 'It is blasphemy to lay a finger on the Healers of Flammermoul, and well you know it.'

Monkshart's hard fingers crushed Maelys's biceps, but he let her go. 'I intended no insult,' he said, bowing low towards the old woman, 'but I must be sure she *is* a healer. That habit can just as easily hide a spy or a traitor, and the Deliverer –'

'She's been doing her work here for days,' Tulitine said coldly, shooing him out of the way. 'If you're so concerned about the Deliverer, you'll let her get on with it.'

Maelys could feel Phrune's eyes on her as if he were trying to burn a hole through her robes, but the old woman took him by the collar and hauled him off. 'And keep your festering acolyte out of her way.'

Monkshart cuffed Phrune over the side of the head. 'Take my personal guard – ten men. Secure the army's war chest plus any surviving battle mancers and devices of the Art. Have the dead stripped of their weapons and valuables. Make sure the horses with the supply wagons don't stampede. And then –'

'Check the dying, Master, for those who may prove useful,' said Phrune.

'Indeed,' said Monkshart and walked away.

For their skins: those who were dying of head injuries only. Maelys couldn't think about Phrune sneaking about in the pile of dead and dying, licking his lips as he relieved the still-living of their skins, or else she would not be able to do her work. It was just one more horror in this most terrible of days.

Maelys was cutting Nish's shirt away from the shaft of the arrow when Tulitine appeared beside her. 'You're in grave danger,' she said softly, so that even the big man holding Nish would not hear. 'You're a threat to their plans. Finish your work then stay out of their way, and keep your face covered at all times, as a good healer would.' She peered into Nish's face. 'What do you think?'

'I'm worried. The wound hasn't bled much, yet he's unconscious and cold.' Maelys took Nish's pulse with her fingers. 'And his heartbeat is weak and fluttery.' She looked up at the old woman. 'I've never dealt with battle wounds before today. What's the matter with him?'

'I can't say. Maybe shock; maybe he's bleeding inside. Bring him to the healers' tent, soldier.' Tulitine touched his arm. 'What's your name?'

He turned towards the tent, walking carefully as though he were carrying the most precious burden in the world. 'I'm Zham, Lady Tulitine.'

'Just Zham?' she said, grinning as though she knew better.

He flushed, lowered his voice. 'My mother called me Zhambellmyne, but . . .'

'But it's a girly name and when you were a kid everyone laughed at you, because you were so huge, and the name was so wrong.'

'Yes, Lady,' he muttered.

'Zham is a good, honourable name, and it fits you perfectly. I like it.'

'Thank you, Lady.'

'I'm no lady, Zham.' He looked away, abashed, and she chuckled throatily. 'You were in the battlefront, I take it?'

'Yes, Lady.'

'Tell me how it went. How was this famous victory achieved?'

He went through it from the beginning as they walked back to the healers' tent. As they paced down an avenue of silent people, all staring at the fallen Deliverer as though all their hopes rested on him, Maelys saw a familiar face in the crowd. It was Timfy, and he'd just opened his mouth to call her name when a hand slapped across it.

Jil shushed him, looking up at Maelys with a mixture of guilt and defiance. Before Maelys could speak, Jil lifted Timfy away and they disappeared into the throng.

Maelys couldn't go after her, but she would try to find Jil later and make peace with her. She was glad they were safe.

Zham carried Nish inside, holding his weight without a quiver while the trestle was scrubbed down with hot water, rinsed clean and wiped off.

'He truly is the Deliverer, Lady Tulitine, for he saved us single-handedly and, even after he took the arrow, the Deliverer refused to give in until he'd given his last order and seen the enemy defeated. I've done a bit of fighting in my time; I know how victory goes. Had it not been for him they would have slain us all, and been molesting –' He broke off, even more abashed. 'I beg your pardon, Lady. I don't hold with that sort of thing.'

'It happens,' said Tulitine. 'This Healer will look after him now.'

'Lay him here, please,' said Maelys. 'On his side.' Zham put him down gently. She cut the rest of the shirt away and began to feel the wound, front and back. 'Thank you, Zham. You can go now.'

He didn't move. 'I –' He wrung his big hands; his broad, peasant's face shone with perspiration. 'I'd rather stay, Lady Healer. He saved my life when the battle madness came on me and I nearly led my friends to ruin. I'm his man now, until I die or he dismisses me.' Zham looked over his shoulder, then lowered his voice. 'And he needs me. Not everyone in this camp is his friend.'

Tulitine looked up sharply. 'What do you know, soldier?'

'Not enough,' he said unhappily, 'but I've heard things, this past week. People talking when they thought no one could overhear.'

'Very well, stay. Hold him on his side, like this. Keep your filthy hands away from the wound.'

Maelys felt Nish's belly. 'I can feel the point of the arrow just under the skin, here at the side. Should I push it through so the head can be cut off?'

Tulitine felt for herself. 'I expect so, though if the arrow has gone through an artery he'll bleed to death once you move it. And if it's cut his intestines, infection will kill him. Ready? Hold him steady, Zham.'

Maelys felt sick at the thought of hurting Nish further, much less of doing something that could cause his death, yet the arrow had to come out. She took a firm grip on the shaft, uncertain how much force to use, then thrust as gently as she could. Nish let out a groan and his eyes moved furiously under their lids. The arrowhead hadn't come through but she couldn't bear to do it again.

Monkshart's face appeared at the flap, but Tulitine stalked across and jerked it shut. 'We can't do our work with you staring. Come back in fifteen minutes and I'll tell you how he is.'

'It'd better be good news,' he growled from outside.

Tulitine returned to the table. 'His back muscle must have tightened around the shaft. It'll hurt less if you're not so gentle.'

Maelys bit her lip, though she knew the old woman was right. This time she thrust as hard as she dared and felt the arrowhead burst through Nish's side. He shrieked and his eyes came open, staring around wildly, but thankfully closed again.

She cut off the arrowhead, wiped away the splinters, then

in one swift movement drew the shaft from his back. Her eyes met Tulitine's.

'If it's his doom to die, Maelys, it won't take long.'

'And there's nothing we can do?'

'Not if he's bleeding inside.'

The giant screwed up his eyes. Maelys held her breath. Even Tulitine was moved by the gravity of the moment. Maelys wiped a smear of blood away from the entry slit. Blood tricked from the gash in his side, though if he were bleeding inside surely there would be more?

'I might as well salve and stitch him,' she said to herself.

'His breathing sounds better,' said Tulitine when Maelys had finished.

'And his pulse is stronger. But could he still . . .?'

'He could. You can't tell with bleeding inside. Sometimes the veins seal over quickly, yet at other times they just keep dribbling blood for hours, or burst open days later. Bandage him and Zham can take him to his tent. We've more work to do.'

Maelys saw Nish settled on a straw mattress there. A trace of colour had come back to his face.

'Monkshart is coming, Lady Healer,' Zham rumbled.

He wasn't as dull-witted as he looked. She ducked out under the canvas, leaving him standing guard, circled the top of the hill and returned to the healers' tent from the other side. The tables were covered in bloody soldiers with such ghastly injuries that she could hardly bear to go back in, but men were suffering and dying for want of skilled hands and she couldn't turn her back on them.

The Defiance dead, numbering more than a thousand, were buried in shallow pits. Then, despite their hundreds of injured, they moved on at dawn the following day. There was no choice, for the mountains of enemy dead were already putrefying in the heat and the stench was unbearable.

381

Maelys travelled with Nish that morning in one of the army's jolting supply wagons. It was stifling under the canopy and, despite her weariness, she would sooner have walked. Once satisfied that Nish was recovering she left him to another healer, for he was coming out of his delirium and she couldn't afford for him to recognise her. He was bound to give her identity away and Monkshart would hear of it.

Over the next two days, Maelys kept feeling that she was being followed, though she never saw anyone suspicious behind her. By that afternoon she'd decided that she was imagining things, until a man stepped out from behind a tree in front of her and crouched down as though he'd dropped something. She looked down as he looked up under her cowl. It was Phrune, and he recognised her at once.

'I thought it had to be you,' he said gleefully. 'I'll be seeing you later, little Maelys.' He drew his stiletto and pointedly flicked a thumb across the blade.

There were people everywhere, so she was safe from immediate attack, and as the quiet little healer, selflessly doing her all for the injured, and especially the Deliverer, she'd earned the respect of everyone in the camp. But she was a threat to Monkshart's plans for Nish and he'd soon find a way to be rid of her.

She didn't move as Phrune oozed away, leering over his shoulder. She watched him until he'd disappeared among the throng around Monkshart's quarters, then slipped into a copse of trees to think. She couldn't stay in the camp – she'd be at risk all the time. It would only take a second to slip a knife into her back. But where was she to go?

Maelys collected the few possessions she'd gleaned since she'd been here: a small pack she'd sewn from torn canvas, a spare set of clothes from one of the young women who'd died in the initial attack, a knife and a few coins of low value, distributed by Monkshart from the captured war chest. The majority of the army's coin, and everything of real worth, had been retained to fund the coming campaign. She also had a dead soldier's water skin and a loaf of bone-hard bread. It was little enough to survive on for the precarious future.

She no longer had any reason to hide her identity from Nish, but each time she approached his tent Phrune was lurking nearby. She ached for her taphloid but wasn't game to go near Phrune's tent. She couldn't find Tulitine to tell her about Phrune; she hadn't seen Jil and Timfy either. It would soon be dark and Maelys began to feel increasingly paranoid, so she slipped her pack under her robes where it wouldn't show and headed out of the camp as if going to relieve herself. No one noticed. It felt as if no one cared.

'Where are you going, Maelys?'

Tulitine seemed to have come out of nowhere. 'Phrune knows who I am.' Maelys explained what had happened.

'I see,' said the old woman. 'And you're running away.'

'You told me to beware of him.'

'I did, but do you really think this is the answer? Where will you go, without friends or coin?'

'What else can I do? If I'm caught, my whole quest fails.'

Tulitine drew her under a tree out of sight of the camp and sat down on the scanty grass. She gestured to the ground beside her and Maelys sat as well, smoothing her gown over her legs.

'You have many fine qualities, Maelys, but some weaknesses that will undermine your quest. Do you know what they are?'

It reminded Maelys of the uncomfortable questions her tutor used to ask her as a young girl when she'd spent the hours daydreaming over one tale or another instead of attending to her lessons. 'It would be easier if you told me . . .'

'Though not as useful as realising it yourself.' Tulitine sighed. 'Very well. You're too biddable, Maelys; too eager to please. If someone asks you to do something, you do it no matter your own feelings. You –'

They'd spoken a little about this on the journey to meet the Defiance. 'The downfall of Clan Nifferlin was my fault and I've got to make up for it.'

'But you only discovered that recently, so it doesn't explain why you're the way you are at all. You're always putting your family's interests above your own. Does it make you feel good to be so self-sacrificing?'

'I have to pay,' Maelys said stubbornly.

'Very well. I can see you're not ready to think about such things. If your mind is made up, I'll bid you farewell, with regret. Help me up, girl.'

Maelys gave Tulitine her hand and drew the old woman to her feet. Tulitine turned away, but Maelys stood where she was, and after a dozen steps, Tulitine turned around. 'What is it, child?'

'It's my taphloid. I told you –'

'That Phrune has it and you want it back.'

'It's everything to me. And . . .'

'And you want me to help you steal it from him, but because of a weakness in your character you can't bear to ask for help.'

Maelys felt like a stupid little girl. 'Yes. Can – can you help me?'

'I could try,' said Tulitine, regarding her sympathetically, 'but I'm not going to, because that would put my own plans at risk. I'm sorry.' She stood there, as if waiting.

Just asking for the favour was hard enough. Maelys couldn't bring herself to argue her case, or, even more mortifyingly, to beg. 'Thanks, anyway,' she said.

'Despite all the things you've done since leaving home, you're full of fear and still have no confidence in yourself. You can do it, Maelys. You'll find the courage you lack if you just look deeply enough inside you.'

Maelys froze in mid-step, then went on without a word.

The only courage she had was the sort one used in an emergency, when there was no other choice, and that was no use here.

'If you don't try you'll always blame yourself,' Tulitine added, then Maelys heard her walking back to the camp.

Maelys went on, trying to think of a way to get her taphloid back, but all foundered on the point Tulitine had put her finger on. Maelys was simply too afraid.

She didn't know where to go or what to do, for this land was a blank map to her, but it was late afternoon and she had to get well clear before nightfall. Maelys trudged across a little plain covered in serrated bluegrass that crept up under the hem of her gown to saw at her calves, through a patch of twisted, spreading trees with leaves that smelled of mint, and onto another plain, a good league from the camp.

By the rising moon she found a cluster of seven upjutting rocks which broke the wind. Sitting with her back to the broadest rock, Maelys rubbed her scratched and blood-streaked calves. She gnawed at the end of her loaf until her jaw ached, washing the gritty residue down with a swig of warm, smelly water from her water skin. She pulled her robes around her, for it was a clear, cool night, pillowed her head on her pack and, despising herself for her cowardice, eventually slept.

She woke with beads of sweat sliding down her back. The sun, though only a handspan above the horizon, was blazing directly on her. After more hard bread and murky water she climbed a hillock to check on her surroundings. The advance guard of the Defiance were already moving northwest, though a long tail stretched back to the camp. Word of the great victory must have spread, for she counted eight small bands of pilgrims moving in to swell their numbers. Further off, carrion birds circled above the unseen battlefield.

Maelys had decided to follow the caravan at a distance,

for the next few days at least. After that, when her food ran out, she would have to find a way to survive in a world where the God-Emperor's spies took note of every traveller to enter the smallest village.

A day later, she was following the trampled path of the caravan through another patch of woodland, treading carefully to avoid the droppings of horses, oxen and ill-mannered people, when she realised that she wasn't the only person shadowing the Defiance. She'd seen that tall, lean figure ahead yesterday afternoon. Maelys had assumed he was going to join the caravan, but he was just as far behind it now.

Losing sight of the fellow, she slipped into the vase-shaped depression formed where five trunks spread from the gnarled base of a tree. Its smooth bark was covered in scribbly marks, like the glyphs of a dead language. Was he one of Phrune's minions, hunting *her*?

She crouched down, feeling for her knife, but saw him further ahead, moving on. He wasn't after her; he was following the caravan. But why keep so far back? A spy could learn nothing from this distance that the whole country didn't already know.

Shortly, peeping out between the trunks, she saw him again, moving slowly and carefully. He had to be up to something. Maelys noted where he made camp that afternoon, in a copse by a rivulet, and once it had grown dark she crept close.

It was the tall, hollow-cheeked supplicant whom Phrune had repeatedly turned away. He was sitting cross-legged on the ground in front of his camp fire, staring into the flames and occasionally rotating a carcass, the size of a large hare, on a spit.

Fat dripped into the fire, which blazed up. A breeze carried the smell of roasting meat to Maelys and she salivated. She'd eaten the last of her dry bread for lunch and, not having found anything edible despite hours of searching, faced the prospect of going to bed hungry and getting up to more of the same.

He didn't look like an assassin, though. He was staring at the dirt between his boots, as if in a deep depression. Maelys was about to turn back to her dismal camp when he called, 'I know you're out there. Either show yourself, or go away and leave me in peace.'

His voice had a bitter edge which matched the downcast look on his face. He'd suffered unjustly, or believed he had. She didn't sense any threat in him though, so after a long hesitation she moved into the circle of fire-light.

'Hello,' Maelys said, uncertainly.

He stared at her. 'The little healer! What are you doing out here, all alone and defenceless?'

'No one would harm me,' she said softly, maintaining the role.

Again his smile displayed that hint of long-endured bitterness. 'Sister, there are people in this world who would eat your living flesh and lap at your flowing blood for the sheer joy of making you suffer. Go back to the Defiance where it's safe, and go quickly.'

'I –'

'I'll escort you, if you wish,' he said softly. 'I would not see you come to harm after your great deeds on the *Deliverer's* behalf.' Sarcasm this time, and she couldn't work out why.

'I – I can't.' She surprised herself by revealing her vulnerability to another, and a stranger at that, but, despite Tulitine's earlier words she felt that she could trust him. If she didn't trust someone she would be lucky to survive.

'Why not?' He indicated the ground.

She sat down with a weary sigh, trying not to look at his dinner. 'I'm not a healer. At least, not a qualified one, and I'm wearing this habit so I won't be recognised.'

He didn't look surprised. 'If it would fit, I'd borrow it from you. Disguise is the only way I'll ever get to plead my case to the Deliverer.'

'What is your case?'

He waved a hand; he didn't plan to tell her. 'You don't look as though you've eaten in days. You're welcome to share my supper.'

'I – I don't –' Her mouth was so thick with saliva she couldn't get the refusal out.

'There's plenty for two.' He prodded the carcass with the point of his knife. Clear juice ran out. 'Besides, I can easily catch another. There are few better hunters in this country than me.'

His words chilled her. What sort of hunter was he and why was he so bitter about the Deliverer? He snapped the backbone and handed her the rear half, which was almost too hot to hold. 'Thank you,' she said, sinking her teeth through the crispy skin into juicy white flesh which, to a half-starved woman, was unbearably delicious.

Neither spoke until they had finished and wiped their hands and faces on handfuls of dry grass. 'Since you're not of the Healing Order, may I see your face? I like to know who I'm sharing my food with.'

She hesitated; but after all, she couldn't hide forever. Maelys drew back her hood. He studied her face as if committing it to memory, then sighed. 'I've a feeling we're after the same thing.'

'What are you talking about? You don't know anything about me. I've never been to this land before.' Why had she given that away?

'We're now on the southern border of Crandor. You must have heard of Crandor, wherever you're from. It's the largest and wealthiest country in the world. At least, it *was* wealthy before the God-Emperor came to power.'

'Of course I've heard of Crandor,' she said mildly, 'and I'm not as far from home as you are.' The native people of Crandor were dark-skinned and filed their teeth to points, and they didn't speak the way he did.

'I'm very far from home, but we were talking about you –

and how you stole the son of the God-Emperor out of his most impregnable dungeon.'

She paled. How could he know that? 'Nonsense!' she cried. 'You're mad.'

'I see you don't deny it. Little sister, the whole world knows about Nish's daring escape from prison and his desperate flight into the mountains with a mysterious raven-haired, *little* woman with a southern accent, who saved him over and again.'

'I haven't heard any such tale.'

'You would have if you'd spent time with the Deliverer's other followers instead of hiding under your healer's robes.'

'Anyway, there are millions of women in the world like me.'

'Not like you, and not *here*. Besides, the village of Tifferfyte saw you drop out of the sky on a stolen flappeter, and the full tale was spread across the world by skeet before those who would use the Deliverer for their own purposes took control. Need I go on?'

'Go on,' she said limply. She had to know what the world was saying about Nish, and her. Though if a man who had never seen her before could recognise her so easily, surely there was nowhere in Crandor she could hope to hide.

'And then the incredible escape from Tifferfyte under the very nose of Seneschal Vomix, using Arts that were never known before. All Crandor knows that tale too, though not just from Monkshart's twisted half-truths. A girl who escaped with you spread the true tale, and even your name. You're Maelys, aren't you?'

No point trying to conceal it any longer, though surely the God-Emperor knew her identity too, and was even now hunting down her family. Nor could she blame Jil for telling the story – to be the bearer of such a tale would feed her and Timfy for weeks. 'I am.'

'So why aren't you standing in the place of honour beside the Deliverer?'

389

'I . . . *like* Nish too much. Monkshart is afraid Nish will become fond of me too, and give up his plan to become the Deliverer. Monkshart wants me dead.'

He shivered. 'Then run for your life, Maelys. He's a dangerous man and, sooner or later . . .'

'But I swore to help Nish become the Deliverer.'

'I'm sure he wouldn't hold you to that promise at the risk of your life.'

'I didn't swear to Nish. He never wanted to become the Deliverer.'

'Really?' he said sourly. 'He looked as though he was loving every minute of his pampered life.'

'He was crushed by his time in prison. It's taken him months to get over it.' She didn't want to say any more. It was none of this man's business and she was beginning to worry about what *he* wanted with Nish. No wonder Nish had yearned to run away. 'Anyhow, he saved us all in the battle.'

'Yes, he did. I doubted him before that, but who could do so afterwards?'

'You didn't give me your name.'

'You can call me Thommel.'

Which implied that he didn't plan to reveal his real name. 'Why are you shadowing the Defiance, *Thommel*?'

He gave a twisted grin, but didn't answer.

'I saw you trying to get an audience with Nish, and Phrune repeatedly refusing you.'

'I don't want to talk about it,' he said coolly, as though she'd trespassed on a forbidden topic.

Thommel was too difficult. She took the hint and stood up, saying formally, 'Thank you for dinner. It was delicious. I hope you find what you're looking for.' She turned away, holding her back straight, though it was impossible to make a dignified exit wearing her tent-like robes.

Thommel sprang up. She shot a glance over her shoulder in case he had ill intentions after all, but he was just standing by the fire, looking anxious.

'I'm sorry. I didn't mean to be rude. We do share a common interest in Nish and . . . if we travelled together, we could watch each other's backs.'

She hesitated, remembering the aunts' childhood warnings about men and their uncontrollable desires. But Nish wasn't like that, and she didn't think Thommel was either.

He added the clincher. 'I've another hare hanging in the tree. For breakfast.'

They followed the caravan for another three days, and Maelys couldn't remember when she'd last eaten so well, which was fortunate because she'd never felt so hungry.

Thommel turned out to be pleasant company after all, except where Nish was mentioned, though, despite Maelys's oblique questioning, he revealed nothing more about himself. He went to every village they passed, to hear the latest news. Maelys wished she could go too but it didn't seem worth the risk. She felt so lonely that she even missed the acerbic company of her mother and aunts.

Everyone knew about the Defiance's great victory, and another attack on its growing force was expected at any time. The caravan was harried every so often by flights of flappeters, though there was no sign of an enemy army. But then, there hadn't been the first time, either.

On their fourth morning together, Maelys and Thommel were sitting on a small pointed hill looking down at the camp as the sun rose, when suddenly people began to run everywhere. She leaned forwards. 'Something must have happened during the night. Something bad.'

'I'd better sneak down and find out.'

Thommel was gone a long time, and returned at a lope. 'Someone tried to assassinate Nish in his bed,' he panted, 'and it wasn't the first time. There was an attempt two days ago as well – by the guard.'

Maelys could feel the blood draining away from her face. 'But you're not saying that Zham –'

391

'It wasn't Zham. Both times it happened when he was off duty. But that's not what's caused the real stir.'

She felt all cold inside. How could it get any worse? 'What is it?'

'Monkshart has gone into an uncontrollable rage; he's stalking the camp like a madman.'

'Thommel, what's going on?'

'Nish fled in the night, with Zham, and no one has the faintest idea where they've gone.'

THIRTY-SIX

The first two days after Nish's injury were a blur of pain and fever accompanied by the strangest dreams: that a small, black-haired woman was tending his wounds, and she had the softest hands he'd ever felt.

Unfortunately, once he regained his wits, Nish discovered that his healer was tall, elderly and dark-skinned, with filed teeth and a brisk, no-nonsense manner, but he kept dreaming about Maelys and often woke, crying out her name. Monkshart came to Nish each time, soothing him and reminding him that Maelys had died in the massacre at Tifferfyte.

He knew it to be true but he didn't want to believe it.

A few days later, Nish was lying awake in the early hours when he heard a rustle outside his tent. The flap was pushed aside, letting in a faint light from the guard's lantern. It wasn't loyal Zham, who was taking the few hours he allowed himself off duty, to sleep.

'Is that you, Monkshart?' There was no answer. Nish tried to turn over, though it proved so exceedingly painful that he stopped halfway.

He could hear heavy breathing, as if the intruder had been running, and smell the rank sweat of a man who hadn't bathed in months. 'Monkshart? Phrune?' No one else ever came into his tent save the tall healer who changed his dressings, and it wouldn't be her at this time of night.

Nish hadn't used his unreliable clearsight in ages, but now the intimation of danger was so strong that, ignoring the pain, he hurled himself sideways off the bed, roaring 'Help!' The dagger missed him by a few hairs, then he struck the floor hard and rolled under the bed. The guard, his face a mask of determined terror, fell to his knees to slash at him in the gloom.

'Help!' Nish shouted. 'Help, help!' He scrabbled the other way, saw a small gap between the tent wall and the ground and tried to roll through it. The stitches popped in his back but he barely felt it. He couldn't think about anything but getting through that gap, though he knew he was too slow.

He was expecting to be stabbed to death when two men burst in through the flap and hurled themselves on the treacherous guard. Tearing the knife from his hand, they dragged him outside and gave him the beating of his life. Nish could hear fists and boots striking flesh for a long time, then a man said, 'He's bleeding bad.'

Not even Monkshart could discover who had corrupted the guard, for in the middle of the beating he'd thrust a hidden dagger into his femoral artery and bled to death in a minute.

Zham was abject when he appeared at the flap, as if it had been his fault for not standing guard twenty-four hours a day. 'I'm sorry, surr,' he said, his broad jaw knotting. 'I was so tired I had to sleep for a few hours. It won't –'

'Zham, it's not your fault,' Nish said wearily, for he ached all over and his back was in agony. The healer redoing his stitches was nowhere near as gentle as the one who still haunted his dreams.

'Of course it's his fault,' Monkshart said coldly from the background. 'He set himself up as your protector and –'

'Monkshart,' Nish gritted. 'Get out of my tent and don't *ever* come back without my express invitation.'

There was a dead silence. The healer stifled a gasp, bent over and busied herself with her stitching.

'Deliverer –' said Monkshart in a strained voice.

'Out, and if you trouble me again I'll set *my* Defiance on you.'

It felt good to humble him; foolhardy but very good. At that moment, if Nish could have crushed Monkshart like a cockroach he would have done it. The tables were turned and from now on he'd be the one giving orders. The astonishing victory in battle had confirmed his authority.

Monkshart's eyes flashed; he ground his teeth together, looking as though he was going to burst with rage. Only with the most enormous effort did he maintain self-control and bow his head as if deferring to his master.

'Surr!' he said formally, then stalked to the flap, flung it open and went out.

'Deliverer,' the healer said quietly, 'You've made an enemy who will never forgive you. And he'll deal with Zham and me for overhearing.'

She wasn't reproaching Nish, though she had a right to. 'I'm sorry,' he said, and he was. 'Gather your gear and go home to your village right away. And thank you, for all you've done for me.'

'Beware, surr,' she added on the way out. 'There's something wrong inside Monkshart.'

Nish's euphoria faded and he began to feel the burst stitches. Why hadn't *he* shown more self-control? His life was difficult enough without making an enemy of his most powerful ally. He should have sent Zham to fetch Monkshart back and made amends, but the pain caught up with him first and he couldn't face it.

Only after the nurse had gone, and Zham had taken up his post, did it occur to Nish to wonder who wanted him dead. And why.

The caravan rolled on without incident apart from nightly attacks by flappeters and other flying creatures, unidentifiable in the darkness. These did little damage, for Monkshart's guards kept close watch now, and bonfires burning on all four sides of the camp gave them good light in which to fire their heavy crossbows. Massed fire had brought one flappeter down, after which the others kept out of range.

Two days after the first attempt on his life, Nish was lying awake listening to his night guards boasting about how easily the latest attack had been beaten off, when something rustled on the canvas floor of his tent. He turned up the wick of his lantern and froze, for what he was looking at couldn't possibly exist.

It was a nylatl, or something horrifyingly like it – a creature he'd fought in ages past and one that had very nearly defeated him. Nylatl had been flesh-formed by the enemy during the war for one purpose alone – to kill as quickly, brutally and terrifyingly as possible. Near the end of the war, once it had been discovered that flesh-formed creatures gave forth an unmistakeable aura which was identifiable from a distance with the Seeking Art, all such beasts had been hunted down and exterminated.

All save this one. He could smell its hot carrion stink, like rotten meat thrown on a hotplate, but Nish couldn't move. The new healer had bound his left arm to his side and strapped him to the bed so he couldn't burst the stitches again.

'Help!' Nish yelled, but he couldn't shout loudly enough. After the first attack, his tent had been set up on its own with twenty paces of open space in every direction, and if his guards were dead he'd have to roar to wake anyone. 'Help!'

The guards burst through the door and froze, staring at this creature out of the Histories. It was the length of a dog, though lower to the ground, with a long fanged mouth, vicious claws on all four feet, and all but the underside was covered in needle-tipped spines which were already oozing venom.

The leading guard, a stocky, scarred, red-faced fellow

who looked like a blacksmith, drew his sword and lunged. The nylatl was quicker.

Arching its back like a cat, it squirted a third of a cup of milky green venom at his eyes. He let out a thin wail, not loud enough to be heard at the nearest tent, staggered sideways and collapsed, clawing at his face, which began to blister like pastry rising in an overly hot oven. The blisters burst to reveal raw red flesh beneath.

The second guard, who was small, wiry and fleet of foot, shielded his eyes with his left arm as he hacked and slashed but, as Nish knew painfully well, nylatl never attacked in the same way twice.

It lost a couple of spines to the guard's blade, then its haunches bunched and it propelled itself at him as if fired from a catapult. He tried to weave out of the way but the nylatl rolled in mid-air, opened its massive jaws and, as it landed on his upper chest, closed them around his throat. Blood fountained across the room.

The nylatl tore through the guard's throat as he went down, exposing veins, sinews and windpipe, then threw its head back and swallowed the chunk of his living flesh. Blood slicked back along its neck as if blown by a high wind. It stood on his chest for a moment but, instead of turning its head, it gave a little jump-jump, rotating in the air, and came down facing Nish. Its glittering eyes fixed on him and he felt its presence in his mind, compelling him as the first one had tried to do, long ago.

Come to me. Come. Come.

Had he not been strapped to the bed, Nish would have gone, for in his weakened state he lacked the strength to resist it. He stared at the beast, knowing it was going to eat his face.

It sprang again, arcing high over the first writhing guard before landing on its four feet and tail. It had halved the distance between it and him. Its gory mouth opened and it appeared to smile, then it propelled itself through the air and thumped onto the wooden bedhead. It teetered back and forth like a child's toy, and on every swing its yawning mouth came so close that he could smell blood and carrion on its breath, and see the ruddy glare in its mesmerising eyes.

As it rocked back the third time, a strand of reeking red saliva oozed from its mouth to drape itself across Nish's forehead, burning like a red-hot wire. His free hand swung up involuntarily, to wipe it away. The nylatl lunged and for a second he thought it was going to tear his fingers off, but it drew back, going *pant-pant* in a way which suggested laughter. It seemed even more malicious than the ones he'd encountered previously, and more intelligent. Was it toying with him?

He heard feet thumping on the hard ground outside. 'Nylatl!' he croaked, 'Look out.'

The nylatl arched its spiny tail up over its head like the sting of a scorpion, then snapped it down as if trying to get him in the throat. Nish tried desperately to get out of its way but the straps held him and one of its spines plunged deep into the muscle of his upper chest, just below the right collarbone.

It hurt far worse than the arrow wound or the burst stitches. The spine must have gone in half the length of a finger and he could feel venom squirting into his flesh, eating into him like hot acid.

'Deliverer?' a man cried hoarsely.

Only Zham could have wielded the huge sword advancing through the flap. A hairy fist, the size of a small melon, followed it. 'Look out,' Nish gasped.

Nish didn't doubt the big man's courage but Zham seemed the last person who could tackle a creature with the lightning reflexes and malicious cunning of a nylatl. Its head swayed back and forth between Nish and Zham as if it couldn't decide whom it most wanted to savage, then it sprang low and fast towards Nish's belly and twisted around to face him, claws ripping through his shirt. It was either

398

going to tear his face off or eat his entrails while he was still alive.

But it didn't. It just crouched there, watching him. Zham lunged and the point of his sword shot out, flicking back and forth too quickly to see. The nylatl tried to swerve away, evidently decided there wasn't time, sprang and landed on the flat of the blade, its scaly feet scrabbling for a purchase. The sword dipped under its weight and Zham swung it away from Nish.

The nylatl clung to the moving sword for a couple of seconds before streaking up the blade towards Zham's unprotected hand. He was going to die the way the two guards had.

Zham spun the sword in mid-air in the centre of the tent, so hard that it blurred like the spinning rotor of an airdreadnought, with a streaked-out red and black clump clinging to the end. The nylatl lost its grip, shot up and struck the ridgepole. It tried to flip over to cling there but missed and hit the floor on its back, where it lay for a second as if dazed.

'It's pretending!' Nish cried as Zham leapt.

As it rolled over, Zham's gigantic boot came down on it as if squashing a cockroach. Putting all his weight on it, he twisted left and right, flattening it against the hard ground. Yellow froth boiled out of its mouth. He kept his weight there while it vainly tried to claw through his boot. Zham ground it into the dirt then sprang backwards.

The sword thudded into the ground, point first. Zham reached out without looking, heaved it free with his left hand, danced backwards and with two quick cuts quartered the dazed and damaged beast. It didn't move again.

Nor did Nish's guards. Both were dead.

Zham's eyes met Nish's. He was breathing heavily, though not as heavily as Nish was. 'Deliverer, I –'

Nish swallowed, then rubbed his burning, throbbing shoulder. 'Don't apologise for not being on duty, Zham. You just saved my life.'

'Surr, I don't think –'

'Lucky you moved into the nearest tent.'

'I swore to protect you,' Zham said simply. He unfastened Nish's straps and pulled back his shirt, though the nylatl's puncture had left only a little circular spot of blood.

'So you did, and I thank you. Would you be so good as to take the bodies out? Then wash your sword. That venom lasts for a long time.' Nish knuckled his shoulder, which made it hurt the more. He'd never felt such pain – it was as if boiling lye had been injected into him – but it did have one benefit. His mind was absolutely clear and he knew what he had to do.

'I'll go and rouse out –'

'Don't go anywhere, Zham. Someone sent that thing after me and I don't know who I can trust, apart from you. Unfasten the strap; help me up. I can't bear to be so helpless.'

Zham did so, then began to drag the bodies out. Nish took up the writing tablet he'd drafted his orations on and began to write a letter to his Defiance. For once the words came quickly and were right the first time.

When it was done he set the tablet on the table beside his bed, dressed and made sure his pack contained everything he needed. Zham returned with a shovel and scooped up the remains of the nylatl.

'Leave it outside, with the bodies. I want everyone to know what happened.'

'Surr?' said Zham.

Nish waved him away, levered his feet to the floor and stood up. The room revolved. He made a grab for the bedside table.

'What are you doing, Deliverer?' said Zham from the flap. 'You can't –'

Nish forced a smile, though it wasn't as carefree as he would have liked. 'How long until the guard changes?'

'Two hours.'

'Then we've got two hours to cover our tracks, assuming Monkshart doesn't decide to check on me in the middle of the night. Get your gear ready. We'll need food and coin.' Nish scooped a pot of salve and a roll of bandage into his pack. 'Take me to the tent where the war chest is held and talk to the guards while I burgle it.' Nish chuckled. 'I feel better already. Let's get moving.'

It was a dark, misty night, and the scattered lanterns were ringed with haloes as Zham led Nish to the treasure tent. Zham stood out the front, chatting to the guards as he often did, though they snapped to attention when they saw Nish.

He shook their hands and spoke briefly to them until the guards at the back of the tent were called around to meet him too, as Nish had known they would be. He exchanged pleasantries with them, then said he was just going to have a leak and walked into the darkness.

He slipped around to the rear of the tent, eased up the canvas and rolled under. The pain of the sting had eased, fortunately. The large war chest and the smaller were locked, of course, but Nish had been an artificer during the war and understood the workings of such mechanical devices. He had the larger chest open in a minute.

He felt around with a stick in case of traps, uncanny or mechanical, then silently scooped a small amount of gold and silver into one of the leather pouches lying nearby. He tied the drawstrings tightly so it wouldn't chink and fastened it to his belt.

The guards were still talking at the front. As he rolled out, more painfully, again Nish felt a momentary dizziness. Moving off into the darkness he coughed twice, as agreed, and shortly Zham appeared. He retrieved their packs from where he'd hidden them, and ten minutes later they were beyond the outer ring of guards and walking as quickly as Nish could manage, due north. Zham could see in the dark almost as well as a cat, evidently, for he wove through the grass and trees without ever tripping or losing his footing.

401

'Monkshart will come after us, won't he, surr?'

'I left a letter to the Defiance, telling them of an urgent mission that I must carry out alone. Monkshart will have to show it to them to explain my disappearance, else the Defiance will fall apart. But once that's done, I'm sure he'll follow us. We've got two hours to cover our tracks. Can you do that, Zham?'

'I'll do my best, surr. I'm a good woodsman.'

Nish felt sure that was an understatement, for Zham's every accomplishment had exceeded his expectations. He followed him into the night, doing exactly as Zham told him.

Nish's mind was on more important matters. Who could have brought the nylatl here, and why did that person want Nish dead? No agent of his father would order such a thing, no matter their ambitions, for if Nish died, Jal-Nish's wrath would be both terrible, widespread and indiscriminate.

It left but one other person, though Nish couldn't bear to think about that.

PART THREE

MISTMURK MOUNTAIN

THIRTY-SEVEN

'Who would want to kill Nish?' Maelys rubbed her goose-pimpled arms, shivering despite the warm morning, and reached into her pack for a cold leg of hare. They'd had a good breakfast an hour ago but she was starving again. 'How would his death benefit anyone?'

'I don't know, but I'm betting he does.' Thommel walked away, making figure-eights around the camp fire and through the trees, then came back. 'Monkshart read out Nish's address to the Defiance. He's gone on a secret mission that he must do alone, after which he will return to lead the Defiance to victory.'

'A secret mission,' she repeated, looking away.

She didn't know much about Nish's vision in the Pit of Possibilities, for they'd been separated before there had been time to discuss it in detail. He had to find a tall but narrow plateau, like a cut-off needle rising out of the rainforest, and climb it to discover whatever was waiting for him at the top. Nish had been transformed by the vision.

Maelys hadn't thought much about it at the time but now it bothered her, for the Pit of Possibilities seemed to have been under Monkshart's control, at least while he was there, and she didn't trust anything he'd had a hand in, or anything that had come out of it. The plateau could be a trap by who-ever wanted to kill Nish, though that seemed unlikely, since it was so far away and difficult to get to. But why else would someone lure him there? To hold the son of the God-Emperor hostage? Again, why so far – unless the plateau was home to powerful forces that could be found nowhere else.

'Maelys?' said Thommel. 'You know where he's gone, don't you?'

'Why should I tell you anything,' she snapped, frustrated that she couldn't work out what was going on, 'since you don't see fit to tell me anything about yourself? Or what you want from my friend Nish.'

'You haven't told me what you *really* want from him either,' he observed. 'Though it conflicts with what I see shining in your eyes. You're in love with him, aren't you?'

'Don't be stupid!' She looked down, flushing again. She had such trouble reading other people, yet her face was an open book to them, and she hated it.

She cursed her sheltered upbringing, her youth and inexperience, and couldn't bear to be dependent on this close-mouthed and alarmingly perceptive fellow. Without food, money and supplies she'd never find the plateau, for as soon as she asked about it she'd come to the notice of the God-Emperor's spies. She had to trust someone and it might as well be him, but she resented it.

'All right!' she muttered. 'But you've got to tell me something about yourself, first.'

He made another figure-eight around the camp fire, his agitation evident in every jerking movement, then sat down and said, 'Very well. I – I met Nish a long time ago, during the war. I helped him and he made me a promise which he never kept.'

'I'm sure there was a good reason.'

He gave her a cynical look, and she knew why. Nish had repeatedly tried to get out of his promise to become the Deliverer, and now he'd fled. Was he totally untrustworthy? She couldn't allow herself to believe it, and yet . . .

'I don't know what his secret mission is, and neither

would Nish want me to talk about his affairs to a stranger. But I do know where he's going.' She described the plateau as Nish had seen it in the Pit. 'He was all aglow after he had the vision. He said it was a lucky place for him.'

Thommel started. 'I know that plateau!' he cried, smiling for the first time. 'I saw it when I was a timber cutter in the rainforest. It's called Thuntunnimoe – Mistmurk Mountain – and it's not that far from here. We could reach it in a fortnight of hard walking.'

'Mistmurk Mountain?' The coincidence of names had to mean something, if it was a coincidence, and she didn't like the sound of it.

Assuming that Nish and Zham would have hidden their tracks, Thommel didn't try to find out which way they'd gone. He set off to the nearest town to buy boy's clothes and an extra pair of boots for Maelys, plus a small sack of flour, a round of cheese and a string of onions. Everything else he planned to get by hunting with his short bow, or by trapping.

Maelys remained at the camp, since the town was in the opposite direction to their destination and she didn't want to take the risk of being recognised again.

After eating she felt vaguely ill, as she had last night. She was sitting by the fire, drinking cup after cup of bitter tea made from a local herb that helped to settle her stomach, when it occurred to her that if she didn't try to get her taphloid back now there was little chance she would ever see it again. The thought of losing it forever to Phrune was too much to bear, and she began to wonder if there might be a way to recover it.

She still had her robes and it would be a simple matter to get back into the camp wearing them, since there were plenty of other healers, though she would have to act right away. Once Monkshart and Phrune set out after Nish, she'd lose the chance.

I'll just go into the camp and see, she thought. And if it

looks impossible, nothing has been lost. It also allowed her to put off the decision for as long as possible. Tulitine was right. She did lack courage.

Within the hour she was in the camp. The Defiance showed no sign of moving on today. The people looked dazed, uncomprehending, milling about in groups which were constantly breaking up and reforming, and everyone who entered the camp was accosted in case they had news of the Deliverer. Maelys was asked three times before she reached the centre of the camp, to which she replied each time with a shake of the head.

She wandered towards Monkshart's large tent. No one took the slightest notice. She circled it twice, feeling her chest tightening at the thought of trying to get inside. If Phrune looked out he would recognise her at once, despite her all-enveloping robes. What if he'd spotted her already?

Maelys followed that thought through, imagining Phrune kneeling over her with his blade, taking the living skin off her in one piece so he could make the perfect body-glove for his master – No! She turned away and plunged back into the crowd, allowing it to carry her along and around the camp like a leaf in a whirlpool.

A disturbance began at the other side of the camp and the crowd surged that way, desperate for news or any kind of diversion. Maelys went with it for a while, until it occurred to her that this might be her chance to get inside Monkshart's tent, if Phrune and his master came out to see what was going on.

She fell back to the rear, then turned and wandered away until she had a clear view of the tent. Yes, there was the tall figure of Monkshart at the entrance, and Phrune a few steps away. Monkshart gestured to Phrune, who hurried after the crowd. Monkshart did not go inside, but walked a few steps, staring at the distant throng. Even from this distance he looked worn. His arms hung limply and his back was bowed. Maelys was pleased to see it.

Now or never. She tried vainly to calm herself, discovered she couldn't, then screwed up her courage as far as it would go and walked around to the back of the tent. No one was looking. She got down on the dry ground, lifted the side and wriggled underneath.

It was divided into a number of rooms inside. She was in a large room, an audience chamber perhaps, with a rug on the ground, several chests in the centre and, beside them, a table made of planks set on trestles. She left this chamber for later. First she had to find Phrune's room. Ah, there it was; the smallest of five. It had a low camp bed, the covers fastidiously arranged, a small chest, a long, knee-high trestle table whose planks were shiny with oil, and a belt which sheathed a number of stilettos. His canvas bag was closed.

Maelys checked it swiftly. It contained nothing but clean clothes. She turned to the chest. It contained several small instruments that might be alchymical devices, plus packets of herbs and powders, and jars of balm. She looked under the bed. Nothing but a spare pair of boots. She checked them. Nothing was hidden inside.

She was about to go to the next room when she heard Phrune plodding back, rather out of breath. 'Just fools fighting over nothing, Master. Come inside and I'll cream you up.'

Monkshart muttered something she didn't catch, in a dead voice. Maelys should have gone under the side at once but she didn't think quickly enough, and when the two entered the outer flap of the tent there was no time to do anything but slip beneath the camp bed and pray that the low-hanging covers would conceal her if they came in.

They did. Maelys could see a sliver of the room through a gap between the covers. Monkshart pulled off his robes then stood while Phrune peeled away the body gloves, inspected them carefully for tears and laid them out over the bed. He then helped Monkshart onto the table. He lay down carefully on his front, wincing. The weeping, corrugated skin covered him all over.

Phrune scooped balm from a jar and began to spread it over Monkshart's legs.

'The scouts saw no sign of the Deliverer,' Monkshart said dully. 'He's concealed his tracks too well; by the time I can scry them out he'll be long gone. Our quest is teetering towards failure, Phrune. How could it have come to this?'

Maelys couldn't hear Phrune's reply over the squelching of the balm.

Monkshart went on. 'He's gone after *her*, hasn't he? After all I've done for him.'

'I expect so, Master.'

'What's the matter with Cryl-Nish? How can he not want to become the Deliverer?'

'He's fatally flawed, Master. I'd say his father has broken him – or else he's a gutless fool whose exploits in the war were a total lie.'

'No – Nish was a hero once; a great man. With his allies, he changed the course of the world.'

'There's no sign of such vision now. You should have held to your original plan – taken his mind and used him as a walking, talking puppet.'

There was a pause while Monkshart turned over, then he said, 'I dare say you're right, and should he ever fall into my hands again that's exactly what I'll do. Unfortunately that doesn't help us now. What does he see in the little wretch, anyway?'

'It'll be her talent between the sheets, Master. The quiet, ugly ones make the best lovers – they have to try harder.' Maelys cringed. 'And after all,' Phrune said slyly, 'Nish hasn't *had it* for ten years. It's not surprising he should become attached to the first little tart who spread her legs for him.'

'I suppose so.' Monkshart's voice hardened. 'But it's not her only appeal, is it?'

'What do you mean, Master?'

'I've been looking into Clan Nifferlin and I don't like what

410

I'm seeing. There's a clan talent. Jal-Nish killed most of the men to be rid of it, but I think she's got it too.'

'But she has no aura. You said –'

'I thought Cryl-Nish had made up those stories about Maelys to protect her, but I've changed my mind since she followed us through the maze. She's got to have a talent: look what she did to Vomix. Have you got that device of hers – what did she call it?'

'She told the boy it was a taphloid.'

'Curious word,' mused Monkshart. 'I've never heard it before.'

Phrune moved and cut off her view, but Maelys heard the rustle of tissue-leather.

'And just the touch of it was agonising to Vomix,' Monkshart went on. 'Can she have enchanted it in some way?'

'I don't think so,' said Phrune. 'I barely touched it, yet it felt as if my aura was being turned inside out – as though my very nature was being forcibly changed. Yet it didn't hurt the boy.'

'The boy has no talent. He's just an ordinary kid with no aura. I don't dare touch it with bare skin – *what did you say*?'

'It seemed to invert my aura, Master. No, it felt as if it was trying to convert my aura into its opposite, and changing me at the same time – transforming the very essence that gives me my talent.' Phrune shuddered ostentatiously. 'Such torment!'

'It's ironic that you should glory in inflicting pain on others, yet be so sensitive to it yourself. It's a weakness, Phrune. You should practise stoicism, as I do. You'll be all the stronger for it.'

'I might not serve you so well, then,' Phrune said sulkily.

'Quite, and we can't have that. Ahh!' said Monkshart. 'Hand me my glove, then stand back. Give me room.'

Phrune fetched the body-glove Monkshart had taken off earlier and moved out of the way. Monkshart held the taphloid in his left hand, in several folds of dangling tissue-leather, turning his hand this way and that. He popped the taphloid open with a covered thumbnail, studied the moon dial inside, made a pass over it with his other hand, then snapped it closed.

'Very, very clever,' said Monkshart.

'What is it, Master?' said Phrune.

'It's designed to conceal an aura – her aura – completely. *That's* why I saw nothing when she came to Tifferfyte, though I looked on all the planes.' He shook his head in wonder, staring at the little device on his palm. 'I've never seen anything like it. This was made by a master crafts-man.'

Maelys, lying under the bed, had a sudden, horrifying thought. What was concealing her aura now? Was it just the nearness of the taphloid? If so, and Phrune went out of the room with it, Monkshart would see her aura at once. She almost choked at the thought. She could feel the blood roaring through her veins, and surely they must notice that too. She would never get out of here alive.

'How does it work?' said Phrune.

'By mimicry, I think. By imitating another person who doesn't have an aura.'

'Does the taphloid enhance her *little* talent, then?' said Phrune.

Monkshart gave a mirthless laugh. 'Your sneer is mis-placed, Phrune. It's designed to suppress Maelys's talent because it's too strong.'

Maelys started, then almost screamed in panic. Had she made a sound? Surely a strong talent meant a strong aura, and the taphloid wouldn't need to be far away before her aura showed up.

'*Suppress* it?' cried Phrune.

'She would have been given the taphloid to conceal her talent as soon as it began to appear, *and* to stunt its devel-opment. That saved her life – no child living so close to

412

Morrelune could have concealed such a strong gift from Jal-Nish.'

'But what *is* her talent?'

'I don't know. The family talent apparently allows them to hide from Jal-Nish's watchers as long as Gatherer itself doesn't actually know about them.'

'We might use such a talent, Master.'

Monkshart recoiled. 'No! It would be too dangerous to me. I daren't risk it. It won't be easy for her to develop her gift anyway, at her age. You've got to start young with that sort of thing. Put the taphloid away.'

He handed it back. Phrune wrapped it in its tissue-leather and hung it around his neck.

'And that's how she was able to control the flappeter, untutored,' Monkshart added. 'The taphloid must have mimicked the dead rider's aura, *around her*, long enough for her to form a bond with it.'

'How could it?' said Phrune. 'His aura would vanish the moment he died.'

'I have no idea,' said Monkshart, shaking his head. He lay down and Phrune began to rub the balm on him again.

It must have happened when I imploded the crystal, *before* I killed the rider, Maelys thought. Afterwards the rider's aura around me must have slowly faded as the taphloid began to work again, *even without its crystal*, and Rurr-shyve became increasingly recalcitrant. No wonder the creature felt that I'd cheated on the contract.

Phrune's voice broke the silence. 'How did the taphloid become so dangerous?'

'By passage through the Mistmurk,' said Monkshart. 'Objects carried through portals between worlds are known to change in unpredictable ways, and the Mistmurk is a minor version of a portal. The Pit of Possibilities is the antithesis of what existed there before the Tifferfyte node was destroyed – a negation of the power of the node, perhaps – and it nullifies all normal powers and forces.'

'Does that always happen when a node is destroyed?'

'Ah – that's the question Jal-Nish most wants answered.'

'And what is the answer, Master?'

'No one knows. Every destroyed node is different. Some are transformed into nothingness, some into a new and opposing force, and some, perhaps, into forces which are the antithesis of each other. I don't think we'll ever know – it would take a mancer's lifetime just to study one destroyed node.'

'But you understood the destroyed Tifferfyte node.'

'Only enough to know why it could reveal the futures. That's why I set it up to spy on Jal-Nish. The Pit should have nullified Maelys's taphloid too, but the abrupt transition from pit to maze, through the Mistmurk, has changed it. It's made the taphloid greater, but more dangerous.'

So that's why she'd seen Jal-Nish using the tears – in the Pit the taphloid had been prevented from suppressing her talent and, because the place had been set up for Monkshart to spy on Jal-Nish, her talent must have shone out and caught that fleeting glimpse of Gatherer.

'And Maelys?' Phrune's voice had a deadly edge. 'What did she see in the Pit, I wonder, with her *special* talent?'

'A very good question, Phrune. More importantly, what are we to do about her?'

'She's a wild card, Master. She keeps interfering, changing the future in unpredictable ways.'

'The wrong ways. You should have dealt with her at once.'

The squelching stopped abruptly. 'I could hardly do that, Master, with hundreds of the Defiance around.'

'Twice before you had the chance to finish her, and failed.' Monkshart sat up and his voice took on a low, silky edge. 'I'm starting to wonder about you, Phrune.'

'Master!' said Phrune with a sharp intake of breath. 'Count the hundreds of ways I've served you, then weigh my few failures against them. Where would you be without my balms and unguents, to say nothing of the body-gloves I've risked my life to provide you? Some donors proved most reluctant to give up their living skin.'

Monkshart sighed. 'Very well. You have served me, Phrune, and I'm grateful for it. Assist me into the gloves, please. I must make plans for the hunt.'

He hopped down from the table and Maelys heard a series of squelches as the body-glove was eased up his balm-covered body. What unfortunate had given his or her young life to ease his pain this time?

'Are you going to take the Defiance with you?' said Phrune when it was done and Monkshart was donning his robes.

'No. We must travel alone, and fast. I'll make arrangements for them to follow, and to be fed titbits about the Deliverer on the way, otherwise they'll soon lose heart and go back to their villages. Should that happen, it won't be so easy to raise them next time.'

'If there is a next time.'

'There must be. I'm wondering if the girl isn't the key to him. Find her and we may find him, sooner or later. Get onto it, Phrune. Learn everything there is to be known about Maelys of Nifferlin, her family and clan. Whatever it costs.'

'And then?'

'Hunt her down, Phrune.'

'Yes, Master. And when I get her?'

'I'll extract what she saw in the Pit.'

'And then, Master?' Phrune sounded uncertain.

Monkshart laughed harshly. 'I'm teasing you, faithful Phrune. You'll take her skin, of course. Then kill her to make sure no one else learns what she saw.'

'Thank you, Master.' Phrune's tongue was lap-lapping at his lips again as he packed away his balms and lotions. He bent to put them in the chest and the taphloid slipped out of his robes, dangling on a chain around his neck. She saw it clearly for the first time, and felt a sudden, overpowering urge to hold it in her hand again.

415

Maelys bit her knuckles to stop herself from crying out, but she must have made a sound, for Phrune's head whipped around. He stole across the room and she was sure he knew she was there. What was she to do? Should she burst out, knife in hand, and go for him? She'd never get away from him *and* Monkshart, but she might just take Phrune with her, and that would be doing the world a service.

She was about to scramble out from under the bed when Phrune walked past the end. What was he doing? She heard the faintest rustle and his feet appeared, parallel to the side wall. He was standing against it as if listening for someone outside. Or searching for an aura?

'Master?' he said softly.

'What is it?' Monkshart said from the adjoining room.

'I just had a fleeting sense of the girl. I think she's still in the camp.'

Monkshart appeared in the doorway. If he came in, and Phrune went out with the taphloid, she was doomed. 'I don't sense any aura nearby, and my senses are stronger than yours . . . but we must leave nothing to chance.'

Maelys's heart was pounding but she tried to hold her nerve. Even if Phrune didn't sense anything he would search the tent, just in case. He could probably hear her thundering heartbeat. He stood there for a long time, then someone spoke outside, not far away, and he went out, creeping on his bare feet.

Monkshart stood in the doorway for a moment, head up in the air as if sensing for something, then went into the adjoining room.

Maelys didn't dare move while Phrune was outside. She waited until he came back, the longest ten minutes of her life, and spoke to Monkshart. A bold warrior or a cunning spy would have lain there until Phrune came into his room, then slit his throat as he slept, or thrust the dagger up into him through the thin mattress. Maelys couldn't do it. Her

416

courage had run out. She felt her way to the side wall of the tent, rolled under it, walked out of the camp and ran for her life.

Thommel was sitting by a small, smokeless fire making tea when she regained the campsite. Maelys checked as soon as she caught sight of him. He would be furious when he discovered what she'd done, and she could hardly blame him, since she'd risked everything for no gain. It didn't occur to her to lie and say she'd just been for a walk. He had to know. Besides, she'd always been a truthful person and couldn't bear to start out with him the way she had with Nish. Look what those lies and deceits had done for her.

'The tea's ready,' Thommel said with a lazy smile as she approached. 'Where have you been?'

Maelys took a deep breath, raising her chin. 'I went back to the camp to see if I could get my taphloid back from Phrune.' She'd told him about its loss previously.

The smile faded. 'You're so brave. After what he's done, I wouldn't have dared.' He stood up, looking anxious. 'Maelys, are you all right?'

'Yes,' she said faintly. 'Why?'

'You're breathing as though you've just run a race, yet you're as white as pastry.' He took her arm. 'Here, sit down. Have some tea. It's good and sweet; I found some honeycomb on the way back.'

She sat down and took the tea, gratefully. 'I'm afraid I've been rather stupid.' She told him what had happened. 'Phrune was so close that I could smell him. I was so afraid, I wanted to scream. What if they'd detected my aura, or I'd left some traces in the tent? I would have ruined everything.' She was still shaking.

He came across to sit beside her, putting an arm across her shoulder. 'I've lost things that are precious to me, too. Of course you had to try to get it back.'

'You're not angry with me?'

417

'You're not my servant. I don't have any right to be angry. But when I think that you could have fallen into their hands, my heart stops beating.'

He hugged her briefly, then moved away and poured himself a mug of tea, for he'd given her his. She sipped the hot sweet drink thoughtfully and her panic began to recede. She'd gotten the wrong impression about Thommel the other day. He was gentle and understanding, and it was good to be sharing the journey with him. She felt safer than she had at any time since she'd left home.

Unlike Nish, Thommel was good-humoured most of the time. His dark side only appeared when Nish's name was mentioned. Thommel believed that Nish had recognised him as soon as he'd appeared in the Defiance camp, and had ordered Monkshart and Phrune to keep him at bay. Whenever she said Nish's name Thommel became bitter and remote.

But what did he want of Nish, and who was Thommel anyway? He wouldn't say, though the name rang falsely in her mind whenever she heard it.

They finished their tea and struck out for Thuntunnimoe at once, though they didn't head directly for it. Thommel was painstaking in covering their tracks, for which Maelys was grateful. Phrune wouldn't give up until he took her skin.

She couldn't stop thinking about that, night and day, nor Monkshart's and Phrune's speculations about destroyed nodes, and what she'd seen in the Pit. If Jal-Nish had a weakness, what could it be? He was afraid that all his work would come to nothing in the end, and perhaps that he'd be undone by the very forces that had made him great in the first place. What forces? The tears? How could they undo him?

Nothing goes to nothing. Monkshart had meant that no power or force could be destroyed, only transmuted into another form and, rarely, its antithesis. He'd been talking

418

about the Tifferfyte node being transformed into the Pit of Possibilities, but surely the principle must also apply to the node whose destruction had created the Profane Tears.

Maelys laboriously followed her chain of logic. The tears had been formed by the destruction of a node in a particular way; they were the distilled essence of that node. But why was Jal-Nish afraid?

Then it struck her, so strongly that it took her breath away. Could the tears and their antithesis have been created at the same time? Was that what he was really afraid of? Maybe that's why he'd captured or killed all the mancers in the world – so no one else could find the antithesis to the tears, wherever it was, and use it to nullify their power.

She was getting a headache, and her idle speculations were no help, so she put them aside for another time and went on to Monkshart's other revelation, that her talent was strong but had been deliberately stunted. It would be very difficult to learn at her age and she couldn't help resenting that.

Two days later they entered the vast, steamy rainforest that ran north and south for fifty leagues, and east-west nearly as far. It was easy walking for the most part, for the gigantic vine-clad trees cut off most of the light and in consequence the leaf-covered ground supported only scattered tree ferns and gigantic, unpleasant-looking fungi. They were constantly slapping mosquitoes, and picking ticks and leeches off each other.

However, in these empty lands, which had been further depopulated by the war, they often walked for days without seeing a soul, and Maelys's spirits rose the further they went. No people meant no watchers for the God-Emperor and, since opening up, Thommel had become pleasant company. He was also a quick and skilled hunter with a short bow, and they'd had fresh meat nearly every day, which was just as well, for Maelys was still ravenous. She was eating more than Thommel, though she often felt ill afterwards and sometimes was weak from hunger a few hours later.

Five or six days into the rainforest, she woke in the middle of the night with her stomach churning as though she'd eaten bad food. Not wanting to disturb Thommel, she got up quietly, slipped out of the circle of the firelight and stumbled a polite distance into the forest before throwing up violently. Maelys raked leaves over the mess with one foot, went back and washed her face, then slipped into her thin bedroll.

She slept at once, but woke not long after, alternately hot and cold, with her belly churning painfully as if two cats were fighting in it. She didn't feel sick this time, but her stomach was in too much turmoil to lie down, so she got up and began to walk back and forth, leaning backwards with her hands folded over her belly because that was the least uncomfortable position.

Her stomach felt hot and swollen. Having helped to look after the clan's animals since an early age, she knew that cattle could suffer from bloat if they ate certain herbs in the wrong season, and if their bellies weren't punctured to let the gas out they would die. Could that be the matter with her? It wasn't a pleasant thought.

'Maelys?' Thommel was lying on his side, supported on one elbow, looking up at her.

'Just a pain in the stomach,' she said, walking the other way. She never wanted to trouble others. 'I'm sure I'll be all right in a –' Her stomach heaved so violently that she couldn't control it and a stream of vomit burst out of her mouth. She fell to hands and knees, retching and retching until there was nothing left to bring up, by which time she could only lie on her side, knees drawn up, gasping.

Thommel crouched beside her, holding her hand. She wanted him to go away; she couldn't bear for anyone to see her in such a state, but was too weak to say so. Maelys just lay there, her stomach churning ever more violently.

420

Despite throwing up everything she'd eaten and drunk, it felt even hotter and more swollen than before.

Eventually she started to feel a little better. Thommel washed her face and hands with a wet cloth and held her up. 'Must have been something I ate,' she whispered.

'But you've eaten the same things as I have.' He sat back. 'You're not pregnant, are you? To *Nish*?'

She wanted to laugh, but couldn't manage it. 'No,' she said faintly. Her throat felt raw.

'Are you sure? It can take time to show –'

'I'm a virgin, Thommel.' Just saying that would have embarrassed her, had it been Nish, but she felt so much more comfortable with Thommel.

'Right,' he said. 'And I don't see how it can be food poisoning, since we've eaten the same things ever since we left, though maybe I've got a stronger stomach. Tell me exactly how you're feeling.'

Maelys described her symptoms. He shook his head.

'I don't understand it. Stand up. I want to look at you.'

He had to help her up, and hold her up once she was on her feet, for her knees were wobbling. He looked her over, pulled up her shirt and felt her stomach, then knelt and put his ear to it.

It tickled and now Maelys did feel uncomfortable. She tried to pull away. 'I'm sure I'll be all right in the morning.'

'Stay there.' He put one arm around her back and pulled her towards him until her belly compressed against the side of his head. Her stomach began to churn even more violently. 'You've got a bug!' He stood up.

'Well, obviously,' she muttered. 'A stomach bug, but I'll soon be over it. I hardly ever get sick.'

'Not this one. Lie down. I've got to get it out.'

THIRTY-EIGHT

She lay down, then lurched up again. 'You're not going to cut me open or puncture me like a bloated cow, are you?'

'Don't be silly,' he said in the infuriatingly soothing way in which healers speak to sick people. 'Wait here. I just need to find the right herb. It's a common one, fortunately.' He thrust a branch into the fire until it was well ablaze and, holding it up, walked into the forest.

Maelys lay down, more worried than before. What did he mean by 'Get it out?' Her stomach was still swelling so she got up, though she could find no position that wasn't acutely uncomfortable.

Thommel was gone for hours and by then she was finding it increasingly difficult to breathe, for her distended belly was squashing her lungs and she could not draw in enough air. What was happening to her? She began to think that she was going to die.

She heard his pounding feet long before he got there. Shortly he burst into the firelight, carrying a blazing strip of bark. The branch must have burned away hours ago. 'Sorry,' he gasped. 'I was looking for slugwort. Usually you see it everywhere, but I must have walked two leagues before I found any.' He threw the bark into the fire and listened to her stomach again.

'Slugwort?' She felt even sicker. 'I haven't a slug inside me?'

422

'Of *course* not,' he said, though he looked more anxious than before. 'Just hang on. I won't be long.' He drew a clump of blue-green herb from his pocket. The tiny, shiny leaves reflected the light in crescents. 'It's tough and I've got to chop it up or it will pass through without doing any good.'

Maelys knew a lot about herb lore but she didn't recognise this one. She sat down, leaned back to ease the pressure on her lungs and watched while he chopped the slugwort finely on a metal plate, going over and over it, then stirred it into a mug of cold tea.

'I'll swirl it around to keep the slugwort suspended, then I want you to drink the lot in a single gulp; all right?'

'Why in a single gulp?' said Maelys, anxious again.

'Just drink it. The sooner you do, the sooner I can get on with it.' He was swirling the contents as he spoke.

'Get on with what?'

'If you're not going to cooperate, I'll have to hold your nose as if you're a little kid.'

Maelys managed a smile, for she'd often done that while helping Aunt Haga dose the small children of the clan for the winter. She nodded and held out her hand obediently. He gave the mug a final swirl and she poured it down in one swallow.

She'd expected it to taste revolting but the herb had no more flavour than grass. It was like drinking a cup of tea leaves, and some stuck to her teeth and the roof of her mouth. She licked them off, swallowed, then felt an agonising pain in her stomach, which began to churn as if a lizard were leaping around inside it.

Maelys reached out blindly, caught Thommel's hand and squeezed it so tightly that he had to clench his jaw. 'What is it? What's the matter with me? Am I going to die?'

Thommel's hesitation was tiny, but it was there. 'Why would you think that?'

'Don't tell me any lies! If there's something badly wrong with me I've got to know.'

423

'You've got a bug inside you, and it's growing fast. Wild meat sometimes has the eggs in it, and if it's not cooked through they can survive.'

She felt sick, disgusted, and very, very cold. 'What kind of a bug?'

'It's called a slurchie. It's not common here; I've only seen it once before. I should have warned you to be careful, and not eat any meat that was still pink inside.'

'That's the way I like it,' she said quietly.

'Me too, but –'

'And when you saw a slurchie before, what happened?'

Thommel paused. 'The man who had it died. How does your stomach feel now?'

'It's still churning, though not as much. But it doesn't hurt any more.'

'Good. That means the herb's working. It numbs the organs to pain. I'd better get to work before . . .' He got up and began to rifle through his pack, pulling things out and tossing them on the ground.

Maelys didn't ask what he was doing, for she didn't think he would tell her. She'd never heard the name slurchie before but it sounded nasty. Thommel had a length of thin cord and was weaving and knotting something on the end, like an open basket about the size of a large lemon. He finished his work, examined it carefully then rolled it into a ball between his palms and came across bearing another mug of water.

He handed her the ball, which had an arm's length of cord trailing from it, but held onto the free end. 'Swallow this with as much water as you can drink.'

'Seriously?'

'Quickly. There's not much time left.'

Maelys didn't see how it could work, or even how she could get the ball down, but she took it into her mouth with half a mug of water and swallowed. The water went down but the string caught in the back of her throat. She gagged

424

and began to heave it up, but Thommel held her mouth open and poured the rest of the mug down her throat, and she felt the string go down further.

He ran for more water. She swallowed it and the ball of cord went the rest of the way. He held onto the end. It felt horrible, the cord running up the back of her throat, and she was constantly suppressing the urge to heave.

'Just keep taking tiny sips if it troubles you,' he said. 'How's your stomach now?'

'Hardly churning at all.'

'Oh!' She'd thought that would be good news but he looked grave. 'Well, I'm sure it'll be all right.'

He didn't sound confident and Maelys, who could only imagine what was going to happen if it wasn't all right, felt sick.

'Lie down, Maelys. Pull your shirt up.'

She lay on her back and drew her shirt up above her stomach. He got down beside her, put his ear to her belly and kept moving it around, listening. He frowned, pushed her left breast up out of the way and listened to the top of her stomach, then did the same to the right. She didn't protest; for the moment he was a healer and she was just a body to him.

'All right,' he said. 'Sit up and turn over. I need you on hands and knees, bum up as high as it will go, head down until your forehead touches the ground.' She complied, feeling most undignified. 'Now, straighten the curve of your back. Your belly's a bit compressed and we don't want that.'

She did so. Her lower back immediately began to ache, but she ignored it.

'Ready?'

'Yes,' she whispered, feeling very afraid. With his free hand he stroked her hair and she felt better. She had confidence in Thommel. If it could be done, he would do it. And if not, well, people often got sick and died for no discernible reason. That was fate.

'Now I'm going to draw out the cord, really slowly. Stay calm and don't move, no matter what happens – or no matter how much it hurts. Can you do that?'

She nodded, almost imperceptibly. He stroked her hair again and she felt a calm descend on her, a kind of peace.

Thommel began to pull on the cord, ever so gently, taking up the slack. Maelys felt vaguely nauseous. The cord grew taut. He drew on it even more carefully, frowned, eased off the tension and pulled it taut again.

'I'm not sure,' he replied to her unasked question. He eased off, pulled taut, eased off, pulled taut. 'Ahhh! I think – yes. I'm sure I've got it.' He pulled harder, drawing a finger-joint length of cord from her mouth. Something flipped back and forth in her lower belly and she felt a twinge of pain. This time it was like a spiny eel thrashing on a line.

Her lower back was throbbing now and it was growing ever harder to hold it straight against the curve of her backbone. The backs of her legs were aching too, and the muscles in her neck. She began to feel shaky. How long was this going to take?

'You're doing well, really well. It won't be long now.'

Unfortunately Maelys knew he was lying; that it had barely started. It was the kind of soothing nonsense healers said all the time, yet it did make her feel better. She wasn't in it alone. Thommel was looking after her.

He eased out a finger's length of cord. The slurchie flipped again, as if it were trying to tie itself in a knot. It was in her upper stomach now, which had not been numbed by the slugwort, for she felt such an agonising pain there that she let out a stifled gasp.

Thommel eased off at once, wrapped the cord around his finger several times, then took her face in his hands and kissed the top of her head. It was just a healer's kiss, nothing in it, but she felt better at once.

'Have you done this before, Thommel?'

'No. Are you afraid that I don't know what I'm doing?'

'I have every confidence in you.'

'I wish I did,' he said under his breath. 'Ready to try again?'

'Yes,' she whispered.

This time it was even worse, but she managed to endure it. It's good pain, she told herself. It proves that whatever he's doing is working.

It went on for an agonisingly long time. Like childbirth in reverse, she imagined, in the moments when she was capable of thinking. It felt as though Thommel was tugging a barbed eel out of her. He got part of it up through the opening between her stomach and throat, but the pain was so great that Maelys shrieked and doubled up, nearly tearing the cord out of Thommel's fingers. He released the tension suddenly, the slurchie slipped back down and when she could think clearly again she knew that he would have to do it all over again.

'I'm sorry, Maelys,' he said, putting his arms around her, and he was, for she saw his tears splash on the leaves below her face. He massaged her lower back and began again, though this time he tied the cord around his wrist and made another turn there each time he'd drawn enough cord out, so the slurchie couldn't slip back.

It was coming up her gullet now, which wasn't numbed at all, and suddenly it no longer felt like good pain. It was agony worse than anything she'd ever imagined. It felt as if her gullet were being shredded.

The slurchie filled it so completely that she could hardly draw breath, for the passage to her lungs was squashed flat. She couldn't breathe; she could feel herself blacking out, her knees giving. She was going to choke to death.

'Hold on, Maelys. Hold on, my love. It's not long now.'

She held on, he pulled harder on the cord and she managed to draw a tiny breath – just enough. The creature's head came up into the back of her throat and cut off her wind again, scoring her as if it were wrapped in brambles.

427

Maelys's consciousness was fading. He was shouting at her but she couldn't make out what he was saying. 'Open your mouth!' he shouted in her ear. 'Open your damned mouth, quick.'

Her jaw was clenched tight. He tugged harder, the head of the slurchie came up into the back of her mouth, she felt herself falling as she fainted from lack of air, then in a panic he jerked too hard and the cord broke.

Thommel let out a cry of despair. Maelys hit the ground with her left cheek, hard enough to feel it, then he was down beside her, crying out as he threw her over onto her back, prised her locked jaw open and thrust one hand into her mouth. Maelys could hear horrible sucking and gasping sounds coming from her, and repulsive gurglings and squelches, followed by a thin squeal like no sound she had ever heard, as Thommel caught the slurchie around the head and in one desperate, agonising heave, ripped it out of her.

Maelys sucked in three breaths worth of air and it was the sweetest she'd ever drawn, though her mouth tasted foul and slimy, and her lips were burning. She tried to spit it out but the slurchie's mucous was so thick that it wouldn't move.

Something popped in her stomach, then it heaved uncontrollably and she threw up all over herself, bringing up a bucketful of watery slime flecked with black ovoid specks. It burned too, though at least it washed away the muck that had coated her mouth and tongue.

Maelys sat up, dripping but too relieved to worry about the spectacle she must make. After what she and Thommel had been through together it didn't matter at all.

He was crouched on his haunches, still holding the squirming, flapping slurchie out in his bloody right hand, and he wore the biggest, most beaming smile she had ever seen. It warmed her.

The creature was enormous – the length of her forearm and outstretched hand. Its small head, which was still burrowed inside the cord basket, was covered in feelers and sucker discs, and what looked like a ring of tiny, transparent teeth. Its black and yellow body was shaped like a stubby eel, with dozens of little legs ending in clinging barbs, and it had a row of raised spines down the centre of its back. The barbs on the front feet had latched on blindly to the cords of the basket, fortunately.

'When it's numbed by slugwort it likes to burrow its head into something, though . . .' Thommel looked up at her, '. . . it doesn't always burrow into the cord basket.'

She knew what he meant. 'And I suppose it can pull out of it, too.'

'So I've heard.'

She didn't need him to say how fortunate she'd been. 'It's so big. How long has it been – in me?'

He shrugged. It jerked in his hand as if trying to get back to Maelys. She pulled away hastily. 'I don't know. A week or two? They grow quickly, feeding on your food, until their needs are more than you can eat. And then they start to eat you, from the inside. Do you want a closer look?'

That explained why she'd been so ravenous, and often felt ill after eating. She shuddered. 'No thanks.'

'I'll get rid of it then.' He got up and went to the fire, unravelling the cord from his wrist. The slurchie began to thrash in his bloody hand; more blood was running down his wrist. He leaned over the fire and tried to shake it off but it dug in its barbs, twisted and pulled its head free of the basket. Its head curled around on itself, squirmed at his palm and dug in.

Thommel let out a cry of pain and lurched backwards, trying to pull it off with his other hand. The barbs on its plump little legs dug in there too and the yellow markings on its back began to flash on and off like a firefly.

For once Thommel's calm self-possession had left him. He was reeling around, panicking as he tried to fling it off, but it wouldn't let go. Maelys scrambled up, picked up a stout stick and stumbled towards him.

'Hold your hands away from you,' she croaked, for the slurchie was flipping back and forth and she was afraid it would go for his mouth or his belly.

He did so. She crept closer, afraid that it might go for her, too. Don't think; just do it. She took careful aim, whacked down with the stick, and her blow tore the sucker mouth off his palm, skin and all. It clung on to his other hand with its barbs, squirming its body around to get a better grip, and she had to whack it again and again until finally a lucky blow knocked it into the coals. She pressed the slurchie down with her stick until it stopped moving and began to char, then raked more coals over it just to make sure.

'Don't know what happened there,' said Thommel, shaking his bleeding hand. 'I just panicked for a moment. Ugh!' He shuddered and held out his arms then, heedless of the vomit and slime all down her front, she went to him.

Things were never the same between them after that, and couldn't be. When Maelys woke in the morning and looked across the embers to Thommel, it felt like she was seeing an old, trusted friend. They did everything together for the rest of the trip and it was a wonderful time, the best Maelys could remember since her childhood. She'd never been friends with a man before and, after all the bitter talk of her mother and aunts, had not imagined that such a thing was possible.

The remainder of the journey proved uneventful, however, and the only blight on it was her lost taphloid. She cursed herself for missing her one opportunity to regain it.

Fifteen days after hearing the news about Nish's flight they stopped on a rock-crowned hill, staring at Thuntunnimoe peak. It stood alone, though many similar peaks rose singly or in scattered clusters out of the rainforest. All were sheer-sided and many needle-narrow, at least in their upper sections, more or less as Nish had described his vision in the pit. It was sunny over the rainforest, with just a few scattered clouds in a washed-out blue sky, but the plateaux were so tall that they created their own weather, and the tops of most were concealed by clinging cloud.

'How can you be sure this is the one?' said Maelys. 'They all look the same.'

'You said Nish kept talking about his luck turning, and riding his fortune while it lasted.'

'Yeees,' she said dubiously.

'In my wood-cutting days I walked around every one of these peaks, searching for the rare timbers that grow nowhere else. The other needle plateaux are circular in outline, or oval, or have ragged edges, but Thuntunnimoe is in the form of a cloverleaf and I always felt lucky when I was here. I *was* lucky.'

'How do you mean?'

'I came to the plateau country searching for the precious red amber tree, whose timber is more valuable than gold. The base of Thuntunnimoe peak is one of only three places on Lauralin the red amber tree grows, and no one knows it's here but me. That'll change once Monkshart follows Nish here, of course. He brings ruin wherever he goes.'

Nish was the one topic she didn't want to raise, for she didn't want Thommel's bitterness to blight their friendship. She assumed there was a good reason for it but since he still hadn't told her and it was his only failing, she made allowances. 'How did you get the timber out?'

'I cut part of the trunk's heart into slices and carried it on my back.'

'All that way?'

'You don't need much. Red amber-wood isn't used as timber – it's too valuable. I stacked the rest carefully so it would season, for I planned to come back for it.'

'But you never did,' she guessed.

'I fell foul of one of Jal-Nish's labour gangs – slave gangs, really – and spent two years of my life on it, though it felt like twenty. They drive you until your bones crack, Maelys.

431

The other slaves were dying all around me and I wanted to die too, just to escape. How I envied Nish, idling his sentence away in a comfortable cell.'

Maelys felt that she had to defend Nish, though she was coming to think that he wasn't the man he'd been made out to be and, guiltily, that Tulitine had been right and her previous feelings for him had just been a romantic infatuation arising from reading his tale so many times as an impressionable child. He didn't compare to Thommel and that troubled her, for even now she only knew one certain way to secure her family's safety.

'It was a stinking hole,' she said mildly. 'I could still smell it on him days after he'd bathed.'

'We slept in stinking holes too, and ate slops.' He wasn't bitter now, just matter-of-fact. 'Then we were whipped awake at dawn, seven days a week, and broke our backs in hard labour, hauling gigantic logs out of the forest.'

'What's red amber-wood used for?' she asked.

'All sorts of things. The wood dust is steeped and mixed into potions, salves and unguents to fight infections; also in the subtlest of perfumes and as the rarest and most tantalising of spices. It's considered to confer good luck; many people also think that having it in their house is a blessing on their family and all their endeavours. I wouldn't know about that, though I was always lucky when I carried some, and I felt cursed as soon as it was taken from me.

'But the greatest value of red amber-wood, from Thuntunnimoe at least, is as a ward against unwanted spells and charms. Perhaps the trees take up something of the native magic of this place as they grow, for red amber-wood from other places is far weaker.

'I would have made my fortune from it, if only . . . Anyway, just a splinter will do, worn on the body. Or burnt in a brazier it will protect a household for a day or two.' Thommel sounded like a fairground spruiker now, though she loved to see him so animated.

'It's not proof against strong Arts – only a king could afford enough red amber-wood for that. But if you could,' he looked over his shoulder then lowered his voice, with an uneasy smile, 'It's said that you could walk past a wisp-watcher carrying a sign, *Death to the Tyrant God-Emperor*, and the watcher wouldn't see you.'

'Really? I could use some of that. Wait a minute!' she cried, staring eagerly at the peak. 'Thommel, if there *is* something uncanny hidden at the top, what if it's surrounded by red amber-wood? Maybe that's how it's been hidden from the God-Emperor all this time.'

He raised an eyebrow and Maelys realised that she'd said too much, and perhaps given Nish's secret away. She prayed that she was right about Thommel, and that he could be trusted.

They trudged across to the base of Thuntunnimoe and circled the peak twice, but found no human footprints save their own. They trekked to the other needle peaks nearby in case Nish had gone to the wrong one, finding no sign there either. A week of agonisingly drawn-out days went by. Nish failed to appear. Finally Maelys was forced to conclude that he'd either been taken or had fallen along the way.

'We'll give him a few more days,' said Thommel. 'I knew where I was going, remember? Let's climb up a bit. We might be able to see something.'

The cloverleaf-shaped peak was somewhat broader at the base, and its cliffed walls were indented by four precipitous clefts, though only one of them looked climbable. They scrambled up it for a hundred spans, struggling on wet, mossy rocks which often moved underfoot, to a point where they could see back over the rainforest.

'Hey!' cried Thommel, staring.

Just a few days' march behind them, a flight of flappeters were circling. Maelys sprang under the fronds of a tree fern, though the flappeters couldn't have seen them from such a distance.

'Only two things could bring such valuable creatures here,' said Thommel, who hadn't moved. 'The Defiance, or Nish.'

'They're circling over a big area,' said Maelys after watching for a while. Her heart leapt. 'They're following Nish.'

'Perhaps,' said Thommel. 'Or the Defiance. And whoever it is, the God-Emperor's forces must be shadowing them.'

So even if Nish did turn up, and found what he was looking for on the plateau, there wouldn't be time to get away with it. What if he were out there now, desperately searching for this peak among dozens of similar ones? That could take weeks, since the cloverleaf shape wasn't apparent from a distance. Was there any way to signal him without the flappeters seeing it?

'Oh, Maelys?' said Thommel.

'Yes?'

'If we do find Nish, please don't say anything.'

'About what?'

'About my meeting him in the war.'

'Why not? That's why you came all this way, *isn't it?*'

'Yes, but it's between me and him, and if he's going to refuse me – well, just don't mention it.'

THIRTY-NINE

Nish and Zham trekked north then west, following a zigzagging path during which Zham had to use every ounce of his bushcraft to throw their pursuers off the track, though Nish couldn't be sure they had. Monkshart would never give him up; he'd exert all his powers to find Nish, and sooner or later he must. Jal-Nish would be equally unrelenting, and how could the Deliverer hide when the whole world was looking for him?

Unfortunately Zham didn't know of any plateau resembling the one Nish was searching for, and Nish was reluctant to tell him the details in case he was captured and the truth tortured out of him. He couldn't send Zham into the towns to ask, for the giant was too easily recognisable.

Nish had to go alone, in disguise, though through judicious questioning in a number of inns he learned that plateau formations like the one he was searching for could be found at just one place in Crandor – deep in the rain-forest fifty or sixty leagues west of Guffeons, not far from the steep rise of the legendary and ill-omened *Wahn Barre*, the Crow Mountains.

Once they reached the sparsely populated rain-forest Nish breathed a little easier, for the chance of accidental discovery was slight here. Conditions were more comfortable, too; it wasn't nearly as hot, though it was stiflingly humid. They were drenched in sweat night and day.

Only one event of note occurred on the journey, and it happened on their third day in the rainforest, late in the afternoon, as they were trekking across a winding valley where the spaces between the tall trees were dotted with head-high patches of aromatic mintbush and thickets of small, red-leaved lotion trees which Zham said were poisonous to humans, though the white gum seeping from their trunks helped wounds to heal more quickly.

He had been stalking a small twisthorn deer through the forest for an hour and had shot it, but it had not yet fallen.

Zham was approaching the thicket where it had taken cover, bow in hand. 'Quiet now, surr, and be careful. Even a small deer can be dangerous –'

He broke off. Nish heard a thin bleat, a furious scrabbling, a grunt, then a thud and more scrabbling.

'Stay back!' Zham hissed, sweeping Nish behind him with one arm. 'No, climb a tree.'

'What is it?' Nish whispered, staying where he was but readying his own sword. He'd defeated lyrinx in hand-to-hand combat; he wasn't going to run away from a wounded deer.

Zham loosened his sword in its scabbard and drew a different arrow. It was short but heavy, with a broad steel head sharp enough to shave with. He fitted it to his compact bow, which could have been carved from the rib of a mammoth, and drew back the twisted cord until his arm quivered under the strain.

Nish felt a twinge of unease. In Zham's hands, that bow could send an arrow in one side of a buffalo and out the other. Perhaps he should have climbed a tree after all. He scanned the area behind him, though none of the nearby trees were climbable.

Something crashed through the head-high band of mintbushes to his left. 'Tusker!' Zham roared. 'Look out!'

He'd whirled and fired before Nish sighted the beast. It burst out of the deep shade, coming low and fast. All he saw was a blurred shadow with red eyes and two pairs of yellow tusks – one pair upcurved, the other pair arcing to the sides – and a foam-covered snout.

The arrow disappeared into its chest and went straight through, for Nish saw bark fly off a buttressed tree root further on, but the tusker kept coming, its hairy trotters making little sound on the soft earth. It was no more than twenty paces away when it swerved towards Nish with an ear-piercing squeal.

Zham had already drawn a second arrow and was nocking it when another tusker shot out of the undergrowth where the rustling had been coming from. It was much bigger than the first; as long as Zham was tall, and the upcurving tusks were almost the length of his bow. There was blood on its snout. Zham turned to face it, putting himself between it and Nish.

Nish couldn't allow him to fight both of them, alone. He heaved out his sword and waited for the smaller tusker to come to him. It was slowing now. Blood ran down its chest from the arrow wound; red foam erupted from its mouth and nostrils with each breath. He didn't understand how it could keep going after that heavy arrow had carved right through it.

The tusker shot around in a curve then leapt forwards, right at him. Nish dragged his sword blade through the air, trying to get it into position and knowing that he was too slow. He caught a foot on something and overbalanced, flailing at the air and realising in the last terrible second that the tusker was going to impale him through the groin or the belly.

He couldn't do anything in time. He was bracing himself for the impact when Zham's sword flashed between Nish and the flying tusker, carving both its right tusks off mid-way and slicing the end off its snout. The bloody tusker slammed into Nish's hip so hard that he was sent flying five or six paces through the air.

He landed heavily on his back and shoulder and the sword jarred out of his hand. The tusker skidded around in a circle and came at him again.

There wasn't time to get up. Nish scrambled for his sword and held it out in front of him, though on his knees he was no higher than it was and at a terrible disadvantage, for he wouldn't be able to move quickly.

He tried to brace himself, to aim the sword for its open mouth, but his numb elbow wouldn't hold the point straight. It carved a bloody streak down the hairy flank of the tusker as it hit him again, though fortunately with its severed tusks – it hadn't yet understood that they were gone. They slammed into his shoulder, knocked him flying and this time the sword skidded out of reach.

Nish looked for help, but Zham was busy with the second tusker. He'd put two arrows in it but it hadn't fallen either. It was circling Zham, who bore a bloody streak on the left thigh.

Nish was dragging himself after his sword when the tusker attacked a third time. It was moving slowly now, wobbling on its feet, with clots of bloody foam oozing from its open mouth. Blood was streaming from its side and dripping from its backside, but it was still deadly.

He was exhausted and felt as though he'd been beaten with hammers. Those days in bed, recovering from the arrow wound, had robbed him of his hard-won strength. He lunged for the sword and forced himself to his feet. It took an effort to hold the blade up this time. Nish felt as weak as a child.

The tusker darted forwards. He swung the sword at it and it propped on its front feet, coughing up clots and regarding him malevolently with its red eyes.

Zham was still busy with the big tusker. It was a matter of endurance now. Nish had to hold out longer than the beast, for if he fell it would savage him with its remaining tusks and teeth until it took its last breath. It came on slowly, stopped, then darted at him. Nish strained his shoulders getting the sword in position, but this time the wobbling point slid into the neat slit below its throat where Zham's arrow had entered.

He forced the sword in, but still the tusker kept coming, its trotters tearing at the earth as it strained to get at him, all the way until it was stopped by the hilt. Nish's feet slipped, he was forced backwards, then suddenly the light went out of its eyes and it toppled sideways. It was dead.

Nish pulled his blade free with an effort, wiped it on the tusker's flank and turned around. Zham bore another streak on his thigh. His tusker was on the ground too, though still kicking. Zham was bent over, panting, and his face was grey.

Then, as Nish wavered towards him, Zham lay down his sword and bowed to his fallen foe. 'You fought nobly for your young, proud beast, and I salute you.'

The tusker's back trotters tore at the earth but it was unable to rise. Zham took his sword, touched the beast on each shoulder and then on the top of the head, then killed it with a single clean thrust between the ribs into its heart.

Zham turned, saw Nish hobbling towards him, and smiled. 'For a minute there I thought I'd let you down, Deliverer.'

'Call me Nish,' Nish said. 'From now on you are my brother, and I know you'll never let me down.'

The big man stood up straight, shocked, and a single tear made its way down his broad cheek. 'Surr,' he said, bowing until his head touched the ground, 'You do me an honour no man can deserve. I cannot –'

Nish raised him up again and embraced him. 'Are you denying the Deliverer?'

'No – of course not, Del – *Nish*.' He pulled away, scrubbed at his eyes with his free arm, and looked Nish over carefully. 'Are you all right?'

'Bruised but unharmed. That was the act of a noble man, Zham.' Nish meant it. Zham might be an uneducated peasant but he possessed more nobility than most of the nobles Nish had met.

'How could I not salute such a stubborn foe?'

'You did not salute the nylatl when you put it down.'

'That was no natural creature . . . Nish. It was an evil thing created by an evil mind.' He turned away, limping badly, hesitated, then came back. 'Surr, Nish,' he said diffidently, 'could you look at my wounds for me?'

The two gashes in his right thigh needed cleaning, for tuskers used their tusks for rooting around in the earth and tearing apart live and dead prey. After he'd washed them carefully, Nish cut a curve through the papery bark of the lotion tree, gathered the thick exudate on his knife blade, spread it over the wounds and bound them up.

'We'll eat well tonight.' He was salivating at the thought of a thick slice of roasted tusker and nicely crisped crackling.

They did better than that, for Zham found the twisthorn deer in the shrubbery. It had been easy prey for the tuskers, though they'd not had time to despoil the body, so they dined on baked venison as well. It was the finest meal Nish had eaten since going to prison.

Nish sighed and glanced across the fire towards Zham, who was carving strips of venison off a shoulder bone, spearing them with the point of his knife and transferring them to his mouth in an unending procession that had been going on for twenty minutes. The wounds troubled him when he moved, though his broad face was unlined and his thoughts seemed focussed on no more than his dinner. Zham didn't talk much, but he didn't seem to have a worry in the world and Nish envied him that inner peace.

For himself, the Defiance's victory over his father's army had rejuvenated him, and this escape allowed him to feel that he'd taken control of his destiny at last, yet it gave him little joy. Why was that? It took him some time to work it out.

He was feeling increasingly guilty about his moral cowardice at Tifferfyte: both his failure to stand up to Monkshart and Phrune over Maelys, and his complicity in allowing the villagers to sacrifice themselves on his behalf. He needed to talk to someone about it and perhaps Zham, after their shared experiences today, might be able to help.

'Do you think I did wrong, Zham?'

'Surr?' Zham paused, a slice of venison halfway to his mouth, looking puzzled. As well he might, for Nish had not previously spoken of his troubles.

'When we fled Tifferfyte, we . . . we couldn't take the villagers with us. They remained behind, fighting to the last man and woman so we could get away.'

'I heard the story from Jil,' said Zham. 'They were believers. They made that sacrifice willingly, as would I.' He resumed eating, though not with the same gusto as previously.

'But I went along with the plan; I hardly protested at all. What's worse, I came to believe that it was right, and that I deserved their sacrifice, because as the Deliverer my life was worth more than theirs. I – I can't come to terms with that, Zham. Was that the first step on the downward path? Am I –?'

Zham shifted on his log, looked down at the shoulder bone, began to carve another slice from it, then abruptly tossed it into the fire and stood up. 'I know you'll always do the right thing, surr. I'm going to turn in now. Good night.'

The following morning Nish tried again, but again Zham avoided the issue, and Nish's eyes. 'I'm sure you'll never let us down, surr,' he said as he rose and heaved the pack on his back. 'We know we can rely on the Deliverer.'

Yet Nish had been a leader of men and knew how to get the best out of them, and deal with their weaknesses too, so he didn't try again. Zham was also a believer, a simple soul, and perhaps he didn't want that belief challenged in any way.

Nish wondered if he had weakened Zham's faith in him.

He was also increasingly troubled by the future he'd seen in the Pit. Nish was coming to question it more every day. Had he, by fleeing so precipitously, done exactly what his father wanted him to? Could the vision he'd seen in the Pit be yet another way of manipulating him, or a malicious joke by his father?

No, that's how Jal-Nish wanted him to think. He wanted Nish to doubt everything he heard, and everyone he met; to cut him off from the world in a prison of his own making.

And the Deliverer's rebellion could fail simply by taking too long to get going, which might also be part of his father's plan. If he *were* close to finding the three things he needed to become invincible and immortal, and to achieve complete mastery of the tears, including the ability to close off their powers to anyone else, everything that delayed the rebellion worked in the God-Emperor's favour.

He sighed and rubbed the itchy scar below his right collarbone where the nylatl had stuck him. Even after all this time the spine wound still troubled him occasionally – a deep, hot ache that spread all the way to the shoulder and temporarily robbed him of strength in that arm. It seemed to be getting worse.

'Well,' said Zham as they slogged to the top of the ridge, then walked out onto a platform of rock that formed a natural lookout among the trees, 'we're here –' He broke off. 'That's a bit of a bugger.'

'What?' Nish said wearily.

He settled on a stone, not too close to the edge, which dropped away sharply into a broad valley covered in forest. They'd been trudging through rainforest for a fortnight and it extended in every direction as if to the ends of the world, save to the west where the distant *Wahn Barre* reared high, jagged and snow-capped even in these northern latitudes.

442

But much closer, standing up out of the rainforest like soot-blackened chimney pipes so high that the tops of most of them were shrouded in cloud, were dozens of tall, cliff-bounded plateaux. Some were half as broad as they were tall; others mere needle-like spires. Some were grouped in clusters while others stood alone, but at least half of them, if viewed from the right angle, could have been the slender, sky-piercing peak he'd seen in that fog-shrouded vision in the Pit of Possibilities.

Nish stared at the vista in dismay. 'How am I supposed to tell the right one?' He tried to recall the details of his vision, but they wouldn't come.

'The plateau country covers a big area,' said Zham. 'Got to be six leagues by four. It'll take ages to check them all.'

Nish didn't answer. A green fly buzzed around his head and he waved it away irritably. 'Well, failing any other way of identifying the right one, that's just what we'll have to do.'

Five days later they were still searching. Nish had crossed seven peaks off his sketch map but there were another ten to go, and the only way to tell was by slogging to the base of each peak and looking up. From that vantage point he could tell instantly that it wasn't the peak he'd seen in the Pit of Possibilities. He'd tried to use clearsight, though without success. It had seldom been available to him since he'd come out of the maze. Nish wondered if he'd damaged it through overuse there.

'This is going to take weeks,' he muttered.

It was late afternoon, it had been raining all day and they were fifty spans up a cleft in the latest pinnacle, where they could see over the rainforest to the next group of peaks. An overhang sheltered them from the rain that fell constantly around the plateaux, even from clear skies, though they were soaked through anyway. Their clothes hadn't been dry in a fortnight and everything smelled mouldy, including his skin, which was peppered with mosquito bites.

443

This peak, like the others, rose sheer for at least a thousand spans of wet, treacherous, unclimbable cliff. The only way up any of the pinnacles, as far as Nish could tell, would be via the precipitous clefts that scored their sides, and even the best of these would be a dangerous climb. Incessant wind shook the writhen trees growing from crevices near the top, gales that could tear an unwary climber off.

Zham was nibbling at a vegetable he'd found on the way. It resembled a doughnut-shaped ear of corn though the individual kernels were like separate bright red teeth. 'Don't have weeks.'

'What . . .?' Nish looked in the direction Zham was staring. A flappeter was hovering over the lookout where they'd stood five days ago, while another was following a track horribly like the path they'd taken to the first pinnacle. His father had found them.

'It looks as though they're tracking us. Well, *you*, I suppose.'

Nish gave Zham a keen glance. 'It does, though I don't see how they could.'

Zham shrugged. He wasn't one to waste time on fruitless speculation. 'Do you want to go to the next peak?'

'Might as well.' So much for fortune turning my way, Nish thought. 'Can we reach it before dark?' He couldn't see the sun through a thick overcast, but night fell with unfamiliar suddenness in these latitudes.

'No. Better camp here.'

'Can we risk a fire?'

Zham frowned. 'Perhaps a small one, deep in that cleft where it won't be seen. But just long enough to cook dinner.'

Unfortunately all the wood was saturated and so rotten that their fingers went right through it, though in the search they discovered a space deep in the cleft where they could sleep in reasonable comfort.

'I'm going to turn in,' said Zham, as he did every night immediately after dinner, as if to forestall uncomfortable discussions or disturbing revelations.

Nish grunted. Zham was a superlative guard and an excellent bushman, but poor company. He was happy to sit in silence for hours. He drifted through life, doing what he was ordered, and didn't seem to want anything more.

Nish pulled his coat around him and leaned against the moist rock, gazing across the forest. What made the plateau he'd seen in the Pit so unique? He couldn't recall, though he still remembered his euphoria when he'd had the vision. It had felt so right for him; so lucky, but now he was going to lose the chance for it, as he'd lost everything else to his all-dominating father. It couldn't be borne. He *couldn't* give in to him.

He sat brooding as darkness fell and the cluster of pinnacles he'd been staring at faded into the black of the night. Nish had lost track of how long he'd been there – it could have been hours – when he became aware of a tiny spark of light in the darkness.

He blinked, then rubbed his eyes, but the spark was still there. And oddly, it seemed to be coming from one peak in the cluster of pinnacles he'd been staring at earlier. He couldn't tell which one.

'Zham?' he said softly.

The big man rolled over in his bedroll, then rose and in one swift movement was beside him. 'What is it?'

'Can you see a light out there?'

'Yup! Coming from one of the pinnacles.' Zham scratched his straw-like hair – Nish could hear his fingernails rasping through it – 'The middle one of that cluster of three we saw earlier, to the left of the main group.'

'Are you certain?'

'I can still see the pinnacles in my mind, as clear as a picture.' Zham counted under his breath. 'Yup, I'm sure.'

Doubtless that was why he was such a good bushman. Nish couldn't have told which pinnacle the light came from. 'And it's at least as high as we are, or we'd never see it for the forest.'

'Higher, I'd say.'

'Is it a camp fire?'

'Could be.'

'Do you think it could be a sign?'

Zham shrugged audibly.

'It's got to be,' Nish said to himself. 'This land is practically uninhabited, and no ordinary person would waste their energy climbing these peaks. So whoever it is, they've come here for the same reason we have – to find what's at the top, and they know which pinnacle it is. They're trying to get there first.'

'Or it's an ambush.'

'It could be, but I've got to take the risk, Zham. Can you find the way there in the darkness?'

'Yup.'

'How long do you think it'll take?'

'Couple of hours.'

A surge of fury went through Nish at the thought that someone was trying to take what was rightfully his, but he controlled it. The light could also be meant to lure him in. 'Let's get going. And when we're near, keep your eyes open for a trap.'

They reached the pinnacle without incident, and the moment he touched the rock and stared up at the peak's outline against the night sky, Nish knew it was the one. A wave of relief swept through him. The vision in the Pit had been right after all. At least, so far.

'This is it, Zham,' he said quietly. 'Can we climb it?'

Zham rubbed his bristly chin. 'We'll have to be mighty careful. They're bound to have guards.'

He moved along until he came to a deep cleft in the rock, like a ravine cutting into the pinnacle. He felt his way inside and at the inner end began to climb. Nish followed him, moving slowly on the wet rock, testing each hand- and foothold before he put his weight on it.

446

'Careful now,' Zham whispered as they edged up a crevice. The mossy stone was hard to get a good grip on. 'I can smell smoke.'

Nish could too. 'Any guards?'

Zham didn't answer, but loosened his sword in its sheath. Nish did the same. He didn't understand how Zham could see to put his feet down, but the big man must have been as clear-sighted as an owl, for he hadn't once slipped or stumbled.

'It's up beyond this rock,' said Zham. 'I don't think there can be many of them. Stay back. Leave the fighting to me.'

Nish was happy to, though he couldn't imagine how one would engage in a sword fight in such a dark, cramped space. Zham crept around the outcrop, drew his monstrous sword, sprang, then let out a cry of astonishment. 'Lady Healer!'

Nish scrambled up after him. The cleft was broader here, the width of a small room, though bounded on either side by sheer rock. The coals of the camp fire revealed two people lying on a banana-shaped patch of sloping ground between the boulders, wrapped in cloaks. The smaller one shot up, brushing the mass of black hair out of her eyes with an achingly familiar movement.

'Maelys!' Nish choked. 'I – they told me you were dead.'

'Monkshart and Phrune tried their hardest.' She scrambled to her feet, her face alight and eyes glowing. He'd never seen her look so lovely.

Zham stirred the fire with his boot and the man beside Maelys sat up, rubbing his eyes.

'I'm Nish,' Nish said, rather abruptly, extending his hand. 'Who are you?'

'You may call me Thommel,' the fellow said, and stood up.

Tall, lean and hollow-cheeked, he reminded Nish vaguely of someone, though he could not think who. Thommel did not put out his hand and Nish took an immediate dislike to

447

him. Thommel and Maelys exchanged glances as if they were the closest of friends, *or even better than friends*. She nodded as if agreeing to something previously discussed, which annoyed Nish too.

'This is Zham,' Nish said. 'Zham, Maelys who helped to rescue me from Mazurhize and saved my life.' Zham was still staring at her with his mouth open. 'Do you know each other?' Nish was feeling more bewildered by the second.

'Surr,' said Zham, gazing at Maelys with sheep-like adoration, 'this is the Lady Healer who cut the arrow out of you after the battle, and tended you afterwards. Don't you remember?'

'I saw you in my fever,' said Nish, 'but when I woke, Monkshart told me it was a hallucination. Why didn't you come back?'

'Tulitine said I was a threat to Monkshart's plans and he must never learn I was among the Defiance. He was always trying to keep us apart, *if you recall*.'

'But . . . how did you get into the camp? Phrune said you were killed in Tifferfyte.'

As she sketched out what had happened since he'd carried her to her room in Tifferfyte, Nish just kept shaking his head. Maelys started forwards, as if to embrace him, then faltered.

'What are you doing *here*?' said Nish.

'When I heard that you'd fled, I had to come after you,' she said softly. 'And Thommel . . . he knew where this pinnacle was. He'd been here before.'

'You told my most secret business to a stranger!' He felt a sudden rush of anger, magnified by the way Thommel was looking at Maelys. What was their relationship, anyway? Their sleeping arrangements looked rather snug. He tried to tell himself that it was none of his business, that he didn't care about her that way and never would, but found it oddly hard to take.

'How else could I find Thuntunnimoe? I was afraid for

you, Nish. The whole world was hunting you and I was your only friend.'

'You and Thommel? How cosy. It's a wonder you had the time.' He couldn't keep the sarcasm out of his voice, though he regretted it instantly.

It wiped the joy off her face. 'And I wonder why I've come all this way for an embittered whiner who can't think about anyone but himself.' She took a deep breath, then added coldly, recklessly, 'Thommel is a decent, honourable man! He's ten times the man you are, and I know I can trust him with my life. While you – after all we'd been through together, you walked away and left me to die. What a fool I was to believe the lying promises of the Deliverer.'

She was right, though it felt as though he'd been smacked in the face with a shovel. 'I – I – Monkshart said you were dead. Phrune said he'd seen you surrounded by the soldiers, and they were slaughtering everyone . . .' He sounded so weak. So craven.

'You knew Monkshart was a murdering swine, and Phrune a despicable liar, and yet you believed them?'

'I –' She looked so disappointed that Nish couldn't go on. Couldn't even try to justify himself, or explain that the soldiers had been coming down the path, that Monkshart and Phrune had stopped him from running up after her. That would sound like an excuse. He couldn't excuse himself, so why would she?

'Phrune drugged me,' said Maelys, 'and carried me up to the village to die. I woke up just as the attack began, and I could smell his reek on me. He was getting ready to skin me alive, and drool over every minute of my agony.'

'Skin you? What are you talking about?'

'You don't even know!' she cried. 'That's the hold Phrune has over his master, you fool. Phrune knows how to make the body-gloves that ease Monkshart's torment, and he makes them from human skin, taken from living people – young people with flawless skin. That's why Phrune said

449

"What a waste" when Monkshart threw the messenger boy into the crater. He'd wasted a beautiful skin. Phrune stalked the villagers of Tifferfyte at night and they couldn't escape; there was no way for them to get through Monkshart's halo of protection.'

Nish's mouth was opening and closing like a stranded fish. He couldn't think of anything to say. Words were quite inadequate to express his mortification, but he had to try. 'I – I'm terribly sorry. I didn't know.'

'Well, now you do. That's the kind of master you follow, Nish. But not me. I'll abandon my duty to my mother and aunts before I help you serve such a monster again.'

'I'm . . . sorry I left you behind. Sorry about everything.' It was the only thing he could think of to say and it wasn't nearly enough. He couldn't face her, much less what he had done.

'I think I'll step down the cleft a bit,' said Zham, who looked as though he'd tasted something unpleasant. 'Coming, Thommel?'

At first Thommel had appeared to be enjoying Nish's mortification, but now he was gazing at his feet, shaking his head. Zham took him by the arm and they passed around the outcrop and down the cleft out of sight.

Nish and Maelys looked at one another, but each turned aside at the same moment. Maelys was wretched, as if all her expectations had been bitterly dashed, and he felt no better. He'd never wanted to hurt her.

And, Nish ruminated, she'd proven her courage and loyalty many times over. She'd followed him all this way, even through the maze, and he couldn't imagine how she'd managed that. She'd tended him after the battle, receiving not a word of thanks for it. She'd undoubtedly lit the camp fire which had shown him the way here. She was an astonishingly clever and persistent woman and he owed her more than he could ever repay.

He had to try, even at the risk of encouraging those

unwelcome feelings which had so disturbed him previously. 'Maelys,' he said, stepping towards her. 'Can we start again?'

After a long pause she nodded stiffly, then gestured to a rock next to the fire. He sat down. Maelys perched on another rock, well back across the fire.

'Why don't you go first?' said Nish. It seemed easier that way.

Maelys told him what had happened to her in Tifferfyte, of all her hopes and fears for him, and her feelings of abandonment after finding herself all alone.

Nish listened in silence, shaking his head. How could he have been duped so easily, even in the emergency of the attack? His admiration for her only grew when she told, baldly, of the escape through the maze, the attack by Phrune, and how she'd found the Defiance with Tulitine. It shamed him to learn of her faithful service as a healer, despite all he'd done to her. Truly, she was as much a hero as the greatest heroes of the Great Tales, and look how he'd treated her.

He could also see how her courage and inner strength had grown in the past month, and for the first time he wondered, if things had turned out differently, if they might have had a chance together. It was too late now. He knew that as soon as she told him about Thommel saving her from the slurchie. Nish didn't think she was falling for Thommel, but he'd acted like a real man and it had shown Nish up for the callow fool he was. Her girlish infatuation with him, and surely that was all it had been, was over. He regretted that now.

After she'd finished, Nish ended up telling her the full tale of what had happened to him over the past month. It helped a little, though not enough. The damage had already been done.

FORTY

This cleft, the main one of the four which formed the cloverleaf shape of the plateau, was wider and deeper than the others, a winding, precipitous ravine choked with fractured rocks and fallen trees, though Thommel thought it could be negotiated most of the way to the top. The uppermost hundred spans appeared extremely steep and difficult, but couldn't be seen clearly due to the cloud.

They began the climb at first light, in a chilly silence. Maelys couldn't bring herself to patch things up with Nish. How dare he judge her, or imply that she was more than friends with Thommel? She wasn't, as it happened, though she might have been. Thommel had made one or two oblique suggestions in that regard but she'd turned them aside, not because she didn't care for him, but because she didn't want to complicate her life even further just now. However it was none of Nish's business if she had been Thommel's lover.

Nish had gone ahead, thankfully, for she could not have borne his eyes on her, judging her. Why was he so upset about her closeness to Thommel? Did Thommel remind Nish of his own failings, or did he think the woodsman was a better and more deserving man, one able to rise above all he'd endured while he, Nish, could not? He was as silent as a spectre. She was grateful for that, too.

The climb proved exhausting and dangerous. The sky

was clear now, save for the clouds gathered at the top of the peak. It wasn't raining as they set out but foaming streams of water flowed down the low points of the ravine, over and under the boulders, constantly splitting and reforming, and becoming little waterfalls at every obstacle.

The shattered rocks were so slippery that Maelys had to test every foot-hold before putting her weight on it. It was already hot and, though the sun did not shine directly into the cleft at this time of year, as the morning heated up it was like climbing in a steam bath.

Above her, Nish stopped to take off his shirt and she wished she could do the same. His pale, scarred back was running with sweat and his knees were wobbly. Several times he caught at Zham's strong arm, but let go as soon as he'd steadied himself, glancing back as if anxious that his weakness had been noted. Maelys pretended she hadn't seen. Though inured to steep climbs from the time she'd taken her first steps, she was struggling too.

They laboured up some fifty spans, stopped just long enough for her screaming muscles to relax into a jelly-like state, then moved up another thirty spans. And so it went on, for hours of the most exhausting labour she'd ever undertaken. Please, please stop, she kept thinking, though Maelys was too proud to ask for a rest. If Nish could do it without complaint, so could she.

At last, when she was so tired that she had to talk herself into taking each step, 'Just one more' and 'Just one more', Thommel stopped suddenly and threw himself down on a rock.

'This must be halfway. Let's take a break.'

Nish lay on his back, gasping, his face scarlet. It was around eleven o'clock. Using dry kindling from his pack and damp wood, Thommel lit a smouldering fire on the steep side of the ravine and boiled water for tea. It tasted like warm, smoky mould.

As they set off, far too soon, it began to drizzle and drip

453

down the back of Maelys's neck. In the airless conditions that only made things more uncomfortable.

The rain became heavier as they climbed, and shortly a cooling breeze began to drift up the cleft. She pulled out her shirt and allowed the breeze to flow over her wet skin. It made a refreshing change from the unceasing heat and humidity she'd been enduring ever since emerging from the maze.

As they climbed higher the whole sky clouded over and the rain became pleasantly chilly though the wind grew ever stronger. By noon it was a blistering updraught, which gusted one way then another so fiercely that Maelys sometimes had to hunch down, clinging to the rock, until the worst had passed. Once her fingers were torn away from their handhold and she was driven sideways into the sheer wall of the cleft. She got up, rubbing her bruised shoulder. No one had noticed; they were struggling on, backs bent and heads bowed, but the gusts blasted the cold rain into their eyes no matter which way they turned.

After another exhausting couple of hours they stopped for lunch. Neither Zham nor Thommel had hunted in days and all they had to eat was flour and water pancakes cooked in the last of their dripping. They proved as tasteless as everything else she'd eaten lately, and quite as mouldy, though at least they were hot. Maelys licked her fingers and pulled her jacket more tightly around her, for the wind at this altitude cut right through her flimsy lowland clothes, and on her wet skin it was freezing.

'I don't like the look of that,' said Zham, staring upwards. A few minutes' climb above them an ever-thickening fog whited everything out.

'How far do we have to go?' Nish asked exhaustedly.

'Another couple of hundred spans,' said Thommel. 'Two hours in these conditions, I dare say.'

'I don't think I can go another minute,' said Nish.

Maelys didn't think she could either, but she said nothing.

It was after two that afternoon when they set off again, into the fog layer which had steadily crept down until it was just above them. Their progress was even slower now, for every surface was thickly coated with either saturated moss or an algal slime, and though Zham was supporting Nish all the way, they had to stop frequently for him to rest. Consequently it was well after four when they climbed over a steep notch in the rock, the fog thinned temporarily and ahead of them the ravine, while still sloping steeply up, opened out until it was about twenty paces across. They could just see the lower sides, though not the top.

'What's that?' said Zham, listening.

The song of the wind had changed. Overlaying the shrill wailing as it streamed over the rocks was a hissing noise, coming from above.

'It's wind rushing through grass or heath,' said Nish, staring up eagerly. 'We're nearly there.'

'Just as well,' said Thommel. 'It's not long to sunset.'

'This is a good place to camp,' said Zham, pulling a fallen branch out of a copse of almost leafless, wind-writhen trees that looked a thousand years old. 'I'll make a fire.'

Yes, please, Maelys thought, but Nish said, 'I've come a long way for this. Let's get to the top and find what we're looking for.'

He plodded on, up and up with Zham, but after a minute Nish stopped suddenly, looking down at his boot. From somewhere above them came a loud wooden clap.

'What was that?' said Thommel.

'I don't know.' Zham sounded worried. 'Extra careful now.'

'I thought I caught my foot on something,' said Nish, 'but there's nothing here.'

They moved up into wind-churned cloud so dense that Maelys couldn't see Nish's feet above her, nor Thommel's head below. She felt as though she was climbing all by herself up a mountain that went on forever.

'I'm at the top,' came Zham's rumbling voice.

At last. The final ten steps were so hard on her knees that she thought she was going to topple backwards into Thommel, but the wind kicked her in the back, lifting the weight off her legs just long enough for Maelys to scramble the last few steps up the cleft and stand on the rim of the plateau, more than a thousand spans, or two thousand vertical paces, above the unseen rainforest.

Nish stood an arm's length away, staring about him into the fog and breathing heavily. He turned and his gaze crossed hers for a moment. Maelys tensed, until she realised that he wasn't even thinking about her. Their fight last night was trivial compared to his expectations of Thuntunnimoe, Mistmurk Mountain: his goal, vision and dream for the past month, and the repository of all his hopes for the future.

All Maelys could see were curved rocks covered in moss mounds, reed-fringed bogs and still grey pools. A faint track led along the edge of the plateau, though it didn't look as though it had been made by humans.

'Where is it?' Nish said, turning around again. 'What is it?'

'Careful,' Zham laid a restraining hand on Nish's shoulder. 'It'd be easy to walk off the edge in the fog.' Nish shook it off.

'Should have brought staffs to feel our way,' muttered Thommel. 'It's always like this up here.'

'How would you know?' Nish said suspiciously. Thommel knew too much and his appearance seemed just a little to convenient.

'You can see the cloud hanging over these peaks from twenty leagues away.'

'Stay here. I'll go down to that copse and cut some timbers.' Zham disappeared down the cleft.

Nish wandered off. The top of the plateau was flat here, and saturated. Maelys stepped the other way and her right foot plunged into a knee-deep pool covered by green strands of algae. Jumping backwards, she emptied the cold water from her boot, put it back on and turned left onto what she thought was rock. Her left foot sank into a bog concealed by floating moss; yellow ooze enveloped her to mid-calf. She went backwards to surer ground near the plateau's rim, swearing under her breath, sat down to clean herself up and decided to wait for Zham.

The fog parted and she saw Nish five or six paces away, treading carefully between the pools. 'This looks safe enough,' he said over his shoulder, went forwards and sank to the waist.

He looked so shocked that Maelys couldn't help herself. All her resentment burst out in a series of giggles that grew louder and more infectious until Thommel began to roar with laughter, and neither of them went to help Nish out.

He pulled himself up onto the edge, scowling and cascading red-brown water. 'Very funny!' he said coldly, took a step to the left and went into another pothole.

This time they did help him, for he'd gone in to the neck and the sides were so slippery that he couldn't climb them.

'You've got to follow those brown streaks,' said Thommel, waving his hand at a series of barely visible meandering marks. 'They're the only places you can be sure to tread safely.'

'How would you know?' Nish said sourly.

'I've climbed some of these peaks before,' Thommel said expressionlessly.

'Really? How come you're only telling us now?'

Thommel shrugged. 'You didn't ask.'

Nish gave him an even sourer look and set off, following one of the brown streaks.

'I think I'll leave you to him,' said Thommel. 'I'm going for a walk.'

'Oh!' said Maelys, already missing the camaraderie of their journey together, though she could understand why he might want to get away for a while.

Thommel headed in the other direction and soon blurred into the fog. Maelys hunched down in a vain attempt to keep

457

out of the wind and waited for Zham to come back. He was so pleasant and uncomplicated; so much easier than Nish.

Shortly he appeared, swinging four wooden staves in one gigantic hand, and whistling. Laying them on the ground, he squatted beside Maelys. She marvelled at his size – he was the biggest man she'd ever seen.

'Last night didn't go the way you were hoping,' he rumbled.

'You can't imagine how much I was looking forward to seeing Nish, and it went all wrong. Stupid man! What's the matter with him?'

'He's afraid.'

'Of *me*?'

'Of who's trying to kill him. Of what he'll find up here. Or if he'll find nothing but ghosts . . .'

He gazed into the drifting fog, which did have a spectral look about it. Maelys sighed. 'I'm so tired.' Without thinking, she settled her head against his upper arm. He didn't move away, or closer. He just allowed her to rest. Of all the men she'd ever met, she knew she was perfectly safe with Zham.

After a few minutes he said, 'We'd better go and find him.'

She sat up, rubbing her cold arms. 'Nish went that away,' she pointed right, 'and Thommel's over there, so we can't go after them both.'

'I'm not concerned for Thommel. He's been here before.'

She got up, wearily. 'What – here on this peak?'

'Yup.'

'How do you know?'

'He knew the way up too well.' He handed her the smallest staff and led the way, probing the ground ahead as he followed the faint marks left in the moss by Nish's boots. 'He knows a lot more than he's telling, does Thommel. Look out!'

Maelys, intent on where she was putting each foot, did not realise the danger off to her right, even when Zham reached back, caught her by the armpit and shoulder and

458

lifted her, legs kicking, right over his head. As he dropped her on solid ground in front of him, something went *snap*! Before she could steady herself, he'd whirled and his long sword was snaking out towards the bizarre creature that had nearly taken her.

Creature or plant? It was like a gigantic green mantrap sprouting from the bog, so broad that she could have lain inside. The edges of its upper and lower jaws, now closed, were covered in overlapping yellow teeth – no, flexible spines – and through the gape she saw a scarlet, ovoid interior coated with glistening mucilage. Yellow vapour seeped from pores on top of the upper jaw. The air took on a disgusting, sulphurous reek that stung her eyes. It smelled as though something had rotted away to hair and bones.

'What is it?' she quavered, scanning the fog in case there were more of them, and spotting another one not ten paces away. She wondered how far it could reach out on its rubbery stalk.

'It's a stink-snapper, a plant that eats animals. It feeds on fish, frogs, birds, insects, and even people if it can catch them. You often see little stink-snappers,' he opened his fingers to form a circle the size of a saucer, 'around the edges of the upland swamps. I've never seen one as big as that, though. Have you got a knife?'

She offered him the little blunt blade Phrune had given her. He tested it, snorted and drew a knife, large enough to butcher a boar and wickedly sharp, from a sheath inside his long boot. 'They lurk just under the water, and all you can see is the tips of the yellow spines. When they sense your footsteps, they shoot up and *snap*. Hold the knife ready and if one gets you, hack your way out, damn quick, and jump in the water! Once that goo starts to work on you, it's too late.'

'Thanks, Zham.' She stowed her old knife in her pack, held out his blade in her right hand and began to prod the ground with the stick.

Shortly they encountered Nish, shivering as he tried to

peer through the swirling fog, and together they began to criss-cross this lobe of the plateau. The plateau was less than a league across, but their progress was so slow that by sunset they hadn't covered a fifth of it.

Nish wouldn't stop even then; he just kept squelching back and forth. Maelys felt for him.

Thommel came tramping back. 'Did you find anything?' Nish asked hopefully.

'I wasn't looking! However I did catch our dinner.' Thommel held up what appeared to be an enormous black slug, the size of his thigh.

'I'm not eating that,' Maelys said, revolted. It brought back memories of the slurchie. Her empty stomach rumbled. 'Er, what is it?'

'All the more for me.' He grinned. 'It's a giant swamp creeper and they're the best eating you'll find up here. Very healthy too. Good for the organs.'

'It looks like an organ from something I wouldn't want to go near,' said Nish.

Thommel glanced at Zham. Zham smacked his lips. 'I haven't tasted one in years. Let's find a camp site.'

'There's no firewood up here,' said Thommel. 'We'll have to go back down the cleft.'

It was really cold now. 'What about the other clefts?' asked Maelys, for they weren't far from the north-western one and the light was fading.

'You'd have to be a mountain climber to get down any of them. Or up.'

They tramped across to the south-eastern cleft, Maelys keeping a careful eye out for stink-snappers. Once or twice she caught a sulphurous whiff and thought one must have been lurking nearby, though she could not see any yellow spines. She clutched her knife more tightly and followed closely on Zham's heels.

They reached the cleft in near darkness and felt their way down the steep pinch to the copse of twisted, aged

460

trees. Between it and the right-hand cliff Zham found a patch of mossy, sloping ground, partially sheltered from the howling updraught. He dragged out dead branches. All the wood was wet but he also carried tinder in his pocket and soon had a cheerful fire going.

'Hurrah!' Thommel said, holding his hands out to the little blaze. 'And we don't have to worry about being seen. There's not an eye on Santhenar that could pierce this fog.'

'Not even the eye in the tears?' Nish said, shivering fitfully. However he collected fallen wood and fed it to the flames until they blazed as high as his shoulders. They gathered around, rubbing their frozen hands.

Thommel got busy skinning and gutting the giant swamp creeper, and ended up with a heavy length of dark brown meat the size of a buffalo fillet. He sliced it lengthways so it would cook more quickly, wrapped it in a cocoon of algae strands, covered that in moss and, once the flames had died down, placed the package in a hole excavated in the coals.

By the time it had cooked Maelys was so hungry, and the roasting smells arising from it were so delicious, that she quite forgot its origins and what it reminded her of. It was a rich, dense meat with a fine texture like liver, though much tastier, and by the time her belly was full she'd put aside the fight of the previous night, and the exhausting day. Thommel was laughing at something Zham had said, and Nish was bright-eyed again. It made her feel good to see him cheerful for once.

'Tomorrow we'll find it,' he said softly. 'Tomorrow pays for everything, Maelys.'

He was up at first light and didn't wait for breakfast. While Maelys was still rubbing the sleep out of her eyes Nish was scrambling up the crevice, the ferocious wind at his back, to disappear into the churning fog. She followed hastily with Zham. 'Coming, Thommel?'

Thommel opened one eye, closed it again and pulled his cloak around him more tightly. 'I'll see you later, Maelys.'

'Thanks for your help!' snapped Nish.

Thommel sat up. 'Your quest is not mine, Deliverer,' he said mildly. 'Would you go out of your way to aid me if I asked it of you?'

Nish hesitated fractionally too long before he said, 'Yes, of course I would.'

Thommel gave him an ironic smile, lay down and closed his eyes again. Nish turned away, looking as though he'd just been shown up.

The fog, oddly, was thinner at the top today and she could see at least thirty paces, though the plateau was a dismal prospect – a series of bogs and ponds, oozes releasing greenish mists, and patches of bare black rock interspersed with circular clusters of brilliantly green moss mounds as much as five or six spans across and waist high to Maelys. At the limit of her vision a stink-snapper, even larger than yesterday's attacker, was sinking into the mire with a small wriggling creature protruding from its jaws.

Nish was following one of the wavering brown streaks, probing ahead with his staff. Zham took up position to Nish's right, and Maelys went beyond him. With the big knife in her right hand and her probing staff in her left, she began the search. Thommel appeared around nine in the morning but didn't join them. He went softly through the mires, head down, hunting with a rude spear made from a knife bound to a short stave.

The fog closed in again, reducing visibility to the length of Maelys's staff. Now every step posed a risk, for she could barely see the ground she was standing on and never knew if the next step would take her into a pool, a mire or the maw of a stink-snapper.

The breeze became a hissing wind which churned the fog but did not blow it away. She was freezing in her damp clothes. This was madness. Whatever Nish was looking for, it could be just paces away and they'd never find it.

'Nish?' she called. Her voice was whipped away by the wind. 'Zham?'

Neither of them answered. With Zham's long legs he could have been at the other side of the plateau by now. Maelys pulled her thin coat around her and stared vainly into the fog. Was that a movement off to her right? 'Zham?' No answer. She heard a splash not far away but had no idea which direction it had come from. 'Thommel? Nish?'

She headed on a few steps. Or was she going back? Everywhere looked the same. Her legs still ached from yesterday's climb and her right thigh was particularly painful. It felt as if she'd strained a muscle. Maelys wanted to lie down and sleep for another ten hours but she couldn't rest here.

She kept on, just walking wherever the brown streaks took her, looking over her shoulder every few steps, for she couldn't escape the feeling that there was someone, or something, behind her. She kept seeing human-sized shapes in the fog but nothing answered her repeated calls.

She must have been walking for hours. She should have reached the other side of the plateau ages ago, even at this slow pace. Or had she been walking in circles all the time? It didn't seem possible that she could be lost – the wretched plateau wasn't a tenth the size of the clan's estate at Nifferlin, and she'd known every part of that.

Something loomed up ahead, taller and broader than a man, though she couldn't make out any definite shape.

'Hello?' she said, trying not to sound afraid.

No reply. The fog swirled and she lost sight of the object. She reached out with her staff but couldn't feel anything. She took a step forwards. Her legs were shaking. The ground squelched and subsided underfoot. She leapt backwards, saw the dark shape again momentarily, then lost it.

Maelys stood still, heart pounding. She couldn't even see the ground now, but she knew something big was in front of her, for she could hear the way the wind shrilled around it. She became aware of how cold she was. Her toes were

463

freezing and her nose felt as if icicles were growing inside it. She could hardly draw breath.

She probed the ground to left and right, found a solid patch and stepped that way. The shrilling faded. She strained her eyes, as if she could penetrate the fog through will alone, but saw nothing. She couldn't find a path to the object either – there was no solid ground that way, just brown-scummed pools and sludgy mires.

'Maelys?'

'Zham!' she cried. 'Where are you?'

'Stay where you are. I'll come to you.'

He kept calling, and she kept answering, and shortly his tree trunk figure loomed up out of the fog.

'Where did you get to?' he said cheerfully, though she could tell he'd been anxious. He put a steadying arm around her and her fears felt silly.

'Walking in circles, I think.'

'Come on. Nish is this way.'

'How do you know?'

'I just do.'

'Have *you* found anything?'

'Not a sausage.' He chuckled. 'But you have, Maelys?'

'I was sure I saw something, much taller than you, a few minutes ago. It was over there but I couldn't get to it . . .'

He reached out with his staff, which was far longer than hers, probing forwards and around. 'Stay here.'

He disappeared into the fog, swinging the staff in front of him. Shortly she heard a splash, a curse. Had he fallen in; had a stink-snapper caught him? Or something worse? 'Zham?'

Zham appeared suddenly from her left, dripping. 'Cursed place.'

'Did you find anything?'

'Nope. Come on.'

Maelys followed him to Nish, who was just five minutes away. Whatever the object had been, she was sure she hadn't imagined it. Nish looked up hopefully as they approached. 'Did you find anything?'

'I didn't,' said Zham, 'though Maelys thinks she saw something –'

'What?' cried Nish so eagerly that she felt for him.

Maelys told him what she'd seen and heard. It sounded flimsy but his face lit up. 'Can you find the place again?'

'I dare say Zham can.'

It didn't turn out to be that easy; even Zham became confused as he tried to retrace his steps to the point where he'd found Maelys.

'Shh!' she said. 'Can you hear that?'

It was the high, unnerving shrilling she'd heard before.

'Definitely something there,' said Zham.

But they couldn't find it – they couldn't tell which direction the sound was coming from.

'It's as if it doesn't want to be found,' Zham said, squelching back and forth over ground they'd covered a dozen times, but there was always water where they wanted to go. 'Look, here's where you were standing before, Maelys.' He indicated two small, foot-shaped depressions in the brilliantly green moss.

'Can't you use clearsight, Nish?' she wondered.

'I've been trying all day but it's not working, as usual. It's never been very reliable, but this time it feels as though something is blocking it.'

Maelys recalled a recent conversation with Thommel. 'Could it be blocked by red amber-wood?'

'Perhaps. I don't know.'

'Well, if something is blocking it, that's good, in a way. At least it confirms that there's something hidden up here.'

Nish scowled. 'Doesn't help if we can't find it.'

Zham had been going back and forth, prodding the ground. He gave an irritated grunt and without warning plunged into a scummy pool up to his chest and began to wade through it, swinging his staff.

'Be careful, Zham,' Maelys cried. 'There could be anything in there –'

The water swirled. Zham let out a muffled cry then stabbed his staff down with full force and held it there. Bubbles burst up all around him; plumes of mud stained the dark water. He swung himself up and over whatever he'd pinned to the bottom, pivoting on the staff, then went on and faded into the fog.

The shrilling resumed, though now it made a lower, more melancholy note. Maelys moved closer to Nish. 'I don't like this plateau,' she said quietly.

'It's not what I imagined either.' He reached out, tentatively, to take her cold hand. 'And yet, I still think there's something up here.'

She held his hand for a while, stiffly, then let it go. 'I hope so.'

'He's been a long time,' Nish said a while later.

'Zham?' Maelys called. Her voice made no impression on the wind. 'Zham!'

'Here!' His shout could have come from anywhere. 'Come on.' There was a note of excitement in his voice.

'He's found it!' Nish cried, plunging recklessly into the water, which came up to his chin. He churned his way across, stumbled on something halfway and his head went under.

Maelys, thinking that some creature had got him, felt for Zham's big knife, though there was little she could do. Nish burst out of the water, turned towards her, eyes staring, then turned the other way and flailed across into the fog.

The windsong dropped to a sobbing moan. She held the knife out, looking this way and that. She didn't like it here, but didn't want to go into the pool either, which was now a muddy brown and looked as thick as soup. Smelly bubbles were popping all over its surface.

She called Nish a couple of times but evidently he couldn't hear her. What if they were both in trouble? If they were it was unlikely she could make any difference, though they had acted recklessly. If she were careful . . .

She didn't want to go into the pool, but she couldn't stand by either. Taking a deep breath, and holding the blade out low, she stepped into the water. It came up to her nose, her eyes; she had to stand on tiptoes to breathe and her boots sank into a deep sludge on the bottom that made it difficult to move. She took one step, then another, feeling an overwhelming urge to shriek, but her mouth was underwater.

Maelys trod on something that gave underfoot, then heaved. She jumped, lost her footing and went under. She tried not to panic but couldn't stop herself. She'd always been afraid of deep water, and even more afraid of creatures that dwelt in dark places where they couldn't be seen. The water was so dark and cold, and she had to close her eyes to keep the mud out.

She went all the way to the bottom and something slapped against her thigh. Flailing madly, she tried to whack it away with the knife but failed to connect. She rolled over, not knowing which way was up and which way was down. Her foot slid through the ooze and she felt hard mud underneath.

Maelys fought the panic. The water wasn't that deep. She should be able to stand up in it. She got her other foot down, propelled herself upright and half waded, half swam until her head popped out of the water and she saw a reedy bank. Sheathing the knife, she caught hold of some bladed reeds with both hands and dragged herself out onto relatively solid ground.

Her hands were bleeding from the sharp edges of the reeds. She wiped them on moss, tore up handfuls of it to clean the mud out of her eyes and stood up. She couldn't see Nish or Zham, though their footprints were clearly visible in the moss, leading straight on.

The sobbing wind was louder now, and more unnerving. This place didn't feel lucky at all. It felt as though something

467

terrible had happened here. She kept going, the feelings growing stronger all the time. And then she saw them.

Nish and Zham stood side by side, staring at something she couldn't make out from here. It wasn't good news, though. Nish's shoulders were slumped; even from behind he looked defeated.

As Maelys came up beside him, the shape she'd seen earlier resolved out of the fog. It was a standing stone – no, a monument, an obelisk cut from a single slab of grey rock. It was at least twice Zham's height, though the top could not be seen, and she saw the blurred outline of writing running up the facing surface. The glyphs weren't clear, since the surface was covered in moss at the bottom and grey-green lichen further up. Feathers of lichen wavered in the wind and a faint mist or steam was rising off the top of the rock. Her scalp prickled.

'That's not it, Nish?'

'No,' Nish said dully. 'It doesn't speak to me at all. The whole journey has been a waste of time.'

It spoke to Maelys, though. It was the monument to a terrible tragedy, though why here where no one would see it? She scraped some of the moss off. The glyphs were clearer in the raw stone. It looked like a script from long ago; one she'd seen in a book of the Histories of ancient times, before her mother had burnt it to keep warm. Unfortunately Maelys hadn't read those Histories first, so the glyphs told her nothing. And, just as curious, the rock was warm.

'Why would it be warm, when everything else up here is cold?'

'I don't know,' said Zham.

'It's a wonder Thommel didn't mention it,' said Nish, 'since he's been here before.'

'It's not easy to find,' rumbled Zham. 'Do you want to go on, Deliverer? There's plenty of plateau left to search. And Maelys needs to get out of the wind.'

'I'm all right,' she said automatically. 'I'm used to the cold.' She shivered. 'Let's finish the job we came so far to do.'

As she went by the obelisk, she stumbled over the top part, which must have been broken off long ago and now lay half buried in the sodden ground, so thickly coated with moss that the memorial glyphs were as unreadable as the memories of those long-dead souls who had erected it. Thinking such melancholy thoughts, she followed Nish and Zham through the barrier pools and they went on with quartering the plateau.

They found nothing. Nish became more downcast as the hours passed and finally, around three in the afternoon, tossed his sword clanging onto a large sloping rock. Something had eaten the moss off it in large, lobed patches, exposing black stone beneath. Nish threw himself down on one of the bare areas, staring morosely into a nearby pool.

'There's nothing here,' he said. 'My vision must have been a lie put into the Pit of Possibilities to mock me. Father is playing games again.' He sprang up, and Maelys couldn't bear to see the torment on his face. 'It's all a lie!' he shouted up into the whirling fog. 'There is no future save the God-Emperor's unending rule, and I was a fool for daring to think otherwise.' His voice cracked. 'A bigger fool for daring to hope.'

He stalked away without either sword or staff, splashing blindly through the bogs and mosses, falling in and heedlessly pulling himself out again. Maelys rose to follow him but Zham laid a hand on her arm. 'Let him go. After coming all this way, you can't blame him.'

'But what if he . . .?' She couldn't say the words in case Nish acted them out. This might push him over the edge.

'He won't harm himself,' said Zham. 'Don't worry.'

'I do worry,' Maelys said softly, but didn't go after him.

After walking for ages, and stumbling into many a bog and pothole, Nish's anguish gave way to a melancholy misery.

He was soaked, and so cold and exhausted that he couldn't find the energy for stronger feelings. He just couldn't take it any more.

Coming to a rock that sloped down in a shelf on the lee side, providing shelter from the wind, he lay on it and tried to make sense of what had been done to him. Did the God-Emperor control the whole world, including the Defiance, Monkshart, and the Pit of Possibilities? Could everything that had happened since he'd been freed from Mazurhize *really* be part of a malicious game, to demonstrate how absolute his father's power was? Nish recoiled from the idea, which smacked of paranoia and allowed no room for hope, but what other explanation was there?

He rubbed the itching spine scar. He could draw no other conclusion. If there truly was no hope, if Father did control the world and they were mere players in his game, why be a pawn? He couldn't fight any more. He felt exhausted; physically, mentally and most of all, morally. The burden was too much for him to bear.

The moment he allowed himself that thought, the long-suppressed temptation grew until it was almost irresistible. Nish could feel himself weakening every second. He wanted what his father offered, more than anything. He always had, though he'd never allowed himself to think about it. But now he did, and why shouldn't he have it? And perhaps . . .

Perhaps there was another way. After all, if anyone could sway his father, curb his excesses and turn him aside from evil, his only surviving son had the best chance of doing it. Yes, it was the only way. Some people, even his friends, might see it as a betrayal, but if he could stand at the right hand of the God-Emperor, and do good at the same time, it would be worth all it had cost him to get there.

Even me, Nish?

It was as if Irisis had spoken in his mind. Nish jumped up, looking around guiltily, longingly, but there was no one in sight.

Use your clearsight, Nish. Is this what you really want?

It had hardly ever worked after he'd come out of the maze, but perhaps he needed to try harder. Nish closed his eyes and was attempting to see with his inner vision, while her voice was still echoing in his mind, when a small rectangular shape appeared out of the fog not far away, near the rim of the southern lobe of the plateau. He began to move towards it, arms out like a sleepwalker. It had to be an illusion, because he'd been back and forth across the area and couldn't have missed anything that big.

It didn't recede as he approached, and when he was close enough he opened his eyes. It was still there, and grew ever clearer, as any real object would. It was an ancient, crumbling wooden hut, listing to the left and looking as though the next puff of wind would blow it over. He caught the faintest spicy whiff but couldn't place it.

Going with trembling steps to the door, Nish rapped on it. There was no answer and his heart sank again, but he pushed it open on its cracked and sagging leather hinges. The floor of the hut was formed from packed earth which the bottom of the door scraped semicircular grooves across as it opened. He stepped inside but it was so dark he couldn't see a thing. He waited until his eyes adjusted. There didn't appear to be anything in the hut but a rude table and chair, and a bed covered in rags.

Until the rags stirred and an acerbic voice he'd never expected to hear again said, 'You took your bloody time, Nish! I expected you nine years ago.'

471

FORTY-ONE

Nish leapt backwards as if he'd been scalded, and shivers broke out across his body. The crusty voice, though rendered hoarse by age and shortness of breath, was unmistakable.

'Xervish? Surr? Is it really you?'

The rags fell away as the figure sat up, slowly and stiffly. 'You always were one for asking stupid questions,' said his old mentor and friend, the former Scrutator Xervish Flydd. 'Of course it's me. Where the devil have you been all this time? On holidays?'

Had anyone else spoken to him that way, Nish would have been mortally offended, but Flydd's acerbity was legendary, and not intended to hurt. Well, not all of the time. When he was angry, Flydd's tongue could flay the hide off a nylatl.

Nish managed a smile. 'I'm afraid I was rather tied up.' He went forwards. Flydd swung his feet onto the floor, the smell of mouldy bedding rising with him.

'Cursed damp place,' said Flydd, coughing. 'Nothing ever dries out. Give me your hand.'

Nish extended his hand. Flydd took it and heaved himself up. 'Let's go outside where I can look at you. The light in here is too dim for my old eyes.'

Outside, the fog had closed in again and visibility was down to a few paces, but it was bright enough to see that the old man had aged shockingly. At the end of the war Flydd had been a vigorous man of sixty-odd years. Yes, he'd been small and skinny, horribly scarred and incredibly ugly, but with such strength, courage and, when he cared to use it, charm, that he'd seemed the best of men. But now . . .

'What are you staring at?' Flydd snapped.

'You've . . . aged, surr,' Nish said softly. Flydd looked positively ancient and was even thinner, if that were possible. His skin was pallid, blotched with age marks and sagging off his bones.

'Of course I've aged. Time doesn't stop just because you want it to. You don't look so fresh yourself.'

Flydd peered at him from eyes that lacked their old sparkle because their centres were clouded by cataracts. Yet he was alive, and sounding just as tough as ever, and a sudden hope surged through Nish. His father had said that all Nish's old friends and allies were dead and, since he'd lied about that, he might have lied about all manner of other things. Why would the all-powerful God-Emperor need to lie . . . unless he wasn't as powerful or secure as he made out? Nish couldn't believe that he'd succumbed to the lie and had nearly given way to what, he saw clearly now, was another of his father's temptations.

'What's so funny?' said Flydd. 'If there's a new joke I'd love to hear it. It's been damned lonely up here these past years.'

Overcome by his feelings, Nish rushed forwards and threw his arms around his old friend. 'Surr,' he said, squeezing him tightly, 'I'm so glad to see you.'

'I'm pleased to see you, too,' said Flydd, pushing him away, 'but you won't see me carrying on about it in such an unseemly fashion. Oh, *all right*!' He embraced Nish briefly then pulled away. 'Let me go, idiot, before you crush my chalky old bones.'

Nish stood back, aware that he was grinning like a loon and not caring. Everything was going to be all right. Flydd never gave up, no matter how hopeless things became; whatever the problem, he always came up with a solution.

Flydd tottered backwards, favouring his right leg, and sank onto a bench against the crumbling wall of the hut. 'You've aged too, Nish. I've never seen you so scrawny. And can your hair be thinning at the front?'

Nish raked it over his forehead with his fingers, then abruptly thrust it back. Surely he wasn't so vain that he cared what this ugly old coot thought?

'What have you been up to all this time?' said Flydd, smiling as if he'd read the thought.

'You don't *know*?' It was hard to believe that there existed a corner of the world where his father's propaganda had not penetrated.

'I reached this bolthole a little over nine years ago, with all my preparations made –'

'What preparations?' said Nish.

'To overthrow your father, of course! To crack you out of prison and begin the revolution. You must have heard – I sent secret messengers so you'd be ready.'

'They must have been caught; I didn't hear a whisper about it. The one thing I heard was that all my old allies were taken or dead, and that my father was all-powerful.'

'But – why did it take so long to get here? I left hints all over the place, ones only you would recognise. You must have found them when my allies finally broke you out . . .'

Nish sat beside him on the bench, which creaked and tilted sideways under his slight weight. 'Xervish, I wasn't freed and Father didn't let me out. I served the whole ten years in the deepest dungeon of Mazurhize, his special prison near Morrelune Palace. You must have heard about that, and how he killed –'

Flydd's gnarled hand came down on his shoulder. 'I heard that Irisis gave up her life to try and save you, and of your promise to the world. And your sentence. But I thought . . .' He shook his head in disbelief. 'It was all planned so carefully.'

'What was, surr?'

'My scheme to free you. It was foolproof, and I couldn't work out why no one came here. Everyone must have been taken, betrayed. *Everyone!* And Jal-Nish has kept it secret all this time, hoping that the prize he wanted most of all – me – would come to find out what had gone wrong. Are you saying that he made you serve the full ten years?'

'With not a moment's remission. Father keeps his promises. Ten agonising years, and I could have been free after the first.' Nish let out a heavy sigh. 'But I'm free now and you're alive. That's all that matters.'

They sat together, staring into the fog with the wind howling in the eaves of the hut. Nish smelt that elusive, spicy scent again.

'Why didn't you go and find out what had gone wrong, Xervish?'

'I waited and waited, but none of my spies or messengers turned up. After a couple of months I knew something had gone wrong, and I was starting down the chasm when I fell and broke my ankle, very badly.' He thrust out his right foot. Its knobbly, blue-veined ankle was much thicker than the other. 'It wouldn't heal properly, and even with all my Arts I couldn't repair it. On bad days I can't put any weight on my ankle, and I couldn't climb down the cleft for any price. I nearly killed myself trying, but I was trapped here, as much a prisoner as you were. I've had no news in all that time.' He looked hopefully at Nish.

'There was no news – no good news, anyway. Even after ten years, Father wouldn't relent.' Nish told Flydd about the confrontation in Morrelune, but didn't mention Irisis in the crystal coffin; he couldn't bear to relive that again. 'Then, a few weeks later I was freed in such an odd way that, even now, I can scarcely believe it happened.' He told the story of his rescue by Fyllis and Maelys.

Flydd gave him a quizzical glance. 'Odd indeed; downright extraordinary. Yet sometimes the desires and deeds of

475

the utterly insignificant can change the course of the future. Are you alone?'

'Maelys is here too, and two others, as I'm sure you know, though I doubt they'll come looking for me in a while. I . . . stormed off.'

Flydd chuckled. 'Ten years older, but no more mature – excellent! Your tantrum will give us the chance to catch up on things.' He rose painfully. 'Stay put, rest your bones. I've a little something inside I've been saving.'

Nish could have sworn he heard the old man's joints creak, though perhaps it was the bench. He leaned back against the wall and closed his eyes, unaccountably weary. No, more than weary, he felt drained to the marrow of his bones, as if the drive that had sustained him all this time had dwindled. That didn't matter now. Flydd would have a solution to all his problems – he always did.

The old man returned carrying a small, squat flask whose pottery bung had been sealed with wax, and two small goblets hand-carved from a golden wood so thin that it glowed translucently even in this murky light. Handing the goblets to Nish, Flydd ran the tip of a knife around the wax, cracked it off and drew the bung, then poured a tot into each goblet.

Nish's eyes watered from the rising fumes. 'I haven't drunk spirits since . . . I don't know when.' He wiped his eyes.

'Then you'll enjoy this. It's a hundred and ninety years old and made by the master himself – Old Shand – or so my vintner told me. Mind you, I never met a wine-seller who wasn't a rogue, no matter how charming they appeared. The first mug goes straight down the spout!' Flydd raised the goblet and poured its contents down his throat without seeming to swallow. 'Ahh! That reminds me of better days.'

Nish sniffed his liqueur; the vapour went up his nose like hot mustard and he also caught a faint, elusive fragrance coming from the wood of the goblet. He tossed the drink down his throat and it burned all the way, then lay in the pit of his empty stomach, seething like soup in a saucepan. It was far stronger than the liqueur Monkshart had given him in Tifferfyte.

'You'll have another, of course,' said Flydd, raising the flask.

Nish scratched the scar from the nylatl's spine, which had become irritatingly itchy lately. 'In a minute. It's very strong.'

'Really?' Flydd gave him a sideways glance. 'I recall you being a legendary drinker, once. After the dreadful home-made grog I pour down my throat each night, this tastes like cordial.'

'You make grog up here? What from?'

'The sweet mucilage from the stink-snapper, mainly, and devilish tricky it is to gather.' Flydd rubbed a long purple scar down his right arm, one of many. 'But when a man must drink, he'll go to any lengths to get it.' He poured himself another goblet, then filled Nish's as well. 'Let's hear the full tale, Nish, and anything else you care to tell me. I'm starved for news. And company.'

The next hour or two passed companionably, assisted by most of the flask of liqueur. 'Monkshart?' said Flydd midway through the tale. 'I've not heard that name before.'

'He served my father during the war. Monkshart saved Father's life, and rescued the tears after the debacle of Gumby Marth, though they crisped his skin like a roast chicken.'

Flydd appeared to be searching his memory. 'It must be Vivimord. He was tall and dark-haired, with a mesmerising charm even then, though abominably ill-disciplined. I never liked the man; never thought he'd amount to anything either. But great suffering changes one – things that once seemed important become irrelevant, while paths that were confused now seem crystal clear.'

Flydd reflected for a while, and Nish felt that his old friend was thinking about his own life. Few had suffered

477

more than he had, and survived. 'Enough of him,' said Flydd. 'Go on.'

Flydd toasted Nish with a goblet when he told of first joining the Defiance, and again after the victorious battle. It felt almost like old times as they sat together and Nish related his tale, up to the point where the nylatl attacked. He choked and couldn't go on.

'What is it, Nish?'

'I've been thinking about what happened ever since, and I can only reach one conclusion. Who would risk Father's wrath to harm me? No one! Therefore only one man could have sent the assassins – Father himself! And that doesn't bear thinking about.'

Flydd looked grave. 'I can scarcely credit it. What, you think you've become too great a danger and he's ordered you killed?'

Nish nodded stiffly.

'I can't see it. Not even Jal-Nish would kill his only surviving son. You're all he has. Go on with the tale.'

Nish told the last of it.

'You've done better than I have,' Flydd said. 'My plans have come to nought and now it's too late.'

It shocked Nish out of his merry state. 'Surely not, surr. Together –'

'I don't have anything left, Nish,' Flydd said gently. 'Look at me. Take a good hard look and tell me what you see.'

Nish turned to his old friend. He looked as if he were reaching for the handle of death's door, and Nish couldn't face it. 'We've both aged, Xervish.'

'But you're still a young man with your best years ahead of you, while I've come to the end of my life and I'm fading fast. I'm going blind, my knees are giving out and my ankle won't support me for more than ten minutes at a time. I haven't been off this peak in nine years and I couldn't climb down now if the greatest prize in the world – a crate of this liqueur – waited at the bottom. Nish, you've got to face the truth, as I have. Every man has his time and I've used mine. I'm sorry that you've come all this way with such expectations, but I can't help you.'

'Then it'll soon be over. We saw flappeters in the west a few days ago.'

'You're safe here, for a while anyway,' said Flydd. 'My hut is built entirely from red amber-wood and I doubt that even the tears could see it without my consent. If a flappeter flew straight over it would see nothing but mire.'

'We searched this area and didn't see a thing.'

'Until I allowed you to. But of course, you can't stay up here for long.'

'Why not?'

'The plateau barely supports me. Five people would eat everything edible within weeks.'

'Then where can I go? What happened to our allies, anyway? Yggur, Malien, Klarm the dwarf scrutator, General Troist, Fyn-Mah?'

Flydd shrugged. 'I've no idea. We separated the day after you were taken, and scattered so Jal-Nish couldn't take all of us at once. I've not heard from anyone else since.'

'Not even Malien, or Yggur?'

Flydd shook his grizzled head.

'But since you survived, others may have too.'

'It's possible, though my feeling is that he took them quickly and put them to death.'

'But I never heard of it, Xervish, and they were among the greatest names of the age. Why wouldn't he make a public spectacle of their deaths?'

'I don't know, but Jal-Nish served under me for years and he was never predictable. Indeed, he would sometimes act out of character so as to make himself more unpredictable. Who knows why he might have kept their deaths a secret? Ah, this will be your friends now.'

Zham was emerging through the fog, followed by Thommel, then Maelys, who must have fallen in another

479

sinkhole, for she was drenched and dripping. The wind outlined her curvy figure through her clothes and Nish caught his breath for a second. Her face lit up as she caught sight of Nish, but then she just stared at Flydd.

Zham came up and ran his fingers along the wall of the hut. 'We walked right past here and saw nothing.' He extended his hand to Flydd. 'My name is Zham, surr, and I've sworn to protect the Deliverer with my life.'

Flydd shook the huge hand. 'Deliverer, eh?' He gave Nish a quizzical glance. 'But then, why not? I'm very pleased to meet you, Zham. You look like my kind of man. My name is Xervish Flydd and I was –'

'I know your name, surr.' Zham bowed awkwardly. 'Everyone does who lived through the war. I saw you once, when I was young. You came to Roros in a metal machine that flew through the air.'

'What I'd give for a thapter now,' said Flydd dreamily. 'They were the most marvellous of all the Aachim's constructs. Alas, all failed when the nodes were destroyed, as did everything great, ingenious and beautiful that had been created or sustained by the Art. I wonder if glorious Shazmak still stands, or if it, too, has fallen into ruin. Everything passes, Zham. Remember that and you'll always be at peace within yourself. Expect nothing to last, for nothing can endure.'

'Save my father, if he gets what he's looking for,' said Nish.

Flydd looked at him sharply but didn't ask what he meant. He was studying Thommel, who was trailing his fingers up and down the timbers of the hut.

Thommel sniffed his fingers and said, 'Precious red amber-wood. No wonder we couldn't see it. My name is Thommel.'

He didn't add 'surr', which Nish felt was disrespectful.

'What do you know about red amber-wood, Thommel?' said Flydd equably as they shook hands.

'I'm a woodcutter nowadays,' Thommel said. 'I used to

480

come to these peaks to gather red amber-wood, but that's a forbidden trade now. Forbidden to me, anyhow.'

'We've all suffered injustice,' said Flydd. 'Our character is shown in the way we face up to it.' He turned to Maelys with the snaggle-toothed smile that transformed his ugly features. 'You're Maelys, and even more lovely than Nish said.' He held out his hand and Maelys took it. 'My name is Xervish Flydd, but you'll call me Xervish. Everyone does,' he lied shamelessly.

'Hel – hello, Xervish.' Stumbling a little over the name, she flushed prettily.

'Come with me, my dear. I want to hear your tale.'

So saying, he handed the flask to Nish. 'If you would be so good as to offer your friends the hospitality of my hut, such as it is. There's food inside.'

Flydd went into the hut and came out with a thick coat made from shiny brown leather with an odd, furry lining. He threw it over Maelys's shoulders then took her by the arm and, without a backward glance, limped off into the mires with her, where they were soon lost to sight.

'The ugly old devil always did have a way with women,' Nish observed, smiling after them. Despite Flydd's words, nothing could dent Nish's mood now. Flydd would find a way out.

He went inside and found a full platter on the table, covered with a woven reed mat, as if Flydd had been expecting them. It contained a pile of green cakes which appeared to have been made from pressed algae, a pot of pickled berries and some dried flesh that could have been fish, fowl or even giant swamp creeper. Nish couldn't tell. He carried it out, plus another three goblets, which he filled with the remainder of the flask.

'He had a way with good food and better drink, too. Shall we?'

To his surprise, Thommel accepted a goblet with good grace, though he waved the platter away. Nish offered it to

Zham, who took one of the algae cakes and put it in his mouth whole. 'Delicious!' he mumbled.

They were, too. Nish couldn't imagine how Flydd had made them from the scant resources of the plateau but, even in the old days, Flydd had never ceased to surprise him.

FORTY-TWO

Maelys had been so anxious about Nish's crushing disappointment, and his state of mind, that her first reaction on seeing him sitting outside the hut with an old man, drinking and talking merrily, was irritation. How dare he enjoy himself when they'd spent the last hours looking for him? But those feelings disappeared as she realised that he'd found what he was looking for at last. His pale skin was lit up by an inner glow.

The existence of the hut, in an area they'd searched thoroughly before, was but a momentary surprise. She'd always known the plateau would be an uncanny place.

But Flydd was a legend from the tales she'd so loved from an early age and she'd imagined him as a powerful, imposing figure, nothing like this wizened, hideous old fellow who looked as though he might die at any moment. Yet once he spoke, she felt as though he was speaking only to her, and when she took his hand she was struck by his charm, his presence and, even in old age, his power.

'Come with me, my dear. I want to hear your tale.'

She pulled his coat tightly about her. It was amazingly warm, though the fur tickled her throat. 'Why?' she said as he gave her his arm and steered her away into the fog, limping badly. 'Surely Nish has told you everything you need to know about me?'

He chuckled. 'Once a scrutator, always a scrutator. When

we ran the world we had to know everything that went on in it, and I never lost the habit. After nine years with only the giant swamp creepers for company, I'm starved for news and human companionship. And, let me be honest, the company of beautiful women.'

She gave him a quick sideways glance which unfortunately he noticed. 'I'm not beautiful, Xervish.'

'Of course you are. And you can't believe that beautiful women would have anything to do with a repulsive old coot like me.'

'I'm innocent of the ways of men, surr,' she said softly, 'but I know what women would see in you.'

'Diplomatically put, Maelys. You and I are going to be great friends.' She must have quivered for he went on quickly, 'Not friends in *that* way. I'm past all that and, besides, your heart belongs to another. But we do have a common interest, which we can talk about later. For now, let's talk about you. Tell me your tale, from the beginning. And you must call me Xervish. I insist.'

'My tale will take a long time, surr.'

'Xervish,' he corrected. 'I have the time. Indeed I have little else. Begin.'

He led her on a meandering path across the plateau but Maelys felt perfectly safe, for he knew every part of it. As they strolled, she told him her tale, leaving out only such parts as were too private, personal or embarrassing.

'Interesting,' he said at the end. 'Now, something Nish mentioned has aroused my curiosity.' She didn't say anything, and shortly he continued. 'That your talent, whatever it may be, is shared by others in your clan, in one way or another. What is your clan name?'

She felt sure Nish would have told him, but said, 'It's Clan Nifferlin . . . Xervish.'

'Nifferlin, Nifferlin, Nifferlin.' He rubbed his seamed temples. 'The scrutators were famed for their memory training and my recall was better than most. While Scrutator for

Einunar, I knew every important family in my realm, and many of those throughout the world, but it all goes in the end.'

'My clan was old, but it wasn't important.'

'Nonsense,' said Flydd. 'Nifferlin – ah, yes. I met two men of your clan when I was travelling in the east, enlisting support for the war, perhaps twelve years ago. I can even remember their names – Rudigo and Pyatre.'

Maelys started, then smiled. It made her feel closer to both of them, and Flydd. 'Rudigo is – was my father. The last I heard, he was dying in Mazurhize, but that was months ago.'

'And Pyatre?'

'My uncle. He disappeared; both my uncles did.'

'Ah,' said Flydd. 'I'm very sorry.'

The injury was so old that it no longer hurt – it was just a loss that could never be made good. 'Not long after that, Seneschal Vomix sent in his troops to raze Nifferlin to the ground. The rest of our clan, at least those who'd survived, fled, but we stayed, living among the wreckage in two rooms that they could never see, hidden by little Fyllis.'

'Extraordinary,' said Flydd, turning to study her more closely. 'And you must have a similar kind of talent. Not the same, but from the same branch.'

'It appears so. Father taught us that such talents were dangerous and had to be suppressed, so I never knew I had one. Fyllis was only little when he went to Mazurhize and I suppose that's why her talent developed normally.' Her heart began to pound. 'Can ... can you help me learn mine?'

'Why are you looking at me so anxiously?'

'Ever since Father had to flee for his life, whenever I've wanted something I've been told I can't have it. Or that it's not for me. Or to get back to work and stop being such a stupid dreamer.' Maelys realised that she was wringing her hands, and put them behind her.

485

'People can be cruel,' said Flydd.

'But it was all my fault.'

'What was?'

She told him about meeting Vomix on the road as a child, and how her foolish, innocent remark had condemned her clan.

'And you feel guilty about that, though you were just a kid?'

'I'll never forgive myself.'

'Yet you're the kind of person who can forgive others for injuries they've done you.' He didn't offer her absolution. He merely said, 'You didn't condemn them. The Nifferlin talent did, and Vomix would surely have found out about it, sooner or later.' He looked away, thinking. 'You will forgive yourself, one day.'

They didn't speak for a while, then Flydd said, 'Tell me everything you know about Monkshart, and Phrune too.'

She did so, and he thanked her, gravely. 'You know more about Monkshart as he is now than anyone, I think, for you've seen him as he really is.'

Maelys was pleased to be able to help him. 'Did you know them, Xervish?'

'Not Phrune. He would not have been of age when the war ended. I've met Monkshart, whom I knew as Vivimord. Nish and I talked about him. What will he do, I wonder?'

Maelys hadn't thought about him lately. Since they'd seen the flappeters she'd been focussed on Nish, and Jal-Nish. 'He'll come.'

'Yes, Monkshart will come. He'll do whatever it takes to get here. He could be here already.'

'What, up here?'

'Not without my knowing, but he may not be far from Thuntunnimoe – what's the matter, Maelys?'

She controlled her heavy breathing with an effort. 'Whenever I think of Phrune and what he nearly did to me, I get such a pain in my chest. I can't seem to draw enough air.'

486

'Breathe slowly, and if you must think about Phrune, don't go over the things he did to you. Think about the times when he was struggling, failing, and terrified. Think of him as a man too afraid to face his own fears or foes, so in malice and bitterness he preys on the innocent when they're helpless.'

Maelys imagined Phrune as she'd seen him coming out of the maze, eyes glazed, speckled with vomit and earless after the sergeant had dealt with him. It helped, just a little.

'Did you also know Tulitine, Xervish?'

'I don't recognise the name, and I don't suppose I'll meet her now. She sounds too old to climb the pinnacle. Pity.'

She took a deep breath, then asked anxiously. 'Will you help me with my talent, surr?'

'Of course, when I have the time. I'd dearly love to read your clan Histories too, but I dare say they're lost.'

'I think so. Mother burned most of the books from the library last winter, to keep warm. Where do you think my talent could have come from?'

'I've no idea. Sometimes such gifts arise spontaneously from a fortunate pairing of mother and father. Others can lie latent for many generations before suddenly rising to the surface in one family, or just one child, then disappearing again. And some families show talent for generation after generation, only to lose it forever. You can never tell. It doesn't matter, does it?'

'I just wondered, since our clan has been all but wiped out to get rid of the talent.'

'The really important question is where your taphloid came from.'

'I don't know. Father gave it to me and told me to keep it secret from everyone, including the aunts. Especially the aunts . . .'

'Describe it.'

She did so, and it roused her longing for the little device, to say nothing of the guilt she felt for being too frightened to

487

do what had needed to be done – slit Phrune's murderous throat and take it back.

'I don't recognise it,' said Flydd, 'but many artisans and mancers crafted cunning devices in the latter stages of the war. No one could keep track of them all, and some were always kept secret. Where is it now?'

'Phrune stole it after we came out of the maze. I'd given it to Jil's little brother and asked him to hand it to Seneschal Vomix, and it turned his aura inside out so agonisingly that his face tore from screaming.' It was another image she'd never forget. 'Vomix couldn't let go of the taphloid. I told you that.'

'It was cleverly done – though I still don't understand quite what it did. And you didn't tell me how you knew to do it.'

'It was a gamble. A guess after he accidentally touched it in the maze while pawing at me, and it hurt him cruelly.'

'One other thing.' Flydd perched his scrawny buttocks on a wet rock and patted the surface beside him.

She sat down. He didn't seem so frightening now. He understood her. 'Yes, Xervish?'

'What do you want from Nish?'

She didn't look away quickly enough, for the blood was already boiling into her cheeks. He took her by the chin and turned her face back to his, and sighed. 'Your mother and aunts didn't send you to save Nish because they cared about him, did they?'

'No,' she whispered, going even redder.

'They sent you on this deadly mission to ensure his gratitude so, if he did rise again, Clan Nifferlin would rise with him.'

'Yes.'

'But gratitude can be difficult to ensure. It's so easy to offend some people, wouldn't you say? Your mother and aunts would have wanted a bond or security to make sure all their efforts, and yours, weren't wasted. But how could they be sure, from so far away? They couldn't. The one person who could form that bond is you, Maelys, but what have you got to offer Nish? Stand up, please.'

She did so, blushing even more furiously as his eyes roved over her, though not in the sordid way of Phrune, or even with the desire she'd seen once or twice on Nish's face, early on, and in Thommel's gaze lately. Flydd's cloudy eyes studied her dispassionately, thoughtfully, and even with a trace of wry amusement.

'They asked you to seduce him and get yourself pregnant with his child, didn't they? Even Jal-Nish, monster that he is, would recognise that bond. It's the one sure way to save Clan Nifferlin.'

'They didn't *ask* me,' Maelys said faintly.

'No, you're not yet of age. You're still subject to their authority. They would have laid it upon you as a solemn and binding duty to the family, which you must carry out no matter the cost to yourself.'

'Yes,' she whispered.

'So what went wrong? You're a lovely girl of good family, desirable in every respect, and Nish is a man who appreciates beautiful women yet has been deprived of a lover for ten years. Why wouldn't he have you?'

'Surr,' she said, trying vainly to prevent the mortifying tears forming, 'you're torturing me.'

'I've got to know what really ails Nish, deep down, and he'll never tell me. I don't wish to hurt you but you're the one person I can ask.'

'I can't say, Xervish.'

'Why not?'

'I just can't. It would be like betraying a confidence.'

'I have to know,' he said sternly. 'I don't want to force you but I will if I have to. And you know I can do it.'

She did, so there was no point denying him. 'All right. It's Irisis!'

'Irisis!' he frowned. 'What do you mean?'

'He's obsessed by her to the point of madness. He can't even think of having another woman, for in his mind Irisis is perfection in every respect, and no one else will do. In his delirium he talked about her as though she was still alive.'

'He's obsessed by a woman *ten years dead*?' Flydd looked grave. 'I knew Irisis well.' He smiled at a memory; momentarily it lit him up from within. 'She was a wonderful woman, but perfection – far from it! She would have been the first person to tell you her faults. What happened when you tried to seduce him? I assume you did try to do your duty?'

'Surr!' she cried. 'I can't – please don't ask me about such things . . .'

'But I am asking you, Maelys, and I must insist that you answer me. This is the most important question anyone has ever put to you. Nish's fate may rest on it, and yours. And your family's.'

'It was wickedly wrong,' she whispered, tears streaming down her cheeks. 'I knew that, despite that it was my duty and I was doing it to save my family. But I had no choice, did I?' He didn't answer, just continued to look into her eyes as if he could read the tiniest falsehood, and shortly she continued. 'I've never been with a man, Xervish, not even a kiss at the midsummer fair, and this was the hardest thing I've ever had to do. But I did my duty. I tried my best, just as my aunt had instructed me in the arts of . . . of seduction.'

She covered her face but he took her hands away and tilted her face up so the misty light fell on it. 'I don't need to know the embarrassing details, but I do need to know how Nish reacted.'

'He went into a cold rage and accused me of trying to steal him away from his beloved, then told me never to come near him again. I felt that I disgusted him; that it made him sick to look at me. It was the most awful moment of my life, Xervish . . . worse than anything that's happened since – even with Phrune.'

Flydd didn't embrace her, or say anything until she had cried herself out, for which Maelys was grateful. She turned her tear-stained face to him. 'I suppose I deserved it –'

'Stupid fool!' He crashed a fist into his palm and swore a series of oaths she'd never heard before. She shrank away. 'Not you, Maelys. This is worse than I could have imagined. Irisis is ten years dead and nothing but mouldering bones in a coffin. What can be the matter with him?'

He got up and splashed through the swamp, limping around and around the rock, heedless of his surroundings. On the third circuit his meandering path took him near a well-hidden stink-snapper, and as he went by it shot up out of the mire, its yellow-spined jaws gaping.

'Xervish!' she yelled as it snapped at his thigh.

He directed a wobbly but well-aimed kick at it, where-upon it withdrew until just the yellow spines were visible. He finished the circuit then came back to sit beside her. 'We're old adversaries, the stink-snappers and I,' he said with a rueful grin, and sat head down, deep in thought.

Maelys didn't want to interrupt his deliberations, but she'd remembered something that could be vital. 'Irisis is more than mouldering bones, Xervish.'

His head jerked up. 'What do you mean?'

'The God-Emperor has her embalmed body in his quarters, with her head sewed back on. He showed it . . . her to Nish, and Nish said she looked just as she did in life. As if she were but sleeping.'

Flydd hooked his bony fingers into claws. 'This is bad, Maelys. Very bad indeed, and I don't know what I'm going to do about it.'

'Are you going to tell him?'

'Tell him what, girl?'

'About . . . you know.' She was flushing again.

'Use the words, Maelys, and they'll begin to lose their power over you.'

There was something about Flydd that made her feel so

491

much better; more confident in herself. 'Are you going to tell him that I . . . was trying to seduce him, so as to get his baby into my belly?'

'No. Why should I?'

'You're his oldest friend. Don't you think he needs to know?'

'He doesn't need me to hold his hand. Besides,' he eyed her up and down again, 'I like you, Maelys. You could be just what he needs.'

A man who's in love with a corpse. She compared it to the way Thommel had cared for her on the journey, always being there when she needed him and asking for nothing in return. And making her laugh, too. 'But is Nish what I need?'

FORTY-THREE

Nish was not exactly drunk but, leaning back against the wall of the hut with a full belly, the liqueur singing warmly through his veins and even an occasional ray of late afternoon sunshine breaking through the fog, he felt pleasantly tipsy. He had absolute faith in Flydd now. Of course he'd think of something. He always did.

Where was Flydd, anyway? He'd gone off with Maelys hours ago. Nish got up, staggered and had to support himself on the wall of the hut. His touch on the crumbling red amber-wood released a drift of its enchanting aroma, which helped clear his head.

He looked around blearily. Zham was slumped against the wall of the hut, snoring. The empty flask lay on the ground on its side, plus another of lesser quality but quite extraordinary flavour. Nish couldn't imagine what Flydd had made it from. Thommel was nowhere to be seen. Out of the shelter of the hut Nish noticed that a strong cross-wind had blown up from the west and the fog was clearing rapidly, as if one of the peak's rare clear days, or nights, was approaching. He could see nearly halfway across the plateau.

Ah, there was Flydd, stalking in from the edge with Maelys on his arm. Nish turned towards him, grinning. 'What is it with you and women, Xervish?' he said jovially, realising that he was slurring his words but not caring.

'You're the ugliest old coot in the world, yet you've always got one on your arm.'

Maelys gave him a disgusted look and moved away, knotting and unknotting her fingers. What was the matter with her? Flydd turned the other way. The last of the fog dispersed and Nish could see for leagues in every direction, even beyond the rainforest east and north to the coast. That smudge on the northern horizon must be the city of Roros, the capital of Crandor and the greatest city in the world.

As Nish rotated to admire the view, the sun dropped below the jagged, threatening peaks of the *Wahn Barre*, and the temperature dropped sharply. He pulled his damp coat around him, the good mood fading.

'I need to talk to you in private,' said Flydd, frowning, 'but clearly now isn't the time. Where's Thommel?'

Nish shrugged. 'I don't know where he went.' He had a vague memory of him taking exception to something Nish had said, but couldn't remember what. 'He's a surly brute. I hope he's up to his neck in the mire.'

'He's warm-hearted, gentle and brave. *He* helped me when I was in trouble,' said Maelys.

Nish had too, though leaving with Monkshart had cancelled those good deeds out and he felt guilty about it. He covered it by sneering, 'I'll bet he did.'

'What's that supposed to mean?' she snapped.

'Nothing,' he muttered, regretting it already. The liqueur had disconnected his brain from his mouth.

She glared at him, hands on hips. 'Thommel is a gentleman, which is more than I can say for you. If it hadn't been for him, you never would have found this place, or Xervish.'

Her casual use of his old friend's first name irritated Nish. He'd known Flydd for years before he'd felt comfortable calling him Xervish. He opened his mouth to snap back but Flydd elbowed him painfully in the ribs.

'Stop bickering and come inside, children. This wind cuts right through to my bones.'

Maelys stirred Zham and they followed Flydd to the hut, Zham carrying the bench for no reason Nish could fathom. There were two lanterns on the wall but Flydd lit a handful of rushlights, which gave the hut a homely glow. It was small and rough-hewn, but more comfortable than Nish had previously thought; far nicer than his cell. The earth floor around the table was strewn with dried rushes. Flydd lit a small fire fuelled with neatly squared blocks of dried peat from a covered stack behind the hut.

Later, with another meal in his belly, his back resting against the wall and warm hands and feet for the first time since he'd climbed to the plateau, Nish's irritability disappeared. He sat there, blinking in the firelight until he found himself drifting off.

He woke suddenly as the door burst open. Thommel was shouting, 'Lights! There are lights *everywhere.*'

'Wha–?' Nish said stupidly, sitting up. The west wind was howling around the corners of the hut, shaking the walls. His head throbbed and he felt as though he was going to throw up. He bit down on the urge. Everyone was shouting at once.

'Enough!' Flydd's voice cut through the babble. 'What lights?'

Thommel was breathing heavily, as if he'd been running. 'Camp fires. Thousands of them, regularly arranged. Like a mighty army.'

'It's the God-Emperor,' said Maelys, unconsciously moving away from the firelight.

'Where are they, Thommel?' said Flydd. 'They must be close or you wouldn't have seen them through the rainforest.'

'They're directly below us, all around the eastern side of Thuntunnimoe. They could be on the other sides as well – I didn't wait to check. And away to the south-east, I saw the glow of camp fires along the river. That must be the Defiance.'

495

'How could the army have found this place? Could the Defiance have led them here?'

'I don't see how,' said Thommel. 'Their fires are a long way off.'

'I walk the rim of the plateau every night,' said Flydd. Outlined against the firelight, he looked like a skin-covered skeleton. 'And every so often the fog thins enough to see down momentarily. If they'd camped around any of the other peaks I would have seen the glow of their fires, but I never have. The army came straight here, so either they followed you or tracked you by some uncanny means.'

'They couldn't have followed us, surr,' said Zham. 'In the first few days we walked up the beds of streams until our boots were rotting.'

'We covered our tracks just as well,' said Maelys. 'And saw no one behind us the whole way, save flappeters a long way back, just after we got here.'

'They tracked one of you,' said Flydd, sitting down. 'Now how could they possibly do that?'

'I have no idea,' said Nish, absently rubbing his scar.

'Why do you keep doing that?' said Flydd irritably.

'It's where the nylatl stung me with one of its tail spines. It's still itchy.'

Flydd shot upright. 'You didn't tell me it had *stung* you. Why would a nylatl sting you when it could have torn your throat out?'

'I don't know.' Nish still felt dull from the drink. 'Now you mention it, it does seem odd.'

'It was just crouching there, staring at him,' said Zham. 'It could have killed him easily, but . . .'

'Maybe it didn't want to,' Flydd mused. 'Yet savage, terrifying killing is the very reason the nylatl were created. Who could have kept one for all this time?'

'What if it wasn't meant to kill?' said Maelys. 'What if the attack was intended to disguise something else?'

'Ahh!' said Flydd. 'That's the answer. The first assassination attempt was intended to fail, Nish, and the assassin to die, so you'd *think* someone – perhaps your own father – was trying to kill you.'

'That doesn't make sense,' said Maelys.

'It does if you're God-Emperor, and paranoid. As the leader of a popular revolution, Nish would be too great a threat, for not even the power of the tears could save Jal-Nish if the entire world turned against him. Nish, you were meant to think that Jal-Nish wanted you dead so you'd assume the real attack, by the nylatl, was another attempt on your life.' He lit a couple of lanterns. 'Give me a look at that scar.'

'What?' said Nish sluggishly.

Flydd tore Nish's shirt open and pressed a fingertip hard against the round purple scar below his right collarbone.

Nish gasped. 'That hurts.'

'Of course it hurts, you damn fool. Part of the spine is still in there. Why didn't you get Zham to take it out?'

'I didn't know it was there. The wound closed over and it had healed by the next day.'

'And you, of all people, weren't suspicious?' growled Flydd. 'You know nylatl wounds never heal cleanly, or quickly. Zham, you'll have a sharp little knife on you.'

Zham drew a small, narrow-bladed dagger from his right boot sheath and handed it over.

'That'll do nicely. Hold still, Nish.'

Nish gritted his teeth. Flydd made a quick cut across the scar, inserted the tip of the blade and levered, and the broken end of a bloody spine appeared. He pinched it between finger and thumb and drew it smoothly out. After rinsing the blood off in a stream of water from a jug, he held it up to the firelight, then his face blackened.

With a swift movement, he dropped the spine into a stone mortar, ground it to powder with a pestle and emptied it into the fire, carefully brushing every last grain of powder out. They sparkled scarlet as they fell into the flames, and Nish felt his unconscious burden ease a trifle.

'You bloody moron!' hissed Flydd, his old face twisted in fury. For all his age, he was still a powerful man and not to be crossed. 'That wasn't a spine, it was a *tracker*. Of course your father wasn't trying to kill you – you're all he's got left. He's happy to see you suffer, for he's endured pain that few people have ever felt and emerged the stronger for it, but he'll protect you with his life. And than means . . .'

He paced across the room, and back. 'The assassination attempts were just decoys to disguise putting the tracker in you. But why do that, when clearly he could have abducted you at any time? Because he's had a new plan ever since you got away from Tifferfyte.'

'What plan?' said Maelys.

'He was there in an air-dreadnought as you fled, remember? And with the tears, he might have read fragments of your vision in the Pit – enough, at least, to realise his chance. You didn't know what was at the end of your vision, but Jal-Nish could have worked it out.

'You wondered why he allowed the Defiance to grow so large, unhindered, and why he took so long to attack. What if he sacrificed the army you destroyed so your rise would be all the more convincing? That's it! He wanted you to lead the Defiance and have a great victory, Nish, because that would coax the last of his old enemies out of hiding. And now you've led him straight to me – the enemy he wants to revenge himself on more than anyone.'

'I – I'm sorry,' said Nish numbly. He'd been used and manipulated from the beginning, and maybe even that great battle victory hadn't been real, although he didn't want to think so. 'It didn't occur to me that –'

Flydd waved a hand. The fury had passed as quickly as it came, though his cloudy eyes had a steely shine in the firelight. 'What does it matter? I'm at the end of my days, anyway. He won't be taking me alive, and I'll do him some damage as I go – as much as I can manage in my feeble state. I just hate to be outwitted so easily.' Shaking his grizzled head, he reached for another flask.

Nish slumped onto the bench. His every small victory was followed by a shattering defeat, and there was no way out of this one.

'What can you do to him, Xervish?' said Maelys. 'I though all power was lost, save the power of the tears?'

'All those Arts which relied on power drawn from nodes failed, yet some of the ancient, more difficult magics linger on, greatly weakened though not destroyed. I haven't wasted *all* my time here in drink and regret – nine years ago I laboured up this peak carrying a pack full of ancient spell books and grimoires.' He waved a hand at a shelf containing half a dozen battered books. Their spines were covered in blue mould. 'I studied them assiduously in the early days, trying to develop new forms of the Art for the final battle.'

'It won't be long,' said Thommel. 'The soldiers could be on the way up already.'

'You couldn't bring an army up that cleft in darkness,' said Flydd.

'He doesn't need an army. Ten soldiers, good climbers, would be more than our match. He must have hundreds of climbers and spies used to working in the dark, and we can't stop them. This is the end.'

'I'm afraid it is, and all we can do is delay it for a few hours.'

'What's the point?' said Thommel dully.

Maelys reached out and touched his arm. He tried to smile at her, to regain what they'd had before, but couldn't manage it.

'If we have to die,' said Flydd, 'defiance in the face of impossible odds is the best way to go out. Our tale will give others hope, assuming they ever hear of it. Besides, you'll be surprised how precious those few extra hours of life become, at the end. You'll do anything to stretch them out . . .'

He fell silent, looking down at the floor, before continuing.

'The cleft you came up is the only one suited to a large force. The other clefts could only be climbed, and then with difficulty, by mountaineers.'

'How can five of us possibly delay them?' said Thommel.

'You'll see in a minute. I put defences in place years ago.'

'Father could attack from the air as well,' said Nish. 'We can't delay that.'

'But the weather will,' said Flydd. 'I chose this place for its natural defences as well as . . . other reasons. The native power of Thuntunnimoe prevents flappeters and other Art-driven beasts, and perhaps even air-dreadnoughts, from descending on us from above. And the updraughts –'

'What is the power of this place? Has it got to do with the obelisk?'

'Not so much the obelisk as what lies beneath it. It's an age-old Charon memorial, I believe, built at a site of native power, an uncanny flame. The obelisk is a memorial to failure – a sign that all endeavours fail in the end, and time undoes all things. That won't please Jal-Nish, of course, since his life's obsession is to change the world in ways that will endure forever.'

He thought about that for a moment. 'The obelisk was built over the cursed flame –'

'I wondered why the stone was so warm,' said Maelys.

'The obelisk is bonded indissolubly to the living rock, sheltering and protecting the cursed flame, not that it matters to us. The flame used to issue from the top in ancient times, as a sign or a warning, but the conduit must have become blocked in ages past. The power of the flame hasn't proven usable by mortal humans, so far . . .'

'But you planned to?'

'I thought I'd found a new way,' said Flydd, 'but I wasn't strong enough. The power was constrained by the builders of the obelisk, deliberately, and it was built to last, well, not forever, but for a very long time.'

'But it's broken. How did that happen?'

'I don't know, but the break hasn't freed the power of the flame. I don't think anything can.'

'You were saying about the updraughts?'

'Oh yes. They gust so wildly that no air-dreadnought could survive them, and they only stop when it's blowing a gale, as now.'

'Do we have a hope of escape, Xervish?' Maelys asked softly. 'Any at all?'

'I'm sorry. There's no way out now.'

'Then what about the ancient Arts you've been studying?' she persisted. 'You must have had a plan to use them.'

'Why do you say that?' Flydd asked mildly.

'I – I devoured the Histories and the tales of the war, from when I was a little girl. Clan Nifferlin had them all in its library, once. I know a lot about you.'

'Do you now?' He bestowed a fond smile on her. 'Then you'll also know that most heroic tales are lies written by rogues for the entertainment of fools.'

'I know no such thing!' she cried hotly. 'Not everything in the tales is truth, for what is truth anyway, when everyone sees a tale differently? But I know you were a great and honourable man –'

'*Were?*' His smile broadened. 'Have you judged me and found me wanting?'

She looked mortified. 'No, of course not, Xervish. I'm sorry.'

He chuckled. 'I'm indulging myself in my last hours by teasing you. But you're right. I chose this plateau carefully, from dozens of possible refuges, because there was an ancient power here which predated the nodes. The broken obelisk is, in part, a monument to the tragic failure of those who died trying to master that power, in days long past.'

'Then what made you think you could do better?'

'Ah, that would be telling. I'll say only that, as my mastery of the old Arts grew, I hoped to draw upon it. But it turned out that the power of Thuntunnimoe had been

501

greatly weakened by the destruction of the nodes, and the old Arts took longer to master than I'd expected. By the time I'd done so I was an old, feeble man, without the strength to draw what I needed. You can't imagine how frustrating it's been to feel the power just beyond my fingertips, yet be too decrepit to use it.

'I also chose Mistmurk Mountain because it offered an escape route, but without power I can't use it. Not only is great power required to open that way, but more is needed to hold it open for the hours it will take to traverse it. All I've got left is the power for one last desperate burst of mancery, to take as many of my enemies as possible with me. Though alas, not the God-Emperor. He knows what a cunning old scoundrel I am and won't risk himself until he's seen my decapitated and quartered body, with the pieces well separated.'

'So we're doomed,' said Nish.

'No, *we're* doomed,' said Thommel, again with that hint of bitterness. 'The God-Emperor will make sure his beloved son is safe. He'll take you back to a life of unimaginable luxury, power and pleasure.'

'I'm not going back.' Nish could feel the temptation tugging at him but had no trouble resisting it now. His father had used him once too often.

'Really?' said Thommel, as if he could read Nish's mind.

'What's that?' said Maelys, cupping her ear. 'It sounds like someone shrieking.'

Fiery pain ran down the length of the nylatl wound, then Nish ran for the door. Zham and Thommel beat him to it and forced their way outside. He followed. The wind was so strong that it lifted him up on tiptoes. The moon was out now, mostly showing its red- and black-blotched face, which touched the bogs and pools with red-tinged reflections. The sky was clear, not a trace of fog or cloud anywhere.

'Stay close by the hut,' hissed Flydd. 'The amber-wood will conceal you here, but not out in the open. If you must go further, put this in your pocket.' He tossed a small chunk of amber-wood to each of them.

Nish sniffed his and thrust it into his pocket. High above, silhouetted against the moon, were a wheeling flock of flappeters.

'Are they spying?' said Maelys.

'Undoubtedly. But something else is going on. I can feel it.'

'What, surr?' said Zham.

One of the flappeters dipped suddenly, shuddered violently then shot away and climbed back towards its fellows. 'It looks as though someone's trying to call it down,' said Flydd.

'What, down here?' said Nish.

'I don't know,' said Flydd. 'There it goes again.'

The flappeter dipped sharply this time, then plunged down at a steep angle towards the centre of the plateau.

'I thought you said they couldn't descend from above the plateau?' said Maelys.

Flydd didn't answer. The flappeter's dive steepened; its rider was standing up in the saddle. It was now hurtling down, the feather-rotors driving it ever faster.

Nish expected it to pull out and come racing towards them but it continued in a straight line and crashed at full speed into the mire, sending gouts of mud flying spans into the air. High above, the remaining flappeters wailed in unison.

Everyone looked shocked. 'I guess that means we're safe for a while,' said Nish.

'He hasn't finished yet, whoever he is,' said Flydd, looking up. 'He's trying again.'

A second beast was now bucking as it, and its rider, tried to fight whatever was attempting to take control of them.

'The call is too strong,' said Flydd. 'Whoever it is, they're determined to prevail.'

'Who could it be?' Maelys said faintly. She was shaking.

503

Instinctively she moved closer to Thommel, who put his arm around her.

Nish looked away. It was none of his business, but he felt a pang for the times they'd shared together and the friendship they might have developed if he hadn't kept her at bay. Despite everything, she'd got under his skin.

The flappeter suddenly dived towards the edge of the plateau, was buffeted perilously close to the cliffs by the updraught then corkscrewed down out of sight. Nish ran to the rim and peered over. The beast was hurtling towards an eroded rock stack jutting up from the side of the pinnacle, halfway to the bottom.

'It seems to be settling,' he said over his shoulder. 'It's in shadow now; I can't see it.'

The others came up behind him. 'It's rising again,' said Zham, whose eyes were keener than Nish's.

Nish made it out now, slowly beating its way up. 'It looks bulkier . . .'

'Carrying two riders,' said Zham.

The flappeter moved out, caught the updraught and shot upwards. 'That's the way to do it,' Maelys said with a professional eye.

'He won't find it easy to get out of the airstream, though,' said Flydd. 'Whoever he is . . .'

As the flappeter neared the top of the cliffs it began to buck and swerve wildly. It was thrown side-on and barely avoided smashing against an overhang, going so close that the rear rider reached out with a long spear to fend the cliff off. The flappeter spun in a circle, then back the other way, the feather-rotors roaring.

'Crash!' said Maelys, standing rigidly erect, unblinking.

The rear rider fended the cliff off again. The flappeter was close now though neither rider showed any sign of seeing them.

'There's a mighty turbulence when the updraught meets the cross-wind,' said Thommel. 'With any luck –'

The front rider thrust his fist through the loop-controller and raw power redly illuminated a banner of mist clinging to the underside of the beast. It let out a screaming wail, caught the updraught and shot up into the clear air above the plateau. Nish heard a shout, 'Down, down!'

It turned around, flutter-flapped inland, flying low where the wind was weakest, then hovered out over the mire. The rear rider slipped over the side, dropped to ground and headed into the swamp.

'What's he doing?' said Nish.

'Heading for the broken obelisk,' Flydd said harshly.

'But he can't do anything there . . . can he?'

'I don't – I *hope* not.'

The flappeter turned in a sweeping circle and began to fly around the edge of the plateau, safely inland from the rim. 'He's searching,' said Zham. 'He knows we're here.'

'He knows all right!' Flydd scowled at Nish, who looked away.

The flappeter was surrounded by a thin yellow nimbus, and Nish could see its open maw and hear its fearful squeals. It was terrified but couldn't break the power controlling it.

The remaining rider now wore a long, funnel-shaped helmet. No, it must have been an Art-enhanced speaking tube, for his voice boomed out and the words were clear, as was the glutinous hiss of his voice.

'Come out, wherever you are! Surrender yourselves to the mercy of the God-Emperor and it will go well with you.'

Behind Nish, Maelys gasped, 'No, it can't be. He's dead.'

It was Seneschal Vomix. The flappeter was thrown upwards and sideways so violently that a gap opened up between Vomix and the saddle. He let out a cry and snatched desperately at the straps with his one hand. The speaking funnel went flying as the flappeter jerked the other way, turned upside down and its feather-rotors missed a couple of beats, but it righted itself and began to climb away, Vomix clinging on with one hand and his legs.

'Should I shoot him?' said Nish, who had his bow in his hands.

'Not unless you know you can kill him,' said Flydd, 'otherwise he'll know where to look for us.'

Nish put an arrow to the string, drew it back and aimed at the wildly bobbing figure. But he lowered the bow. Once he would have been sure he could do it, though it was a difficult shot in the moonlight and he was out of practice. 'Zham's a better shot than I am.'

'I wouldn't risk it either,' said Zham. 'But I don't think we'll need to . . .'

'Go back!' Nish heard Vomix roar, but the beast ignored him.

It was buffeted this way and that across the sky, flung upside down again then plunged sideways over the edge of the plateau, feather-rotors beating furiously to avoid the cliff. It spiralled down, out of control, before slamming hard into the top of a rock stack hundreds of spans below them. The rider fell off and lay beside the flappeter, which kicked feebly then went still.

'Is he alive?' said Maelys.

'I think so,' said Zham. 'But the flappeter isn't!'

'He's hunting me. And he won't give up until he gets me!'

'He hasn't come all this way just for you,' said Nish.

'Vomix must be in disgrace,' mused Flydd. 'He's desperate to make up for his previous blunders and recover his position, else he would never have risked his precious skin. He'll have to climb all the way up from that rock stack now, and he won't be quick. It would take immense power to seize control of a flappeter from so far away, and aftersickness must be crippling him. He'll never force another flappeter down. He won't have the strength.'

'What difference does it make *to us*?' said Thommel, giving Nish another black look. 'Nish led the enemy here, yet he's the only one who's going to survive.'

'We can't be taken,' said Flydd. 'That would give Jal-Nish

506

the victory he so desperately craves. Come inside. We've got to make plans.' They went in to the fire and he continued, 'Since we have no hope of escape, I propose we make a pact – to fight to the death, but if we're going to be captured, *we jump*. That's my plan, anyway, but I have nothing to lose. What say you?'

'I'll not give the God-Emperor the satisfaction of tormenting me,' Thommel said bleakly. 'But first, Nish, you'll hear what I have to say!'

Nish blinked. 'What are you talking about?'

'The fact that you don't remember makes it even worse. But then, after breaking your solemn undertaking to the world, any word you'd given to a child would be meaningless.'

'If you've got a grievance, man, spit the damn thing out!' snapped Flydd.

'My clan was robbed of their heritage by the enemy when I was little,' said Thommel. 'Even my parents gave up and walked away, for they didn't have the courage to fight and die for what was theirs.'

'If they had, you wouldn't have lived to be here now,' said Flydd, pulling the bung of a flask with a satisfying pop.

'In the circumstances that's no consolation,' Thommel said dryly. 'And since the war ended, the brutal favourites of the God-Emperor have been given my heritage. All my life I've slaved to gather enough coin to fight them for what was mine, yet every time I've been knocked down again. And all my troubles began with him.' He prodded Nish in the chest.

'With *me*?' said Nish.

'A few years before the war ended, you fell from the collapsed bag of an air-floater into a teeming work camp near Nilkerrand, on the other side of Lauralin. It was a brutal place. You would have been slain within minutes had not a boy looked after you, and his family taken you in at the risk of their own lives. And in return, you promised the boy that one day you would help him regain his heritage.'

'You're Colm!' Nish cried, memories of that terrible time flooding back. 'The first time I met you I thought you looked familiar.'

'Day after day, month after month, I waited for you. I kept hearing great tales about your heroic deeds and your valour. People queued up to say what a noble and honourable man you were. I believed in you. I hero-worshipped you, and I *knew* you'd come back one day to honour your word. But you never did.'

'I'm very sorry, but there was a war on,' said Nish, feeling hot in the face. 'And the moment it ended, I was sent to prison.'

'I know and I understand,' said Colm, and it was as if the apology, or the confrontation, had lifted the weight from his shoulders. 'I know everything about you, Nish. But that's not the real reason, is it?'

Nish didn't know what to say. He wanted to make an excuse but Maelys was looking at him and only the naked truth would do. 'No,' he said finally. 'No it's not. The truth is, I'd forgotten the boy and the promise. I – I'm really sorry, Colm.'

Colm acknowledged it with the faintest of smiles, though Nish didn't think the obligation had been wiped away. 'The boy couldn't understand, for it was his dream and his faith that were broken. But I'm a grown man. I know you couldn't come back, Nish, and there was nothing you could have done if you had, not while the enemy occupied the lands of my heritage.'

'Then why put me through all this?'

'For the boy. The dreamer. He had to hear you say it.'

'I do keep my promises, Colm. I –'

'In the circumstances,' Colm said soberly, 'I won't hold you to it, though if we should survive . . .' He offered Nish his hand and Nish took it.

Now he turned to Maelys, who was staring at him as if she knew just what he was going to say. Colm's smile faded.

He reached out to her. 'I'm really sorry, Maelys. The past few weeks with you, they've been the best I can remember. You're a true friend and I even dared to think – well, never mind. There's no future for us, and no way out. When it comes to the end, and if we are going to be taken, I – I – I'm jumping with Flydd.'

He lowered his head. He was shaking. Maelys moved in beside him and took his arm but it didn't seem to help.

'I'll follow the Deliverer wherever he leads,' said Zham after a long pause, though his fists were knotted at his sides and he was very rigid.

Nish felt for him; for all of them. 'I've sent men into battle, knowing they were going to die, but I can't order any man to take his own life. Zham, at the end it's every man for himself and you must do what's best for you, not me. My folly brought Father here, after all.'

'I'll go with you all the way, surr,' Zham said gruffly.

Everyone was looking at Nish expectantly. Jumping with Flydd was the one blow he could strike at the God-Emperor, though surely it would be a futile one. Would it weaken his father's grip on the world, or make it harsher?

As he stood there, he could almost feel Jal-Nish trying to influence him, using Gatherer to wake the long-buried compulsion he'd put on Nish many years ago.

Come to me, Cryl-Nish, and all will be forgiven. I swore never to bend, but things have changed and I must bend with them. Do you think I achieved all this for myself? *I did it for you, Son. You're all I have left, so come, bend the knee and I'll raise you up to sit at my right hand. You'll have everything you could ever want. Even the deepest desire of your heart can be yours, if you will come.*

How he wanted to. Nish didn't want to die either, and what if his father *could* give him the deepest desire of his heart? What if Jal-Nish could replace that loss which still burned Nish every day? He wanted it so desperately.

Nish looked up. Everyone was staring at him. He'd let

them down, unwittingly betrayed them, and he had to make up for it.

'I'm with you, Xervish,' Nish said, without knowing if he was. Could he really take the ultimate step and plunge over the cliff when his deepest desire was on offer? Or would he see his friends die one after another, then betray their memory?

FORTY-FOUR

They were all looking at Maelys now and she didn't know what to say. Their situation was hopeless, and falling into Vomix's hands was unthinkable, but Flydd's path wasn't one she could follow. She'd considered that way out months ago, and rejected it.

'I can't do it,' she said quietly. 'Not even if the alternative is to be taken, tortured or even . . .' She shivered, closed her eyes. Her eyelids fluttered. 'No! Life is precious and it's wrong to take your own –'

Nish began to say something but Flydd held up a hand. 'Say no more. I admire you all the more for staying true to your conscience, whatever it costs you. None of us will seek to persuade you otherwise, though you've made a harder decision than we have. We've a few hours to prepare ourselves; at most, until dawn, and I suggest we each do so according to our inclination. I plan to walk the rim of the plateau, *alone*, as I do every night, then get splendidly, roaringly drunk.'

He nodded to them, checked that the protective amberwood was still in his pocket, and went out.

Maelys made sure she had hers as well. Colm was trying to catch her eye and she wanted to go to his calm, reliable solidity, but if these were to be her last hours of freedom there were things she needed to settle with Nish first. 'Later, Colm,' she said softly.

Nish touched her on the shoulder. 'Would you walk with me for a bit?'

Her gut tightened at the thought of what she must say to him but it had to be done. She offered him her arm as if they were the best of friends and nothing bad had ever happened between them.

Flydd was visible in the moonlight, shuffling along the rim of the plateau to their left, so they turned the other way. The cross-wind was even stronger now. Maelys, who was on the right, kept well clear of the edge.

'Nish, I'm sorry I was so angry on the way up,' she began. 'I should have tried harder –'

'It doesn't matter now,' he said. 'In my last hours, I've got bigger problems to worry about than a trifling misunderstanding.'

Maelys bit her lip. It wasn't trifling to her and she had to get it out. And once she did, she needed Nish to acknowledge her apology and offer one in return, though she didn't think he was going to. Why were his problems always more important than hers? Because he was the son of the most powerful man in the world, and her clan had been reduced to beggary. No, Clan Nifferlin were proud, whatever their state, and she didn't have to take it. What had she ever seen in him?

'What problems?' she said, then realised that he'd been waiting for her to ask. Stupid, stupid man.

'Ones that I can't even talk to Flydd about, or it'll destroy all the faith he's ever had in me.'

But it doesn't matter about my faith in you, because you don't care a fig for me, despite all I've done for you. Why am I putting myself through this? But because she still felt for him, and in a few hours it would all be over, Maelys said, 'What is it, Nish?'

He let go of her arm and went to the brink, staring down. She edged after him, afraid that a sudden gust would hurl them over. Far below, the camp fires of Jal-Nish's mighty

512

army twinkled around the base of the cliffs like an arc of fireflies. Were they already on the way up, or would Jal-Nish wait until the last possible moment, to draw out the tension until everyone snapped?

'Father is getting to me,' said Nish. 'He's found a way into my mind.'

That was one problem she hadn't anticipated. 'What, *now*?'

'A while ago, just before we made our choices. He was only there for a minute or two, and I know it hurt him to stay that long, but he'll be back.'

As she turned to face him, the wind stripped away her last vestiges of warmth. She hugged her thin coat around her, though it made no difference. 'What does he want?'

'What Father has always wanted. For me to acknowledge him as my liege and swear to serve him.'

'And the price?'

'He'll give me everything I've ever dreamed of – power, wealth, authority . . .'

Nish flushed. He'd left something out – the most important something. 'I meant the price you have to pay,' said Maelys.

He turned away, cold sweat glistening on his brow. 'Becoming like him.'

'Are you prepared to pay that price?' she said, so softly that the shrieking wind carried her words away and she had to repeat herself.

He looked every way but at her. 'It's so very tempting. You can't imagine how much I've always wanted to be an important man, a leader, someone people looked up to. I know it's weak of me but –'

'Can't I?' she said, deliberately softly this time.

He didn't hear, or ignored her. 'I can resist those temptations, just. But –'

Her inner chill deepened and she fought the urge to block her ears, for she knew what he was going to say and

513

couldn't bear to hear it. Horror spread though her veins like her blood crystallising to ice.

'Father has offered me the deepest desire of my heart,' he whispered.

Don't say a thing. Don't ask what he means – just turn away and run as fast as you can. But she didn't. 'What *is* the deepest desire of your heart, Nish?' His eyes were like pools of despair, or longing. She couldn't tell which, in the dim light.

'To have the love of my life back again. And I don't know what to do.'

She wanted to smack him until he came to his senses. His obsession had driven him over the edge. She took him by the arms and shook him, unable to contain her anger any longer. 'Why are you telling me this, Nish? What do you expect me to say – that it could actually happen? It can't, and we both know it.'

He didn't answer, though she thought his cheeks grew a trifle darker. No, no, no! Surely he wasn't asking for her approval? 'And you'd betray everything you've ever fought for, as well as the faith of all those people who've suffered and died for the Deliverer, *for a dead woman*?' she hissed.

'You don't understand. You can't understand.'

Maelys lost it. 'How would you know what I understand? You've never taken the time to bother with me. And what's so special about you? What makes your feelings so unique, so elevated, so *noble*?' She spat the words out. 'You're sick, Nish, and I'm not listening to another word of it. Go to your precious father, or stay, but stop whining and begging us to sanction your choices. What kind of a man are you anyway? You're no better than Monkshart, or . . . *or Vomix!*'

She turned to stalk away before she lost what little remained of her dignity, until out of the corner of her eye she saw Nish squeezing his skull between the heels of his hands and reeling about, dangerously close to the edge. Momentarily she thought he was putting on an act, but the pain on his face was unmistakable. She caught him by the arm and dragged him away.

'He's back,' Nish mumbled through a locked jaw. 'He's back and I can't get rid of him. It hurts; it hurts.' His eyes were staring into infinity. 'Oh, Irisis,' he whispered. 'Irisis, Irisis, Irisis.'

Maelys shook him, but couldn't break the trance, or possession. She slapped his face; it made no difference. Taking his head between her hands, she roared, 'Get out of his head, Jal-Nish,' right in his face.

Nish's head jerked. She let go; his eyes focussed on her and he slowly took his hands away. 'I don't know what you did, but he's gone. I feel like a normal man again.' He put his arms around her and hugged her tightly; like a brother would.

It didn't mean he cared for her, nor did it erase what she'd just seen. It was too late, anyway, and it no longer mattered, since she'd never be doing her duty with him now. She felt only relief, and pulled away before he did. 'Come on.'

They walked a third of the way around the cloverleaf-shaped rim in silence. Maelys saw army camp fires all the way. Once a flappeter shot up over the cliff not far ahead, bucking wildly as it rode the updraughts. Its rider seemed to be scanning the centre of the plateau with night glasses, but shortly it banked, curving away and down again without showing signs of seeing them.

After watching it out of sight, Nish said, 'Please don't say anything to Flydd, or the others. It's my private torment. I'd die if they knew.'

'Do you mean about Irisis, or your father tempting you?'

'Both. But mainly Irisis.'

After a long hesitation she said reluctantly, 'All right.' It didn't matter now. Let him take it to the grave, if that's what he really planned to do. 'Irisis is dead, Nish. You do understand that.'

'Of course I do! I saw her slain.'

'And the dead can't come back to life. No power can restore a life once it's been lost. So this obsession of yours –' At the expression on his face she hastily rephrased. 'What I meant was, your father can't give Irisis back to you, so how can he have any hold over you?'

'I know that, but when he's in my head I can't see it. Father is the very prince of deceivers . . . No, wait! I've just seen the way.'

Maelys clenched her fists. He was further gone than she'd thought; totally delusional. 'Nish, Irisis is dead –'

'I'm not talking about Irisis,' he said impatiently. 'I'm talking about Xervish. It's the answer – the one way out of here. Come on!' He raced off.

She ran after him, catching him as they reached the hut. Nish thrust the door wide. Flydd, who was warming a goblet by the peat fire, looked up sharply. Zham lay on the floor in the shadows, asleep, while Colm was sitting at the table, shaving a length of red amber-wood into curls. He glanced at Nish, then her, and must have read the gulf between them for he gave Maelys a sympathetic smile.

She went across and sat beside him, saying quietly, 'It's over, Colm. I'm done with him. I'm free – until Jal-Nish comes.'

Colm began to say something but was drowned out by Nish who, after standing uncertainly for a while, said, 'Surr! I've found the answer – *renewal*.'

'What are you talking about, *boy*?' growled Flydd, sniffing his goblet.

Nish flushed. 'Rejuvenation of a mancer's ageing body by the Secret Art. It would give you the strength to use the escape –'

'I know what renewal is,' Flydd snapped. 'And what it does. It's one of the most degrading Arts of all. All mancers who cast the renewal spell upon themselves were either corrupt beforehand or corrupted by taking it, and long ago I swore a solemn oath that I would never resort to it. When a man grows old, he dies, thus making room for the young. That's been the way of the world since time began.'

'People have accused me of offering hope to the world, Xervish,' Nish said quietly, though with a determination he'd lacked previously, 'then breaking my word. And they were right. I did make that solemn declaration ten years ago, in memory of Irisis, yet I was going to repudiate my oath because I was too afraid. Afraid to hope and have hope dashed. Afraid to try. Rather, I chose to slink away like a craven cur, until others, better than me, forced me to *remember my duty.*'

Flydd's scarred and death-like face grew black as he listened, and at the end he exploded. 'You miserable little worm! You snivelling, puling wretch! You dare to lecture me, a former scrutator, on my duty? I'm not so feeble that I can't flog you until you beg for mercy like the whining little turd you are. I damn well might.'

Colm and Zham came to their feet. Nish took a step backwards and Maelys could see his resolve weakening under his old friend's fury. To her own surprise she moved in beside Nish and, standing shoulder to shoulder, took a deep breath. Her knees were shaking. She'd been taught to respect legitimate authority and she'd never met anyone with as much natural authority as Flydd, but he was wrong. If renewal was the only hope left, he had to be convinced to take it, for the whole world was at stake.

'I know a thing about duty, Xervish, and I say Nish is right. If you flog him, you'll have to flog me too.' Her voice cracked. She'd seen men, and once a woman, flogged by Vomix's troops in the market square, and still flinched when she thought about it.

'Go and check the clefts!' snarled Flydd, with such ferocity that even Zham and Colm took involuntary steps backwards. 'Now!' They went out, most reluctantly. When

517

they were gone Flydd went on, 'I'll flog you too, Maelys, if that's what it takes to convince him. I will *not* take renewal!'

Maelys screwed her eyes shut. She couldn't believe he was serious, not at such a time as this, and after her demure upbringing it was unthinkable to defy such a great and powerful figure, but she had to find a way. After lecturing Flydd as she had, backing down would make a hypocrite out of her. She must persist, no matter the consequences.

She straightened her back, tilted up her chin and looked him fair in the eye. 'Do what you will, Xervish, for I cannot turn my back on what I know to be right.'

They went eye to eye for a minute or two, which was even harder, for Flydd was a master of that game who had broken scrutators at it, and his cloudy eyes gave nothing away. But Maelys could not give in either, and though her knees were wobbling like clock pendulums, and her belly felt as though a full-grown slurchie was gnawing through it, she had to hold her nerve. Only Flydd could save them now, so he must take renewal.

Eventually he gave a mocking laugh, as though the camaraderie they'd shared earlier had been coldly calculated; meaningless. 'Surely you don't think you can best *me* at this mind game, you silly little girl?'

Nish's teeth were chattering. He'd seen Flydd at the height of his powers and doubtless knew just what he could do, but Maelys put Nish's fears out of mind. Why would Flydd resort to taunts unless his own resolve was weakening? She chose to think so, anyway. Hers was, too. The pressure was too much and she was going to crack. She had to take the assault to him now, while she could.

She tightened her will another notch and stepped forwards until she was standing breast to chest, staring up into his eyes and willing him to look away. They held that pose for several minutes, the longest of her life. Flydd grinned crookedly, but it looked a trifle forced and that gave her hope.

'Maybe I am a silly little girl, but I'm not going to give up, Xervish.'

His cloudy eyes drifted fractionally so that his gaze circled around hers. He *was* weakening. She went up on her toes and his eyes were slow to follow hers. Flydd was no longer staring directly into her eyes, but rather in the vicinity of her lower lashes. She chose to interpret that as a weakening, that he'd lowered his eyes, and peered directly into them.

Again his gaze slid almost imperceptibly down, and she knew she had him. 'You broke,' she said softly, not crowing, for it was not that kind of victory.

After a draining eternity he said, 'I broke.' He bowed his head, panting. 'And you, my dear, sweet Maelys, belong with the very bravest foes I've ever encountered. You're a formidable gir– young woman, and such strength deserves its audience. Do you realise what you're asking, when you ask me to take renewal?'

'No, Xervish, I have no idea.'

'If you did, you'd be less eager to put me through it. The renewal spell is ancient, yet little used by even the most greedy mancers, for it kills as many as survive it, and some who do survive wish they hadn't. Self-harm and suicide are common among those to survive renewal, while many have been crippled or driven out of their wits by it.'

He was right. How little she knew or understood.

Flydd went on. 'It's one of the most excruciatingly painful spells ever used upon a human being. So painful that I who, as you see written upon my body, suffered brutal tortures as a young man, have nightmares thinking about it.

'And even if I could summon the power to work such a desperate and dangerous spell, *and it succeeded*, I'd still be trapped on this pinnacle without allies, for Jal-Nish will fall upon the Defiance any day now and wipe them out to the last woman and the last child. So what's the point of putting myself through the agony?'

No one spoke. Maelys was quelled. How could she require him to suffer such pain for such a slim chance of success? Their cause was lost, and she'd made her choice, but what right did she have to impose her will on him? Why not let the old man end his life with whatever dignity he had left? Because that would mean letting Jal-Nish win, and she could not.

'Because your giving up would put out the lights forever, Xervish. There's no hope for the world unless we create it, here and now. Think of the young people who will one day take your place; think of the children. Would you have them grow up in a world without hope, if we had the means, or even the slenderest chance, of offering hope to them? We must try, Xervish.' She reached out her small hand to his scarred one, and he took it. 'We can do no less.'

'Is there hope, though? Is there any at all?'

'Just a grain, surr,' said Nish. 'It's the tiniest flicker, but it does exist. Maelys saw it in the Pit of Possibilities and I believe her.'

'I'd like to believe,' said Flydd. He turned to Maelys. 'Well?'

'I saw into the God-Emperor's mind when he was looking into the tears.'

'Are you sure he didn't *let* you in?'

'I – Yes, I'm sure. He does have a weakness, and he's afraid. He hasn't robbed the world of all its Arts. Most, but not all. He hasn't crushed all his enemies yet. And as Monkshart told Nish, *nothing goes to nothing.*'

'Nothing goes to nothing,' Flydd mused. 'Indeed not. And everything has its antithesis.'

Maelys started, for it reminded her of her speculations after escaping from Monkshart's tent.

'That's right,' she cried. 'Monkshart and Phrune talked about it but they never followed the idea through.'

'And you did?' said Flydd, looking puzzled.

'Yes, and if that's true, then somewhere in the world –

hidden, transmuted perhaps – there must lie the antithesis to the tears, something that can be used to nullify their power.'

Suddenly the light came back to Flydd's rheumy eyes and he laughed, with just a tinge of bitter irony this time. 'Only one person on Santhenar could know that. A calculating, inscrutable, relentless foe that in a hundred years no one has ever set eyes upon; the power who established the Council of Scrutators for an unknown purpose so long ago. And the one in whose name I was flogged until half the flesh had been scoured from my bones.'

He looked around the hut, studying them one by one as if weighing up their fitness. 'Very well, Maelys, I will do as you ask. I will attempt the renewal spell. And if I should survive it, and we get away, which can't and won't happen, I will lead you on the long hunt to find this terrible foe. I'll take you south towards the frigid pole, across the Frozen Sea to the forbidden Island of Noom, and there we'll climb the Tower of a Thousand Steps where, *if you dare*, you may put that question to the Numinator.'

FORTY-FIVE

Zham had appeared at the door but did not interrupt. Nish shivered at Flydd's words, and Maelys wondered what he knew that she did not.

'What's the Numinator?' she said.

'I don't know,' said Nish, 'and I'm not sure I want to.'

'Nish, if you know something, can't you just say so?'

'No one knows about the Numinator, Maelys,' said Flydd. 'Not even the head of the Council of Scrutators, when it was the most powerful body in the world, could say whether the Numinator was man, woman, beast or alien, or what its purpose was. We knew only that the Council answered to the Numinator which had created it, and how savagely it punished all who tried to pry into its affairs.'

'How come it hasn't taken down the God-Emperor, then?' said Nish. 'Or he it, if Father truly is all-powerful?'

'I don't know,' said Flydd. 'Perhaps he has. Or perhaps they've reached some accommodation; or a stalemate.'

'Either way, it's been very quiet,' said Nish.

'Everything about the Numinator has been kept quiet; I doubt that forty people, living or dead, have ever heard the name.'

'So even if we succeed in all these impossible challenges,' said Maelys, 'and reach the Tower of a Thousand Steps on the Island of Noom, the Numinator could slay us out of hand?'

'He, she or it could.' Flydd was staring into space again. 'But the Numinator might also have been hurt by the destruction of the nodes; perhaps even humbled.' A vengeful smile crept across his face, and Maelys shuddered. He had depths she couldn't imagine.

He snapped back to the present. 'There's no time for speculation. You've required me to take renewal, and I will. The preparations are arduous, the after-effects long and brutal, and we'll be undone if Jal-Nish arrives when I'm still laid low with aftersickness. It's late. What news from the watch, Zham?'

'They're not waiting until dawn, Mr Xervish, surr,' said Zham. 'There's movement at the camp fires and a line of torches around the south-east cleft.'

Flydd cursed. 'How long do you think they'll take?'

'It took us eight hours in daylight, not counting rest stops. Even his most reckless climbers couldn't do it in under ten hours at night. Though an advance guard might already be on their way.'

'I dare say they are, though he won't attack until he's got a strong force in place,' said Flydd. 'Jal-Nish knows that Nish came here to meet one of his great enemies. He's probably guessed that it's me and knows I'm not weaponless. He won't want to lose the element of surprise by sending a handful of scouts who could be destroyed with a single blast.'

'Could you destroy them with a single blast?' said Maelys, remembering tales of the great mancers of olden times. And she'd taken him on without a thought.

'In my present state I'd be hard-pressed to stop a one-legged tortoise, but fear makes your enemies greater, and Jal-Nish has always feared me.'

'Let's say we've got six hours, just to be safe,' said Nish. 'Can you work the renewal spell in that time, Xervish, and recover from it?'

Flydd's eyes went to the grimoires and spell books on his

rudely carved bookshelf. 'I have no idea – I haven't done it before.'

'But you do know how?'

'Well – I've seen it done. As a young man, not yet out of prenticeship, I assisted my master to take renewal.'

'How did it go?' asked Maelys.

'It took us prentices a week to scrape his organs off the ceiling.'

He sat down, staring at the rush-strewn floor between his feet, breathing heavily. No one spoke. *You could die just as horribly*, Maelys thought, *and I forced you into it.* She wanted to stop him, but backing out now would have been cowardice, so she dug her nails into her palms and waited.

Finally Flydd raised his head. 'Nish, the four ways must be watched, and since there are only three of you, one will have to run back and forth.'

'There's four of us, Xervish.'

'But to cast the spell I require an assistant; and to watch over me while it takes its painful course, an observer. And since Maelys was so kind as to urge renewal on me, I choose her.'

'It's no less dangerous than guarding the ways up, Maelys,' he said quickly. 'Don't think for a minute I'm offering you the easy alternative because you're a girl. I've chosen you because you have healing skills; and because you alone among us aren't trained in combat. And also,' he said with a thin smile, 'because I want you to know exactly what you've put me through. I'm a vengeful man. Petty, and vengeful. Let's begin.'

Reaching up onto a shelf, he took down a folded sheet of paper. 'I haven't wasted my nine years here. Long ago I prepared an array of defences in case the worst happened, and this plan sets them out.' He handed the paper to Nish. 'Get a lantern and read it outside – I've got to get on without interruption. Take some more amber-wood; you'll need all the concealment you can carry.' He scooped chips and shavings from the table. 'It might even conceal you from Gatherer, as long as the tears are a long way away.'

'But not from the eyes of ordinary soldiers?' said Nish, handing chips to Colm and Zham. Colm shook his head. He already had a pocketful.

'No, unfortunately. Nor from the tears if Jal-Nish gets onto the plateau.'

Nish, Colm and Zham checked their weapons and went out. Flydd lifted the lid of a box behind the door and removed four large packets of food wrapped in woven reeds. He opened the first – strips of dried swamp creeper flesh, from the colour – and wolfed them down with gasping gulps from a water jug. When he'd consumed the lot, enough to feed the five of them, he held the empty jug out and began on the second packet, more of the green biscuits.

'Are you all right?' said Maelys uneasily, not taking the jug.

'Water!' He crammed a lump of biscuit in his mouth sideways. 'Renewal is the most draining spell of all and one can't eat for days afterwards. And besides –' He shook the jug at her. 'Just fill the damn thing.'

She scurried out and scooped it full at the nearest rivulet. By the time she returned, Flydd's stomach was bulging like a pregnant woman's. He was at the table, reading a blackened grimoire which was charred at the edges, as if it had been rescued from a fire. She handed him the jug, which he drained in a single long swallow, then let it fall to the earth floor. She stood by the fire, waiting for him to tell her what to do. After five minutes he was still turning the pages so she said, 'Xervish, how would you have me prepare?'

'By holding your bloody tongue.'

She did so for another while, then couldn't stand it any longer. 'Are you angry with me?'

He stood up suddenly, treading on the jug and kicking it out of the way. 'Of course I'm angry. I'm a proud old man, set in my ways, and you've forced me to a path I swore never to take. Renewal is utterly abhorrent to me; I've never

525

felt anything but contempt for those mancers who've taken it, whatever their justification. I feel like a hypocrite.'

How little she'd known what she was asking. But she hadn't taken the choice from him – how could she? He'd made the decision for himself. 'Why did you choose me?'

'I told you – petty revenge.'

'I've never thought of you as a petty man.'

He smiled thinly. 'And after knowing me for half a day, little Maelys can read all the quirks of my character. Isn't she a clever one!'

How could she have thought to bandy words with him? 'But –'

'Will you shut up! I can't think for your foolish chatter.'

She shut up, feeling bruised. He turned the pages back and forth, settled on one and began to read. His lips moved as if he were rehearsing lines, then he placed a dried rush in the book and closed it.

'I also chose you for the inner strength you displayed a while back, and your unwavering courage.'

She thought he was being sarcastic again. 'It wavers all the time, Xervish.'

'Not the way mine does; *or Nish's,*' he said meaningfully. 'Besides, I may have to draw strength from you to complete the spell, since my body is so cursedly frail.'

She didn't think it was quite as frail as he made out, but said, 'I'll do whatever I can.'

'Splendid!' he said with fake joviality. 'Let's begin.' Opening a small flat wooden case which she hadn't noticed on the table, he fingered something inside, then drew it out between finger and thumb.

The crystal, about the size of one of her finger joints, was a pale translucent red, though as it warmed to his touch it gave out the faintest inner glow. The box held four more crystals, each a different shape and colour, but dull.

Seeing her staring at the box, he said, 'I don't have to explain about powered crystals, do I?'

'Er –'

'Any crystals charged before the nodes were destroyed will retain that power for a long time, though once it's drawn upon the crystal becomes useless.'

'I do know that much. Where did you get them?'

'I'd hidden three of them in a secret place long ago, in case the worst happened. After Jal-Nish came to power I walked halfway across Lauralin, hunted all the way, to recover them.' He paused for a long moment, lost in memories. 'That story, were it ever told, would rival one of the lesser Great Tales of ancient times. The other two crystals I bought later, at the most fantastic cost – a mancer's ransom, in fact. The fewer such crystals are left, the more valuable the remaining ones become. Keep silent while I recite the spell, then wait.'

After a pause she said, 'I don't know what you want me to do.'

'Stand by and be ready to hand me the second crystal, though I pray I won't need it. Assuming that renewal gives me the strength to use them, *at least* three crystals, and maybe four, will be required to force the barrier for our escape, then hold the shadow realm open for the hours it will take to traverse it. Not to mention keeping at bay the phantasms which stalk that place, hungering for the flesh-and-blood prey which offer their only hope of escape from the shadow realm, like blood-sucking leeches hitching a ride out of the endless slough to the undefended feasting grounds.'

He sounded almost lyrical as he spoke but an abrupt hand gesture told her to ask no more questions. 'Put out the lights; cover your eyes from the crystal and keep out of its sphere of influence. *Now!*'

He began to take his clothes off. Maelys stared at his scrawny and horribly scarred chest, which looked as though the surplus flesh had been gouged off with a red-hot spoon, then hastily turned away.

She didn't see him cast the spell on himself, for she had her back turned, blowing out the second lantern, though she heard guttural whispers in a language she did not know. A brilliant red flare cast her wavering shadow on the wall for a few seconds, then began to fade. Flydd gasped, in pain.

Mindful of his orders, she turned carefully, shielding her eyes from the flare, only to see him falling. Steaming blood dripped from the fingers of his right hand, where the crystal had given up all its power in a moment. Now colourless, cloudy and dark, it lay on the floor in fragments.

'Xervish!' She ran the five steps to him but didn't get there in time. He hit the floor with a hollow thump. His heels drummed, rustling the rushes, and he lay still.

The egg-shaped floating flare drifted up towards the ceiling, slowly fading. She knelt beside Flydd in its dim red light, afraid that the onset of the spell had killed him, but found a faint pulse in his neck. His eyes were staring glassily, like a dead man's. She went to close them with her fingertips but his bony arm snapped up, cracking painfully into her wrist and knocking it away.

'Don't – touch –'

The flare dwindled to a point of dull red below the central roof beam, directly above them. Flydd had gone so rigid that she could hear his joints cracking. His teeth ground together and liquids gurgled in his distended belly, which bulged up as if he'd swallowed a watermelon, then all was still save for the wind shaking the walls of the hut.

The minutes ticked by. Maelys crouched beside Flydd in numb terror. Why hadn't he told her what was going to happen? Was the spell working properly? If it went wrong, how would she know, and what was she supposed to do then? Were Jal-Nish's climbers creeping up the clefts, even now?

Half an hour might have gone by before anything changed, then the red point of light went blue. A speck formed at its base and swelled until it resembled a large dangling soap bubble. It wobbled back and forth, expanding at the bottom, broke off and drifted down towards them.

Maelys was crouched by Flydd, watching the bubble fall and wondering what it meant, when his arm snapped out again, whacking her painfully across the nose and knocking her backwards. She didn't realise that he was protecting her until the bubble landed on his face.

It went flat and the curved edges rolled out in all directions, stretching to enclose his head, then extending down his neck and trunk, and across his shoulders and underneath, until his whole body had been enveloped. Again the light faded, though not completely this time. Not enough to conceal what was happening to him, unfortunately.

It began with little blisters forming on his face, thousands of them, until no patch of skin was unaffected. The blisters expanded, linking into a continuous swelling which spread across his head and inflated with fluid, lifting the skin away from his flesh in one bloody piece, hair and all. The same process was extending down his body. She averted her eyes.

Flydd's fingers clenched and unclenched. He writhed, went rigid, writhed again and rose slightly off the floor as the blisters grew and combined beneath him. In a few minutes he was enclosed in a transparent balloon of inflated skin, beneath which the raw flesh bubbled and wept red trails until eddies in the blister fluid rendered it opaque.

The only parts of him unchanged were his eyes, staring sightlessly up until the blister closed them off, then his mouth and nostrils as well. He no longer bore any resemblance to Flydd. He was just one gigantic, human-shaped blister almost as big as Zham.

Something popped beneath him, releasing a nauseating stench. Maelys didn't dare move in case he called on her, so she held her nose and endured it. The blue pinprick of light below the roof beam turned green and faded until she could barely make out the shape of the blister, though what she could see was alarming enough.

It was undulating, waves rippling through the fluid from one end of his body to the other. It swelled at his feet, but shrank again. Pulses ran down and back up. His knees inflated; the blister fluid whirled there like water going down a plughole, then went still.

Nothing else happened for a long time. Maelys's own knees were aching. So was her back. She settled against a chair and waited. And waited. She was half asleep when the door was thrust open and Nish burst in. He took two strides into the room then stopped abruptly, staring at the elongated blob on the floor.

'Is that –?' He couldn't finish. 'What's he doing, Maelys?'

'Xervish used the first crystal to cast the renewal spell, and this is what happened. That's all I know.'

Nish made a gagging sound. 'Is – is *this* how it's supposed to go?'

'I have no idea. He didn't tell me anything.'

He cursed softly, his chest rising and falling. Water dropped from his coat, forming muddy puddles on the earth floor.

'Is there any sight of the enemy?' she asked.

'No sight. No sound. They could be up to any devilry and we won't know until they fall on us.' He looked down at her. 'Three of us can't stop them. There's no way out.'

'We mustn't give up hope, Nish.' Even in her own ears she sounded unconvincing. Nish gave her a desperate, white-eyed look and went out.

Maelys resumed her watch, though nothing happened apart from an occasional swirl within the blister. An hour later Nish returned, inspected the amorphous shape on the floor and retreated without saying anything. Maelys was really worried now. Half the mancers who had attempted renewal didn't survive it, Flydd had said, and surely most had been stronger and less frail than he. Were those faint movements within the blister his death agonies?

Without warning, his distended stomach inflated even more, bulging to the left then the right as if there were wrestling twins inside, and slowly began to shrink until it was as flat as it had been when she'd first met him; then even flatter. It went concave and hard, outlining the stringy muscles of his belly. The bubble pulled in at the sides but grew at either end; there were more roilings, churnings, bulges and depressions, and more unpleasant smells.

A spasm racked him from one end to the other; the bubble churned more violently than ever, and the fold which had closed off Flydd's mouth parted with a sticky hiss. 'Crrr!' he said, an agonised crackle. 'Ccccrrri –'

She went to her knees again, reaching for him but, remembering his earlier warning, drew back before she touched the bubble. 'Xervish, what is it?'

'Crrr – crrrrr –'

The second crystal! She sprang up, snatched the blue crystal from the case and carefully slid it between his balloon-like fingers. Flydd tried to raise it but the bubble was now so taut that he could not bend his elbow.

The fold over his mouth parted again. He made an urgent sound she could not decipher, 'Wa! Wa!' and it wasn't until he'd said it a third time that she realised he meant, 'Away!'

Fool! She sprang backwards and was turning aside when the crystal went off, dazzlingly bright. Shards punctured his finger blisters, which spurted fluid like pricked sausages in a frying pan but quickly sealed over again.

Flydd let out a hoarse, crackly scream. Beneath the body-blister, bulges and depressions undulated in all directions. His legs lengthened suddenly as if propelled by bands of rubber, before whipping back to thick, stumpy limbs no longer than her forearm.

Maelys put her hand over her mouth. The spell was going wrong. He was going to end up a monstrosity. His legs lengthened again, but much further this time, until the base of his blister-feet touched the wall, before shrinking once more. His head flattened, became pointed, then sucked in on the left side.

His chest bulged like a beer barrel before flattening like a board; every other part of him went through bizarre transformations, each accompanied by hisses and crackly gasps, and revolting stenches.

The blister swelled all over before finally contracting until a normal man's form was revealed, rather larger than Flydd's original shape and size, though the fluid within it remained blood-coloured and opaque. He became as rigid as a post, remained that way for several minutes, and stretched out his hand again.

'Crrr – crrrrr –'

Her heart gave a leap. The renewal must have gone very wrong if he needed a third crystal, and it only left two to crack the barrier and hold open the path through the shadow realm, whatever that was. Two wouldn't be enough. Even if he survived renewal they wouldn't be able to escape now.

There was no choice but to go on. When she turned back with the green crystal the blister was contracting again, but this time it went all the way down as the fluid was drawn into Flydd's tissues. It shrank tight on his torso, thickened, darkened then tore and began to peel away like week-old sunburn, exposing new pink skin beneath, as smooth as a baby's.

The body it clothed was that of a mature man in middle age, though he wasn't the scrawny runt Flydd had been. This fellow was of average height or taller but with muscular thighs, big feet and broad shoulders. The blister still covered his face and she couldn't make out any details there, though he looked in good health. She breathed out. Flydd had come through and, if renewal was nearly done, he might not need to use the third crystal after all.

She slipped it between his extended fingers – the blisters hadn't collapsed there either – and turned away at once, though this time the flash was barely visible. He'd required hardly any power.

But then blood began to trickle down his fingers, and her own blood seemed to harden in her veins. What had gone wrong? He dropped the shattered fragments of the green crystal and reached out to her again.

'Crrr – crrrrr –'

FORTY-SIX

Nish sat on the bench outside the hut, handed the lantern to Zham and unfolded Flydd's plan of the defences. The wind tried to tear it out of his hands. Zham held the lantern close, shielding Nish from the worst of it. Colm stood on his other side, the hostility gone, though Nish didn't think they could ever be friends. Still, it didn't matter now.

The plan showed the cloverleaf outline of the plateau top, with the four clefts between the lobes clearly marked, as well as the hut near the rim of the southern lobe. Other markings were explained in a series of annotations, in Flydd's small, neat hand.

'The side walls of the clefts are sheer,' Nish read, 'but skilled climbers with ropes and irons could make their way up the steep broken stone in the inner ends. The clefts are protected with trip lines a hundred spans below the top, which set off wooden clappers by the hut –' He looked up. 'That's what I heard as we came up yesterday. Bloody Flydd! He knew we were here, yet he let us wander around like geese for a full day.'

'Get on with it,' said Colm.

Nish read on. '– giving a warning so there's time to drop fire pots onto the peat walls in the three narrow clefts.'

'Peat walls?' said Colm.

Nish squinted at the plan. 'The inner ends of those clefts

are walled off below the top with oil-soaked peat blocks that can be set on fire to delay an attack.'

'Clever,' said Zham. 'They won't be able to climb around a burning wall, and if they try to pull it down it'll collapse on them.'

'What about the main cleft?' said Zham. 'It doesn't have a wall.'

Nish frowned at the plan. 'It just says to hurl the barrels down onto the rocks.'

'What barrels?'

'They're stored in hollows to right and left of the cleft.'

'What's in them?' said Colm.

'It doesn't say. Oil, I suppose.'

'I don't see what good oil would be,' said Colm, 'but let's get it done.'

'Better to wait until we hear the clappers,' said Zham. 'If it rains, the oil will wash away before morning. Let's start doing the rounds of the clefts.'

'I'm so tired!' Nish was huddled in a depression near the main cleft, out of the wind. They'd been tramping from one cleft to another for hours, keeping watch. There had been no sign of the enemy and he was wet, cold and exhausted. In the olden days he could have endured it without complaint but he felt a lesser man now . . .

'You must stay awake, surr,' said Zham, shaking him. 'It won't be long.'

The faintest mist had risen, just enough to create a halo around the moon. Even in the dim light his eyes looked bloodshot, but his back was held as straight as ever. Perhaps straighter. Zham was a simple man whose faith in Nish was absolute. His oath had sustained him through every trial so far and it drove him now. If he felt doubt or fear, it was carefully hidden.

Zham's hand caught Nish as he swayed backwards. 'Sorry!' Nish said, horrified that he'd dozed off. During the

535

war, a sentry would have been executed for sleeping on watch, but the greater shame was letting one's comrades down.

Zham was staring straight ahead, his big jaw working, stolidly refusing to judge, which made it worse. Nish forced himself to his feet. 'I'll go back to the hut and see how they're going. Can you –?'

'I'll do the rounds again, and get Colm's report from the other side.'

'Thanks, Zham.' Nish reached up to clap him on the shoulder, then turned away to slosh down the churned track to the hut, praying that Flydd's renewal would show progress this time.

It didn't.

Maelys forced herself to stay calm. 'What's gone wrong, Xervish?'

'Crrr – crrrrr –'

She stumbled to the crystal case, extracted the sulphur yellow crystal, the second last, and slid it into his fingers, which were still sausage-like. They clenched around the crystal, he reached across to slip it into his right hand, and his left hand reached out to her again.

'What is it, Xervish? Do you want the last crystal?' They were doomed either way.

The renewed, unfamiliar Flydd was squealing deep in his throat and reaching for her hand, but she couldn't work out what he wanted. Alarmed, she backed away, remembering the warning and afraid of his touch, but his squealing grew more urgent. He reached out to her. Could he be trying to tell her something, or was the thing inside the blister not Flydd at all? What if she touched him and caused the spell to go wrong?

What if she didn't help him and renewal failed? She had to take the risk. How could he hope to complete the spell when he was in such pain?

Taking a deep breath, she touched his left index finger with her own. He snatched at her hand, his bloated fingers compressing around hers with a hiss as the remaining fluid was squeezed back into his tissues. He was much stronger now; his grip crushed her hand.

A boiling surge ran through her fingers and up her arm, followed by a dizzying wrench that had her staggering and fending off the floor with her free hand. Letting out a tormented cry, he tried to push her away.

Maelys attempted to pull free, seized by a sudden panic, but his left hand had locked around hers and a line of heat was running from her midriff, along her arm and into her fingers, growing stronger all the time. The centre of her chest, surrounding her heart, grew so hot, tight and painful that she couldn't stand upright.

As she hit the floor, the lines of fire were like molten tin being pumped down her veins. Her fingers were burning now; she could feel the heat streaming from her into Flydd, and as it did her chest cooled; her racing heart began to beat more slowly. And more slowly still.

The coolness continued down her arm into her throbbing fingers, but her chest muscles were stiffening with cold, her heartbeat slowing to a murmur. Another wave of dizziness swept through her . . .

She woke up lying on the floor on the other side of the hut, her head and shoulder aching as if she'd crashed hard into something.

Or been thrown.

'Maelys?' Nish was standing in the doorway, still dripping.

She sat up, which really hurt. Her fingers were covered in flakes of skin; Flydd's old skin.

'It's as bad as it could be,' she croaked brushing it off. 'Four crystals gone and I still don't know if it's done. He had to draw on *me*, Nish, though he'd warned me not to come near while the spell was still active. He took something from me and now my head feels strange. I don't know what's happening and I'm really, really afraid. Should I have kept him at bay? Have I made things worse?'

His larynx bobbed up and down; his mouth opened and closed. 'Maybe it's all part of the spell. We've got to keep faith.' He didn't sound as though he believed it.

'But he used *four* crystals, Nish! He hoped he could do it with one. Flydd said at least three were needed for our escape, so without them –'

'Get a grip on yourself!' he snapped, then added with a heroic attempt at calm, 'No one in the world is better in a tight situation than Xervish. Trust him. Believe in him. We've still got time. There's no sign of them yet –'

Maelys thought she'd heard something outside. 'What's that?'

'I didn't hear anything.'

The sound came again, a faint *clack-clack*, followed by running feet and a low, urgent cry of, 'Nish! Nish!'

Before Nish could reach the door it slammed back against the wall and Zham was framed in the opening. 'They're coming!'

FORTY-SEVEN

Nish's tiredness vanished. 'Where?'

'North-west cleft,' said Zham, his mighty chest heaving.

'How many?'

'I don't know, but the clappers just went off.'

Nish said, 'It's all up to you, Maelys,' and turned to the door.

'No, it's up to Flydd,' she said softly. 'I can't do any more.'

He ran out. 'We'd better fire the peat walls, Zham.'

'All of them, surr?'

Nish splashed down the track after Zham. He, Zham and Colm had inspected the defences earlier. Flydd had cunningly built the peat barriers, walls a good two spans high, at the narrowest and steepest parts of the three narrow clefts, where it was impossible to climb around them. A knotted rope, fixed to the rim of the plateau, could be tossed over to assist climbing down to each wall, and bladders of oil were concealed nearby to ensure a good blaze.

Once fired, the peat walls would hold a small force off for an hour or two, since peat burned slowly, though after that the walls would collapse.

All depended on how many climbers came up each cleft. If Vomix had sent just a few, they probably wouldn't risk their lives trying to get past the burning walls in case all were lost, which would leave a gap in the attack plan. But if each cleft held a dozen or more troops, their leaders would order the most reckless soldiers to pull the burning wall down from below, and shelter under their shields. His father wouldn't care if a few men fell to their deaths as long as enough survived to carry out the attack plan.

What would that plan be? First, guard the four clefts so no one could escape, and make sure they couldn't get away in a home-made air-floater. Then secure the rim so they couldn't leap to their deaths, though that would take a sizeable force.

To be sure, the attack must wait for dawn, by which time hundreds of soldiers would have climbed the main cleft. Sunrise was still some way off, but could he, Nish, afford to wait? No, he had to give Flydd as much time as possible, for even if the renewal spell worked perfectly he'd suffer cruelly from aftersickness. The soldiers must be approaching the peat walls now and if they got past all was lost. Nish felt a spasm of panic and struggled to control it.

'Do it!' he said hoarsely. 'Run! I'll take the south-western cleft. Signal Colm to fire the north-western one, and you do the north-eastern. Then come back to the main cleft.'

Zham lit one of the lanterns and waved it in a great circle on the end of his arm, the pre-arranged signal. Nish was already running around the lobe of the plateau. It would be further than cutting directly through the marshes, but would be quicker, since the footing along the rim was solid rock or hard-packed earth. After a minute or two he made out Colm's answering lantern wave from the other side, a moving halo through the wind-churned ground mist.

Watching the light as he ran, Nish's toe snagged on something and he hit the ground so hard that his sword jarred out of its scabbard, clanging on rock. He skidded into a puddle, mud splashed into his eyes and he flailed blindly for his weapon. Not now, not *now*! What if they were already tearing down the peat barrier?

Panic again. He didn't recall being quite so prone to it in

the old days, but since getting out of prison it had been his greatest failing – apart from despair.

Think! The sword couldn't be more than half a span away and it had probably flown forwards. He came to his knees, felt in the most likely place and there it was – cold, comforting steel under his hand. He slid it back into its sheath and limped to the cleft.

At the top he scanned the misty gloom to left and right, in case the enemy were already up, but saw and heard nothing, nor from the cleft either. This one was just a gash into the plateau, like a thin wedge cut deep into a cake. It would make the climb up even more difficult for the enemy; would make it harder to fire the peat wall, too. Nish marvelled that Flydd had been able to build them at all in such precipitous terrain.

He peered over the edge but saw only impenetrable darkness. The clapper warning had gone off in the north-western cleft, though he must assume that there would be coordinated attacks from all four clefts.

He couldn't see the peat barrier in the moon shadow, though he knew where it was, some ten spans below. Unfortunately he couldn't fire it from here. He'd have to go down the knotted rope with the bladder of oil slung over his shoulder, to make sure the oil ended up on the peat.

Nish searched the darkness for any sign that the other walls were on fire. He'd not see flames from here – wet peat wouldn't blaze high, as dry firewood did – but might glimpse a glow. He saw nothing. What if Zham had fallen in the swamp, or been taken by one of the stink-snappers?

Stop it! Just get the job done. Nish felt for the oil bladder under its concealing moss, checked that he had the flint striker as well, then lowered the rope. Still no sign of the enemy, nor any sound. He'd eased over the edge and was hanging from the first knot in the drizzling rain when he smelt something.

It was the reek of sweaty, unwashed bodies, carried to him

on the updraught, so they weren't far below. What if they'd torn through the wall already? He wouldn't see them among the dark rocks, looking down, though he'd be clearly outlined against the sky. They'd grab him before he saw them.

There wasn't time to worry about it. If they'd crossed the wall, all was lost anyway, so he had to go down and make sure. It took all the courage he had. The thought of walking tamely into his father's clutches and being sent back to prison couldn't be borne.

He went down facing outwards, the better to see, lowering himself hand over hand from one knot to the next, and as his fingers closed around each knot his terror grew until his stomach became a clenched fist of pain. Every second he expected to be struck down by an unseen blow, or for big, callused hands to grasp hold of him.

He didn't try to will the pain away, or ignore it. Nish used it to focus his mind on one thing only: defeating the enemy. He would go on, no matter what. He would master his fears and do his best, and if that failed, so be it.

A projection in the stone gouged along his backbone, though he barely noticed. His heels struck a knob; he lifted his feet forwards, went down to the next knot, then the one below that, holding his breath, expecting the blow. It didn't fall. Hands didn't grasp him out of the darkness, and after a couple more knots a dark wall rose in front of him and his feet settled on steeply sloping rock. He was at the base of the peat barrier; he was in time.

He reached out to feel its comforting, fibrous solidity. Flydd had built it well, chiselling out the steeply sloping rock to make a sound foundation. The wall was a third of a span through at the top, thicker at the base, and as solid as stone when he leaned his weight on it. Nish settled the oil bladder on his back and began to pull himself up the rope, pushing at the barrier with his feet. He was just below the top when he heard the *tap-clink* of a climbing iron being knocked into a crevice, then someone spoke.

'What the blazes is this?' There came a thump, as if the soldier had laid into the wall with his sword. 'It's like it's made of cheese.'

'Toss a grapple iron over it and be quick,' hissed another man, a sergeant from the authority in his voice. 'That last cliff has cost us time and if we're late the whole troop pays. You know what Vomix is like.'

He'd survived that dive over the cliff on the flappeter, then. Nish shivered, drew back against the rock face so he couldn't be seen and twisted the bung of the oil bladder. It rotated in place. He pulled a little harder, but it didn't budge.

Rope whirred through the air and a grappling iron struck the upslope wall of the peat barrier. He caught a faint gleam of silver as the rope pulled taut and the soldier tested it with a couple of quick heaves. It held.

Nish jerked furiously at the bung, which came free with an audible pop.

'What's that?' hissed the soldier.

'A guard, drinking on duty,' said the sergeant. 'Quiet now.'

Nish crept along the top of the wall, pouring the thin, volatile oil onto the damp peat and fretting that there wouldn't be enough to set it alight. He could hear boots scrabbling on the peat, the soldier coming up rapidly. Too rapidly. Nish dropped the bladder at the other end of the wall, allowing the remaining oil to drain out. There wasn't time to light it; the soldier was halfway up. He should have cut the rope at once.

Heaving out his sword, he slashed wildly at the rope, burying the blade deep in the peat. The rope parted but the soldier, lightning fast, threw a brawny arm onto the top of the wall and swung from it. Before Nish's sluggish reflexes could wrench the embedded blade free, the man had the other arm over and was pulling himself up.

There was no choice; no time to think. Nish had to clear the wall before he could fire it. He wrenched, twisted and the blade came free in a cascade of peat chunks as the soldier rolled over and onto the wall.

'He's on the wall. Get another grapple up there,' roared the sergeant.

Nish slashed at the soldier's head. The soldier ducked then flung his sword up, the blade sliding along Nish's and striking the hilt so hard that it nearly tore the sword out of his hand. Nish's blade went sideways with a clang and a drifting spark. His arms wheeled as he tried to avoid going over the edge onto the swords of the troops below. By the time he'd recovered, the soldier was on his feet and the advantage had been lost.

Nish had been a skilled swordsman, once. He'd single-handedly slain a number of the alien lyrinx, which were much bigger and faster than men. His muscles remembered the moves but he was too slow for this crack soldier.

Nish went backwards, parrying for his life, the soldier thrusting and cutting like the expert he was. Nish stumbled; the soldier swung his blade out then prepared to bring it back in a blow that would take Nish's head off his shoulders. He couldn't get out of the way, nor get his blade into defensive position in time. He stumbled backwards, the moonlight shone on his face and the soldier stopped his blade in mid-air with a wrench that went all the way up to his shoulder.

'Surr!' he cried to the sergeant. 'It's the son of the God-Emperor.'

The sergeant let out a whoop. 'Bring him down, but don't harm a hair of his head. Signaller, signal for the *luminal*.'

Nish had no idea what a luminal was and didn't wait to find out. While the soldier was still off-balance he thrust his own blade up into the man's groin. It burst with a spray of fluid and the soldier doubled over, dropping his blade on the wall. He slid sideways, landed on the edge and fell onto the soldiers below.

The sergeant was roaring and bellowing at his men. Another grappling iron flew up and over the far end of the wall. Nish fumbled the flint striker out of his pocket, touched it to the peat and struck it. A feeble spark jumped but went out.

The iron caught hold on the back of the wall and the rope was jerked tight. Nish snapped the flint striker again and again, with no success. A soldier was already coming up the rope; another was close behind. Nish ran along the wall, hacked the line apart and snapped his striker a few more times, fruitlessly. The drifting sparks did not catch.

The troops now hit on a better approach. Four of them had hammered spikes into the peat and hung onto them, allowing other soldiers to scramble onto their shoulders and reach up to grab the top of the wall at the same time. If he attacked one, the others could spring onto the wall. Nish raised his blade high and hacked down at the fallen blade on the wall with all his strength. There was a mighty clang; a flurry of sparks landed on the oil-soaked peat and it caught. As the soldiers tried to scramble onto the wall, the oil blazed up beneath their fingers.

It gave Nish his chance. He dashed through the growing flames, slashing at the soldiers' arms, and the combination of fire and attack proved too much. Two lost their grip and fell back. A third leapt to safety. The fourth made it onto the wall, sleeves blazing, but before he could come to his feet or beat the fire out Nish swept down on him, swung his blade hard and took the soldier's round head off his stubby neck. Blood fountained all over him.

Nish sheathed his red sword. Flames were swirling around his wet boots and pants as he scrambled down the back of the barrier and began to climb the knotted rope. By the time he looked down again the whole of the wall was on fire and the troops could be seen as a cluster of shadows a few spans below it. He must have been clearly visible climbing the rope but they had no way to bring him down without harming him.

He reached the top and rolled onto the plateau, noting with grim pleasure the glows coming from the north-western

545

and north-eastern clefts. However he'd only gone a few steps when a flare ignited high above the centre of the plateau, brighter than any light he'd ever seen.

A brilliantly sparking and sputtering sphere of uncanny force, the luminal lit up the surface of the plateau as brightly as daylight. It had to be a creation of the tears – no other Art could have focussed such power – and since the God-Emperor held the tears tightly to him and allowed no one else to use them, Nish knew that his father had taken personal charge. The real battle was about to begin.

The attack by the main force must be swarming up the south-eastern cleft not far from the hut, and that way lay undefended. What if he'd left it too late? The clapperboards could have been going for ten minutes and there would have been no one to hear them. How long had he spent here? Nish couldn't tell. Ten or fifteen minutes, plus another ten coming across. If he sprinted all the way back, heedless of the dangers of the cliff track, it would take at least five minutes to reach the main cleft. That could be too late.

He bolted, pounding along the muddy track Flydd had worn in nine years of nightly wandering, splashing through puddles, skidding on mossy rocks and leaping over broader pools fringed with stubby rushes.

He kept glancing over his shoulder at the sky. He didn't think the luminal could have been conjured from a vast distance – no, Jal-Nish was up there somewhere, probably hanging silently in the night sky from his favoured air-dreadnought, shielded from view by his Arts until the moment when he burst upon them in an overwhelming display of power.

That was the one thing Nish could be sure of. When his father finally came to the attack it would be at the moment when victory was assured, and he would make a display of it that the whole world would talk about. It wasn't just the victory that mattered; the display of power was equally important. His father had learned that lesson from the scrutators at an early age.

Nish skidded to a stop beside the hut, before realising that there was no point going in to check on Flydd yet again. He ran on, looking fearfully down the cliff whenever the path skirted the edge, expecting to see lights everywhere. There were none, not even where the camp fires had been at the base of the pinnacle, earlier.

Surely that could only mean one thing – that the entire army was on the way up after all. He reached the cleft just ahead of Zham, who was charging along the rim path like a buffalo, and almost as unstoppable. There was no sign of Colm but he'd had a much longer run, on a winding, treacherous path between the bogs and stink-snapper pools.

'Surr!' cried Zham, staring in horror.

Nish looked down. He was drenched in the blood of the soldier he'd killed. 'It's not mine. Come on.'

He hurled Flydd's moss-covered timbers off the small stack of barrels on the right side of the cleft. Zham began to do the same to the left. Nish had just heaved the first barrel above his head when Zham, who was already at the edge with his, stifled a cry.

Stumbling under the weight, Nish looked over. Down where the cleft opened out before the last precipitous ascent stood hundreds of soldiers clad in the distinctive beetle-shell armour of the God-Emperor's Imperial Militia. More soldiers were forming up below them, as far as he could see, but they weren't looking up. They were watching a man who had his back to the plateau and was speaking in a thick, hissing voice that cut through the howling wind. It was Seneschal Vomix, alive and seemingly unharmed by the earlier crash.

A soldier in the front ranks raised his right arm. Vomix broke off, turning slowly and deliberately, and the light of the luminal was so bright that, even from this distance, Nish could see every detail of his face, ravaged from the time Timfy had innocently placed the taphloid in his hand.

Vomix's nose was a flattened blob, several front teeth were missing and long, ragged scars ran around and across his cheeks, as if his face had been torn off with a giant hand, ripped into three pieces and rudely sewn back on again. His right arm ended in a knobbly stump.

Vomix saw Nish standing at the edge of the cliff and his burst mouth peeled open in the most sickening travesty of a smile. He snapped his stump towards Nish, three times.

Dozens of soldiers rose from concealment against the upper slopes above Vomix, clad in dark grey uniforms that blended perfectly into the black rocks and deep shadows formed by the luminal. They began to move up the cliff-bound slope, the only way onto the plateau, and two people couldn't defend it.

FORTY-EIGHT

'It'd take a shipload of burning oil to hold that force back,' Zham said wearily. Nonetheless, he hurled his barrel towards the rocks above the camouflaged soldiers and ran back for another.

Nish wasn't hopeful either, especially when Zham's barrel struck the rocks and burst open, splattering its contents everywhere. It wasn't oil, but something thick and sticky that looked no use at all. But as the clots of red-brown gunk, connected by stretching strands, wheeled through the air, they left yellow fuming trails behind. A small clot landed on the wrist of one of the soldiers, who tried to wipe it away with his other hand but began to scream as his skin came off in red strips.

Another soldier, walking through a wavering yellow band of fumes, stopped as if he'd walked into a wall then began to vomit uncontrollably. Soon others were doing the same. Nish hastily hurled his barrel to shatter on the sharp rocks above the leading group of armoured soldiers, and ran for another.

By the time he returned, Vomix was scrabbling up the slope, surrounded by a flickering green nimbus, presumably some kind of defensive shield, and roaring at his troops.

'Go at them. Any dog who falters in courage will die at my hand, while those who win through to capture the son of the God-Emperor will be rewarded beyond their dreams.'

There was something odd about him though. The nimbus drew right in and for a fleeting instant he looked haggard and sunken-cheeked. The climb, on top of his previous injuries, must have been too much for him.

Many of the camouflaged troops had fallen but the armoured ones were lowering their visors and scrambling purposefully up the steep climb. Nish and Zham hurled another two barrels. The burning mucilage, which Nish suspected had been made from the goo inside the stink-snappers, mixed with some reeking substance of unknown source, had little effect on the armoured troops, but the yellow miasma was bringing them down.

A burly soldier strode boldly into a hanging yellow cloud and came out the other side, seemingly unharmed. However his footsteps became slower and slower until he stopped with one foot in the air. He abruptly doubled over, straightened up again and tried to tear off his helm, but didn't manage it in time. Streams of vomit burst out through the mouth, nose and eye holes, to ooze down his iridescent chest plate.

'On, you cowardly cur!' roared Vomix, standing in the yellow cloud but evidently protected by his green nimbus.

The soldier ripped his helm off, wiped his face and tried to struggle on, but doubled over again and began to bring up green and black muck from the pit of his stomach. He cast a fearful glance over his shoulder at Vomix, took another step but stumbled, fell to his knees and could not go on.

Vomix snapped his fingers at a sergeant, then pointed to the soldier. The sergeant shook his head. Vomix swelled with rage; the nimbus flickered in and out, creating an illusion that his body was stretching and contracting, then he smashed the sergeant down with a mailed fist and with his sword carved the stricken soldier's head from his body.

Seneschal Vomix held the head up, still pouring blood, urging the troops on with threats and curses. On they climbed into the spreading yellow murk, spewing and vomiting blood, and falling down.

Oh for a crossbow. Nish, shocked by Vomix's casual viciousness to the proud Imperial Militia, would have shot him without a qualm. If he could treat them so badly, the horrors he must have visited on ordinary folk would be unimaginable.

Vomix looked up and they locked eyes. He gave a sick leer, thrust his forefinger into the head's windpipe, rotated it to face Nish and held it high, taunting him. Again the nimbus flickered, and Vomix appeared to stretch and contract, but there was something else odd about him. What was it? Nish tried to see with clearsight but it couldn't penetrate the nimbus.

Nish swayed; Zham jerked him away from the edge. Zham had two barrels under his other arm and passed one across. 'You might just get him from over there, surr.'

He indicated the cliffed edge of the cleft further out. Zham carefully tapped in the end of his own barrel with a stone, then hastily poured the mucilaginous mess along the edge of the cleft until he'd treated the entire length of the way up. Within seconds, in contact with the air, yellow fumes began to issue forth.

Nish crept out along the rim where the cliff fell away, moss-covered and unclimbable, for hundreds of spans into the darkness, to a point where it overlooked the wider part of the cleft where the troops had gathered. Vomix was keeping well back so he couldn't be targeted, though Nish thought that, with a little luck, he might splatter some of the contents of his barrel on him from here.

He peered over. Vomix was stalking back and forth, roaring orders, increasingly frustrated at the inability of the Imperial Militia to pass through the miasma. He looked barely in control and his attacks on the stricken troops grew ever more vicious. Three more soldiers now lay headless before him and Vomix had hacked the third to pieces after he fell.

The soldiers at the front were retching and struggling on,

and falling. None had yet passed through the yellow murk that hugged the steep ascent and, as Nish watched, Zham pegged another barrel into the defile they'd have to pass through in the final climb.

Putting down his own barrel, Nish carefully tapped in the end. Vomix, almost incoherent with rage, kept casting anxious glances at the sky in the direction of the luminal, and well he might. The God-Emperor's retribution fell swift and hard on those who failed him, whatever their rank, and Vomix had notably failed once. Another defeat would see him broken to a common soldier, or slave, or even sent to Jal-Nish's torture chambers. Nish hoped so. It was only fitting that his father's most vicious lieutenant should die as he had lived.

Vomix broke off from his ranting to raise his sword, intending to decapitate another collapsed soldier, and Nish saw his chance. He stood up, held his breath as he raised the gently fuming barrel and, aiming it with a focus born of cold fury, hurled it hard and high.

A sergeant of the Imperial Militia standing behind Vomix glanced up and saw it coming but, oddly, said not a word. Vomix's sword hacked through the unfortunate soldier's neck, then the sergeant stepped smartly out of the way as the tumbling barrel slammed upside down onto the back of Vomix's head.

He collapsed onto his knees, gasping and gurgling as the mucilage streaming down his head and shoulders began to fume, but not one soldier of the Imperial Militia moved to aid him. The sergeant looked up, his eyes locked with Nish's, then jerked his head in acknowledgement.

The Imperial Militia were not entirely without honour. The momentary truce was over and they'd be after him the instant they could get past the miasma, though it could be hours before that was possible. And, thankfully, even if Vomix survived, he would be in no shape to lead his men for a very long time.

But Nish was immediately proven wrong. Vomix lurched to his feet, tore the barrel off and with a frantic snap of the fingers, a sound that echoed like a whip crack, forced the green nimbus down until it disappeared into his skin. His whole head and shoulders were foaming; his ravaged face appeared to be peeling apart in bloody strips. He thrust both hands high and let out a scream of pain and rage, as if calling power into himself from the sky.

The Imperial Militia turned to stare as one, for he was stretching and shrinking again. He drew his clenched fists in, striking himself above the heart, emitted a great roar of agony, then seemed to literally burst apart.

Bloody skin, fuming rags, fragments of armour and boot leather flew in all directions, trailing smoke. What remained of him fell to his knees, clawed at the moss-covered rocks beneath his feet, then, as naked as the day he was born, lunged for the sky again.

Nish nearly fell off the cliff in shock. It was like Flydd's transformation in reverse, for what had been revealed was not Vomix at all, but a taller and more strongly built man, one whose skin was red, cracked and weeping all over, save where the burning mucilage had etched away the corrugated layers of his face to reveal raw flesh beneath. A man with long dark hair, now falling out in sticky clumps, an arching prow of a nose, and a fanatic, almost maniacal gleam in his dark eyes.

'It's Monkshart!' Zham said in astonishment.

Monkshart had transfigured himself into the very image of Vomix, and the change must have been of astonishing perfection, to fool not just the officers and troops of the army but its accompanying mancers as well.

To perform such a feat after calling down the flappeter would have taken more power than most mancers could summon. But the illusion had been failing under the strain, and that's why the nimbus had been flickering, almost revealing Monkshart's true form. Aftersickness must have been hurting him cruelly and only a man of iron will could have endured it for so long.

Monkshart swayed on his feet, wiped a streak of raw sloughing skin off his right cheek with the back of a raw hand, shuddered, then directed such a look of rage at Nish that he reeled.

The officers suddenly woke up to what had happened. 'It's Monkshart!' one shouted. 'Take him in the name of Jal-Nish, the God-Emperor.'

The Imperial Militia went for Monkshart but the green nimbus expanded until it was spans wide all around, and they bounced harmlessly off it. Monkshart appeared to summon the last of his strength, expanded the nimbus even further, then stumbled downslope and hurled himself into the steep part of the gully. The flickering, fading nimbus bounced once, twice, slowed then drifted down like a balloon, carrying him out of sight.

Nish didn't see how the zealot would be able to summon the strength to do anything further. However, Jal-Nish was surely keeping watch from on high and would move to the next phase of the attack as soon as he could come close enough to swing it into action. Nish scanned the sky but couldn't see anything save the luminal. He turned away. Zham was throwing the last of the barrels over.

'Save one,' Nish yelled, 'just in case.' But it was too late. The last barrel was gone.

Suddenly the wind reversed direction and a churning fog swept in, reducing the brilliant glare of the luminal to an eerie glow that appeared to come from every direction at once.

Nish stood on the edge for a moment, wondering how much time they'd gained and remembering the look on Monkshart's face. He, Nish, had made a life-long enemy, though that wasn't what bothered him most. Monkshart had driven himself too hard. The rages were getting worse, and lasting longer. What would happen if they drove such a powerful, charismatic man over the edge into insanity?

Zham tapped his shoulder. 'We'd better get to the hut. Mr Xervish might be done by now.'

How touching his faith was. Nish didn't have much left but he followed the giant. By the time he reached the hut he could only see the outline of the luminal, though he couldn't tell whether it had faded or the fog had thickened. However, the God-Emperor might be able to see via other Arts and Nish didn't want to give away the location of the hut, which hopefully was still shielded by the red amberwood.

Inside it was nearly as dark, and more gloomy. The lantern was guttering, the fire just a few glowing coals which picked out the renewed Flydd lying on his back on the floor, his chest rising and falling minutely. The last of the old skin was shredding off his face, hands and legs.

Beneath it Nish saw a muscular man of middle height and uncertain age – fifty at the most – with wavy, iron grey hair receding at the temples. His olive skin was baby-smooth, apart from several faint small scars in roughly the same places as Flydd's most prominent scars had been. In other respects he resembled Flydd not at all. His eyes were staring straight up, though Nish could not make out their colour.

'Xervish?' said Nish.

The full lips parted and the barest wisp of voice issued forth, a whispery croak, though deeper than Flydd's voice. 'More time.'

Nish glanced at Zham, who was hanging back, then Maelys, crouched by the fire. Her skin had a greenish tinge, there were beads of sweat on her brow and upper lip, and if she hadn't supported herself on her arms she would have fallen over.

Outside, the luminal brightened momentarily; Nish heard a distant grumble of thunder.

'Deliverer?' said Zham, head cocked as if trying to distinguish a different sound over the howling wind.

Another grumble of thunder came, closer this time, though surely that wasn't what was bothering him. No, it was a faint *blatt-blatt*. Nish looked out.

The fog had thinned again. The luminal had faded to an eclipsed globe but now a storm cloud was forming above the plateau, a gigantic thunderhead condensing out of the empty air. Was his father using weather mancery to create a downpour that would wash away the gunk from the barrels and allow his ground troops to storm the plateau? Doubtless it would wash some of his soldiers away as well, though that wouldn't bother Jal-Nish.

Where was he? He had to be near, surely? Nish strained his eyes upwards, and when the lightning flashed he caught a faint, crystalline ripple, like light reflecting off cut glass as it moved, but the thunderhead grew until it covered the centre of the sky and he didn't see another flash.

Jal-Nish was there, though; Nish knew it. His father was waiting like a gigantic, deformed spider for the moment when his prey was helpless.

The drizzle had stopped and it was now warmer than at any time since they'd reached the plateau. Nish began to sweat in his coat, though, oddly, his exposed skin had a dry, itchy feel and he could feel his hair rising up from the top of his head. Lightning flashed out over the mire, illuminating Zham, whose short hair was also streaming upwards, and in the darkness between flashes tiny sparks were discharging from the tips.

'I don't like it, surr,' said Zham, rubbing his left hand through his hair and creating a flurry of sparks. 'There's something not right about this storm.'

'Nor I, Zham. It's unnatural.'

'Is it the God-Emperor's doing?'

'That's what I'm thinking.'

A quadruple flash of lightning curving down over each of the clefts was accompanied by ear-shattering thunder, then gusting waves of heat. Nish's cheeks grew hot. Sweat trails were trickling down his chest and back, and the itching was almost unbearable. He pressed his palms to his ears but couldn't stop them ringing.

'I wish it would storm proper,' muttered Zham. 'I can't bear the waiting.'

It had only been a few minutes but Nish couldn't stand it either. 'That's what Father wants,' he said in a leathery croak. 'To provoke us.'

'I wish it would rain.'

'So do I.'

'Maybe he's enjoying tormenting us,' said Zham.

'That goes without saying.'

A flash of lightning struck the swamp not far away, hurling mud and burning plant fragments in all directions. A speck of scalding mud struck Nish on the cheekbone. He smacked it off, rubbing furiously at the burn. Steam rose from the swamp.

Now more lightning struck, and more, viciously and violently, dozens of strokes at once until they lit up the plateau more brightly than the luminal had done. Nish was so dazzled that he could barely see; his ears ached as if they'd been pummelled by flailing fists.

Zham jerked him back into the doorway. 'This isn't right, surr. He's out of control.'

Nish felt it too. It was the wildest storm he'd ever seen; a rage against them. The thunderhead had gone a boiling black and now covered the sky, save only for a paler rim around the horizon. The air was warmer and stickier than ever, though not a drop of rain had fallen. Nish longed for cooling rain yet exulted that it wasn't happening. It was as if Mistmurk Mountain were defying his father, and Jal-Nish couldn't bear it.

The display continued, growing ever more furious and the lightning strikes more menacing, until the plateau was thick with wavering steam trails from boiling bogs and blasted pools. Then the lightning stopped abruptly, as if Jal-Nish had tired of the game – or formed a better plan.

The air was steamy now, whirling about in wild, choking eddies, but Nish lost sight of them as the night went black. The luminal was a bare outline and the sinking moon could not penetrate the cloud. Dawn must be close, though there was not a trace of light in the eastern sky.

'What now?' muttered Zham, creeping out a few steps. 'There's that noise again . . .'

Blatt-blatt, blatt-blatt.

It was the faintest red flash, dim lantern light reflecting from a pair of globular eyes, that warned Nish. He threw himself sideways just in time, the beast's claws skimming through his short hair, and landed hard on hip and shoulder. He was rolling over, trying to free his sword, when Zham gasped.

Nish kicked the door wide, for the light. Something huge, bat-like and bloated had hold of Zham by the back of the neck and one shoulder. Great wings were beating furiously; the creature's already distended belly now inflated to several times its former size, lifting Zham's feet off the ground. The canine, sharp-toothed muzzle was arching over his head, down towards his eyes.

Zham tried to hold it off with his forearms but his struggles became increasingly feeble, as if it had injected a fast-acting venom. Another of the creatures darted at Nish, *blatt-blatt, blatt-blatt.* He came up off the ground in a rush, swinging his sword wildly, and a lucky stroke hacked through its left wing. It rolled over and spun head-first into the ground. Nish went for the other one. He couldn't reach its wings but the bloated belly hanging above Zham's head made a tempting target and he thrust the sword at it.

It went straight through thin, leathery skin, air hissed out and a spark from Zham's hair ignited it in a roiling blast of orange fire that blew the creature to squealing pieces. Zham fell to the ground, hair smoking, and didn't move. Nish felt the hairs on his sword arm shrivelling from the blast, and his cheeks stinging.

Something scratched at his heels and he swung the sword around blindly, momentarily dazzled. The other bladder-bat had dragged itself across the ground towards him, inflating its body until it began to lift, and its remaining wing had touched him. His sword carved through its belly and it went limp, though this time the gas didn't ignite.

The luminal began to glow again and he made out dozens of bladder-bats, whirling down from an aperture in the centre of the storm cloud. He couldn't fight them all, alone. He began to back towards the door but trod on Zham, who was sitting up, wiping at the claw marks in his neck and shoulder, then a puncture on his forearm, with a chunk of moss. His hair was frizzled, his cheeks blistered from the explosion and his eyes were streaming.

'It numbed me for a minute. I could hardly move. You saved my life, surr.'

'They're coming,' said Nish. 'Dozens of them.'

He put up his sword. Bladder-bat fluids ran down the blade onto his fingers, which began to go numb. Nish tore up a clump of moss and scrubbed the sword clean, then prepared to fight for his life.

But these bladder-bats were in trouble. Though their abdomens were deflated, they were having trouble descending through the wild, corkscrewing winds near the edge of the plateau. The leading one folded its wings and plummeted down at him, but before it reached halfway a gust sent it spinning, whipped its span-long wings out to their fullest extent then tore them off.

A second bladder-bat had gone out wide, away from the edge of the plateau, and now came gliding in towards the hut, though as soon as it struck the updraught near the cliffs its wings collapsed as if their bones had shattered. It inflated its abdomen furiously but could not generate lift in time and slammed into the ridgepole of the hut with such force that it broke its neck.

It slid down the roof towards Nish, who batted it out of

the way with his sword. It was surprisingly light for such a large creature. It must have had hollow bones.

He dispatched the last of that flight with a weary flick, but seconds later another flight of five raced in wingtip to wingtip. Nish and Zham put their backs to the wall and wove a barrier of steel between themselves and the bladder-bats, working desperately to keep them out.

They weren't going for Nish, but making coordinated strikes at Zham, trying to lure him away from the wall so they could attack on all sides. Zham was still sluggish from the venom and Nish was weakening rapidly as he struggled to defend a man twice his size. He'd forgotten how exhausting a few minutes of battle could be. He could barely hold his sword up.

Bladder-bats now littered the ground around them, many dead, others trying to drag their way across the ground to attack, though on the ground they were helpless creatures, easily put down.

Another group of three hurtled in low over the centre of the plateau where the updraughts were less fierce, and began to beat across the mires at reed height. Nish was despairing of being able to deal with three at once when the water swirled, *snap*, *snap*. The maw of a stink-snapper closed and began to withdraw back into the mire. The remaining bladder-bats scattered and Nish didn't see what became of them.

But the attack was far from over. As a blush of pink spread across the eastern horizon, he heard the distinctive *thup-thup* of a flappeter's feather-rotors. Shortly a flight of ten appeared, circling the plateau, their riders urging them in.

The flappeters turned towards the rim with evident reluctance, fighting the vicious updraughts with their feather-rotors twisting and buckling, sending the beasts plunging towards the cliffs before they recovered and darted out to safer air.

'Ten flappeters,' said Zham, dazedly. 'We can't fight ten of them.'

'That's almost all Father's got left, I'd say, and he'll risk them reluctantly. But risk them he will if there's no alternative. He was never loath to break a precious thing in pursuit of something he wanted more.'

'I think we should move away from the hut,' said Zham. 'Just in case they see us and it gives Flydd's location away.'

There was a good chance that Jal-Nish already knew, for the bladder-bats had come straight for them, though if they weren't magical creatures they might have seen him and Zham without being able to communicate it to the God-Emperor.

'Good idea,' said Nish. They went out towards the main cleft, keeping close to the rim where the turbulence was greatest.

Something flashed in the thunderhead. It wasn't lightning, but white light focussed to a pinpoint, followed by a rolling echo that sounded as if there were words in it, harsh orders. Nish couldn't make them out.

There came an almighty ground-shaking thump, as if something massive had fallen a long way away. Blue light jagged down from the clouds towards the centre of the plateau, followed by a long, echoing boom. Nish couldn't see anything out there, though.

The leading rider hauled his beast in their direction. Had the flappeter seen him? Nish couldn't be sure – the red amber-wood was supposed to conceal them, but if they'd seen through it his father must be close by, wielding Gatherer. The flappeter fought its rider for a minute or two, until he raised a stubby rod in his right hand and pressed it to the nub at the back of the beast's skull.

It jerked convulsively, the feather-rotors missing a beat and its back arching up until its tail almost touched the back of its head. Curving around in a great circle which took it a league out over the rainforest, it turned and raced towards them.

Nish wearily raised his sword, though nothing save an

561

exceptionally long and well-aimed spear would be any good against a racing flappeter. The beast hurtled towards them, its feather-rotors a blur, clearly planning to use its momentum to cleave straight through the turbulence.

'Leave this one to me, surr,' said Zham, pushing Nish out of the way.

He sprang forwards towards the edge of the cliff, his great sword held out and up. He looked as solid as one of the giant trees in the rainforest below, though next to a flappeter even Zham was small, and it was coming so fast that it would smash right through him, or drive his shattered body through the low rocks behind them.

Zham crouched abruptly. What was he up to?

Nish suddenly realised that it wasn't attacking at all. It was coming straight for *him*, as the first one had, that night in the Defiance camp before the battle. Its intention must be to snatch him, then fly inland and climb through the air over the marshes, which Jal-Nish was now calming with his weather Arts.

As Nish stumbled backwards, Zham sprang up into the path of the flappeter. It saw him just as it entered the zone of the updraught. It baulked instinctively at the obstacle, reared up but lost way and was caught side-on in the boiling wind. The flappeter was flung upside down, then stopped dead in the air. The rotor shaft appeared to lock under the strain but the feather-rotors kept spinning until they twisted the shaft right out of the creature's back in a sticky spray of scales, flesh and horny carapace. The rider, screaming in sympathetic agony, tried to leap to safety but couldn't get free of the saddle in time. The flappeter crashed upside down onto the edge of the cliff, stoving the rider's head in and breaking its own back, then lay there, kicking and screeching, until Zham darted across and severed its head from its body.

'Well done, Zham,' Nish said, putting a hand on the big man's shoulder. 'I never would have thought of that.'

'I always try to think of a way to avoid fighting, first.'

After that, not even the most furious flashes and thundering orders from above could induce the other flappeters to approach. Jal-Nish's flesh-formed creatures were ingenious and deadly, but that wasn't enough to overcome the plateau's natural defences. Flydd had chosen his lair well.

'Is that it?' Zham said hopefully as the remaining flappeters curved away towards the forest. 'Have we beaten him?'

'Never. He'll wait, and in an hour or two his troops will be able to pass our burning barriers . . .'

'What are you thinking, Nish?'

'That he'll beat us if we give him time. We've got to force Father's hand and make him attack now, before he's ready. Before his troops can get here.'

'How will that help?'

'Maybe it won't, but it can't make things worse. Keep watch. This is our final hour – it's all or nothing now.' He shook his fist at the black sky, shouting, 'I defy *you*, Father, and I'll win, for you don't have the courage to face me.'

A growl of thunder made the cloud swirl. Nish shivered then went into the hut.

Flydd – it was almost impossible to think of him as Flydd, because he looked so different – was sitting up now, holding a wooden mug of water to his lips. His hands barely had the strength to keep it there.

'Surr!' said Nish. 'Your renewal worked!'

'Did it?' croaked Flydd. 'I don't – know.'

'Of course it did,' Nish said uneasily. 'Surr, that wasn't Vomix we saw before, it was Monkshart, under an illusion . . .' He trailed off, looking around the dark hut. 'Where's Maelys?'

'Sent – her out.'

'You what?'

'Renewal – took four – crystals.' Flydd could barely get the words out. 'Had to have – more power.'

563

'When, Xervish?

'After flash and boom. Had – idea. Sent her – obelisk – charge crystal – flame.'

A chill made its way up Nish's spine. 'But that was Monkshart on the flappeter, earlier, not Vomix. So the other rider must have been . . .'

'Phrune,' Flydd gasped.

Maelys's nemesis, and she didn't know he was there.

FORTY-NINE

Maelys had been moistening Flydd's mouth with water, careful not to let him swallow any since his renewed stomach would not be able to take it yet, when the plateau shook. A blue flash came through the doorway, followed by a distant, echoing boom.

'What – that?' croaked Flydd.

She went to the door. 'I can't see anything save Nish and Zham over by the rim, halfway to the main cleft. They're staring up at a flight of flappeters – looks as though they're going to attack. I can't see Colm.'

'Boom?' said Flydd. 'Obelisk?'

'What? Oh, I don't know where the sound came from, though I can see a blue flicker out in the mire. I can't make out the obelisk, but the flicker comes from that direction. What is it, Xervish?'

'Take – last crystal.'

'What do you mean?'

'To cursed – flame. Obelisk.'

'But . . . you said no one can get to the power contained beneath the obelisk.'

'Jal-Nish – destroy – so can – can – come down. Chance. Take crystal. Go. *Go!*'

Maelys's mouth went dry. 'I don't know what you want me to do. What is the cursed flame? Is it safe to go near it?'

'Charge crystal – flame. Only chance. Go . . .' His head slumped forwards and his eyes closed.

Maelys felt dreadfully afraid. She didn't know enough – no, she didn't know *anything* save that the obelisk was deadly and the flame cursed. How was she to charge the last crystal?

She would have seized upon any excuse to remain here, but she'd pressured Flydd to take renewal against his sworn oath, so how could she back out now?

Maelys got the crystal out of the box – it was the size of her thumbnail and perfectly clear, like diamond, though it had no sparkle – put it in a secure pocket and turned to Flydd. 'I'm off, then.'

His head was still slumped; he looked asleep or unconscious, but he wheezed, 'Take – amber-wood coat. All rests – on you. Hurry!'

Hanging on a hook behind the door was a long coat made from thousands of little shaped pieces of amber-wood threaded on knotted cords. The pieces made up an intricate, swirling design which she couldn't identify in the dim light. The detailed work would have helped Flydd pass the endless, solitary hours, though perhaps the design had a purpose, too.

The coat came down to her heels and had a hood as well. She put it on and fastened the amber-wood toggles. It was light but warm, and the fragrance released by the wood was overpowering. As soon as she'd fastened the last toggle she felt an amazing sense of security – as if she'd just been removed from the physical world. The coat was greater than the sum of its parts. But would it hide her from the direct gaze of Gatherer?

She took a lantern, though Maelys did not light it, and ran out. On the rim, Nish and Zham had their swords up and a flappeter was heading in towards them. Maelys froze, one foot in the air, but there was no time to make sure they were safe. She grabbed her staff and scuttled into the mire towards the obelisk.

She hoped she'd meet Colm on the way – she'd feel so much safer looking for the cursed flame with him – but there was no sign of him. What if he'd been caught; killed?

She had no trouble finding the obelisk this time, for its covering of grey lichen shone silvery in the faint light of the luminal, and she could hear the wind howling around it. She even found a way to get to the obelisk without plunging up to her nose in a dark pool. The stone looked as though it had been struck by a bolt of lightning. Half of the moss and lichen had been charred off and it was tilted at an angle of fifty degrees. At the point where its base had been bonded to the living rock she found a neat, triangular hole, not much wider than her shoulders, from which a stream of warm, musty air issued.

Only now did she remember the second rider – the one who had dropped from Vomix's flappeter and headed into the mires. Had he been coming to the obelisk? She had seen no footmarks in the moonlight, though walking in this country rarely left good tracks. Even moss soon sprang back up to obliterate them.

She checked all around but saw no sign of him. Nonetheless, she wasn't going to be taken unawares. Crouching low, Maelys lit the lantern, unshuttered it a fraction and inspected the triangular hole. A small stream of water swirled into it from the nearest pool.

Hot air gushed up. The cursed flame *had* to be down there, protected by the obelisk until Jal-Nish had, evidently, toppled it with Reaper. Had he done so to destroy the power here, or because this monument to the ultimate failure of all endeavours gave the lie to his own life's purpose?

Thump! This time the impact felt closer. It shook the plateau, churning the water in the nearby pool and sending a surge past her into the triangular hole. The obelisk moved a little further towards the horizontal. Another shock and it must fall, which would close the hole again.

Something went whistling and hissing through the air

high above, though at first she couldn't believe what she was seeing. It looked like a gigantic cable snaking across the sky, running up from the far edge of the plateau, its coils slowly straightening as though a winch in the clouds, whence it originated, drew it tight. Jal-Nish was definitely here now.

Maelys didn't wait to see what he was going to do. She put her feet into the hole, lowered them as far as they would go and wriggled in, supporting herself on the edges with her forearms while she peered down. She couldn't see much, for the lantern's rays were at the wrong angle, but there appeared to be a fall of about a span onto a flat rock. She picked up the lantern, took a deep breath and dropped.

The flat rock was covered in a yellow growth. Her feet went from under her and she landed on her bottom, which was just as well, as the surface was only a few paces across. It was the foundation stone for the obelisk, and extended straight down into darkness on all sides. If she'd slipped . . .

Water showered on her head. She wiped her face and looked around. A hole in the centre of the stone was blocked with debris. To her left across the gap Maelys made out another triangular opening, this time in a gently sloping rock face, about the size of the surface she was sitting on. The hole looked like the top of a tight triangular staircase and warm air wafted from the opening, though there was no way to get to it except by jumping the gap and she wasn't sure she could do it.

But everything depended on her, so she had to get across.

It wasn't a difficult jump for an athlete, or even a fool-hardy youth, but it looked an awfully long way to a bookish girl who preferred reading about adventures to having them. If she missed she'd fall and break her neck. If she landed on top of the stairs the result would probably be the same.

What if she sprang for the stair hole but held the staff out above her head so she couldn't fall through? It might work, though the impact would probably tear her hands off.

Maelys swiftly unknotted the cords from the bottom of

Flydd's coat, plaited them into two short lengths of rope and tied it around her wrists. She bound the other ends to the staff, then stood up and scuffed the slime off the rock with the side of her boot to get a better footing. She estimated the jump, moved the staff so it wouldn't hit the wall, and flexed her legs.

It looked such a long way. She wasn't sure she could jump that far from a standing start. In fact, she was sure she couldn't. Maelys flexed again. The gap looked even wider.

Just go! She tied the lantern to her belt and tried to jump; she bent her knees and sprang almost all the way up, but baulked at the last second. She was too much of a coward. Maelys tried to talk herself into the jump, but thinking about it only made it worse. She could imagine all the things that might go wrong, fatally.

So don't think about it. Just do it. Jump. *Now!*

Maelys jumped, though as soon as her feet left the ground she imagined the staff breaking under her weight. The jump was almost perfect – her feet passed through the sides of the stair hole, her thigh and shoulder scraped along its edge, then the staff whacked down on top. Her weight tore her hands off the staff, just as she'd expected, and she hung from the creaking, splintered wood by the plaited ropes.

The staff held, just, though it took a long, painful time to untie her right wrist one-handed. Maelys hadn't thought about that difficulty beforehand. She slid along until she could get her feet onto the top step, then untied her left wrist and manoeuvred the staff in. Holding out the lantern, she began to make her way down the triangular stair.

It was incredibly steep and coated with slippery yellow fungi, as well as silver marks like gigantic snail trails. She couldn't see how far down the stair went, though it was a lot further than her lantern's rays extended.

The howling of the wind dwindled as Maelys descended. She looked up after a few minutes and couldn't see the way out, but what she could see, clinging to the undersides of the stairs, were hundreds, no thousands of swamp creepers, their glistening antennae stirring in the light like white eggs on black stalks.

She went down hastily and after a few minutes reached a landing beside a level floor. Maelys vaguely made out walls in the distance, though she could not tell if they had been smoothed by human hand, as the floor must have been, or were the walls of caves.

The nearby wall and ceiling were covered with finger-thick crusts of dried mucous as well as sticky, ropy webs too thick to have been made by any spider she'd ever heard of, while every corner, angle and hollow was clotted with swamp creepers, stirring and crawling over each other until the squelching sounds were magnified ten thousand times.

The stair continued down, but the air coming up it was cool, while the floor was blood-warm, so Maelys guessed that the cursed flame lay somewhere on this level. She stepped onto the floor, shuttered her lantern and looked for any other source of light.

There, in the far distance, she caught the faintest wavering blue glow. She opened the shutter a fraction, went three steps and came to a fresh, muddy footprint on the dusty floor. It wasn't large enough to be Colm's, so it had to belong to the second rider and she must assume that he was nearby. He was probably going to the flame as well.

Resisting her urge to panic, Maelys shuttered the lantern and moved twenty steps to her left in case her light had been seen. She couldn't hear anything above the squelching of the swamp creepers gliding on their mucous tracks. She could smell them, too, a sickly spiciness that contrasted unpleasantly with the bouquet of the amber-wood.

Maelys went carefully towards the glow, which became a blue flame issuing knee-high from a star-shaped fissure in the middle of a large block of stone itself rising chest-high from the floor.

The outsides of the block had been roughly shaped, though the makers did not appear to have had any particular form in mind. It was wedge-shaped, about three spans long and one-and-a-half spans wide at the broad end, tapering to just half a span at its narrowest. It was shaped something like a coffin, though one that would have fitted a giant.

The top of the block was coated with soot, plus sugar-sized crystals of sulphur and salts condensed from the flame. Shiny bituminous trails had once oozed outwards from the fissure, though these had set hard and cracked. The sides of the block held more unreadable glyphs, and yet more were carved into the walls and roof, though the latter were blurred to unintelligibility by layers of swamp creeper crusts.

That was all she saw in the dim light, and there was no time to speculate about the inscriptions. She got out Flydd's crystal and was moving towards the cursed flame, wondering what the curse was and how she was supposed to recharge the crystal at a flame anyway, when she smelt an unpleasantly familiar oily odour.

Instantly, a set of plump fingers fixed around the back of her neck and her worst nightmare rewoke. She dropped her staff, though she kept hold of the crystal.

'Perfect timing, little Maelys.' Phrune pressed his slick lips to her ear. 'My master is dying at Nish's hand and only one thing can save him – a blood sacrifice at the cursed flame. There's no better blood than virgin's blood. I'll fill a small bucket from you, and then I'll have the skin I should have taken from you in Tifferfyte, you vicious little bitch.'

FIFTY

'Can't go – after Maelys,' said Flydd. 'God-Emperor – coming.'

'I went without her once,' said Nish. 'I'm not doing it again. Zham?'

He was at the door. 'Surr?'

'Help me get him dressed. I've got to go after Maelys and we can't leave Flydd now. You'll have to take him to the escape way and wait for me.'

Zham gathered up Flydd's clothes. Fortunately the garments had been loose. He drew Flydd's pants up his muscular legs and tied them at the waist. The shirt barely met around his broad chest. Flydd's old boots were far too small, but Nish found a pair of leather sandals that he was able to cram onto the large, broad feet and buckle up, then they helped him to stand.

'Find a pack, Zham. Fill it with food and drink, as much as you can cram in.'

Flydd was swaying where he stood. Nish held him up. 'Xervish, where's the escape way?'

'Rope,' slurred Flydd. 'Hidden rope ladder – behind hut – over cliff. Must rest.'

It was taking too long. 'Get him down, Zham,' cried Nish, frantically checking his sword and bow. It could be too late already. 'I've got to fly.'

Another gigantic thump, somewhere in the distance, shook the ground and the hut.

'Surr!' cried Zham from the door. 'Quick!'

Nish couldn't let go of Flydd, so he lurched him to the door, looked up and gaped.

A gigantic grappling iron or five-fluked anchor, the size of a horse and cart, had been fired from the clouds. It had hooked over the rim of the plateau not far from the hut, and now the loops of cable trailing in the air after it, wavering in the wild updraughts, were being pulled tight.

Another grappling iron, fired off to their left, shook the ground as it buried itself in the rocks beyond the north-western cleft. Waist-thick cables trailed in the air towards the far side of the plateau from a third anchor.

The cables were slowly pulled up into the base of the cloud until they went iron-taut, though Nish could not see what they were attached to. Colm came limping around the cliff edge, covered in mud and old blood, his notched sword in hand. By the look of him, he'd faced a tougher opponent at his cleft.

'Is this it?' he said in a flat voice.

'Yes.'

Nish let the bow fall to the ground, realising that he must fail Maelys again. There was no point going after her now, for the raw power of Gatherer, this close, would penetrate all illusions and he would be seen before he got ten paces. Maelys would have to take her chances, which Nish felt were a lot better than his.

Colm raised the sword. 'Then I'm ready for it. I'm sick of waiting. Where's Maelys?'

Nish explained, wearily.

'And you let her go?' Colm cried frantically, shaking Nish. 'What kind of a man are you, Deliverer?'

Zham peeled them apart with his free hand. 'We weren't here, Colm. We were over there by the rim, fighting flap-peters and other beasts, and didn't see her go.' He stared up at the base of the cloud, which was black and roiling, and swallowed. 'The God-Emperor is coming. There's nothing we can do for her.'

'And without that crystal we've got no hope of getting away,' Nish added.

Colm crouched down and put his head in his hands. 'Ah Maelys, Maelys.' He stood up. 'Is this the end? Must we go over the cliff, then?'

'Not yet,' rumbled Zham. 'Have faith. She could be on her way back with the charged crystal already.'

'I can't see her,' said Colm, springing up and staring into the mires. 'But you're right. We must have faith, for her sake.'

The base of the cloud stirred, then something oval, flat and glassy sent it whirling out of the way. It looked like the base of a platter, hundreds of spans long and many spans thick. The ropes slackened momentarily but tightened again; the base jerked down another half span; then another.

Slender white columns ran up from its ends, sides and middle into the clouds, as if it were suspended from something. Now on the glass base there appeared the most astonishing building Nish had ever seen. Indeed, he wasn't sure that it was a building.

A series of arching shells, dazzlingly white, rose from blood-red foundations built upon the glass, but the shells were not held up by beams, columns or any other structure – they simply soared a good fifty spans into the sky, supported by each other.

And now, as the structure, or craft, jerked lower, he saw that the white columns were topped by tiers of long arching wings like horizontal sails fixed to each other by struts and taut wires. The lowest tier consisted of four such wings. Above the gaps between them stood a tier of three; above that, two; and, highest of all, one, so the wings formed an open roof.

'It's a sky palace,' said Zham in wonder.

As good a name as any, Nish thought. The white palace

slowly descended, shuddering in the wind but held against it by the tension of the cables. The gale whistled shrilly through them.

'How can such a weighty craft move through the air?' said Colm.

'It defies the very principles of flight,' said Nish, who had studied such matters in the days when air-floaters had first been invented, 'and all natural laws – intentionally so, I'd say. It's a demonstration. It's meant to show the world that, with the power of Gatherer and Reaper, Father can transcend all natural laws. That he truly is a god.' He felt a touch of awe that his own father, who had not been a great mancer, could have achieved such mastery of the Art.

'Then we'd better hope Flydd's escape plan works.' Colm turned to frown at him. 'I assume *this* is Flydd.'

'I – am – Xervish – Flydd,' said the renewed Flydd, as if trying to convince himself.

Without warning, blasts of white fire speared down towards each of the four clefts in the plateau. Shouts echoed up from the main cleft, nearest the hut.

Nish and Colm exchanged glances. 'He's cleared the barriers,' said Nish. 'His army will be here in minutes. We'd better get going.'

The sky palace was now held rock-steady in the howling gale, hanging just a few spans above the mires. A white railing swung aside and a set of silver stairs extended out and down to one of the paths.

A pair of white-armour-clad soldiers appeared, the God-Emperor's Imperial Guard in their field uniforms. They marched down the steps to inspect the land below. The guard on the right gestured with a gloved hand towards the hut. The great windlasses spun, the cables creaked, and the sky palace began to creep in their direction.

The first soldiers appeared from the main cleft, followed by a handful from the south-western one which Nish had fired. Soon squads of troops were advancing across the plateau and around the rim paths, their armour sparking. Even if Maelys had charged the crystal, she'd never get through to them now.

'Come on!' Nish said hoarsely, dragging Flydd behind the hut. They were finished but he was going to fight to the very end. The others followed close behind. 'He said there's a hidden rope ladder.'

Everyone began to feel among the rocks, save Flydd. 'Need – time.'

'There is no more time, Xervish,' cried Nish. 'That's the God-Emperor out there and if you don't do something we're all doomed.'

'Doom – time,' mumbled Flydd.

Colm began searching the mossy edge of the cliff. Zham was walking backwards parallel to the cliff, dragging his sword hilt across the ground. 'It's here!'

He groped between the rocks and pulled up a moss-covered rope ladder, one end of which was fixed to a ring buried in the rock. 'Looks half rotten,' he said to himself, then shrugged, went to the cliff and tossed the free end over. He peered down. 'There's a hollow in the cliff below here. Could be a cave or tunnel.'

'If it isn't,' said Colm dryly, 'we'd better keep going down when the ladder ends.'

A searing blast smashed the amber-wood hut into a wave of whirling, smouldering splinters that battered against them before being swept over the cliff. The blast would have carried Zham with it had he not been hanging onto the ladder. He slipped, went half over, then moved down out of sight.

The sky palace stopped about fifty spans from where the hut door had been. The white staircase extended again and Nish's heart clenched painfully, for at the top of it, dressed all in black and flanked by his tall guards, stood his father.

'There's no way to escape, Cryl-Nish,' Jal-Nish called, smiling thinly beneath the half-mask. He strode towards

Nish. 'There never was; never will be. This has all been a game. You can either play it against me and lose every time, or play with me and win. Which is it to be?'

Nish assessed the chance of escape. None. Colm was heading for the ladder and might get down, but Jal-Nish would take Nish and Flydd before they could reach the ladder. And without a competent, empowered Flydd they had no hope anyway.

'Xervish?' said Nish, desperately.

'Need – time,' said Flydd dully.

'You'll have all the time you could wish for, Xervish,' said Jal-Nish, stopping where the hut had been and examining Flydd dispassionately. 'I can't believe you, of all people, were taken in by that renewal spell. It has a false step in it. Surely you knew that?'

'Step . . .?' said Flydd.

'It was put there in ancient times to ensure that only the truly deserving could successfully take the path of renewal. Any great mancer would have recognised the falsehood, but you always were flawed, Flydd.'

'Time,' said Flydd, more strongly.

'You'll have all the time you can endure.' Jal-Nish turned away to face Nish. 'Cryl-Nish, my only son –'

'Time!' said Flydd.

Suddenly Nish realised what he was saying. He whipped up his sword and sent it spinning at his father. 'Go!' he roared.

The sword vanished in a flash of fire, forming a shower of molten metal that had Jal-Nish and his soldiers reeling backwards.

Nish caught Flydd's arm and bolted for the ladder. He thrust Flydd's foot onto the top rung, pushed him down, then followed as quickly as he could, though before his head dropped below the edge of the cliff his father had recovered and the sky palace began creeping towards them.

The ladder was bouncing and banging around in the

updraught, each thump against the cliff tearing skin off Nish's knuckles. Down about twenty rungs he saw a streaming curtain of moss and algae partly covering an opening in the cliff. He reached it and Zham's huge hands pulled Nish in and set him on the floor.

He couldn't hear the sky palace coming over the howling gale, but it wouldn't be long. As his eyes adjusted to the dark, Nish looked towards the back of the cave, which ended in a flat wall with two half columns carved in the rock at either side, like pillars framing a doorway.

Outside, the great cables whined as the nearby anchor was released, lowered and, with a crunch of shattered rock, hooked on further down the cliff. The sky palace crept over the edge and out, dropped to their level then pulled back in, illuminating the cave with its reflected whiteness. This time, though, the staircase didn't extend.

Instead, a glittering plank slid out until it parted the moss curtains at the entrance. It was narrow but Jal-Nish trod it confidently, as if there wasn't a drop of a thousand spans to either side and the treacherous updraughts whirling all about. Perhaps with the tears he could even control gravity's pull on him.

And he had the tears, or one of them, dangling from a chain around his neck. Nish couldn't tell which one. Jal-Nish stopped just outside, his greying hair stirring in the wind, condensed moisture dripping off the platinum mask. Nish couldn't breathe. Flydd was still mumbling, but to no effect. It was too late. Jal-Nish stepped through the moss curtain, his real hand caressing the tear, the restored arm hanging stiffly at his side.

'Gatherer?' Nish said limply.

'No, Son. It's time for Reaper.'

FIFTY-ONE

Maelys felt a shriek of raw, living terror building up inside her, and this time she didn't try to suppress it, because she'd remembered Phrune's one weakness and if she didn't act on it instantly she was dead. She let it out, screaming so loudly and shrilly that it tore at her healing throat where it had been scored by the barbs of the slurchie.

Phrune clapped his hands over his ear holes, trying to block out the high-pitched sounds which caused him so much pain. Instantly, Maelys punched him in the larynx. Her father had once told her that it was a good way to disable an attacker.

Phrune fell to his knees, gasping, though he could still draw air. She hadn't hit him hard enough. He began to struggle to his feet. She kicked them from under him then grabbed her staff and thumped him over the head with it.

There was no time to think. Maelys sprang up onto the centre of the slab and held the clear crystal in the cursed flame, praying that it was the right thing to do. The flame was only warm, but a shock ran up her arm, then her muscles contracted violently, hurling her backwards. She landed on the flat top of the slab, tingling all over and unable to get up, for her muscles wouldn't obey her.

Phrune pushed himself to his feet, looking like a mutilated, malevolent death's head, and let out an incongruous giggle. 'It's the *cursed* flame, Maelys. Are you really that

579

stupid? Yes, you must be. You can't get up; can't move. You've doomed yourself. What bliss you're going to give me as I take your skin and offer your blood to my master.'

He turned away into the gloom beyond the direct rays of the cursed flame. Maelys heard scuffling and shortly he reappeared, hauling the limp form of Monkshart.

The zealot was naked, his ruined skin weeping from hundreds of inflamed cracks, but his head, neck and shoulders were a bloody, grotesque mess. Almost all the carefully tended long hair had fallen out and his face looked as though it had been boiled in acid. The corrugated, bark-like skin there was gone apart from a few residual tiles standing above raw flesh. His eyes were swollen closed and he was barely breathing.

Phrune saw the expression in her eyes as she looked at the ruin that had once been a man.

'Nish attacked him, after all my master did for him. But he'll pay.'

Phrune hauled Monkshart into a cavity Maelys hadn't noticed, under the broad end of the slab, and scuffling indicated that he'd dragged him beneath the star-shaped hole through which the cursed flame issued.

Phrune's head popped up above the other end of the slab. 'Are you ready to be sacrificed, Maelys? Of course you are, but you can't say so, can you? You can't move, for the kiss of the flame has paralysed you. What a pity you didn't take the trouble to find out first.'

Maelys tried to wiggle her toes, and found that she could move them a little. She attempted the same with her hand, the one that had gone into the flame. It didn't budge, though she caught a faint diamond-clear flicker between her fingers, as if some of the brightness of the cursed flame had been trapped within the crystal. It didn't help her; she had no idea how to use that power.

Her arm was completely dead but she *could* move the fingers of her other hand. Perhaps the amber-wood had helped. Unfortunately, she couldn't think of a way to use it either.

Phrune clambered up and started to unfasten the toggles of the amber-wood coat, but his oily fingers were shaking in his excitement and kept fumbling. Monkshart let out a piteous groan from beneath the slab.

Phrune cried, 'Sorry, Master,' then hacked the cords apart with his ever-ready stiletto, scattering amber-wood everywhere.

'Flydd must have come to a pretty pass if he has to make himself a coat out of wood,' he sneered.

He didn't know it was amber-wood. Not that it helped.

Monkshart moaned. 'Master, what is it?' said Phrune.

'Piiittt,' said Monkshart.

'What, Master?'

Monkshart said nothing. Phrune looked over the side, head cocked. 'Ah, yes. What did you see in the Pit of Possibilities, Maelys?'

She didn't answer, thinking that he'd have to keep her alive until she told him, and if she could just hold out –

In an instant he was beside her, gripping her nose with his slippery fingers. 'You're not a pretty girl, Maelys, but you'll be hideous when I cut your nose off.' He pressed the blade up against her nostrils. 'Be quick. My master is dying and I won't tolerate delay.'

Maelys couldn't waste time, either. If she didn't get the crystal back to Flydd soon, it would be too late. 'I saw Jal-Nish with the tears,' she said. 'He was close to reaching his ultimate goals.'

'What goals?' Phrune's eyes glistened in the blue light of the flame.

'He needs but three things to become invulnerable: perfect knowledge of the tears; complete mastery of himself; and a clear understanding of the Art by which he uses Gatherer and Reaper. And he's close to gaining all three . . .'

'But that's not all, is it? What else did you see?'

She didn't want to reveal their solitary hope of undermining the God-Emperor but the blade was cutting into her nostrils. One slash and her nose would be gone, and she couldn't bear that even if she was going to die. 'He's afraid.'

Phrune sighed. 'Ahh!' and it was echoed from under the slab. 'What is he afraid of?'

Maelys couldn't think of any convincing lie. She wished she could resist him but felt too afraid. 'We believe that somewhere, at the moment the tears were formed, their antithesis was also created – the one thing that could undermine their power.'

Phrune went very still, save for his dark, flickering tongue. 'Where is this *antithesis*?' he hissed. 'What is it?'

'I have no idea. But if an enemy –'

Monkshart made a grunting sound and Phrune interjected. 'That's all we need!' He favoured her with his sick grin. 'Now *my* time begins.'

He began to strip off Maelys's clothes, carefully, though not out of any concern for her. He didn't want to risk an accidental nick that would damage her beautiful skin. He had her naked in a minute, then began to run his hands all over her, gloating over the fineness of the body-glove he was going to make from her.

She tried to restrain her disgust, to pretend to raw, incoherent terror, and that wasn't hard at all. Let him think that she was helpless and there might be a chance, for she'd had an idea.

He eased her into position until her backside was over the star-shaped hole, the cursed flame licking warmly against her buttocks. It tickled but did not burn, but what was it doing to her? She didn't feel any shock this time, so that must have come from holding the crystal in the flame.

'Your blood runs down through the star hole,' said Phrune, 'where it is sanctified and transformed by the cursed flame. Every drop that drips on my master's cruelly burned face will restore him.'

Monkshart groaned again. Phrune flicked the blade against the pad of his thumb, several times, frowned, then took out an oiled sharpening stone and began to hone the edge.

While he was thus occupied, Maelys's groping fingers gathered a piece of amber-wood and poked it beneath her buttocks until it fell into the flame. Feeling a surge of heat, she gathered more amber-wood and awkwardly did the same with it. She thought it was doing some good, because she could move this arm further now, and some life was even coming back to the hand she'd put into the flame. But would it be enough? He didn't need the skin from her face and neck, for Monkshart didn't wear tissue-leathers there. Phrune could indulge his lust for pain and suffering all he liked, before draining her blood for his master.

Maelys felt cold inside and out, despite the warmth of the chamber. Her feet were freezing; her pulse ticked slowly in her temples, counting the remaining seconds of her life away. She was afraid to move too soon in case she missed her chance; afraid to wait too long in case he did something irrevocable. She was scared of the cursed flame licking at her buttocks and terrified of Monkshart groaning softly beneath the slab. He smelt like freshly butchered meat.

Phrune finished honing, wiped the blade, laid the sharpening stone on the slab and climbed up. He moved along on hands and knees until he was straddling Maelys, and she began to fear that he'd begin with rape. He laughed at the look on her face, then settled back on his haunches.

'I wouldn't touch you in that way for any reward.' Phrune's mouth puckered in disgust, then he reached forwards with the knife. Her nerves shrank from the blade but her body couldn't move. He pricked her throat and his tongue went slither-slap across his lips. Even his eyes seemed to be drooling. She had to do something *right now*.

What if she thrust a finger into his eye and tried to gouge it out? She didn't think she could reach that far, for her upper arm and shoulder had little strength yet. Not enough to hurt him.

Then he leaned forwards, deliberately bringing his repulsive face close to hers, and the tissue-wrapped taphloid slipped from his shirt, swinging below his bruised throat. He licked his lips again and bent over her, concentrating on the first cut.

Maelys saw her only chance, and she took it. Her good hand shot out, clawed the tissue off the taphloid and thrust it through his obscenely plump lips. She ground it into his mouth, holding it there with the heel of her hand.

He reared backwards and dropped the knife, whose point went a finger width into the flesh of her left hip before clattering to the slab. Blood welled out, running underneath her and into the flame, which burned blisteringly hot for a second. Monkshart cried out in pain, or exultation.

Phrune was leaning back on his haunches, squealing as his cheeks inflated and his lips swelled to several times their normal size and turned a vivid plum purple. Bubbles of blood formed in his right nostril, then his left eye and both ear holes. He began scrabbling at his mouth with his fingers, trying to claw the taphloid out, but his lips were already so swollen that he couldn't force his fingers in.

Great shudders racked him. His eyes went red; a scream burst through his lips; the taphloid was forced out, to bounce against his throat, every impact creating a circular red swelling.

Maelys felt her upper arm unfreezing, which had to be due to the amber-wood. She gathered all she could reach, raked it into the hole and, as the flame singed her buttocks, felt the paralysis fading.

She hastily rolled off the table before her blood healed Monkshart further, landing hard on her bottom. Her legs were still partly numb but she managed to pull herself to her feet, holding the rough side of the slab, and dressed painfully. Ebbing blood stained her pants along the hip.

Phrune was still crouched on the slab but his head had swollen so much it looked about to explode. The skin along his jawline began to tear in his agony. He looked down at the star hole and tried to smile, but was in too much pain.

Blood trickled from his mouth. He pressed his lips tightly together to contain it. Falling to his hands and knees, he crawled forwards to the hole, saying in gurgling dribbles, 'Master . . . my last service . . .'

A red mouthful poured out, splashing on the stone and running into the cursed flame, which blazed as high as the ceiling, fleetingly revealing something of the size and magnificence of the ancient chamber, before dying down again. Directly above him, a pyramidal conduit led up into darkness, perhaps to the obelisk itself.

Phrune gagged and one hand slipped over the edge of the slab, but he recovered and directed the next mouthful into the flame. He gasped, his eyes protruded; he spat a few stringy drops into the blaze then fell forwards, his head thudding to the slab beside the hole.

His back arched and enough blood to fill a saucepan poured out of him, then a series of clots the size of fried eggs, followed by something white that oozed out and flopped into the hole like a thick white worm, or a piece of intestine.

Maelys felt sick. She couldn't bear to look at him; at what she'd done to him. She wanted to run away but the crystal still had to be charged at the flame, and Phrune was in the way. He was shrunken now. His formerly plump skin had gone saggy and transparent. One hand kept twitching, sliding back and forth across the slab, but there was no life in his eyes.

She tried to heave him out of the way but he toppled off, hitting the floor with a flabby splat. She winced, then fed the rest of the amber-wood into the flame, hoping it would overcome the curse sufficiently for her to try again.

Taking a deep breath, she put her hand, holding the crystal, into the flame. It was hotter now, unpleasantly so, but she held her hand there for the count of thirty, until the tingling began again. Had she recharged the crystal? She couldn't tell, though it was brighter than before.

The taphloid still hung from his neck. She wiped it on Phrune's shirt then pulled the chain over his head, wrapped it and put it in her pocket. She'd have to scrub both taphloid and chain before she could bear to put it on.

Monkshart's feet scrabbled on the floor. Surely he wasn't recovering already? Maelys stumbled into the nearest shadows, concealing her clenched fist inside her pocket, for the crystal was growing brighter every second. So much flame had been trapped there that its light was making her fingers glow red. She dared not let him see. Maelys wasn't game to take Monkshart on, whatever his condition.

He crawled out from under the slab and stood up, shakily. His eyes were open. The last ruined skin of his face was flaking off to reveal smooth, olive-dark skin that looked too young for a man of his age. Breathing raspily, he scooped congealed blood from the floor under the flame and rubbed it all over his body, even on the soles of his feet. By the time he'd finished, the skin he'd treated first was already flaking off.

He scoured the rest away with the backs of his hands, then held his arms out in front of him as if he couldn't see and took a few halting steps, holding onto the edge of the slab with both hands.

'Phrune?' he said in a wispy voice. 'Phrune, faithful friend, where are you?'

Phrune did not answer. Monkshart continued around the slab, blind eyes searching the darkness. One foot kicked the body. He crouched down, painfully, and felt around and along it.

'Phrune?' he whispered, stroking his acolyte's swollen face, his bloody, lacerated mouth. *'Phrune!'*

The cry hinted at such depths of anguish that it sent a shudder down Maelys's spine. They were monsters both, yet they had depended on each other – perhaps even loved each other in some twisted way, and she was moved by his agony, and his loss.

Monkshart prostrated himself over the body of the smaller man, weeping. 'Phrune, Phrune, what will I ever do without you?'

He picked Phrune up, holding him in his arms with the younger man's arms and legs flopping like the limbs of a cloth doll. A dribble of blood must have run into the hole then, for the cursed flame flared high again and in the sudden brightness Maelys saw that Monkshart was weeping. Tears of blood were oozing from his swollen eyes and falling onto Phrune's cheek.

He stood there for such a long time that she was tempted to sneak around behind him and attack. She knew she should; one swift blow with the knife and his troubles would be over. And hers as well.

She was trying to find strength for the terrible, cold-blooded deed when something reminded her of the futures she'd seen in the Pit, and she faltered. What if this evil man were the key to Santhenar's future – a good future? How could she tell? Her blow might usher in a worse world than the one she lived in now.

Monkshart let out another wrenching cry and the opportunity was lost as he fell to his knees and pushed Phrune's still body under the slab. Monkshart scrambled on top and, with the fallen stiletto, carved a curving line across his own great chest, allowing his blood to fall directly into the flame.

This time it flared so high that it shrivelled the mucous crusts on the high ceiling. Monkshart's wound soon scabbed over, however, and once it did, he half scrambled, half fell off and crawled in to Phrune. Shortly he gave a third anguished wail and came out again, his long head darting around wildly, his blind eyes open and staring.

Maelys eased back into the shadows, for he was looking for her and she knew he was bent on a terrible revenge.

'You'll pay for this, Maelys Nifferlin,' he said in a voice as thick as the curdled blood on the floor. 'I know Black Arts that can make a corpse scream in agony, that can torment even a bodiless spirit and cause lifeless bones to chatter in terror. You'll pay and pay, and keep on paying a hundred years after your agonising death.'

He turned towards the shadows where she hid, trembling in every limb, opening his clenched fists into hooked claws. The cursed flame was burning in him and right through him now. He glowed in the dark; flames dripped like burning water from his knuckles and elbows, and the tip of his long nose.

Maelys couldn't move; couldn't speak, for she was frozen with terror. Even in the darkness he could see her, yet he was blind. She didn't have the stamina to outrun him; certainly couldn't hide from him.

He began to stalk her, an awful smile on his lips – like mad, frozen rage. His head was covered in Phrune's dried blood. Bloodstains ran down his chest and patches of flaking skin were stuck all over him. He looked like a week-dead corpse that had been brought back to life, and nothing could stop him. Nothing!

He was just a few paces away when there came another colossal thump, like the one Maelys had heard earlier. Monkshart stopped, one foot in the air, took another step, then stopped again, head cocked. She made out a whistling sound from high above.

Monkshart looked blindly into the darkness, head tilted up. 'He comes!'

Maelys edged backwards, trying not to make a sound. Her mouth was as dry as the crusts that had fallen from the ceiling.

'I'll be back for you, Maelys.' Monkshart turned aside, trod on her staff, picked it up and tap-tapped his way into the darkness away from the triangular stairs.

She wasn't game to run after him now and attack him while his back was turned. She had no courage left. Making sure the crystal was secure, Maelys headed back the way she had come. It had been a stroke of luck remembering that amber-wood was blessed as well as lucky, and a bigger one that its virtue had countered the curse of the flame sufficiently to remove her paralysis. But maybe that was the fortune of the amber-wood. She'd burned enough of it for a lifetime of good luck.

Maelys prayed that hers would hold long enough for her to get back to the hut, and that she could do something to help her friends when she got there, though even once she climbed out into the fresh, wind-whipped air of the mire she couldn't get the smell of Phrune's blood out of her nostrils.

FIFTY-TWO

In the cavern, the God-Emperor was silent for a long time. He appeared to be consulting Reaper, though about what, Nish could not imagine. His father's power passed all comprehension. Finally Jal-Nish smiled thinly behind his mask. 'It's seems there's more going on here than I'd thought. Where is the other one – the girl?'

'Are you telling me you don't know, Father?' said Nish. 'Surely you're not admitting to a weakness?'

'Spare me your third-rate taunts, Son; you've never had the ability to sting me. You might as well say, for I can soon find out by calling to Gatherer. Not all the amber-wood in the world can hide her from me, this close.'

Nish knew it to be true, but he didn't think his father could see into Maelys's heart with the tears, and so he risked a lie. 'She broke during the horror of Flydd's renewal and fled into the mires. We were fighting your bladder-bats and flappeters at the time and didn't see her go.'

'My Imperial Guard will soon take her, unless the stink-snappers get her first. It makes no difference, either way.' Jal-Nish surveyed them each in turn, first Nish, then Zham, Colm and finally Flydd, and not even Flydd could hold the God-Emperor's adamantine gaze. 'I've reconsidered.'

Nish looked sceptical. 'Yes, I know you believe that I never go back on a threat,' his father went on, 'but a man can change his mind. Indeed, when circumstances change, he must change with them, or fail. And so, because I do admire the courage you've shown, and your boldness and tenacity, I will offer each of you a choice. Save you, Flydd. You're *mine*! But that lingering pleasure I plan to keep till last.'

Nish didn't believe his father for a moment. This had to be another of his malicious games.

Jal-Nish slipped his hand into Reaper and Nish heard the windlasses whirr and the cables creak. Through the mossy curtain he could see the sky palace moving away until it was just a speck in the distance, connected to the cave only by the greatly lengthened and perilous plank.

'For our privacy,' said the God-Emperor. 'Cryl-Nish, you will be first. You have one last chance, but I'm not going to make a song and dance of it like some villain in a melo-drama. I'll put it simply. I want you by my side. You're all I have now – you *are* all, aren't you? If you've got a child into the belly of this Maelys girl, say the word and I'll recover her from the mires in an instant.'

Nish considered lying and saying that he had made Maelys pregnant, to save her, but what if she had escaped? If Jal-Nish discovered that he'd lied, it would condemn her. 'I've not touched her in that way, Father.'

'Really?' said Jal-Nish. 'Then what about the hundreds of girls Vivimord plied you with while you were *playing* at being the Deliverer? Surely you've impregnated one or two of them?'

His father had always belittled Nish's efforts. Perhaps that was why he so craved success, greatness, adulation. But he answered truthfully. 'I've had intimate relations with no one since my escape from Mazurhize.'

'You astound me. Why ever not? Surely you haven't lost –'

'I desired every one of them, Father. My lust was like a live animal inside me, gnawing at my vitals, but I would not give in to Monkshart and let him manipulate me so crudely.'

Jal-Nish considered that, head to one side. 'There's more to you than I'd thought. Very well, I have a proposition for you.'

'Yes?' Nish said hoarsely, feeling his heart making wild, erratic thumps. 'What is it this time?'

Jal-Nish took a deep breath, didn't speak for a long moment, then said hastily, as if it had taken all his courage, 'Come back to me, Cryl-Nish. Serve me willingly, because you care for your father.' He held up his hand as Nish opened his mouth to speak.

'No, allow me to finish. I've done evil, Son. Terrible, terrible evil, for a long time. I admit it and I wish to make amends. With you by my side, helping to show me the right path, the path you've largely followed since your salutary flogging at the manufactory, I hope and pray that I can make amends. Well, what do you say?'

Of all appeals his father might have made, this was the least expected, and Nish didn't know how to respond. The offer tempted him unbearably, because it expressed the line of his own earlier thoughts. For a long time he'd clung to the hope that if he joined his father he could turn him aside from evil. How Nish wanted to. And if he gained power and respect for himself that way, surely that would be a path to greatness he could feel proud of?

Nish was about to say yes when his eye fell upon his father's hand, still partly enveloped in Reaper as he fondled the Profane Tear with which he had caused so much suffering. No, Nish thought, this is wrong. Father is the very God of Liars and he's lying to me now.

Or was he? What if he were sincere? Nish couldn't believe that Jal-Nish *was* sincere, but anything was possible with his father. How was he to decide?

He looked around the cavern but the faces of his companions were no help. If only Irisis were here, he thought foolishly. She would know in an instant. He tried to conjure up her image but this time nothing came. He could only rely on his judgement, and he was dreadfully afraid that he was going to make the wrong choice.

Nish wanted desperately to take up his father's offer. He

yearned for it, but was afraid he wanted it for all the wrong reasons: not for the hope of turning an evil man to good, but rather for the acclamation he, Nish, would gain if he did so. For the glory, the power, the respect, and also for the possibility that Jal-Nish really could give him what he wanted most in all the world.

In the moment of that realisation, Nish knew his father was lying, manipulating him, and he had to refuse his offer. It hurt bitterly, but there was no choice.

'You're playing with my mind, Father, for the most cynical of motives. I know what you're thinking and it's not about making amends for the evil you've done. You'd say anything to get me back, but you'll never change. You're a monster and you'll be a monster until the day you die. I cannot serve you.'

This time Jal-Nish's expression didn't flicker, though his back grew ramrod-stiff. 'Never tell a man that you know what he is thinking – clearly you have no idea, for my plea was heartfelt. But if I must go forward alone, so be it.' He waved a hand in dismissal and paced to the opening of the cave, then out onto the plank, where he stood swaying in the wind.

Suddenly, awfully, and with perfect clarity, Nish's clearsight told him that he'd been wrong. Jal-Nish had been sincere after all. He *had* been prepared to change, and had hoped desperately that his only son would help him do so. Nish couldn't imagine what might have caused such a transformation, but he had to seize the opportunity to wrest some good out of this monster.

He started forwards, then stopped, realising that it was too late. His father was a proud man. What must it have cost him to humble himself in such an appeal? And how much more humiliating to be rejected so coldly?

It would only reinforce the darker side of his father, his grim view about the faithlessness of humanity in general and his family in particular, and most of all his selfish, disrespectful son. Jal-Nish, despite his demeanour, was shattered. He'd really believed that Nish would come to him this time, but rejection would turn his father irrevocably to the dark side of his nature. The offer would never be repeated.

What a fool I am, Nish thought. Father is right. I am unworthy.

He was belabouring himself thus when stone squealed at the back of the cave and a door grated open on the flat surface between the half-columns. Stale air gushed out, laden with dust, and before it had cleared a man stood swaying in the opening. He staggered through and the door slammed shut.

Nish didn't recognise the intruder at first. He was very tall, with an elongated head completely bare of hair, as if it had recently fallen out. His olive-dark skin was baby-smooth but swollen and streaked with stains that might have been dried blood, and his face was flushed as if he were burning up with fever. He had a beaked nose, black, swollen eye sockets and eyes that stared straight ahead, unblinking, as if he were blind. He was clad in pale robes thickly covered in grey dust and more rusty bloodstains.

Jal-Nish parted the moss curtain and stepped into the cavern entrance, his grim face transformed. 'Vivimord! This is a pleasure.' He was actually smiling.

Vivimord, or Monkshart, did not smile. He moved as wearily as an old man, as if the events of the past hours had drained him to the dregs. 'It's been a long time, Jal-Nish.' He shuffled forwards and held out his hand.

Nish didn't think his father would take it, but he did.

'You look terrible,' said Jal-Nish. 'Aftersickness?'

Vivimord nodded. 'Taking on the persona of Vomix, then calling down your flappeter to carry me up here, took more power than I had at my disposal. It began to consume me from the inside; and then I suffered an unexpected attack which nearly finished me.' He related the story of Nish's barrel of mucilage.

'He's a man with an innovative mind, my son,' said Jal-Nish, again studying Nish thoughtfully. 'But you survived?'

'Faithful Phrune hauled me all the way to the cursed flame – thank you for breaching its age-old defences, Jal-Nish, else I'd be dead hours ago – and there shed his own life's blood into the fire to cure me of my afflictions. I'll miss his service.'

'He served his purpose,' said Jal-Nish indifferently. 'So, what of you, Vivimord? Do you still hold to your notion of turning my son into the Deliverer and toppling me?'

'I do,' said Vivimord, 'though it grows ever more unlikely that I'll succeed.'

'You rate yourself lower than I do, but . . .' Jal-Nish's cheek spasmed and he seemed to be going through an inner struggle, as if the rejection of his previous appeal made it impossible to try again. He went on in a rush, 'I've never had more need of an ally, and you were ever my closest friend. You were more a son to me than that treacherous little worm who cares not a jot for his family.' He slashed his stiff arm towards Nish. 'You're the only man I ever truly trusted, Vivimord, and I need you now. There's a growing threat in the void and not even with the tears can I face it alone.'

It hurt. Nish could never have imagined that his father's words would cut him so. He went to his knees, holding his head in his hands and cursing his folly.

Vivimord looked as though he'd anticipated the appeal; moreover, that he'd been moved by it. 'Ah, old friend, would that I could. But you forget – I know everything about you. I know all the evil you've done to get where you are today. Shocking evil and dreadful betrayals.'

Jal-Nish bowed his head. 'I have. I acknowledge it.'

'I know how much you've gained; or should I say, how little. And what it's cost you.'

'Aye,' said Jal-Nish. 'It's cost me. It's cost me every single thing I ever cared about.'

'And yet you can't turn your back on what you've done.'

'I might have done.' Jal-Nish glanced at Nish. 'I tried, but it came to nothing and I cannot try again.'

'Not for any price?' Vivimord said compassionately.

'Alas not,' said Jal-Nish.

'I thought that would be your answer, and here is mine. But for one thing alone, I would come back to you, Jal-Nish. And you know what that thing is.'

'My declaring myself as God-Emperor.'

'Emperor I could take, for that is what you are – emperor of the world, and I admire you for having the foresight to aspire to such heights, and the strength to seize Santhenar at the critical moment. But no man may declare himself a god. That is a matter of personal faith on which I cannot yield.'

'I know and understand, but even if I were of a mind to give up the title, I cannot. You understand the basis of power, Vivimord. The moment I denied my godhead, every jackal on Santhenar would fall on me, and even with the tears I could not keep them all at bay. It would be a fatal sign of weakness from which I would never recover.'

'I thought you were better than that. I confess I'm disappointed, Jal-Nish. '

Jal-Nish laughed harshly. 'Are you? Are you really? At least I'm not a mealy-mouthed hypocrite. You forget that I know where all *your* bodies are buried, Vivimord, and there's an awful lot of them. I know how you appeased Phrune, allowing him to slake his sordid and murderous lusts on the innocent because you couldn't do without him. Or *wouldn't*. And I know about the things you do in your ungovernable rages –'

Vivimord clenched his fists; pale flames dripped from his knuckles and his face grew ever more inflamed, as if a fire were burning inside him. 'That affliction comes from the touch of the tears, Jal-Nish. While I was saving them *for you*.'

'Does it? Or were the tears a convenient excuse? You always had to control everything around you, yet you could never control yourself.'

596

Vivimord tried to do so now, but couldn't. He shuddered with fury, then snapped, 'Why should *you* have it all? You're not half the man I am.'

'You show your real colours, Vivimord. Envy burns you, doesn't it? That's why I let you go, despite all you meant to me. So, you're challenging me. Must we fight, then?'

'We must, though not today.'

'If we must fight, it will be now,' said Jal-Nish, regretfully. 'I love my few friends despite their weaknesses, but you've declared yourself my enemy and I can't allow any enemy to walk away and recover his strength.'

He was reaching for Reaper when Vivimord flung out his hand, blue fire jagging from his fingertips. 'I may be at death's door but the cursed flame burns strong in me, thanks to Phrune's sacrifice. Let the chaos within Reaper turn against you, false God-Emperor! Fall!'

Jal-Nish recoiled as if he'd been burned and fell sideways to the floor of the cave, the tear slipping from around his neck and wobbling across the floor into a bed of moss. Vivimord thrust out his arm and the pale, dripping fire shot out like water from a hose, setting the damp moss ablaze between Jal-Nish and Reaper. Vivimord swung his arm, pointing, and the door at the back of the cave opened to a shoulder-wide crack.

'Run, Deliverer,' he said hoarsely. 'This is your chance. You'll not get another.'

Jal-Nish got up and raised his hand. 'I don't need to touch Reaper to draw *some* power from it.' He gestured and the door began to grind shut.

Vivimord stopped it with a finger gesture and the two mancers strove against each other for a minute or two, though neither had the strength to prevail and the door remained ajar. Despite Jal-Nish's words, it was clear that without the touch of the tears his power was greatly weakened.

It was their chance. Flydd lurched towards the door. Colm

and Zham followed. Nish was starting after them when his father, who stood near the mossy entrance, looked up sharply.

'Hello?' He turned towards Vivimord, rapped out, 'Truce,' then turned his back, as if knowing that he would not be struck down from behind.

After a long hesitation punctuated by convulsive jerks of his fingers, Vivimord overcame the temptation. His lips moved, 'Truce,' though Nish couldn't hear the word over the sound of the wind.

Jal-Nish stepped out through the moss curtain, saying, 'The last of the crew has come. Can you also think to bring me down, Maelys of Nifferlin?'

Nish froze, then, ignoring Vivimord's gasped, 'Run, you fool!' turned back to the entrance. The burning moss had gone out.

Maelys was coming down the rope ladder, which was swinging wildly back and forth in the updraught. She let out a cry as it slammed against the wet cliff, cracking her knuckles between the rock and the rope, then clung desperately to the rungs as the wind lifted the ladder almost to the horizontal before slamming it back. She managed to swing around this time and take the impact on shoulder and hip, though she almost lost her grip. She wrapped her arms around and through the rungs and hung on grimly, eyes closed, but Nish knew she wouldn't survive another such impact.

'Go up, Maelys!' he said hoarsely. 'There's nothing you can do.'

She wouldn't have heard him over the sound of the wind, and she had her back to the entrance so she hadn't seen Jal-Nish either, though she must know he was here. She hung limply on the rope for a moment, took a deep, sobbing breath, then straightened her back and continued down.

Maelys turned when she was just a rung above the plank, searching for a safe way to get off the ladder and inside, then

598

froze when she saw Jal-Nish standing by the entrance, swaying on the balls of his feet like a sailor on the deck of a ship.

He took hold of the ladder, holding it still for her. She moved down stiffly; her feet settled on the plank.

'Come in,' he said, gesturing with his good hand. 'Join your friends.' Jal-Nish moved sideways in the entrance to give her room, the curtain of moss sweeping wetly across his shoulders.

'Fly, Maelys!' cried Nish.

Maelys looked past him to Zham and Colm, who had gathered inside the curtain and were also urging her to go back. Flydd had managed to stumble halfway before falling to his knees.

Maelys came inside. Nish didn't dare say anything that might give away what she'd gone for. Could she have succeeded after all?

She was spattered with dried blood, and streaked with dust and green moss stains. Her eyes were as hollow as her cheeks. She looked as if she'd been to the depths of the abyss and back.

'What happened to you out –?' began Colm.

Zham brought his weight down on Colm's toes and he broke off.

'Phrune caught me and . . . took me to the cursed flame.' She shuddered involuntarily. 'I – I – managed to kill him, but he gave his blood to the flame, to save his master's life.' Maelys glanced at Vivimord, whose blind eyes were on her, then away hastily. 'It was a terrible death,' she said softly. 'I'll never get over it.'

Vivimord went as rigid as a poker. 'Nor I,' he rasped. His jaw knotted and for a moment Nish thought he was going to give way to his affliction and strike her down, but the zealot managed to control himself this time. 'I'll deal with you later,' he spat, then turned to Jal-Nish. 'Truce over?'

Jal-Nish nodded. He waved his hand. The door between the columns slammed shut and disappeared. 'Truce over.'

The cavern suddenly went dark save for the faint outline of Jal-Nish near the entrance. Now Vivimord became an outline too, as the green nimbus of before surrounded him. Reaper, lying half buried in the damp moss, appeared to shimmer as it reflected the zealot's glow. Jal-Nish moved his hand again and a transparent barrier sealed off Nish, Flydd, Colm and Zham, who had retreated to the rear of the cavern. Another small hemisphere trapped Maelys against the side wall. Nish presumed it was to protect them.

A struggle ensued, full of long tense silences as the two mancers manoeuvred for position in the gloom, then sudden violent flashes which lit up the cave as they used unknown powers on each other. Vivimord kept moving so as to keep himself between Jal-Nish and Reaper, though the zealot maintained his distance from the deadly tear. After what it had done to him long ago, Nish understood why he kept away.

Without the direct power of Reaper at Jal-Nish's disposal, he and Vivimord seemed evenly matched. The zealot, with the cursed flame burning within him, might have had the edge in power had he been well enough to use it, but he moved ever more stiffly and often stumbled. His ordeals had greatly weakened him.

As the battle raged on, Nish noticed that Flydd was probing the stone wall where the door had opened, then running his hands over the transparent barrier. Flydd shook his head.

'You can't open it, surr?'

'Not – without power.'

'Do you think Maelys –?' Flydd gave a violent shake of the head and Nish broke off. His father might still overhear.

Maelys, about ten paces away in her bubble, was also fingering its clear curved wall. Not finding any weakness, she stood with her nose pressed to the barrier, watching the combatants. A blast of blue fire from Vivimord was accompanied by a roar that made the wall oscillate like a soap bubble. She jumped backwards, then came forwards again, staring out.

Both mancers were staggering now. Jal-Nish was bent over, gasping for breath. Vivimord stood upright, keeping his back to Reaper, but could barely move. It looked as if his joints were freezing up.

Maelys turned away from them, putting her hand down her front as if to scratch herself, but lifted something over her head. Nish couldn't see what she held, but she thrust her hand out, pushing it hard into the barrier, and to his amazement it tore open. She forced through, her face a mask of terrified resolve. As Nish stared at Maelys, she took three steps to Jal-Nish, who stood side-on to her, and before he had realised the danger she whacked her open hand against his bare neck.

Jal-Nish convulsed and a coruscating red and black aura, a reversal or corruption of his own, flickered into existence around him, dazzlingly bright, then abruptly pulled back in. He smashed Maelys out of the way with his stiff arm and reeled off, holding his face in his hands and crying out in agony. She'd touched him with her taphloid.

Vivimord's head whipped from side to side, as if the senses which replaced his sight hadn't told him what had happened, then threw out his arm to destroy the presumptuous God-Emperor. Nish caught his breath – despite everything, this wasn't how his father should fall. And was Vivimord any better?

Maelys, lying on the floor of the cavern where she'd fallen, drew her arm back and tossed her taphloid at Vivimord. It whirled through the air on its chain and struck him on the right cheek. The green nimbus flared then shrank to nothing; a patch of skin the size of an egg blistered and bulged out like a black mole. Letting out a thin scream, Vivimord fell down, right on Reaper. He convulsed until he bent double and shot to his feet again, his robes smouldering across his chest and belly, the cloth falling away there to reveal his skin bubbling like crackling on a roast pig.

Nish, scenting the hope of escape after all, forced at the barrier but it didn't give. 'Maelys!' he screamed, gesturing at her to break it with the taphloid.

She didn't see him. She was watching the two mancers, mouth open. Vivimord was on his knees by the wall, his face screwed up in agony. Jal-Nish was lurching in circles, the deadly aura flickering in and out, though Nish noticed that every wobbling circle took him closer to the tears.

Vivimord hit him with blue fire again, knocking Jal-Nish backwards into the wall. He slumped to the floor but managed to raise his hand for one final burst of power which hurled Vivimord backwards through the mossy curtain. He landed on the springy plank, bounced high, struck again and, deliberately, rolled over the edge.

The transparent barrier faded to nothing. Nish ran to the entrance, getting there just before his father. It didn't seem like Vivimord to commit suicide, and he hadn't.

He was whirling his hands in front of his face as he fell, evidently performing summoning mancery, then flung them out as a flock of Jal-Nish's bladder-bats materialised below him. He caught one by the legs, swinging around in a falling spiral as it inflated to several times its former size, then slowly drifted down out of sight.

Jal-Nish lurched out after him and stood on the plank, his arms hanging limply, panting. He stared after his former friend, then beckoned and the distant sky palace began to grind back towards the cave on its contracting plank. Jal-Nish turned towards Reaper but his corrupted aura flared brilliantly. He gasped and doubled over, shaking his head as if to clear it.

Maelys got up, slowly and painfully, retrieved her taphloid from the floor and hung it around her neck. Had she succeeded in recharging the crystal after all?

Nish felt a surge of impossible hope, but if they had any

chance at all they had to strike now while his father was still weak, and while the inverted aura prevented him from taking up Reaper again. Even now, Jal-Nish was far from powerless. He, Nish, had to create a diversion so she could get the crystal to Flydd, unseen.

His mind raced. What could he do? He had no weapon, nor any way to attack his father. No plea would make any difference now. Neither would Jal-Nish listen if Nish were to agree to go back to him. It was too late for that.

Could he shock Jal-Nish by playing on his greatest fear? Nish dared not reveal that Maelys had seen him in the Pit of Possibilities, for that would doom her instantly, but . . .

'I know what you're most afraid of, Father,' he said. It didn't come out as well as he'd thought. It sounded like something one child would say to another in the school-yard.

Flydd made a grunting sound in his throat, as if trying to cut Nish off, but Nish ignored him. They had only one tiny chance and he had to take it, whatever the cost later. Assuming there was a later.

Jal-Nish didn't react at all. 'Another of your silly games, Cryl-Nish?'

Flydd made another urgent grunt. Nish had to say it now or he'd never be able to. 'It's the antithesis to the tears!' he burst out. 'The one thing that can unmake them and take all your power with it. We're going to find it and tear you down, Father.'

Jal-Nish jerked so violently that the platinum mask slipped sideways, revealing his ruined mouth and scarred chin. His one eye stared at Nish for a moment, then he thumped the mask back into place, saying hoarsely, 'I have no weakness. There is *no* antithesis to the tears.'

From the corner of his eye, Nish saw Maelys ease something from her pocket, her hand glowing faintly red. She'd done it! They had one last chance, if she could get the crystal to Flydd without Jal-Nish seeing.

But Jal-Nish raised his good hand. 'I see what you're about, Son, and it won't work. I know what *you're* most afraid of, Maelys of Nifferlin.'

Maelys's clenched hand, which had been creeping out towards Flydd's, froze. The red glow pulsed in her fist, as if synchronised to her heartbeat. 'Afraid of?' she croaked.

Jal-Nish made a pass in the air and a floating ball of mist appeared between them, just above head height. 'Look into the mist,' he said.

'Don't look,' said Flydd. 'Whatever he shows you, it'll be a lie.'

She looked, and so did Nish. The mist cleared to a globe of darkness within which the faintest shadows moved. A dull yellow light grew in the centre, revealing a horribly familiar cell – Nish's dungeon cell in Mazurhize, or another exactly like it. It contained four people: three middle-aged women slumped against one wall, and someone, much smaller, clinging desperately to the bars.

'Mother!' Maelys cried in anguish. 'Fyllis?'

It was the beautiful blonde-haired little girl who had rescued Nish from Mazurhize, but she looked gaunt, her hair was lifeless and her eyes were staring vacantly through the bars. The women didn't move.

'It's a lie,' Flydd repeated. 'All a lie, Maelys.'

'No,' said Maelys. 'He has them; I know it.'

'Give up the crystal, Maelys,' said Jal-Nish, 'and I promise you'll see your family again.'

'Because I'll be in that cell with them.'

'You're a clever, brave girl who has given your all for my son, worthless though he is. I recognise your courage. Hand me the crystal and I'll allow you your freedom, and your family's. I'll even rebuild Nifferlin Manor and restore it to you.'

Why doesn't Father strike her down and take the crystal? Nish wondered. Was he enjoying the game, or was he too weak now – too afraid that Flydd would get the crystal first and crush him with its flame-fed power?

'But if you don't,' Jal-Nish went on, 'your family will feel the longest and most terrible excruciations my torturers can devise, and your little sister will suffer equally with them.'

Maelys closed her eyes, swaying on her feet. Nish knew what she was going through, for he'd endured the agony of his father's bitter choices many times. 'Don't give in to him,' he said softly, though who was he to say it? In her place . . .

Maelys looked up at Fyllis, whose mouth was gaping as she stared through the bars, then turned away from Flydd. 'I can't do it, Xervish,' she said. 'I'm so sorry.'

Flydd groaned and reached out a hand.

Maelys took a step towards Jal-Nish, staring into his eye. She opened her hand and the crystal, lying on her palm, lit up the cavern with diamond-clear beams of flame-fed light. Nish felt a shiver pass down his spine at the raw power it held.

The moment was drawn out; time hardly seemed to be passing at all. His father was staring at it too. Nish saw him swallow. It threatened him, in his weakened state.

Flydd had fallen to his knees again. Zham and Colm were at the rear of the cavern, by the closed door, too far away to help. This was Nish's own moment of choice. No one else could do anything. It was up to him. His father wasn't even looking at him. Dare he try? It would mean sacrificing Maelys's family and destroying her faith in him forever. But surely, if it was their only chance to overthrow his father, he had to take it.

Maelys took another step forwards, and another.

Yes, he would take it. He must, whatever the consequences. Nish sprang at her, tore the crystal from her hand and in one movement tossed it to Flydd, praying that his old friend had the wit to catch it.

Flydd fumbled the crystal but caught it on the second attempt. He stood upright, crying out in exultation, then clenched the crystal in his fist and raised it high. Jal-Nish hadn't moved. He was as stiff as a plank and his thick hair was standing up on his head. He was afraid of his old enemy and it did Nish's heart good to see it.

Flydd strained for a minute or two, his face went red and the muscles of his square jaw stood out, but the closed door behind him did not budge. He groaned and his hand fell to his side.

Jal-Nish let his breath out, then laughed mockingly. The corrupted red and black aura which had so weakened him was gone; he wasn't afraid now. He'd won and everyone knew it.

'What's the matter?' said Nish desperately, turning to Jal-Nish. 'What have you done to the flame crystal?'

'Show me,' said Jal-Nish, walking across and picking Reaper up out of its bed of moss.

Flydd held out his hand. The crystal lay on his palm, burning with trapped fire.

Jal-Nish hung Reaper about his neck and caressed the shimmering quicksilver tear. 'That crystal has power to open any barrier, *for one who can use it.*'

'What – what do you mean?' said Nish.

'Oh, this is the most delicious irony I've ever tasted,' Jal-Nish gloated. 'Flydd always swore that he'd never take renewal – indeed, that it was the ultimate corruption. Yet he repudiated that vow, seduced by the thought of being young and hale again, and having back what the scrutators' torturers rightly cut from him. Perhaps he thought to rival me, even overthrow me. Fool! He knew the renewal spell often goes wrong, yet took no precautions to prevent it.

'Renewal has stripped Flydd of his talent for the Art. He's not a mancer any more, just the most ordinary of men, and even if that crystal held all the power of Gatherer and Reaper, he couldn't force a worm back into its hole with it. He's mine, and so are you, Cryl-Nish. If you'd come willingly, you could have had it all. Now you'll get nothing – any of you.'

Maelys directed a hate-filled glare at Nish for his betrayal, then fell to her knees and wept.

GEOMANCER

Volume One of The Well of Echoes

Ian Irvine

Two hundred years ago the Charon fought for their lives against the creatures of the Void. Hunted and afraid, the last of the Charon sought to cross the Forbidding and take refuge on the human world of Santhenar.

In the battle that followed the power of the Charon was broken and humanity saved – but every victory comes at a price . . . For in that battle the Forbidding was destroyed. Now the forces that slaughtered the Charon have emerged from the Void, and Santhenar's people fight a desperate battle for survival.

But there is yet hope. For in the Secret Arts there lies hidden a strength as perilous and deadly as anything the Void commands. And it is the destiny of one woman to wield that power – to become a warrior, a leader, a saviour . . . a Geomancer

A SHADOW ON THE GLASS

Volume One of The View from the Mirror

Ian Irvine

Once there were three worlds, each with their own people. Then, fleeing out of the void, on the edge of extinction, came the Charon. And the balance changed forever.

Karen, a sensitive with a troubled past, is forced to steal an ancient relic in payment for a debt. But she is not told that the relic is the Mirror of Aachan, a twisted, deceitful thing that remembers everything it has seen.

Llian, meanwhile, a brilliant chronicler, is expelled from his college for uncovering a perilous mystery.

Thrown together by fate, Karen and Llian are hunted across a world at war, for the Mirror contains a secret of incredible power.

THE DARKNESS THAT COMES BEFORE

The Prince of Nothing, Book One

R. Scott Bakker

A score of centuries has passed since the First Apocalypse and the thoughts of men have turned, inevitably, to more worldly concerns . . .

A veteran sorcerer and spy seeks news of an ancient enemy. A military genius plots to conquer the known world for his Emperor but dreams of the throne for himself. The spiritual leader of the Thousand Temples seeks a Holy War to cleanse the land of the infidel. An exiled barbarian chieftain seeks vengeance against the man who disgraced him. And into this world steps a man like no other, seeking to bind all – man and woman, emperor and slave – to his own mysterious ends.

But the fate of men – even great men – means little when the world itself may soon be torn asunder. Behind the politics, beneath the religious fervour, a dark and ancient evil is reawakening. After two thousand years, the No-God is returning. The Second Apocalypse is nigh. And one cannot raise walls against what has been forgotten . . .